Georg Ebers

Uarda

e-artnow 2020

Georg Ebers

Uarda

Historical Novel - A Romance of Ancient Egypt

Translator: Clara Bell

e-artnow, 2020
Contact: info@e-artnow.org

ISBN 978-80-273-0872-9

Contents

PREFACE. 13

PREFACE TO THE FIFTH GERMAN EDITION. 15

CHAPTER 1. 16

CHAPTER II. 21

CHAPTER III. 27

CHAPTER IV. 31

CHAPTER V. 38

CHAPTER VI. 47

CHAPTER VII. 55

CHAPTER VIII. 62

CHAPTER IX. 70

CHAPTER X. 76

CHAPTER XI. 81

CHAPTER XII. 85

CHAPTER XIII. 90

CHAPTER XIV. 94

CHAPTER XV. 99

CHAPTER XVI. 104

CHAPTER XVII. 109

CHAPTER XVIII. 115

CHAPTER XIX. 121

CHAPTER XX. 125

CHAPTER XXI. 129

CHAPTER XXII. 135

CHAPTER XXIII. 142

CHAPTER XXIV. 148

CHAPTER XXV. 152

CHAPTER XXVI. 158

CHAPTER XXVII. 166

CHAPTER XXVIII. 171

CHAPTER XXIX. 179

CHAPTER XXX. 186

CHAPTER XXXI. 195

CHAPTER XXXII. 200

CHAPTER XXXIII. 203

CHAPTER XXXIV. 211

CHAPTER XXXV. 219

CHAPTER XXXVI. 222

CHAPTER XXXVII.   228
CHAPTER XXXVIII.   232
CHAPTER XXXIX.   238
CHAPTER XL.   243
CHAPTER XLI.   248
CHAPTER XLII   254
CHAPTER XLIII.   257
CHAPTER XLIV.   262
CHAPTER XLV.   266
CHAPTER XLVI.   271
CHAPTER XLVII.   275
Footnotes   277

PREFACE.

In the winter of 1873 I spent some weeks in one of the tombs of the Necropolis of Thebes in order to study the monuments of that solemn city of the dead; and during my long rides in the silent desert the germ was developed whence this book has since grown. The leisure of mind and body required to write it was given me through a long but not disabling illness.

In the first instance I intended to elucidate this story-like my "Egyptian Princess" —with numerous and extensive notes placed at the end; but I was led to give up this plan from finding that it would lead me to the repetition of much that I had written in the notes to that earlier work.

The numerous notes to the former novel had a threefold purpose. In the first place they served to explain the text; in the second they were a guarantee of the care with which I had striven to depict the archaeological details in all their individuality from the records of the monuments and of Classic Authors; and thirdly I hoped to supply the reader who desired further knowledge of the period with some guide to his studies.

In the present work I shall venture to content myself with the simple statement that I have introduced nothing as proper to Egypt and to the period of Rameses that cannot be proved by some authority; the numerous monuments which have descended to us from the time of the Rameses, in fact enable the enquirer to understand much of the aspect and arrangement of Egyptian life, and to follow it step try step through the details of religious, public, and private life, even of particular individuals. The same remark cannot be made in regard to their mental life, and here many an anachronism will slip in, many things will appear modern, and show the coloring of the Christian mode of thought.

Every part of this book is intelligible without the aid of notes; but, for the reader who seeks for further enlightenment, I have added some foot-notes, and have not neglected to mention such works as afford more detailed information on the subjects mentioned in the narrative.

The reader who wishes to follow the mind of the author in this work should not trouble himself with the notes as he reads, but merely at the beginning of each chapter read over the notes which belong to the foregoing one. Every glance at the foot-notes must necessarily disturb and injure the development of the tale as a work of art. The story stands here as it flowed from one fount, and was supplied with notes only after its completion.

A narrative of Herodotus combined with the Epos of Pentaur, of which so many copies have been handed down to us, forms the foundation of the story.

The treason of the Regent related by the Father of history is referable perhaps to the reign of the third and not of the second Rameses. But it is by no means certain that the Halicarnassian writer was in this case misinformed; and in this fiction no history will be inculcated, only as a background shall I offer a sketch of the time of Sesostris, from a picturesque point of view, but with the nearest possible approach to truth. It is true that to this end nothing has been neglected that could be learnt from the monuments or the papyri; still the book is only a romance, a poetic fiction, in which I wish all the facts derived from history and all the costume drawn from the monuments to be regarded as incidental, and the emotions of the actors in the story as what I attach importance to.

But I must be allowed to make one observation. From studying the conventional mode of execution of ancient Egyptian art-which was strictly subject to the hieratic laws of type and proportion-we have accustomed ourselves to imagine the inhabitants of the Nile-valley in the time of the Pharaohs as tall and haggard men with little distinction of individual physiognomy, and recently a great painter has sought to represent them under this aspect in a modern picture. This is an error; the Egyptians, in spite of their aversion to foreigners and their strong attachment to their native soil, were one of the most intellectual and active people of antiquity; and he who would represent them as they lived, and to that end copies the forms which remain painted on the walls of the temples and sepulchres, is the accomplice of those priestly corrupters of art who compelled the painters and sculptors of the Pharaonic era to abandon truth to nature in favor of their sacred laws of proportion.

13

He who desires to paint the ancient Egyptians with truth and fidelity, must regard it in some sort as an act of enfranchisement; that is to say, he must release the conventional forms from those fetters which were peculiar to their art and altogether foreign to their real life. Indeed, works of sculpture remain to us of the time of the first pyramid, which represent men with the truth of nature, unfettered by the sacred canon. We can recall the so-called "Village Judge" of Bulaq, the "Scribe" now in Paris, and a few figures in bronze in different museums, as well as the noble and characteristic busts of all epochs, which amply prove how great the variety of individual physiognomy, and, with that, of individual character was among the Egyptians. Alma Tadelna in London and Gustav Richter in Berlin have, as painters, treated Egyptian subjects in a manner which the poet recognizes and accepts with delight.

Many earlier witnesses than the late writer Flavius Vopiscus might be referred to who show us the Egyptians as an industrious and peaceful people, passionately devoted it is true to all that pertains to the other world, but also enjoying the gifts of life to the fullest extent, nay sometimes to excess.

Real men, such as we see around us in actual life, not silhouettes constructed to the old priestly scale such as the monuments show us-real living men dwelt by the old Nile-stream; and the poet who would represent them must courageously seize on types out of the daily life of modern men that surround him, without fear of deviating too far from reality, and, placing them in their own long past time, color them only and clothe them to correspond with it.

I have discussed the authorities for the conception of love which I have ascribed to the ancients in the preface to the second edition of "An Egyptian Princess."

With these lines I send Uarda into the world; and in them I add my thanks to those dear friends in whose beautiful home, embowered in green, bird-haunted woods, I have so often refreshed my spirit and recovered my strength, where I now write the last words of this book.

Rheinbollerhutte, September 22, 1876.
GEORG EBERS.

PREFACE TO THE FIFTH GERMAN EDITION.

The earlier editions of "Uarda" were published in such rapid succession, that no extensive changes in the stereotyped text could be made; but from the first issue, I have not ceased to correct it, and can now present to the public this new fifth edition as a "revised" one.

Having felt a constantly increasing affection for "Uarda" during the time I was writing, the friendly and comprehensive attention bestowed upon it by our greatest critics and the favorable reception it met with in the various classes of society, afforded me the utmost pleasure.

I owe the most sincere gratitude to the honored gentlemen, who called my attention to certain errors, and among them will name particularly Professor Paul Ascherson of Berlin, and Dr. C. Rohrbach of Gotha. Both will find their remarks regarding mistakes in the geographical location of plants, heeded in this new edition.

The notes, after mature deliberation, have been placed at the foot of the pages instead of at the end of the book.

So many criticisms concerning the title "Uarda" have recently reached my ears, that, rather by way of explanation than apology, I will here repeat what I said in the preface to the third edition.

This title has its own history, and the more difficult it would be for me to defend it, the more ready I am to allow an advocate to speak for me, an advocate who bears a name no less distinguished than that of G. E. Lessing, who says:

"Nanine? (by Voltaire, 1749). What sort of title is that? What thoughts does it awake? Neither more nor less than a title should arouse. A title must not be a bill of fare. The less it betrays of the contents, the better it is. Author and spectator are both satisfied, and the ancients rarely gave their comedies anything but insignificant names."

This may be the case with "Uarda," whose character is less prominent than some others, it is true, but whose sorrows direct the destinies of my other heroes and heroines.

Why should I conceal the fact? The character of "Uarda" and the present story have grown out of the memory of a Fellah girl, half child, half maiden, whom I saw suffer and die in a hut at Abu el Qurnah in the Necropolis of Thebes.

I still persist in the conviction I have so frequently expressed, the conviction that the fundamental traits of the life of the soul have undergone very trivial modifications among civilized nations in all times and ages, but will endeavor to explain the contrary opinion, held by my opponents, by calling attention to the circumstance, that the expression of these emotions show considerable variations among different peoples, and at different epochs. I believe that Juvenal, one of the ancient writers who best understood human nature, was right in saying:

"Nil erit ulterius, quod nostris moribus addat
Posteritas: eadem cupient facientque minores."

Leipsic, October 15th, 1877.

15

CHAPTER 1.

By the walls of Thebes-the old city of a hundred gates-the Nile spreads to a broad river; the heights, which follow the stream on both sides, here take a more decided outline; solitary, almost cone-shaped peaks stand out sharply from the level background of the many-colored. limestone hills, on which no palm-tree flourishes and in which no humble desert-plant can strike root. Rocky crevasses and gorges cut more or less deeply into the mountain range, and up to its ridge extends the desert, destructive of all life, with sand and stones, with rocky cliffs and reef-like, desert hills.

Behind the eastern range the desert spreads to the Red Sea; behind the western it stretches without limit, into infinity. In the belief of the Egyptians beyond it lay the region of the dead.

Between these two ranges of hills, which serve as walls or ramparts to keep back the desert-sand, flows the fresh and bounteous Nile, bestowing blessing and abundance; at once the father and the cradle of millions of beings. On each shore spreads the wide plain of black and fruit-ful soil, and in the depths many-shaped creatures, in coats of mail or scales, swarm and find subsistence.

The lotos floats on the mirror of the waters, and among the papyrus reeds by the shore water-fowl innumerable build their nests. Between the river and the mountain-range lie fields, which after the seed-time are of a shining blue-green, and towards the time of harvest glow like gold. Near the brooks and water-wheels here and there stands a shady sycamore; and date-palms, carefully tended, group themselves in groves. The fruitful plain, watered and manured every year by the inundation, lies at the foot of the sandy desert-hills behind it, and stands out like a garden flower-bed from the gravel-path.

In the fourteenth century before Christ-for to so remote a date we must direct the thoughts of the reader-impassable limits had been set by the hand of man, in many places in Thebes, to the inroads of the water; high dykes of stone and embankments protected the streets and squares, the temples and the palaces, from the overflow.

Canals that could be tightly closed up led from the dykes to the land within, and smaller branch-cuttings to the gardens of Thebes.

On the right, the eastern bank of the Nile, rose the buildings of the far-famed residence of the Pharaohs. Close by the river stood the immense and gaudy Temples of the city of Amon; behind these and at a short distance from the Eastern hills-indeed at their very foot and partly even on the soil of the desert-were the palaces of the King and nobles, and the shady streets in which the high narrow houses of the citizens stood in close rows.

Life was gay and busy in the streets of the capital of the Pharaohs.

The western shore of the Nile showed a quite different scene. Here too there was no lack of stately buildings or thronging men; but while on the farther side of the river there was a compact mass of houses, and the citizens went cheerfully and openly about their day's work, on this side there were solitary splendid structures, round which little houses and huts seemed to cling as children cling to the protection of a mother. And these buildings lay in detached groups.

Any one climbing the hill and looking down would form the notion that there lay below him a number of neighboring villages, each with its lordly manor house. Looking from the plain up to the precipice of the western hills, hundreds of closed portals could be seen, some solitary, others closely ranged in rows; a great number of them towards the foot of the slope, yet more half-way up, and a few at a considerable height.

And even more dissimilar were the slow-moving, solemn groups in the roadways on this side, and the cheerful, confused throng yonder. There, on the eastern shore, all were in eager pursuit of labor or recreation, stirred by pleasure or by grief, active in deed and speech; here, in the west, little was spoken, a spell seemed to check the footstep of the wanderer, a pale hand to sadden the bright glance of every eye, and to banish the smile from every lip.

And yet many a gaily-dressed bark stopped at the shore, there was no lack of minstrel bands, grand processions passed on to the western heights; but the Nile boats bore the dead, the songs sung here were songs of lamentation, and the processions consisted of mourners following the sarcophagus.

We are standing on the soil of the City of the Dead of Thebes.

Nevertheless even here nothing is wanting for return and revival, for to the Egyptian his dead died not. He closed his eyes, he bore him to the Necropolis, to the house of the embalmer, or Kolchytes, and then to the grave; but he knew that the souls of the departed lived on; that the justified absorbed into Osiris floated over the Heavens in the vessel of the Sun; that they appeared on earth in the form they choose to take upon them, and that they might exert influence on the current of the lives of the survivors. So he took care to give a worthy interment to his dead, above all to have the body embalmed so as to endure long: and had fixed times to bring fresh offerings for the dead of flesh and fowl, with drink-offerings and sweet-smelling essences, and vegetables and flowers.

Neither at the obsequies nor at the offerings might the ministers of the gods be absent, and the silent City of the Dead was regarded as a favored sanctuary in which to establish schools and dwellings for the learned.

So it came to pass that in the temples and on the site Of the Necropolis, large communities of priests dwelt together, and close to the extensive embalming houses lived numerous Kolchytes, who handed down the secrets of their art from father to son.

Besides these there were other manufactories and shops. In the former, sarcophagi of stone and of wood, linen bands for enveloping mummies, and amulets for decorating them, were made; in the latter, merchants kept spices and essences, flowers, fruits, vegetables and pastry for sale. Calves, gazelles, goats, geese and other fowl, were fed on enclosed meadow-plats, and the mourners betook themselves thither to select what they needed from among the beasts pronounced by the priests to be clean for sacrifice, and to have them sealed with the sacred seal. Many bought only part of a victim at the shambles-the poor could not even do this. They bought only colored cakes in the shape of beasts, which symbolically took the place of the calves and geese which their means were unable to procure. In the handsomest shops sat servants of the priests, who received forms written on rolls of papyrus which were filled up in the writing room of the temple with those sacred verses which the departed spirit must know and repeat to ward off the evil genius of the deep, to open the gate of the under world, and to be held righteous before Osiris and the forty-two assessors of the subterranean court of justice.

What took place within the temples was concealed from view, for each was surrounded by a high enclosing wall with lofty, carefully-closed portals, which were only opened when a chorus of priests came out to sing a pious hymn, in the morning to Horus the rising god, and in the evening to Tum the descending god.[1]

As soon as the evening hymn of the priests was heard, the Necropolis was deserted, for the mourners and those who were visiting the graves were required by this time to return to their boats and to quit the City of the Dead. Crowds of men who had marched in the processions of the west bank hastened in disorder to the shore, driven on by the body of watchmen who took it in turns to do this duty and to protect the graves against robbers. The merchants closed their booths, the embalmers and workmen ended their day's work and retired to their houses, the priests returned to the temples, and the inns were filled with guests, who had come hither on long pilgrimages from a distance, and who preferred passing the night in the vicinity of the dead whom they had come to visit, to going across to the bustling noisy city farther shore.

The voices of the singers and of the wailing women were hushed, even the song of the sailors on the numberless ferry boats from the western shore to Thebes died away, its faint echo was now and then borne across on the evening air, and at last all was still.

A cloudless sky spread over the silent City of the Dead, now and then darkened for an instant by the swiftly passing shade of a bat returning to its home in a cave or cleft of the rock after flying the whole evening near the Nile to catch flies, to drink, and so prepare itself for the next day's sleep. From time to time black forms with long shadows glided over the still illuminated plain-the jackals, who at this hour frequented the shore to slake their thirst, and often fearlessly showed themselves in troops in the vicinity of the pens of geese and goats.

It was forbidden to hunt these robbers, as they were accounted sacred to the god Anubis, the tutelary of sepulchres; and indeed they did little mischief, for they found abundant food in the tombs.[2]

The remnants of the meat offerings from the altars were consumed by them; to the perfect satisfaction of the devotees, who, when they found that by the following day the meat had disappeared, believed that it had been accepted and taken away by the spirits of the underworld.

They also did the duty of trusty watchers, for they were a dangerous foe for any intruder who, under the shadow of the night, might attempt to violate a grave.

Thus-on that summer evening of the year 1352 B.C., when we invite the reader to accompany us to the Necropolis of Thebes-after the priests' hymn had died away, all was still in the City of the Dead.

The soldiers on guard were already returning from their first round when suddenly, on the north side of the Necropolis, a dog barked loudly; soon a second took up the cry, a third, a fourth. The captain of the watch called to his men to halt, and, as the cry of the dogs spread and grew louder every minute, commanded them to march towards the north.

The little troop had reached the high dyke which divided the west bank of the Nile from a branch canal, and looked from thence over the plain as far as the river and to the north of the Necropolis. Once more the word to "halt" was given, and as the guard perceived the glare of torches in the direction where the dogs were barking loudest, they hurried forward and came up with the author of the disturbance near the Pylon of the temple erected by Seti I., the deceased father of the reigning King Rameses II.[3]

The moon was up, and her pale light flooded the stately structure, while the walls glowed with the ruddy smoky light of the torches which flared in the hands of black attendants.

A man of sturdy build, in sumptuous dress, was knocking at the brass-covered temple door with the metal handle of a whip, so violently that the blows rang far and loud through the night. Near him stood a litter, and a chariot, to which were harnessed two fine horses. In the litter sat a young woman, and in the carriage, next to the driver, was the tall figure of a lady. Several men of the upper classes and many servants stood around the litter and the chariot. Few words were exchanged; the whole attention of the strangely lighted groups seemed concentrated on the temple-gate. The darkness concealed the features of individuals, but the mingled light of the moon and the torches was enough to reveal to the gate-keeper, who looked down on the party from a tower of the Pylon, that it was composed of persons of the highest rank; nay, perhaps of the royal family.

He called aloud to the one who knocked, and asked him what was his will.

He looked up, and in a voice so rough and imperious, that the lady in the litter shrank in horror as its tones suddenly violated the place of the dead, he cried out —"How long are we to wait here for you-you dirty hound? Come down and open the door and then ask questions. If the torch-light is not bright enough to show you who is waiting, I will score our name on your shoulders with my whip, and teach you how to receive princely visitors."

While the porter muttered an unintelligible answer and came down the steps within to open the door, the lady in the chariot turned to her impatient companion and said in a pleasant but yet decided voice, "You forget, Paaker, that you are back again in Egypt, and that here you have to deal not with the wild Schasu —[A Semitic race of robbers in the cast of Egypt.] —but with friendly priests of whom we have to solicit a favor. We have always had to lament your roughness, which seems to me very ill-suited to the unusual circumstances under which we approach this sanctuary."

Although these words were spoken in a tone rather of regret than of blame, they wounded the sensibilities of the person addressed; his wide nostrils began to twitch ominously, he clenched his right hand over the handle of his whip, and, while he seemed to be bowing humbly, he struck such a heavy blow on the bare leg of a slave who was standing near to him, an old Ethiopian, that he shuddered as if from sudden cold, though-knowing his lord only too well-he let no cry of pain escape him. Meanwhile the gate-keeper had opened the door, and with him a tall young priest stepped out into the open air to ask the will of the intruders.

Paaker would have seized the opportunity of speaking, but the lady in the chariot interposed and said:

"I am Bent-Anat, the daughter of the King, and this lady in the litter is Nefert, the wife of the noble Mena, the charioteer of my father. We were going in company with these gentlemen to the north-west valley of the Necropolis to see the new works there. You know the narrow pass in the rocks which leads up the gorge. On the way home I myself held the reins and I had the misfortune to drive over a girl who sat by the road with a basket full of flowers, and to hurt her-to hurt her very badly I am afraid. The wife of Mena with her own hands bound up the child, and then she carried her to her father's house-he is a paraschites —[One who opened the bodies of the dead to prepare them for being embalmed.] —Pinem is his name. I know not whether he is known to you."

"Thou hast been into his house, Princess?"

"Indeed, I was obliged, holy father," she replied, "I know of course that I have defiled myself by crossing the threshold of these people, but —"

"But," cried the wife of Mena, raising herself in her litter, "Bent-Anat can in a day be purified by thee or by her house-priest, while she can hardly-or perhaps never-restore the child whole and sound again to the unhappy father."

"Still, the den of a paraschites is above every thing unclean," said the chamberlain Penbesa, master of the ceremonies to the princess, interrupting the wife of Mena, "and I did not conceal my opinion when Bent-Anat announced her intention of visiting the accursed hole in person. I suggested," he continued, turning to the priest, "that she should let the girl be taken home, and send a royal present to the father."

"And the princess?" asked the priest.

"She acted, as she always does, on her own judgment," replied the master of the ceremonies.

"And that always hits on the right course," cried the wife of Mena.

"Would to God it were so!" said the princess in a subdued voice. Then she continued, addressing the priest, "Thou knowest the will of the Gods and the hearts of men, holy father, and I myself know that I give alms willingly and help the poor even when there is none to plead for them but their poverty. But after what has occurred here, and to these unhappy people, it is I who come as a suppliant."

"Thou?" said the chamberlain.

"I," answered the princess with decision. The priest who up to this moment had remained a silent witness of the scene raised his right hand as in blessing and spoke.

"Thou hast done well. The Hathors fashioned thy heart and the Lady of Truth guides it. Thou hast broken in on our night-prayers to request us to send a doctor to the injured girl?"[4]

"Thou hast said."

"I will ask the high-priest to send the best leech for outward wounds immediately to the child. But where is the house of the paraschites Pinem? I do not know it."

"Northwards from the terrace of Hatasu —[A great queen of the 18th dynasty and guardian of two Pharaohs] —close to —; but I will charge one of my attendants to conduct the leech. Besides, I want to know early in the morning how the child is doing. —Paaker."

The rough visitor, whom we already know, thus called upon, bowed to the earth, his arms hanging by his sides, and asked:

"What dost thou command?"

"I appoint you guide to the physician," said the princess. "It will be easy to the king's pioneer to find the little half-hidden house again —[5] besides, you share my guilt, for," she added, turning to the priest, "I confess that the misfortune happened because I would try with my horses to overtake Paaker's Syrian racers, which he declared to be swifter than the Egyptian horses. It was a mad race."

"And Amon be praised that it ended as it did," exclaimed the master of the ceremonies. "Packer's chariot lies dashed in pieces in the valley, and his best horse is badly hurt."

"He will see to him when he has taken the physician to the house of the paraschites," said the princess. "Dost thou know, Penbesa-thou anxious guardian of a thoughtless girl-that to-day for the first time I am glad that my father is at the war in distant Satiland?"—[Asia].

"He would not have welcomed us kindly!" said the master of the ceremonies, laughing.

"But the leech, the leech!" cried Bent-Anat. "Packer, it is settled then. You will conduct him, and bring us to-morrow morning news of the wounded girl."

Paaker bowed; the princess bowed her head; the priest and his companions, who meanwhile had come out of the temple and joined him, raised their hands in blessing, and the belated procession moved towards the Nile.

Paaker remained alone with his two slaves; the commission with which the princess had charged him greatly displeased him. So long as the moonlight enabled him to distinguish the litter of Mena's wife, he gazed after it; then he endeavored to recollect the position of the hut of the paraschites. The captain of the watch still stood with the guard at the gate of the temple.

"Do you know the dwelling of Pinem the paraschites?" asked Paaker.

"What do you want with him?"

"That is no concern of yours," retorted Paaker.

"Lout!" exclaimed the captain, "left face and forwards, my men."

"Halt!" cried Paaker in a rage. "I am the king's chief pioneer."

"Then you will all the more easily find the way back by which you came. March."

The words were followed by a peal of many-voiced laughter: the re-echoing insult so con-founded Paaker that he dropped his whip on the ground. The slave, whom a short time since he had struck with it, humbly picked it up and then followed his lord into the fore court of the temple. Both attributed the titter, which they still could hear without being able to detect its origin, to wandering spirits. But the mocking tones had been heard too by the old gate-keeper, and the laughers were better known to him than to the king's pioneer; he strode with heavy steps to the door of the temple through the black shadow of the pylon, and striking blindly before him called out—

"Ah! you good-for-nothing brood of Seth."[6]

"You gallows-birds and brood of hell—I am coming."

The giggling ceased; a few youthful figures appeared in the moonlight, the old man pursued them panting, and, after a short chase, a troop of youths fled back through the temple gate.

The door-keeper had succeeded in catching one miscreant, a boy of thirteen, and held him so tight by the ear that his pretty head seemed to have grown in a horizontal direction from his shoulders.

"I will take you before the school-master, you plague-of-locusts, you swarm of bats!" cried the old man out of breath. But the dozen of school-boys, who had availed themselves of the opportunity to break out of bounds, gathered coaxing round him, with words of repentance, though every eye sparkled with delight at the fun they had had, and of which no one could deprive them; and when the biggest of them took the old man's chin, and promised to give him the wine which his mother was to send him next day for the week's use, the porter let go his prisoner-who tried to rub the pain out of his burning ear-and cried out in harsher tones than before:

"You will pay me, will you, to let you off! Do you think I will let your tricks pass? You little know this old man. I will complain to the Gods, not to the school-master; and as for your wine, youngster, I will offer it as a libation, that heaven may forgive you."

CHAPTER II.

The temple where, in the fore-court, Paaker was waiting, and where the priest had disappeared to call the leech, was called the "House of Seti" — [It is still standing and known as the temple of Qurnah.] —and was one of the largest in the City of the Dead. Only that magnificent building of the time of the deposed royal race of the reigning king's grandfather-that temple which had been founded by Thotmes III., and whose gate-way Amenophis III. had adorned with immense colossal statues —[That which stands to the north is the famous musical statue, or Pillar of Memmon] —exceeded it in the extent of its plan; in every other respect it held the pre-eminence among the sanctuaries of the Necropolis. Rameses I. had founded it shortly after he succeeded in seizing the Egyptian throne; and his yet greater son Seti carried on the erection, in which the service of the dead for the Manes of the members of the new royal family was conducted, and the high festivals held in honor of the Gods of the under-world. Great sums had been expended for its establishment, for the maintenance of the priesthood of its sanctuary, and the support of the institutions connected with it. These were intended to be equal to the great original foundations of priestly learning at Heliopolis and Memphis; they were regulated on the same pattern, and with the object of raising the new royal residence of Upper Egypt, namely Thebes, above the capitals of Lower Egypt in regard to philosophical distinction.

One of the most important of these foundations was a very celebrated school of learning.[7]

First there was the high-school, in which priests, physicians, judges, mathematicians, astronomers, grammarians, and other learned men, not only had the benefit of instruction, but, subsequently, when they had won admission to the highest ranks of learning, and attained the dignity of "Scribes," were maintained at the cost of the king, and enabled to pursue their philosophical speculations and researches, in freedom from all care, and in the society of fellow-workers of equal birth and identical interests.

An extensive library, in which thousands of papyrus-rolls were preserved, and to which a manufactory of papyrus was attached, was at the disposal of the learned; and some of them were intrusted with the education of the younger disciples, who had been prepared in the elementary school, which was also dependent on the House-or university-of Seti. The lower school was open to every son of a free citizen, and was often frequented by several hundred boys, who also found night-quarters there. The parents were of course required either to pay for their maintenance, or to send due supplies of provisions for the keep of their children at school.

In a separate building lived the temple-boarders, a few sons of the noblest families, who were brought up by the priests at a great expense to their parents.

Seti I., the founder of this establishment, had had his own sons, not excepting Rameses, his successor, educated here.

The elementary schools were strictly ruled, and the rod played so large a part in them, that a pedagogue could record this saying: "The scholar's ears are at his back: when he is flogged then he hears."

Those youths who wished to pass up from the lower to the high-school had to undergo an examination. The student, when he had passed it, could choose a master from among the learned of the higher grades, who undertook to be his philosophical guide, and to whom he remained attached all his life through, as a client to his patron. He could obtain the degree of "Scribe" and qualify for public office by a second examination.

Near to these schools of learning there stood also a school of art, in which instruction was given to students who desired to devote themselves to architecture, sculpture, or painting; in these also the learner might choose his master.

Every teacher in these institutions belonged to the priesthood of the House of Seti. It consisted of more than eight hundred members, divided into five classes, and conducted by three so-called Prophets.

The first prophet was the high-priest of the House of Seti, and at the same time the superior of all the thousands of upper and under servants of the divinities which belonged to the City of the Dead of Thebes.

The temple of Seti proper was a massive structure of limestone. A row of Sphinxes led from the Nile to the surrounding wall, and to the first vast pro-pylon, which formed the entrance to a broad fore-court, enclosed on the two sides by colonnades, and beyond which stood a second gate-way. When he had passed through this door, which stood between two towers, in shape like truncated pyramids, the stranger came to a second court resembling the first, closed at the farther end by a noble row of pillars, which formed part of the central temple itself.

The innermost and last was dimly lighted by a few lamps.

Behind the temple of Seti stood large square structures of brick of the Nile mud, which however had a handsome and decorative effect, as the humble material of which they were constructed was plastered with lime, and that again was painted with colored pictures and hieroglyphic inscriptions.

The internal arrangement of all these houses was the same. In the midst was an open court, on to which opened the doors of the rooms of the priests and philosophers. On each side of the court was a shady, covered colonnade of wood, and in the midst a tank with ornamental plants. In the upper story were the apartments for the scholars, and instruction was usually given in the paved courtyard strewn with mats.

The most imposing was the house of the chief prophets; it was distinguished by its waving standards and stood about a hundred paces behind the temple of Seti, between a well kept grove and a clear lake-the sacred tank of the temple; but they only occupied it while fulfilling their office, while the splendid houses which they lived in with their wives and children, lay on the other side of the river, in Thebes proper.

The untimely visit to the temple could not remain unobserved by the colony of sages. Just as ants when a hand breaks in on their dwelling, hurry restlessly hither and thither, so an unwonted stir had agitated, not the school-boys only, but the teachers and the priests. They collected in groups near the outer walls, asking questions and hazarding guesses. A messenger from the king had arrived-the princess Bent-Anat had been attacked by the Kolchytes-and a wag among the school-boys who had got out, declared that Paaker, the king's pioneer, had been brought into the temple by force to be made to learn to write better. As the subject of the joke had formerly been a pupil of the House of Seti, and many delectable stories of his errors in penmanship still survived in the memory of the later generation of scholars, this information was received with joyful applause; and it seemed to have a glimmer of probability, in spite of the apparent contradiction that Paaker filled one of the highest offices near the king, when a grave young priest declared that he had seen the pioneer in the forecourt of the temple.

The lively discussion, the laughter and shouting of the boys at such an unwonted hour, was not unobserved by the chief priest.

This remarkable prelate, Ameni the son of Nebket, a scion of an old and noble family, was far more than merely the independent head of the temple-brotherhood, among whom he was prominent for his power and wisdom; for all the priesthood in the length and breadth of the land acknowledged his supremacy, asked his advice in difficult cases, and never resisted the decisions in spiritual matters which emanated from the House of Seti-that is to say, from Ameni. He was the embodiment of the priestly idea; and if at times he made heavy-nay extraordinary-demands on individual fraternities, they were submitted to, for it was known by experience that the indirect roads which he ordered them to follow all converged on one goal, namely the exaltation of the power and dignity of the hierarchy. The king appreciated this remarkable man, and had long endeavored to attach him to the court, as keeper of the royal seal; but Ameni was not to be induced to give up his apparently modest position; for he contemned all outward show and ostentatious titles; he ventured sometimes to oppose a decided resistance to the measures of the Pharaoh,[8] and was not minded to give up his unlimited control of the priests for the sake of a limited dominion over what seemed to him petty external concerns, in the service of a king who was only too independent and hard to influence.

He regularly arranged his mode and habits of life in an exceptional way.

Eight days out of ten he remained in the temple entrusted to his charge; two he devoted to his family, who lived on the other bank of the Nile; but he let no one, not even those nearest to him, know what portion of the ten days he gave up to recreation. He required only four hours of sleep. This he usually took in a dark room which no sound could reach, and in the middle of the day; never at night, when the coolness and quiet seemed to add to his powers of work, and when from time to time he could give himself up to the study of the starry heavens.

All the ceremonials that his position required of him, the cleansing, purification, shaving, and fasting he fulfilled with painful exactitude, and the outer bespoke the inner man.

Ameni was entering on his fiftieth year; his figure was tall, and had escaped altogether the stoutness to which at that age the Oriental is liable. The shape of his smoothly-shaven head was symmetrical and of a long oval; his forehead was neither broad nor high, but his profile was unusually delicate, and his face striking; his lips were thin and dry, and his large and piercing eyes, though neither fiery nor brilliant, and usually cast down to the ground under his thick eyebrows, were raised with a full, clear, dispassionate gaze when it was necessary to see and to examine.

The poet of the House of Seti, the young Pentaur, who knew these eyes, had celebrated them in song, and had likened them to a well-disciplined army which the general allows to rest before and after the battle, so that they may march in full strength to victory in the fight.

The refined deliberateness of his nature had in it much that was royal as well as priestly; it was partly intrinsic and born with him, partly the result of his own mental self-control. He had many enemies, but calumny seldom dared to attack the high character of Amemi.

The high-priest looked up in astonishment, as the disturbance in the court of the temple broke in on his studies.

The room in which he was sitting was spacious and cool; the lower part of the walls was lined with earthenware tiles, the upper half plastered and painted. But little was visible of the masterpieces of the artists of the establishment, for almost everywhere they were concealed by wooden closets and shelves, in which were papyrus-rolls and wax-tablets. A large table, a couch covered with a panther's skin, a footstool in front of it, and on it a crescent-shaped support for the head, made of ivory,[9] several seats, a stand with beakers and jugs, and another with flasks of all sizes, saucers, and boxes, composed the furniture of the room, which was lighted by three lamps, shaped like birds and filled with kiki oil. —[Castor oil, which was used in the lamps.]

Ameni wore a fine pleated robe of snow-white linen, which reached to his ankles, round his hips was a scarf adorned with fringes, which in front formed an apron, with broad, stiffened ends which fell to his knees; a wide belt of white and silver brocade confined the drapery of his robe. Round his throat and far down on his bare breast hung a necklace more than a span deep, composed of pearls and agates, and his upper arm was covered with broad gold bracelets. He rose from the ebony seat with lion's feet, on which he sat, and beckoned to a servant who squatted by one of the walls of the sitting-room. He rose and without any word of command from his master, he silently and carefully placed on the high-priest's bare head a long and thick curled wig,[10] and threw a leopard-skin, with its head and claws overlaid with gold-leaf, over his shoulders. A second servant held a metal mirror before Ameni, in which he cast a look as he settled the panther-skin and head-gear.

A third servant was handing him the crosier, the insignia of his dignity as a prelate, when a priest entered and announced the scribe Pentaur.

Ameni nodded, and the young priest who had talked with the princess Bent-Anat at the temple-gate came into the room.

Pentaur knelt and kissed the hand of the prelate, who gave him his blessing, and in a clear sweet voice, and rather formal and unfamiliar language-as if he were reading rather than speaking, said:

"Rise, my son; your visit will save me a walk at this untimely hour, since you can inform me of what disturbs the disciples in our temple. Speak."

"Little of consequence has occurred, holy father," replied Pentaur. "Nor would I have disturbed thee at this hour, but that a quite unnecessary tumult has been raised by the youths; and that the princess Bent-Anat appeared in person to request the aid of a physician. The unusual hour and the retinue that followed her —"

"Is the daughter of Pharaoh sick?" asked the prelate.

"No, father. She is well-even to wantonness, since-wishing to prove the swiftness of her horses-she ran over the daughter of the paraschites Pinem. Noble-hearted as she is, she herself carried the sorely-wounded girl to her house."

"She entered the dwelling of the unclean."

"Thou hast said."

"And she now asks to be purified?"

"I thought I might venture to absolve her, father, for the purest humanity led her to the act, which was no doubt a breach of discipline, but —"

"But," asked the high-priest in a grave voice and he raised his eyes which he had hitherto on the ground.

"But," said the young priest, and now his eyes fell, "which can surely be no crime. When Ra —[The Egyptian Sun-god.] —in his golden bark sails across the heavens, his light falls as freely and as bountifully on the hut of the despised poor as on the Palace of the Pharaohs; and shall the tender human heart withhold its pure light-which is benevolence-from the wretched, only because they are base?"

"It is the poet Pentaur that speaks," said the prelate, "and not the priest to whom the privilege was given to be initiated into the highest grade of the sages, and whom I call my brother and my equal. I have no advantage over you, young man, but perishable learning, which the past has won for you as much as for me-nothing but certain perceptions and experiences that offer nothing new, to the world, but teach us, indeed, that it is our part to maintain all that is ancient in living efficacy and practice. That which you promised a few weeks since, I many years ago vowed to the Gods; to guard knowledge as the exclusive possession of the initiated. Like fire, it serves those who know its uses to the noblest ends, but in the hands of children-and the people, the mob, can never ripen into manhood-it is a destroying brand, raging and unextinguishable, devouring all around it, and destroying all that has been built and beautified by the past. And how can we remain the Sages and continue to develop and absorb all learning within the shelter of our temples, not only without endangering the weak, but for their benefit? You know and have sworn to act after that knowledge. To bind the crowd to the faith and the institutions of the fathers is your duty-is the duty of every priest. Times have changed, my son; under the old kings the fire, of which I spoke figuratively to you-the poet-was enclosed in brazen walls which the people passed stupidly by. Now I see breaches in the old fortifications; the eyes of the uninitiated have been sharpened, and one tells the other what he fancies he has spied, though half-blinded, through the glowing rifts."

A slight emotion had given energy to the tones of the speaker, and while he held the poet spell-bound with his piercing glance he continued:

"We curse and expel any one of the initiated who enlarges these breaches; we punish even the friend who idly neglects to repair and close them with beaten brass!"

"My father!" cried Pentaur, raising his head in astonishment while the blood mounted to his cheeks. The high-priest went up to him and laid both hands on his shoulders.

They were of equal height and of equally symmetrical build; even the outline of their features was similar. Nevertheless no one would have taken them to be even distantly related; their countenances were so infinitely unlike in expression.

On the face of one were stamped a strong will and the power of firmly guiding his life and commanding himself; on the other, an amiable desire to overlook the faults and defects of the world, and to contemplate life as it painted itself in the transfiguring magic-mirror of his poet's soul. Frankness and enjoyment spoke in his sparkling eye, but the subtle smile on his lips when he was engaged in a discussion, or when his soul was stirred, betrayed that Pentaur, far from childlike carelessness, had fought many a severe mental battle, and had tasted the dark waters of doubt.

At this moment mingled feelings were struggling in his soul. He felt as if he must withstand the speaker; and yet the powerful presence of the other exercised so strong an influence over his mind, long trained to submission, that he was silent, and a pious thrill passed through him when Ameni's hands were laid on his shoulders.

"I blame you," said the high-priest, while he firmly held the young man, "nay, to my sorrow I must chastise you; and yet," he said, stepping back and taking his right hand, "I rejoice in the necessity, for I love you and honor you, as one whom the Unnameable has blessed with high gifts and destined to great things. Man leaves a weed to grow unheeded or roots it up but you are a noble tree, and I am like the gardener who has forgotten to provide it with a prop, and who is now thankful to have detected a bend that reminds him of his neglect. You look at me enquiringly, and I can see in your eyes that I seem to you a severe judge. Of what are you accused? You have suffered an institution of the past to be set aside. It does not matter-so the short-sighted and heedless think; but I say to you, you have doubly transgressed, because the wrong-doer was the king's daughter, whom all look up to, great and small, and whose actions may serve as an example to the people. On whom then must a breach of the ancient institutions lie with the darkest stain if not on the highest in rank? In a few days it will be said the paraschites are men even as we are, and the old law to avoid them as unclean is folly. And will the reflections of the people, think you, end there, when it is so easy for them to say that he who errs in one point may as well fail in all? In questions of faith, my son, nothing is insignificant. If we open one tower to the enemy he is master of the whole fortress. In these unsettled times our sacred lore is like a chariot on the declivity of a precipice, and under the wheels thereof a stone. A child takes away the stone, and the chariot rolls down into the abyss and is dashed to pieces. Imagine the princess to be that child, and the stone a loaf that she would fain give to feed a beggar. Would you then give it to her if your father and your mother and all that is dear and precious to you were in the chariot? Answer not! the princess will visit the paraschites again to-morrow. You must await her in the man's hut, and there inform her that she has transgressed and must crave to be purified by us. For this time you are excused from any further punishment.

"Heaven has bestowed on you a gifted soul. Strive for that which is wanting to you-the strength to subdue, to crush for One-and you know that One-all things else-even the misguiding voice of your heart, the treacherous voice of your judgment. —But stay! send leeches to the house of the paraschites, and desire them to treat the injured girl as though she were the queen herself. Who knows where the man dwells?"

"The princess," replied Pentaur, "has left Paaker, the king's pioneer, behind in the temple to conduct the leeches to the house of Pinem."

The grave high-priest smiled and said. "Paaker! to attend the daughter of a paraschites."

Pentaur half beseechingly and half in fun raised his eyes which he had kept cast down. "And Pentaur," he murmured, "the gardener's son! who is to refuse absolution to the king's daughter!"

"Pentaur, the minister of the Gods-Pentaur, the priest-has not to do with the daughter of the king, but with the transgressor of the sacred institutions," replied Ameni gravely. "Let Paaker know I wish to speak with him."

The poet bowed low and quitted the room, the high priest muttered to himself: "He is not yet what he should be, and speech is of no effect with him."

For a while he was silent, walking to and fro in meditation; then he said half aloud, "And the boy is destined to great things. What gifts of the Gods doth he lack? He has the faculty of learning-of thinking-of feeling-of winning all hearts, even mine. He keeps himself undefiled and separate —" suddenly the prelate paused and struck his hand on the back of a chair that stood by him. "I have it; he has not yet felt the fire of ambition. We will light it for his profit and our own."

CHAPTER III.

Pentauer hastened to execute the commands of the high-priest. He sent a servant to escort Paaker, who was waiting in the forecourt, into the presence of Ameni while he himself repaired to the physicians to impress on them the most watchful care of the unfortunate girl.

Many proficients in the healing arts were brought up in the house of Seti, but few used to remain after passing the examination for the degree of Scribe.[11]

The most gifted were sent to Heliopolis, where flourished, in the great "Hall of the Ancients," the most celebrated medical faculty of the whole country, whence they returned to Thebes, endowed with the highest honors in surgery, in ocular treatment, or in any other branch of their profession, and became physicians to the king or made a living by imparting their learning and by being called in to consult on serious cases.

Naturally most of the doctors lived on the east bank of the Nile, in Thebes proper, and even in private houses with their families; but each was attached to a priestly college.

Whoever required a physician sent for him, not to his own house, but to a temple. There a statement was required of the complaint from which the sick was suffering, and it was left to the principal medical staff of the sanctuary to select that of the healing art whose special knowledge appeared to him to be suited for the treatment of the case.

Like all priests, the physicians lived on the income which came to them from their landed property, from the gifts of the king, the contributions of the laity, and the share which was given them of the state-revenues; they expected no honorarium from their patients, but the restored sick seldom neglected making a present to the sanctuary whence a physician had come to them, and it was not unusual for the priestly leech to make the recovery of the sufferer conditional on certain gifts to be offered to the temple.

The medical knowledge of the Egyptians was, according to every indication, very considerable; but it was natural that physicians, who stood by the bed of sickness as "ordained servants of the Divinity," should not be satisfied with a rational treatment of the sufferer, and should rather think that they could not dispense with the mystical effects of prayers and vows.

Among the professors of medicine in the House of Seti there were men of the most different gifts and bent of mind; but Pentaur was not for a moment in doubt as to which should be entrusted with the treatment of the girl who had been run over, and for whom he felt the greatest sympathy.

The one he chose was the grandson of a celebrated leech, long since dead, whose name of Nebsecht he had inherited, and a beloved school-friend and old comrade of Pentaur.

This young man had from his earliest years shown high and hereditary talent for the profession to which he had devoted himself; he had selected surgery[12] for his special province at Heliopolis, and would certainly have attained the dignity of teacher there if an impediment in his speech had not debarred him from the viva voce recitation of formulas and prayers.

This circumstance, which was deeply lamented by his parents and tutors, was in fact, in the best opinions, an advantage to him; for it often happens that apparent superiority does us damage, and that from apparent defect springs the saving of our life.

Thus, while the companions of Nebsecht were employed in declaiming or in singing, he, thanks to his fettered tongue, could give himself up to his inherited and almost passionate love of observing organic life; and his teachers indulged up to a certain point his innate spirit of investigation, and derived benefit from his knowledge of the human and animal structures, and from the dexterity of his handling.

His deep aversion for the magical part of his profession would have brought him heavy punishment, nay very likely would have cost him expulsion from the craft, if he had ever given it expression in any form. But Nebsecht's was the silent and reserved nature of the learned man, who free from all desire of external recognition, finds a rich satisfaction in the delights of investigation; and he regarded every demand on him to give proof of his capacity, as a vexatious but unavoidable intrusion on his unassuming but laborious and fruitful investigations.

Nebsecht was dearer and nearer to Pentaur than any other of his associates.

He admired his learning and skill; and when the slightly-built surgeon, who was indefatigable in his wanderings, roved through the thickets by the Nile, the desert, or the mountain range, the young poet-priest accompanied him with pleasure and with great benefit to himself, for his companion observed a thousand things to which without him he would have remained for ever blind; and the objects around him, which were known to him only by their shapes, derived connection and significance from the explanations of the naturalist, whose intractable tongue moved freely when it was required to expound to his friend the peculiarities of organic beings whose development he had been the first to detect.

The poet was dear in the sight of Nebsecht, and he loved Pentaur, who possessed all the gifts he lacked; manly beauty, childlike lightness of heart, the frankest openness, artistic power, and the gift of expressing in word and song every emotion that stirred his soul. The poet was as a novice in the order in which Nebsecht was master, but quite capable of understanding its most difficult points; so it happened that Nebsecht attached greater value to his judgment than to that of his own colleagues, who showed themselves fettered by prejudice, while Pentaur's decision always was free and unbiassed.

The naturalist's room lay on the ground floor, and had no living-rooms above it, being under one of the granaries attached to the temple. It was as large as a public hall, and yet Pentaur, making his way towards the silent owner of the room, found it everywhere strewed with thick bundles of every variety of plant, with cages of palm-twigs piled four or five high, and a number of jars, large and small, covered with perforated paper. Within these prisons moved all sorts of living creatures, from the jerboa, the lizard of the Nile, and a light-colored species of owl, to numerous specimens of frogs, snakes, scorpions and beetles.

On the solitary table in the middle of the room, near to a writing-stand, lay bones of animals, with various sharp flints and bronze knives.

In a corner of this room lay a mat, on which stood a wooden head-prop, indicating that the naturalist was in the habit of sleeping on it.

When Pentaur's step was heard on the threshold of this strange abode, its owner pushed a rather large object under the table, threw a cover over it, and hid a sharp flint scalpel[13] fixed into a wooden handle, which he had just been using, in the folds of his robe-as a school-boy might hide some forbidden game from his master. Then he crossed his arms, to give himself the aspect of a man who is dreaming in harmless idleness.

The solitary lamp, which was fixed on a high stand near his chair, shed a scanty light, which, however, sufficed to show him his trusted friend Pentaur, who had disturbed Nebsecht in his prohibited occupations. Nebsecht nodded to him as he entered, and, when he had seen who it was, said:

"You need not have frightened me so!" Then he drew out from under the table the object he had hidden —a living rabbit fastened down to a board-and continued his interrupted observations on the body, which he had opened and fastened back with wooden pins while the heart continued to beat.

He took no further notice of Pentaur, who for some time silently watched the investigator; then he laid his hand on his shoulder and said:

"Lock your door more carefully, when you are busy with forbidden things."

"They took-they took away the bar of the door lately," stammered the naturalist, "when they caught me dissecting the hand of the forger Ptahmes." —[The law sentenced forgers to lose a hand.]

"The mummy of the poor man will find its right hand wanting," answered the poet.

"He will not want it out there."

"Did you bury the least bit of an image in his grave?"[14]

"Nonsense."

"You go very far, Nebsecht, and are not foreseeing, 'He who needlessly hurts an innocent animal shall be served in the same way by the spirits of the netherworld,' says the law; but I see what you will say. You hold it lawful to put a beast to pain, when you can thereby increase that knowledge by which you alleviate the sufferings of man, and enrich —"

"And do not you?"

A gentle smile passed over Pentaur's face; leaned over the animal and said:

"How curious! the little beast still lives and breathes; a man would have long been dead under such treatment. His organism is perhaps of a more precious, subtle, and so more fragile nature?"

Nebsecht shrugged his shoulders.

"Perhaps!" he said.

"I thought you must know."

"I —how should I?" asked the leech. "I have told you-they would not even let me try to find out how the hand of a forger moves."

"Consider, the scripture tells us the passage of the soul depends on the preservation of the body."

Nebsecht looked up with his cunning little eyes and shrugging his shoulders, said:

"Then no doubt it is so: however these things do not concern me. Do what you like with the souls of men; I seek to know something of their bodies, and patch them when they are damaged as well as may be."

"Nay-Toth be praised, at least you need not deny that you are master in that art."[15]

"Who is master," asked Nebsecht, "excepting God? I can do nothing, nothing at all, and guide my instruments with hardly more certainty than a sculptor condemned to work in the dark."

"Something like the blind Resu then," said Pentaur smiling, "who understood painting better than all the painters who could see."

"In my operations there is a 'better' and a 'worse;'" said Nebsecht, "but there is nothing 'good.'"

"Then we must be satisfied with the 'better,' and I have come to claim it," said Pentaur.

"Are you ill?"

"Isis be praised, I feel so well that I could uproot a palm-tree, but I would ask you to visit a sick girl. The princess Bent-Anat —"

"The royal family has its own physicians."

"Let me speak! the princess Bent-Anat has run over a young girl, and the poor child is seriously hurt."

"Indeed," said the student reflectively. "Is she over there in the city, or here in the Necropolis?"

"Here. She is in fact the daughter of a paraschites."

"Of a paraschites?" exclaimed Nebsecht, once more slipping the rabbit under the table, "then I will go."

"You curious fellow. I believe you expect to find something strange among the unclean folk."

"That is my affair; but I will go. What is the man's name?"

"Pinem."

"There will be nothing to be done with him," muttered the student, "however-who knows?"

With these words he rose, and opening a tightly closed flask he dropped some strychnine on the nose and in the mouth of the rabbit, which immediately ceased to breathe. Then he laid it in a box and said, "I am ready."

"But you cannot go out of doors in this stained dress."

The physician nodded assent, and took from a chest a clean robe, which he was about to throw on over the other! but Pentaur hindered him. "First take off your working dress," he said laughing. "I will help you. But, by Besa, you have as many coats as an onion."[16]

Pentaur was known as a mighty laugher among his companions, and his loud voice rung in the quiet room, when he discovered that his friend was about to put a third clean robe over two dirty ones, and wear no less than three dresses at once.

Nebsecht laughed too, and said, "Now I know why my clothes were so heavy, and felt so intolerably hot at noon. While I get rid of my superfluous clothing, will you go and ask the high-priest if I have leave to quit the temple."

"He commissioned me to send a leech to the paraschites, and added that the girl was to be treated like a queen."

"Ameni? and did he know that we have to do with a paraschites?"

"Certainly."

"Then I shall begin to believe that broken limbs may be set with vows-aye, vows! You know I cannot go alone to the sick, because my leather tongue is unable to recite the sentences or to wring rich offerings for the temple from the dying. Go, while I undress, to the prophet Gagabu and beg him to send the pastophorus Teta, who usually accompanies me."

"I would seek a young assistant rather than that blind old man."

"Not at all. I should be glad if he would stay at home, and only let his tongue creep after me like an eel or a slug. Head and heart have nothing to do with his wordy operations, and they go on like an ox treading out corn."[17]

"It is true," said Pentaur; "just lately I saw the old man singing out his litanies by a sick-bed, and all the time quietly counting the dates, of which they had given him a whole sack-full."

"He will be unwilling to go to the paraschites, who is poor, and he would sooner seize the whole brood of scorpions yonder than take a piece of bread from the hand of the unclean. Tell him to come and fetch me, and drink some wine. There stands three days' allowance; in this hot weather it dims my sight."

"Does the paraschites live to the north or south of the Necropolis?"

"I think to the north. Paaker, the king's pioneer, will show you the way."

"He!" exclaimed the student, laughing. "What day in the calendar is this, then?[18]

The child of a paraschites is to be tended like a princess, and a leech have a noble to guide him, like the Pharaoh himself! I ought to have kept on my three robes!"

"The night is warm," said Pentaur.

"But Paaker has strange ways with him. Only the day before yesterday I was called to a poor boy whose collar bone he had simply smashed with his stick. If I had been the princess's horse I would rather have trodden him down than a poor little girl."

"So would I," said Pentaur laughing, and left the room to request The second prophet Gagabu, who was also the head of the medical staff of the House of Seti, to send the blind pastophorus[19] Teta, with his friend as singer of the litany.

CHAPTER IV.

Pentaur knew where to seek Gagabu, for he himself had been invited to the banquet which the prophet had prepared in honor of two sages who had lately come to the House of Seti from the university of Chennu.[20]

In an open court, surrounded by gaily-painted wooden pillars, and lighted by many lamps, sat the feasting priests in two long rows on comfortable armchairs. Before each stood a little table, and servants were occupied in supplying them with the dishes and drinks, which were laid out on a splendid table in the middle of the court. Joints of gazelle,[21] roast geese and ducks, meat pasties, artichokes, asparagus and other vegetables, and various cakes and sweetmeats were carried to the guests, and their beakers well-filled with the choice wines of which there was never any lack in the lofts of the House of Seti.[22]

In the spaces between the guests stood servants with metal bowls, in which they might wash their hands, and towels of fine linen.

When their hunger was appeased, the wine flowed more freely, and each guest was decked with sweetly-smelling flowers, whose odor was supposed to add to the vivacity of the conversation.

Many of the sharers in this feast wore long, snowwhite garments, and were of the class of the Initiated into the mysteries of the faith, as well as chiefs of the different orders of priests of the House of Seti.

The second prophet, Gagabu, who was to-day charged with the conduct of the feast by Ameni-who on such occasions only showed himself for a few minutes-was a short, stout man with a bald and almost spherical head. His features were those of a man of advancing years, but well-formed, and his smoothly-shaven, plump cheeks were well-rounded. His grey eyes looked out cheerfully and observantly, but had a vivid sparkle when he was excited and began to twitch his thick, sensual mouth.

Close by him stood the vacant, highly-ornamented chair of the high-priest, and next to him sat the priests arrived from Chennu, two tall, dark-colored old men. The remainder of the company was arranged in the order of precedency, which they held in the priests' colleges, and which bore no relation to their respective ages.

But strictly as the guests were divided with reference to their rank, they mixed without distinction in the conversation.

"We know how to value our call to Thebes," said the elder of the strangers from Chennu, Tuauf, whose essays were frequently used in the schools —[Some of them are still in existence] —"for while, on one hand, it brings us into the neighborhood of the Pharaoh, where life, happiness, and safety flourish, on the other it procures us the honor of counting ourselves among your number; for, though the university of Chennu in former times was so happy as to bring up many great men, whom she could call her own, she can no longer compare with the House of Seti. Even Heliopolis and Memphis are behind you; and if I, my humble self, nevertheless venture boldly among you, it is because I ascribe your success as much to the active influence of the Divinity in your temple, which may promote my acquirements and achievements, as to your great gifts and your industry, in which I will not be behind you. I have already seen your high-priest Ameni-what a man! And who does not know thy name, Gagabu, or thine, Meriapu?"

"And which of you," asked the other new-comer, "may we greet as the author of the most beautiful hymn to Amon, which was ever sung in the land of the Sycamore? Which of you is Pentaur?"

"The empty chair yonder," answered Gagabu, pointing to a seat at the lower end of the table, "is his. He is the youngest of us all, but a great future awaits him."

"And his songs," added the elder of the strangers. "Without doubt," replied the chief of the haruspices —[One of the orders of priests in the Egyptian hierarchy] —an old man with a large grey curly head, that seemed too heavy for his thin neck, which stretched forward-perhaps from the habit of constantly watching for signs-while his prominent eyes glowed with a fanatical gleam. "Without doubt the Gods have granted great gifts to our young friend, but it remains to be proved how he will use them. I perceive a certain freedom of thought in the youth, which pains me deeply. Although in his poems his flexible style certainly follows the prescribed forms, his ideas transcend all tradition; and even in the hymns intended for the ears of the people I find turns of thought, which might well be called treason to the mysteries which only a few months ago he swore to keep secret. For instance he says-and we sing-and the laity hear —

> "One only art Thou, Thou Creator of beings;
> And Thou only makest all that is created.

And again —

> He is one only, Alone, without equal;
> Dwelling alone in the holiest of holies."[23]

Such passages as these ought not to be sung in public, at least in times like ours, when new ideas come in upon us from abroad, like the swarms of locusts from the East."

"Spoken to my very soul!" cried the treasurer of the temple, "Ameni initiated this boy too early into the mysteries."

"In my opinion, and I am his teacher," said Gagabu, "our brotherhood may be proud of a member who adds so brilliantly to the fame of our temple. The people hear the hymns without looking closely at the meaning of the words. I never saw the congregation more devout, than when the beautiful and deeply-felt song of praise was sung at the feast of the stairs."[24]

"Pentaur was always thy favorite," said the former speaker. "Thou wouldst not permit in any one else many things that are allowed to him. His hymns are nevertheless to me and to many others a dangerous performance; and canst thou dispute the fact that we have grounds for grave anxiety, and that things happen and circumstances grow up around us which hinder us, and at last may perhaps crush us, if we do not, while there is yet time, inflexibly oppose them?"

"Thou bringest sand to the desert, and sugar to sprinkle over honey," exclaimed Gagabu, and his lips began to twitch. "Nothing is now as it ought to be, and there will be a hard battle to fight; not with the sword, but with this-and this." And the impatient man touched his forehead and his lips. "And who is there more competent than my disciple? There is the champion of our cause, a second cap of Hor, that overthrew the evil one with winged sunbeams, and you come and would clip his wings and blunt his claws! Alas, alas, my lords! will you never understand that a lion roars louder than a cat, and the sun shines brighter than an oil-lamp? Let Pentuar alone, I say; or you will do as the man did, who, for fear of the toothache, had his sound teeth drawn. Alas, alas, in the years to come we shall have to bite deep into the flesh, till the blood flows, if we wish to escape being eaten up ourselves!"

"The enemy is not unknown to us also," said the elder priest from Chennu, "although we, on the remote southern frontier of the kingdom, have escaped many evils that in the north have eaten into our body like a cancer. Here foreigners are now hardly looked upon at all as unclean and devilish." —["Typhonisch," belonging to Typhon or Seth. —Translator.]

"Hardly?" exclaimed the chief of the haruspices; "they are invited, caressed, and honored. Like dust, when the simoon blows through the chinks of a wooden house, they crowd into the houses and temples, taint our manners and language;[25] nay, on the throne of the successors of Ra sits a descendant —"

"Presumptuous man!" cried the voice of the high-priest, who at this instant entered the hall, "Hold your tongue, and be not so bold as to wag it against him who is our king, and wields the sceptre in this kingdom as the Vicar of Ra."

The speaker bowed and was silent, then he and all the company rose to greet Ameni, who bowed to them all with polite dignity, took his seat, and turning to Gagabu asked him carelessly:

"I find you all in most unpriestly excitement; what has disturbed your equanimity?"

"We were discussing the overwhelming influx of foreigners into Egypt, and the necessity of opposing some resistance to them."

"You will find me one of the foremost in the attempt," replied Ameni. "We have endured much already, and news has arrived from the north, which grieves me deeply."

"Have our troops sustained a defeat?"

"They continue to be victorious, but thousands of our countrymen have fallen victims in the fight or on the march. Rameses demands fresh reinforcements. The pioneer, Paaker, has brought me a letter from our brethren who accompany the king, and delivered a document from him to the Regent, which contains the order to send to him fifty thousand fighting men: and as the whole of the soldier-caste and all the auxiliaries are already under arms, the bondmen of the temple, who till our acres, are to be levied, and sent into Asia."

A murmur of disapproval arose at these words. The chief of the haruspices stamped his foot, and Gagabu asked:

"What do you mean to do?"

"To prepare to obey the commands of the king," answered Ameni, "and to call the heads of the temples of the city of Anion here without delay to hold a council. Each must first in his holy of holies seek good counsel of the Celestials. When we have come to a conclusion, we must next win the Viceroy over to our side. Who yesterday assisted at his prayers?"

"It was my turn," said the chief of the haruspices.

"Follow me to my abode, when the meal is over." commanded Ameni. "But why is our poet missing from our circle?"

At this moment Pentaur came into the hall, and while he bowed easily and with dignity to the company and low before Ameni, he prayed him to grant that the pastophorus Teta should accompany the leech Nebsecht to visit the daughter of the paraschites.

Ameni nodded consent and exclaimed: "They must make haste. Paaker waits for them at the great gate, and will accompany them in my chariot."

As soon as Pentaur had left the party of feasters, the old priest from Chennu exclaimed, as he turned to Ameni:

"Indeed, holy father, just such a one and no other had I pictured your poet. He is like the Sun-god, and his demeanor is that of a prince. He is no doubt of noble birth."

"His father is a homely gardener," said the highpriest, "who indeed tills the land apportioned to him with industry and prudence, but is of humble birth and rough exterior. He sent Pentaur to the school at an early age, and we have brought up the wonderfully gifted boy to be what he now is."

"What office does he fill here in the temple?"

"He instructs the elder pupils of the high-school in grammar and eloquence; he is also an excellent observer of the starry heavens, and a most skilled interpreter of dreams," replied Gagabu. "But here he is again. To whom is Paaker conducting our stammering physician and his assistant?"

"To the daughter of the paraschites, who has been run over," answered Pentaur. "But what a rough fellow this pioneer is. His voice hurts my ears, and he spoke to our leeches as if they had been his slaves."

"He was vexed with the commission the princess had devolved on him," said the high-priest benevolently, "and his unamiable disposition is hardly mitigated by his real piety."

"And yet," said an old priest, "his brother, who left us some years ago, and who had chosen me for his guide and teacher, was a particularly loveable and docile youth."

"And his father," said Ameni, "was one of the most superior energetic, and withal subtle-minded of men."

"Then he has derived his bad peculiarities from his mother?"

"By no means. She is a timid, amiable, soft-hearted woman."

"But must the child always resemble its parents?" asked Pentaur. "Among the sons of the sacred bull, sometimes not one bears the distinguishing mark of his father."

"And if Paaker's father were indeed an Apis," Gagabu laughing, "according to your view the pioneer himself belongs, alas! to the peasant's stable."

Pentaur did not contradict him, but said with a smile:

"Since he left the school bench, where his school-fellows called him the wild ass on account of his unruliness, he has remained always the same. He was stronger than most of them, and yet they knew no greater pleasure than putting him in a rage."

"Children are so cruel!" said Ameni. "They judge only by appearances, and never enquire into the causes of them. The deficient are as guilty in their eyes as the idle, and Paaker could put forward small claims to their indulgence. I encourage freedom and merriment," he continued turning to the priests from Cheraw, "among our disciples, for in fettering the fresh enjoyment of youth we lame our best assistant. The excrescences on the natural growth of boys cannot be more surely or painlessly extirpated than in their wild games. The school-boy is the school-boy's best tutor."

"But Paaker," said the priest Meriapu, "was not improved by the provocations of his companions. Constant contests with them increased that roughness which now makes him the terror of his subordinates and alienates all affection."

"He is the most unhappy of all the many youths, who were intrusted to my care," said Ameni, "and I believe I know why-he never had a childlike disposition, even when in years he was still a child, and the Gods had denied him the heavenly gift of good humor. Youth should be modest, and he was assertive from his childhood. He took the sport of his companions for earnest, and his father, who was unwise only as a tutor, encouraged him to resistance instead of to forbearance, in the idea that he thus would be steeled to the hard life of a Mohar."[26]

"I have often heard the deeds of the Mohar spoken of," said the old priest from Chennu, "yet I do not exactly know what his office requires of him."

"He has to wander among the ignorant and insolent people of hostile provinces, and to inform himself of the kind and number of the population, to investigate the direction of the mountains, valleys, and rivers, to set forth his observations, and to deliver them to the house of war,[27] so that the march of the troops may be guided by them."

"The Mohar then must be equally skilled as a warrior and as a Scribe."

"As thou sayest; and Paaker's father was not a hero only, but at the same time a writer, whose close and clear information depicted the country through which he had travelled as plainly as if it were seen from a mountain height. He was the first who took the title of Mohar. The king held him in such high esteem, that he was inferior to no one but the king himself, and the minister of the house of war."

"Was he of noble race?"

"Of one of the oldest and noblest in the country. His father was the noble warrior Assa," answered the haruspex, "and he therefore, after he himself had attained the highest consideration and vast wealth, escorted home the niece of the King Hor-em-lieb, who would have had a claim to the throne, as well as the Regent, if the grandfather of the present Rameses had not seized it from the old family by violence."

"Be careful of your words," said Ameni, interrupting the rash old man. "Rameses I. was and is the grandfather of our sovereign, and in the king's veins, from his mother's side, flows the blood of the legitimate descendants of the Sun-god."

"But fuller and purer in those of the Regent the haruspex ventured to retort.

"But Rameses wears the crown," cried Ameni, "and will continue to wear it so long as it pleases the Gods. Reflect-your hairs are grey, and seditious words are like sparks, which are borne by the wind, but which, if they fall, may set our home in a blaze. Continue your feasting, my lords; but I would request you to speak no more this evening of the king and his new decree. You, Pentaur, fulfil my orders to-morrow morning with energy and prudence."

The high-priest bowed and left the feast.

As soon as the door was shut behind him, the old priest from Chennu spoke.

"What we have learned concerning the pioneer of the king, a man who holds so high an office, surprises me. Does he distinguish himself by a special acuteness?"

"He was a steady learner, but of moderate ability."

"Is the rank of Mohar then as high as that of a prince of the empire?"

"By no means."

"How then is it —?"

"It is, as it is," interrupted Gagabu. "The son of the vine-dresser has his mouth full of grapes, and the child of the door-keeper opens the lock with words."

"Never mind," said an old priest who had hitherto kept silence. "Paaker earned for himself the post of Mohar, and possesses many praiseworthy qualities. He is indefatigable and faithful, quails before no danger, and has always been earnestly devout from his boyhood. When the other scholars carried their pocket-money to the fruit-sellers and confectioners at the temple-gates, he would buy geese, and, when his mother sent him a handsome sum, young gazelles, to offer to the Gods on the altars. No noble in the land owns a greater treasure of charms and images of the Gods than he. To the present time he is the most pious of men, and the offerings for the dead, which he brings in the name of his late father, may be said to be positively kingly."

"We owe him gratitude for these gifts," said the treasurer, "and the high honor he pays his father, even after his death, is exceptional and far-famed."

"He emulates him in every respect," sneered Gagabu; "and though he does not resemble him in any feature, grows more and more like him. But unfortunately, it is as the goose resembles the swan, or the owl resembles the eagle. For his father's noble pride he has overbearing haughtiness; for kindly severity, rude harshness; for dignity, conceit; for perseverance, obstinacy. Devout he is, and we profit by his gifts. The treasurer may rejoice over them, and the dates off a crooked tree taste as well as those off a straight one. But if I were the Divinity I should prize them no higher than a hoopoe's crest; for He, who sees into the heart of the giver-alas! what does he see! Storms and darkness are of the dominion of Seth, and in there-in there —" and the old man struck his broad breast "all is wrath and tumult, and there is not a gleam of the calm blue heaven of Ra, that shines soft and pure in the soul of the pious; no, not a spot as large as this wheaten-cake."

"Hast thou then sounded to the depths of his soul?" asked the haruspex.

"As this beaker!" exclaimed Gagabu, and he touched the rim of an empty drinking-vessel. "For fifteen years without ceasing. The man has been of service to us, is so still, and will continue to be. Our leeches extract salves from bitter gall and deadly poisons; and folks like these —"

"Hatred speaks in thee," said the haruspex, interrupting the indignant old man.

"Hatred!" he retorted, and his lips quivered. "Hatred?" and he struck his breast with his clenched hand. "It is true, it is no stranger to this old heart. But open thine ears, O haruspex, and all you others too shall hear. I recognize two sorts of hatred. The one is between man and man; that I have gagged, smothered, killed, annihilated-with what efforts, the Gods know. In past years I have certainly tasted its bitterness, and served it like a wasp, which, though it knows that in stinging it must die, yet uses its sting. But now I am old in years, that is in knowledge, and I know that of all the powerful impulses which stir our hearts, one only comes solely from Seth, one only belongs wholly to the Evil one and that is hatred to man and man. Covetousness may lead to industry, sensual appetites may beget noble fruit, but hatred is a devastator, and in the soul that it occupies all that is noble grows not upwards and towards the light, but downwards to the earth and to darkness. Everything may be forgiven by the Gods, save only hatred between man and man. But there is another sort of hatred that is pleasing to the Gods, and which you must cherish if you would not miss their presence in your souls; that is, hatred for all that hinders the growth of light and goodness and purity-the hatred of Horus for Seth. The Gods would punish me if I hated Paaker whose father was dear to me; but the spirits of darkness would possess the old heart in my breast if it were devoid of horror for the covetous and sordid devotee, who would fain buy earthly joys of the Gods with gifts of beasts and wine, as men exchange an ass for a robe, in whose soul seethe dark promptings. Paaker's gifts can no more be pleasing to the Celestials than a cask of attar of roses would please thee, haruspex, in which scorpions, centipedes, and venomous snakes were swimming. I have long led this man's prayers, and never have I heard him crave for noble gifts, but a thousand times for the injury of the men he hates."

"In the holiest prayers that come down to us from the past," said the haruspex, "the Gods are entreated to throw our enemies under our feet; and, besides, I have often heard Paaker pray fervently for the bliss of his parents."

"You are a priest and one of the initiated," cried Gagabu, "and you know not-or will not seem to know-that by the enemies for whose overthrow we pray, are meant only the demons of darkness and the outlandish peoples by whom Egypt is endangered! Paaker prayed for his parents? Ay, and so will he for his children, for they will be his future as his fore fathers are his past. If he had a wife, his offerings would be for her too, for she would be the half of his own present."

"In spite of all this," said the haruspex Septah, "you are too hard in your judgment of Paaker, for although he was born under a lucky sign, the Hathors denied him all that makes youth happy. The enemy for whose destruction he prays is Mena, the king's charioteer, and, indeed, he must have been of superhuman magnanimity or of unmanly feebleness, if he could have wished well to the man who robbed him of the beautiful wife who was destined for him."

"How could that happen?" asked the priest from Chennu. "A betrothal is sacred."[28]

"Paaker," replied Septah, "was attached with all the strength of his ungoverned but passionate and faithful heart to his cousin Nefert, the sweetest maid in Thebes, the daughter of Katuti, his mother's sister; and she was promised to him to wife. Then his father, whom he accompanied on his marches, was mortally wounded in Syria. The king stood by his death-bed, and granting his last request, invested his son with his rank and office: Paaker brought the mummy of his father home to Thebes, gave him princely interment, and then before the time of mourning was over, hastened back to Syria, where, while the king returned to Egypt, it was his duty to reconnoitre the new possessions. At last he could quit the scene of war with the hope of marrying Nefert. He rode his horse to death the sooner to reach the goal of his desires; but when he reached Tanis, the city of Rameses, the news met him that his affianced cousin had been given to another, the handsomest and bravest man in Thebes-the noble Mena. The more precious a thing is that we hope to possess, the more we are justified in complaining of him who contests our claim, and can win it from us. Paaker's blood must have been as cold as a frog's if he could have forgiven Mena instead of hating him, and the cattle he has offered to the Gods to bring down their wrath on the head of the traitor may be counted by hundreds."

"And if you accept them, knowing why they are offered, you do unwisely and wrongly," exclaimed Gagabu. "If I were a layman, I would take good care not to worship a Divinity who condescends to serve the foulest human fiends for a reward. But the omniscient Spirit, that rules the world in accordance with eternal laws, knows nothing of these sacrifices, which only tickle the nostrils of the evil one. The treasurer rejoices when a beautiful spotless heifer is driven in among our herds. But Seth rubs his red hands[29] with delight that he accepts it. My friends, I have heard the vows which Paaker has poured out over our pure altars, like hogwash that men set before swine. Pestilence and boils has he called down on Mena, and barrenness and heartache on the poor sweet woman; and I really cannot blame her for preferring a bat-tle-horse to a hippopotamus —a Mena to a Paaker."

"Yet the Immortals must have thought his remonstrances less unjustifiable, and have stricter views as to the inviolable nature of a betrothal than you," said the treasurer, "for Nefert, during four years of married life, has passed only a few weeks with her wandering husband, and remains childless. It is hard to me to understand how you, Gagabu, who so often absolve where we condemn, can so relentlessly judge so great a benefactor to our temple."

"And I fail to comprehend," exclaimed the old man, "how you-you who so willingly condemn, can so weakly excuse this-this-call him what you will."

"He is indispensable to us at this time," said the haruspex.

"Granted," said Gagabu, lowering his tone. "And I think still to make use of him, as the high-priest has done in past years with the best effect when dangers have threatened us; and a dirty road serves when it makes for the goal. The Gods themselves often permit safety to come from what is evil, but shall we therefore call evil good-or say the hideous is beautiful? Make use of the king's pioneer as you will, but do not, because you are indebted to him for gifts, neglect to judge him according to his imaginings and deeds if you would deserve your title of the Initiated and the Enlightened. Let him bring his cattle into our temple and pour his gold into our treasury, but do not defile your souls with the thought that the offerings of such a heart and such a hand are pleasing to the Divinity. Above all," and the voice of the old man had a heart-felt impressiveness, "Above all, do not flatter the erring man-and this is what you do, with the idea that he is walking in the right way; for your, for our first duty, O my friends, is always this-to guide the souls of those who trust in us to goodness and truth."

"Oh, my master!" cried Pentaur, "how tender is thy severity."

"I have shown the hideous sores of this man's soul," said the old man, as he rose to quit the hall. "Your praise will aggravate them, your blame will tend to heal them. Nay, if you are not content to do your duty, old Gagabu will come some day with his knife, and will throw the sick man down and cut out the canker."

During this speech the haruspex had frequently shrugged his shoulders. Now he said, turning to the priests from Chennu —

"Gagabu is a foolish, hot-headed old man, and you have heard from his lips just such a sermon as the young scribes keep by them when they enter on the duties of the care of souls. His sentiments are excellent, but he easily overlooks small things for the sake of great ones. Ameni would tell you that ten souls, no, nor a hundred, do not matter when the safety of the whole is in question."

CHAPTER V.

The night during which the Princess Bent-Anat and her followers had knocked at the gate of the House of Seti was past.

The fruitful freshness of the dawn gave way to the heat, which began to pour down from the deep blue cloudless vault of heaven. The eye could no longer gaze at the mighty globe of light whose rays pierced the fine white dust which hung over the declivity of the hills that enclosed the city of the dead on the west. The limestone rocks showed with blinding clearness, the atmosphere quivered as if heated over a flame; each minute the shadows grew shorter and their outlines sharper.

All the beasts which we saw peopling the Necropolis in the evening had now withdrawn into their lurking places; only man defied the heat of the summer day. Undisturbed he accomplished his daily work, and only laid his tools aside for a moment, with a sigh, when a cooling breath blew across the overflowing stream and fanned his brow.

The harbor or clock where those landed who crossed from eastern Thebes was crowded with barks and boats waiting to return.

The crews of rowers and steersmen who were attached to priestly brotherhoods or noble houses, were enjoying a rest till the parties they had brought across the Nile drew towards them again in long processions.

Under a wide-spreading sycamore a vendor of eatables, spirituous drinks, and acids for cooling the water, had set up his stall, and close to him, a crowd of boatmen, and drivers shouted and disputed as they passed the time in eager games at morra.[30]

Many sailors lay on the decks of the vessels, others on the shore; here in the thin shade of a palm tree, there in the full blaze of the sun, from those burning rays they protected themselves by spreading the cotton cloths, which served them for cloaks, over their faces.

Between the sleepers passed bondmen and slaves, brown and black, in long files one behind the other, bending under the weight of heavy burdens, which had to be conveyed to their destination at the temples for sacrifice, or to the dealers in various wares. Builders dragged blocks of stone, which had come from the quarries of Chennu and Suan,[31] on sledges to the site of a new temple; laborers poured water under the runners, that the heavily loaded and dried wood should not take fire.

All these working men were driven with sticks by their overseers, and sang at their labor; but the voices of the leaders sounded muffled and hoarse, though, when after their frugal meal they enjoyed an hour of repose, they might be heard loud enough. Their parched throats refused to sing in the noontide of their labor.

Thick clouds of gnats followed these tormented gangs, who with dull and spirit-broken endurance suffered alike the stings of the insects and the blows of their driver. The gnats pursued them to the very heart of the City of the dead, where they joined themselves to the flies and wasps, which swarmed in countless crowds around the slaughter houses, cooks' shops, stalls of fried fish, and booths of meat, vegetable, honey, cakes and drinks, which were doing a brisk business in spite of the noontide heat and the oppressive atmosphere heated and filled with a mixture of odors.

The nearer one got to the Libyan frontier, the quieter it became, and the silence of death reigned in the broad north-west valley, where in the southern slope the father of the reigning king had caused his tomb to be hewn, and where the stone-mason of the Pharaoh had prepared a rock tomb for him.

A newly made road led into this rocky gorge, whose steep yellow and brown walls seemed scorched by the sun in many blackened spots, and looked like a ghostly array of shades that had risen from the tombs in the night and remained there.

At the entrance of this valley some blocks of stone formed a sort of doorway, and through this, indifferent to the heat of day, a small but brilliant troop of the men was passing.

Four slender youths as staff bearers led the procession, each clothed only with an apron and a flowing head-cloth of gold brocade; the mid-day sun played on their smooth, moist, red-brown skins, and their supple naked feet hardly stirred the stones on the road.

Behind them followed an elegant, two-wheeled chariot, with two prancing brown horses bearing tufts of red and blue feathers on their noble heads, and seeming by the bearing of their arched necks and flowing tails to express their pride in the gorgeous housings, richly embroidered in silver, purple, and blue and golden ornaments, which they wore–and even more in their beautiful, royal charioteer, Bent-Anat, the daughter of Rameses, at whose lightest word they pricked their ears, and whose little hand guided them with a scarcely perceptible touch.

Two young men dressed like the other runners followed the chariot, and kept the rays of the sun off the face of their mistress with large fans of snow-white ostrich feathers fastened to long wands.

By the side of Bent-Anat, so long as the road was wide enough to allow of it, was carried Nefert, the wife of Mena, in her gilt litter, borne by eight tawny bearers, who, running with a swift and equally measured step, did not remain far behind the trotting horses of the princess and her fan-bearers.

Both the women, whom we now see for the first time in daylight, were of remarkable but altogether different beauty.

The wife of Mena had preserved the appearance of a maiden; her large almond-shaped eyes had a dreamy surprised look out from under her long eyelashes, and her figure of hardly the middle-height had acquired a little stoutness without losing its youthful grace. No drop of foreign blood flowed in her veins, as could be seen in the color of her skin, which was of that fresh and equal line which holds a medium between golden yellow and bronze brown–and which to this day is so charming in the maidens of Abyssinia–in her straight nose, her well-formed brow, in her smooth but thick black hair, and in the fineness of her hands and feet, which were ornamented with circles of gold.

The maiden princess next to her had hardly reached her nineteenth year, and yet something of a womanly self-consciousness betrayed itself in her demeanor. Her stature was by almost a head taller than that of her friend, her skin was fairer, her blue eyes kind and frank, without tricks of glance, but clear and honest, her profile was noble but sharply cut, and resembled that of her father, as a landscape in the mild and softening light of the moon resembles the same landscape in the broad clear light of day. The scarcely perceptible aquiline of her nose, she inherited from her Semitic ancestors,[32] as well as the slightly waving abundance of her brown hair, over which she wore a blue and white striped silk kerchief; its carefully-pleated folds were held in place by a gold ring, from which in front a horned urarus[33] raised its head crowned with a disk of rubies. From her left temple a large tress, plaited with gold thread, hung down to her waist, the sign of her royal birth. She wore a purple dress of fine, almost transparent stuff, that was confined with a gold belt and straps. Round her throat was fastened a necklace like a collar, made of pearls and costly stones, and hanging low down on her well-formed bosom.

Behind the princess stood her charioteer, an old officer of noble birth.

Three litters followed the chariot of the princess, and in each sat two officers of the court; then came a dozen of slaves ready for any service, and lastly a crowd of wand-bearers to drive off the idle populace, and of lightly-armed soldiers, who–dressed only in the apron and head-cloth —each bore a dagger-shaped sword in his girdle, an axe in his right hand, and in his left; in token of his peaceful service, a palm-branch.

Like dolphins round a ship, little girls in long shirt-shaped garments swarmed round the whole length of the advancing procession, bearing water-jars on their steady heads, and at a sign from any one who was thirsty were ready to give him a drink. With steps as light as the gazelle they often outran the horses, and nothing could be more graceful than the action with which the taller ones bent over with the water-jars held in both arms to the drinker.

The courtiers, cooled and shaded by waving fans, and hardly perceiving the noontide heat, conversed at their ease about indifferent matters, and the princess pitied the poor horses, who were tormented as they ran, by annoying gadflies; while the runners and soldiers, the litter-bearers and fan-bearers, the girls with their jars and the panting slaves, were compelled to exert themselves under the rays of the mid-day sun in the service of their masters, till their sinews threatened to crack and their lungs to burst their bodies.

At a spot where the road widened, and where, to the right, lay the steep cross-valley where the last kings of the dethroned race were interred, the procession stopped at a sign from Paaker, who preceded the princess, and who drove his fiery black Syrian horses with so heavy a hand that the bloody foam fell from their bits.

When the Mohar had given the reins into the hand of a servant, he sprang from his chariot, and after the usual form of obeisance said to the princess:

"In this valley lies the loathsome den of the people, to whom thou, O princess, dost deign to do such high honor. Permit me to go forward as guide to thy party."

"We will go on foot," said the princess, "and leave our followers behind here."

Paaker bowed, Bent-Anat threw the reins to her charioteer and sprang to the ground, the wife of Mena and the courtiers left their litters, and the fan-bearers and chamberlains were about to accompany their mistress on foot into the little valley, when she turned round and ordered, "Remain behind, all of you. Only Paaker and Nefert need go with me."

The princess hastened forward into the gorge, which was oppressive with the noon-tide heat; but she moderated her steps as soon as she observed that the frailer Nefert found it difficult to follow her.

At a bend in the road Paaker stood still, and with him Bent-Anat and Nefert. Neither of them had spoken a word during their walk. The valley was perfectly still and deserted; on the highest pinnacles of the cliff, which rose perpendicularly to the right, sat a long row of vultures, as motionless as if the mid-day heat had taken all strength out of their wings.

Paaker bowed before them as being the sacred animals of the Great Goddess of Thebes,[34] and the two women silently followed his example.

"There," said the Mohar, pointing to two huts close to the left cliff of the valley, built of bricks made of dried Nile-mud, "there, the neatest, next the cave in the rock."

Bent-Anat went towards the solitary hovel with a beating heart; Paaker let the ladies go first. A few steps brought them to an ill-constructed fence of canestalks, palm-branches, briars and straw, roughly thrown together. A heart-rending cry of pain from within the hut trembled in the air and arrested the steps of the two women. Nefert staggered and clung to her stronger companion, whose beating heart she seemed to hear. Both stood a few minutes as if spellbound, then the princess called Paaker, and said:

"You go first into the house."

Paaker bowed to the ground.

"I will call the man out," he said, "but how dare we step over his threshold. Thou knowest such a proceeding will defile us."

Nefert looked pleadingly at Bent-Anat, but the princess repeated her command.

"Go before me; I have no fear of defilement." The Mohar still hesitated.

"Wilt thou provoke the Gods? —and defile thyself?" But the princess let him say no more; she signed to Nefert, who raised her hands in horror and aversion; so, with a shrug of her shoulders, she left her companion behind with the Mohar, and stepped through an opening in the hedge into a little court, where lay two brown goats; a donkey with his forelegs tied together stood by, and a few hens were scattering the dust about in a vain search for food.

Soon she stood, alone, before the door of the paraschites' hovel. No one perceived her, but she could not take her eyes-accustomed only to scenes of order and splendor-from the gloomy but wonderfully strange picture, which riveted her attention and her sympathy. At last she went up to the doorway, which was too low for her tall figure. Her heart shrunk painfully within her, and she would have wished to grow smaller, and, instead of shining in splendor, to have found herself wrapped in a beggar's robe.

Could she step into this hovel decked with gold and jewels as if in mockery? —like a tyrant who should feast at a groaning table and compel the starving to look on at the banquet. Her delicate perception made her feel what trenchant discord her appearance offered to all that surrounded her, and the discord pained her; for she could not conceal from herself that misery and external meanness were here entitled to give the key-note and that her magnificence derived no especial grandeur from contrast with all these modest accessories, amid dust, gloom, and suffering, but rather became disproportionate and hideous, like a giant among pigmies.

She had already gone too far to turn back, or she would willingly have done so. The longer she gazed into the but, the more deeply she felt the impotence of her princely power, the nothingness of the splendid gifts with which she approached it, and that she might not tread the dusty floor of this wretched hovel but in all humility, and to crave a pardon.

The room into which she looked was low but not very small, and obtained from two cross lights a strange and unequal illumination; on one side the light came through the door, and on the other through an opening in the time-worn ceiling of the room, which had never before harbored so many and such different guests.

All attention was concentrated on a group, which was clearly lighted up from the doorway.

On the dusty floor of the room cowered an old woman, with dark weather-beaten features and tangled hair that had long been grey. Her black-blue cotton shirt was open over her withered bosom, and showed a blue star tattooed upon it.

In her lap she supported with her hands the head of a girl, whose slender body lay motionless on a narrow, ragged mat. The little white feet of the sick girl almost touched the threshold. Near to them squatted a benevolent-looking old man, who wore only a coarse apron, and sitting all in a heap, bent forward now and then, rubbing the child's feet with his lean hands and muttering a few words to himself.

The sufferer wore nothing but a short petticoat of coarse light-blue stuff. Her face, half resting on the lap of the old woman, was graceful and regular in form, her eyes were half shut-like those of a child, whose soul is wrapped in some sweet dream-but from her finely chiselled lips there escaped from time to time a painful, almost convulsive sob.

An abundance of soft, but disordered reddish fair hair, in which clung a few withered flowers, fell over the lap of the old woman and on to the mat where she lay. Her cheeks were white and rosy-red, and when the young surgeon Nebsecht-who sat by her side, near his blind, stupid companion, the litany-singer —lifted the ragged cloth that had been thrown over her bosom, which had been crushed by the chariot wheel, or when she lifted her slender arm, it was seen that she had the shining fairness of those daughters of the north who not unfrequently came to Thebes among the king's prisoners of war.

The two physicians sent hither from the House of Seti sat on the left side of the maiden on a little carpet. From time to time one or the other laid his hand over the heart of the sufferer, or listened to her breathing, or opened his case of medicaments, and moistened the compress on her wounded breast with a white ointment.

In a wide circle close to the wall of the room crouched several women, young and old, friends of the paraschites, who from time to time gave expression to their deep sympathy by a piercing cry of lamentation. One of them rose at regular intervals to fill the earthen bowl by the side of the physician with fresh water. As often as the sudden coolness of a fresh compress on her hot bosom startled the sick girl, she opened her eyes, but always soon to close them again for longer interval, and turned them at first in surprise, and then with gentle reverence, towards a particular spot.

These glances had hitherto been unobserved by him to whom they were directed.

Leaning against the wall on the right hand side of the room, dressed in his long, snow-white priest's robe, Pentaur stood awaiting the princess. His head-dress touched the ceiling, and the narrow streak of light, which fell through the opening in the roof, streamed on his handsome head and his breast, while all around him was veiled in twilight gloom.

Once more the suffering girl looked up, and her glance this time met the eye of the young priest, who immediately raised his hand, and half-mechanically, in a low voice, uttered the words of blessing; and then once more fixed his gaze on the dingy floor, and pursued his own reflections.

Some hours since he had come hither, obedient to the orders of Ameni, to impress on the princess that she had defiled herself by touching a paraschites, and could only be cleansed again by the hand of the priests.

He had crossed the threshold of the paraschites most reluctantly, and the thought that he, of all men, had been selected to censure a deed of the noblest humanity, and to bring her who had done it to judgment, weighed upon him as a calamity.

In his intercourse with his friend Nebsecht, Pentaur had thrown off many fetters, and given place to many thoughts that his master would have held sinful and presumptuous; but at the same time he acknowledged the sanctity of the old institutions, which were upheld by those whom he had learned to regard as the divinely-appointed guardians of the spiritual possessions of God's people; nor was he wholly free from the pride of caste and the haughtiness which, with prudent intent, were inculcated in the priests. He held the common man, who put forth his strength to win a maintenance for his belongings by honest bodily labor-the merchant-the artizan-the peasant, nay even the warrior, as far beneath the godly brotherhood who strove for only spiritual ends; and most of all he scorned the idler, given up to sensual enjoyments.

He held him unclean who had been branded by the law; and how should it have been otherwise? These people, who at the embalming of the dead opened the body of the deceased, had become despised for their office of mutilating the sacred temple of the soul; but no paraschites chose his calling of his own free will. —[Diodorus I, 91] —It was handed down from father to son, and he who was born a paraschites-so he was taught-had to expiate an old guilt with which his soul had long ago burdened itself in a former existence, within another body, and which had deprived it of absolution in the nether world. It had passed through various animal forms, and now began a new human course in the body of a paraschites, once more to stand after death in the presence of the judges of the under-world.

Pentaur had crossed the threshold of the man he despised with aversion; the man himself, sitting at the feet of the suffering girl, had exclaimed as he saw the priest approaching the hovel:

"Yet another white robe! Does misfortune cleanse the unclean?"

Pentaur had not answered the old man, who on his part took no further notice of him, while he rubbed the girl's feet by order of the leech; and his hands impelled by tender anxiety untiringly continued the same movement, as the water-wheel in the Nile keeps up without intermission its steady motion in the stream.

"Does misfortune cleanse the unclean?" Pentaur asked himself. "Does it indeed possess a purifying efficacy, and is it possible that the Gods, who gave to fire the power of refining metals and to the winds power to sweep the clouds from the sky, should desire that a man-made in their own image-that a man should be tainted from his birth to his death with an indelible stain?"

He looked at the face of the paraschites, and it seemed to him to resemble that of his father. This startled him!

And when he noticed how the woman, in whose lap the girl's head was resting, bent over the injured bosom of the child to catch her breathing, which she feared had come to a stand-still —with the anguish of a dove that is struck down by a hawk-he remembered a moment in his own childhood, when he had lain trembling with fever on his little bed. What then had happened to him, or had gone on around him, he had long forgotten, but one image was deeply imprinted on his soul, that of the face of his mother bending over him in deadly anguish, but who had gazed on her sick boy not more tenderly, or more anxiously, than this despised woman on her suffering child.

"There is only one utterly unselfish, utterly pure and utterly divine love," said he to himself, "and that is the love of Isis for Horus-the love of a mother for her child. If these people were indeed so foul as to defile every thing they touch, how would this pure, this tender, holy impulse show itself even in them in all its beauty and perfection?"

"Still," he continued, "the Celestials have implanted maternal love in the breast of the lioness, of the typhonic river-horse of the Nile."

He looked compassionately at the wife of the paraschites.

He saw her dark face as she turned it away from the sick girl. She had felt her breathe, and a smile of happiness lighted up her old features; she nodded first to the surgeon, and then with a deep sigh of relief to her husband, who, while he did not cease the movement of his left hand, held up his right hand in prayer to heaven, and his wife did the same.

It seemed to Pentaur that he could see the souls of these two, floating above the youthful creature in holy union as they joined their hands; and again he thought of his parents' house, of the hour when his sweet, only sister died. His mother had thrown herself weeping on the pale form, but his father had stamped his foot and had thrown back his head, sobbing and striking his forehead with his fist.

"How piously submissive and thankful are these unclean ones!" thought Pentaur; and repugnance for the old laws began to take root in his heart. "Maternal love may exist in the hyaena, but to seek and find God pertains only to man, who has a noble aim. Up to the limits of eternity-and God is eternal! —thought is denied to animals; they cannot even smile. Even men cannot smile at first, for only physical life-an animal soul-dwells in them; but soon a share of the world's soul-beaming intelligence-works within them, and first shows itself in the smile of a child, which is as pure as the light and the truth from which it comes. The child of the paraschites smiles like any other creature born of woman, but how few aged men there are, even among the initiated, who can smile as innocently and brightly as this woman who has grown grey under open ill-treatment."

Deep sympathy began to fill his heart, and he knelt down by the side of the poor child, raised her arm, and prayed fervently to that One who had created the heavens and who rules the world-to that One, whom the mysteries of faith forbade him to name; and not to the innumerable gods, whom the people worshipped, and who to him were nothing but incarnations of the attributes of the One and only God of the initiated-of whom he was one-who was thus brought down to the comprehension of the laity.

He raised his soul to God in passionate emotion; but he prayed, not for the child before him and for her recovery, but rather for the whole despised race, and for its release from the old ban, for the enlightenment of his own soul, imprisoned in doubts, and for strength to fulfil his hard task with discretion.

The gaze of the sufferer followed him as he took up his former position.

The prayer had refreshed his soul and restored him to cheerfulness of spirit. He began to reflect what conduct he must observe towards the princess.

He had not met Bent-Anat for the first time yesterday; on the contrary, he had frequently seen her in holiday processions, and at the high festivals in the Necropolis, and like all his young companions had admired her proud beauty-admired it as the distant light of the stars, or the evening-glow on the horizon.

Now he must approach this lady with words of reproof.

He pictured to himself the moment when he must advance to meet her, and could not help thinking of his little tutor Chufu, above whom he towered by two heads while he was still a boy, and who used to call up his admonitions to him from below. It was true, he himself was tall and slim, but he felt as if to-day he were to play the part towards Bent-Anat of the much-laughed-at little tutor.

His sense of the comic was touched, and asserted itself at this serious moment, and with such melancholy surroundings. Life is rich in contrasts, and a susceptible and highly-strung human soul would break down like a bridge under the measured tread of soldiers, if it were allowed to let the burden of the heaviest thoughts and strongest feelings work upon it in undisturbed monotony; but just as in music every key-note has its harmonies, so when we cause one chord of our heart to vibrate for long, all sorts of strange notes respond and clang, often those which we least expect.

Pentaur's glance flew round the one low, over-filled room of the paraschites' hut, and like a lightning flash the thought, "How will the princess and her train find room here?" flew through his mind.

His fancy was lively, and vividly brought before him how the daughter of the Pharaoh with a crown on her proud head would bustle into the silent chamber, how the chattering courtiers would follow her, and how the women by the walls, the physicians by the side of the sick girl, the sleek white cat from the chest where she sat, would rise and throng round her. There must be frightful confusion. Then he imagined how the smart lords and ladies would keep themselves far from the unclean, hold their slender hands over their mouths and noses, and suggest to the old folks how they ought to behave to the princess who condescended to bless them with her presence. The old woman must lay down the head that rested in her bosom, the paraschites must drop the feet he so anxiously rubbed, on the floor, to rise and kiss the dust before Bent-Anat. Whereupon-the "mind's eye" of the young priest seemed to see it all-the courtiers fled before him, pushing each other, and all crowded together into a corner, and at last the princess threw a few silver or gold rings into the laps of the father and mother, and perhaps to the girl too, and he seemed to hear the courtiers all cry out: "Hail to the gracious daughter of the Sun!"—to hear the joyful exclamations of the crowd of women-to see the gorgeous apparition leave the hut of the despised people, and then to see, instead of the lovely sick child who still breathed audibly, a silent corpse on the crumpled mat, and in the place of the two tender nurses at her head and feet, two heart-broken, loud-lamenting wretches.

Pentaur's hot spirit was full of wrath. As soon as the noisy cortege appeared actually in sight he would place himself in the doorway, forbid the princess to enter, and receive her with strong words.

She could hardly come hither out of human kindness.

"She wants variety," said he to himself, "something new at Court; for there is little going on there now the king tarries with the troops in a distant country; it tickles the vanity of the great to find themselves once in a while in contact with the small, and it is well to have your goodness of heart spoken of by the people. If a little misfortune opportunely happens, it is not worth the trouble to inquire whether the form of our benevolence does more good or mischief to such wretched people."

He ground his teeth angrily, and thought no more of the defilement which might threaten Bent-Anat from the paraschites, but exclusively, on the contrary, of the impending desecration by the princess of the holy feelings astir in this silent room.

Excited as he was to fanaticism, his condemning lips could not fail to find vigorous and impressive words.

He stood drawn to his full height and drawing his breath deeply, like a spirit of light who holds his weapon raised to annihilate a demon of darkness, and he looked out into the valley to perceive from afar the cry of the runners and the rattle of the wheels of the gay train he expected.

And he saw the doorway darkened by a lowly, bending figure, who, with folded arms, glided into the room and sank down silently by the side of the sick girl. The physicians and the old people moved as if to rise; but she signed to them without opening her lips, and with moist, expressive eyes, to keep their places; she looked long and lovingly in the face of the wounded girl, stroked her white arm, and turning to the old woman softly whispered to her

"How pretty she is!"

The paraschites' wife nodded assent, and the girl smiled and moved her lips as though she had caught the words and wished to speak.

Bent-Anat took a rose from her hair and laid it on her bosom.

The paraschites, who had not taken his hands from the feet of the sick child, but who had followed every movement of the princess, now whispered, "May Hathor requite thee, who gave thee thy beauty."

The princess turned to him and said, "Forgive the sorrow, I have caused you."

The old man stood up, letting the feet of the sick girl fall, and asked in a clear loud voice: "Art thou Bent-Anat?"

"Yes, I am," replied the princess, bowing her head low, and in so gentle a voice, that it seemed as though she were ashamed of her proud name.

The eyes of the old man flashed. Then he said softly but decisively:

"Leave my hut then, it will defile thee."

"Not till you have forgiven me for that which I did unintentionally."

"Unintentionally! I believe thee," replied the paraschites. "The hoofs of thy horse became unclean when they trod on this white breast. Look here —" and he lifted the cloth from the girl's bosom, and showed her the deep red wound, "Look here-here is the first rose you laid on my grandchild's bosom, and the second-there it goes."

The paraschites raised his arm to fling the flower through the door of his hut. But Pentaur had approached him, and with a grasp of iron held the old man's hand.

"Stay," he cried in an eager tone, moderated however for the sake of the sick girl. "The third rose, which this noble hand has offered you, your sick heart and silly head have not even perceived. And yet you must know it if only from your need, your longing for it. The fair blossom of pure benevolence is laid on your child's heart, and at your very feet, by this proud princess. Not with gold, but with humility. And whoever the daughter of Rameses approaches as her equal, bows before her, even if he were the first prince in the Land of Egypt. Indeed, the Gods shall not forget this deed of Bent-Anat. And you-forgive, if you desire to be forgiven that guilt, which you bear as an inheritance from your fathers, and for your own sins."

The paraschites bowed his head at these words, and when he raised it the anger had vanished from his well-cut features. He rubbed his wrist, which had been squeezed by Pentaur's iron fingers, and said in a tone which betrayed all the bitterness of his feelings:

"Thy hand is hard, Priest, and thy words hit like the strokes of a hammer. This fair lady is good and loving, and I know; that she did not drive her horse intentionally over this poor girl, who is my grandchild and not my daughter. If she were thy wife or the wife of the leech there, or the child of the poor woman yonder, who supports life by collecting the feet and feathers of the fowls that are slaughtered for sacrifice, I would not only forgive her, but console her for having made herself like to me; fate would have made her a murderess without any fault of her own, just as it stamped me as unclean while I was still at my mother's breast. Aye —I would comfort her; and yet I am not very sensitive. Ye holy three of Thebes! —[The triad of Thebes: Anion, Muth and Chunsu.] —how should I be? Great and small get out of my way that I may not touch them, and every day when I have done what it is my business to do they throw stones at me.[35]

"The fulfilment of duty-which brings a living to other men, which makes their happiness, and at the same time earns them honor, brings me every day fresh disgrace and painful sores. But I complain to no man, and must forgive-forgive-forgive, till at last all that men do to me seems quite natural and unavoidable, and I take it all like the scorching of the sun in summer, and the dust that the west wind blows into my face. It does not make me happy, but what can I do? I forgive all —"

The voice of the paraschites had softened, and Bent-Anat, who looked down on him with emotion, interrupted him, exclaiming with deep feeling:

"And so you will forgive me? —poor man!"

The old man looked steadily, not at her, but at Pentaur, while he replied: "Poor man! aye, truly, poor man. You have driven me out of the world in which you live, and so I made a world for myself in this hut. I do not belong to you, and if I forget it, you drive me out as an intruder-nay as a wolf, who breaks into your fold; but you belong just as little to me, only when you play the wolf and fall upon me, I must bear it!"

"The princess came to your hut as a suppliant, and with the wish of doing you some good," said Pentaur.

"May the avenging Gods reckon it to her, when they visit on her the crimes of her father against me! Perhaps it may bring me to prison, but it must come out. Seven sons were mine, and Rameses took them all from me and sent them to death; the child of the youngest, this girl, the light of my eyes, his daughter has brought to her death. Three of my boys the king left to die of thirst by the Tenat,[36] which is to join the Nile to the Red Sea, three were killed by the Ethiopians, and the last, the star of my hopes, by this time is eaten by the hyaenas of the north."

At these words the old woman, in whose lap the head of the girl rested, broke out into a loud cry, in which she was joined by all the other women.

The sufferer started up frightened, and opened her eyes.

"For whom are you wailing?" she asked feebly. "For your poor father," said the old woman.

The girl smiled like a child who detects some well-meant deceit, and said:

"Was not my father here, with you? He is here, in Thebes, and looked at me, and kissed me, and said that he is bringing home plunder, and that a good time is coming for you. The gold ring that he gave me I was fastening into my dress, when the chariot passed over me. I was just pulling the knots, when all grew black before my eyes, and I saw and heard nothing more. Undo it, grandmother, the ring is for you; I meant to bring it to you. You must buy a beast for sacrifice with it, and wine for grandfather, and eye salve[37] for yourself, and sticks of mastic,[38] which you have so long lead to do without."

The paraschites seemed to drink these words from the mouth of his grandchild. Again he lifted his hand in prayer, again Pentaur observed that his glance met that of his wife, and a large, warm tear fell from his old eyes on to his callous hand. Then he sank down, for he thought the sick child was deluded by a dream. But there were the knots in her dress.

With a trembling hand he untied them, and a gold ring rolled out on the floor.

Bent-Anat picked it up, and gave it to the paraschites. "I came here in a lucky hour," she said, "for you have recovered your son and your child will live."

"She will live," repeated the surgeon, who had remained a silent witness of all that had occurred.

"She will stay with us," murmured the old man, and then said, as he approached the princess on his knees, and looked up at her beseechingly with tearful eyes:

"Pardon me as I pardon thee; and if a pious wish may not turn to a curse from the lips of the unclean, let me bless thee."

"I thank you," said Bent-Anat, towards whom the old man raised his hand in blessing.

Then she turned to Nebsecht, and ordered him to take anxious care of the sick girl; she bent over her, kissed her forehead, laid her gold bracelet by her side, and signing to Pentaur left the hut with him.

CHAPTER VI.

During the occurrence we have described, the king's pioneer and the young wife of Mena were obliged to wait for the princess.

The sun stood in the meridian, when Bent-Anat had gone into the hovel of the paraschites.

The bare limestone rocks on each side of the valley and the sandy soil between, shone with a vivid whiteness that hurt the eyes; not a hand's breadth of shade was anywhere to be seen, and the fan-beaters of the two, who were waiting there, had, by command of the princess, staid behind with the chariot and litters.

For a time they stood silently near each other, then the fair Nefert said, wearily closing her almond-shaped eyes:

"How long Bent-Anat stays in the but of the unclean! I am perishing here. What shall we do?"

"Stay!" said Paaker, turning his back on the lady; and mounting a block of stone by the side of the gorge, he cast a practised glance all round, and returned to Nefert: "I have found a shady spot," he said, "out there."

Mena's wife followed with her eyes the indication of his hand, and shook her head. The gold ornaments on her head-dress rattled gently as she did so, and a cold shiver passed over her slim body in spite of the midday heat.

"Sechet is raging in the sky," said Paaker.[39]

"Let us avail ourselves of the shady spot, small though it be. At this hour of the day many are struck with sickness."

"I know it," said Nefert, covering her neck with her hand. Then she went towards two blocks of stone which leaned against each other, and between them afforded the spot of shade, not many feet wide, which Paaker had pointed out as a shelter from the sun. Paaker preceded her, and rolled a flat piece of limestone, inlaid by nature with nodules of flint, under the stone pavilion, crushed a few scorpions which had taken refuge there, spread his head-cloth over the hard seat, and said, "Here you are sheltered."

Nefert sank down on the stone and watched the Mohar, who slowly and silently paced backwards and forward in front of her. This incessant to and fro of her companion at last became unendurable to her sensitive and irritated nerves, and suddenly raising her head from her hand, on which she had rested it, she exclaimed

"Pray stand still."

The pioneer obeyed instantly, and looked, as he stood with his back to her, towards the hovel of the paraschites.

After a short time Nefert said, "Say something to me!"

The Mohar turned his full face towards her, and she was frightened at the wild fire that glowed in the glance with which he gazed at her.

Nefert's eyes fell, and Paaker, saying:

"I would rather remain silent," recommenced his walk, till Nefert called to him again and said,

"I know you are angry with me; but I was but a child when I was betrothed to you. I liked you too, and when in our games your mother called me your little wife, I was really glad, and used to think how fine it would be when I might call all your possessions mine, the house you would have so splendidly restored for me after your father's death, the noble gardens, the fine horses in their stables, and all the male and female slaves!"

Paaker laughed, but the laugh sounded so forced and scornful that it cut Nefert to the heart, and she went on, as if begging for indulgence:

"It was said that you were angry with us; and now you will take my words as if I had cared only for your wealth; but I said, I liked you. Do you no longer remember how I cried with you over your tales of the bad boys in the school; and over your father's severity? Then my uncle died; —then you went to Asia."

"And you," interrupted Paaker, hardly and drily, "you broke your bethrothal vows, and became the wife of the charioteer Mena. I know it all; of what use is talking?"

"Because it grieves me that you should be angry, and your good mother avoid our house. If only you could know what it is when love seizes one, and one can no longer even think alone, but only near, and with, and in the very arms of another; when one's beating heart throbs in one's very temples, and even in one's dreams one sees nothing-but one only."

"And do I not know it?" cried Paaker, placing himself close before her with his arms crossed. "Do I not know it? and you it was who taught me to know it. When I thought of you, not blood, but burning fire, coursed in my veins, and now you have filled them with poison; and here in this breast, in which your image dwelt, as lovely as that of Hathor in her holy of holies, all is like that sea in Syria which is called the Dead Sea, in which every thing that tries to live presently dies and perishes."

Paaker's eyes rolled as he spoke, and his voice sounded hoarsely as he went on.

"But Mena was near to the king-nearer than I, and your mother —"

"My mother!" —Nefert interrupted the angry Mohar. "My mother did not choose my husband. I saw him driving the chariot, and to me he resembled the Sun God, and he observed me, and looked at me, and his glance pierced deep into my heart like a spear; and when, at the festival of the king's birthday, he spoke to me, it was just as if Hathor had thrown round me a web of sweet, sounding sunbeams. And it was the same with Mena; he himself has told me so since I have been his wife. For your sake my mother rejected his suit, but I grew pale and dull with longing for him, and he lost his bright spirit, and was so melancholy that the king remarked it, and asked what weighed on his heart-for Rameses loves him as his own son. Then Mena confessed to the Pharaoh that it was love that dimmed his eye and weakened his strong hand; and then the king himself courted me for his faithful servant, and my mother gave way, and we were made man and wife, and all the joys of the justified in the fields of Aalu[40] are shallow and feeble by the side of the bliss which we two have known-not like mortal men, but like the celestial gods."

Up to this point Nefert had fixed her large eyes on the sky, like a glorified soul; but now her gaze fell, and she said softly —

"But the Cheta[41] disturbed our happiness, for the king took Mena with him to the war. Fifteen times did the moon, rise upon our happiness, and then —"

"And then the Gods heard my prayer, and accepted my offerings," said Paaker, with a trembling voice, "and tore the robber of my joys from you, and scorched your heart and his with desire. Do you think you can tell me anything I do not know? Once again for fifteen days was Mena yours, and now he has not returned again from the war which is raging hotly in Asia."

"But he will return," cried the young wife.

"Or possibly not," laughed Paaker. "The Cheta, carry sharp weapons, and there are many vultures in Lebanon, who perhaps at this hour are tearing his flesh as he tore my heart."

Nefert rose at these words, her sensitive spirit bruised as with stones thrown by a brutal hand, and attempted to leave her shady refuge to follow the princess into the house of the parascllites; but her feet refused to bear her, and she sank back trembling on her stone seat. She tried to find words, but her tongue was powerless. Her powers of resistance forsook her in her unutterable and soul-felt distress-heart-wrung, forsaken and provoked.

A variety of painful sensations raised a hot vehement storm in her bosom, which checked her breath, and at last found relief in a passionate and convulsive weeping that shook her whole body. She saw nothing more, she heard nothing more, she only shed tears and felt herself miserable. Paaker stood over her in silence.

There are trees in the tropics, on which white blossoms hang close by the withered fruit, there are days when the pale moon shows itself near the clear bright sun; —and it is given to the soul of man to feel love and hatred, both at the same time, and to direct both to the same end.

Nefert's tears fell as dew, her sobs as manna on the soul of Paaker, which hungered and thirsted for revenge. Her pain was joy to him, and yet the sight of her beauty filled him with passion, his gaze lingered spell-bound on her graceful form; he would have given all the bliss of heaven once, only once, to hold her in his arms–once, only once, to hear a word of love from her lips.

After some minutes Nefert's tears grew less violent. With a weary, almost indifferent gaze she looked at the Mohar, still standing before her, and said in a soft tone of entreaty:

'My tongue is parched, fetch me a little water."

"The princess may come out at any moment," replied Paaker.

"But I am fainting," said Nefert, and began again to cry gently.

Paaker shrugged his shoulders, and went farther into the valley, which he knew as well as his father's house; for in it was the tomb of his mother's ancestors, in which, as a boy, he had put up prayers at every full and new moon, and laid gifts on the altar.

The hut of the paraschites was prohibited to him, but he knew that scarcely a hundred paces from the spot where Nefert was sitting, lived an old woman of evil repute, in whose hole in the rock he could not fail to find a drink of water.

He hastened forward, half intoxicated with had seen and felt within the last few minutes.

The door, which at night closed the cave against the intrusions of the plunder-seeking jackals, was wide open, and the old woman sat outside under a ragged piece of brown sail-cloth, fastened at one end to the rock and at the other to two posts of rough wood. She was sorting a heap of dark and light-colored roots, which lay in her lap. Near her was a wheel, which turned in a high wooden fork. A wryneck made fast to it by a little chain, and by springing from spoke to spoke kept it in continual motion. —[From Theocritus' idyl: The Sorceress.] —A large black cat crouched beside her, and smelt at some ravens' and owls' heads, from which the eyes had not long since been extracted.

Two sparrow-hawks sat huddled up over the door of the cave, out of which came the sharp odor of burning juniper-berries; this was intended to render the various emanations rising from the different strange substances, which were collected and preserved there, innocuous.

As Paaker approached the cavern the old woman called out to some one within:

"Is the wax cooking?"

An unintelligible murmur was heard in answer.

Then throw in the ape's eyes,[42] and the ibis feathers, and the scraps of linen with the black signs on them. Stir it all a little; now put out the fire,

"Take the jug and fetch some water–make haste, here comes a stranger."

A sooty-black negro woman, with a piece of torn colorless stuff hanging round her hips, set a large clay-jar on her grey woolly matted hair, and without looking at him, went past Paaker, who was now close to the cave.

The old woman, a tall figure bent with years, with a sharply-cut and wrinkled face, that might once have been handsome, made her preparations for receiving the visitor by tying a gaudy kerchief over her head, fastening her blue cotton garment round her throat, and flinging a fibre mat over the birds' heads.

Paaker called out to her, but she feigned to be deaf and not to hear his voice. Only when he stood quite close to her, did she raise her shrewd, twinkling eyes, and cry out:

"A lucky day! a white day that brings a noble guest and high honor."

"Get up," commanded Paaker, not giving her any greeting, but throwing a silver ring among the roots that lay in her lap,[43] "and give me in exchange for good money some water in a clean vessel."

"Fine pure silver," said the old woman, while she held the ring, which she had quickly picked out from the roots, close to her eyes; "it is too much for mere water, and too little for my good liquors."

"Don't chatter, hussy, but make haste," cried Paaker, taking another ring from his money-bag and throwing it into her lap.

"Thou hast an open hand," said the old woman, speaking in the dialect of the upper classes; "many doors must be open to thee, for money is a pass-key that turns any lock. Would'st thou have water for thy good money? Shall it protect thee against noxious beasts? —shall it help thee to reach down a star? Shall it guide thee to secret paths? —It is thy duty to lead the way. Shall it make heat cold, or cold warm? Shall it give thee the power of reading hearts, or shall it beget beautiful dreams? Wilt thou drink of the water of knowledge and see whether thy friend or thine enemy-ha! if thine enemy shall die? Would'st thou a drink to strengthen thy memory? Shall the water make thee invisible? or remove the 6th toe from thy left foot?"

"You know me?" asked Paaker.

"How should I?" said the old woman, "but my eyes are sharp, and I can prepare good waters for great and small."

"Mere babble!" exclaimed Paaker, impatiently clutching at the whip in his girdle; "make haste, for the lady for whom —"

"Dost thou want the water for a lady?" interrupted the old woman. "Who would have thought it? —old men certainly ask for my philters much oftener than young ones-but I can serve thee."

With these words the old woman went into the cave, and soon returned with a thin cylindrical flask of alabaster in her hand.

"This is the drink," she said, giving the phial to Paaker. "Pour half into water, and offer it to the lady. If it does not succeed at first, it is certain the second time. A child may drink the water and it will not hurt him, or if an old man takes it, it makes him gay. Ah, I know the taste of it!" and she moistened her lips with the white fluid. "It can hurt no one, but I will take no more of it, or old Hekt will be tormented with love and longing for thee; and that would ill please the rich young lord, ha! ha! If the drink is in vain I am paid enough, if it takes effect thou shalt bring me three more gold rings; and thou wilt return, I know it well."

Paaker had listened motionless to the old woman, and siezed the flask eagerly, as if bidding defiance to some adversary; he put it in his money bag, threw a few more rings at the feet of the witch, and once more hastily demanded a bowl of Nile-water.

"Is my lord in such a hurry?" muttered the old woman, once more going into the cave. "He asks if I know him? him certainly I do? but the darling? who can it be hereabouts? perhaps little Uarda at the paraschites yonder. She is pretty enough; but she is lying on a mat, run over and dying. We must see what my lord means. He would have pleased me well enough, if I were young; but he will reach the goal, for he is resolute and spares no one."

While she muttered these and similar words, she filled a graceful cup of glazed earthenware with filtered Nile-water, which she poured out of a large porous clay jar, and laid a laurel leaf, on which was scratched two hearts linked together by seven strokes, on the surface of the limpid fluid. Then she stepped out into the air again.

As Paaker took the vessel from her looked at the laurel leaf, she said:

"This indeed binds hearts; three is the husband, four is the wife, seven is the chachach, charcharachacha." —[This jargon is fund in a magic-papyrus at Berlin.]

The old woman sang this spell not without skill; but the Mohar appeared not to listen to her jargon. He descended carefully into the valley, and directed his steps to the resting place of the wife of Mena.

By the side of a rock, which hill him from Nefert, he paused, set the cup on a flat block of stone, and drew the flask with the philter out of his girdle.

His fingers trembled, but a thousand voices seemed to surge up and cry:

"Take it! —do it! —put in the drink! —now or never." He felt like a solitary traveller, who finds on his road the last will of a relation whose possessions he had hoped for, but which disinherits him. Shall he surrender it to the judge, or shall he destroy it.

Paaker was not merely outwardly devout; hitherto he had in everything intended to act according to the prescriptions of the religion of his fathers. Adultery was a heavy sin; but had not he an older right to Nefert than the king's charioteer?

He who followed the black arts of magic, should, according to the law, be punished by death, and the old woman had a bad name for her evil arts; but he had not sought her for the sake of the philter. Was it not possible that the Manes of his forefathers, that the Gods themselves, moved by his prayers and offerings, had put him in possession by an accident-which was almost a miracle-of the magic potion efficacy he never for an instant doubted?

Paaker's associates held him to be a man of quick decision, and, in fact, in difficult cases he could act with unusual rapidity, but what guided him in these cases, was not the swift-winged judgment of a prepared and well-schooled brain, but usually only resulted from the outcome of a play of question and answer.

Amulets of the most various kinds hung round his neck, and from his girdle, all consecrated by priests, and of special sanctity or the highest efficacy.

There was the lapis lazuli eye, which hung to his girdle by a gold chain; When he threw it on the ground, so as to lie on the earth, if its engraved side turned to heaven, and its smooth side lay on the ground, he said "yes;" in the other case, on the contrary, "no." In his purse lay always a statuette of the god Apheru, who opened roads; this he threw down at cross-roads, and followed the direction which the pointed snout of the image indicated. He frequently called into council the seal-ring of his deceased father, an old family possession, which the chief priests of Abydos had laid upon the holiest of the fourteen graves of Osiris, and endowed with miraculous power. It consisted of a gold ring with a broad signet, on which could be read the name of Thotmes III., who had long since been deified, and from whom Paaker's ancestors had derived it. If it were desirable to consult the ring, the Mohar touched with the point of his bronze dagger the engraved sign of the name, below which were represented three objects sacred to the Gods, and three that were, on the contrary, profane. If he hit one of the former, he concluded that his father-who was gone to Osiris-concurred in his design; in the contrary case he was careful to postpone it. Often he pressed the ring to his heart, and awaited the first living creature that he might meet, regarding it as a messenger from his father; —if it came to him from the right hand as an encouragement, if from the left as a warning.

By degrees he had reduced these questionings to a system. All that he found in nature he referred to himself and the current of his life. It was at once touching, and pitiful, to see how closely he lived with the Manes of his dead. His lively, but not exalted fancy, wherever he gave it play, presented to the eye of his soul the image of his father and of an elder brother who had died early, always in the same spot, and almost tangibly distinct.

But he never conjured up the remembrance of the beloved dead in order to think of them in silent melancholy-that sweet blossom of the thorny wreath of sorrow; only for selfish ends. The appeal to the Manes of his father he had found especially efficacious in certain desires and difficulties; calling on the Manes of his brother was potent in certain others; and so he turned from one to the other with the precision of a carpenter, who rarely doubts whether he should give the preference to a hatchet or a saw.

These doings he held to be well pleasing to the Gods, and as he was convinced that the spirits of his dead had, after their justification, passed into Osiris that is to say, as atoms forming part of the great world-soul, at this time had a share in the direction of the universe-he sacrificed to them not only in the family catacomb, but also in the temples of the Necropolis dedicated to the worship of ancestors, and with special preference in the House of Seti.

He accepted advice, nay even blame, from Ameni and the other priests under his direction; and so lived full of a virtuous pride in being one of the most zealous devotees in the land, and one of the most pleasing to the Gods, a belief on which his pastors never threw any doubt.

Attended and guided at every step by supernatural powers, he wanted no friend and no confidant. In the field, as in Thebes, he stood apart, and passed among his comrades for a reserved man, rough and proud, but with a strong will.

He had the power of calling up the image of his lost love with as much vividness as the forms of the dead, and indulged in this magic, not only through a hundred still nights, but in long rides and drives through silent wastes.

Such visions were commonly followed by a vehement and boiling overflow of his hatred against the charioteer, and a whole series of fervent prayers for his destruction.

When Paaker set the cup of water for Nefert on the flat stone and felt for the philter, his soul was so full of desire that there was no room for hatred; still he could not altogether exclude the idea that he would commit a great crime by making use of a magic drink. Before pouring the fateful drops into the water, he would consult the oracle of the ring. The dagger touched none of the holy symbols of the inscription on the signet, and in other circumstances he would, without going any farther, have given up his project.

But this time he unwillingly returned it to its sheath, pressed the gold ring to his heart, muttered the name of his brother in Osiris, and awaited the first living creature that might come towards him.

He had not long to wait, from the mountain slope opposite to him rose, with heavy, slow wing-strokes, two light-colored vultures.

In anxious suspense he followed their flight, as they rose, higher and higher. For a moment they poised motionless, borne up by the air, circled round each other, then wheeled to the left and vanished behind the mountains, denying him the fulfilment of his desire.

He hastily grasped the phial to fling it from him, but the surging passion in his veins had deprived him of his self-control. Nefert's image stood before him as if beckoning him; a mysterious power clenched his fingers close and yet closer round the phial, and with the same defiance which he showed to his associates, he poured half of the philter into the cup and approached his victim.

Nefert had meanwhile left her shady retreat and come towards him.

She silently accepted the water he offered her, and drank it with delight, to the very dregs.

"'Thank you," she said, when she had recovered breath after her eager draught.

"That has done me good! How fresh and acid the water tastes; but your hand shakes, and you are heated by your quick run for me-poor man."

With these words she looked at him with a peculiar expressive glance of her large eyes, and gave him her right hand, which he pressed wildly to his lips.

"That will do," she said smiling; "here comes the princess with a priest, out of the hovel of the unclean. With what frightful words you terrified me just now. It is true I gave you just cause to be angry with me; but now you are kind again-do you hear? —and will bring your mother again to see mine. Not a word. I shall see, whether cousin Paaker refuses me obedience."

She threatened him playfully with her finger, and then growing grave she added, with a look that pierced Paaker's heart with pain, and yet with ecstasy, "Let us leave off quarrelling. It is so much better when people are kind to each other."

After these words she walked towards the house of the paraschites, while Paaker pressed his hands to his breast, and murmured:

"The drink is working, and she will be mine. I thank ye-ye Immortals!"

But this thanksgiving, which hitherto he had never failed to utter when any good fortune had befallen him, to-day died on his lips. Close before him he saw the goal of his desires; there, under his eyes, lay the magic spring longed for for years. A few steps farther, and he might slake at its copious stream his thirst both for love and for revenge.

While he followed the wife of Mena, and replaced the phial carefully in his girdle, so as to lose no drop of the precious fluid which, according to the prescription of the old woman, he needed to use again, warning voices spoke in his breast, to which he usually listened as to a fatherly admonition; but at this moment he mocked at them, and even gave outward expression to the mood that ruled him-for he flung up his right hand like a drunken man, who turns away from the preacher of morality on his way to the wine-cask; and yet passion held him so closely ensnared, that the thought that he should live through the swift moments which would change him from an honest man into a criminal, hardly dawned, darkly on his soul. He had hitherto dared to indulge his desire for love and revenge in thought only, and had left it to the Gods to act for themselves; now he had taken his cause out of the hand of the Celestials, and gone into action without them, and in spite of them.

The sorceress Hekt passed him; she wanted to see the woman for whom she had given him the philter. He perceived her and shuddered, but soon the old woman vanished among the rocks muttering.

"Look at the fellow with six toes. He makes himself comfortable with the heritage of Assa."

In the middle of the valley walked Nefert and the pioneer, with the princess Bent-Anat and Pentaur who accompanied her.

When these two had come out of the hut of the paraschites, they stood opposite each other in silence. The royal maiden pressed her hand to her heart, and, like one who is thirsty, drank in the pure air of the mountain valley with deeply drawn breath; she felt as if released from some overwhelming burden, as if delivered from some frightful danger.

At last she turned to her companion, who gazed earnestly at the ground.

"What an hour!" she said.

Pentaur's tall figure did not move, but he bowed his head in assent, as if he were in a dream. Bent-Anat now saw him for the first time in fall daylight; her large eyes rested on him with admiration, and she asked:

"Art thou the priest, who yesterday, after my first visit to this house, so readily restored me to cleanness?"

"I am he," replied Pentaur.

"I recognized thy voice, and I am grateful to thee, for it was thou that didst strengthen my courage to follow the impulse of my heart, in spite of my spiritual guides, and to come here again. Thou wilt defend me if others blame me."

"I came here to pronounce thee unclean."

"Then thou hast changed thy mind?" asked Bent-Anat, and a smile of contempt curled her lips.

"I follow a high injunction, that commands us to keep the old institutions sacred. If touching a paraschites, it is said, does not defile a princess, whom then can it defile? for whose garment is more spotless than hers?"

"But this is a good man with all his meanness," interrupted Bent-Anat, "and in spite of the disgrace, which is the bread of life to him as honor is to us. May the nine great Gods forgive me! but he who is in there is loving, pious and brave, and pleases me-and thou, thou, who didst think yesterday to purge away the taint of his touch with a word-what prompts thee today to cast him with the lepers?"

"The admonition of an enlightened man, never to give up any link of the old institutions; because thereby the already weakened chain may be broken, and fall rattling to the ground."

"Then thou condemnest me to uncleanness for the sake of all old superstition, and of the populace, but not for my actions? Thou art silent? Answer me now, if thou art such a one as I took the for, freely and sincerely; for it concerns the peace of my soul." Pentaur breathed hard; and then from the depths of his soul, tormented by doubts, these deeply-felt words forced themselves as if wrung from him; at first softly, but louder as he went on.

"Thou dost compel me to say what I had better not even think; but rather will I sin against obedience than against truth, the pure daughter of the Sun, whose aspect, Bent-Anat, thou dost wear. Whether the paraschites is unclean by birth or not, who am I that I should decide? But to me this man appeared-as to thee-as one moved by the same pure and holy emotions as stir and bless me and mine, and thee and every soul born of woman; and I believe that the impressions of this hour have touched thy soul as well as mine, not to taint, but to purify. If I am wrong, may the many-named Gods forgive me, Whose breath lives and works in the paraschites as well as in thee and me, in Whom I believe, and to Whom I will ever address my humble songs, louder and more joyfully, as I learn that all that lives and breathes, that weeps and rejoices, is the image of their sublime nature, and born to equal joy and equal sorrow."

Pentaur had raised his eyes to heaven; now they met the proud and joyful radiance of the princess' glance, while she frankly offered him her hand. He humbly kissed her robe, but she said:

"Nay-not so. Lay thy hand in blessing on mine. Thou art a man and a true priest. Now I can be satisfied to be regarded as unclean, for my father also desires that, by us especially, the institutions of the past that have so long continued should be respected, for the sake of the people. Let us pray in common to the Gods, that these poor people may be released from the old ban. How beautiful the world might be, if men would but let man remain what the Celestials have made him. But Paaker and poor Nefert are waiting in the scorching sun-come, follow me."

She went forward, but after a few steps she turned round to him, and asked:

"What is thy name?"

"Pentaur."

"Thou then art the poet of the House of Seti?"

"They call me so."

Bent-Anat stood still a moment, gazing full at him as at a kinsman whom we meet for the first time face to face, and said:

"The Gods have given thee great gifts, for thy glance reaches farther and pierces deeper than that of other men; and thou canst say in words what we can only feel —I follow thee willingly!"

Pentaur blushed like a boy, and said, while Paaker and Nefert came nearer to them:

"Till to-day life lay before me as if in twilight; but this moment shows it me in another light. I have seen its deepest shadows; and," he added in a low tone "how glorious its light can be."

CHAPTER VII.

An hour later, Bent-Anat and her train of followers stood before the gate of the House of Seti.

Swift as a ball thrown from a man's hand, a runner had sprung forward and hurried on to announce the approach of the princess to the chief priest. She stood alone in her chariot, in advance of all her companions, for Pentaur had found a place with Paaker. At the gate of the temple they were met by the head of the haruspices.

The great doors of the pylon were wide open, and afforded a view into the forecourt of the sanctuary, paved with polished squares of stone, and surrounded on three sides with colonnades. The walls and architraves, the pillars and the fluted cornice, which slightly curved in over the court, were gorgeous with many colored figures and painted decorations. In the middle stood a great sacrificial altar, on which burned logs of cedar wood, whilst fragrant balls of Kyphi[44] were consumed by the flames, filling the wide space with their heavy perfume. Around, in semi-circular array, stood more than a hundred white-robed priests, who all turned to face the approaching princess, and sang heart-rending songs of lamentation.

Many of the inhabitants of the Necropolis had collected on either side of the lines of sphinxes, between which the princess drove up to the Sanctuary. But none asked what these songs of lamentation might signify, for about this sacred place lamentation and mystery for ever lingered. "Hail to the child of Rameses!" —"All hail to the daughter of the Sun!" rang from a thousand throats; and the assembled multitude bowed almost to the earth at the approach of the royal maiden.

At the pylon, the princess descended from her chariot, and preceded by the chief of the haruspices, who had gravely and silently greeted her, passed on to the door of the temple. But as she prepared to cross the forecourt, suddenly, without warning, the priests' chant swelled to a terrible, almost thundering loudness, the clear, shrill voice of the Temple scholars rising in passionate lament, supported by the deep and threatening roll of the basses.

Bent-Anat started and checked her steps. Then she walked on again.

But on the threshold of the door, Ameni, in full pontifical robes, stood before her in the way, his crozier extended as though to forbid her entrance.

"The advent of the daughter of Rameses in her purity," he cried in loud and passionate tones, "augurs blessing to this sanctuary; but this abode of the Gods closes its portals on the unclean, be they slaves or princes. In the name of the Immortals, from whom thou art descended, I ask thee, Bent-Anat, art thou clean, or hast thou, through the touch of the unclean, defiled thyself and contaminated thy royal hand?"

Deep scarlet flushed the maiden's cheeks, there was a rushing sound in her ears as of a stormy sea surging close beside her, and her bosom rose and fell in passionate emotion. The kingly blood in her veins boiled wildly; she felt that an unworthy part had been assigned to her in a carefully-premeditated scene; she forgot her resolution to accuse herself of uncleanness, and already her lips were parted in vehement protest against the priestly assumption that so deeply stirred her to rebellion, when Ameni, who placed himself directly in front of the Princess, raised his eyes, and turned them full upon her with all the depths of their indwelling earnestness.

The words died away, and Bent-Anat stood silent, but she endured the gaze, and returned it proudly and defiantly.

The blue veins started in Ameni's forehead; yet he repressed the resentment which was gathering like thunder clouds in his soul, and said, with a voice that gradually deviated more and more from its usual moderation:

"For the second time the Gods demand through me, their representative: Hast thou entered this holy place in order that the Celestials may purge thee of the defilement that stains thy body and soul?"

"My father will communicate the answer to thee," replied Bent-Anat shortly and proudly.

"Not to me," returned Ameni, "but to the Gods, in whose name I now command thee to quit this sanctuary, which is defiled by thy presence."

Bent-Anat's whole form quivered. "I will go," she said with sullen dignity.

She turned to recross the gateway of the Pylon. At the first step her glance met the eye of the poet. As one to whom it is vouchsafed to stand and gaze at some great prodigy, so Pentaur had stood opposite the royal maiden, uneasy and yet fascinated, agitated, yet with secretly uplifted soul. Her deed seemed to him of boundless audacity, and yet one suited to her true and noble nature. By her side, Ameni, his revered and admired master, sank into insignificance; and when she turned to leave the temple, his hand was raised indeed to hold her back, but as his glance met hers, his hand refused its office, and sought instead to still the throbbing of his overflowing heart.

The experienced priest, meanwhile, read the features of these two guileless beings like an open book. A quickly-formed tie, he felt, linked their souls, and the look which he saw them exchange startled him. The rebellious princess had glanced at the poet as though claiming approbation for her triumph, and Pentaur's eyes had responded to the appeal.

One instant Ameni paused. Then he cried: "Bent-Anat!"

The princess turned to the priest, and looked at him gravely and enquiringly.

Ameni took a step forward, and stood between her and the poet.

"Thou wouldst challenge the Gods to combat," he said sternly. "That is bold; but such daring it seems to me has grown up in thee because thou canst count on an ally, who stands scarcely farther from the Immortals than I myself. Hear this: —to thee, the misguided child, much may be forgiven. But a servant of the Divinity," and with these words he turned a threatening glance on Pentaur —"a priest, who in the war of free-will against law becomes a deserter, who forgets his duty and his oath-he will not long stand beside thee to support thee, for he-even though every God had blessed him with the richest gifts-he is damned. We drive him from among us, we curse him, we —"

At these words Bent-Anat looked now at Ameni, trembling with excitement, now at Pentaur standing opposite to her. Her face was red and white by turns, as light and shade chase each other on the ground when at noon-day a palm-grove is stirred by a storm.

The poet took a step towards her.

She felt that if he spoke it would be to defend all that she had done, and to ruin himself. A deep sympathy, a nameless anguish seized her soul, and before Pentaur could open his lips, she had sunk slowly down before Ameni, saying in low tones:

"I have sinned and defiled myself; thou hast said it-as Pentaur said it by the hut of the paraschites. Restore me to cleanness, Ameni, for I am unclean."

Like a flame that is crushed out by a hand, so the fire in the high-priest's eye was extinguished. Graciously, almost lovingly, he looked down on the princess, blessed her and conducted her before the holy of holies, there had clouds of incense wafted round her, anointed her with the nine holy oils, and commanded her to return to the royal castle.

Yet, said he, her guilt was not expiated; she should shortly learn by what prayers and exercises she might attain once more to perfect purity before the Gods, of whom he purposed to enquire in the holy place.

During all these ceremonies the priests stationed in the forecourt continued their lamentations.

The people standing before the temple listened to the priest's chant, and interrupted it from time to time with ringing cries of wailing, for already a dark rumor of what was going on within had spread among the multitude.

The sun was going down. The visitors to the Necropolis must soon be leaving it, and Bent-Anat, for whose appearance the people impatiently waited, would not show herself. One and another said the princess had been cursed, because she had taken remedies to the fair and injured Uarda, who was known to many of them.

Among the curious who had flocked together were many embalmers, laborers, and humble folk, who lived in the Necropolis. The mutinous and refractory temper of the Egyptians, which brought such heavy suffering on them under their later foreign rulers, was aroused, and rising with every minute. They reviled the pride of the priests, and their senseless, worthless, institutions. A drunken soldier, who soon reeled back into the tavern which he had but just left, distinguished himself as ringleader, and was the first to pick up a heavy stone to fling at the huge brass-plated temple gates. A few boys followed his example with shouts, and law-abiding men even, urged by the clamor of fanatical women, let themselves be led away to stone-flinging and words of abuse.

Within the House of Seti the priests' chant went on uninterruptedly; but at last, when the noise of the crowd grew louder, the great gate was thrown open, and with a solemn step Ameni, in full robes, and followed by twenty pastophori —[An order of priests] —who bore images of the Gods and holy symbols on their shoulders-Ameni walked into the midst of the crowd.

All were silent.

"Wherefore do you disturb our worship?" he asked loudly and calmly.

A roar of confused cries answered him, in which the frequently repeated name of Bent-Anat could alone be distinguished.

Ameni preserved his immoveable composure, and, raising his crozier, he cried —

"Make way for the daughter of Rameses, who sought and has found purification from the Gods, who behold the guilt of the highest as of the lowest among you. They reward the pious, but they punish the offender. Kneel down and let us pray that they may forgive you, and bless both you and your children."

Ameni took the holy Sistrum[45] from one of the attendant pastophori, and held it on high; the priests behind him raised a solemn hymn, and the crowd sank on their knees; nor did they move till the chant ceased and the high-priest again cried out:

"The Immortals bless you by me their servant. Leave this spot and make way for the daughter of Rameses."

With these words he withdrew into the temple, and the patrol, without meeting with any opposition, cleared the road guarded by Sphinxes which led to the Nile.

As Bent-Anat mounted her chariot Ameni said "Thou art the child of kings. The house of thy father rests on the shoulders of the people. Loosen the old laws which hold them subject, and the people will conduct themselves like these fools."

Ameni retired. Bent-Anat slowly arranged the reins in her hand, her eyes resting the while on the poet, who, leaning against a door-post, gazed at her in beatitude. She let her whip fall to the ground, that he might pick it up and restore it to her, but he did not observe it. A runner sprang forward and handed it to the princess, whose horses started off, tossing themselves and neighing.

Pentaur remained as if spell-bound, standing by the pillar, till the rattle of the departing wheels on the flag-way of the Avenue of Sphinxes had altogether died away, and the reflection of the glowing sunset painted the eastern hills with soft and rosy hues.

The far-sounding clang of a brass gong roused the poet from his ecstasy. It was the tomtom calling him to duty, to the lecture on rhetoric which at this hour he had to deliver to the young priests. He laid his left hand to his heart, and pressed his right hand to his forehead, as if to collect in its grasp his wandering thoughts; then silently and mechanically he went towards the open court in which his disciples awaited him. But instead of, as usual, considering on the way the subject he was to treat, his spirit and heart were occupied with the occurrences of the last few hours. One image reigned supreme in his imagination, filling it with delight-it was that of the fairest woman, who, radiant in her royal dignity and trembling with pride, had thrown herself in the dust for his sake. He felt as if her action had invested her whole being with a new and princely worth, as if her glance had brought light to his inmost soul, he seemed to breathe a freer air, to be borne onward on winged feet.

In such a mood he appeared before his hearers. When he found himself confronting all the the well-known faces, he remembered what it was he was called upon to do. He supported himself against the wall of the court, and opened the papyrus-roll handed to him by his favorite pupil, the young Anana. It was the book which twenty-four hours ago he had promised to begin upon. He looked now upon the characters that covered it, and felt that he was unable to read a word.

With a powerful effort he collected himself, and looking upwards tried to find the thread he had cut at the end of yesterday's lecture, and intended to resume to-day; but between yesterday and to-day, as it seemed to him, lay a vast sea whose roaring surges stunned his memory and powers of thought.

His scholars, squatting cross-legged on reed mats before him, gazed in astonishment on their silent master who was usually so ready of speech, and looked enquiringly at each other. A young priest whispered to his neighbor, "He is praying —" and Anana noticed with silent anxiety the strong hand of his teacher clutching the manuscript so tightly that the slight material of which it consisted threatened to split.

At last Pentaur looked down; he had found a subject. While he was looking upwards his gaze fell on the opposite wall, and the painted name of the king with the accompanying title "the good God" met his eye. Starting from these words he put this question to his hearers, "How do we apprehend the Goodness of the Divinity?"

He challenged one priest after another to treat this subject as if he were standing before his future congregation.

Several disciples rose, and spoke with more or less truth and feeling. At last it came to Anana's turn, who, in well-chosen words, praised the purpose-full beauty of animate and inanimate creation, in which the goodness of Amon[46] of Ra,[47] and Ptah,[48] as well as of the other Gods, finds expression.

Pentaur listened to the youth with folded arms, now looking at him enquiringly, now adding approbation. Then taking up the thread of the discourse when it was ended, he began himself to speak.

Like obedient falcons at the call of the falconer, thoughts rushed down into his mind, and the divine passion awakened in his breast glowed and shone through his inspired language that soared every moment on freer and stronger wings. Melting into pathos, exulting in rapture, he praised the splendor of nature; and the words flowed from his lips like a limpid crystal-clear stream as he glorified the eternal order of things, and the incomprehensible wisdom and care of the Creator-the One, who is one alone, and great and without equal.

"So incomparable," he said in conclusion, "is the home which God has given us. All that He-the One-has created is penetrated with His own essence, and bears witness to His Goodness. He who knows how to find Him sees Him everywhere, and lives at every instant in the enjoyment of His glory. Seek Him, and when ye have found Him fall down and sing praises before Him. But praise the Highest, not only in gratitude for the splendor of that which he has created, but for having given us the capacity for delight in his work. Ascend the mountain peaks and look on the distant country, worship when the sunset glows with rubies, and the dawn with roses, go out in the nighttime, and look at the stars as they travel in eternal, unerring, immeasurable, and endless circles on silver barks through the blue vault of heaven, stand by the cradle of the child, by the buds of the flowers, and see how the mother bends over the one, and the bright dew-drops fall on the other. But would you know where the stream of divine goodness is most freely poured out, where the grace of the Creator bestows the richest gifts, and where His holiest altars are prepared? In your own heart; so long as it is pure and full of love. In such a heart, nature is reflected as in a magic mirror, on whose surface the Beautiful shines in three-fold beauty. There the eye can reach far away over stream, and meadow, and hill, and take in the whole circle of the earth; there the morning and evening-red shine, not like roses and rubies, but like the very cheeks of the Goddess of Beauty; there the stars circle on, not in silence, but with the mighty voices of the pure eternal harmonies of heaven; there the child smiles like an infant-god, and the bud unfolds to magic flowers; finally, there thankfulness grows broader and devotion grows deeper, and we throw ourselves into the arms of a God, who-as I imagine his glory-is a God to whom the sublime nine great Gods pray as miserable and helpless suppliants."

The tomtom which announced the end of the hour interrupted him.

Pentaur ceased speaking with a deep sigh, and for a minute not a scholar moved.

At last the poet laid the papyrus roll out of his hand, wiped the sweat from his hot brow, and walked slowly towards the gate of the court, which led into the sacred grove of the temple. He had hardly crossed the threshold when he felt a hand laid upon his shoulder.

He looked round. Behind him stood Ameni. "You fascinated your hearers, my friend," said the high-priest, coldly; "it is a pity that only the Harp was wanting."

Ameni's words fell on the agitated spirit of the poet like ice on the breast of a man in fever. He knew this tone in his master's voice, for thus he was accustomed to reprove bad scholars and erring priests; but to him he had never yet so spoken.

"It certainly would seem," continued the high-priest, bitterly, "as if in your intoxication you had forgotten what it becomes the teacher to utter in the lecture-hall. Only a few weeks since you swore on my hands to guard the mysteries, and this day you have offered the great secret of the Unnameable one, the most sacred possession of the initiated, like some cheap ware in the open market."

"Thou cuttest with knives," said Pentaur.

"May they prove sharp, and extirpate the undeveloped canker, the rank weed from your soul," cried the high-priest. "You are young, too young; not like the tender fruit-tree that lets itself be trained aright, and brought to perfection, but like the green fruit on the ground, which will turn to poison for the children who pick it up-yea even though it fall from a sacred tree. Gagabu and I received you among us, against the opinion of the majority of the initiated. We gainsaid all those who doubted your ripeness because of your youth; and you swore to me, gratefully and enthusiastically, to guard the mysteries and the law. To-day for the first time I set you on the battle-field of life beyond the peaceful shelter of the schools. And how have you defended the standard that it was incumbent on you to uphold and maintain?"

"I did that which seemed to me to be right and true," answered Pentaur deeply moved.

"Right is the same for you as for us-what the law prescribes; and what is truth?"

"None has lifted her veil," said Pentaur, "but my soul is the offspring of the soul-filled body of the All; a portion of the infallible spirit of the Divinity stirs in my breast, and if it shows itself potent in me —"

"How easily we may mistake the flattering voice of self-love for that of the Divinity!"

"Cannot the Divinity which works and speaks in me-as in thee-as in each of us-recognize himself and his own voice?"

"If the crowd were to hear you," Ameni interrupted him, "each would set himself on his little throne, would proclaim the voice of the god within him as his guide, tear the law to shreds, and let the fragments fly to the desert on the east wind."

"I am one of the elect whom thou thyself hast taught to seek and to find the One. The light which I gaze on and am blest, would strike the crowd —I do not deny it-with blindness —"

"And nevertheless you blind our disciples with the dangerous glare-"

"I am educating them for future sages."

"And that with the hot overflow of a heart intoxicated with love!"

"Ameni!"

"I stand before you, uninvited, as your teacher, who reproves you out of the law, which always and everywhere is wiser than the individual, whose defender the king-among his highest titles-boasts of being, and to which the sage bows as much as the common man whom we bring up to blind belief—I stand before you as your father, who has loved you from a child, and expected from none of his disciples more than from you; and who will therefore neither lose you nor abandon the hope he has set upon you —

"Make ready to leave our quiet house early tomorrow morning. You have forfeited your office of teacher. You shall now go into the school of life, and make yourself fit for the honored rank of the initiated which, by my error, was bestowed on you too soon. You must leave your scholars without any leave-taking, however hard it may appear to you. After the star of Sothis[49] has risen come for your instructions. You must in these next months try to lead the priesthood in the temple of Hatasu, and in that post to win back my confidence which you have thrown away. No remonstrance; to-night you will receive my blessing, and our authority-you must greet the rising sun from the terrace of the new scene of your labors. May the Unnameable stamp the law upon your soul!"

Ameni returned to his room.

He walked restlessly to and fro.

On a little table lay a mirror; he looked into the clear metal pane, and laid it back in its place again, as if he had seen some strange and displeasing countenance.

The events of the last few hours had moved him deeply, and shaken his confidence in his unerring judgment of men and things.

The priests on the other bank of the Nile were Bent-Anat's counsellors, and he had heard the princess spoken of as a devout and gifted maiden. Her incautious breach of the sacred institutions had seemed to him to offer a welcome opportunity for humiliating —a member of the royal family.

Now he told himself that he had undervalued this young creature that he had behaved clumsily, perhaps foolishly, to her; for he did not for a moment conceal from himself that her sudden change of demeanor resulted much more from the warm flow of her sympathy, or perhaps of her, affection, than from any recognition of her guilt, and he could not utilize her transgression with safety to himself, unless she felt herself guilty.

Nor was he of so great a nature as to be wholly free from vanity, and his vanity had been deeply wounded by the haughty resistance of the princess.

When he commanded Pentaur to meet the princess with words of reproof, he had hoped to awaken his ambition through the proud sense of power over the mighty ones of the earth.

And now?

How had his gifted admirer, the most hopeful of all his disciples, stood the test.

The one ideal of his life, the unlimited dominion of the priestly idea over the minds of men, and of the priesthood over the king himself, had hitherto remained unintelligible to this singular young man.

He must learn to understand it.

"Here, as the least among a hundred who are his superiors, all the powers of resistance of his soaring soul have been roused," said Ameni to himself. "In the temple of Hatasu he will have to rule over the inferior orders of slaughterers of victims and incense-burners; and, by requiring obedience, will learn to estimate the necessity of it. The rebel, to whom a throne devolves, becomes a tyrant!"

"Pentuar's poet soul," so he continued to reflect "has quickly yielded itself a prisoner to the charm of Bent-Anat; and what woman could resist this highly favored being, who is radiant in beauty as Ra-Harmachis, and from whose lips flows speech as sweet as Techuti's. They ought never to meet again, for no tie must bind him to the house of Rameses."

Again he paced to and fro, and murmured:

"How is this? Two of my disciples have towered above their fellows, in genius and gifts, like palm trees above their undergrowth. I brought them up to succeed me, to inherit my labors and my hopes.

"Mesu fell away;[50] and Pentaur may follow him. Must my aim be an unworthy one because it does not attract the noblest? Not so. Each feels himself made of better stuff than his companions in destiny, constitutes his own law, and fears to see the great expended in trifles; but I think otherwise; like a brook of ferruginous water from Lebanon, I mix with the great stream, and tinge it with my color."

Thinking thus Ameni stood still.

Then he called to one of the so-called "holy fathers," his private secretary, and said:

"Draw up at once a document, to be sent to all the priests'-colleges in the land. Inform them that the daughter of Rameses has lapsed seriously from the law, and defiled herself, and direct that public-you hear me public-prayers shall be put up for her purification in every temple. Lay the letter before me to be signed within in hour. But no! Give me your reed and palette; I will myself draw up the instructions."

The "holy father" gave him writing materials, and retired into the background. Ameni muttered: "The King will do us some unheard-of violence! Well, this writing may be the first arrow in opposition to his lance."

CHAPTER VIII.

The moon was risen over the city of the living that lay opposite the Necropolis of Thebes.

The evening song had died away in the temples, that stood about a mile from the Nile, connected with each other by avenues of sphinxes and pylons; but in the streets of the city life seemed only just really awake.

The coolness, which had succeeded the heat of the summer day, tempted the citizens out into the air, in front of their doors or on the roofs and turrets of their houses; or at the tavern-tables, where they listened to the tales of the story-tellers while they refreshed them selves with beer, wine, and the sweet juice of fruits. Many simple folks squatted in circular groups on the ground, and joined in the burden of songs which were led by an appointed singer, to the sound of a tabor and flute.

To the south of the temple of Amon stood the king's palace, and near it, in more or less extensive gardens, rose the houses of the magnates of the kingdom, among which, one was distinguished by it splendor and extent.

Paaker, the king's pioneer, had caused it to be erected after the death of his father, in the place of the more homely dwelling of his ancestors, when he hoped to bring home his cousin, and install her as its mistress. A few yards further to the east was another stately though older and less splendid house, which Mena, the king's charioteer, had inherited from his father, and which was inhabited by his wife Nefert and her mother Isatuti, while he himself, in the distant Syrian land, shared the tent of the king, as being his body-guard. Before the door of each house stood servants bearing torches, and awaiting the long deferred return home of their masters.

The gate, which gave admission to Paaker's plot of ground through the wall which surrounded it, was disproportionately, almost ostentatiously, high and decorated with various paintings. On the right hand and on the left, two cedar-trunks were erected as masts to carry standards; he had had them felled for the purpose on Lebanon, and forwarded by ship to Pelusium on the north-east coast of Egypt. Thence they were conveyed by the Nile to Thebes.

On passing through the gate one entered a wide, paved court-yard, at the sides of which walks extended, closed in at the back, and with roofs supported on slender painted wooden columns. Here stood the pioneer's horses and chariots, here dwelt his slaves, and here the necessary store of produce for the month's requirements was kept.

In the farther wall of this store-court was a very high doorway, that led into a large garden with rows of well-tended trees and trellised vines, clumps of shrubs, flowers, and beds of vegetables. Palms, sycamores, and acacia-trees, figs, pomegranates, and jasmine throve here particularly well-for Paaker's mother, Setchem, superintended the labors of the gardeners; and in the large tank in the midst there was never any lack of water for watering the beds and the roots of the trees, as it was always supplied by two canals, into which wheels turned by oxen poured water day and night from the Nile-stream.

On the right side of this plot of ground rose the one-storied dwelling house, its length stretching into distant perspective, as it consisted of a single row of living and bedrooms. Almost every room had its own door, that opened into a veranda supported by colored wooden columns, and which extended the whole length of the garden side of the house. This building was joined at a right angle by a row of store-rooms, in which the garden-produce in fruits and vegetables, the wine-jars, and the possessions of the house in woven stuffs, skins, leather, and other property were kept.

In a chamber of strong masonry lay safely locked up the vast riches accumulated by Paaker's father and by himself, in gold and silver rings, vessels and figures of beasts. Nor was there lack of bars of copper and of precious stones, particularly of lapis-lazuli and malachite.

In the middle of the garden stood a handsomely decorated kiosk, and a chapel with images of the Gods; in the background stood the statues of Paaker's ancestors in the form of Osiris wrapped in mummy-cloths.[51]

The faces, which were likenesses, alone distinguished these statues from each other.

The left side of the store-yard was veiled in gloom, yet the moonlight revealed numerous dark figures clothed only with aprons, the slaves of the king's pioneer, who squatted on the ground in groups of five or six, or lay near each other on thin mats of palm-bast, their hard beds.

Not far from the gate, on the right side of the court, a few lamps lighted up a group of dusky men, the officers of Paaker's household, who wore short, shirt-shaped, white garments, and who sat on a carpet round a table hardly two feet high. They were eating their evening-meal, consisting of a roasted antelope, and large flat cakes of bread. Slaves waited on them, and filled their earthen beakers with yellow beer. The steward cut up the great roast on the table, offered the intendant of the gardens a piece of antelope-leg, and said:[52]

"My arms ache; the mob of slaves get more and more dirty and refractory."

"I notice it in the palm-trees," said the gardener, "you want so many cudgels that their crowns will soon be as bare as a moulting bird."

"We should do as the master does," said the head-groom, "and get sticks of ebony-they last a hundred years."

"At any rate longer than men's bones," laughed the chief neat-herd, who had come in to town from the pioneer's country estate, bringing with him animals for sacrifices, butter and cheese. "If we were all to follow the master's example, we should soon have none but cripples in the servant's house."

"Out there lies the lad whose collar-bone he broke yesterday," said the steward, "it is a pity, for he was a clever mat-platter. The old lord hit softer."

"You ought to know!" cried a small voice, that sounded mockingly behind the feasters.

They looked and laughed when they recognized the strange guest, who had approached them unobserved.

The new comer was a deformed little man about as big as a five-year-old boy, with a big head and oldish but uncommonly sharply-cut features.

The noblest Egyptians kept house-dwarfs for sport, and this little wight served the wife of Mena in this capacity. He was called Nemu, or "the dwarf," and his sharp tongue made him much feared, though he was a favorite, for he passed for a very clever fellow and was a good tale-teller.

"Make room for me, my lords," said the little man. "I take very little room, and your beer and roast is in little danger from me, for my maw is no bigger than a fly's head."

"But your gall is as big as that of a Nile-horse," cried the cook.

"It grows," said the dwarf laughing, "when a turn-spit and spoon-wielder like you turns up. There —I will sit here."

"You are welcome," said the steward, "what do you bring?"

"Myself."

"Then you bring nothing great."

"Else I should not suit you either!" retorted the dwarf. "But seriously, my lady mother, the noble Katuti, and the Regent, who just now is visiting us, sent me here to ask you whether Paaker is not yet returned. He accompanied the princess and Nefert to the City of the Dead, and the ladies are not yet come in. We begin to be anxious, for it is already late."

The steward looked up at the starry sky and said: "The moon is already tolerably high, and my lord meant to be home before sun-down."

"The meal was ready," sighed the cook. "I shall have to go to work again if he does not remain all night."

"How should he?" asked the steward. "He is with the princess Bent-Anat."

"And my mistress," added the dwarf.

"What will they say to each other," laughed gardener; "your chief litter-bearer declared that yesterday on the way to the City of the Dead they did not speak a word to each other."

"Can you blame the lord if he is angry with the lady who was betrothed to him, and then was wed to another? When I think of the moment when he learnt Nefert's breach of faith I turn hot and cold."

"Care the less for that," sneered the dwarf, "since you must be hot in summer and cold in winter."

"It is not evening all day," cried the head groom. "Paaker never forgets an injury, and we shall live to see him pay Mena-high as he is-for the affront he has offered him."

"My lady Katuti," interrupted Nemu, "stores up the arrears of her son-in-law."

"Besides, she has long wished to renew the old friendship with your house, and the Regent too preaches peace. Give me a piece of bread, steward. I am hungry!"

"The sacks, into which Mena's arrears flow seem to be empty," laughed the cook.

"Empty! empty! much like your wit!" answered the dwarf. "Give me a bit of roast meat, steward; and you slaves bring me a drink of beer."

"You just now said your maw was no bigger than a fly's head," cried the cook, "and now you devour meat like the crocodiles in the sacred tank of Seeland. You must come from a world of upside-down, where the men are as small as flies, and the flies as big as the giants of the past."

"Yet, I might be much bigger," mumbled the dwarf while he munched on unconcernedly, "perhaps as big as your spite which grudges me the third bit of meat, which the steward-may Zefa bless him with great possessions-is cutting out of the back of the antelope."

"There, take it, you glutton, but let out your girdle," said the steward laughing, "I had cut the slice for myself, and admire your sharp nose."

"All noses," said the dwarf, "they teach the knowing better than any haruspex what is inside a man."

"How is that?" cried the gardener.

"Only try to display your wisdom," laughed the steward; "for, if you want to talk, you must at last leave off eating."

"The two may be combined," said the dwarf. "Listen then! A hooked nose, which I compare to a vulture's beak, is never found together with a submissive spirit. Think of the Pharaoh and all his haughty race. The Regent, on the contrary, has a straight, well-shaped, medium-sized nose, like the statue of Amon in the temple, and he is an upright soul, and as good as the Gods. He is neither overbearing nor submissive beyond just what is right; he holds neither with the great nor yet with the mean, but with men of our stamp. There's the king for us!"

"A king of noses!" exclaimed the cook, "I prefer the eagle Rameses. But what do you say to the nose of your mistress Nefert?"

"It is delicate and slender and moves with every thought like the leaves of flowers in a breath of wind, and her heart is exactly like it."

"And Paaker?" asked the head groom.

"He has a large short nose with wide open nostrils. When Seth whirls up the sand, and a grain of it flies up his nose, he waxes angry-so it is Paaker's nose, and that only, which is answerable for all your blue bruises. His mother Setchem, the sister of my lady Katuti, has a little roundish soft —"

"You pigmy," cried the steward interrupting the speaker, "we have fed you and let you abuse people to your heart's content, but if you wag your sharp tongue against our mistress, I will take you by the girdle and fling you to the sky, so that the stars may remain sticking to your crooked hump."

At these words the dwarf rose, turned to go, and said indifferently: "I would pick the stars carefully off my back, and send you the finest of the planets in return for your juicy bit of roast. But here come the chariots. Farewell! my lords, when the vulture's beak seizes one of you and carries you off to the war in Syria, remember the words of the little Nemu who knows men and noses."

The pioneer's chariot rattled through the high gates into the court of his house, the dogs in their leashes howled joyfully, the head groom hastened towards Paaker and took the reins in his charge, the steward accompanied him, and the head cook retired into the kitchen to make ready a fresh meal for his master.

Before Paaker had reached the garden-gate, from the pylon of the enormous temple of Amon, was heard first the far-sounding clang of hard-struck plates of brass, and then the many-voiced chant of a solemn hymn.

The Mohar stood still, looked up to heaven, called to his servants —"The divine star Sothis is risen!" threw himself on the earth, and lifted his wards the star in prayer.

The slaves and officers immediately followed his example.

No circumstance in nature remained unobserved by the priestly guides of the Egyptian people. Every phenomenon on earth or in the starry heavens was greeted by them as the manifestation of a divinity, and they surrounded the life of the inhabitants of the Nile-valley —from morning to evening-from the beginning of the inundation to the days of drought-with a web of chants and sacrifices, of processions and festivals, which inseparably knit the human individual to the Divinity and its earthly representatives the priesthood.

For many minutes the lord and his servants remained on their knees in silence, their eyes fixed on the sacred star, and listening to the pious chant of the priests.

As it died away Paaker rose. All around him still lay on the earth; only one naked figure, strongly lighted by the clear moonlight, stood motionless by a pillar near the slaves' quarters.

The pioneer gave a sign, the attendants rose; but Paaker went with hasty steps to the man who had disdained the act of devotion, which he had so earnestly performed, and cried:

"Steward, a hundred strokes on the soles of the feet of this scoffer."

The officer thus addressed bowed and said: "My lord, the surgeon commanded the mat-weaver not to move and he cannot lift his arm. He is suffering great pain. Thou didst break his collar-bone yesterday.

"It served him right!" said Paaker, raising his voice so much that the injured man could not fail to hear it. Then he turned his back upon him, and entered the garden; here he called the chief butler, and said: "Give the slaves beer for their night draught-to all of them, and plenty."

A few minutes later he stood before his mother, whom he found on the roof of the house, which was decorated with leafy plants, just as she gave her two-years'-old grand daughter, the child of her youngest son, into the arms of her nurse, that she might take her to bed.

Paaker greeted the worthy matron with reverence. She was a woman of a friendly, homely aspect; several little dogs were fawning at her feet. Her son put aside the leaping favorites of the widow, whom they amused through many long hours of loneliness, and turned to take the child in his arms from those of the attendant. But the little one struggled with such loud cries, and could not be pacified, that Paaker set it down on the ground, and involuntarily exclaimed:

"The naughty little thing!"

"She has been sweet and good the whole afternoon," said his mother Setchem. "She sees you so seldom."

"May be," replied Paaker; "still I know this-the dogs love me, but no child will come to me."

"You have such hard hands."

"Take the squalling brat away," said Paaker to the nurse. "Mother, I want to speak to you."

Setchem quieted the child, gave it many kisses, and sent it to bed; then she went up to her son, stroked his cheeks, and said:

"If the little one were your own, she would go to you at once, and teach you that a child is the greatest blessing which the Gods bestow on us mortals." Paaker smiled and said: "I know what you are aiming at-but leave it for the present, for I have something important to communicate to you."

"Well?" asked Setchem.

"To-day for the first time since-you know when, I have spoken to Nefert. The past may be forgotten. You long for your sister; go to her, I have nothing more to say against it."

Setchem looked at her son with undisguised astonishment; her eyes which easily filled with tears, now overflowed, and she hesitatingly asked: "Can I believe my ears; child, have you? —"

"I have a wish," said Paaker firmly, "that you should knit once more the old ties of affection with your relations; the estrangement has lasted long enough."

"Much too long!" cried Setchem.

The pioneer looked in silence at the ground, and obeyed his mother's sign to sit down beside her.

"I knew," she said, taking his hand, "that this day would bring us joy; for I dreamt of your father in Osiris, and when I was being carried to the temple, I was met, first by a white cow, and then by a wedding procession. The white ram of Anion, too, touched the wheat-cakes that I offered him." —[It boded death to Germanicus when the Apis refused to eat out of his hand.]

"Those are lucky presages," said Paaker in a tone of conviction.

"And let us hasten to seize with gratitude that which the Gods set before us," cried Setchem with joyful emotion. "I will go to-morrow to my sister and tell her that we shall live together in our old affection, and share both good and evil; we are both of the same race, and I know that, as order and cleanliness preserve a house from ruin and rejoice the stranger, so nothing but unity can keep up the happiness of the family and its appearance before people. What is bygone is bygone, and let it be forgotten. There are many women in Thebes besides Nefert, and a hundred nobles in the land would esteem themselves happy to win you for a son-in-law."

Paaker rose, and began thoughtfully pacing the broad space, while Setchem went on speaking.

"I know," she said, "that I have touched a wound in thy heart; but it is already closing, and it will heal when you are happier even than the charioteer Mena, and need no longer hate him. Nefert is good, but she is delicate and not clever, and scarcely equal to the management of so large a household as ours. Ere long I too shall be wrapped in mummy-cloths, and then if duty calls you into Syria some prudent housewife must take my place. It is no small matter. Your grandfather Assa often would say that a house well-conducted in every detail was a mark of a family owning an unspotted race, and living with wise liberality and secure solidity, in which each had his assigned place, his allotted duty to fulfil, and his fixed rights to demand. How often have I prayed to the Hathors that they may send you a wife after my own heart."

"A Setchem I shall never find!" said Paaker kissing his mother's forehead, "women of your sort are dying out."

"Flatterer!" laughed Setchem, shaking her finger at her son. But it is true. Those who are now growing up dress and smarten themselves with stuffs from Kaft —[Phoenicia] —mix their language with Syrian words, and leave the steward and housekeeper free when they themselves ought to command. Even my sister Katuti, and Nefert —

"Nefert is different from other women," interrupted Paaker, "and if you had brought her up she would know how to manage a house as well as how to ornament it."

Setchem looked at her son in surprise; then she said, half to herself: "Yes, yes, she is a sweet child; it is impossible for any one to be angry with her who looks into her eyes. And yet I was cruel to her because you were hurt by her, and because-but you know. But now you have forgiven, I forgive her, willingly, her and her husband."

Paaker's brow clouded, and while he paused in front of his mother he said with all the peculiar harshness of his voice:

"He shall pine away in the desert, and the hyaenas of the North shall tear his unburied corpse."

At these words Setchem covered her face with her veil, and clasped her hands tightly over the amulets hanging round her neck. Then she said softly:

"How terrible you can be! I know well that you hate the charioteer, for I have seen the seven arrows over your couch over which is written 'Death to Mena.'"

"That is a Syrian charm which a man turns against any one whom he desires to destroy. How black you look! Yes, it is a charm that is hateful to the Gods, and that gives the evil one power over him that uses it. Leave it to them to punish the criminal, for Osiris withdraws his favor from those who choose the fiend for their ally."

"My sacrifices," replied Paaker, "secure me the favor of the Gods; but Mena behaved to me like a vile robber, and I only return to him the evil that belongs to him. Enough of this! and if you love me, never again utter the name of my enemy before me. I have forgiven Nefert and her mother-that may satisfy you."

Setchem shook her head, and said: "What will it lead to! The war cannot last for ever, and if Mena returns the reconciliation of to-day will turn to all the more bitter enmity. I see only one remedy. Follow my advice, and let me find you a wife worthy of you."

"Not now!" exclaimed Paaker impatiently. "In a few days I must go again into the enemy's country, and do not wish to leave my wife, like Mena, to lead the life of a widow during my existence. Why urge it? my brother's wife and children are with you-that might satisfy you."

"The Gods know how I love them," answered Setchem; "but your brother Horns is the younger, and you the elder, to whom the inheritance belongs. Your little niece is a delightful plaything, but in your son I should see at once the future stay of our race, the future head of the family; brought up to my mind and your father's; for all is sacred to me that my dead husband wished. He rejoiced in your early betrothal to Nefert, and hoped that a son of his eldest son should continue the race of Assa."

"It shall be by no fault of mine that any wish of his remains unfulfilled. The stars are high, mother; sleep well, and if to-morrow you visit Nefert and your sister, say to them that the doors of my house are open to them. But stay! Katuti's steward has offered to sell a herd of cattle to ours, although the stock on Mena's land can be but small. What does this mean?"

"You know my sister," replied Setchem. "She manages Mena's possessions, has many requirements, tries to vie with the greatest in splendor, sees the governor often in her house, her son is no doubt extravagant-and so the most necessary things may often be wanting."

Paaker shrugged his shoulders, once more embraced his mother and left her.

Soon after, he was standing in the spacious room in which he was accustomed to sit and to sleep when he was in Thebes. The walls of this room were whitewashed and decorated with pious glyphic writing, which framed in the door and the windows opening into the garden.

In the middle of the farther wall was a couch in the form of a lion. The upper end of it imitated a lion's head, and the foot, its curling tail; a finely dressed lion's skin was spread over the bell, and a headrest of ebony, decorated with pious texts, stood on a high foot-step, ready for the sleeper.

Above the bed various costly weapons and whips were elegantly displayed, and below them the seven arrows over which Setchem had read the words "Death to Mena." They were written across a sentence which enjoined feeding the hungry, giving drink to the thirsty, and clothing the naked; with loving-kindness, alike to the great and the humble.

A niche by the side of the bed-head was closed with a curtain of purple stuff.

In each corner of the room stood a statue; three of them symbolized the triad of Thebes-Anion, Muth, and Chunsu-and the fourth the dead father of the pioneer. In front of each was a small altar for offerings, with a hollow in it, in which was an odoriferous essence. On a wooden stand were little images of the Gods and amulets in great number, and in several painted chests lay the clothes, the ornaments and the papers of the master. In the midst of the chamber stood a table and several stool-shaped seats.

When Paaker entered the room he found it lighted with lamps, and a large dog sprang joyfully to meet him. He let him spring upon him, threw him to the ground, let him once more rush upon him, and then kissed his clever head.

Before his bed an old negro of powerful build lay in deep sleep. Paaker shoved him with his foot and called to him as he awoke —

"I am hungry."

The grey-headed black man rose slowly, and left the room.

As soon as he was alone Paaker drew the philter from his girdle, looked at it tenderly, and put it in a box, in which there were several flasks of holy oils for sacrifice. He was accustomed every evening to fill the hollows in the altars with fresh essences, and to prostrate himself in prayer before the images of the Gods. To-day he stood before the statue of his father, kissed its feet, and murmured: "Thy will shall be done. —The woman whom thou didst intend for me shall indeed be mine-thy eldest son's."

Then he walked to and fro and thought over the events of the day.

At last he stood still, with his arms crossed, and looked defiantly at the holy images; like a traveller who drives away a false guide, and thinks to find the road by himself.

His eye fell on the arrows over his bed; he smiled, and striking his broad breast with his fist, he exclaimed, "I —I —I —"

His hound, who thought his master meant to call him, rushed up to him. He pushed him off and said —"If you meet a hyaena in the desert, you fall upon it without waiting till it is touched by my lance-and if the Gods, my masters, delay, I myself will defend my right; but thou," he continued turning to the image of his father, "thou wilt support me."

This soliloquy was interrupted by the slaves who brought in his meal.

Paaker glanced at the various dishes which the cook had prepared for him, and asked: "How often shall I command that not a variety, but only one large dish shall be dressed for me? And the wine?"

"Thou art used never to touch it?" answered the old negro.

"But to-day I wish for some," said the pioneer. "Bring one of the old jars of red wine of Kakem."

The slaves looked at each other in astonishment; the wine was brought, and Paaker emptied beaker after beaker. When the servants had left him, the boldest among them said: "Usually the master eats like a lion, and drinks like a midge, but to-day —"

"Hold your tongue!" cried his companion, "and come into the court, for Paaker has sent us out beer. The Hathors must have met him."

The occurrences of the day must indeed have taken deep hold on the inmost soul of the pioneer; for he, the most sober of all the warriors of Rameses, to whom intoxication was un-known, and who avoided the banquets of his associates-now sat at the midnight hours, alone at his table, and toped till his weary head grew heavy.

He collected himself, went towards his couch and drew the curtain which concealed the niche at the head of the bed. A female figure, with the head-dress and attributes of the Goddess Hathor, made of painted limestone, revealed itself.

Her countenance had the features of the wife of Mena.

The king, four years since, had ordered a sculptor to execute a sacred image with the lovely features of the newly-married bride of his charioteer, and Paaker had succeeded in having a duplicate made.

He now knelt down on the couch, gazed on the image with moist eyes, looked cautiously around to see if he was alone, leaned forward, pressed a kiss to the delicate, cold stone lips; laid down and went to sleep without undressing himself, and leaving the lamps to burn themselves out.

Restless dreams disturbed his spirit, and when the dawn grew grey, he screamed out, tor-mented by a hideous vision, so pitifully, that the old negro, who had laid himself near the dog at the foot of his bed, sprang up alarmed, and while the dog howled, called him by his name to wake him.

Paaker awoke with a dull head-ache. The vision which had tormented him stood vividly before his mind, and he endeavored to retain it that he might summon a haruspex to interpret it. After the morbid fancies of the preceding evening he felt sad and depressed.

The morning-hymn rang into his room with a warning voice from the temple of Amon; he cast off evil thoughts, and resolved once more to resign the conduct of his fate to the Gods, and to renounce all the arts of magic.

As he was accustomed, he got into the bath that was ready for him. While splashing in the tepid water he thought with ever increasing eagerness of Nefert and of the philter which at first he had meant not to offer to her, but which actually was given to her by his hand, and which might by this time have begun to exercise its charm.

Love placed rosy pictures-hatred set blood-red images before his eyes. He strove to free himself from the temptations, which more and more tightly closed in upon him, but it was with him as with a man who has fallen into a bog, who, the more vehemently he tries to escape from the mire, sinks the deeper.

As the sun rose, so rose his vital energy and his self-confidence, and when he prepared to quit his dwelling, in his most costly clothing, he had arrived once more at the decision of the night before, and had again resolved to fight for his purpose, without-and if need were-against the Gods.

The Mohar had chosen his road, and he never turned back when once he had begun a journey.

CHAPTER IX.

It was noon: the rays of the sun found no way into the narrow shady streets of the city of Thebes, but they blazed with scorching heat on the broad dyke-road which led to the king's castle, and which at this hour was usually almost deserted.

To-day it was thronged with foot-passengers and chariots, with riders and litter-bearers.

Here and there negroes poured water on the road out of skins, but the dust was so deep, that, in spite of this, it shrouded the streets and the passengers in a dry cloud, which extended not only over the city, but down to the harbor where the boats of the inhabitants of the Necropolis landed their freight.

The city of the Pharaohs was in unwonted agitation, for the storm-swift breath of rumor had spread some news which excited both alarm and hope in the huts of the poor as well as in the palaces of the great.

In the early morning three mounted messengers had arrived from the king's camp with heavy letter-bags, and had dismounted at the Regent's palace.[53]

As after a long drought the inhabitants of a village gaze up at the black thunder-cloud that gathers above their heads promising the refreshing rain-but that may also send the kindling lightning-flash or the destroying hail-storm —so the hopes and the fears of the citizens were centred on the news which came but rarely and at irregular intervals from the scene of war; for there was scarcely a house in the huge city which had not sent a father, a son, or a relative to the fighting hosts of the king in the distant northeast.

And though the couriers from the camp were much oftener the heralds of tears than of joy; though the written rolls which they brought told more often of death and wounds than of promotion, royal favors, and conquered spoil, yet they were expected with soul-felt longing and received with shouts of joy.

Great and small hurried after their arrival to the Regent's palace, and the scribes-who distributed the letters and read the news which was intended for public communication, and the lists of those who had fallen or perished-were closely besieged with enquirers.

Man has nothing harder to endure than uncertainty, and generally, when in suspense, looks forward to bad rather than to good news. And the bearers of ill ride faster than the messengers of weal.

The Regent Ani resided in a building adjoining the king's palace. His business-quarters surrounded an immensely wide court, and consisted of a great number of rooms opening on to this court, in which numerous scribes worked with their chief. On the farther side was a large, veranda-like hall open at the front, with a roof supported by pillars.

Here Ani was accustomed to hold courts of justice, and to receive officers, messengers, and petitioners. To-day he sat, visible to all comers, on a costly throne in this hall, surrounded by his numerous followers, and overlooking the crowd of people whom the guardians of the peace guided with long staves, admitting them in troops into the court of the "High Gate," and then again conducting them out.

What he saw and heard was nothing joyful, for from each group surrounding a scribe arose a cry of woe. Few and far between were those who had to tell of the rich booty that had fallen to their friends.

An invisible web woven of wailing and tears seemed to envelope the assembly.

Here men were lamenting and casting dust upon their heads, there women were rending their clothes, shrieking loudly, and crying as they waved their veils "oh, my husband! oh, my father! oh, my brother!"

Parents who had received the news of the death of their son fell on each other's neck weeping; old men plucked out their grey hair and beard; young women beat their forehead and breast, or implored the scribes who read out the lists to let them see for themselves the name of the beloved one who was for ever torn from them.

The passionate stirring of a soul, whether it be the result of joy or of sorrow, among us moderns covers its features with a veil, which it had no need of among the ancients.

Where the loudest laments sounded, a restless little being might be seen hurrying from group to group; it was Nemu, Katuti's dwarf, whom we know.

Now he stood near a woman of the better class, dissolved in tears because her husband had fallen in the last battle.

"Can you read?" he asked her; "up there on the architrave is the name of Rameses, with all his titles. Dispenser of life,' he is called. Aye indeed; he can create-widows; for he has all the husbands killed."

Before the astonished woman could reply, he stood by a man sunk in woe, and pulling his robe, said "Finer fellows than your son have never been seen in Thebes. Let your youngest starve, or beat him to a cripple, else he also will be dragged off to Syria; for Rameses needs much good Egyptian meat for the Syrian vultures."

The old man, who had hitherto stood there in silent despair, clenched his fist. The dwarf pointed to the Regent, and said: "If he there wielded the sceptre, there would be fewer orphans and beggars by the Nile. To-day its sacred waters are still sweet, but soon it will taste as salt as the north sea with all the tears that have been shed on its banks."

It almost seemed as if the Regent had heard these words, for he rose from his seat and lifted his hands like a man who is lamenting.

Many of the bystanders observed this action; and loud cries of anguish filled the wide court-yard, which was soon cleared by soldiers to make room for other troops of people who were thronging in.

While these gathered round the scribes, the Regent Ani sat with quiet dignity on the throne, surrounded by his suite and his secretaries, and held audiences.

He was a man at the close of his fortieth year and the favorite cousin of the king.

Rameses I., the grandfather of the reigning monarch, had deposed the legitimate royal family, and usurped the sceptre of the Pharaohs. He descended from a Semitic race who had remained in Egypt at the time of the expulsion of the Hyksos,[54] and had distinguished itself by warlike talents under Thotmes and Amenophis. After his death he was succeeded by his son Seti, who sought to earn a legitimate claim to the throne by marrying Tuaa, the grand-daughter of Amenophis III. She presented him with an only son, whom he named after his father Rameses. This prince might lay claim to perfect legitimacy through his mother, who descended directly from the old house of sovereigns; for in Egypt a noble family-even that of the Pharaohs-might be perpetuated through women.

Seti proclaimed Rameses partner of his throne, so as to remove all doubt as to the validity of his position. The young nephew of his wife Tuaa, the Regent Ani, who was a few years younger than Rameses, he caused to be brought up in the House of Seti, and treated him like his own son, while the other members of the dethroned royal family were robbed of their possessions or removed altogether.

Ani proved himself a faithful servant to Seti, and to his son, and was trusted as a brother by the warlike and magnanimous Rameses, who however never disguised from himself the fact that the blood in his own veins was less purely royal than that which flowed in his cousin's.

It was required of the race of the Pharaohs of Egypt that it should be descended from the Sun-god Ra, and the Pharaoh could boast of this high descent only through his mother-Ani through both parents.

But Rameses sat on the throne, held the sceptre with a strong hand, and thirteen young sons promised to his house the lordship over Egypt to all eternity.

When, after the death of his warlike father, he went to fresh conquests in the north, he appointed Ani, who had proved himself worthy as governor of the province of Kush, to the regency of the kingdom.

A vehement character often over estimates the man who is endowed with a quieter tempera-ment, into whose nature he cannot throw himself, and whose excellences he is unable to imitate;

so it happened that the deliberate and passionless nature of his cousin impressed the fiery and warlike Rameses.

Ani appeared to be devoid of ambition, or the spirit of enterprise; he accepted the dignity that was laid upon him with apparent reluctance, and seemed a particularly safe person, because he had lost both wife and child, and could boast of no heir.

He was a man of more than middle height; his features were remarkably regular-even beautifully, cut, but smooth and with little expression. His clear blue eyes and thin lips gave no evidence of the emotions that filled his heart; on the contrary, his countenance wore a soft smile that could adapt itself to haughtiness, to humility, and to a variety of shades of feeling, but which could never be entirely banished from his face.

He had listened with affable condescension to the complaint of a landed proprietor, whose cattle had been driven off for the king's army, and had promised that his case should be enquired into. The plundered man was leaving full of hope; but when the scribe who sat at the feet of the Regent enquired to whom the investigation of this encroachment of the troops should be entrusted, Ani said: "Each one must bring a victim to the war; it must remain among the things that are done, and cannot be undone."

The Nomarch —[Chief of a Nome or district.] —of Suan, in the southern part of the country, asked for funds for a necessary, new embankment. The Regent listened to his eager representation with benevolence, nay with expressions of sympathy; but assured him that the war absorbed all the funds of the state, that the chests were empty; still he felt inclined-even if they had not failed-to sacrifice a part of his own income to preserve the endangered arable land of his faithful province of Suan, to which he desired greeting.

As soon as the Nomarch had left him, he commanded that a considerable sum should be taken out of the Treasury, and sent after the petitioner.

From time to time in the middle of conversation, he arose, and made a gesture of lamentation, to show to the assembled mourners in the court that he sympathized in the losses which had fallen on them.

The sun had already passed the meridian, when a disturbance, accompanied by loud cries, took possession of the masses of people, who stood round the scribes in the palace court.

Many men and women were streaming together towards one spot, and even the most impassive of the Thebans present turned their attention to an incident so unusual in this place.

A detachment of constabulary made a way through the crushing and yelling mob, and another division of Lybian police led a prisoner towards a side gate of the court. Before they could reach it, a messenger came up with them, from the Regent, who desired to be informed as to what happened.

The head of the officers of public safety followed him, and with eager excitement informed Ani, who was waiting for him, that a tiny man, the dwarf of the Lady Katuti, had for several hours been going about in the court, and endeavoring to poison the minds of the citizens with seditious speeches.

Ani ordered that the misguided man should be thrown into the dungeon; but so soon as the chief officer had left him, he commanded his secretary to have the dwarf brought into his presence before sundown.

While he was giving this order an excitement of another kind seized the assembled multitude.

As the sea parted and stood on the right hand and on the left of the Hebrews, so that no wave wetted the foot of the pursued fugitives, so the crowd of people of their own free will, but as if in reverent submission to some high command, parted and formed a broad way, through which walked the high-priest of the House of Seti, as, full robed and accompanied by some of the "holy fathers," he now entered the court.

The Regent went to meet him, bowed before him, and then withdrew to the back of the hall with him alone. "It is nevertheless incredible," said Ameni, "that our serfs are to follow the militia!"

"Rameses requires soldiers-to conquer," replied the Regent.

"And we bread-to live," exclaimed the priest.

"Nevertheless I am commanded, at once, before the seed-time, to levy the temple-serfs. I regret the order, but the king is the will, and I am only the hand."

"The hand, which he makes use of to sequester ancient rights, and to open a way to the desert over the fruitful land."[55]

"Your acres will not long remain unprovided for. Rameses will win new victories with the increased army, and the help of the Gods."

"The Gods! whom he insults!"

"After the conclusion of peace he will reconcile the Gods by doubly rich gifts. He hopes confidently for an early end to the war, and writes to me that after the next battle he wins he intends to offer terms to the Cheta. A plan of the king's is also spoken of-to marry again, and, indeed, the daughter of the Cheta King Chetasar."

Up to this moment the Regent had kept his eyes cast down. Now he raised them, smiling, as if he would fain enjoy Ameni's satisfaction, and asked:

"What dost thou say to this project?"

"I say," returned Ameni, and his voice, usually so stern, took a tone of amusement, "I say that Rameses seems to think that the blood of thy cousin and of his mother, which gives him his right to the throne, is incapable of pollution."

"It is the blood of the Sun-god!"

"Which runs but half pure in his veins, but wholly pure in thine."

The Regent made a deprecatory gesture, and said softly, with a smile which resembled that of a dead man:

"We are not alone."

"No one is here," said Ameni, "who can hear us; and what I say is known to every child."

"But if it came to the king's ears —" whispered Ani, "he —"

"He would perceive how unwise it is to derogate from the ancient rights of those on whom it is incumbent to prove the purity of blood of the sovereign of this land. However, Rameses sits on the throne; may life bloom for him, with health and strength!" —[A formula which even in private letters constantly follows the name of the Pharaoh.]

The Regent bowed, and then asked:

"Do you propose to obey the demand of the Pharaoh without delay?"

"He is the king. Our council, which will meet in a few days, can only determine how, and not whether we shall fulfil his command."

"You will retard the departure of the serfs, and Rameses requires them at once. The bloody labor of the war demands new tools."

"And the peace will perhaps demand a new master, who understands how to employ the sons of the land to its greatest advantage —a genuine son of Ra."

The Regent stood opposite the high-priest, motionless as an image cast in bronze, and re-mained silent; but Ameni lowered his staff before him as before a god, and then went into the fore part of the hall.

When Ani followed him, a soft smile played as usual upon his countenance, and full of dignity he took his seat on the throne.

"Art thou at an end of thy communications?" he asked the high-priest.

"It remains for me to inform you all," replied Ameni with a louder voice, to be heard by all the assembled dignitaries, "that the princess Bent-Anat yesterday morning committed a heavy sin, and that in all the temples in the land the Gods shall be entreated with offerings to take her uncleanness from her."

Again a shadow passed over the smile on the Regent's countenance. He looked meditatively on the ground, and then said:

"To-morrow I will visit the House of Seti; till then I beg that this affair may be left to rest."

Ameni bowed, and the Regent left the hall to withdraw to a wing of the king's palace, in which he dwelt.

On his writing-table lay sealed papers. He knew that they contained important news for him; but he loved to do violence to his curiosity, to test his resolution, and like an epicure to reserve the best dish till the last.

He now glanced first at some unimportant letters. A dumb negro, who squatted at his feet, burned the papyrus rolls which his master gave him in a brazier. A secretary made notes of the short facts which Ani called out to him, and the ground work was laid of the answers to the different letters.

At a sign from his master this functionary quitted the room, and Ani then slowly opened a letter from the king, whose address: "To my brother Ani," showed that it contained, not public, but private information.

On these lines, as he well knew, hung his future life, and the road it should follow.

With a smile, that was meant to conceal even from himself his deep inward agitation, he broke the wax which sealed the short manuscript in the royal hand.

"What relates to Egypt, and my concern for my country, and the happy issue of the war," wrote the Pharaoh, "I have written to you by the hand of my secretary; but these words are for the brother, who desires to be my son, and I write to him myself. The lordly essence of the Divinity which dwells in me, readily brings a quick 'Yes' or 'No' to my lips, and it decides for the best. Now you demand my daughter Bent-Anat to wife, and I should not be Rameses if I did not freely confess that before I had read the last words of your letter, a vehement 'No' rushed to my lips. I caused the stars to be consulted, and the entrails of the victims to be examined, and they were adverse to your request; and yet I could not refuse you, for you are dear to me, and your blood is royal as my own. Even more royal, an old friend said, and warned me against your ambition and your exaltation. Then my heart changed, for I were not Seti's son if I allow myself to injure a friend through idle apprehensions; and he who stands so high that men fear that he may try to rise above Rameses, seems to me to be worthy of Bent-Anat. Woo her, and, should she consent freely, the marriage may be celebrated on the day when I return home. You are young enough to make a wife happy, and your mature wisdom will guard my child from misfortune. Bent-Anat shall know that her father, and king, encourages your suit; but pray too to the Hathors, that they may influence Bent-Anat's heart in your favor, for to her decision we must both submit."

The Regent had changed color several times while reading this letter. Now he laid it on the table with a shrug of his shoulders, stood up, clasped his hand behind him, and, with his eyes cast meditatively on the floor, leaned against one of the pillars which supported the beams of the roof.

The longer he thought, the less amiable his expression became. "A pill sweetened with honey,[56] such as they give to women," he muttered to himself. Then he went back to the table, read the king's letter through once more, and said: "One may learn from it how to deny by granting, and at the same time not to forget to give it a brilliant show of magnanimity. Rameses knows his daughter. She is a girl like any other, and will take good care not to choose a man twice as old as herself, and who might be her father. Rameses will 'submit' — I am to I submit!' And to what? to the judgment and the choice of a wilful child!"

With these words he threw the letter so vehemently on to the table, that it slipped off on to the floor.

The mute slave picked it up, and laid it carefully on the table again, while his master threw a ball into a silver bason.

Several attendants rushed into the room, and Ani ordered them to bring to him the captive dwarf of the Lady Katuti. His soul rose in indignation against the king, who in his remote camp-tent could fancy he had made him happy by a proof of his highest favor. When we are plotting against a man we are inclined to regard him as an enemy, and if he offers us a rose we believe it to be for the sake, not of the perfume, but of the thorns.

The dwarf Nemu was brought before the Regent and threw himself on the ground at his feet.

Ani ordered the attendants to leave him, and said to the little man

74

"You compelled me to put you in prison. Stand up!" The dwarf rose and said, "Be thanked-for my arrest too."

The Regent looked at him in astonishment; but Nemu went on half humbly, half in fun, "I feared for my life, but thou hast not only not shortened it, but hast prolonged it; for in the solitude of the dungeon time seemed long, and the minutes grown to hours."

"Keep your wit for the ladies," replied the Regent. "Did I not know that you meant well, and acted in accordance with the Lady Katuti's fancy, I would send you to the quarries."

"My hands," mumbled the dwarf, "could only break stones for a game of draughts; but my tongue is like the water, which makes one peasant rich, and carries away the fields of another."

"We shall know how to dam it up."

"For my lady and for thee it will always flow the right way," said the dwarf. "I showed the complaining citizens who it is that slaughters their flesh and blood, and from whom to look for peace and content. I poured caustic into their wounds, and praised the physician."

"But unasked and recklessly," interrupted Ani; "otherwise you have shown yourself capable, and I am willing to spare you for a future time. But overbusy friends are more damaging than intelligent enemies. When I need your services I will call for you. Till then avoid speech. Now go to your mistress, and carry to Katuti this letter which has arrived for her."

"Hail to Ani, the son of the Sun!" cried the dwarf kissing the Regent's foot. "Have I no letter to carry to my mistress Nefert?"

"Greet her from me," replied the Regent. "Tell Katuti I will visit her after the next meal. The king's charioteer has not written, yet I hear that he is well. Go now, and be silent and discreet."

The dwarf quitted the room, and Ani went into an airy hall, in which his luxurious meal was laid out, consisting of many dishes prepared with special care. His appetite was gone, but he tasted of every dish, and gave the steward, who attended on him, his opinion of each.

Meanwhile he thought of the king's letter, of Bent-Anat, and whether it would be advisable to expose himself to a rejection on her part.

After the meal he gave himself up to his body-servant, who carefully shaved, painted, dressed, and decorated him, and then held the mirror before him.

He considered the reflection with anxious observation, and when he seated himself in his litter to be borne to the house of his friend Katuti, he said to himself that he still might claim to be called a handsome man.

If he paid his court to Bent-Anat —if she listened to his suit-what then?

He would refer it to Katuti, who always knew how to say a decisive word when he, entangled in a hundred pros and cons, feared to venture on a final step.

By her advice he had sought to wed the princess, as a fresh mark of honor-as an addition to his revenues-as a pledge for his personal safety. His heart had never been more or less attached to her than to any other beautiful woman in Egypt. Now her proud and noble personality stood before his inward eye, and he felt as if he must look up to it as to a vision high out of his reach. It vexed him that he had followed Katuti's advice, and he began to wish his suit had been repulsed. Marriage with Bent-Anat seemed to him beset with difficulties. His mood was that of a man who craves some brilliant position, though he knows that its requirements are beyond his powers-that of an ambitious soul to whom kingly honors are offered on condition that he will never remove a heavy crown from his head. If indeed another plan should succeed, if-and his eyes flashed eagerly-if fate set him on the seat of Rameses, then the alliance with Bent-Anat would lose its terrors; there would he be her absolute King and Lord and Master, and no one could require him to account for what he might be to her, or vouchsafe to her.

CHAPTER X.

During the events we have described the house of the charioteer Mena had not remained free from visitors.

It resembled the neighboring estate of Paaker, though the buildings were less new, the gay paint on the pillars and walls was faded, and the large garden lacked careful attention. In the vicinity of the house only, a few well-kept beds blazed with splendid flowers, and the open colonnade, which was occupied by Katuti and her daughter, was furnished with royal magnificence.

The elegantly carved seats were made of ivory, the tables of ebony, and they, as well as the couches, had gilt feet. The artistically worked Syrian drinking vessels on the sideboard, tables, and consoles were of many forms; beautiful vases full of flowers stood everywhere; rare perfumes rose from alabaster cups, and the foot sank in the thick pile of the carpets which covered the floor.

And over the apparently careless arrangement of these various objects there reigned a peculiar charm, an indescribably fascinating something.

Stretched at full-length on a couch, and playing with a silky-haired white cat, lay the fair Nefert-fanned to coolness by a negro-girl —while her mother Katuti nodded a last farewell to her sister Setchem and to Paaker.

Both had crossed this threshold for the first time for four years, that is since the marriage of Mena with Nefert, and the old enmity seemed now to have given way to heartfelt reconciliation and mutual understanding.

After the pioneer and his mother had disappeared behind the pomegranate shrubs at the entrance of the garden, Katuti turned to her daughter and said:

"Who would have thought it yesterday? I believe Paaker loves you still."

Nefert colored, and exclaimed softly, while she hit the kitten gently with her fan —

"Mother!"

Katuti smiled.

She was a tall woman of noble demeanor, whose sharp but delicately-cut features and sparkling eyes could still assert some pretensions to feminine beauty. She wore a long robe, which reached below her ankles; it was of costly material, but dark in color, and of a studied simplicity. Instead of the ornaments in bracelets, anklets, ear and finger-rings, in necklaces and clasps, which most of the Egyptian ladies-and indeed her own sister and daughter-were accustomed to wear, she had only fresh flowers, which were never wanting in the garden of her son-in-law. Only a plain gold diadem, the badge of her royal descent, always rested, from early morning till late at night, on her high brow-for a woman too high, though nobly formed-and confined the long blue-black hair, which fell unbraided down her back, as if its owner contemned the vain labor of arranging it artistically. But nothing in her exterior was unpremeditated, and the unbejewelled wearer of the diadem, in her plain dress, and with her royal figure, was everywhere sure of being observed, and of finding imitators of her dress, and indeed of her demeanor.

And yet Katuti had long lived in need; aye at the very hour when we first make her acquaintance, she had little of her own, but lived on the estate of her son-in-law as his guest, and as the administrator of his possessions; and before the marriage of her daughter she had lived with her children in a house belonging to her sister Setchem.

She had been the wife of her own brother,[57] who had died young, and who had squandered the greatest part of the possessions which had been left to him by the new royal family, in an extravagant love of display.

When she became a widow, she was received as a sister with her children by her brother-in-law, Paaker's father. She lived in a house of her own, enjoyed the income of an estate assigned to her by the old Mohar, and left to her son-in-law the care of educating her son, a handsome and overbearing lad, with all the claims and pretensions of a youth of distinction.

Such great benefits would have oppressed and disgraced the proud Katuti, if she had been content with them and in every way agreed with the giver. But this was by no means the case; rather, she believed that she might pretend to a more brilliant outward position, felt herself hurt when her heedless son, while he attended school, was warned to work more seriously, as he would by and by have to rely on his own skill and his own strength. And it had wounded her when occasionally her brother-in-law had suggested economy, and had reminded her, in his straightforward way, of her narrow means, and the uncertain future of her children.

At this she was deeply offended, for she ventured to say that her relatives could never, with all their gifts, compensate for the insults they heaped upon her; and thus taught them by experience that we quarrel with no one more readily than with the benefactor whom we can never repay for all the good he bestows on us.

Nevertheless, when her brother-in-law asked the hand of her daughter for his son, she willingly gave her consent.

Nefert and Paaker had grown up together, and by this union she foresaw that she could secure her own future and that of her children.

Shortly after the death of the Mohar, the charioteer Mena had proposed for Nefert's hand, but would have been refused if the king himself had not supported the suit of his favorite officer. After the wedding, she retired with Nefert to Mena's house, and undertook, while he was at the war, to manage his great estates, which however had been greatly burthened with debt by his father.

Fate put the means into her hands of indemnifying herself and her children for many past privations, and she availed herself of them to gratify her innate desire to be esteemed and admired; to obtain admission for her son, splendidly equipped, into a company of chariot-warriors of the highest class; and to surround her daughter with princely magnificence.

When the Regent, who had been a friend of her late husband, removed into the palace of the Pharaohs, he made her advances, and the clever and decided woman knew how to make herself at first agreeable, and finally indispensable, to the vacillating man.

She availed herself of the circumstance that she, as well as he, was descended from the old royal house to pique his ambition, and to open to him a view, which even to think of, he would have considered forbidden as a crime, before he became intimate with her.

Ani's suit for the hand of the princess Bent-Anat was Katuti's work. She hoped that the Pharoah would refuse, and personally offend the Regent, and so make him more inclined to tread the dangerous road which she was endeavoring to smooth for him. The dwarf Nemu was her pliant tool.

She had not initiated him into her projects by any words; he however gave utterance to every impulse of her mind in free language, which was punished only with blows from a fan, and, only the day before, had been so audacious as to say that if the Pharoah were called Ani instead of Rameses, Katuti would be not a queen but a goddess for she would then have not to obey, but rather to guide, the Pharaoh, who indeed himself was related to the Immortals.

Katuti did not observe her daughter's blush, for she was looking anxiously out at the garden gate, and said:

"Where can Nemu be! There must be some news arrived for us from the army."

"Mena has not written for so long," Nefert said softly. "Ah! here is the steward!"

Katuti turned to the officer, who had entered the veranda through a side door:

"What do you bring," she asked.

"The dealer Abscha," was the answer, "presses for payment. The new Syrian chariot and the purple cloth —"

"Sell some corn," ordered Katuti.

"Impossible, for the tribute to the temples is not yet paid, and already so much has been delivered to the dealers that scarcely enough remains over for the maintenance of the household and for sowing."

"Then pay with beasts."

"But, madam," said the steward sorrowfully, "only yesterday, we again sold a herd to the Mohar; and the water-wheels must be turned, and the corn must be thrashed, and we need beasts for sacrifice, and milk, butter, and cheese, for the use of the house, and dung for firing."[58]

Katuti looked thoughtfully at the ground.

"It must be," she said presently. "Ride to Hermonthis, and say to the keeper of the stud that he must have ten of Mena's golden bays driven over here."

"I have already spoken to him," said the steward, "but he maintains that Mena strictly forbade him to part with even one of the horses, for he is proud of the stock. Only for the chariot of the lady Nefert."

"I require obedience," said Katuti decidedly and cutting short the steward's words, "and I expect the horses to-morrow."

"But the stud-master is a daring man, whom Mena looks upon as indispensable, and he —"

"I command here, and not the absent," cried Katuti enraged, "and I require the horses in spite of the former orders of my son-in-law."

Nefert, during this conversation, pulled herself up from her indolent attitude. On hearing the last words she rose from her couch, and said, with a decision which surprised even her mother —

"The orders of my husband must be obeyed. The horses that Mena loves shall stay in their stalls. Take this armlet that the king gave me; it is worth more than twenty horses."

The steward examined the trinket, richly set with precious stones, and looked enquiringly at Katuti. She shrugged her shoulders, nodded consent, and said —

"Abscha shall hold it as a pledge till Mena's booty arrives. For a year your husband has sent nothing of importance."

When the steward was gone, Nefert stretched herself again on her couch and said wearily:

"I thought we were rich."

"We might be," said Katuti bitterly; but as she perceived that Nefert's cheeks again were glowing, she said amiably, "Our high rank imposes great duties on us. Princely blood flows in our veins, and the eyes of the people are turned on the wife of the most brilliant hero in the king's army. They shall not say that she is neglected by her husband. How long Mena remains away!"

"I hear a noise in the court," said Nefert. "The Regent is coming."

Katuti turned again towards the garden.

A breathless slave rushed in, and announced that Bent-Anat, the daughter of the king, had dismounted at the gate, and was approaching the garden with the prince Rameri.

Nefert left her couch, and went with her mother to meet the exalted visitors.

As the mother and daughter bowed to kiss the robe of the princess, Bent-Anat signed them back from her. "Keep farther from me," she said; "the priests have not yet entirely absolved me from my uncleanness."

"And in spite of them thou art clean in the sight of Ra!" exclaimed the boy who accompanied her, her brother of seventeen, who was brought up at the House of Seti, which however he was to leave in a few weeks-and he kissed her.

"I shall complain to Ameni of this wild boy," said Bent-Anat smiling. "He would positively accompany me. Your husband, Nefert, is his model, and I had no peace in the house, for we came to bring you good news."

"From Mena?" asked the young wife, pressing her hand to her heart.

"As you say," returned Bent-Anat. "My father praises his ability, and writes that he, before all others, will have his choice at the dividing of the spoil."

Nefert threw a triumphant glance at her mother, and Katuti drew a deep breath.

Bent-Anat stroked Nefert's cheeks like those of a child. Then she turned to Katuti, led her into the garden, and begged her to aid her, who had so early lost her mother, with her advice in a weighty matter.

"My father," she continued, after a few introductory words, "informs me that the Regent Ani desires me for his wife, and advises me to reward the fidelity of the worthy man with my hand. He advises it, you understand-he does not command."

"And thou?" asked Katuti.

"And I," replied Bent-Anat decidedly, "must refuse him."

"Thou must!"

Bent-Anat made a sign of assent and went on:

"It is quite clear to me. I can do nothing else."

"Then thou dost not need my counsel, since even thy father, I well know, will not be able to alter thy decision."

"Not God even," said Anat firmly. "But you are Ani's friend, and as I esteem him, I would save him from this humiliation. Endeavor to persuade him to give up his suit. I will meet him as though I knew nothing of his letter to my father."

Katuti looked down reflectively. Then she said —"The Regent certainly likes very well to pass his hours of leisure with me gossiping or playing draughts, but I do not know that I should dare to speak to him of so grave a matter."

"Marriage-projects are women's affairs," said Bent-Anat, smiling.

"But the marriage of a princess is a state event," replied the widow. "In this case it is true the uncle[59] only courts his niece, who is dear to him, and who he hopes will make the second half of his life the brightest. Ani is kind and without severity. Thou would'st win in him a husband, who would wait on thy looks, and bow willingly to thy strong will."

Bent-Anat's eyes flashed, and she hastily exclaimed: "That is exactly what forces the decisive irrevocable 'No' to my lips. Do you think that because I am as proud as my mother, and resolute like my father, that I wish for a husband whom I could govern and lead as I would? How little you know me! I will be obeyed by my dogs, my servants, my officers, if the Gods so will it, by my children. Abject beings, who will kiss my feet, I meet on every road, and can buy by the hundred, if I wish it, in the slave market. I may be courted twenty times, and reject twenty suitors, but not because I fear that they might bend my pride and my will; on the contrary, because I feel them increased. The man to whom I could wish to offer my hand must be of a loftier stamp, must be greater, firmer, and better than I, and I will flutter after the mighty wing-strokes of his spirit, and smile at my own weakness, and glory in admiring his superiority."

Katuti listened to the maiden with the smile by which the experienced love to signify their superiority over the visionary.

"Ancient times may have produced such men," she said. "But if in these days thou thinkest to find one, thou wilt wear the lock of youth,[60] till thou art grey. Our thinkers are no heroes, and our heroes are no sages. Here come thy brother and Nefert."

"Will you persuade Ani to give up his suit!" said the princess urgently.

"I will endeavor to do so, for thy sake," replied Katuti. Then, turning half to the young Rameri and half to his sister, she said:

"The chief of the House of Seti, Ameni, was in his youth such a man as thou paintest, Bent-Anat. Tell us, thou son of Rameses, that art growing up under the young sycamores, which shall some day over-shadow the land-whom dost thou esteem the highest among thy companions? Is there one among them, who is conspicuous above them all for a lofty spirit and strength of intellect?"

The young Rameri looked gaily at the speaker, and said laughing: "We are all much alike, and do more or less willingly what we are compelled, and by preference every thing that we ought not."

"A mighty soul —a youth, who promises to be a second Snefru, a Thotmes, or even an Amem? Dost thou know none such in the House of Seti?" asked the widow. "Oh yes!" cried Rameri with eager certainty.

"And he is —?" asked Katuti.

"Pentaur, the poet," exclaimed the youth. Bent-Anat's face glowed with scarlet color, while her, brother went on to explain.

"He is noble and of a lofty soul, and all the Gods dwell in him when he speaks. Formerly we used to go to sleep in the lecture-hall; but his words carry us away, and if we do not take in the full meaning of his thoughts, yet we feel that they are genuine and noble."

Bent-Anat breathed quicker at these words, and her eyes hung on the boy's lips.

"You know him, Bent-Anat," continued Rameri. "He was with you at the paraschites' house, and in the temple-court when Ameni pronounced you unclean. He is as tall and handsome as the God Mentli, and I feel that he is one of those whom we can never forget when once we have seen them. Yesterday, after you had left the temple, he spoke as he never spoke before; he poured fire into our souls. Do not laugh, Katuti, I feel it burning still. This morning we were informed that he had been sent from the temple, who knows where-and had left us a message of farewell. It was not thought at all necessary to communicate the reason to us; but we know more than the masters think. He did not reprove you strongly enough, Bent-Anat, and therefore he is driven out of the House of Seti. We have agreed to combine to ask for him to be recalled; Anana is drawing up a letter to the chief priest, which we shall all subscribe. It would turn out badly for one alone, but they cannot be at all of us at once. Very likely they will have the sense to recall him. If not, we shall all complain to our fathers, and they are not the meanest in the land."

"It is a complete rebellion," cried Katuti. "Take care, you lordlings; Ameni and the other prophets are not to be trifled with."

"Nor we either," said Rameri laughing, "If Pentaur is kept in banishment, I shall appeal to my father to place me at the school at Heliopolis or Chennu, and the others will follow me. Come, Bent-Anat, I must be back in the trap before sunset. Excuse me, Katuti, so we call the school. Here comes your little Nemu."

The brother and sister left the garden.

As soon as the ladies, who accompanied them, had turned their backs, Bent-Anat grasped her brother's hand with unaccustomed warmth, and said:

"Avoid all imprudence; but your demand is just, and I will help you with all my heart."

CHAPTER XI.

As soon as Bent-Anat had quitted Mena's domain, the dwarf Nemu entered the garden with a letter, and briefly related his adventures; but in such a comical fashion that both the ladies laughed, and Katuti, with a lively gaiety, which was usually foreign to her, while she warned him, at the same time praised his acuteness. She looked at the seal of the letter and said:

"This is a lucky day; it has brought us great things, and the promise of greater things in the future." Nefert came close up to her and said imploringly: "Open the letter, and see if there is nothing in it from him."

Katuti unfastened the wax, looked through the letter with a hasty glance, stroked the cheek of her child, and said:

"Perhaps your brother has written for him; I see no line in his handwriting."

Nefert on her side glanced at the letter, but not to read it, only to seek some trace of the well-known handwriting of her husband.

Like all the Egyptian women of good family she could read, and during the first two years of her married life she had often-very often-had the opportunity of puzzling, and yet rejoicing, over the feeble signs which the iron hand of the charioteer had scrawled on the papyrus for her whose slender fingers could guide the reed pen with firmness and decision.

She examined the letter, and at last said, with tears in her eyes:

"Nothing! I will go to my room, mother."

Katuti kissed her and said, "Hear first what your brother writes."

But Nefert shook her head, turned away in silence, and disappeared into the house.

Katuti was not very friendly to her son-in-law, but her heart clung to her handsome, reckless son, the very image of her lost husband, the favorite of women, and the gayest youth among the young nobles who composed the chariot-guard of the king.

How fully he had written to-day —he who weilded the reed-pen so laboriously.

This really was a letter; while, usually, he only asked in the fewest words for fresh funds for the gratification of his extravagant tastes.

This time she might look for thanks, for not long since he must have received a considerable supply, which she had abstracted from the income of the possessions entrusted to her by her son-in-law.

She began to read.

The cheerfulness, with which she had met the dwarf, was insincere, and had resembled the brilliant colors of the rainbow, which gleam over the stagnant waters of a bog. A stone falls into the pool, the colors vanish, dim mists rise up, and it becomes foul and clouded.

The news which her son's letter contained fell, indeed, like a block of stone on Katuti's soul.

Our deepest sorrows always flow from the same source as might have filled us with joy, and those wounds burn the fiercest which are inflicted by a hand we love.

The farther Katuti went in the lamentably incorrect epistle-which she could only decipher with difficulty-which her darling had written to her, the paler grew her face, which she several times covered with her trembling hands, from which the letter dropped.

Nemu squatted on the earth near her, and followed all her movements.

When she sprang forward with a heart-piercing scream, and pressed her forehead to a rough palmtrunk, he crept up to her, kissed her feet, and exclaimed with a depth of feeling that overcame even Katuti, who was accustomed to hear only gay or bitter speeches from the lips of her jester —

"Mistress! lady! what has happened?"

Katuti collected herself, turned to him, and tried to speak; but her pale lips remained closed, and her eyes gazed dimly into vacancy as though a catalepsy had seized her.

"Mistress! Mistress!" cried the dwarf again, with growing agitation. "What is the matter? shall I call thy daughter?"

Katuti made a sign with her hand, and cried feebly: "The wretches! the reprobates!"

Her breath began to come quickly, the blood mounted to her cheeks and her flashing eyes; she trod upon the letter, and wept so loud and passionately, that the dwarf, who had never before seen tears in her eyes, raised himself timidly, and said in mild reproach: "Katuti!"

She laughed bitterly, and said with a trembling voice:

"Why do you call my name so loud! it is disgraced and degraded. How the nobles and the ladies will rejoice! Now envy can point at us with spiteful joy-and a minute ago I was praising this day! They say one should exhibit one's happiness in the streets, and conceal one's misery; on the contrary, on the contrary! Even the Gods should not know of one's hopes and joys, for they too are envious and spiteful!"

Again she leaned her head against the palm-tree. "Thou speakest of shame, and not of death," said Nemu, "and I learned from thee that one should give nothing up for lost excepting the dead."

These words had a powerful effect on the agitated woman. Quickly and vehemently she turned upon the dwarf saying.

"You are clever, and faithful too, so listen! but if you were Amon himself there is nothing to be done —"

"We must try," said Nemu, and his sharp eyes met those of his mistress.

"Speak," he said, "and trust me. Perhaps I can be of no use; but that I can be silent thou knowest."

"Before long the children in the streets will talk of what this tells me," said Katuti, laughing with bitterness, "only Nefert must know nothing of what has happened-nothing, mind; what is that? the Regent coming! quick, fly; tell him I am suddenly taken ill, very ill; I cannot see him, not now! No one is to be admitted-no one, do you hear?"

The dwarf went.

When he came back after he had fulfilled his errand, he found his mistress still in a fever of excitement.

"Listen," she said; "first the smaller matter, then the frightful, the unspeakable. Rameses loads Mena with marks of his favor. It came to a division of the spoils of war for the year; a great heap of treasure lay ready for each of his followers, and the charioteer had to choose before all the others."

"Well?" said the dwarf.

"Well!" echoed Katuti. "Well! how did the worthy householder care for his belongings at home, how did he seek to relieve his indebted estate? It is disgraceful, hideous! He passed by the silver, the gold, the jewels, with a laugh; and took the captive daughter of the Danaid princes, and led her into his tent."

"Shameful!" muttered the dwarf.

"Poor, poor Nefert!" cried Katuti, covering her face with her hands.

"And what more?" asked Nemu hastily.

"That," said Katuti, "that is-but I will keep calm-quite calm and quiet. You know my son. He is heedless, but he loves me and his sister more than anything in the world. I, fool as I was, to persuade him to economy, had vividly described our evil plight, and after that disgraceful conduct of Mena he thought of us and of our anxieties. His share of the booty was small, and could not help us. His comrades threw dice for the shares they had obtained-he staked his to win more for us. He lost-all-all-and at last against an enormous sum, still thinking of us, and only of us, he staked the mummy of his dead father.[61]

He lost. If he does not redeem the pledge before the expiration of the third month, he will fall into infamy, the mummy will belong to the winner, and disgrace and ignominy will be my lot and his."

Katuti pressed her hands on her face, the dwarf muttered to himself, "The gambler and hypocrite!" When his mistress had grown calmer, he said:

"It is horrible, yet all is not lost. How much is the debt?"

It sounded like a heavy curse, when Katuti replied, "Thirty Babylonian talents." —[£7000 sterling in 1881.]

The dwarf cried out, as if an asp had stung him. "Who dared to bid against such a mad stake?"

"The Lady Hathor's son, Antef," answered Katuti, "who has already gambled away the inheritance of his fathers, in Thebes."

"He will not remit one grain of wheat of his claim," cried the dwarf. "And Mena?"

"How could my son turn to him after what had happened? The poor child implores me to ask the assistance of the Regent."

"Of the Regent?" said the dwarf, shaking his big head. "Impossible!"

"I know, as matters now stand; but his place, his name."

"Mistress," said the dwarf, and deep purpose rang in the words, "do not spoil the future for the sake of the present. If thy son loses his honor under King Rameses, the future King, Ani, may restore it to him. If the Regent now renders you all an important service, he will regard you as amply paid when our efforts have succeeded, and he sits on the throne. He lets himself be led by thee now because thou hast no need of his help, and dost seem to work only for his sake, and for his elevation. As soon as thou hast appealed to him, and he has assisted thee, all thy confidence and freedom will be gone, and the more difficult he finds it to raise so large a sum of money at once, the angrier he will be to think that thou art making use of him. Thou knowest his circumstances."

"He is in debt," said Katuti. "I know that."

"Thou should'st know it," cried the dwarf, "for thou thyself hast forced him to enormous expenses. He has won the people of Thebes with dazzling festive displays; as guardian of Apis[62] he gave a large donation to Memphis; he bestowed thousands on the leaders of the troops sent into Ethiopia, which were equipped by him; what his spies cost him at, the camp of the king, thou knowest. He has borrowed sums of money from most of the rich men in the country, and that is well, for so many creditors are so many allies. The Regent is a bad debtor; but the king Ani, they reckon, will be a grateful payer."

Katuti looked at the dwarf in astonishment. "You know men!" she said.

"To my sorrow!" replied Nemu. "Do not apply to the Regent, and before thou dost sacrifice the labor of years, and thy future greatness, and that of those near to thee, sacrifice thy son's honor."

"And my husband's, and my own?" exclaimed Katuti. "How can you know what that is! Honor is a word that the slave may utter, but whose meaning he can never comprehend; you rub the weals that are raised on you by blows; to me every finger pointed at me in scorn makes a wound like an ashwood lance with a poisoned tip of brass. Oh ye holy Gods! who can help us?"

The miserable woman pressed her hands over her eyes, as if to shut out the sight of her own disgrace. The dwarf looked at her compassionately, and said in a changed tone:

"Dost thou remember the diamond which fell out of Nefert's handsomest ring? We hunted for it, and could not find it. Next day, as I was going through the room, I trod on something hard; I stooped down and found the stone. What the noble organ of sight, the eye, overlooked, the callous despised sole of the foot found; and perhaps the small slave, Nemu, who knows nothing of honor, may succeed in finding a mode of escape which is not revealed to the lofty soul of his mistress!"

"What are you thinking of?" asked Katuti.

"Escape," answered the dwarf. "Is it true that thy sister Setchem has visited thee, and that you are reconciled?"

"She offered me her hand, and I took it?"

"Then go to her. Men are never more helpful than after a reconciliation. The enmity they have driven out, seems to leave as it were a freshly-healed wound which must be touched with caution; and Setchem is of thy own blood, and kind-hearted."

"She is not rich," replied Katuti. "Every palm in her garden comes from her husband, and belongs to her children."

"Paaker, too, was with you?"

"Certainly only by the entreaty of his mother-he hates my son-in-law."

"I know it," muttered the dwarf, "but if Nefert would ask him?"

The widow drew herself up indignantly. She felt that she had allowed the dwarf too much freedom, and ordered him to leave her alone.

Nemu kissed her robe and asked timidly:

"Shall I forget that thou hast trusted me, or am I permitted to consider further as to thy son's safety?" Katuti stood for a moment undecided, then she said:

"You were clever enough to find what I carelessly dropped; perhaps some God may show you what I ought to do. Now leave me."

"Wilt thou want me early to-morrow?"

"No."

"Then I will go to the Necropolis, and offer a sacrifice."

"Go!" said Katuti, and went towards the house with the fatal letter in her hand.

Nemu stayed behind alone; he looked thoughtfully at the ground, murmuring to himself.

"She must not lose her honor; not at present, or indeed all will be lost. What is this honor? We all come into the world without it, and most of us go to the grave without knowing it, and very good folks notwithstanding. Only a few who are rich and idle weave it in with the homely stuff of their souls, as the Kuschites do their hair with grease and oils, till it forms a cap of which, though it disfigures them, they are so proud that they would rather have their ears cut off than the monstrous thing. I see, I see-but before I open my mouth I will go to my mother. She knows more than twenty prophets."

CHAPTER XII.

Before the sun had risen the next morning, Nemu got himself ferried over the Nile, with the small white ass which Mena's deceased father had given him many years before. He availed himself of the cool hour which precedes the rising of the sun for his ride through the Necropolis.

Well acquainted as he was with every stock and stone, he avoided the high roads which led to the goal of his expedition, and trotted towards the hill which divides the valley of the royal tombs from the plain of the Nile.

Before him opened a noble amphitheatre of lofty lime-stone peaks, the background of the stately terrace-temple which the proud ancestress of two kings of the fallen family, the great Hatasu, had erected to their memory, and to the Goddess Hathor.

Nemu left the sanctuary to his left, and rode up the steep hill-path which was the nearest way from the plain to the valley of the tombs.

Below him lay a bird's eye view of the terrace-building of Hatasu, and before him, still slumbering in cool dawn, was the Necropolis with its houses and temples and colossal statues, the broad Nile glistening with white sails under the morning mist; and, in the distant east, rosy with the coming sun, stood Thebes and her gigantic temples.

But the dwarf saw nothing of the glorious panorama that lay at his feet; absorbed in thought, and stooping over the neck of his ass, he let the panting beast climb and rest at its pleasure.

When he had reached half the height of the hill, he perceived the sound of footsteps coming nearer and nearer to him.

The vigorous walker had soon reached him, and bid him good morning, which he civilly returned.

The hill-path was narrow, and when Nemu observed that the man who followed him was a priest, he drew up his donkey on a level spot, and said reverently:

"Pass on, holy father; for thy two feet carry thee quicker than my four."

"A sufferer needs my help," replied the leech Nebsecht, Pentaur's friend, whom we have already seen in the House of Seti, and by the bed of the paraschites' daughter; and he hastened on so as to gain on the slow pace of the rider.

Then rose the glowing disk of the sun above the eastern horizon, and from the sanctuaries below the travellers rose up the pious many-voiced chant of praise.

Nemu slipped off his ass, and assumed an attitude of prayer; the priest did the same; but while the dwarf devoutly fixed his eyes on the new birth of the Sun-God from the eastern range, the priest's eyes wandered to the earth, and his raised hand fell to pick up a rare fossil shell which lay on the path.

In a few minutes Nebsecht rose, and Nemu followed him.

"It is a fine morning," said the dwarf; "the holy fathers down there seem more cheerful to-day than usual."

The surgeon laughed assent. "Do you belong to the Necropolis?" he said. "Who here keeps dwarfs?"

"No one," answered the little man. "But I will ask thee a question. Who that lives here behind the hill is of so much importance, that a leech from the House of Seti sacrifices his night's rest for him?"

"The one I visit is mean, but the suffering is great," answered Nebsecht.

Nemu looked at him with admiration, and muttered, "That is noble, that is — —" but he did not finish his speech; he struck his brow and exclaimed, "You are going, by the desire of the Princess Bent-Anat, to the child of the paraschites that was run over. I guessed as much. The food must have an excellent after-taste, if a gentleman rises so early to eat it. How is the poor child doing?"

There was so much warmth in these last words that Nebsecht, who had thought the dwarf's reproach uncalled for, answered in a friendly tone:

"Not so badly; she may be saved."

"The Gods be praised!" exclaimed Nemu, while the priest passed on.

Nebsecht went up and down the hillside at a redoubled pace, and had long taken his place by the couch of the wounded Uarda in the hovel of the paraschites, when Nemu drew near to the abode of his Mother Hekt, from whom Paaker had received the philter.

The old woman sat before the door of her cave. Near her lay a board, fitted with cross pieces, between which a little boy was stretched in such a way that they touched his head and his feet.

Hekt understood the art of making dwarfs; playthings in human form were well paid for, and the child on the rack, with his pretty little face, promised to be a valuable article.

As soon as the sorceress saw some one approaching, she stooped over the child, took him up board and all in her arms, and carried him into the cave. Then she said sternly:

"If you move, little one, I will flog you. Now let me tie you."

"Don't tie me," said the child, "I will be good and lie still."

"Stretch yourself out," ordered the old woman, and tied the child with a rope to the board. "If you are quiet, I'll give you a honey-cake by-and-bye, and let you play with the young chickens."

The child was quiet, and a soft smile of delight and hope sparkled in his pretty eyes. His little hand caught the dress of the old woman, and with the sweetest coaxing tone, which God bestows on the innocent voices of children, he said:

"I will be as still as a mouse, and no one shall know that I am here; but if you give me the honeycake you will untie me for a little, and let me go to Uarda."

"She is ill! —what do you want there?"

"I would take her the cake," said the child, and his eyes glistened with tears.

The old woman touched the child's chin with her finger, and some mysterious power prompted her to bend over him to kiss him. But before her lips had touched his face she turned away, and said, in a hard tone:

"Lie still! by and bye we will see." Then she stooped, and threw a brown sack over the child. She went back into the open air, greeted Nemu, entertained him with milk, bread and honey, gave him news of the girl who had been run over, for he seemed to take her misfortune very much to heart, and finally asked:

"What brings you here? The Nile was still narrow when you last found your way to me, and now it has been falling some time.[63]

Are you sent by your mistress, or do you want my help? All the world is alike. No one goes to see any one else unless he wants to make use of him. What shall I give you?"

"I want nothing," said the dwarf, "but —"

"You are commissioned by a third person," said the witch, laughing. "It is the same thing. Whoever wants a thing for some one else only thinks of his own interest."

"May be," said Nemu. "At any rate your words show that you have not grown less wise since I saw you last-and I am glad of it, for I want your advice."

"Advice is cheap. What is going on out there?" Nemu related to his mother shortly, clearly, and without reserve, what was plotting in his mistress's house, and the frightful disgrace with which she was threatened through her son.

The old woman shook her grey head thoughtfully several times: but she let the little man go on to the end of his story without interrupting him. Then she asked, and her eyes flashed as she spoke:

"And you really believe that you will succeed in putting the sparrow on the eagle's perch-Ani on the throne of Rameses?"

"The troops fighting in Ethiopia are for us," cried Nemu. "The priests declare themselves against the king, and recognize in Ani the genuine blood of Ra."

"That is much," said the old woman.

"And many dogs are the death of the gazelle," said Nemu laughing.

"But Rameses is not a gazelle to run, but a lion," said the old woman gravely. "You are playing a high game."

"We know it," answered Nemu. "But it is for high stakes-there is much to win."

"And all to lose," muttered the old woman, passing her fingers round her scraggy neck. "Well, do as you please-it is all the same to me who it is sends the young to be killed, and drives the old folks' cattle from the field. What do they want with me?"

"No one has sent me," answered the dwarf. "I come of my own free fancy to ask you what Katuti must do to save her son and her house from dishonor."

"Hm!" hummed the witch, looking at Nemu while she raised herself on her stick. "What has come to you that you take the fate of these great people to heart as if it were your own?"

The dwarf reddened, and answered hesitatingly, "Katuti is a good mistress, and, if things go well with her, there may be windfalls for you and me."

Hekt shook her head doubtfully.

"A loaf for you perhaps, and a crumb for me!" she said. "There is more than that in your mind, and I can read your heart as if you were a ripped up raven. You are one of those who can never keep their fingers at rest, and must knead everybody's dough; must push, and drive and stir something. Every jacket is too tight for you. If you were three feet taller, and the son of a priest, you might have gone far. High you will go, and high you will end; as the friend of a king-or on the gallows."

The old woman laughed; but Nemu bit his lips, and said:

"If you had sent me to school, and if I were not the son of a witch, and a dwarf, I would play with men as they have played with me; for I am cleverer than all of them, and none of their plans are hidden from me. A hundred roads lie before me, when they don't know whether to go out or in; and where they rush heedlessly forwards I see the abyss that they are running to."

"And nevertheless you come to me?" said the old woman sarcastically.

"I want your advice," said Nemu seriously. "Four eyes see more than one, and the impartial looker-on sees clearer than the player; besides you are bound to help me."

The old woman laughed loud in astonishment. "Bound!" she said, "I? and to what if you please?"

"To help me," replied the dwarf, half in entreaty, and half in reproach. "You deprived me of my growth, and reduced me to a cripple."

"Because no one is better off than you dwarfs," interrupted the witch.

Nemu shook his head, and answered sadly —

"You have often said so-and perhaps for many others, who are born in misery like me-perhaps-you are right; but for me-you have spoilt my life; you have crippled not my body only but my soul, and have condemned me to sufferings that are nameless and unutterable."

The dwarf's big head sank on his breast, and with his left hand he pressed his heart.

The old woman went up to him kindly.

"What ails you?" she asked, "I thought it was well with you in Mena's house."

"You thought so?" cried the dwarf. "You who show me as in a mirror what I am, and how mysterious powers throng and stir in me? You made me what I am by your arts; you sold me to the treasurer of Rameses, and he gave me to the father of Mena, his brother-in-law. Fifteen years ago! I was a young man then, a youth like any other, only more passionate, more restless, and fiery than they. I was given as a plaything to the young Mena, and he harnessed me to his little chariot, and dressed me out with ribbons and feathers, and flogged me when I did not go fast enough. How the girl-for whom I would have given my life-the porter's daughter, laughed when I, dressed up in motley, hopped panting in front of the chariot and the young lord's whip whistled in my ears wringing the sweat from my brow, and the blood from my broken heart. Then Mena's father died, the boy, went to school, and I waited on the wife of his steward, whom Katuti banished to Hermonthis. That was a time! The little daughter of the house made a doll of me,[64] laid me in the cradle, and made me shut my eyes and pretend to sleep, while love and hatred, and great projects were strong within me. If I tried to resist they beat me with rods; and when once, in a rage, I forgot myself, and hit little Mertitefs hard, Mena, who came in, hung me up in the store-room to a nail by my girdle, and left me to swing there; he said he had forgotten to take me down again. The rats fell upon me; here are the scars, these little white spots here-look! They perhaps will some day wear out, but the wounds that my spirit received in those hours have not yet ceased to bleed. Then Mena married Nefert, and, with her, his mother-in-law, Katuti, came into the house. She took me from the steward, I became indispensable to her; she treats me like a man, she values my intelligence and listens to my advice-therefore I will make her great, and with her, and through her, I will wax mighty. If Ani mounts the throne, we wilt guide him-you, and I, and she! Rameses must fall, and with him Mena, the boy who degraded my body and poisoned my soul!"

During this speech the old woman had stood in silence opposite the dwarf. Now she sat down on her rough wooden seat, and said, while she proceeded to pluck a lapwing:

"Now I understand you; you wish to be revenged. You hope to rise high, and I am to whet your knife, and hold the ladder for you. Poor little man! there, sit down-drink a gulp of milk to cool you, and listen to my advice. Katuti wants a great deal of money to escape dishonor. She need only pick it up-it lies at her door." The dwarf looked at the witch in astonishment.

"The Mohar Paaker is her sister Setchem's son. Is he not?"

"As you say."

"Katuti's daughter Nefert is the wife of your master Mena, and another would like to tempt the neglected little hen into his yard."

"You mean Paaker, to whom Nefert was promised before she went after Mena."

"Paaker was with me the day before yesterday."

"With you?"

"Yes, with me, with old Hekt-to buy a love philter. I gave him one, and as I was curious I went after him, saw him give the water to the little lady, and found out her name."

"And Nefert drank the magic drink?" asked the dwarf horrified. "Vinegar and turnip juice," laughed the old witch. "A lord who comes to me to win a wife is ripe for any thing. Let Nefert ask Paaker for the money, and the young scapegrace's debts are paid."

"Katuti is proud, and repulsed me severely when I proposed this."

"Then she must sue to Paaker herself for the money. Go back to him, make him hope that Nefert is inclined to him, tell him what distresses the ladies, and if he refuses, but only if he refuses, let him see that you know something of the little dose."

The dwarf looked meditatively on the ground, and then said, looking admiringly at the old woman: "That is the right thing."

"You will find out the lie without my telling you," mumbled the witch; "your business is not perhaps such a bad one as it seemed to me at first. Katuti may thank the ne'er-do-well who staked his father's corpse. You don't understand me? Well, if you are really the sharpest of them all over there, what must the others be?"

"You mean that people will speak well of my mistress for sacrificing so large a sum for the sake —?"

"Whose sake? why speak well of her?" cried the old woman impatiently. "Here we deal with other things, with actual facts. There stands Paaker-there the wife of Mena. If the Mohar sacrifices a fortune for Nefert, he will be her master, and Katuti will not stand in his way; she knows well enough why her nephew pays for her. But some one else stops the way, and that is Mena. It is worth while to get him out of the way. The charioteer stands close to the Pharaoh, and the noose that is flung at one may easily fall round the neck of the other too. Make the Mohar your ally, and it may easily happen that your rat-bites may be paid for with mortal wounds, and Rameses who, if you marched against him openly, might blow you to the ground, may be hit by a lance thrown from an ambush. When the throne is clear, the weak legs of the Regent may succeed in clambering up to it with the help of the priests. Here you sit-open-mouthed; and I have told you nothing that you might not have found out for yourself."

"You are a perfect cask of wisdom!" exclaimed the dwarf.

"And now you will go away," said Hekt, "and reveal your schemes to your mistress and the Regent, and they will be astonished at your cleverness. To-day you still know that I have shown you what you have to do; to-morrow you will have forgotten it; and the day after to-morrow you will believe yourself possessed by the inspiration of the nine great Gods. I know that; but I cannot give anything for nothing. You live by your smallness, another makes his living with his hard hands, I earn my scanty bread by the thoughts of my brain. Listen! when you have half won Paaker, and Ani shows himself inclined to make use of him, then say to him that I may know a secret—and I do know one, I alone—which may make the Mohar the sport of his wishes, and that I may be disposed to sell it."

"That shall be done! certainly, mother," cried the dwarf. "What do you wish for?"

"Very little," said the old woman. "Only a permit that makes me free to do and to practise whatever I please, unmolested even by the priests, and to receive an honorable burial after my death."

"The Regent will hardly agree to that; for he must avoid everything that may offend the servants of the Gods."

"And do everything," retorted the old woman, "that can degrade Rameses in their sight. Ani, do you hear, need not write me a new license, but only renew the old one granted to me by Rameses when I cured his favorite horse. They burnt it with my other possessions, when they plundered my house, and denounced me and my belongings for sorcery. The permit of Rameses is what I want, nothing more."

"You shall have it," said the dwarf. "Good-by; I am charged to look into the tomb of our house, and see whether the offerings for the dead are regularly set out; to pour out fresh essences and have various things renewed. When Sechet has ceased to rage, and it is cooler, I shall come by here again, for I should like to call on the paraschites, and see how the poor child is."

CHAPTER XIII.

During this conversation two men had been busily occupied, in front of the paraschites' hut, in driving piles into the earth, and stretching a torn linen cloth upon them.

One of them, old Pinem, whom we have seen tending his grandchild, requested the other from time to time to consider the sick girl and to work less noisily.

After they had finished their simple task, and spread a couch of fresh straw under the awning, they too sat down on the earth, and looked at the hut before which the surgeon Nebsecht was sitting waiting till the sleeping girl should wake.

"Who is that?" asked the leech of the old man, pointing to his young companion, a tall sunburnt soldier with a bushy red beard.

"My son," replied the paraschites, "who is just returned from Syria."

"Uarda's father?" asked Nebsecht.

The soldier nodded assent, and said with a rough voice, but not without cordiality.

"No one could guess it by looking at us-she is so white and rosy. Her mother was a foreigner, and she has turned out as delicate as she was. I am afraid to touch her with my little finger-and there comes a chariot over the brittle doll, and does not quite crush her, for she is still alive."

"Without the help of this holy father," said the paraschites, approaching the surgeon, and kissing his robe, "you would never have seen her alive again. May the Gods reward thee for what thou hast done for its poor folks!"

"And we can pay too," cried the soldier, slapping a full purse that hung at his gridle. "We have taken plunder in Syria, and I will buy a calf, and give it to thy temple."

"Offer a beast of dough, rather."[65] replied Nebsecht, "and if you wish to show yourself grateful to me, give the money to your father, so that he may feed and nurse your child in accordance with my instructions."

"Hm," murmured the soldier; he took the purse from his girdle, flourished it in his hand, and said, as he handed it to the paraschites:

"I should have liked to drink it! but take it, father, for the child and my mother."

While the old man hesitatingly put out his hand for the rich gift, the soldier recollected himself and said, opening the purse:

"Let me take out a few rings, for to-day I cannot go dry. I have two or three comrades lodging in the red Tavern. That is right. There-take the rest of the rubbish."

Nebsecht nodded approvingly at the soldier, and he, as his father gratefully kissed the surgeon's hand, exclaimed:

"Make the little one sound, holy father! It, is all over with gifts and offerings, for I have nothing left; but there are two iron fists and a breast like the wall of a fortress. If at any time thou dost want help, call me, and I will protect thee against twenty enemies. Thou hast saved my child-good! Life for life. I sign myself thy blood-ally—there."

With these words he drew his poniard out of his girdle. He scratched his arm, and let a few drops of his blood run down on a stone at the feet of Nebsecht —"Look," he said. "There is my bond, Kaschta has signed himself thine, and thou canst dispose of my life as of thine own. What I have said, I have said."

"I am a man of peace," Nebsecht stammered, "And my white robe protects me. But I believe our patient is awake."

The physician rose, and entered the hut.

Uarda's pretty head lay on her grandmother's lap, and her large blue eyes turned contentedly on the priest.

"She might get up and go out into the air," said the old woman. "She has slept long and soundly." The surgeon examined her pulse, and her wound, on which green leaves were laid.

"Excellent," he said; "who gave you this healing herb?"

The old woman shuddered, and hesitated; but Uarda said fearlessly; "Old Hekt, who lives over there in the black cave."

"The witch!" muttered Nebsecht. "But we will let the leaves remain; if they do good, it is no matter where they came from."

"Hekt tasted the drops thou didst give her," said the old woman, "and agreed that they were good."

"Then we are satisfied with each other," answered Nebsecht, with a smile of amusement. "We will carry you now into the open air, little maid; for the air in here is as heavy as lead, and your damaged lung requires lighter nourishment."

"Yes, let me go out," said the girl. "It is well that thou hast not brought back the other with thee, who tormented me with his vows."

"You mean blind Teta," said Nebsecht, "he will not come again; but the young priest who soothed your father, when he repulsed the princess, will visit you. He is kindly disposed, and you should-you should —"

"Pentaur will come?" said the girl eagerly.

"Before midday. But how do you know his name?"

"I know him," said Uarda decidedly.

The surgeon looked at her surprised.

"You must not talk any more," he said, "for your cheeks are glowing, and the fever may return. We have arranged a tent for you, and now we will carry you into the open air."

"Not yet," said the girl. "Grandmother, do my hair for me, it is so heavy."

With these words she endeavored to part her mass of long reddish-brown hair with her slender hands, and to free it from the straws that had got entangled in it.

"Lie still," said the surgeon, in a warning voice.

"But it is so heavy," said the sick girl, smiling and showing Nebsecht her abundant wealth of golden hair as if it were a fatiguing burden. "Come, grandmother, and help me."

The old woman leaned over the child, and combed her long locks carefully with a coarse comb made of grey horn, gently disengaged the straws from the golden tangle, and at last laid two thick long plaits on her granddaughter's shoulders.

Nebsecht knew that every movement of the wounded girl might do mischief, and his impulse was to stop the old woman's proceedings, but his tongue seemed spell-bound. Surprised, motionless, and with crimson cheeks, he stood opposite the girl, and his eyes followed every movement of her hands with anxious observation.

She did not notice him.

When the old woman laid down the comb Uarda drew a long breath.

"Grandmother," she said, "give me the mirror." The old woman brought a shard of dimly glazed, baked clay. The girl turned to the light, contemplated the undefined reflection for a moment, and said:

"I have not seen a flower for so long, grandmother."

"Wait, child," she replied; she took from a jug the rose, which the princess had laid on the bosom of her grandchild, and offered it to her. Before Uarda could take it, the withered petals fell, and dropped upon her. The surgeon stooped, gathered them up, and put them into the child's hand.

"How good you are!" she said; "I am called Uarda-like this flower-and I love roses and the fresh air. Will you carry me out now?"

Nebsecht called the paraschites, who came into the hut with his son, and they carried the girl out into the air, and laid her under the humble tent they had contrived for her. The soldier's knees trembled while he held the light burden of his daughter's weight in his strong hands, and he sighed when he laid her down on the mat.

"How blue the sky is!" cried Uarda. "Ah! grandfather has watered my pomegranate, I thought so! and there come my doves! give me some corn in my hand, grandmother. How pleased they are."

The graceful birds, with black rings round their reddish-grey necks, flew confidingly to her, and took the corn that she playfully laid between her lips.

Nebsecht looked on with astonishment at this pretty play. He felt as if a new world had opened to him, and some new sense, hitherto unknown to him, had been revealed to him within his breast. He silently sat down in front of the but, and drew the picture of a rose on the sand with a reed-stem that he picked up.

Perfect stillness was around him; the doves even had flown up, and settled on the roof. Presently the dog barked, steps approached; Uarda lifted herself up and said:

"Grandmother, it is the priest Pentaur."

"Who told you?" asked the old woman.

"I know it," answered the girl decidedly, and in a few moments a sonorous voice cried: "Good day to you. How is your invalid?"

Pentaur was soon standing by Uarda; pleased to hear Nebsecht's good report, and with the sweet face of the girl. He had some flowers in his hand, that a happy maiden had laid on the altar of the Goddess Hathor, which he had served since the previous day, and he gave them to the sick girl, who took them with a blush, and held them between her clasped hands.

"The great Goddess whom I serve sends you these," said Pentaur, "and they will bring you healing. Continue to resemble them. You are pure and fair like them, and your course henceforth may be like theirs. As the sun gives life to the grey horizon, so you bring joy to this dark but. Preserve your innocence, and wherever you go you will bring love, as flowers spring in every spot that is trodden by the golden foot of Hathor.[66]

May her blessing rest upon you!"

He had spoken the last words half to the old couple and half to Uarda, and was already turning to depart when, behind a heap of dried reeds that lay close to the awning over the girl, the bitter cry of a child was heard, and a little boy came forward who held, as high as he could reach, a little cake, of which the dog, who seemed to know him well, had snatched half.

"How do you come here, Scherau?" the paraschites asked the weeping boy; the unfortunate child that Hekt was bringing up as a dwarf.

"I wanted," sobbed the little one, "to bring the cake to Uarda. She is ill—I had so much—"

"Poor child," said the paraschites, stroking the boy's hair; "there-give it to Uarda."

Scherau went up to the sick girl, knelt down by her, and whispered with streaming eyes:

"Take it! It is good, and very sweet, and if I get another cake, and Hekt will let me out, I will bring it to you.

"Thank you, good little Scherau," said Uarda, kissing the child. Then she turned to Pentaur and said:

"For weeks he has had nothing but papyrus-pith, and lotus-bread, and now he brings me the cake which grandmother gave old Hekt yesterday."

The child blushed all over, and stammered:

"It is only half-but I did not touch it. Your dog bit out this piece, and this."

He touched the honey with the tip of his finger, and put it to his lips. "I was a long time behind the reeds there, for I did not like to come out because of the strangers there." He pointed to Nebsecht and Pentaur. "But now I must go home," he cried.

The child was going, but Pentaur stopped him, seized him, lifted him up in his arms and kissed him; saying, as he turned to Nebsecht:

"They were wise, who represented Horus-the symbol of the triumph of good over evil and of purity over the impure-in the form of a child. Bless you, my little friend; be good, and always give away what you have to make others happy. It will not make your house rich-but it will your heart!"

Scherau clung to the priest, and involuntarily raised his little hand to stroke Pentaur's cheek. An unknown tenderness had filled his little heart, and he felt as if he must throw his arms round the poet's neck and cry upon his breast.

But Pentaur set him down on the ground, and he trotted down into the valley. There he paused. The sun was high in the heavens, and he must return to the witch's cave and his board, but he would so much like to go a little farther-only as far as to the king's tomb, which was quite near.

Close by the door of this tomb was a thatch of palm-branches, and under this the sculptor Batau, a very aged man, was accustomed to rest. The old man was deaf, but he passed for the best artist of his time, and with justice; he had designed the beautiful pictures and hieroglyphic inscriptions in Seti's splendid buildings at Abydos and Thebes, as well as in the tomb of that prince, and he was now working at the decoration of the walls in the grave of Rameses.

Scherau had often crept close up to him, and thoughtfully watched him at work, and then tried himself to make animal and human figures out of a bit of clay.

One day the old man had observed him.

The sculptor had silently taken his humble attempt out of his hand, and had returned it to him with a smile of encouragement.

From that time a peculiar tie had sprung up between the two. Scherau would venture to sit down by the sculptor, and try to imitate his finished images. Not a word was exchanged between them, but often the deaf old man would destroy the boy's works, often on the contrary improve them with a touch of his own hand, and not seldom nod at him to encourage him.

When he staid away the old man missed his pupil, and Scherau's happiest hours were those which he passed at his side.

He was not forbidden to take some clay home with him. There, when the old woman's back was turned, he moulded a variety of images which he destroyed as soon as they were finished.

While he lay on his rack his hands were left free, and he tried to reproduce the various forms which lived in his imagination, he forgot the present in his artistic attempts, and his bitter lot acquired a flavor of the sweetest enjoyment.

But to-day it was too late; he must give up his visit to the tomb of Rameses.

Once more he looked back at the hut, and then hurried into the dark cave.

CHAPTER XIV.

Pentauer also soon quitted the but of the paraschites.

Lost in meditation, he went along the hill-path which led to the temple which Ameni had put under his direction.[67]

He foresaw many disturbed and anxious hours in the immediate future.

The sanctuary of which he was the superior, had been dedicated to her own memory, and to the goddess Hathor, by Hatasu,[68] a great queen of the dethroned dynasty.

The priests who served it were endowed with peculiar chartered privileges, which hitherto had been strictly respected. Their dignity was hereditary, going down from father to son, and they had the right of choosing their director from among themselves.

Now their chief priest Rui was ill and dying, and Ameni, under whose jurisdiction they came, had, without consulting them, sent the young poet Pentaur to fill his place.

They had received the intruder most unwillingly, and combined strongly against him when it became evident that he was disposed to establish a severe rule and to abolish many abuses which had become established customs.

They had devolved the greeting of the rising sun on the temple-servants; Pentaur required that the younger ones at least should take part in chanting the morning hymn, and himself led the choir. They had trafficked with the offerings laid on the altar of the Goddess; the new master repressed this abuse, as well as the extortions of which they were guilty towards women in sorrow, who visited the temple of Hathor in greater number than any other sanctuary.

The poet-brought up in the temple of Seti to self-control, order, exactitude, and decent customs, deeply penetrated with a sense of the dignity of his position, and accustomed to struggle with special zeal against indolence of body and spirit-was disgusted with the slothful life and fraudulent dealings of his subordinates; and the deeper insight which yesterday's experience had given him into the poverty and sorrow of human existence, made him resolve with increased warmth that he would awake them to a new life.

The conviction that the lazy herd whom he commanded was called upon to pour consolation into a thousand sorrowing hearts, to dry innumerable tears, and to clothe the dry sticks of despair with the fresh verdure of hope, urged him to strong measures.

Yesterday he had seen how, with calm indifference, they had listened to the deserted wife, the betrayed maiden, to the woman, who implored the withheld blessing of children, to the anxious mother, the forlorn widow-and sought only to take advantage of sorrow, to extort gifts for the Goddess, or better still for their own pockets or belly.

Now he was nearing the scene of his new labors.

There stood the reverend building, rising stately from the valley on four terraces handsomely and singularly divided, and resting on the western side against the high amphitheatre of yellow cliffs.

On the closely-joined foundation stones gigantic hawks were carved in relief, each with the emblem of life, and symbolized Horus, the son of the Goddess, who brings all that fades to fresh bloom, and all that dies to resurrection.

On each terrace stood a hall open to the east, and supported on two and twenty archaic pillars.[69]

On their inner walls elegant pictures and inscriptions in the finest sculptured work recorded, for the benefit of posterity, the great things that Hatasu had done with the help of the Gods of Thebes.

There were the ships which she had to send to Punt[70] to enrich Egypt with the treasures of the east; there the wonders brought to Thebes from Arabia might be seen; there were delineated the houses of the inhabitants of the land of frankincense, and all the fishes of the Red Sea, in distinct and characteristic outline.

On the third and fourth terraces were the small adjoining rooms of Hatasu and her brothers Thotmes II. and III., which were built against the rock, and entered by granite doorways. In them purifications were accomplished, the images of the Goddess worshipped, and the more distinguished worshippers admitted to confess. The sacred cows of the Goddess were kept in a side-building.

As Pentaur approached the great gate of the terrace-temple, he became the witness of a scene which filled him with resentment.

A woman implored to be admitted into the forecourt, to pray at the altar of the Goddess for her husband, who was very ill, but the sleek gate-keeper drove her back with rough words.

"It is written up," said he, pointing to the inscription over the gate, "only the purified may set their foot across this threshold, and you cannot be purified but by the smoke of incense."

"Then swing the censer for me," said the woman, and take this silver ring-it is all I have."

"A silver ring!" cried the porter, indignantly. "Shall the goddess be impoverished for your sake! The grains of Anta, that would be used in purifying you, would cost ten times as much."

"But I have no more," replied the woman, "my husband, for whom I come to pray, is ill; he cannot work, and my children —"

"You fatten them up and deprive the goddess of her due," cried the gate-keeper. "Three rings down, or I shut the gate."

"Be merciful," said the woman, weeping. "What will become of us if Hathor does not help my husband?"

"Will our goddess fetch the doctor?" asked the porter. "She has something to do besides curing sick starvelings. Besides, that is not her office. Go to Imhotep or to Chunsu the counsellor, or to the great Techuti herself, who helps the sick. There is no quack medicine to be got here."

"I only want comfort in my trouble," said the woman.

"Comfort!" laughed the gate-keeper, measuring the comely young woman with his eye. "That you may have cheaper."

The woman turned pale, and drew back from the hand the man stretched out towards her.

At this moment Pentaur, full of wrath, stepped between them.

He raised his hand in blessing over the woman, who bent low before him, and said, "Whoever calls fervently on the Divinity is near to him. You are pure. Enter."

As soon as she had disappeared within the temple, the priest turned to the gate-keeper and exclaimed: "Is this how you serve the goddess, is this how you take advantage of a heart-wrung woman? Give me the keys of this gate. Your office is taken from you, and early to-morrow you go out in the fields, and keep the geese of Hathor."

The porter threw himself on his knees with loud outcries; but Pentaur turned his back upon him, entered the sanctuary, and mounted the steps which led to his dwelling on the third terrace.

A few priests whom he passed turned their backs upon him, others looked down at their dinners, eating noisily, and making as if they did not see him. They had combined strongly, and were determined to expel the inconvenient intruder at any price.

Having reached his room, which had been splendidly decorated for his predecessor, Pentaur laid aside his new insignia, comparing sorrowfully the past and the present.

To what an exchange Ameni had condemned him! Here, wherever he looked, he met with sulkiness and aversion; while, when he walked through the courts of the House of Seti, a hundred boys would hurry towards him, and cling affectionately to his robe. Honored there by great and small, his every word had had its value; and when each day he gave utterance to his thoughts, what he bestowed came back to him refined by earnest discourse with his associates and superiors, and he gained new treasures for his inner life.

"What is rare," thought he, "is full of charm; and yet how hard it is to do without what is habitual!" The occurrences of the last few days passed before his mental sight. Bent-Anat's image appeared before him, and took a more and more distinct and captivating form. His heart began to beat wildly, the blood rushed faster through his veins; he hid his face in his hands, and recalled every glance, every word from her lips.

"I follow thee willingly," she had said to him before the hut of the paraschites. Now he asked himself whether he were worthy of such a follower.

He had indeed broken through the old bonds, but not to disgrace the house that was dear to him, only to let new light into its dim chambers.

"To do what we have earnestly felt to be right," said he to himself, "may seem worthy of punishment to men, but cannot before God."

He sighed and walked out into the terrace in a mood of lofty excitement, and fully resolved to do here nothing but what was right, to lay the foundation of all that was good.

"We men," thought he, "prepare sorrow when we come into the world, and lamentation when we leave it; and so it is our duty in the intermediate time to fight with suffering, and to sow the seeds of joy. There are many tears here to be wiped away. To work then!" The poet found none of his subordinates on the upper terrace. They had all met in the forecourt of the temple, and were listening to the gate-keeper's tale, and seemed to sympathize with his angry complaint-against whom Pentaur well knew.

With a firm step he went towards them and said:

"I have expelled this man from among us, for he is a disgrace to us. To-morrow he quits the temple."

"I will go at once," replied the gate-keeper defiantly, "and in behalf of the holy fathers (here he cast a significant glance at the priests), ask the high-priest Ameni if the unclean are henceforth to be permitted to enter this sanctuary."

He was already approaching the gate, but Pentaur stepped before him, saying resolutely:

"You will remain here and keep the geese to-morrow, day after to-morrow, and until I choose to pardon you." The gate-keeper looked enquiringly at the priests. Not one moved.

"Go back into your house," said Pentaur, going closer to him.

The porter obeyed.

Pentaur locked the door of the little room, gave the key to one of the temple-servants, and said: "Perform his duty, watch the man, and if he escapes you will go after the geese to-morrow too. See, my friends, how many worshippers kneel there before our altars-go and fulfil your office. I will wait in the confessional to receive complaints, and to administer comfort."

The priests separated and went to the votaries. Pentaur once more mounted the steps, and sat down in the narrow confessional which was closed by a curtain; on its wall the picture of Hatasu was to be seen, drawing the milk of eternal life from the udders of the cow Hathor.

He had hardly taken his place when a temple-servant announced the arrival of a veiled lady. The bearers of her litter were thickly veiled, and she had requested to be conducted to the confession chamber. The servant handed Pentaur a token by which the high-priest of the great temple of Anion, on the other bank of the Nile, granted her the privilege of entering the inner rooms of the temple with the Rechiu, and to communicate with all priests, even with the highest of the initiated.

The poet withdrew behind a curtain, and awaited the stranger with a disquiet that seemed to him all the more singular that he had frequently found himself in a similar position. Even the noblest dignitaries had often been transferred to him by Ameni when they had come to the temple to have their visions interpreted.

A tall female figure entered the still, sultry stone room, sank on her knees, and put up a long and absorbed prayer before the figure of Hathor. Pentaur also, seen by no one, lifted his hands, and fervently addressed himself to the omnipresent spirit with a prayer for strength and purity.

Just as his arms fell the lady raised her head. It was as though the prayers of the two souls had united to mount upwards together.

The veiled lady rose and dropped her veil.

It was Bent-Anat.

In the agitation of her soul she had sought the goddess Hathor, who guides the beating heart of woman and spins the threads which bind man and wife.

"High mistress of heaven! many-named and beautiful!" she began to pray aloud, "golden Hathor! who knowest grief and ecstasy-the present and the future-draw near to thy child, and guide the spirit of thy servant, that he may advise me well. I am the daughter of a father who is great and noble and truthful as one of the Gods. He advises me-he will never compel me-to yield to a man whom I can never love. Nay, another has met me, humble in birth but noble in spirit and in gifts —"

Thus far, Pentaur, incapable of speech, had overheard the princess.

Ought he to remain concealed and hear all her secret, or should he step forth and show himself to her? His pride called loudly to him: "Now she will speak your name; you are the chosen one of the fairest and noblest." But another voice to which he had accustomed himself to listen in severe self-discipline made itself heard, and said —"Let her say nothing in ignorance, that she need be ashamed of if she knew."

He blushed for her; —he opened the curtain and went forward into the presence of Bent-Anat.

The Princess drew back startled.

"Art thou Pentaur," she asked, "or one of the Immortals?"

"I am Pentaur," he answered firmly, "a man with all the weakness of his race, but with a desire for what is good. Linger here and pour out thy soul to our Goddess; my whole life shall be a prayer for thee."

The poet looked full at her; then he turned quickly, as if to avoid a danger, towards the door of the confessional.

Bent-Anat called his name, and he stayed his steps:

"The daughter of Rameses," she said, "need offer no justification of her appearance here, but the maiden Bent-Anat," and she colored as she spoke, "expected to find, not thee, but the old priest Rui, and she desired his advice. Now leave me to pray."

Bent-Anat sank on her knees, and Pentaur went out into the open air.

When the princess too had left the confessional, loud voices were heard on the south side of the terrace on which they stood.

She hastened towards the parapet.

"Hail to Pentaur!" was shouted up from below. The poet rushed forward, and placed himself near the princess. Both looked down into the valley, and could be seen by all.

"Hail, hail! Pentaur," was called doubly loud, "Hail to our teacher! come back to the House of Seti. Down with the persecutors of Pentaur-down with our oppressors!"

At the head of the youths, who, so soon as they had found out whither the poet had been exiled, had escaped to tell him that they were faithful to him, stood the prince Rameri, who nodded triumphantly to his sister, and Anana stepped forward to inform the honored teacher in a solemn and well-studied speech, that, in the event of Ameni refusing to recall him, they had decided requesting their fathers to place them at another school.

The young sage spoke well, and Bent-Anat followed his words, not without approbation; but Pentaur's face grew darker, and before his favorite disciple had ended his speech he interrupted him sternly.

His voice was at first reproachful, and then complaining, and loud as he spoke, only sorrow rang in his tones, and not anger.

"In truth," he concluded, "every word that I have spoken to you I could but find it in me to regret, if it has contributed to encourage you to this mad act. You were born in palaces; learn to obey, that later you may know how to command. Back to your school! You hesitate? Then I will come out against you with the watchman, and drive you back, for you do me and yourselves small honor by such a proof of affection. Go back to the school you belong to."

The school-boys dared make no answer, but surprised and disenchanted turned to go home.

Bent-Anat cast down her eyes as she met those of her brother, who shrugged his shoulders, and then she looked half shyly, half respectfully, at the poet; but soon again her eyes turned to the plain below, for thick dust-clouds whirled across it, the sound of hoofs and the rattle of wheels became audible, and at the same moment the chariot of Septah, the chief haruspex, and a vehicle with the heavily-armed guard of the House of Seti, stopped near the terrace.

The angry old man sprang quickly to the ground, called the host of escaped pupils to him in a stern voice, ordered the guard to drive them back to the school, and hurried up to the temple gates like a vigorous youth. The priests received him with the deepest reverence, and at once laid their complaints before him.

He heard them willingly, but did not let them discuss the matter; then, though with some difficulty, he quickly mounted the steps, down which Bent-Anat came towards him.

The princess felt that she would divert all the blame and misunderstanding to herself, if Septah recognized her; her hand involuntarily reached for her veil, but she drew it back quickly, looked with quiet dignity into the old man's eyes, which flashed with anger, and proudly passed by him. The haruspex bowed, but without giving her his blessing, and when he met Pentaur on the second terrace, ordered that the temple should be cleared of worshippers.

This was done in a few minutes, and the priests were witnesses of the most painful, scene which had occurred for years in their quiet sanctuary.

The head of the haruspices of the House of Seti was the most determined adversary of the poet who had so early been initiated into the mysteries, and whose keen intellect often shook those very ramparts which the zealous old man had, from conviction, labored to strengthen from his youth up. The vexatious occurrences, of which he had been a witness at the House of Seti, and here also but a few minutes since, he regarded as the consequence of the unbridled license of an ill-regulated imagination, and in stern language he called Pentaur to account for the "revolt" of the school-boys.

"And besides our boys," he exclaimed, "you have led the daughter of Rameses astray. She was not yet purged of her uncleanness, and yet you tempt her to an assignation, not even in the stranger's quarters-but in the holy house of this pure Divinity." Undeserved praise is dangerous to the weak; unjust blame may turn even the strong from the right way. Pentaur indignantly repelled the accusations of the old man, called them unworthy of his age, his position, and his name, and for fear that his anger might carry him too far, turned his back upon him; but the haruspex ordered him to remain, and in his presence questioned the priests, who unanimously accused the poet of having admitted to the temple another unpurified woman besides Bent-Anat, and of having expelled the gate-keeper and thrown him into prison for opposing the crime.

The haruspex ordered that the "ill-used man" should be set at liberty.

Pentaur resisted this command, asserted his right to govern in this temple, and with a trembling voice requested Septah to quit the place.

The haruspex showed him Ameni's ring, by which, during his residence in Thebes, he made him his plenipotentiary, degraded Pentaur from his dignity, but ordered him not to quit the sanctuary till further notice, and then finally departed from the temple of Hatasu.

Pentaur had yielded in silence to the signet of his chief, and returned to the confessional in which he had met Bent-Anat. He felt his soul shaken to its very foundations, his thoughts were confused, his feelings struggling with each other; he shivered, and when he heard the laughter of the priests and the gatekeeper, who were triumphing in their easy victory, he started and shuddered like a man who in passing a mirror should see a brand of disgrace on his brow.

But by degrees he recovered himself, his spirit grew clearer, and when he left the little room to look towards the east-where, on the farther shore, rose the palace where Bent-Anat must be —a deep contempt for his enemies filled his soul, and a proud feeling of renewed manly energy. He did not conceal from himself that he had enemies; that a time of struggle was beginning for him; but he looked forward to it like a young hero to the morning of his first battle.

CHAPTER XV.

The afternoon shadows were already growing long, when a splendid chariot drew up to the gates of the terrace-temple. Paaker, the chief pioneer, stood up in it, driving his handsome and fiery Syrian horses. Behind him stood an Ethiopian slave, and his big dog followed the swift team with his tongue out.

As he approached the temple he heard himself called, and checked the pace of his horses. A tiny man hurried up to him, and, as soon as he had recognized in him the dwarf Nemu, he cried angrily:

"Is it for you, you rascal, that I stop my drive? What do you want?"

"To crave," said the little man, bowing humbly, "that, when thy business in the city of the dead is finished, thou wilt carry me back to Thebes."

"You are Mena's dwarf?" asked the pioneer.

"By no means," replied Nemu. "I belong to his neglected wife, the lady Nefert. I can only cover the road very slowly with my little legs, while the hoofs of your horses devour the way-as a crocodile does his prey."

"Get up!" said Paaker. "Did you come here on foot?"

"No, my lord," replied Nemu, "on an ass; but a demon entered into the beast, and has struck it with sickness. I had to leave it on the road. The beasts of Anubis will have a better supper than we to-night."

"Things are not done handsomely then at your mistress's house?" asked Paaker.

"We still have bread," replied Nemu, "and the Nile is full of water. Much meat is not neces-sary for women and dwarfs, but our last cattle take a form which is too hard for human teeth."

The pioneer did not understand the joke, and looked enquiringly at the dwarf.

"The form of money," said the little man, "and that cannot be chewed; soon that will be gone too, and then the point will be to find a recipe for making nutritious cakes out of earth, water, and palm-leaves. It makes very little difference to me, a dwarf does not need much-but the poor tender lady!"

Paaker touched his horses with such a violent stroke of his whip that they reared high, and it took all his strength to control their spirit.

"The horses' jaws will be broken," muttered the slave behind. "What a shame with such fine beasts!"

"Have you to pay for them?" growled Paaker. Then he turned again to the dwarf, and asked: "Why does Mena let the ladies want?"

"He no longer cares for his wife," replied the dwarf, casting his eyes down sadly. "At the last division of the spoil he passed by the gold and silver; and took a foreign woman into his tent. Evil demons have blinded him, for where is there a woman fairer than Nefert?"

"You love your mistress."

"As my very eyes!"

During this conversation they had arrived at the terrace-temple. Paaker threw the reins to the slave, ordered him to wait with Nemu, and turned to the gate-keeper to explain to him, with the help of a handful of gold, his desire of being conducted to Pentaur, the chief of the temple.

The gate-keeper, swinging a censer before him with a hasty action, admitted him into the sanctuary. "You will find him on the third terrace," he said, "but he is no longer our superior."

"They said so in the temple of Seti, whence I have just come," replied Paaker.

The porter shrugged his shoulders with a sneer, and said: "The palm-tree that is quickly set up falls down more quickly still." Then he desired a servant to conduct the stranger to Pentaur.

The poet recognized the Mohar at once, asked his will, and learned that he was come to have a wonderful vision interpreted by him.

Paaker explained before relating his dream, that he did not ask this service for nothing; and when the priest's countenance darkened he added:

"I will send a fine beast for sacrifice to the Goddess if the interpretation is favorable."

"And in the opposite case?" asked Pentaur, who, in the House of Seti, never would have anything whatever to do with the payments of the worshippers or the offerings of the devout.

"I will offer a sheep," replied Paaker, who did not perceive the subtle irony that lurked in Pentaur's words, and who was accustomed to pay for the gifts of the Divinity in proportion to their value to himself.

Pentaur thought of the verdict which Gagabu, only two evenings since, had passed on the Mohar, and it occurred to him that he would test how far the man's superstition would lead him. So he asked, while he suppressed a smile:

"And if I can foretell nothing bad, but also nothing actually good?" —

"An antelope, and four geese," answered Paaker promptly.

"But if I were altogether disinclined to put myself at your service?" asked Pentaur. "If I thought it unworthy of a priest to let the Gods be paid in proportion to their favors towards a particular person, like corrupt officials; if I now showed you-you-and I have known you from a school-boy, that there are things that cannot be bought with inherited wealth?"

The pioneer drew back astonished and angry, but Pentaur continued calmly —

"I stand here as the minister of the Divinity; and nevertheless, I see by your countenance, that you were on the point of lowering yourself by showing to me your violent and extortionate spirit.

"The Immortals send us dreams, not to give us a foretaste of joy or caution us against danger, but to remind us so to prepare our souls that we may submit quietly to suffer evil, and with heartfelt gratitude accept the good; and so gain from each profit for the inner life. I will not interpret your dream! Come without gifts, but with a humble heart, and with longing for inward purification, and I will pray to the Gods that they may enlighten me, and give you such interpretation of even evil dreams that they may be fruitful in blessing.

"Leave me, and quit the temple!"

Paaker ground his teeth with rage; but he controlled himself, and only said as he slowly withdrew:

"If your office had not already been taken from you, the insolence with which you have dismissed me might have cost you your place. We shall meet again, and then you shall learn that inherited wealth in the right hand is worth more than you will like."

"Another enemy!" thought the poet, when he found himself alone and stood erect in the glad consciousness of having done right.

During Paaker's interview with the poet, the dwarf Nemu had chatted to the porter, and had learned from him all that had previously occurred.

Paaker mounted his chariot pale with rage, and whipped on his horses before the dwarf had clambered up the step; but the slave seized the little man, and set him carefully on his feet behind his master.

"The villian, the scoundrel! he shall repent it-Pentaur is he called! the hound!" muttered the pioneer to himself.

The dwarf lost none of his words, and when he caught the name of Pentaur he called to the pioneer, and said —

"They have appointed a scoundrel to be the superior of this temple; his name is Pentaur. He was expelled from the temple of Seti for his immorality, and now he has stirred up the younger scholars to rebellion, and invited unclean women into the temple. My lips hardly dare repeat it, but the gate-keeper swore it was true-that the chief haruspex from the House of Seti found him in conference with Bent-Anat, the king's daughter, and at once deprived him of his office."

"With Bent-Anat?" replied the pioneer, and muttered, before the dwarf could find time to answer, "Indeed, with Bent-Anat!" and he recalled the day before yesterday, when the princess had remained so long with the priest in the hovel of the parashites, while he had talked to Nefert and visited the old witch.

"I should not care to be in the priest's skin," observed Nemu, "for though Rameses is far away, the Regent Ani is near enough. He is a gentleman who seldom pounces, but even the dove won't allow itself to be attacked in is own nest."

100

Paaker looked enquiringly at Nemu.

"I know," said the dwarf "Ani has asked Rameses' consent to marry his daughter."

"He has already asked it," continued the dwarf as Paaker smiled incredulously, "and the king is not disinclined to give it. He likes making marriages-as thou must know pretty well."

"I?" said Paaker, surprised.

"He forced Katuti to give her daughter as wife to the charioteer. That I know from herself. She can prove it to thee."

Paaker shook his head in denial, but the dwarf continued eagerly, "Yes, yes! Katuti would have had thee for her son-in-law, and it was the king, not she, who broke off the betrothal. Thou must at the same time have been inscribed in the black books of the high gate, for Rameses used many hard names for thee. One of us is like a mouse behind the curtain, which knows a good deal."

Paaker suddenly brought his horses to a stand-still, threw the reins to the slave, sprang from the chariot, called the dwarf to his side, and said:

"We will walk from here to the river, and you shall tell me all you know; but if an untrue word passes your lips I will have you eaten by my dogs."

"I know thou canst keep thy word," gasped the little man. "But go a little slower if thou wilt, for I am quite out of breath. Let Katuti herself tell thee how it all came about. Rameses compelled her to give her daughter to the charioteer. I do not know what he said of thee, but it was not complimentary. My poor mistress! she let herself be caught by the dandy, the ladies' man-and now she may weep and wail. When I pass the great gates of thy house with Katuti, she often sighs and complains bitterly. And with good reason, for it soon will be all over with our noble estate, and we must seek an asylum far away among the Amu in the low lands; for the nobles will soon avoid us as outcasts. Thou mayst be glad that thou hast not linked thy fate to ours; but I have a faithful heart, and will share my mistress's trouble."

"You speak riddles," said Paaker, "what have they to fear?"

The dwarf now related how Nefert's brother had gambled away the mummy of his father, how enormous was the sum he had lost, and that degradation must overtake Katuti, and her daughter with her.

"Who can save them," he whimpered. "Her shameless husband squanders his inheritance and his prize-money. Katuti is poor, and the little words 'Give me!' scare away friends as the cry of a hawk scares the chickens. My poor mistress!"

"It is a large sum," muttered Paaker to himself. "It is enormous!" sighed the dwarf, "and where is it to be found in these hard times? It would have been different with us, if-ah if—. And it would be a form of madness which I do not believe in, that Nefert should still care for her braggart husband. She thinks as much of thee as of him."

Paaker looked at the dwarf half incredulous and half threatening.

"Ay-of thee," repeated Nemu. "Since our excursion to the Necropolis the day before yesterday it was-she speaks only of thee, praising thy ability, and thy strong manly spirit. It is as if some charm obliged her to think of thee."

The pioneer began to walk so fast that his small companion once more had to ask him to moderate his steps.

They gained the shore in silence, where Paaker's boat was waiting, which also conveyed his chariot. He lay down in the little cabin, called the dwarf to him, and said:

"I am Katuti's nearest relative; we are now reconciled; why does she not turn to me in her difficulty?"

"Because she is proud, and thy blood flows in her veins. Sooner would she die with her child-she said so-than ask thee, against whom she sinned, for an 'alms'."

"She did think of me then?"

"At once; nor did she doubt thy generosity. She esteems thee highly —I repeat it; and if an arrow from a Cheta's bow or a visitation of the Gods attained Mena, she would joyfully place her child in thine arms, and Nefert believe me has not forgotten her playfellow. The day before yesterday, when she came home from the Necropolis, and before the letter had come from the camp, she was full of thee —[71] nay called to thee in her dreams; I know it from Kandake, her black maid." The pioneer looked down and said:

"How extraordinary! and the same night I had a vision in which your mistress appeared to me; the insolent priest in the temple of Hathor should have interpreted it to me."

"And he refused? the fool! but other folks understand dreams, and I am not the worst of them-Ask thy servant. Ninety-nine times out of a hundred my interpretations come true. How was the vision?"

"I stood by the Nile," said Paaker, casting down his eyes and drawing lines with his whip through the wool of the cabin rug. "The water was still, and I saw Nefert standing on the farther bank, and beckoning to me. I called to her, and she stepped on the water, which bore her up as if it were this carpet. She went over the water dry-foot as if it were the stony wilderness. A wonderful sight! She came nearer to me, and nearer, and already I had tried to take her hand, when she ducked under like a swan. I went into the water to seize her, and when she came up again I clasped her in my arms; but then the strangest thing happened-she flowed away, she dissolved like the snow on the Syrian hills, when you take it in your hand, and yet it was not the same, for her hair turned to water-lilies, and her eyes to blue fishes that swam away merrily, and her lips to twigs of coral that sank at once, and from her body grew a crocodile, with a head like Mena, that laughed and gnashed its teeth at me. Then I was seized with blind fury; I threw myself upon him with a drawn sword, he fastened his teeth in my flesh, I pierced his throat with my weapon; the Nile was dark with our streaming blood, and so we fought and fought-it lasted an eternity-till I awoke."

Paaker drew a deep breath as he ceased speaking; as if his wild dream tormented him again.

The dwarf had listened with eager attention, but several minutes passed before he spoke.

"A strange dream," he said, "but the interpretation as to the future is not hard to find. Nefert is striving to reach thee, she longs to be thine, but if thou dost fancy that she is already in thy grasp she will elude thee; thy hopes will melt like ice, slip away like sand, if thou dost not know how to put the crocodile out of the way."

At this moment the boat struck the landing-place. The pioneer started up, and cried, "We have reached the end!"

"We have reached the end," echoed the little man with meaning. "There is only a narrow bridge to step over."

When they both stood on the shore, the dwarf said,

"I have to thank thee for thy hospitality, and when I can serve thee command me."

"Come here," cried the pioneer, and drew Nemu away with him under the shade of a sycamore veiled in the half light of the departing sun.

"What do you mean by a bridge which we must step over? I do not understand the flowers of speech, and desire plain language."

The dwarf reflected for a moment; and then asked, "Shall I say nakedly and openly what I mean, and will you not be angry?"

"Speak!"

"Mena is the crocodile. Put him out of the world, and you will have passed the bridge; then Nefert will be thine-if thou wilt listen to me."

"What shall I do?"

"Put the charioteer out of the world."

Paaker's gesture seemed to convey that that was a thing that had long been decided on, and he turned his face, for a good omen, so that the rising moon should be on his right hand.

The dwarf went on.

"Secure Nefert, so that she may not vanish like her image in the dream, before you reach the goal; that is to say, ransom the honor of your future mother and wife, for how could you take an outcast into your house?"

Paaker looked thoughtfully at the ground.

"May I inform my mistress that thou wilt save her?" asked Nemu. "I may? —Then all will be well, for he who will devote a fortune to love will not hesitate to devote a reed lance with a brass point to it to his love and his hatred together."

CHAPTER XVI.

The sun had set, and darkness covered the City of the Dead, but the moon shone above the valley of the kings' tombs, and the projecting masses of the rocky walls of the chasm threw sharply-defined shadows. A weird silence lay upon the desert, where yet far more life was stirring than in the noonday hour, for now bats darted like black silken threads through the night air, owls hovered aloft on wide-spread wings, small troops of jackals slipped by, one following the other up the mountain slopes. From time to time their hideous yell, or the whining laugh of the hyena, broke the stillness of the night.

Nor was human life yet at rest in the valley of tombs. A faint light glimmered in the cave of the sorceress Hekt, and in front of the paraschites' but a fire was burning, which the grandmother of the sick Uarda now and then fed with pieces of dry manure. Two men were seated in front of the hut, and gazed in silence on the thin flame, whose impure light was almost quenched by the clearer glow of the moon; whilst the third, Uarda's father, disembowelled a large ram, whose head he had already cut off.

"How the jackals howl!" said the old paraschites, drawing as he spoke the torn brown cotton cloth, which he had put on as a protection against the night air and the dew, closer round his bare shoulders.

"They scent the fresh meat," answered the physician, Nebsecht. "Throw them the entrails, when you have done; the legs and back you can roast. Be careful how you cut out the heart-the heart, soldier. There it is! What a great beast."

Nebsecht took the ram's heart in his hand, and gazed at it with the deepest attention, whilst the old paraschites watched him anxiously. At length:

"I promised," he said, "to do for you what you wish, if you restore the little one to health; but you ask for what is impossible."

"Impossible?" said the physician, "why, impossible? You open the corpses, you go in and out of the house of the embalmer. Get possession of one of the canopi,[72] lay this heart in it, and take out in its stead the heart of a human being. No one-no one will notice it. Nor need you do it to-morrow, or the day after to-morrow even. Your son can buy a ram to kill every day with my money till the right moment comes. Your granddaughter will soon grow strong on a good meat-diet. Take courage!"

"I am not afraid of the danger," said the old man, "but how can I venture to steal from a dead man his life in the other world? And then-in shame and misery have I lived, and for many a year-no man has numbered them for me-have I obeyed the commandments, that I may be found righteous in that world to come, and in the fields of Aalu, and in the Sun-bark find compensation for all that I have suffered here. You are good and friendly. Why, for the sake of a whim, should you sacrifice the future bliss of a man, who in all his long life has never known happiness, and who has never done you any harm?"

"What I want with the heart," replied the physician, "you cannot understand, but in procuring it for me, you will be furthering a great and useful purpose. I have no whims, for I am no idler. And as to what concerns your salvation, have no anxiety. I am a priest, and take your deed and its consequences upon myself; upon myself, do you understand? I tell you, as a priest, that what I demand of you is right, and if the judge of the dead shall enquire, 'Why didst thou take the heart of a human being out of the Kanopus?' then reply-reply to him thus, 'Because Nebsecht, the priest, commanded me, and promised himself to answer for the deed.'"

The old man gazed thoughtfully on the ground, and the physician continued still more urgently:

"If you fulfil my wish, then-then I swear to you that, when you die, I will take care that your mummy is provided with all the amulets, and I myself will write you a book of the Entrance into Day, and have it wound within your mummy-cloth, as is done with the great.[73]

That will give you power over all demons, and you will be admitted to the hall of the twofold justice, which punishes and rewards, and your award will be bliss."

"But the theft of a heart will make the weight of my sins heavy, when my own heart is weighed," sighed the old man.

Nebsecht considered for a moment, and then said: "I will give you a written paper, in which I will certify that it was I who commanded the theft. You will sew it up in a little bag, carry it on your breast, and have it laid with you in the grave. Then when Techuti, the agent of the soul, receives your justification before Osiris and the judges of the dead, give him the writing. He will read it aloud, and you will be accounted just."[74]

"I am not learned in writing," muttered the paraschites with a slight mistrust that made itself felt in his voice.

"But I swear to you by the nine great Gods, that I will write nothing on the paper but what I have promised you. I will confess that I, the priest Nebsecht, commanded you to take the heart, and that your guilt is mine."

"Let me have the writing then," murmured the old man.

The physician wiped the perspiration from his forehead, and gave the paraschites his hand. "To-morrow you shall have it," he said, "and I will not leave your granddaughter till she is well again."

The soldier engaged in cutting up the ram, had heard nothing of this conversation. Now he ran a wooden spit through the legs, and held them over the fire to roast them. The jackals howled louder as the smell of the melting fat filled the air, and the old man, as he looked on, forgot the terrible task he had undertaken. For a year past, no meat had been tasted in his house.

The physician Nebsecht, himself eating nothing but a piece of bread, looked on at the feasters. They tore the meat from the bones, and the soldier, especially, devoured the costly and unwonted meal like some ravenous animal. He could be heard chewing like a horse in the manger, and a feeling of disgust filled the physician's soul.

"Sensual beings," he murmured to himself, "animals with consciousness! And yet human beings. Strange! They languish bound in the fetters of the world of sense, and yet how much more ardently they desire that which transcends sense than we-how much more real it is to them than to us!"

"Will you have some meat?" cried the soldier, who had remarked that Nebsecht's lips moved, and tearing a piece of meat from the bone of the joint he was devouring, he held it out to the physician. Nebsecht shrank back; the greedy look, the glistening teeth, the dark, rough features of the man terrified him. And he thought of the white and fragile form of the sick girl lying within on the mat, and a question escaped his lips.

"Is the maiden, is Uarda, your own child?" he said.

The soldier struck himself on the breast. "So sure as the king Rameses is the son of Seti," he answered. The men had finished their meal, and the flat cakes of bread which the wife of the paraschites gave them, and on which they had wiped their hands from the fat, were consumed, when the soldier, in whose slow brain the physician's question still lingered, said, sighing deeply:

"Her mother was a stranger; she laid the white dove in the raven's nest."

"Of what country was your wife a native?" asked the physician.

"That I do not know," replied the soldier.

"Did you never enquire about the family of your own wife?"

"Certainly I did: but how could she have answered me? But it is a long and strange story."

"Relate it to me," said Nebsecht, "the night is long, and I like listening better than talking. But first I will see after our patient."

When the physician had satisfied himself that Uarda was sleeping quietly and breathing regularly, he seated himself again by the paraschites and his son, and the soldier began:

"It all happened long ago. King Seti still lived, but Rameses already reigned in his stead, when I came home from the north. They had sent me to the workmen, who were building the fortifications in Zoan, the town of Rameses. —[The Rameses of the Bible. Exodus i. ii.] —I was set over six men, Amus —[Semites] —of the Hebrew race, over whom Rameses kept such a tight hand.[75]

Amongst the workmen there were sons of rich cattle-holders, for in levying the people it was never: 'What have you?' but 'Of what race are you?' The fortifications and the canal which was to join the Nile and the Red Sea had to be completed, and the king, to whom be long life, health, and prosperity, took the youth of Egypt with him to the wars, and left the work to the Amus, who are connected by race with his enemies in the east. One lives well in Goshen, for it is a fine country, with more than enough of corn and grass and vegetables and fish and fowls, and I always had of the best, for amongst my six people were two mother's darlings, whose parents sent me many a piece of silver. Every one loves his children, but the Hebrews love them more tenderly than other people. We had daily our appointed tale of bricks to deliver, and when the sun burnt hot, I used to help the lads, and I did more in an hour than they did in three, for I am strong and was still stronger then than I am now.

"Then came the time when I was relieved. I was ordered to return to Thebes, to the prisoners of war who were building the great temple of Amon over yonder, and as I had brought home some money, and it would take a good while to finish the great dwelling of the king of the Gods, I thought of taking a wife; but no Egyptian. Of daughters of paraschites there were plenty; but I wanted to get away out of my father's accursed caste, and the other girls here, as I knew, were afraid of our uncleanness. In the low country I had done better, and many an Amu and Schasu woman had gladly come to my tent. From the beginning I had set my mind on an Asiatic.

"Many a time maidens taken prisoners in war were brought to be sold, but either they did not please me, or they were too dear. Meantime my money melted away, for we enjoyed life in the time of rest which followed the working hours. There were dancers too in plenty, in the foreign quarter.

"Well, it was just at the time of the holy feast of Amon-Chem, that a new transport of prisoners of war arrived, and amongst them many women, who were sold publicly to the highest bidder. The young and beautiful ones were paid for high, but even the older ones were too dear for me.

"Quite at the last a blind woman was led forward, and a withered-looking woman who was dumb, as the auctioneer, who generally praised up the merits of the prisoners, informed the buyers. The blind woman had strong hands, and was bought by a tavern-keeper, for whom she turns the handmill to this day; the dumb woman held a child in her arms, and no one could tell whether she was young or old. She looked as though she already lay in her coffin, and the little one as though he would go under the grass before her. And her hair was red, burning red, the very color of Typhon. Her white pale face looked neither bad nor good, only weary, weary to death. On her withered white arms blue veins ran like dark cords, her hands hung feebly down, and in them hung the child. If a wind were to rise, I thought to myself, it would blow her away, and the little one with her.

"The auctioneer asked for a bid. All were silent, for the dumb shadow was of no use for work; she was half-dead, and a burial costs money.

"So passed several minutes. Then the auctioneer stepped up to her, and gave her a blow with his whip, that she might rouse herself up, and appear less miserable to the buyers. She shivered like a person in a fever, pressed the child closer to her, and looked round at every one as though seeking for help-and me full in the face. What happened now was a real wonder, for her eyes were bigger than any that I ever saw, and a demon dwelt in them that had power over me and ruled me to the end, and that day it bewitched me for the first time.

"It was not hot and I had drunk nothing, and yet I acted against my own will and better judgment when, as her eyes fell upon me, I bid all that I possessed in order to buy her. I might have had her cheaper! My companions laughed at me, the auctioneer shrugged his shoulders as he took my money, but I took the child on my arm, helped the woman up, carried her in a boat over the Nile, loaded a stone-cart with my miserable property, and drove her like a block of lime home to the old people.

"My mother shook her head, and my father looked as if he thought me mad; but neither of them said a word. They made up a bed for her, and on my spare nights I built that ruined thing hard by-it was a tidy hut once. Soon my mother grew fond of the child. It was quite small, and we called it Pennu —[Pennu is the name for the mouse in old Egyptian] —because it was so pretty, like a little mouse. I kept away from the foreign quarter, and saved my wages, and bought a goat, which lived in front of our door when I took the woman to her own hut.

"She was dumb, but not deaf, only she did not understand our language; but the demon in her eyes spoke for her and understood what I said. She comprehended everything, and could say everything with her eyes; but best of all she knew how to thank one. No high-priest who at the great hill festival praises the Gods in long hymns for their gifts can return thanks so earnestly with his lips as she with her dumb eyes. And when she wished to pray, then it seemed as though the demon in her look was mightier than ever.

"At first I used to be impatient enough when she leaned so feebly against the wall, or when the child cried and disturbed my sleep; but she had only to look up, and the demon pressed my heart together and persuaded me that the crying was really a song. Pennu cried more sweetly too than other children, and he had such soft, white, pretty little fingers.

"One day he had been crying for a long time, At last I bent down over him, and was going to scold him, but he seized me by the beard. It was pretty to see! Afterwards he was for ever wanting to pull me about, and his mother noticed that that pleased me, for when I brought home anything good, an egg or a flower or a cake, she used to hold him up and place his little hands on my beard.

"Yes, in a few months the woman had learnt to hold him up high in her arms, for with care and quiet she had grown stronger. White she always remained and delicate, but she grew younger and more beautiful from day to day; she can hardly have numbered twenty years when I bought her. What she was called I never heard; nor did we give her any name. She was 'the woman,' and so we called her.

"Eight moons passed by, and then the little Mouse died. I wept as she did, and as I bent over the little corpse and let my tears have free course, and thought-now he can never lift up his pretty little finger to you again; then I felt for the first time the woman's soft hand on my cheek. She stroked my rough beard as a child might, and with that looked at me so gratefully that I felt as though king Pharaoh had all at once made me a present of both Upper and Lower Egypt.

"When the Mouse was buried she got weaker again, but my mother took good care of her. I lived with her, like a father with his child. She was always friendly, but if I approached her, and tried to show her any fondness, she would look at me, and the demon in her eyes drove me back, and I let her alone.

"She grew healthier and stronger and more and more beautiful, so beautiful that I kept her hidden, and was consumed by the longing to make her my wife. A good housewife she never became, to be sure; her hands were so tender, and she did not even know how to milk the goat. My mother did that and everything else for her.

"In the daytime she stayed in her hut and worked, for she was very skillful at woman's work, and wove lace as fine as cobwebs, which my mother sold that she might bring home perfumes with the proceeds. She was very fond of them, and of flowers too; and Uarda in there takes after her.

"In the evening, when the folk from the other side had left the City of the Dead, she would often walk down the valley here, thoughtful and often looking up at the moon, which she was especially fond of.

"One evening in the winter-time I came home. It was already dark, and I expected to find her in front of the door. All at once, about a hundred steps behind old Hekt's cave, I heard a troop of jackals barking so furiously that I said to myself directly they had attacked a human being, and I knew too who it was, though no one had told me, and the woman could not call or cry out. Frantic with terror, I tore a firebrand from the hearth and the stake to which the goat was fastened out of the ground, rushed to her help, drove away the beasts, and carried her back senseless to the hut. My mother helped me, and we called her back to life. When we were alone, I wept like a child for joy at her escape, and she let me kiss her, and then she became my wife, three years after I had bought her.

"She bore me a little maid, that she herself named Uarda; for she showed us a rose, and then pointed to the child, and we understood her without words.

"Soon afterwards she died.

"You are a priest, but I tell you that when I am summoned before Osiris, if I am admitted amongst the blessed, I will ask whether I shall meet my wife, and if the doorkeeper says no, he may thrust me back, and I will go down cheerfully to the damned, if I find her again there."

"And did no sign ever betray her origin?" asked the physician.

The soldier had hidden his face in his hand; he was weeping aloud, and did not hear the question. But, the paraschites answered:

"She was the child of some great personage, for in her clothes we found a golden jewel with a precious stone inscribed with strange characters. It is very costly, and my wife is keeping it for the little one."

CHAPTER XVII.

In the earliest glimmer of dawn the following clay, the physician Nebsecht having satisfied himself as to the state of the sick girl, left the paraschites' hut and made his way in deepest thought to the 'Terrace Temple of Hatasu, to find his friend Pentaur and compose the writing which he had promised to the old man.

As the sun arose in radiance he reached the sanctuary. He expected to hear the morning song of the priests, but all was silent. He knocked and the porter, still half-asleep, opened the door.

Nebsecht enquired for the chief of the Temple. "He died in the night," said the man yawning.

"What do you say?" cried the physician in sudden terror, "who is dead?"

"Our good old chief, Rui."

Nebsecht breathed again, and asked for Pentaur.

"You belong to the House of Seti," said the doorkeeper, "and you do not know that he is deposed from his office? The holy fathers have refused to celebrate the birth of Ra with him. He sings for himself now, alone up on the watch-tower. There you will find him."

Nebsecht strode quickly up the stairs. Several of the priests placed themselves together in groups as soon as they saw him, and began singing. He paid no heed to them, however, but hastened on to the uppermost terrace, where he found his friend occupied in writing.

Soon he learnt all that had happened, and wrathfully he cried: "You are too honest for those wise gentlemen in the House of Seti, and too pure and zealous for the rabble here. I knew it, I knew what would come of it if they introduced you to the mysteries. For us initiated there remains only the choice between lying and silence."

"The old error!" said Pentaur, "we know that the Godhead is One, we name it, 'The All,' 'The Veil of the All,' or simply 'Ra.' But under the name Ra we understand something different than is known to the common herd; for to us, the Universe is God, and in each of its parts we recognize a manifestation of that highest being without whom nothing is, in the heights above or in the depths below."

"To me you can say everything, for I also am initiated," interrupted Nebsecht.

"But neither from the laity do I withhold it," cried Pentaur, "only to those who are incapable of understanding the whole, do I show the different parts. Am I a liar if I do not say, 'I speak,' but 'my mouth speaks,' if I affirm, 'Your eye sees,' when it is you yourself who are the seer. When the light of the only One manifests itself, then I fervently render thanks to him in hymns, and the most luminous of his forms I name Ra. When I look upon yonder green fields, I call upon the faithful to give thanks to Rennut, that is, that active manifestation of the One, through which the corn attains to its ripe maturity. Am I filled with wonder at the bounteous gifts with which that divine stream whose origin is hidden, blesses our land, then I adore the One as the God Hapi, the secret one. Whether we view the sun, the harvest, or the Nile, whether we contemplate with admiration the unity and harmony of the visible or invisible world, still it is always with the Only, the All-embracing One we have to do, to whom we also ourselves belong as those of his manifestations in which lie places his self-consciousness. The imagination of the multitude is limited...."

"And so we lions,[76] give them the morsel that we can devour at one gulp, finely chopped up, and diluted with broth as if for the weak stomach of a sick man."

"Not so; we only feel it our duty to temper and sweeten the sharp potion, which for men even is almost too strong, before we offer it to the children, the babes in spirit. The sages of old veiled indeed the highest truths in allegorical forms, in symbols, and finally in a beautiful and richly-colored mythos, but they brought them near to the multitude shrouded it is true but still discernible."

"Discernible?" said the physician, "discernible? Why then the veil?"

"And do you imagine that the multitude could look the naked truth in the face,[77] and not despair?"

"Can I, can any one who looks straight forward, and strives to see the truth and nothing but the truth?" cried the physician. "We both of us know that things only are, to us, such as they picture themselves in the prepared mirror of our souls. I see grey, grey, and white, white, and have accustomed myself in my yearning after knowledge, not to attribute the smallest part to my own idiosyncrasy, if such indeed there be existing in my empty breast. You look straight onwards as I do, but in you each idea is transfigured, for in your soul invisible shaping powers are at work, which set the crooked straight, clothe the commonplace with charm, the repulsive with beauty. You are a poet, an artist; I only seek for truth."

"Only?" said Pentaur, "it is just on account of that effort that I esteem you so highly, and, as you already know, I also desire nothing but the truth."

"I know, I know," said the physician nodding, "but our ways run side by side without ever touching, and our final goal is the reading of a riddle, of which there are many solutions. You believe yourself to have found the right one, and perhaps none exists."

"Then let us content ourselves with the nearest and the most beautiful," said Pentaur.

"The most beautiful?" cried Nebsecht indignantly. "Is that monster, whom you call God, beautiful-the giant who for ever regenerates himself that he may devour himself again? God is the All, you say, who suffices to himself. Eternal he is and shall be, because all that goes forth from him is absorbed by him again, and the great niggard bestows no grain of sand, no ray of light, no breath of wind, without reclaiming it for his household, which is ruled by no design, no reason, no goodness, but by a tyrannical necessity, whose slave he himself is. The coward hides behind the cloud of incomprehensibility, and can be revealed only by himself—I would I could strip him of the veil! Thus I see the thing that you call God!"

"A ghastly picture," said Pentaur, "because you forget that we recognize reason to be the essence of the All, the penetrating and moving power of the universe which is manifested in the harmonious working together of its parts, and in ourselves also, since we are formed out of its substance, and inspired with its soul."

"Is the warfare of life in any way reasonable?" asked Nebsecht. "Is this eternal destruction in order to build up again especially well-designed and wise? And with this introduction of reason into the All, you provide yourself with a self-devised ruler, who terribly resembles the gracious masters and mistresses that you exhibit to the people."

"Only apparently," answered Pentaur, "only because that which transcends sense is communicable through the medium of the senses alone. When God manifests himself as the wisdom of the world, we call him 'the Word,' 'He, who covers his limbs with names,' as the sacred Text expresses itself, is the power which gives to things their distinctive forms; the scarabaeus, 'which enters life as its own son' reminds us of the ever self-renewing creative power which causes you to call our merciful and benevolent God a monster, but which you can deny as little as you can the happy choice of the type; for, as you know, there are only male scarabei, and this animal reproduces itself."

Nebsecht smiled. "If all the doctrines of the mysteries," he said, "have no more truth than this happily chosen image, they are in a bad way. These beetles have for years been my friends and companions. I know their family life, and I can assure you that there are males and females amongst them as amongst cats, apes, and human beings. Your 'good God' I do not know, and what I least comprehend in thinking it over quietly is the circumstance that you distinguish a good and evil principle in the world. If the All is indeed God, if God as the scriptures teach, is goodness, and if besides him is nothing at all, where is a place to be found for evil?"

"You talk like a school-boy," said Pentaur indignantly. "All that is, is good and reasonable in itself, but the infinite One, who prescribes his own laws and his own paths, grants to the finite its continuance through continual renewal, and in the changing forms of the finite progresses for evermore. What we call evil, darkness, wickedness, is in itself divine, good, reasonable, and clear; but it appears in another light to our clouded minds, because we perceive the way only and not the goal, the details only, and not the whole. Even so, superficial listeners blame the music, in which a discord is heard, which the harper has only evoked from the strings that his hearers may more deeply feel the purity of the succeeding harmony; even so, a fool blames the painter who has colored his board with black, and does not wait for the completion of the picture which shall be thrown into clearer relief by the dark background; even so, a child chides the noble tree, whose fruit rots, that a new life may spring up from its kernel. Apparent evil is but an antechamber to higher bliss, as every sunset is but veiled by night, and will soon show itself again as the red dawn of a new day."

"How convincing all that sounds!" answered the physician, "all, even the terrible, wins charm from your lips; but I could invert your proposition, and declare that it is evil that rules the world, and sometimes gives us one drop of sweet content, in order that we may more keenly feel the bitterness of life. You see harmony and goodness in everything. I have observed that passion awakens life, that all existence is a conflict, that one being devours another."

"And do you not feel the beauty of visible creation, and does not the immutable law in everything fill you with admiration and humility?"

"For beauty," replied Nebsecht, "I have never sought; the organ is somehow wanting in me to understand it of myself, though I willingly allow you to mediate between us. But of law in nature I fully appreciate the worth, for that is the veritable soul of the universe. You call the One 'Temt,' that is to say the total-the unity which is reached by the addition of many units; and that pleases me, for the elements of the universe and the powers which prescribe the paths of life are strictly defined by measure and number-but irrespective of beauty or benevolence."

"Such views," cried Pentaur troubled, "are the result of your strange studies. You kill and destroy, in order, as you yourself say, to come upon the track of the secrets of life. Look out upon nature, develop the faculty which you declare to be wanting, in you, and the beauty of creation will teach you without my assistance that you are praying to a false god."

"I do not pray," said Nebsecht, "for the law which moves the world is as little affected by prayers as the current of the sands in your hour-glass. Who tells you that I do not seek to come upon the track of the first beginning of things? I proved to you just now that I know more about the origin of Scarabei than you do. I have killed many an animal, not only to study its organism, but also to investigate how it has built up its form. But precisely in this work my organ for beauty has become blunt rather than keen. I tell you that the beginning of things is not more attractive to contemplate than their death and decomposition."

Pentaur looked at the physician enquiringly.

"I also for once," continued Nebsecht, "will speak in figures. Look at this wine, how pure it is, how fragrant; and yet it was trodden from the grape by the brawny feet of the vintagers. And those full ears of corn! They gleam golden yellow, and will yield us snow-white meal when they are ground, and yet they grew from a rotting seed. Lately you were praising to me the beauty of the great Hall of Columns nearly completed in the Temple of Amon over yonder in Thebes.[78]

How posterity will admire it! I saw that Hall arise. There lay masses of freestone in wild confusion, dust in heaps that took away my breath, and three months since I was sent over there, because above a hundred workmen engaged in stone-polishing under the burning sun had been beaten to death. Were I a poet like you, I would show you a hundred similar pictures, in which you would not find much beauty. In the meantime, we have enough to do in observing the existing order of things, and investigating the laws by which it is governed."

"I have never clearly understood your efforts, and have difficulty in comprehending why you did not turn to the science of the haruspices," said Pentaur. "Do you then believe that the changing, and-owing to the conditions by which they are surrounded-the dependent life of plants and animals is governed by law, rule, and numbers like the movement of the stars?"

"What a question! Is the strong and mighty hand, which compels yonder heavenly bodies to roll onward in their carefully-appointed orbits, not delicate enough to prescribe the conditions of the flight of the bird, and the beating of the human heart?"

"There we are again with the heart," said the poet smiling, "are you any nearer your aim?"

The physician became very grave. "Perhaps tomorrow even," he said, "I may have what I need. You have your palette there with red and black color, and a writing reed. May I use this sheet of papyrus?"

"Of course; but first tell me...."

"Do not ask; you would not approve of my scheme, and there would only be a fresh dispute."

"I think," said the poet, laying his hand on his friend's shoulder, "that we have no reason to fear disputes. So far they have been the cement, the refreshing dew of our friendship."

"So long as they treated of ideas only, and not of deeds."

"You intend to get possession of a human heart!" cried the poet. "Think of what you are doing! The heart is the vessel of that effluence of the universal soul, which lives in us."

"Are you so sure of that?" cried the physician with some irritation, "then give me the proof. Have you ever examined a heart, has any one member of my profession done so? The hearts of criminals and prisoners of war even are declared sacred from touch, and when we stand helpless by a patient, and see our medicines work harm as often as good, why is it? Only because we physicians are expected to work as blindly as an astronomer, if he were required to look at the stars through a board. At Heliopolis I entreated the great Urma Rahotep, the truly learned chief of our craft, and who held me in esteem, to allow me to examine the heart of a dead Amu; but he refused me, because the great Sechet leads virtuous Semites also into the fields of the blessed.[79]

And then followed all the old scruples: that to cut up the heart of a beast even is sinful, because it also is the vehicle of a soul, perhaps a condemned and miserable human soul, which before it can return to the One, must undergo purification by passing through the bodies of animals. I was not satisfied, and declared to him that my great-grandfather Nebsecht, before he wrote his treatise on the heart, must certainly have examined such an organ. Then he answered me that the divinity had revealed to him what he had written, and therefore his work had been accepted amongst the sacred writings of Toth,[80] which stood fast and unassailable as the laws of the world; he wished to give me peace for quiet work, and I also, he said, might be a chosen spirit, the divinity might perhaps vouchsafe revelations to me too. I was young at that time, and spent my nights in prayer, but I only wasted away, and my spirit grew darker instead of clearer. Then I killed in secret-first a fowl, then rats, then a rabbit, and cut up their hearts, and followed the vessels that lead out of them, and know little more now than I did at first; but I must get to the bottom of the truth, and I must have a human heart."

"What will that do for you?" asked Pentaur; "you cannot hope to perceive the invisible and the infinite with your human eyes?"

"Do you know my great-grandfather's treatise?"

"A little," answered the poet; "he said that wherever he laid his finger, whether on the head, the hands, or the stomach, he everywhere met with the heart, because its vessels go into all the members, and the heart is the meeting point of all these vessels. Then Nebsecht proceeds to state how these are distributed in the different members, and shows-is it not so? —that the various mental states, such as anger, grief, aversion, and also the ordinary use of the word heart, declare entirely for his view."

"That is it. We have already discussed it, and I believe that he is right, so far as the blood is concerned, and the animal sensations. But the pure and luminous intelligence in us-that has another seat," and the physician struck his broad but low forehead with his hand. "I have observed heads by the hundred down at the place of execution, and I have also removed the top of the skulls of living animals. But now let me write, before we are disturbed."[81]

The physician took the reed, moistened it with black color prepared from burnt papyrus, and in elegant hieratic characters[82] wrote the paper for the paraschites, in which he confessed to having impelled him to the theft of a heart, and in the most binding manner declared himself willing to take the old man's guilt upon himself before Osiris and the judges of the dead.

When he had finished, Pentaur held out his hand for the paper, but Nebsecht folded it together, placed it in a little bag in which lay an amulet that his dying mother had hung round his neck, and said, breathing deeply:

"That is done. Farewell, Pentaur."

But the poet held the physician back; he spoke to him with the warmest words, and conjured him to abandon his enterprise. His prayers, however, had no power to touch Nebsecht, who only strove forcibly to disengage his finger from Pentaur's strong hand, which held him as in a clasp of iron. The excited poet did not remark that he was hurting his friend, until after a new and vain attempt at freeing himself, Nebsecht cried out in pain, "You are crushing my finger!"

A smile passed over the poet's face, he loosened his hold on the physician, and stroked the reddened hand like a mother who strives to divert her child from pain.

"Don't be angry with me, Nebsecht," he said, "you know my unlucky fists, and to-day they really ought to hold you fast, for you have too mad a purpose on hand."

"Mad?" said the physician, whilst he smiled in his turn. "It may be so; but do you not know that we Egyptians all have a peculiar tenderness for our follies, and are ready to sacrifice house and land to them?"

"Our own house and our own land," cried the poet: and then added seriously, "but not the existence, not the happiness of another."

"Have I not told you that I do not look upon the heart as the seat of our intelligence? So far as I am concerned, I would as soon be buried with a ram's heart as with my own."

"I do not speak of the plundered dead, but of the living," said the poet. "If the deed of the paraschites is discovered, he is undone, and you would only have saved that sweet child in the hut behind there, to fling her into deeper misery."

Nebsecht looked at the other with as much astonishment and dismay, as if he had been awakened from sleep by bad tidings. Then he cried: "All that I have, I would share with the old man and Uarda."

"And who would protect her?"

"Her father."

"That rough drunkard who to-morrow or the day after may be sent no one knows where."

"He is a good fellow," said the physician interrupting his friend, and stammering violently. "But who 'would do anything to the child? She is so so.... She is so charming, so perfectly-sweet and lovely."

With these last words he cast down his eyes and reddened like a girl.

"You understand that," he said, "better than I do; yes, and you also think her beautiful! Strange! you must not laugh if I confess—I am but a man like every one else-when I confess, that I believe I have at length discovered in myself the missing organ for beauty of form-not believe merely, but truly have discovered it, for it has not only spoken, but cried, raged, till I felt a rushing in my ears, and for the first time was attracted more by the sufferer than by suffering. I have sat in the hut as though spell-bound, and gazed at her hair, at her eyes, at how she breathed. They must long since have missed me at the House of Seti, perhaps discovered all my preparations, when seeking me in my room! For two days and nights I have allowed myself to be drawn away from my work, for the sake of this child. Were I one of the laity, whom you would approach, I should say that demons had bewitched me. But it is not that,"—and with these words the physician's eyes flamed up—"it is not that! The animal in me, the low instincts of which the heart is the organ, and which swelled my breast at her bedside, they have mastered the pure and fine emotions here-here in this brain; and in the very moment when I hoped to know as the God knows whom you call the Prince of knowledge, in that moment I must learn that the animal in me is stronger than that which I call my God."

The physician, agitated and excited, had fixed his eyes on the ground during these last words, and hardly noticed the poet, who listened to him wondering and full of sympathy. For a time both were silent; then Pentaur laid his hand on his friend's hand, and said cordially:

"My soul is no stranger to what you feel, and heart and head, if I may use your own words, have known a like emotion. But I know that what we feel, although it may be foreign to our usual sensations, is loftier and more precious than these, not lower. Not the animal, Nebsecht, is it that you feel in yourself, but God. Goodness is the most beautiful attribute of the divine, and you have always been well-disposed towards great and small; but I ask you, have you ever before felt so irresistibly impelled to pour out an ocean of goodness on another being, whether for Uarda you would not more joyfully and more self-forgetfully sacrifice all that you have, and all that you are, than to father and mother and your oldest friend?"

Nebsecht nodded assentingly.

"Well then," cried Pentaur, "follow your new and godlike emotion, be good to Uarda and do not sacrifice her to your vain wishes. My poor friend! With your-enquiries into the secrets of life, you have never looked round upon itself, which spreads open and inviting before our eyes. Do you imagine that the maiden who can thus inflame the calmest thinker in Thebes, will not be coveted by a hundred of the common herd when her protector fails her? Need I tell you that amongst the dancers in the foreign quarter nine out of ten are the daughters of outlawed parents? Can you endure the thought that by your hand innocence may be consigned to vice, the rose trodden under foot in the mud? Is the human heart that you desire, worth an Uarda? Now go, and to-morrow come again to me your friend who understands how to sympathize with all you feel, and to whom you have approached so much the nearer to-day that you have learned to share his purest happiness."

Pentaur held out his hand to the physician, who held it some time, then went thoughtfully and lingeringly, unmindful of the burning glow of the mid-day sun, over the mountain into the valley of the king's graves towards the hut of the paraschites.

Here he found the soldier with his daughter. "Where is the old man?" he asked anxiously.

"He has gone to his work in the house of the embalmer," was the answer. "If anything should happen to him he bade me tell you not to forget the writing and the book. He was as though out of his mind when he left us, and put the ram's heart in his bag and took it with him. Do you remain with the little one; my mother is at work, and I must go with the prisoners of war to Harmontis."

CHAPTER XVIII.

While the two friends from the House of Seti were engaged in conversation, Katuti restlessly paced the large open hall of her son-in-law's house, in which we have already seen her. A snow-white cat followed her steps, now playing with the hem of her long plain dress, and now turning to a large stand on which the dwarf Nemu sat in a heap; where formerly a silver statue had stood, which a few months previously had been sold.

He liked this place, for it put him in a position to look into the eyes of his mistress and other frill-grown people. "If you have betrayed me! If you have deceived me!" said Katuti with a threatening gesture as she passed his perch.

"Put me on a hook to angle for a crocodile if I have. But I am curious to know how he will offer you the money."

"You swore to me," interrupted his mistress with feverish agitation, "that you had not used my name in asking Paaker to save us?"

"A thousand times I swear it," said the little man.

"Shall I repeat all our conversation? I tell thee he will sacrifice his land, and his house-great gate and all, for one friendly glance from Nefert's eyes."

"If only Mena loved her as he does!" sighed the widow, and then again she walked up and down the hall in silence, while the dwarf looked out at the garden entrance. Suddenly she paused in front of Nemu, and said so hoarsely that Nemu shuddered:

"I wish she were a widow." "The little man made a gesture as if to protect himself from the evil eye, but at the same instant he slipped down from his pedestal, and exclaimed:

"There is a chariot, and I hear his big dog barking. It is he. Shall I call Nefert?"

"No!" said Katuti in a low voice, and she clutched at the back of a chair as if for support.

The dwarf shrugged his shoulders, and slunk behind a clump of ornamental plants, and a few minutes later Paaker stood in the presence of Katuti, who greeted him, with quiet dignity and self-possession.

Not a feature of her finely-cut face betrayed her inward agitation, and after the Mohar had greeted her she said with rather patronizing friendliness:

"I thought that you would come. Take a seat. Your heart is like your father's; now that you are friends with us again it is not by halves."

Paaker had come to offer his aunt the sum which was necessary for the redemption of her husband's mummy. He had doubted for a long time whether he should not leave this to his mother, but reserve partly and partly vanity had kept him from doing so. He liked to display his wealth, and Katuti should learn what he could do, what a son-in-law she had rejected.

He would have preferred to send the gold, which he had resolved to give away, by the hand of one of his slaves, like a tributary prince. But that could not be done so he put on his finger a ring set with a valuable stone, which king Seti I., had given to his father, and added various clasps and bracelets to his dress.

When, before leaving the house, he looked at himself in a mirror, he said to himself with some satisfaction, that he, as he stood, was worth as much as the whole of Mena's estates.

Since his conversation with Nemu, and the dwarf's interpretation of his dream, the path which he must tread to reach his aim had been plain before him. Nefert's mother must be won with the gold which would save her from disgrace, and Mena must be sent to the other world. He relied chiefly on his own reckless obstinacy-which he liked to call firm determination-Nemu's cunning, and the love-philter.

He now approached Katuti with the certainty of success, like a merchant who means to acquire some costly object, and feels that he is rich enough to pay for it. But his aunt's proud and dignified manner confounded him.

He had pictured her quite otherwise, spirit-broken, and suppliant; and he had expected, and hoped to earn, Nefert's thanks as well as her mother's by his generosity. Mena's pretty wife was however absent, and Katuti did not send for her even after he had enquired after her health.

The widow made no advances, and some time passed in indifferent conversation, till Paaker abruptly informed her that he had heard of her son's reckless conduct, and had decided, as being his mother's nearest relation, to preserve her from the degradation that threatened her. For the sake of his bluntness, which she took for honesty, Katuti forgave the magnificence of his dress, which under the circumstances certainly seemed ill-chosen; she thanked him with dignity, but warmly, more for the sake of her children than for her own; for life she said was opening before them, while for her it was drawing to its close.

"You are still at a good time of life," said Paaker.

"Perhaps at the best," replied the widow, "at any rate from my point of view; regarding life as I do as a charge, a heavy responsibility."

"The administration of this involved estate must give you many, anxious hours-that I understand." Katuti nodded, and then said sadly:

"I could bear it all, if I were not condemned to see my poor child being brought to misery without being able to help her or advise her. You once would willingly have married her, and I ask you, was there a maiden in Thebes-nay in all Egypt-to compare with her for beauty? Was she not worthy to be loved, and is she not so still? Does she deserve that her husband should leave her to starve, neglect her, and take a strange woman into his tent as if he had repudiated her? I see what you feel about it! You throw all the blame on me. Your heart says: 'Why did she break off our betrothal,' and your right feeling tells you that you would have given her a happier lot."

With these words Katuti took her nephew's hand, and went on with increasing warmth.

"We know you to-day for the most magnanimous man in Thebes, for you have requited injustice with an immense benefaction; but even as a boy you were kind and noble. Your father's wish has always been dear and sacred to me, for during his lifetime he always behaved to us as an affectionate brother, and I would sooner have sown the seeds of sorrow for myself than for your mother, my beloved sister. I brought up my child—I guarded her jealously-for the young hero who was absent, proving his valor in Syria-for you and for you only. Then your father died, my sole stay and protector."

"I know it all!" interrupted Paaker looking gloomily at the floor.

"Who should have told you?" said the widow. "For your mother, when that had happened which seemed incredible, forbid us her house, and shut her ears. The king himself urged Mena's suit, for he loves him as his own son, and when I represented your prior claim he commanded; — and who may resist the commands of the sovereign of two worlds, the Son of Ra? Kings have short memories; how often did your father hazard his life for him, how many wounds had he received in his service. For your father's sake he might have spared you such an affront, and such pain."

"And have I myself served him, or not?" asked the pioneer flushing darkly.

"He knows you less," returned Katuti apologetically. Then she changed her tone to one of sympathy, and went on:

"How was it that you, young as you were, aroused his dissatisfaction, his dislike, nay his —"

"His what?" asked the pioneer, trembling with excitement.

"Let that pass!" said the widow soothingly. "The favor and disfavor of kings are as those of the Gods. Men rejoice in the one or bow to the other."

"What feeling have I aroused in Rameses besides dissatisfaction, and dislike? I insist on knowing!" said Paaker with increasing vehemence.

"You alarm me," the widow declared. "And in speaking ill of you, his only motive was to raise his favorite in Nefert's estimation."

"Tell me what he said!" cried the pioneer; cold drops stood on his brown forehead, and his glaring eyes showed the white eye-balls.

Katuti quailed before him, and drew back, but he followed her, seized her arm, and said huskily:

"What did he say?"

"Paaker!" cried the widow in pain and indignation. "Let me go. It is better for you that I should not repeat the words with which Rameses sought to turn Nefert's heart from you. Let me go, and remember to whom you are speaking."

But Paaker gripped her elbow the tighter, and urgently repeated his question.

"Shame upon you!" cried Katuti, "you are hurting me; let me go! You will not till you have heard what he said? Have your own way then, but the words are forced from me! He said that if he did not know your mother Setchem for an honest woman, he never would have believed you were your father's son-for you were no more like him than an owl to an eagle."

Paaker took his hand from Katuti's arm. "And so-and so —" he muttered with pale lips.

"Nefert took your part, and I too, but in vain. Do not take the words too hardly. Your father was a man without an equal, and Rameses cannot forget that we are related to the old royal house. His grandfather, his father, and himself are usurpers, and there is one now living who has a better right to the throne than he has."

"The Regent Ani!" exclaimed Paaker decisively. Katuti nodded, she went up to the pioneer and said in a whisper:

"I put myself in your hands, though I know they may be raised against me. But you are my natural ally, for that same act of Rameses that disgraced and injured you, made me a partner in the designs of Ani. The king robbed you of your bride, me of my daughter. He filled your soul with hatred for your arrogant rival, and mine with passionate regret for the lost happiness of my child. I feel the blood of Hatasu in my veins, and my spirit is high enough to govern men. It was I who roused the sleeping ambition of the Regent —I who directed his gaze to the throne to which he was destined by the Gods. The ministers of the Gods, the priests, are favorably disposed to us; we have —"

At this moment there was a commotion in the garden, and a breathless slave rushed in exclaiming "The Regent is at the gate!"

Paaker stood in stupid perplexity, but he collected himself with an effort and would have gone, but Katuti detained him.

"I will go forward to meet Ani," she said. "He will be rejoiced to see you, for he esteems you highly and was a friend of your father's."

As soon as Katuti had left the hall, the dwarf Nemu crept out of his hiding-place, placed himself in front of Paaker, and asked boldly:

"Well? Did I give thee good advice yesterday, or no?"

Put Paaker did not answer him, he pushed him aside with his foot, and walked up and down in deep thought.

Katuti met the Regent half way down the garden. He held a manuscript roll in his hand, and greeted her from afar with a friendly wave of his hand.

The widow looked at him with astonishment.

It seemed to her that he had grown taller and younger since the last time she had seen him.

"Hail to your highness!" she cried, half in joke half reverently, and she raised her hands in supplication, as if he already wore the double crown of Upper and Lower Egypt. "Have the nine Gods met you? have the Hathors kissed you in your slumbers? This is a white day —a lucky day —I read it in your face!" "That is reading a cipher!" said Ani gaily, but with dignity. "Read this despatch."

Katuti took the roll from his hand, read it through, and then returned it.

"The troops you equipped have conquered the allied armies of the Ethiopians," she said gravely, "and are bringing their prince in fetters to Thebes, with endless treasure, and ten thousand prisoners! The Gods be praised!"

"And above all things I thank the Gods that my general Scheschenk-my foster-brother and friend-is returning well and unwounded from the war. I think, Katuti, that the figures in our dreams are this day taking forms of flesh and blood!"

"They are growing to the stature of heroes!" cried the widow. "And you yourself, my lord, have been stirred by the breath of the Divinity. You walk like the worthy son of Ra, the Courage of Menth beams in your eyes, and you smile like the victorious Horus."

"Patience, patience my friend," said Ani, moderating the eagerness of the widow; "now, more than ever, we must cling to my principle of over-estimating the strength of our opponents, and underrating our own. Nothing has succeeded on which I had counted, and on the contrary many things have justified my fears that they would fail. The beginning of the end is hardly dawning on us."

"But successes, like misfortunes, never come singly," replied Katuti.

"I agree with you," said Ani. "The events of life seem to me to fall in groups. Every misfortune brings its fellow with it-like every piece of luck. Can you tell me of a second success?"

"Women win no battles," said the widow smiling. "But they win allies, and I have gained a powerful one."

"A God or an army?" asked Ani.

"Something between the two," she replied. "Paaker, the king's chief pioneer, has joined us;" and she briefly related to Ani the history of her nephew's love and hatred.

Ani listened in silence; then he said with an expression of much disquiet and anxiety:

"This man is a follower of Rameses, and must shortly return to him. Many may guess at our projects, but every additional person who knows them may be come a traitor. You are urging me, forcing me, forward too soon. A thousand well-prepared enemies are less dangerous than one untrustworthy ally —"

"Paaker is secured to us," replied Katuti positively. "Who will answer for him?" asked Ani.

"His life shall be in your hand," replied Katuti gravely. "My shrewd little dwarf Nemu knows that he has committed some secret crime, which the law punishes by death."

The Regent's countenance cleared.

"That alters the matter," he said with satisfaction. "Has he committed a murder?"

"No," said Katuti, "but Nemu has sworn to reveal to you alone all that he knows. He is wholly devoted to us."

"Well and good," said Ani thoughtfully, "but he too is imprudent-much too imprudent. You are like a rider, who to win a wager urges his horse to leap over spears. If he falls on the points, it is he that suffers; you let him lie there, and go on your way."

"Or are impaled at the same time as the noble horse," said Katuti gravely. "You have more to win, and at the same time more to lose than we; but the meanest clings to life; and I must tell you, Ani, that I work for you, not to win any thing through your success, but because you are as dear to me as a brother, and because I see in you the embodiment of my father's claims which have been trampled on."

Ani gave her his hand and asked:

"Did you also as my friend speak to Bent-Anat? Do I interpret your silence rightly?"

Katuti sadly shook her head; but Ani went on: "Yesterday that would have decided me to give her up; but to-day my courage has risen, and if the Hathors be my friends I may yet win her."

With these words he went in advance of the widow into the hall, where Paaker was still walking uneasily up and down.

The pioneer bowed low before the Regent, who returned the greeting with a half-haughty, half-familiar wave of the hand, and when he had seated himself in an arm-chair politely addressed Paaker as the son of a friend, and a relation of his family.

"All the world," he said, "speaks of your reckless courage. Men like you are rare; I have none such attached to me. I wish you stood nearer to me; but Rameses will not part with you, although-although-In point of fact your office has two aspects; it requires the daring of a soldier, and the dexterity of a scribe. No one denies that you have the first, but the second-the sword and the reed-pen are very different weapons, one requires supple fingers, the other a sturdy fist. The king used to complain of your reports-is he better satisfied with them now?"

"I hope so," replied the Mohar; "my brother Horus is a practised writer, and accompanies me in my journeys."

"That is well," said Ani. "If I had the management of affairs I should treble your staff, and give you four-five-six scribes under you, who should be entirely at your command, and to whom you could give the materials for the reports to be sent out. Your office demands that you should be both brave and circumspect; these characteristics are rarely united; but there are scriveners by hundreds in the temples."

"So it seems to me," said Paaker.

Ani looked down meditatively, and continued—"Rameses is fond of comparing you with your father. That is unfair, for he-who is now with the justified-was without an equal; at once the bravest of heroes and the most skilful of scribes. You are judged unjustly; and it grieves me all the more that you belong, through your mother, to my poor but royal house. We will see whether I cannot succeed in putting you in the right place. For the present you are required in Syria almost as soon as you have got home. You have shown that you are a man who does not fear death, and who can render good service, and you might now enjoy your wealth in peace with your wife."

"I am alone," said Paaker.

"Then, if you come home again, let Katuti seek you out the prettiest wife in Egypt," said the Regent smiling. "She sees herself every day in her mirror, and must be a connoisseur in the charms of women."

Ani rose with these words, bowed to Paaker with studied friendliness, gave his hand to Katuti, and said as he left the hall:

"Send me to-day the-the handkerchief-by the dwarf Nemu."

When he was already in the garden, he turned once more and said to Paaker

"Some friends are supping with me to-day; pray let me see you too."

The pioneer bowed; he dimly perceived that he was entangled in invisible toils. Up to the present moment he had been proud of his devotion to his calling, of his duties as Mohar; and now he had discovered that the king, whose chain of honor hung round his neck, undervalued him, and perhaps only suffered him to fill his arduous and dangerous post for the sake of his father, while he, notwithstanding the temptations offered him in Thebes by his wealth, had accepted it willingly and disinterestedly. He knew that his skill with the pen was small, but that was no reason why he should be despised; often had he wished that he could reconstitute his office exactly as Ani had suggested, but his petition to be allowed a secretary had been rejected by Rameses. What he spied out, he was told was to be kept secret, and no one could be responsible for the secrecy of another.

As his brother Horus grew up, he had followed him as his obedient assistant, even after he had married a wife, who, with her child, remained in Thebes under the care of Setchem.

He was now filling Paaker's place in Syria during his absence; badly enough, as the pioneer thought, and yet not without credit; for the fellow knew how to write smooth words with a graceful pen.

Paaker, accustomed to solitude, became absorbed in thought, forgetting everything that surrounded him; even the widow herself, who had sunk on to a couch, and was observing him in silence.

He gazed into vacancy, while a crowd of sensations rushed confusedly through his brain. He thought himself cruelly ill-used, and he felt too that it was incumbent on him to become the instrument of a terrible fate to some other person. All was dim 'and chaotic in his mind, his love merged in his hatred; only one thing was clear and unclouded by doubt, and that was his strong conviction that Nefert would be his.

The Gods indeed were in deep disgrace with him. How much he had expended upon them-and with what a grudging hand they had rewarded him; he knew of but one indemnification for his wasted life, and in that he believed so firmly that he counted on it as if it were capital which he had invested in sound securities. But at this moment his resentful feelings embittered the sweet dream of hope, and he strove in vain for calmness and clear-sightedness; when such cross-roads as these met, no amulet, no divining rod could guide him; here he must think for himself, and beat his own road before he could walk in it; and yet he could think out no plan, and arrive at no decision.

He grasped his burning forehead in his hands, and started from his brooding reverie, to remember where he was, to recall his conversation with the mother of the woman he loved, and her saying that she was capable of guiding men.

"She perhaps may be able to think for me," he muttered to himself. "Action suits me better."

He slowly went up to her and said:

"So it is settled then—we are confederates."

"Against Rameses, and for Ani," she replied, giving him her slender hand.

"In a few days I start for Syria, meanwhile you can make up your mind what commissions you have to give me. The money for your son shall be conveyed to you to-day before sunset. May I not pay my respects to Nefert?"

"Not now, she is praying in the temple."

"But to-morrow?"

"Willingly, my dear friend. She will be delighted to see you, and to thank you."

"Farewell, Katuti."

"Call me mother," said the widow, and she waved her veil to him as a last farewell.

CHAPTER XIX.

As soon as Paaker had disappeared behind the shrubs, Katuti struck a little sheet of metal, a slave appeared, and Katuti asked her whether Nefert had returned from the temple.

"Her litter is just now at the side gate," was the answer.

"I await her here," said the widow. The slave went away, and a few minutes later Nefert entered the hall.

"You want me?" she said; and after kissing her mother she sank upon her couch. "I am tired," she exclaimed, "Nemu, take a fan and keep the flies off me."

The dwarf sat down on a cushion by her couch, and began to wave the semi-circular fan of ostrich-feathers; but Katuti put him aside and said:

"You can leave us for the present; we want to speak to each other in private."

The dwarf shrugged his shoulders and got up, but Nefert looked at her mother with an irresistible appeal.

"Let him stay," she said, as pathetically as if her whole happiness depended upon it. "The flies torment me so, and Nemu always holds his tongue."

She patted the dwarf's big head as if he were a lap-dog, and called the white cat, which with a graceful leap sprang on to her shoulder and stood there with its back arched, to be stroked by her slender fingers.

Nemu looked enquiringly at his mistress, but Katuti turned to her daughter, and said in a warning voice:

"I have very serious things to discuss with you."

"Indeed?" said her daughter, "but I cannot be stung by the flies all the same. Of course, if you wish it —"

"Nemu may stay then," said Katuti, and her voice had the tone of that of a nurse who gives way to a naughty child. "Besides, he knows what I have to talk about."

"There now!" said Nefert, kissing the head of the white cat, and she gave the fan back to the dwarf.

The widow looked at her daughter with sincere compassion, she went up to her and looked for the thousandth time in admiration at her pretty face.

"Poor child," she sighed, "how willingly I would spare you the frightful news which sooner or later you must hear-must bear. Leave off your foolish play with the cat, I have things of the most hideous gravity to tell you."

"Speak on," replied Nefert. "To-day I cannot fear the worst. Mena's star, the haruspex told me, stands under the sign of happiness, and I enquired of the oracle in the temple of Besa, and heard that my husband is prospering. I have prayed in the temple till I am quite content. Only speak! —I know my brother's letter from the camp had no good news in it; the evening before last I saw you had been crying, and yesterday you did not look well; even the pomegranate flowers in your hair did not suit you."

"Your brother," sighed Katuti, "has occasioned me great trouble, and we might through him have suffered deep dishonor —"

"We-dishonor?" exclaimed Nefert, and she nervously clutched at the cat.

"Your brother lost enormous sums at play; to recover them he pledged the mummy of your father —"

"Horrible!" cried Nefert. "We must appeal at once to the king; —I will write to him myself; for Mena's sake he will hear me. Rameses is great and noble, and will not let a house that is faithfully devoted to him fall into disgrace through the reckless folly of a boy. Certainly I will write to him."

She said this in a voice of most childlike confidence, and desired Nemu to wave the fan more gently, as if this concern were settled.

In Katuti's heart surprise and indignation at the unnatural indifference of her daughter were struggling together; but she withheld all blame, and said carelessly:

"We are already released, for my nephew Paaker, as soon as he heard what threatened us, offered me his help; freely and unprompted, from pure goodness of heart and attachment."

"How good of Paaker!" cried Nefert. "He was so fond of me, and you know, mother, I always stood up for him. No doubt it was for my sake that he behaved so generously!"

The young wife laughed, and pulling the cat's face close to her own, held her nose to its cool little nose, stared into its green eyes, and said, imitating childish talk:

"There now, pussy-how kind people are to your little mistress."

Katuti was vexed daughter's childish impulses.

"It seems to me," she said, "that you might leave off playing and trifling when I am talking of such serious matters. I have long since observed that the fate of the house to which your father and mother belong is a matter of perfect indifference to you; and yet you would have to seek shelter and protection under its roof if your husband —"

"Well, mother?" asked Nefert breathing more quickly.

As soon as Katuti perceived her daughter's agitation she regretted that she had not more gently led up to the news she had to break to her; for she loved her daughter, and knew that it would give her keen pain.

So she went on more sympathetically:

"You boasted in joke that people are good to you, and it is true; you win hearts by your mere being-by only being what you are. And Mena too loved you tenderly; but 'absence,' says the proverb, 'is the one real enemy,' and Mena —"

"What has Mena done?" Once more Nefert interrupted her mother, and her nostrils quivered.

"Mena," said Katuti, decidedly, "has violated the truth and esteem which he owes you-he has trodden them under foot, and —"

"Mena?" exclaimed the young wife with flashing eyes; she flung the cat on the floor, and sprang from her couch.

"Yes-Mena," said Katuti firmly. "Your brother writes that he would have neither silver nor gold for his spoil, but took the fair daughter of the prince of the Danaids into his tent. The ignoble wretch!"

"Ignoble wretch!" cried Nefert, and two or three times she repeated her mother's last words. Katuti drew back in horror, for her gentle, docile, childlike daughter stood before her absolutely transfigured beyond all recognition.

She looked like a beautiful demon of revenge; her eyes sparkled, her breath came quickly, her limbs quivered, and with extraordinary strength and rapidity she seized the dwarf by the hand, led him to the door of one of the rooms which opened out of the hall, threw it open, pushed the little man over the threshold, and closed it sharply upon him; then with white lips she came up to her mother.

"An ignoble wretch did you call him?" she cried out with a hoarse husky voice, "an ignoble wretch! Take back your words, mother, take back your words, or —"

Katuti turned paler and paler, and said soothingly:

"The words may sound hard, but he has broken faith with you, and openly dishonored you."

"And shall I believe it?" said Nefert with a scornful laugh. "Shall I believe it, because a scoundrel has written it, who has pawned his father's body and the honor of big family; because it is told you by that noble and brave gentleman! why a box on the ears from Mena would be the death of him. Look at me, mother, here are my eyes, and if that table there were Mena's tent, and you were Mena, and you took the fairest woman living by the hand and led her into it, and these eyes saw it-aye, over and over again —I would laugh at it-as I laugh at it now; and I should say, 'Who knows what he may have to give her, or to say to her,' and not for one instant would I doubt his truth; for your son is false and Mena is true. Osiris broke faith with Isis-but Mena may be favored by a hundred women-he will take none to his tent but me!"

"Keep your belief," said Katuti bitterly, "but leave me mine."

"Yours?" said Nefert, and her flushed cheeks turned pale again. "What do you believe? You listen to the worst and basest things that can be said of a man who has overloaded you with benefits! A wretch, bah! an ignoble wretch? Is that what you call a man who lets you dispose of his estate as you please!"

"Nefert," cried Katuti angrily, "I will —"

"Do what you will," interrupted her indignant daughter, "but do not vilify the generous man who has never hindered you from throwing away his property on your son's debts and your own ambition. Since the day before yesterday I have learned that we are not rich; and I have reflected, and I have asked myself what has become of our corn and our cattle, of our sheep and the rents from the farmers. The wretch's estate was not so contemptible; but I tell you plainly I should be unworthy to be the wife of the noble Mena if I allowed any one to vilify his name under his own roof. Hold to your belief, by all means, but one of us must quit this house-you or I."

At these words Nefert broke into passionate sobs, threw herself on her knees by her couch, hid her face in the cushions, and wept convulsively and without intermission.

Katuti stood behind her, startled, trembling, and not knowing what to say. Was this her gentle, dreamy daughter? Had ever a daughter dared to speak thus to her mother? But was she right or was Nefert? This question was the pressing one; she knelt down by the side of the young wife, put her arm round her, drew her head against her bosom, and whispered pitifully:

"You cruel, hard-hearted child; forgive your poor, miserable mother, and do not make the measure of her wretchedness overflow."

Then Nefert rose, kissed her mother's hand, and went silently into her own room.

Katuti remained alone; she felt as if a dead hand held her heart in its icy grasp, and she muttered to herself:

"Ani is right-nothing turns to good excepting that from which we expect the worst."

She held her hand to her head, as if she had heard something too strange to be believed. Her heart went after her daughter, but instead of sympathizing with her she collected all her courage, and deliberately recalled all the reproaches that Nefert had heaped upon her. She did not spare herself a single word, and finally she murmured to herself: "She can spoil every thing. For Mena's sake she will sacrifice me and the whole world; Mena and Rameses are one, and if she discovers what we are plotting she will betray us without a moment's hesitation. Hitherto all has gone on without her seeing it, but to-day something has been unsealed in her-an eye, a tongue, an ear, which have hitherto been closed. She is like a deaf and dumb person, who by a sudden fright is restored to speech and hearing. My favorite child will become the spy of my actions, and my judge."

She gave no utterance to the last words, but she seemed to hear them with her inmost ear; the voice that could speak to her thus, startled and frightened her, and solitude was in itself a torture; she called the dwarf, and desired him to have her litter prepared, as she intended going to the temple, and visiting the wounded who had been sent home from Syria.

"And the handkerchief for the Regent?" asked the little man.

"It was a pretext," said Katuti. "He wishes to speak to you about the matter which you know of with regard to Paaker. What is it?"

"Do not ask," replied Nemu, "I ought not to betray it. By Besa, who protects us dwarfs, it is better that thou shouldst never know it."

"For to-day I have learned enough that is new to me," retorted Katuti. "Now go to Ani, and if you are able to throw Paaker entirely into his power-good —I will give-but what have I to give away? I will be grateful to you; and when we have gained our end I will set you free and make you rich."

Nemu kissed her robe, and said in a low voice: "What is the end?"

"You know what Ani is striving for," answered the widow. "And I have but one wish!"

"And that is?"

"To see Paaker in Mena's place."

"Then our wishes are the same," said the dwarf and he left the Hall.

Katuti looked after him and muttered:

"It must be so. For if every thing remains as it was and Mena comes home and demands a reckoning–it is not to be thought of! It must not be!"

CHAPTER XX.

As Nemu, on his way back from his visit to Ani, approached his mistress's house, he was detained by a boy, who desired him to follow him to the stranger's quarter. Seeing him hesitate, the messenger showed him the ring of his mother Hekt, who had come into the town on business, and wanted to speak with him.

Nemu was tired, for he was not accustomed to walking; his ass was dead, and Katuti could not afford to give him another. Half of Mena's beasts had been sold, and the remainder barely sufficed for the field-labor.

At the corners of the busiest streets, and on the market-places, stood boys with asses which they hired out for a small sum;[83] but Nemu had parted with his last money for a garment and a new wig, so that he might appear worthily attired before the Regent. In former times his pocket had never been empty, for Mena had thrown him many a ring of silver, or even of gold, but his restless and ambitious spirit wasted no regrets on lost luxuries. He remembered those years of superfluity with contempt, and as he puffed and panted on his way through the dust, he felt himself swell with satisfaction.

The Regent had admitted him to a private interview, and the little man had soon succeeded in riveting his attention; Ani had laughed till the tears rolled down his cheeks at Nemu's description of Paaker's wild passion, and he had proved himself in earnest over the dwarf's further communications, and had met his demands half-way. Nemu felt like a duck hatched on dry land, and put for the first time into water; like a bird hatched in a cage, and that for the first time is allowed to spread its wings and fly. He would have swum or have flown willingly to death if circumstances had not set a limit to his zeal and energy.

Bathed in sweat and coated with dust, he at last reached the gay tent in the stranger's quarter, where the sorceress Hekt was accustomed to alight when she came over to Thebes.

He was considering far-reaching projects, dreaming of possibilities, devising subtle plans-rejecting them as too subtle, and supplying their place with others more feasible and less dangerous; altogether the little diplomatist had no mind for the motley tribes which here surrounded him. He had passed the temple in which the people of Kaft adored their goddess Astarte, and the sanctuary of Seth, where they sacrificed to Baal, without letting himself be disturbed by the dancing devotees or the noise of cymbals and music which issued from their enclosures. The tents and slightly-built wooden houses of the dancing girls did not tempt him. Besides their inhabitants, who in the evening tricked themselves out in tinsel finery to lure the youth of Thebes into extravagance and folly, and spent their days in sleeping till sun-down, only the gambling booths drove a brisk business; and the guard of police had much trouble to restrain the soldier, who had staked and lost all his prize money, or the sailor, who thought himself cheated, from such outbreaks of rage and despair as must end in bloodshed. Drunken men lay in front of the taverns, and others were doing their utmost, by repeatedly draining their beakers, to follow their example.

Nothing was yet to be seen of the various musicians, jugglers, fire-eaters, serpent-charmers, and conjurers, who in the evening displayed their skill in this part of the town, which at all times had the aspect of a never ceasing fair. But these delights, which Nemu had passed a thousand times, had never had any temptation for him. Women and gambling were not to his taste; that which could be had simply for the taking, without trouble or exertion, offered no charms to his fancy, he had no fear of the ridicule of the dancing-women, and their associates-indeed, he occasionally sought them, for he enjoyed a war of words, and he was of opinion that no one in Thebes could beat him at having the last word. Other people, indeed, shared this opinion, and not long before Paaker's steward had said of Nemu:

"Our tongues are cudgels, but the little one's is a dagger."

The destination of the dwarf was a very large and gaudy tent, not in any way distinguished from a dozen others in its neighborhood. The opening which led into it was wide, but at present closed by a hanging of coarse stuff.

Nemu squeezed himself in between the edge of the tent and the yielding door, and found himself in an almost circular tent with many angles, and with its cone-shaped roof supported on a pole by way of a pillar.

Pieces of shabby carpet lay on the dusty soil that was the floor of the tent, and on these squatted some gaily-clad girls, whom an old woman was busily engaged in dressing. She painted the finger and toenails of the fair ones with orange-colored Hennah, blackened their brows and eye-lashes with Mestem —[Antimony.] —to give brilliancy to their glance, painted their cheeks with white and red, and anointed their hair with scented oil.

It was very hot in the tent, and not one of the girls spoke a word; they sat perfectly still before the old woman, and did not stir a finger, excepting now and then to take up one of the porous clay pitchers, which stood on the ground, for a draught of water, or to put a pill of Kyphi between their painted lips.

Various musical instruments leaned against the walls of the tent, hand-drums, pipes and lutes and four tambourines lay on the ground; on the vellum of one slept a cat, whose graceful kittens played with the bells in the hoop of another.

An old negro-woman went in and out of the little back-door of the tent, pursued by flies and gnats, while she cleared away a variety of earthen dishes with the remains of food-pomegranate-peelings, breadcrumbs, and garlic-tops —which had been lying on one of the carpets for some hours since the girls had finished their dinner.

Old Hekt sat apart from the girls on a painted trunk, and she was saying, as she took a parcel from her wallet:

"Here, take this incense, and burn six seeds of it, and the vermin will all disappear —" she pointed to the flies that swarmed round the platter in her hand. "If you like I will drive away the mice too and draw the snakes out of their holes better than the priests."[84]

"Keep your magic to yourself," said a girl in a husky voice. "Since you muttered your words over me, and gave me that drink to make me grow slight and lissom again, I have been shaken to pieces with a cough at night, and turn faint when I am dancing."

"But look how slender you have grown," answered Hekt, "and your cough will soon be well."

"When I am dead," whispered the girl to the old woman. "I know that most of us end so."

The witch shrugged her shoulders, and perceiving the dwarf she rose from her seat.

The girls too noticed the little man, and set up the indescribable cry, something like the cackle of hens, which is peculiar to Eastern women when something tickles their fancy. Nemu was well known to them, for his mother always stayed in their tent whenever she came to Thebes, and the gayest of them cried out:

"You are grown, little man, since the last time you were here."

"So are you," said the dwarf sharply; "but only as far as big words are concerned."

"And you are as wicked as you are small," retorted the girl.

"Then my wickedness is small too," said the dwarf laughing, "for I am little enough! Good morning, girls-may Besa help your beauty. Good day, mother-you sent for me?"

The old woman nodded; the dwarf perched himself on the chest beside her, and they began to whisper together.

"How dusty and tired you are," said Hekt. I do believe you have come on foot in the burning sun."

"My ass is dead," replied Nemu, "and I have no money to hire a steed."

"A foretaste of future splendor," said the old woman with a sneer. "What have you succeeded in doing?"

"Paaker has saved us," replied Nemu, "and I have just come from a long interview with the Regent."

"Well?"

"He will renew your letter of freedom, if you will put Paaker into his power."

"Good-good. I wish he would make up his mind to come and seek me-in disguise, of course —I would —"

126

"He is very timid, and it would not suggest to him anything so unpracticable."

"Hm —" said Hekt, "perhaps you are right, for when we have to demand a good deal it is best only to ask for what is feasible. One rash request often altogether spoils the patron's inclination for granting favors."

"What else has occurred?"

"The Regent's army has conquered the Ethiopians, and is coming home with rich spoils."

"People may be bought with treasure," muttered the old woman, "I good-good!"

"Paaker's sword is sharpened; I would give no more for my master's life, than I have in my pocket-and you know why I came on foot through the dust."

"Well, you can ride home again," replied his mother, giving the little man a small silver ring. "Has the pioneer seen Nefert again?"

"Strange things have happened," said the dwarf, and he told his mother what had taken place between Katuti and Nefert. Nemu was a good listener, and had not forgotten a word of what he had heard.

The old woman listened to his story with the most eager attention.

"Well, well," she muttered, "here is another extraordinary thing. What is common to all men is generally disgustingly similar in the palace and in the hovel. Mothers are everywhere she-apes, who with pleasure let themselves be tormented to death by their children, who repay them badly enough, and the wives generally open their ears wide if any one can tell them of some misbehavior of their husbands! But that is not the way with your mistress."

The old woman looked thoughtful, and then she continued:

"In point of fact this can be easily explained, and is not at all more extraordinary than it is that those tired girls should sit yawning. You told me once that it was a pretty sight to see the mother and daughter side by side in their chariot when they go to a festival or the Panegyrai; Katuti, you said, took care that the colors of their dresses and the flowers in their hair should harmonize. For which of them is the dress first chosen on such occasions?"

"Always for the lady Katuti, who never wears any but certain colors," replied Nemu quickly.

"You see," said the witch laughing, "Indeed it must be so. That mother always thinks of herself first, and of the objects she wishes to gain; but they hang high, and she treads down everything that is in her way-even her own child-to reach them. She will contrive that Paaker shall be the ruin of Mena, as sure as I have ears to hear with, for that woman is capable of playing any tricks with her daughter, and would marry her to that lame dog yonder if it would advance her ambitious schemes."

"But Nefert!" said Nemu. "You should have seen her. The dove became a lioness."

"Because she loves Mena as much as her mother loves herself," answered Hekt. "As the poets say, 'she is full of him.' It is really true of her, there is no room for any thing else. She cares for one only, and woe to those who come between him and her!"

"I have seen other women in love," said Nemu, "but —"

"But," exclaimed the old witch with such a sharp laugh that the girls all looked up, "they behaved differently to Nefert —I believe you, for there is not one in a thousand that loves as she does. It is a sickness that gives raging pain-like a poisoned arrow in an open wound, and devours all that is near it like a fire-brand, and is harder to cure than the disease which is killing that coughing wench. To be possessed by that demon of anguish is to suffer the torture of the damned-or else," and her voice sank to softness, "to be more blest than the Gods, happy as they are. I know —I know it all; for I was once one of the possessed, one of a thousand, and even now —"

"Well?" asked the dwarf.

"Folly!" muttered the witch, stretching herself as if awaking from sleep. "Madness! He-is long since dead, and if he were not it would be all the same to me. All men are alike, and Mena will be like the rest."

"But Paaker surely is governed by the demon you describe?" asked the dwarf.

"May be," replied his mother; "but he is self-willed to madness. He would simply give his life for the thing because it is denied him. If your mistress Nefert were his, perhaps he might be easier; but what is the use of chattering? I must go over to the gold tent, where everyone goes now who has any money in their purse, to speak to the mistress —"

"What do you want with her?" interrupted Nemu. "Little Uarda over there," said the old woman, "will soon be quite well again. You have seen her lately; is she not grown beautiful, wonderfully beautiful? Now I shall see what the good woman will offer me if I take Uarda to her? the girl is as light-footed as a gazelle, and with good training would learn to dance in a very few weeks."

Nemu turned perfectly white.

"That you shall not do," said he positively.

"And why not?" asked the old woman, "if it pays well."

"Because I forbid it," said the dwarf in a choked voice.

"Bless me," laughed the woman; "you want to play my lady Nefert, and expect me to take the part of her mother Katuti. But, seriously, having seen the child again, have you any fancy for her?"

"Yes," replied Nemu. "If we gain our end, Katuti will make me free, and make me rich. Then I will buy Pinem's grandchild, and take her for my wife. I will build a house near the hall of justice, and give the complainants and defendants private advice, like the hunch-back Sent, who now drives through the streets in his own chariot."

"Hm —" said his mother, "that might have done very well, but perhaps it is too late. When the child had fever she talked about the young priest who was sent from the House of Seti by Ameni. He is a fine tall fellow, and took a great interest in her; he is a gardener's son, named Pentaur."

"Pentaur?" said the dwarf. "Pentaur? He has the haughty air and the expression of the old Mohar, and would be sure to rise; but they are going to break his proud neck for him."

"So much the better," said the old woman. "Uarda would be just the wife for you, she is good and steady, and no one knows —"

"What?" said Nemu.

"Who her mother was-for she was not one of us. She came here from foreign parts, and when she died she left a trinket with strange letters on it. We must show it to one of the prisoners of war, after you have got her safe; perhaps they could make out the queer inscription. She comes of a good stock, that I am certain; for Uarda is the very living image of her mother, and as soon as she was born, she looked like the child of a great man. You smile, you idiot! Why thousands of infants have been in my hands, and if one was brought to me wrapped in rags I could tell if its parents were noble or base-born. The shape of the foot shows it-and other marks. Uarda may stay where she is, and I will help you. If anything new occurs let me know."

CHAPTER XXI.

When Nemu, riding on an ass this time, reached home, he found neither his mistress nor Nefert within.

The former was gone, first to the temple, and then into the town; Nefert, obeying an irresistible impulse, had gone to her royal friend Bent-Anat.

The king's palace was more like a little town than a house. The wing in which the Regent resided, and which we have already visited, lay away from the river; while the part of the building which was used by the royal family commanded the Nile.

It offered a splendid, and at the same time a pleasing prospect to the ships which sailed by at its foot, for it stood, not a huge and solitary mass in the midst of the surrounding gardens, but in picturesque groups of various outline. On each side of a large structure, which contained the state rooms and banqueting hall, three rows of pavilions of different sizes extended in symmetrical order. They were connected with each other by colonnades, or by little bridges, under which flowed canals, that watered the gardens and gave the palace-grounds the aspect of a town built on islands.

The principal part of the castle of the Pharaohs was constructed of light Nile-mud bricks and elegantly carved woodwork, but the extensive walls which surrounded it were ornamented and fortified with towers, in front of which heavily armed soldiers stood on guard.

The walls and pillars, the galleries and colonnades, even the roofs, blazed in many colored paints, and at every gate stood tall masts, from which red and blue flags fluttered when the king was residing there. Now they stood up with only their brass spikes, which were intended to intercept and conduct the lightning. —[According to an inscription first interpreted by Dumichen.]

To the right of the principal building, and entirely surrounded with thick plantations of trees, stood the houses of the royal ladies, some mirrored in the lake which they surrounded at a greater or less distance. In this part of the grounds were the king's storehouses in endless rows, while behind the centre building, in which the Pharaoh resided, stood the barracks for his body guard and the treasuries. The left wing was occupied by the officers of the household, the innumerable servants and the horses and chariots of the sovereign.

In spite of the absence of the king himself, brisk activity reigned in the palace of Rameses, for a hundred gardeners watered the turf, the flower-borders, the shrubs and trees; companies of guards passed hither and thither; horses were being trained and broken; and the princess's wing was as full as a beehive of servants and maids, officers and priests.

Nefert was well known in this part of the palace. The gate-keepers let her litter pass unchallenged, with low bows; once in the garden, a lord in waiting received her, and conducted her to the chamberlain, who, after a short delay, introduced her into the sitting-room of the king's favorite daughter.

Bent-Anat's apartment was on the first floor of the pavilion, next to the king's residence. Her dead mother had inhabited these pleasant rooms, and when the princess was grown up it made the king happy to feel that she was near him; so the beautiful house of the wife who had too early departed, was given up to her, and at the same time, as she was his eldest daughter, many privileges were conceded to her, which hitherto none but queens had enjoyed.

The large room, in which Nefert found the princess, commanded the river. A doorway, closed with light curtains, opened on to a long balcony with a finely-worked balustrade of copper-gilt, to which clung a climbing rose with pink flowers.

When Nefert entered the room, Bent-Anat was just having the rustling curtain drawn aside by her waiting-women; for the sun was setting, and at that hour she loved to sit on the balcony, as it grew cooler, and watch with devout meditation the departure of Ra, who, as the grey-haired Turn, vanished behind the western horizon of the Necropolis in the evening to bestow the blessing of light on the under-world.

Nefert's apartment was far more elegantly appointed than the princess's; her mother and Mena had surrounded her with a thousand pretty trifles. Her carpets were made of sky-blue and silver brocade from Damascus, the seats and couches were covered with stuff embroidered in feathers by the Ethiopian women, which looked like the breasts of birds. The images of the Goddess Hathor, which stood on the house-altar, were of an imitation of emerald, which was called Mafkat, and the other little figures, which were placed near their patroness, were of lapis-lazuli, malachite, agate and bronze, overlaid with gold. On her toilet-table stood a collection of salve-boxes, and cups of ebony and ivory finely carved, and everything was arranged with the utmost taste, and exactly suited Nefert herself.

Bent-Anat's room also suited the owner.

It was high and airy, and its furniture consisted in costly but simple necessaries; the lower part of the wall was lined with cool tiles of white and violet earthen ware, on each of which was pictured a star, and which, all together, formed a tasteful pattern. Above these the walls were covered with a beautiful dark green material brought from Sais, and the same stuff was used to cover the long divans by the wall. Chairs and stools, made of cane, stood round a very large table in the middle of this room, out of which several others opened; all handsome, comfortable, and harmonious in aspect, but all betraying that their mistress took small pleasure in trifling decorations. But her chief delight was in finely-grown plants, of which rare and magnificent specimens, artistically arranged on stands, stood in the corners of many of the rooms. In others there were tall obelisks of ebony, which bore saucers for incense, which all the Egyptians loved, and which was prescribed by their physicians to purify and perfume their dwellings. Her simple bedroom would have suited a prince who loved floriculture, quite as well as a princess.

Before all things Bent-Anat loved air and light. The curtains of her windows and doors were only closed when the position of the sun absolutely required it; while in Nefert's rooms, from morning till evening, a dim twilight was maintained.

The princess went affectionately towards the charioteer's wife, who bowed low before her at the threshold; she took her chin with her right hand, kissed her delicate narrow forehead, and said:

"Sweet creature! At last you have come uninvited to see lonely me! It is the first time since our men went away to the war. If Rameses' daughter commands there is no escape; and you come; but of your own free will —"

Nefert raised her large eyes, moist with tears, with an imploring look, and her glance was so pathetic that Bent-Anat interrupted herself, and taking both her hands, exclaimed:

"Do you know who must have eyes exactly like yours? I mean the Goddess from whose tears, when they fall on the earth, flowers spring."

Nefert's eyes fell and she blushed deeply.

"I wish," she murmured, "that my eyes might close for ever, for I am very unhappy." And two large tears rolled down her cheeks.

"What has happened to you, my darling?" asked the princess sympathetically, and she drew her towards her, putting her arm round her like a sick child.

Nefert glanced anxiously at the chamberlain, and the ladies in waiting who had entered the room with her, and Bent-Anat understood the look; she requested her attendants to withdraw, and when she was alone with her sad little friend —"Speak now," she said. "What saddens your heart? how comes this melancholy expression on your dear baby face? Tell me, and I will comfort you, and you shall be my bright thoughtless plaything once more."

"Thy plaything!" answered Nefert, and a flash of displeasure sparkled in her eyes. "Thou art right to call me so, for I deserve no better name. I have submitted all my life to be nothing but the plaything of others."

"But, Nefert, I do not know you again," cried Bent-Anat. "Is this my gentle amiable dreamer?"

"That is the word I wanted," said Nefert in a low tone. "I slept, and dreamed, and dreamed on-till Mena awoke me; and when he left me I went to sleep again, and for two whole years

I have lain dreaming; but to-day I have been torn from my dreams so suddenly and roughly, that I shall never find any rest again."

While she spoke, heavy tears fell slowly one after another over her cheeks.

Bent-Anat felt what she saw and heard as deeply as if Nefert were her own suffering child. She lovingly drew the young wife down by her side on the divan, and insisted on Nefert's letting her know all that troubled her spirit.

Katuti's daughter had in the last few hours felt like one born blind, and who suddenly receives his sight. He looks at the brightness of the sun, and the manifold forms of the creation around him, but the beams of the day-star blind its eyes, and the new forms, which he has sought to guess at in his mind, and which throng round him in their rude reality, shock him and pain him. To-day, for the first time, she had asked herself wherefore her mother, and not she herself, was called upon to control the house of which she nevertheless was called the mistress, and the answer had rung in her ears: "Because Mena thinks you incapable of thought and action." He had often called her his little rose, and she felt now that she was neither more nor less than a flower that blossoms and fades, and only charms the eye by its color and beauty.

"My mother," she said to Bent-Anat, "no doubt loves me, but she has managed badly for Mena, very badly; and I, miserable idiot, slept and dreamed of Mena, and saw and heard nothing of what was happening to his-to our-inheritance. Now my mother is afraid of my husband, and those whom we fear, says my uncle, we cannot love, and we are always ready to believe evil of those we do not love. So she lends an ear to those people who blame Mena, and say of him that he has driven me out of his heart, and has taken a strange woman to his tent. But it is false and a lie; and I cannot and will not countenance my own mother even, if she embitters and mars what is left to me-what supports me-the breath and blood of my life-my love, my fervent love for my husband."

Bent-Anat had listened to her without interrupting her; she sat by her for a time in silence. Then she said:

"Come out into the gallery; then I will tell you what I think, and perhaps Toth may pour some helpful counsel into my mind. I love you, and I know you well, and though I am not wise, I have my eyes open and a strong hand. Take it, come with me on to the balcony."

A refreshing breeze met the two women as they stepped out into the air. It was evening, and a reviving coolness had succeeded the heat of the day. The buildings and houses already cast long shadows, and numberless boats, with the visitors returning from the Necropolis, crowded the stream that rolled its swollen flood majestically northwards.

Close below lay the verdant garden, which sent odors from the rose-beds up to the princess's balcony. A famous artist had laid it out in the time of Hatasu, and the picture which he had in his mind, when he sowed the seeds and planted the young shoots, was now realized, many decades after his death. He had thought of planning a carpet, on which the palace should seem to stand. Tiny streams, in bends and curves, formed the outline of the design, and the shapes they enclosed were filled with plants of every size, form, and color; beautiful plats of fresh green turf everywhere represented the groundwork of the pattern, and flower-beds and clumps of shrubs stood out from them in harmonious mixtures of colors, while the tall and rare trees, of which Hatasu's ships had brought several from Arabia, gave dignity and impressiveness to the whole.

Clear drops sparkled on leaf and flower and blade, for, only a short time before, the garden by Bent-Anat's house had been freshly watered. The Nile beyond surrounded an island, where flourished the well-kept sacred grove of Anion.

The Necropolis on the farther side of the river was also well seen from Bent-Anat's balcony. There stood in long perspective the rows of sphinxes, which led from the landing-place of the festal barges to the gigantic buildings of Amenophis III. with its colossi-the hugest in Thebes-to the House of Seti, and to the temple of Hatasu. There lay the long workshops of the embalmers and closely-packed homes of the inhabitants of the City of the Dead. In the farthest west rose the Libyan mountains with their innumerable graves, and the valley of the kings' tombs took a wide curve behind, concealed by a spur of the hills.

The two women looked in silence towards the west. The sun was near the horizon-now it touched it, now it sank behind the hills; and as the heavens flushed with hues like living gold, blazing rubies, and liquid garnet and amethyst, the evening chant rang out from all the temples, and the friends sank on their knees, hid their faces in the bower-rose garlands that clung to the trellis, and prayed with full hearts.

When they rose night was spreading over the landscape, for the twilight is short in Thebes. Here and there a rosy cloud fluttered across the darkening sky, and faded gradually as the evening star appeared.

"I am content," said Bent-Anat. "And you? have you recovered your peace of mind?"

Nefert shook her head. The princess drew her on to a seat, and sank down beside her. Then she began again "Your heart is sore, poor child; they have spoilt the past for you, and you dread the future. Let me be frank with you, even if it gives you pain. You are sick, and I must cure you. Will you listen to me?"

"Speak on," said Nefert.

"Speech does not suit me so well as action," replied the princess; "but I believe I know what you need, and can help you. You love your husband; duty calls him from you, and you feel lonely and neglected; that is quite natural. But those whom I love, my father and my brothers, are also gone to the war; my mother is long since dead; the noble woman, whom the king left to be my companion, was laid low a few weeks since by sickness. Look what a half-abandoned spot my house is! Which is the lonelier do you think, you or I?"

"I," said Nefert. "For no one is so lonely as a wife parted from the husband her heart longs after."

"But you trust Mena's love for you?" asked Bent-Anat.

Nefert pressed her hand to her heart and nodded assent:

"And he will return, and with him your happiness."

"I hope so," said Nefert softly.

"And he who hopes," said Bent Anat, "possesses already the joys of the future. Tell me, would you have changed places with the Gods so long as Mena was with you? No! Then you are most fortunate, for blissful memories-the joys of the past-are yours at any rate. What is the present? I speak of it, and it is no more. Now, I ask you, what joys can I look forward to, and what certain happiness am I justified in hoping for?

"Thou dost not love any one," replied Nefert. "Thou dost follow thy own course, calm and undeviating as the moon above us. The highest joys are unknown to thee, but for the same reason thou dost not know the bitterest pain."

"What pain?" asked the princess.

"The torment of a heart consumed by the fires of Sechet," replied Nefert.

The princess looked thoughtfully at the ground, then she turned her eyes eagerly on her friend.

"You are mistaken," she said; "I know what love and longing are. But you need only wait till a feast day to wear the jewel that is your own, while my treasure is no more mine than a pearl that I see gleaming at the bottom of the sea."

"Thou canst love!" exclaimed Nefert with joyful excitement. "Oh! I thank Hathor that at last she has touched thy heart. The daughter of Rameses need not even send for the diver to fetch the jewel out of the sea; at a sign from her the pearl will rise of itself, and lie on the sand at her slender feet."

Bent-Anat smiled and kissed Nefert's brow.

"How it excites you," she said, "and stirs your heart and tongue! If two strings are tuned in harmony, and one is struck, the other sounds, my music master tells me. I believe you would listen to me till morning if I only talked to you about my love. But it was not for that we came out on the balcony. Now listen! I am as lonely as you, I love less happily than you, the

House of Seti threatens me with evil times-and yet I can preserve my full confidence in life and my joy in existence. How can you explain this?"

"We are so very different," said Nefert.

"True," replied Bent-Anat, "but we are both young, both women, and both wish to do right. My mother died, and I have had no one to guide me, for I who for the most part need some one to lead me can already command, and be obeyed. You had a mother to bring you up, who, when you were still a child, was proud of her pretty little daughter, and let her-as it became her so well-dream and play, without warning her against the dangerous propensity. Then Mena courted you. You love him truly, and in four long years he has been with you but a month or two; your mother remained with you, and you hardly observed that she was managing your own house for you, and took all the trouble of the household. You had a great pastime of your own-your thoughts of Mena, and scope for a thousand dreams in your distant love. I know it, Nefert; all that you have seen and heard and felt in these twenty months has centred in him and him alone. Nor is it wrong in itself. The rose tree here, which clings to my balcony, delights us both; but if the gardener did not frequently prune it and tie it with palm-bast, in this soil, which forces everything to rapid growth, it would soon shoot up so high that it would cover door and window, and I should sit in darkness. Throw this handkerchief over your shoulders, for the dew falls as it grows cooler, and listen to me a little longer! —The beautiful passion of love and fidelity has grown unchecked in your dreamy nature to such a height, that it darkens your spirit and your judgment. Love, a true love, it seems to me, should be a noble fruit-tree, and not a rank weed. I do not blame you, for she who should have been the gardener did not heed-and would not heed-what was happening. Look, Nefert, so long as I wore the lock of youth, I too did what I fancied —I never found any pleasure in dreaming, but in wild games with my brothers, in horses and in falconry; they often said I had the spirit of a boy, and indeed I would willingly have been a boy."

"Not I —never!" said Nefert.

"You are just a rose-my dearest," said Bent-Anat. "Well! when I was fifteen I was so discontented, so insubordinate and full of all sorts of wild behavior, so dissatisfied in spite of all the kindness and love that surrounded me-but I will tell you what happened. It is four years ago, shortly before your wedding with Mena; my father called me to play draughts.[85]

You know how certainly he could beat the most skilful antagonist; but that day his thoughts were wandering, and I won the game twice following. Full of insolent delight, I jumped up and kissed his great handsome forehead, and cried 'The sublime God, the hero, under whose feet the strange nations writhe, to whom the priests and the people pray-is beaten by a girl!' He smiled gently, and answered 'The Lords of Heaven are often outdone by the Ladies, and Necheb, the lady of victory, is a woman. Then he grew graver, and said: 'You call me a God, my child, but in this only do I feel truly godlike, that at every moment I strive to the utmost to prove myself useful by my labors; here restraining, there promoting, as is needful. Godlike I can never be but by doing or producing something great! These words, Nefert, fell like seeds in my soul. At last I knew what it was that was wanting to me; and when, a few weeks later, my father and your husband took the field with a hundred thousand fighting men, I resolved to be worthy of my godlike father, and in my little circle to be of use too! You do not know all that is done in the houses behind there, under my direction. Three hundred girls spin pure flax, and weave it into bands of linen for the wounds of the soldiers; numbers of children, and old women, gather plants on the mountains, and others sort them according to the instructions of a physician; in the kitchens no banquets are prepared, but fruits are preserved in sugar for the loved ones, and the sick in the camp. Joints of meat are salted, dried, and smoked for the army on its march through the desert. The butler no longer thinks of drinking-bouts, but brings me wine in great stone jars; we pour it into well-closed skins for the soldiers, and the best sorts we put into strong flasks, carefully sealed with pitch, that they may perform the journey uninjured, and warm and rejoice the hearts of our heroes. All that, and much more, I manage and arrange, and my days pass in hard work. The Gods send me no bright visions in the night, for after utter fatigue —I sleep soundly. But I know that I am of use. I can hold my head proudly, because in some degree I resemble my great father; and if the king thinks of me at all I know he can rejoice in the doings of his child. That is the end of it, Nefert-and I only say, Come and join me, work with me, prove yourself of use, and compel Mena to think of his wife, not with affection only, but with pride." Nefert let her head sink slowly on Bent-Anat's bosom, threw her arms round her neck, and wept like a child. At last she composed herself and said humbly:

"Take me to school, and teach me to be useful." "I knew," said the princess smiling, "that you only needed a guiding hand. Believe me, you will soon learn to couple content and longing. But now hear this! At present go home to your mother, for it is late; and meet her lovingly, for that is the will of the Gods. To-morrow morning I will go to see you, and beg Katuti to let you come to me as companion in the place of my lost friend. The day after to-morrow you will come to me in the palace. You can live in the rooms of my departed friend and begin, as she had done, to help me in my work. May these hours be blest to you!"

CHAPTER XXII.

At the time of this conversation the leech Nebsecht still lingered in front of the hovel of the paraschites, and waited with growing impatience for the old man's return.

At first he trembled for him; then he entirely forgot the danger into which he had thrown him, and only hoped for the fulfilment of his desires, and for wonderful revelations through his investigations of the human heart.

For some minutes he gave himself up to scientific considerations; but he became more and more agitated by anxiety for the paraschites, and by the exciting vicinity of Uarda.

For hours he had been alone with her, for her father and grandmother could no longer stop away from their occupations. The former must go to escort prisoners of war to Hermonthis, and the old woman, since her granddaughter had been old enough to undertake the small duties of the household, had been one of the wailing-women, who, with hair all dishevelled, accompanied the corpse on its way to the grave, weeping, and lamenting, and casting Nile-mud on their forehead and breast. Uarda still lay, when the sun was sinking, in front of the hut.

She looked weary and pale. Her long hair had come undone, and once more got entangled with the straw of her humble couch. If Nebsecht went near her to feel her pulse or to speak to her she carefully turned her face from him.

Nevertheless when the sun disappeared behind the rocks he bent over her once more, and said:

"It is growing cool; shall I carry you indoors?"

"Let me alone," she said crossly. "I am hot, keep farther away. I am no longer ill, and could go indoors by myself if I wished; but grandmother will be here directly."

Nebsecht rose, and sat down on a hen-coop that was some paces from Uarda, and asked stammering, "Shall I go farther off?"

"Do as you please," she answered. "You are not kind," he said sadly.

"You sit looking at me," said Uarda, "I cannot bear it; and I am uneasy-for grandfather was quite different this morning from his usual self, and talked strangely about dying, and about the great price that was asked of him for curing me. Then he begged me never to forget him, and was so excited and so strange. He is so long away; I wish he were here, with me."

And with these words Uarda began to cry silently. A nameless anxiety for the paraschites seized Nebsecht, and it struck him to the heart that he had demanded a human life in return for the mere fulfilment of a duty. He knew the law well enough, and knew that the old man would be compelled without respite or delay to empty the cup of poison if he were found guilty of the theft of a human heart.

It was dark: Uarda ceased weeping and said to the surgeon:

"Can it be possible that he has gone into the city to borrow the great sum of money that thou-or thy temple-demanded for thy medicine? But there is the princess's golden bracelet, and half of father's prize, and in the chest two years' wages that grandmother had earned by wailing he untouched. Is all that not enough?"

The girl's last question was full of resentment and reproach, and Nebsecht, whose perfect sincerity was part of his very being, was silent, as he would not venture to say yes. He had asked more in return for his help than gold or silver. Now he remembered Pentaur's warning, and when the jackals began to bark he took up the fire-stick,[86] and lighted some fuel that was lying ready. Then he asked himself what Uarda's fate would be without her grandparents, and a strange plan which had floated vaguely before him for some hours, began now to take a distinct outline and intelligible form. He determined if the old man did not return to ask the kolchytes or embalmers to admit him into their guild-and for the sake of his adroitness they were not likely to refuse him-then he would make Uarda his wife, and live apart from the world, for her, for his studies, and for his new calling, in which he hoped to learn a great deal. What did he care for comfort and proprieties, for recognition from his fellow-men, and a superior position!

He could hope to advance more quickly along the new stony path than on the old beaten track. The impulse to communicate his acquired knowledge to others he did not feel. Knowledge in itself amply satisfied him, and he thought no more of his ties to the House of Seti. For three whole days he had not changed his garments, no razor had touched his chin or his scalp, not a drop of water had wetted his hands or his feet. He felt half bewildered and almost as if he had already become an embalmer, nay even a paraschites, one of the most despised of human beings. This self-degradation had an infinite charm, for it brought him down to the level of Uarda, and she, lying near him, sick and anxious, with her dishevelled hair, exactly suited the future which he painted to himself.

"Do you hear nothing?" Uarda asked suddenly. He listened. In the valley there was a barking of dogs, and soon the paraschites and his wife appeared, and, at the door of their hut, took leave of old Hekt, who had met them on her return from Thebes.

"You have been gone a long time," cried Uarda, when her grandmother once more stood before her. "I have been so frightened."

"The doctor was with you," said the old woman going into the house to prepare their simple meal, while the paraschites knelt down by his granddaughter, and caressed her tenderly, but yet with respect, as if he were her faithful servant rather than her blood-relation.

Then he rose, and gave to Nebsecht, who was trembling with excitement, the bag of coarse linen which he was in the habit of carrying tied to him by a narrow belt.

"The heart is in that," he whispered to the leech; "take it out, and give me back the bag, for my knife is in it, and I want it."

Nebsecht took the heart out of the covering with trembling hands and laid it carefully down. Then he felt in the breast of his dress, and going up to the paraschites he whispered:

"Here, take the writing, hang it round your neck, and when you die I will have the book of scripture wrapped up in your mummy cloths like a great man. But that is not enough. The property that I inherited is in the hands of my brother, who is a good man of business, and I have not touched the interest for ten years. I will send it to you, and you and your wife shall enjoy an old age free from care."

The paraschites had taken the little bag with the strip of papyrus, and heard the leech to the end. Then he turned from him saying: "Keep thy money; we are quits. That is if the child gets well," he added humbly.

"She is already half cured," stammered Nebsecht. "But why will you-why won't you accept —"

"Because till to day I have never begged nor borrowed," said the paraschites, "and I will not begin in my old age. Life for life. But what I have done this day not Rameses with all his treasure could repay."

Nebsecht looked down, and knew not how to answer the old man.

His wife now came out; she set a bowl of lentils that she had hastily warmed before the two men, with radishes and onions,[87] then she helped Uarda, who did not need to be carried, into the house, and invited Nebsecht to share their meal. He accepted her invitation, for he had eaten nothing since the previous evening.

When the old woman had once more disappeared indoors, he asked the paraschites:

"Whose heart is it that you have brought me, and how did it come into your hands?"

"Tell me first," said the other, "why thou hast laid such a heavy sin upon my soul?"

"Because I want to investigate the structure of the human heart," said Nebsecht, "so that, when I meet with diseased hearts, I may be able to cure them."

The paraschites looked for a long time at the ground in silence; then he said:

"Art thou speaking the truth?"

"Yes," replied the leech with convincing emphasis. "I am glad," said the old man, "for thou givest help to the poor."

"As willingly as to the rich!" exclaimed Nebsecht. "But tell me now where you got the heart."

"I went into the house of the embalmer," said the old man, after he had selected a few large flints, to which, with crafty blows, he gave the shape of knives, "and there I found three bodies in which I had to make the eight prescribed incisions with my flint-knife. When the dead lie there undressed on the wooden bench they all look alike, and the begger lies as still as the favorite son of a king. But I knew very well who lay before me. The strong old body in the middle of the table was the corpse of the Superior of the temple of Hatasu, and beyond, close by each other, were laid a stone-mason of the Necropolis, and a poor girl from the strangers' quarter, who had died of consumption-two miserable wasted figures. I had known the Prophet well, for I had met him a hundred times in his gilt litter, and we always called him Rui, the rich. I did my duty by all three, I was driven away with the usual stoning, and then I arranged the inward parts of the bodies with my mates. Those of the Prophet are to be preserved later in an alabaster canopus,[88] those of the mason and the girl were put back in their bodies.

"Then I went up to the three bodies, and I asked myself, to which I should do such a wrong as to rob him of his heart. I turned to the two poor ones, and I hastily went up to the sinning girl. Then I heard the voice of the demon that cried out in my heart 'The girl was poor and despised like you while she walked on Seb,[89] perhaps she may find compensation and peace in the other world if you do not mutilate her; and when I turned to the mason's lean corpse, and looked at his hands, which were harder and rougher than my own, the demon whispered the same. Then I stood before the strong, stout corpse of the prophet Rui, who died of apoplexy, and I remembered the honor and the riches that he had enjoyed on earth, and that he at least for a time had known happiness and ease. And as soon as I was alone, I slipped my hand into the bag, and changed the sheep's heart for his.

"Perhaps I am doubly guilty for playing such an accursed trick with the heart of a high-priest; but Rui's body will be hung round with a hundred amulets, Scarabaei[90] will be placed over his heart, and holy oil and sacred sentences will preserve him from all the fiends on his road to Amenti—[Underworld]—while no one will devote helping talismans to the poor. And then! thou hast sworn, in that world, in the hall of judgment, to take my guilt on thyself."

Nebsecht gave the old man his hand.

"That I will," said he, "and I should have chosen as you did. Now take this draught, divide it in four parts, and give it to Uarda for four evenings following. Begin this evening, and by the day after to-morrow I think she will be quite well. I will come again and look after her. Now go to rest, and let me stay a while out here; before the star of Isis is extinguished I will be gone, for they have long been expecting me at the temple."

When the paraschites came out of his but the next morning, Nebsecht had vanished; but a blood-stained cloth that lay by the remains of the fire showed the old man that the impatient investigator had examined the heart of the high-priest during the night, and perhaps cut it up.

Terror fell upon him, and in agony of mind he threw himself on his knees as the golden bark of the Sun-God appeared on the horizon, and he prayed fervently, first for Uarda, and then for the salvation of his imperilled soul.

He rose encouraged, convinced himself that his granddaughter was progressing towards recovery, bid farewell to his wife, took his flint knife and his bronze hook,[91] and went to the house of the embalmer to follow his dismal calling.

The group of buildings in which the greater number of the corpses from Thebes went through the processes of mummifying, lay on the bare desert-land at some distance from his hovel, southwards from the House of Seti at the foot of the mountain. They occupied by themselves a fairly large space, enclosed by a rough wall of dried mud-bricks.

The bodies were brought in through the great gate towards the Nile, and delivered to the kolchytes—[The whole guild of embalmers]—while the priests, paraschites, and tariclleutes—[Salter of the bodies]—bearers and assistants, who here did their daily work, as well as innumerable water-carriers who came up from the Nile, loaded with skins, found their way into the establishment by a side gate.

At the farthest northern building of wood, with a separate gate, in which the orders of the bereaved were taken, and often indeed those of men still in active life, who thought to provide betimes for their suitable interment.

The crowd in this house was considerable. About fifty men and women were moving in it at the present moment, all of different ranks, and not only from Thebes but from many smaller towns of Upper Egypt, to make purchases or to give commissions to the functionaries who were busy here.

This bazaar of the dead was well supplied, for coffins of every form stood up against the walls, from the simplest chest to the richly gilt and painted coffer, in form resembling a mummy. On wooden shelves lay endless rolls of coarse and fine linen, in which the limbs of the mummies were enveloped, and which were manufactured by the people of the embalming establishment under the protection of the tutelar goddesses of weavers, Neith, Isis and Nephthys, though some were ordered from a distance, particularly from Sais.

There was free choice for the visitors of this pattern-room in the matter of mummy-cases and cloths, as well as of necklets, scarabaei, statuettes, Uza-eyes, girdles, head-rests, triangles, split-rings, staves, and other symbolic objects, which were attached to the dead as sacred amulets, or bound up in the wrappings.

There were innumerable stamps of baked clay, which were buried in the earth to show any one who might dispute the limits, how far each grave extended, images of the gods, which were laid in the sand to purify and sanctify it-for by nature it belonged to Seth-Typhon —as well as the figures called Schebti, which were either enclosed several together in little boxes, or laid separately in the grave; it was supposed that they would help the dead to till the fields of the blessed with the pick-axe, plough, and seed-bag which they carried on their shoulders.

The widow and the steward of the wealthy Superior of the temple of Hatasu, and with them a priest of high rank, were in eager discussion with the officials of the embalming-House, and were selecting the most costly of the patterns of mummy-cases which were offered to their inspection, the finest linen, and amulets of malachite, and lapis-lazuli, of blood-stone, carnelian and green felspar, as well as the most elegant alabaster canopi for the deceased; his body was to be enclosed first in a sort of case of papier-mache, and then in a wooden and a stone coffin. They wrote his name on a wax tablet which was ready for the purpose, with those of his parents, his wife and children, and all his titles; they ordered what verses should be written on his coffin, what on the papyrus-rolls to be enclosed in it, and what should be set out above his name. With regard to the inscription on the walls of the tomb, the pedestal of the statue to be placed there and the face of the stele —[Stone tablet with round pediment.] —to be erected in it, yet further particulars would be given; a priest of the temple of Seti was charged to write them, and to draw up a catalogue of the rich offerings of the survivors. The last could be done later, when, after the division of the property, the amount of the fortune he had left could be ascertained. The mere mummifying of the body with the finest oils and essences, cloths, amulets, and cases, would cost a talent of silver, without the stone sarcophagus.

The widow wore a long mourning robe, her forehead was lightly daubed with Nile-mud, and in the midst of her chaffering with the functionaries of the embalming-house, whose prices she complained of as enormous and rapacious, from time to time she broke out into a loud wail of grief-as the occasion demanded.

More modest citizens finished their commissions sooner, though it was not unusual for the income of a whole year to be sacrificed for the embalming of the head of a household-the father or the mother of a family. The mummifying of the poor was cheap, and that of the poorest had to be provided by the kolchytes as a tribute to the king, to whom also they were obliged to pay a tax in linen from their looms.

This place of business was carefully separated from the rest of the establishment, which none but those who were engaged in the processes carried on there were on any account permitted to enter. The kolchytes formed a closely-limited guild at the head of which stood a certain number of priests, and from among them the masters of the many thousand members were chosen. This guild was highly respected, even the taricheutes, who were entrusted with the actual work of embalming, could venture to mix with the other citizens, although in Thebes itself people always avoided them with a certain horror; only the paraschites, whose duty it was to open the body, bore the whole curse of uncleanness. Certainly the place where these people fulfilled their office was dismal enough.

The stone chamber in which the bodies were opened, and the halls in which they were prepared with salt, had adjoining them a variety of laboratories and depositaries for drugs and preparations of every description.

In a court-yard, protected from the rays of the sun only by an awning, was a large walled bason, containing a solution of natron, in which the bodies were salted, and they were then dried in a stone vault, artificially supplied with hot air.

The little wooden houses of the weavers, as well as the work-shops of the case-joiners and decorators, stood in numbers round the pattern-room; but the farthest off, and much the largest of the buildings of the establishment, was a very long low structure, solidly built of stone and well roofed in, where the prepared bodies were enveloped in their cerements, tricked out in amulets, and made ready for their journey to the next world. What took place in this building-into which the laity were admitted, but never for more than a few minutes-was to the last degree mysterious, for here the gods themselves appeared to be engaged with the mortal bodies.

Out of the windows which opened on the street, recitations, hymns, and lamentations sounded night and day. The priests who fulfilled their office here wore masks like the divinities of the under-world. Many were the representatives of Anubis, with the jackal-head, assisted by boys with masks of the so-called child-Horus. At the head of each mummy stood or squatted a wailing-woman with the emblems of Nephthys, and one at its feet with those of Isis.

Every separate limb of the deceased was dedicated to a particular divinity by the aid of holy oils, charms, and sentences; a specially prepared cloth was wrapped round each muscle, every drug and every bandage owed its origin to some divinity, and the confusion of sounds, of disguised figures, and of various perfumes, had a stupefying effect on those who visited this chamber. It need not be said that the whole embalming establishment and its neighborhood was enveloped in a cloud of powerful resinous fumes, of sweet attar, of lasting musk, and pungent spices.

When the wind blew from the west it was wafted across the Nile to Thebes, and this was regarded as an evil omen, for from the south-west comes the wind that enfeebles the energy of men-the fatal simoon.

In the court of the pattern-house stood several groups of citizens from Thebes, gathered round different individuals, to whom they were expressing their sympathy. A new-comer, the superintendent of the victims of the temple of Anion, who seemed to be known to many and was greeted with respect, announced, even before he went to condole with Rui's widow, in a tone full of horror at what had happened, that an omen, significant of the greatest misfortune, had occurred in Thebes, in a spot no less sacred than the very temple of Anion himself.

Many inquisitive listeners stood round him while he related that the Regent Ani, in his joy at the victory of his troops in Ethiopia, had distributed wine with a lavish hand to the garrison of Thebes, and also to the watchmen of the temple of Anion, and that, while the people were carousing, wolves[92] had broken into the stable of the sacred rams. Some were killed, but the noblest ram, which Rameses himself had sent as a gift from Mendes when he set out for the war-the magnificent beast which Amon had chosen as the tenement of his spirit, was found, torn in pieces, by the soldiers, who immediately terrified the whole city with the news. At the same hour news had come from Memphis that the sacred bull Apis was dead.

All the people who had collected round the priest, broke out into a far-sounding cry of woe, in which he himself and Rui's widow vehemently joined.

The buyers and functionaries rushed out of the pattern-room, and from the mummy-house the taricheutes, paraschites and assistants; the weavers left their looms, and all, as soon as they had learned what had happened, took part in the lamentations, howling and wailing, tearing their hair and covering their faces with dust.

The noise was loud and distracting, and when its violence diminished, and the work-people went back to their business, the east wind brought the echo of the cries of the dwellers in the Necropolis, perhaps too, those of the citizens of Thebes itself.

"Bad news," said the inspector of the victims, "cannot fail to reach us soon from the king and the army; he will regret the death of the ram which we called by his name more than that of Apis. It is a bad —a very bad omen."

"My lost husband Rui, who rests in Osiris, foresaw it all," said the widow. "If only I dared to speak I could tell a good deal that many might find unpleasant."

The inspector of sacrifices smiled, for he knew that the late superior of the temple of Hatasu had been an adherent of the old royal family, and he replied:

"The Sun of Rameses may be for a time covered with clouds, but neither those who fear it nor those who desire it will live to see its setting."

The priest coldly saluted the lady, and went into the house of a weaver in which he had business, and the widow got into her litter which was waiting at the gate.

The old paraschites Pinem had joined with his fellows in the lamentation for the sacred beasts, and was now sitting on the hard pavement of the dissecting room to eat his morsel of food-for it was noon.

The stone room in which he was eating his meal was badly lighted; the daylight came through a small opening in the roof, over which the sun stood perpendicularly, and a shaft of bright rays, in which danced the whirling motes, shot down through the twilight on to the stone pavement. Mummy-cases leaned against all the walls, and on smooth polished slabs lay bodies covered with coarse cloths. A rat scudded now and then across the floor, and from the wide cracks between the stones sluggish scorpions crawled out.

The old paraschites was long since blunted to the horror which pervaded this locality. He had spread a coarse napkin, and carefully laid on it the provisions which his wife had put into his satchel; first half a cake of bread, then a little salt, and finally a radish.

But the bag was not yet empty.

He put his hand in and found a piece of meat wrapped up in two cabbage-leaves. Old Hekt had brought a leg of a gazelle from Thebes for Uarda, and he now saw that the women had put a piece of it into his little sack for his refreshment. He looked at the gift with emotion, but he did not venture to touch it, for he felt as if in doing so he should be robbing the sick girl. While eating the bread and the radish he contemplated the piece of meat as if it were some costly jewel, and when a fly dared to settle on it he drove it off indignantly.

At last he tasted the meat, and thought of many former noon-day meals, and how he had often found a flower in the satchel, that Uarda had placed there to please him, with the bread. His kind old eyes filled with tears, and his whole heart swelled with gratitude and love. He looked up, and his glance fell on the table, and he asked himself how he would have felt if instead of the old priest, robbed of his heart, the sunshine of his old age, his granddaughter, were lying there motionless. A cold shiver ran over him, and he felt that his own heart would not have been too great a price to pay for her recovery. And yet! In the course of his long life he had experienced so much suffering and wrong, that he could not imagine any hope of a better lot in the other world. Then he drew out the bond Nebsecht had given him, held it up with both hands, as if to show it to the Immortals, and particularly to the judges in the hall of truth and judgment, that they might not reckon with him for the crime he had committed-not for himself but for another-and that they might not refuse to justify Rui, whom he had robbed of his heart.

While he thus lifted his soul in devotion, matters were getting warm outside the dissecting room. He thought he heard his name spoken, and scarcely had he raised his head to listen when a taricheut came in and desired him to follow him.

In front of the rooms, filled with resinous odors and incense, in which the actual process of embalming was carried on, a number of taricheutes were standing and looking at an object in an alabaster bowl. The knees of the old man knocked together as he recognized the heart of the beast which he had substituted for that of the Prophet.

The chief of the taricheutes asked him whether he had opened the body of the dead priest. Pinem stammered out "Yes." Whether this was his heart? The old man nodded affirmatively.

The taricheutes looked at each other, whispered together; then one of them went away, and returned soon with the inspector of victims from the temple of Anion, whom he had found in the house of the weaver, and the chief of the kolchytes.

"Show me the heart," said the superintendent of the sacrifices as he approached the vase. "I can decide in the dark if you have seen rightly. I examine a hundred animals every day. Give it here! —By all the Gods of Heaven and Hell that is the heart of a ram!"

"It was found in the breast of Rui," said one of the taricheutes decisively. "It was opened yesterday in the presence of us all by this old paraschites."

"It is extraordinary," said the priest of Anion. "And incredible. But perhaps an exchange was effected. —Did you slaughter any victims here yesterday or —?"

"We are purifying ourselves," the chief of the kolchytes interrupted, "for the great festival of the valley, and for ten days no beast can have been killed here for food; besides, the stables and slaughterhouses are a long way from this, on the other side of the linen-factories."

"It is strange!" replied the priest. "Preserve this heart carefully, kolchytes: or, better still, let it be enclosed in a case. We will take it over to the chief prophet of Anion. It would seem that some miracle has happened."

"The heart belongs to the Necropolis," answered the chief kolchytes, "and it would therefore be more fitting if we took it to the chief priest of the temple of Seti, Ameni."

"You command here!" said the other. "Let us go." In a few minutes the priest of Anion and the chief of the kolchytes were being carried towards the valley in their litters. A taricheut followed them, who sat on a seat between two asses, and carefully carried a casket of ivory, in which reposed the ram's heart.

The old paraschites watched the priests disappear behind the tamarisk bushes. He longed to run after them, and tell them everything.

His conscience quaked with self reproach, and if his sluggish intelligence did not enable him to take in at a glance all the results that his deed might entail, he still could guess that he had sown a seed whence deceit of every kind must grow. He felt as if he had fallen altogether into sin and falsehood, and that the goddess of truth, whom he had all his life honestly served, had reproachfully turned her back on him. After what had happened never could he hope to be pronounced a "truth-speaker" by the judges of the dead. Lost, thrown away, was the aim and end of a long life, rich in self-denial and prayer! His soul shed tears of blood, a wild sighing sounded in his ears, which saddened his spirit, and when he went back to his work again, and wanted to remove the soles of the feet[93] from a body, his hand trembled so that he could not hold the knife.

CHAPTER XXIII.

The news of the end of the sacred ram of Anion, and of the death of the bull Apis of Memphis, had reached the House of Seti, and was received there with loud lamentation, in which all its inhabitants joined, from the chief haruspex down to the smallest boy in the school-courts.

The superior of the institution, Ameni, had been for three days in Thebes, and was expected to return to-day. His arrival was looked for with anxiety and excitement by many. The chief of the haruspices was eager for it that he might hand over the imprisoned scholars to condign punishment, and complain to him of Pentaur and Bent-Anat; the initiated knew that important transactions must have been concluded on the farther side of the Nile; and the rebellious disciples knew that now stern justice would be dealt to them.

The insurrectionary troop were locked into an open court upon bread and water, and as the usual room of detention of the establishment was too small for them all, for two nights they had had to sleep in a loft on thin straw mats. The young spirits were excited to the highest pitch, but each expressed his feelings in quite a different manner.

Bent-Anat's brother, Rameses' son, Rameri, had experienced the same treatment as his fellows, whom yesterday he had led into every sort of mischief, with even more audacity than usual, but to-day he hung his head.

In a corner of the court sat Anana, Pentaur's favorite scholar, hiding his face in his hands which rested on his knees. Rameri went up to him, touched his shoulders and said:

"We have played the game, and now must bear the consequences for good and for evil. Are you not ashamed of yourself, old boy? Your eyes are wet, and the drops here on your hands have not fallen from the clouds. You who are seventeen, and in a few months will be a scribe and a grown man!"

Anana looked at the prince, dried his eyes quickly; and said:

"I was the ring-leader. Ameni will turn me out of the place, and I must return disgraced to my poor mother, who has no one in the world but me."

"Poor fellow!" said Rameri kindly. "It was striking at random! If only our attempt had done Pentaur any good!"

"We have done him harm, on the contrary," said Anana vehemently, "and have behaved like fools!" Rameri nodded in full assent, looked thoughtful for a moment, and then said:

"Do you know, Anana, that you were not the ringleader? The trick was planned in this crazy brain; I take the whole blame on my own shoulders. I am the son of Rameses, and Ameni will be less hard on me than on you."

"He will examine us all," replied Anana, "and I will be punished sooner than tell a lie." Rameri colored.

"Have you ever known my tongue sin against the lovely daughter of Ra?" he exclaimed. "But look here! did I stir up Antef, Hapi, Sent and all the others or no? Who but I advised you to find out Pentaur? Did I threaten to beg my father to take me from the school of Seti or not? I was the instigator of the mischief, I pulled the wires, and if we are questioned let me speak first. Not one of you is to mention Anana's name; do you hear? not one of you, and if they flog us or deprive us of our food we all stick to this, that I was guilty of all the mischief."

"You are a brave fellow!" said the son of the chief priest of Anion, shaking his right hand, while Anana held his left.

The prince freed himself laughing from their grasp.

"Now the old man may come home," he exclaimed, "we are ready for him. But all the same I will ask my father to send me to Chennu, as sure as my name is Rameri, if they do not recall Pentaur."

"He treated us like school-boys!" said the eldest of the young malefactors.

"And with reason," replied Rameri, "I respect him all the more for it. You all think I am a careless dog-but I have my own ideas, and I will speak the words of wisdom."

With these words he looked round on his companions with comical gravity, and continued-imitating Ameni's manner:

"Great men are distinguished from little men by this-they scorn and contemn all which flatters their vanity, or seems to them for the moment desirable, or even useful, if it is not compatible with the laws which they recognize, or conducive to some great end which they have set before them; even though that end may not be reached till after their death.

"I have learned this, partly from my father, but partly I have thought it out for myself; and now I ask you, could Pentaur as 'a great man' have dealt with us better?"

"You have put into words exactly what I myself have thought ever since yesterday," cried Anana. "We have behaved like babies, and instead of carrying our point we have brought ourselves and Pentaur into disgrace."

The rattle of an approaching chariot was now audible, and Rameri exclaimed, interrupting Anana, "It is he. Courage, boys! I am the guilty one. He will not dare to have me thrashed-but he will stab me with looks!"

Ameni descended quickly from his chariot. The gate-keeper informed him that the chief of the kolchytes, and the inspector of victims from the temple of Anion, desired to speak with him.

"They must wait," said the Prophet shortly. "Show them meanwhile into the garden pavilion. Where is the chief haruspex?"

He had hardly spoken when the vigorous old man for whom he was enquiring hurried to meet him, to make him acquainted with all that had occurred in his absence. But the high-priest had already heard in Thebes all that his colleague was anxious to tell him.

When Ameni was absent from the House of Seti, he caused accurate information to be brought to him every morning of what had taken place there.

Now when the old man began his story he interrupted him.

"I know everything," he said. "The disciples cling to Pentaur, and have committed a folly for his sake, and you met the princess Bent-Anat with him in the temple of Hatasu, to which he had admitted a woman of low rank before she had been purified. These are grave matters, and must be seriously considered, but not to-day. Make yourself easy; Pentaur will not escape punishment; but for to-day we must recall him to this temple, for we have need of him to-morrow for the solemnity of the feast of the valley. No one shall meet him as an enemy till he is condemned; I desire this of you, and charge you to repeat it to the others."

The haruspex endeavored to represent to his superior what a scandal would arise from this untimely clemency; but Ameni did not allow him to talk, he demanded his ring back, called a young priest, delivered the precious signet into his charge, and desired him to get into his chariot that was waiting at the door, and carry to Pentaur the command, in his name, to return to the temple of Seti.

The haruspex submitted, though deeply vexed, and asked whether the guilty boys were also to go unpunished.

"No more than Pentaur," answered Ameni. "But can you call this school-boy's trick guilt? Leave the children to their fun, and their imprudence. The educator is the destroyer, if he always and only keeps his eyes open, and cannot close them at the right moment. Before life demands of us the exercise of serious duties we have a mighty over-abundance of vigor at our disposal; the child exhausts it in play, and the boy in building wonder-castles with the hammer and chisel of his fancy, in inventing follies. You shake your head, Septah! but I tell you, the audacious tricks of the boy are the fore-runners of the deeds of the man. I shall let one only of the boys suffer for what is past, and I should let him even go unpunished if I had not other pressing reasons for keeping him away from our festival."

The haruspex did not contradict his chief; for he knew that when Ameni's eyes flashed so suddenly, and his demeanor, usually so measured, was as restless as at present, something serious was brewing.

The high-priest understood what was passing in Septah's mind.

"You do not understand me now," said he. "But this evening, at the meeting of the initiated, you shall know all. Great events are stirring. The brethren in the temple of Anion, on the other shore, have fallen off from what must always be the Holiest to us white-robed priests, and will stand in our way when the time for action is arrived. At the feast of the valley we shall stand in competition with the brethren from Thebes. All Thebes will be present at the solemn service, and it must be proved which knows how to serve the Divinity most worthily, they or we. We must avail ourselves of all our resources, and Pentaur we certainly cannot do without. He must fill the function of Cherheb[94] for to-morrow only; the day after he must be brought to judgment. Among the rebellious boys are our best singers, and particularly young Anana, who leads the voices of the choir-boys.

"I will examine the silly fellows at once. Rameri-Rameses' son-was among the young miscreants?"

"He seems to have been the ring-leader," answered Septah.

Ameni looked at the old man with a significant smile, and said:

"The royal family are covering themselves with honor! His eldest daughter must be kept far from the temple and the gathering of the pious, as being unclean and refractory, and we shall be obliged to expel his son too from our college. You look horrified, but I say to you that the time for action is come. More of this, this evening. Now, one question: Has the news of the death of the ram of Anion reached you? Yes? Rameses himself presented him to the God, and they gave it his name. A bad omen."

"And Apis too is dead!" The haruspex threw up his arms in lamentation.

"His Divine spirit has returned to God," replied Ameni. "Now we have much to do. Before all things we must prove ourselves equal to those in Thebes over there, and win the people over to our side. The panegyric prepared by us for to-morrow must offer some great novelty. The Regent Ani grants us a rich contribution, and —"

"And," interrupted Septah, "our thaumaturgists understand things very differently from those of the house of Anion, who feast while we practise."

Ameni nodded assent, and said with a smile: "Also we are more indispensable than they to the people. They show them the path of life, but we smooth the way of death. It is easier to find the way without a guide in the day-light than in the dark. We are more than a match for the priests of Anion."

"So long as you are our leader, certainly," cried the haruspex.

"And so long as the temple has no lack of men of your temper!" added Ameni, half to Septah, and half to the second prophet of the temple, sturdy old Gagabu, who had come into the room.

Both accompanied him into the garden, where the two priests were awaiting him with the miraculous heart.

Ameni greeted the priest from the temple of Anion with dignified friendliness, the head kolchytes with distant reserve, listened to their story, looked at the heart which lay in the box, with Septah and Gagabu, touched it delicately with the tips of his fingers, carefully examining the object, which diffused a strong perfume of spices; then he said earnestly:

"If this, in your opinion, kolchytes, is not a human heart, and if in yours, my brother of the temple of Anion, it is a ram's heart, and if it was found in the body of Rui, who is gone to Osiris, we here have a mystery which only the Gods can solve. Follow me into the great court. Let the gong be sounded, Gagabu, four times, for I wish to call all the brethren together."

The gong rang in loud waves of sound to the farthest limits of the group of buildings. The initiated, the fathers, the temple-servants, and the scholars streamed in, and in a few minutes were all collected. Not a man was wanting, for at the four strokes of the rarely-sounded alarum every dweller in the House of Seti was expected to appear in the court of the temple. Even the leech Nebsecht came; for he feared that the unusual summons announced the outbreak of a fire.

Ameni ordered the assembly to arrange itself in a procession, informed his astonished hearers that in the breast of the deceased prophet Rui, a ram's heart, instead of a man's, had been found, and desired them all to follow his instructions. Each one, he said, was to fall on his knees and pray, while he would carry the heart into the holiest of holies, and enquire of the Gods what this wonder might portend to the faithful.

Ameni, with the heart in his hand, placed himself at the head of the procession, and disappeared behind the veil of the sanctuary, the initiated prayed in the vestibule, in front of it; the priests and scholars in the vast court, which was closed on the west by the stately colonnade and the main gateway to the temple.

For fully an hour Ameni remained in the silent holy of holies, from which thick clouds of incense rolled out, and then he reappeared with a golden vase set with precious stones. His tall figure was now resplendent with rich ornaments, and a priest, who walked before him, held the vessel high above his head.

Ameni's eyes seemed spell-bound to the vase, and he followed it, supporting himself by his crozier, with humble inflections.

The initiated bowed their heads till they touched the pavement, and the priests and scholars bent their faces down to the earth, when they beheld their haughty master so filled with humility and devotion. The worshippers did not raise themselves till Ameni had reached the middle of the court and ascended the steps of the altar, on which the vase with the heart was now placed, and they listened to the slow and solemn accents of the high-priest which sounded clearly through the whole court.

"Fall down again and worship! wonder, pray, and adore! The noble inspector of sacrifices of the temple of Anion has not been deceived in his judgment; a ram's heart was in fact found in the pious breast of Rui. I heard distinctly the voice of the Divinity in the sanctuary, and strange indeed was the speech that met my ear. Wolves tore the sacred ram of Anion in his sanctuary on the other bank of the river, but the heart of the divine beast found its way into the bosom of the saintly Rui. A great miracle has been worked, and the Gods have shown a wonderful sign. The spirit of the Highest liked not to dwell in the body of this not perfectly holy ram, and seeking a purer abiding-place found it in the breast of our Rui; and now in this consecrated vase. In this the heart shall be preserved till a new ram offered by a worthy hand enters the herd of Anion. This heart shall be preserved with the most sacred relics, it has the property of healing many diseases, and the significant words seem favorable which stood written in the midst of the vapor of incense, and which I will repeat to you word for word, 'That which is high shall rise higher, and that which exalts itself, shall soon fall down.' Rise, pastophori! hasten to fetch the holy images, bring them out, place the sacred heart at the head of the procession, and let us march round the walls of the temple with hymns of praise. Ye temple-servants, seize your staves, and spread in every part of the city the news of the miracle which the Divinity has vouchsafed to us."

After the procession had marched round the temple and dispersed, the priest of Anion took leave of Ameni; he bowed deeply and formally before him, and with a coolness that was almost malicious said:

"We, in the temple of Anion, shall know how to appreciate what you heard in the holy of holies. The miracle has occurred, and the king shall learn how it came to pass, and in what words it was announced."

"In the words of the Most High," said the high priest with dignity; he bowed to the other, and turned to a group of priests, who were discussing the great event of the day.

Ameni enquired of them as to the preparations for the festival of the morrow, and then desired the chief haruspex to call the refractory pupils together in the school-court. The old man informed him that Pentaur had returned, and he followed his superior to the released prisoners, who, prepared for the worst, and expecting severe punishment, nevertheless shook with laughter when Rameri suggested that, if by chance they were condemned to kneel upon peas, they should get them cooked first.

"It will be long asparagus"[95]

Each feared the worst, and when the high-priest stood before them even Rameri's mirth was quite quelled, for though Ameni looked neither angry nor threatening, his appearance commanded respect, and each one recognized in him a judge against whose verdict no remonstrance was to be thought of.

To their infinite astonishment Ameni spoke kindly to the thoughtless boys, praised the motive of their action-their attachment to a highly-endowed teacher-but then clearly and deliberately laid before them the folly of the means they had employed to attain their end, and at what a cost. "Only think," he continued, turning to the prince, "if your father sent a general, who he thought would be better in a different place, from Syria to Kusch, and his troops therefore all went over to the enemy! How would you like that?"

So for some minutes he continued to blame and warn them, and he ended his speech by promising, in consideration of the great miracle that gave that day a special sanctity, to exercise unwonted clemency. For the sake of example, he said, he could not let them pass altogether unpunished, and he now asked them which of them had been the instigator of the deed; he and he only should suffer punishment.

He had hardly clone speaking, when prince Rameri stepped forward, and said modestly:

"We acknowledge, holy father, that we have played a foolish trick; and I lament it doubly because I devised it, and made the others follow me. I love Pentaur, and next to thee there is no one like him in the sanctuary."

Ameni's countenance grew dark, and he answered with displeasure:

"No judgment is allowed to pupils as to their teachers-nor to you. If you were not the son of the king, who rules Egypt as Ra, I would punish your temerity with stripes. My hands are tied with regard to you, and yet they must be everywhere and always at work if the hundreds committed to my care are to be kept from harm."

"Nay, punish me!" cried Rameri. "If I commit a folly I am ready to bear the consequences."

Ameni looked pleased at the vehement boy, and would willingly have shaken him by the hand and stroked his curly head, but the penance he proposed for Rameri was to serve a great end, and Ameni would not allow any overflow of emotion to hinder him in the execution of a well considered design. So he answered the prince with grave determination:

"I must and will punish you-and I do so by requesting you to leave the House of Seti this very day."

The prince turned pale. But Ameni went on more kindly:

"I do not expel you with ignominy from among us —I only bid you a friendly farewell. In a few weeks you would in any case have left the college, and by the king's command have transferred your blooming life, health, and strength to the exercising ground of the chariot-brigade. No punishment for you but this lies in my power. Now give me your hand; you will make a fine man, and perhaps a great warrior."

The prince stood in astonishment before Ameni, and did not take his offered hand. Then the priest went up to him, and said:

"You said you were ready to take the consequences of your folly, and a prince's word must be kept. Before sunset we will conduct you to the gate of the temple."

Ameni turned his back on the boys, and left the school-court.

Rameri looked after him. Utter whiteness had overspread his blooming face, and the blood had left even his lips. None of his companions approached him, for each felt that what was passing in his soul at this moment would brook no careless intrusion. No one spoke a word; they all looked at him.

He soon observed this, and tried to collect himself, and then he said in a low tone while he held out his hands to Anana and another friend:

"Am I then so bad that I must be driven out from among you all like this-that such a blow must be inflicted on my father?"

"You refused Ameni your hand!" answered Anana. "Go to him, offer him your hand, beg him to be less severe, and perhaps he will let you remain."

Rameri answered only "No." But that "No" was so decided that all who knew him understood that it was final.

Before the sun set he had left the school. Ameni gave him his blessing; he told him that if he himself ever had to command he would understand his severity, and allowed the other scholars to accompany him as far as the Nile. Pentaur parted from him tenderly at the gate.

When Rameri was alone in the cabin of his gilt bark with his tutor, he felt his eyes swimming in tears.

"Your highness is surely not weeping?" asked the official.

"Why?" asked the prince sharply.

"I thought I saw tears on your highness' cheeks."

"Tears of joy that I am out of the trap," cried Rameri; he sprang on shore, and in a few minutes he was with his sister in the palace.

CHAPTER XXIV.

This eventful day had brought much that was unexpected to our friends in Thebes, as well as to those who lived in the Necropolis.

The Lady Katuti had risen early after a sleepless night. Nefert had come in late, had excused her delay by shortly explaining to her mother that she had been detained by Bent-Anat, and had then affectionately offered her brow for a kiss of "good-night."

When the widow was about to withdraw to her sleeping-room, and Nemu had lighted her lamp, she remembered the secret which was to deliver Paaker into Ani's hands. She ordered the dwarf to impart to her what he knew, and the little man told her at last, after sincere efforts at resistance-for he feared for his mother's safety-that Paaker had administered half of a love-philter to Nefert, and that the remainder was still in his hands.

A few hours since this information would have filled Katuti with indignation and disgust; now, though she blamed the Mohar, she asked eagerly whether such a drink could be proved to have any actual effect.

"Not a doubt of it," said the dwarf, "if the whole were taken, but Nefert only had half of it."

At a late hour Katuti was still pacing her bedroom, thinking of Paaker's insane devotion, of Mena's faithlessness, and of Nefert's altered demeanor; and when she went to bed, a thousand conjectures, fears, and anxieties tormented her, while she was distressed at the change which had come over Nefert's love to her mother, a sentiment which of all others should be the most sacred, and the most secure against all shock.

Soon after sunrise she went into the little temple attached to the house, and made an offering to the statue, which, under the form of Osiris, represented her lost husband; then she went to the temple of Anion, where she also prayed a while, and nevertheless, on her return home, found that her daughter had not yet made her appearance in the hall where they usually breakfasted together.

Katuti preferred to be undisturbed during the early morning hours, and therefore did not interfere with her daughter's disposition to sleep far into the day in her carefully-darkened room.

When the widow went to the temple Nefert was accustomed to take a cup of milk in bed, then she would let herself be dressed, and when her mother returned, she would find her in the veranda or hall, which is so well known to the reader.

To-day however Katuti had to breakfast alone; but when she had eaten a few mouthfuls she prepared Nefert's breakfast —a white cake and a little wine in a small silver beaker, carefully guarded from dust and insects by a napkin thrown over it-and went into her daughter's room.

She was startled at finding it empty, but she was informed that Nefert had gone earlier than was her wont to the temple, in her litter.

With a heavy sigh she returned to the veranda, and there received her nephew Paaker, who had come to enquire after the health of his relatives, followed by a slave, who carried two magnificent bunches of flowers, and by the great dog which had formerly belonged to his father. One bouquet he said had been cut for Nefert, and the other for her mother.[96]

Katuti had taken quite a new interest in Paaker since she had heard of his procuring the philter.

No other young man of the rank to which they belonged, would have allowed himself to be so mastered by his passion for a woman as this Paaker was, who went straight to his aim with stubborn determination, and shunned no means that might lead to it. The pioneer, who had grown up under her eyes, whose weaknesses she knew, and whom she was accustomed to look down upon, suddenly appeared to her as a different man-almost a stranger-as the deliverer of his friends, and the merciless antagonist of his enemies.

These reflections had passed rapidly through her mind. Now her eyes rested on the sturdy, strongly-knit figure of her nephew, and it struck her that he bore no resemblance to his tall, handsome father. Often had she admired her brother-in-law's slender hand, that nevertheless could so effectually wield a sword, but that of his son was broad and ignoble in form.

While Paaker was telling her that he must shortly leave for Syria, she involuntarily observed the action of this hand, which often went cautiously to his girdle as if he had something concealed there; this was the oval phial with the rest of the philter. Katuti observed it, and her cheeks flushed when it occurred to her to guess what he had there.

The pioneer could not but observe Katuti's agitation, and he said in a tone of sympathy:

"I perceive that you are in pain, or in trouble. The master of Mena's stud at Hermonthis has no doubt been with you-No? He came to me yesterday, and asked me to allow him to join my troops. He is very angry with you, because he has been obliged to sell some of Mena's gold-bays. I have bought the finest of them. They are splendid creatures! Now he wants to go to his master 'to open his eyes,' as he says. Lie down a little while, aunt, you are very pale."

Katuti did not follow this prescription; on the contrary she smiled, and said in a voice half of anger and half of pity:

"The old fool firmly believes that the weal or woe of the family depends on the gold-bays. He would like to go with you? To open Mena's eyes? No one has yet tried to bind them!"

Katuti spoke the last words in a low tone, and her glance fell. Paaker also looked down, and was silent; but he soon recovered his presence of mind, and said:

"If Nefert is to be long absent, I will go."

"No-no, stay," cried the widow. "She wished to see you, and must soon come in. There are her cake and her wine waiting for her."

With these words she took the napkin off the breakfast-table, held up the beaker in her hand, and then said, with the cloth still in her hand:

"I will leave you a moment, and see if Nefert is not yet come home."

Hardly had she left the veranda when Paaker, having convinced himself that no one could see him, snatched the flask from his girdle, and, with a short invocation to his father in Osiris, poured its whole contents into the beaker, which thus was filled to the very brim. A few minutes later Nefert and her mother entered the hall.

Paaker took up the nosegay, which his slave had laid down on a seat, and timidly approached the young woman, who walked in with such an aspect of decision and self-confidence, that her mother looked at her in astonishment, while Paaker felt as if she had never before appeared so beautiful and brilliant. Was it possible that she should love her husband, when his breach of faith troubled her so little? Did her heart still belong to another? Or had the love-philter set him in the place of Mena? Yes! yes! for how warmly she greeted him. She put out her hand to him while he was still quite far off, let it rest in his, thanked him with feeling, and praised his fidelity and generosity.

Then she went up to the table, begged Paaker to sit down with her, broke her cake, and enquired for her aunt Setchern, Paaker's mother.

Katuti and Paaker watched all her movements with beating hearts.

Now she took up the beaker, and lifted it to her lips, but set it down again to answer Paaker's remark that she was breakfasting late.

"I have hitherto been a real lazy-bones," she said with a blush. "But this morning I got up early, to go and pray in the temple in the fresh dawn. You know what has happened to the sacred ram of Amion. It is a frightful occurrence. The priests were all in the greatest agitation, but the venerable Bek el Chunsu received me himself, and interpreted my dream, and now my spirit is light and contented."

"And you did all this without me?" said Katuti in gentle reproof.

"I would not disturb you," replied Nefert. "Besides," she added coloring, "you never take me to the city and the temple in the morning."

Again she took up the wine-cup and looked into it, but without drinking any, went on:

"Would you like to hear what I dreamed, Paaker? It was a strange vision."

The pioneer could hardly breathe for expectation, still he begged her to tell her dream.

"Only think," said Nefert, pushing the beaker on the smooth table, which was wet with a few drops which she had spilt, "I dreamed of the Neha-tree, down there in the great tub, which your father brought me from Punt, when I was a little child, and which since then has grown quite a tall tree. There is no tree in the garden I love so much, for it always reminds me of your father, who was so kind to me, and whom I can never forget!"

Paaker bowed assent.

Nefert looked at him, and interrupted her story when she observed his crimson cheeks.

"It is very hot! Would you like some wine to drink-or some water?"

With these words she raised the wine-cup, and drank about half of the contents; then she shuddered, and while her pretty face took a comical expression, she turned to her mother, who was seated behind her and held the beaker towards her.

"The wine is quite sour to-day!" she said. "Taste it, mother."

Katuti took the little silver-cup in her hand, and gravely put it to her lips, but without wetting them. A smile passed over her face, and her eyes met those of the pioneer, who stared at her in horror. The picture flashed before her mind of herself languishing for the pioneer, and of his terror at her affection for him! Her selfish and intriguing spirit was free from coarseness, and yet she could have laughed with all her heart even while engaged in the most shameful deed of her whole life. She gave the wine back to her daughter, saying good-humoredly:

"I have tasted sweeter, but acid is refreshing in this heat."

"That is true," said the wife of Mena; she emptied the cup to the bottom, and then went on, as if refreshed, "But I will tell you the rest of my dream. I saw the Neha-tree, which your father gave me, quite plainly; nay I could have declared that I smelt its perfume, but the interpreter assured me that we never smell in our dreams. I went up to the beautiful tree in admiration. Then suddenly a hundred axes appeared in the air, wielded by unseen hands, and struck the poor tree with such violence that the branches one by one fell to the ground, and at last the trunk itself was felled. If you think it grieved me you are mistaken. On the contrary, I was delighted with the flashing hatchets and the flying splinters. When at last nothing was left but the roots in the tub of earth, I perceived that the tree was rising to new life. Suddenly my arms became strong, my feet active, and I fetched quantities of water from the tank, poured it over the roots, and when, at last, I could exert myself no longer, a tender green shoot showed itself on the wounded root, a bud appeared, a green leaf unfolded itself, a juicy stem sprouted quickly, it became a firm trunk, sent out branches and twigs, and these became covered with leaves and flowers, white, red and blue; then various birds came and settled on the top of the tree, and sang. Ah! my heart sang louder than the birds at that moment, and I said to myself that without me the tree would have been dead, and that it owed its life to me."

"A beautiful dream," said Katuti; "that reminds me of your girlhood, when you would be awake half the night inventing all sorts of tales. What interpretation did the priest give you?"

"He promised me many things," said Nefert, "and he gave me the assurance that the happiness to which I am predestined shall revive in fresh beauty after many interruptions."

"And Paaker's father gave you the Neha-tree?" asked Katuti, leaving the veranda as she spoke and walking out into the garden.

"My father brought it to Thebes from the far cast," said Paaker, in confirmation of the widow's parting words.

"And that is exactly what makes me so happy," said Nefert. "For your father was as kind, and as dear to me as if he had been my own. Do you remember when we were sailing round the pond, and the boat upset, and you pulled me senseless out of the water? Never shall I forget the expression with which the great man looked at me when I woke up in its arms; such wise true eyes no one ever had but he."

"He was good, and he loved you very much," said Paaker, recalling, for his part, the moment when he had dared to press a kiss on the lips of the sweet unconscious child.

"And I am so glad," Nefert went on, "that the day has come at last when we can talk of him together again, and when the old grudge that lay so heavy in my heart is all forgotten. How good you are to us, I have already learned; my heart overflows with gratitude to you, when I remember my childhood, and I can never forget that I was indebted to you for all that was bright and happy in it. Only look at the big dog-poor Descher! —how he rubs against me, and shows that he has not forgotten me! Whatever comes from your house fills my mind with pleasant memories."

"We all love you dearly," said Paaker looking at her tenderly.

"And how sweet it was in your garden!" cried Nefert. "The nosegay here that you have brought me shall be placed in water, and preserved a long time, as greeting from the place in which once I could play carelessly, and dream so happily."

With these words she pressed the flowers to her lips; Paaker sprang forward, seized her hand, and covered it with burning kisses.

Nefert started and drew away her hand, but he put out his arm to clasp her to him. He had touched her with his trembling hand, when loud voices were heard in the garden, and Nemu hurried in to announce he arrival of the princess Bent-Anat.

At the same moment Katuti appeared, and in a few minutes the princess herself.

Paaker retreated, and quitted the room before Nefert had time to express her indignation. He staggered to his chariot like a drunken man. He supposed himself beloved by Mena's wife, his heart was full of triumph, he proposed rewarding Hekt with gold, and went to the palace without delay to crave of Ani a mission to Syria. There it should be brought to the test-he or Mena.

CHAPTER XXV.

While Nefert, frozen with horror, could not find a word of greeting for her royal friend, Bent-Anat with native dignity laid before the widow her choice of Nefert to fill the place of her lost companion, and desired that Mena's wife should go to the palace that very day.

She had never before spoken thus to Katuti, and Katuti could not overlook the fact that Bent-Anat had intentionally given up her old confidential tone.

"Nefert has complained of me to her," thought she to herself, "and she considers me no longer worthy of her former friendly kindness."

She was vexed and hurt, and though she understood the danger which threatened her, now her daughter's eyes were opened, still the thought of losing her child inflicted a painful wound. It was this which filled her eyes with tears, and sincere sorrow trembled in her voice as she replied:

"Thou hast required the better half of my life at my hand; but thou hast but to command, and I to obey." Bent-Anat waved her hand proudly, as if to confirm the widow's statement; but Nefert went up to her mother, threw her arms round her neck, and wept upon her shoulder.

Tears glistened even in the princess's eyes when Katuti at last led her daughter towards her, and pressed yet one more kiss on her forehead.

Bent-Anat took Nefert's hand, and did not release it, while she requested the widow to give her daughter's dresses and ornaments into the charge of the slaves and waiting-women whom she would send for them.

"And do not forget the case with the dried flowers, and my amulets, and the images of the Gods," said Nefert. "And I should like to have the Neha tree which my uncle gave me."

Her white cat was playing at her feet with Paaker's flowers, which she had dropped on the floor, and when she saw her she took her up and kissed her.

"Bring the little creature with you," said Bent-Anat. "It was your favorite plaything."

"No," replied Nefert coloring.

The princess understood her, pressed her hand, and said while she pointed to Nemu:

"The dwarf is your own too: shall he come with you?"

"I will give him to my mother," said Nefert. She let the little man kiss her robe and her feet, once more embraced Katuti, and quitted the garden with her royal friend.

As soon as Katuti was alone, she hastened into the little chapel in which the figures of her ancestors stood, apart from those of Mena. She threw herself down before the statue of her husband, half weeping, half thankful.

This parting had indeed fallen heavily on her soul, but at the same time it released her from a mountain of anxiety that had oppressed her breast. Since yesterday she had felt like one who walks along the edge of a precipice, and whose enemy is close at his heels; and the sense of freedom from the ever threatening danger, soon got the upperhand of her maternal grief. The abyss in front of her had suddenly closed; the road to the goal of her efforts lay before her smooth and firm beneath her feet.

The widow, usually so dignified, hastily and eagerly walked down the garden path, and for the first time since that luckless letter from the camp had reached her, she could look calmly and clearly at the position of affairs, and reflect on the measures which Ani must take in the immediate future. She told herself that all was well, and that the time for prompt and rapid action was now come.

When the messengers came from the princess she superintended the packing of the various objects which Nefert wished to have, with calm deliberation, and then sent her dwarf to Ani, to beg that he would visit her. But before Nemu had left Mena's grounds he saw the out-runners of the Regent, his chariot, and the troop of guards following him.

Very soon Katuti and her noble friend were walking up and down in the garden, while she related to him how Bent-Anat had taken Nefert from her, and repeated to him all that she had planned and considered during the last hour.

"You have the genius of a man," said Ani; "and this time you do not urge me in vain. Ameni is ready to act, Paaker is to-day collecting his troops, to-morrow he will assist at the feast of the Valley, and the next day he goes to Syria."

"He has been with you?" Katuti asked.

"He came to the palace on leaving your house," replied Ani, "with glowing cheeks, and resolved to the utmost; though he does not dream that I hold him in my hand."

Thus speaking they entered the veranda, in which Nemu had remained, and he now hid himself as usual behind the ornamental shrubs to overhear them. They sat down near each other, by Nefert's breakfast table, and Ani asked Katuti whether the dwarf had told her his mother's secret. Katuti feigned ignorance, listened to the story of the love-philter, and played the part of the alarmed mother very cleverly. The Regent was of opinion, while he tried to soothe her, that there was no real love-potion in the case; but the widow exclaimed:

"Now I understand, now for the first time I comprehend my daughter. Paaker must have poured the drink into her wine, for she had no sooner drunk it this morning than she was quite altered her words to Paaker had quite a tender ring in them; and if he placed himself so cheerfully at your disposal it is because he believes himself certainly to be beloved by my daughter. The old witch's potion was effectual."

"There certainly are such drinks —" said Ani thoughtfully. "But will they only win hearts to young men! If that is the case, the old woman's trade is a bad one, for youth is in itself a charm to attract love. If I were only as young as Paaker! You laugh at the sighs of a man-say at once of an old man! Well, yes, I am old, for the prime of life lies behind me. And yet Katuti, my friend, wisest of women-explain to me one thing. When I was young I was loved by many and admired many women, but not one of them-not even my wife, who died young, was more to me than a toy, a plaything; and now when I stretch out my hand for a girl, whose father I might very well be-not for her own sake, but simply to serve my purpose-and she refuses me, I feel as much disturbed, as much a fool as-as that dealer in love-philters, Paaker."

"Have you spoken to Bent-Anat?" asked Katuti.

"And heard again from her own lips the refusal she had sent me through you. You see my spirit has suffered!"

"And on what pretext did she reject your suit?" asked the widow.

"Pretext!" cried Ani. "Bent-Anat and pretext! It must be owned that she has kingly pride, and not Ma —[The Goddess of Truth] —herself is more truthful than she. That I should have to confess it! When I think of her, our plots seem to me unutterably pitiful. My veins contain, indeed, many drops of the blood of Thotmes, and though the experience of life has taught me to stoop low, still the stooping hurts me. I have never known the happy feeling of satisfaction with my lot and my work; for I have always had a greater position than I could fill, and constantly done less than I ought to have done. In order not to look always resentful, I always wear a smile. I have nothing left of the face I was born with but the mere skin, and always wear a mask. I serve him whose master I believe I ought to be by birth; I hate Rameses, who, sincerely or no, calls me his brother; and while I stand as if I were the bulwark of his authority I am diligently undermining it. My whole existence is a lie."

"But it will be truth," cried Katuti, "as soon as the Gods allow you to be-as you are-the real king of this country."

"Strange!" said Ani smiling, Ameni, "this very day, used almost exactly the same words. The wisdom of priests, and that of women, have much in common, and they fight with the same weapons. You use words instead of swords, traps instead of lances, and you cast not our bodies, but our souls, into irons."

"Do you blame or praise us for it?" said the widow. "We are in any case not impotent allies, and therefore, it seems to me, desirable ones."

"Indeed you are," said Ani smiling. "Not a tear is shed in the land, whether it is shed for joy or for sorrow, for which in the first instance a priest or a woman is not responsible. Seriously, Katuti-in nine great events out of ten you women have a hand in the game. You gave the first impulse to all that is plotting here, and I will confess to you that, regardless of all consequences, I should in a few hours have given up my pretensions to the throne, if that woman Bent-Anat had said 'yes' instead of 'no.'"

"You make me believe," said Katuti, "that the weaker sex are gifted with stronger wills than the nobler. In marrying us you style us, 'the mistress of the house,' and if the elders of the citizens grow infirm, in this country it is not the sons but the daughters that must be their mainstay. But we women have our weaknesses, and chief of these is curiosity. —May I ask on what ground Bent-Anat dismissed you?"

"You know so much that you may know all," replied Ani. "She admitted me to speak to her alone. It was yet early, and she had come from the temple, where the weak old prophet had absolved her from uncleanness; she met me, bright, beautiful and proud, strong and radiant as a Goddess, and a princess. My heart throbbed as if I were a boy, and while she was showing me her flowers I said to myself: 'You are come to obtain through her another claim to the throne.' And yet I felt that, if she consented to be mine, I would remain the true brother, the faithful Regent of Rameses, and enjoy happiness and peace by her side before it was too late. If she refused me then I resolved that fate must take its way, and, instead of peace and love, it must be war for the crown snatched from my fathers. I tried to woo her, but she cut my words short, said I was a noble man, and a worthy suitor but —"

"There came the but."

"Yes-in the form of a very frank 'no.' I asked her reasons. She begged me to be content with the 'no;' then I pressed her harder, till she interrupted me, and owned with proud decision that she preferred some one else. I wished to learn the name of the happy man-that she refused. Then my blood began to boil, and my desire to win her increased; but I had to leave her, rejected, and with a fresh, burning, poisoned wound in my heart."

"You are jealous!" said Katuti, "and do you know of whom?"

"No," replied Ani. "But I hope to find out through you. What I feel it is impossible for me to express. But one thing I know, and that is this, that I entered the palace a vacillating man-that I left it firmly resolved. I now rush straight onwards, never again to turn back. From this time forward you will no longer have to drive me onward, but rather to hold me back; and, as if the Gods had meant to show that they would stand by me, I found the high-priest Ameni, and the chief pioneer Paaker waiting for me in my house. Ameni will act for me in Egypt, Paaker in Syria. My victorious troops from Ethiopia will enter Thebes to-morrow morning, on their return home in triumph, as if the king were at their head, and will then take part in the Feast of the Valley. Later we will send them into the north, and post them in the fortresses which protect Egypt against enemies coming from the east Tanis, Daphne, Pelusium, Migdol. Rameses, as you know, requires that we should drill the serfs of the temples, and send them to him as auxiliaries. I will send him half of the body-guard, the other half shall serve my own purposes. The garrison of Memphis, which is devoted to Rameses, shall be sent to Nubia, and shall be relieved by troops that are faithful to me. The people of Thebes are led by the priests, and tomorrow Ameni will point out to them who is their legitimate king, who will put an end to the war and release them from taxes. The children of Rameses will be excluded from the solemnities, for Ameni, in spite of the chief-priest of Anion, still pronounces Bent-Anat unclean. Young Rameri has been doing wrong and Ameni, who has some other great scheme in his mind, has forbidden him the temple of Seti; that will work on the crowd! You know how things are going on in Syria: Rameses has suffered much at the hands of the Cheta and their allies; whole legions are weary of eternally lying in the field, and if things came to extremities would join us; but, perhaps, especially if Paaker acquits himself well, we may be victorious without fighting. Above all things now we must act rapidly."

"I no longer recognize the timid, cautious lover of delay!" exclaimed Katuti.

"Because now prudent hesitation would be want of prudence," said Ani.

"And if the king should get timely information as to what is happening here?" said Katuti.

"I said so!" exclaimed Ani; "we are exchanging parts."

"You are mistaken," said Katuti. "I also am for pressing forwards; but I would remind you of a necessary precaution. No letters but yours must reach the camp for the next few weeks."

"Once more you and the priests are of one mind," said Ani laughing; "for Ameni gave me the same counsel. Whatever letters are sent across the frontier between Pelusium and the Red Sea will be detained. Only my letters-in which I complain of the piratical sons of the desert who fall upon the messengers-will reach the king."

"That is wise," said the widow; "let the seaports of the Red Sea be watched too, and the public writers. When you are king, you can distinguish those who are affected for or against you."

Ani shook his head and replied:

"That would put me in a difficult position; for it I were to punish those who are now faithful to their king, and exalt the others, I should have to govern with unfaithful servants, and turn away the faithful ones. You need not color, my kind friend, for we are kin, and my concerns are yours."

Katuti took the hand he offered her and said:

"It is so. And I ask no further reward than to see my father's house once more in the enjoyment of its rights."

"Perhaps we shall achieve it," said Ani; "but in a short time if-if-Reflect, Katuti; try to find out, ask your daughter to help you to the utmost. Who is it that she-you know whom I mean-Who is it that Bent-Anat loves?"

The widow started, for Ani had spoken the last words with a vehemence very foreign to his usual courtliness, but soon she smiled and repeated to the Regent the names of the few young nobles who had not followed the king, and remained in Thebes. "Can it be Chamus?" at last she said, "he is at the camp, it is true, but nevertheless —"

At this instant Nemu, who had not lost a word of the conversation, came in as if straight from the garden and said:

"Pardon me, my lady; but I have heard a strange thing."

"Speak," said Katuti.

"The high and mighty princess Bent-Anat, the daughter of Rameses, is said to have an open love-affair with a young priest of the House of Seti."

"You barefaced scoundrel!" exclaimed Ani, and his eyes sparkled with rage. "Prove what you say, or you lose your tongue."

"I am willing to lose it as a slanderer and traitor according to the law," said the little man abjectly, and yet with a malicious laugh; "but this time I shall keep it, for I can vouch for what I say. You both know that Bent-Anat was pronounced unclean because she stayed for an hour and more in the house of a paraschites. She had an assignation there with the priest. At a second, in the temple of Hatasu, they were surprised by Septah, the chief of the haruspices of the House of Seti."

"Who is the priest?" asked Ani with apparent calmness.

"A low-born man," replied Nemu, "to whom a free education was given at the House of Seti, and who is well known as a verse-maker and interpreter of dreams. His name is Pentaur, and it certainly must be admitted that he is handsome and dignified. He is line for line the image of the pioneer Paaker's late father. Didst thou ever see him, my lord?"

The Regent looked gloomily at the floor and nodded that he had. But Katuti cried out; "Fool that I am! the dwarf is right! I saw how she blushed when her brother told her how the boys had rebelled on his account against Ameni. It is Pentaur and none other!"

"Good!" said Ani, "we will see."

With these words he took leave of Katuti, who, as he disappeared in the garden, muttered to herself: "He was wonderfully clear and decided to-day; but jealousy is already blinding him and will soon make him feel that he cannot get on without my sharp eyes."

Nemu had slipped out after the Regent.

He called to him from behind a fig-tree, and hastily whispered, while he bowed with deep respect:

"My mother knows a great deal, most noble highness! The sacred Ibis[97] wades through the fen when it goes in search of prey, and why shouldst thou not stoop to pick up gold out of the dust? I know how thou couldst speak with the old woman without being seen."

"Speak," said Ani.

"Throw her into prison for a day, hear what she has to say, and then release her-with gifts if she is of service to you-if not, with blows. But thou wilt learn something important from her that she obstinately refused to tell me even."

"We will see!" replied the Regent. He threw a ring of gold to the dwarf and got into his chariot.

So large a crowd had collected in the vicinity of the palace, that Ani apprehended mischief, and ordered his charioteer to check the pace of the horses, and sent a few police-soldiers to the support of the out-runners; but good news seemed to await him, for at the gate of the castle he heard the unmistakable acclamations of the crowd, and in the palace court he found a messenger from the temple of Seti, commissioned by Ameni to communicate to him and to the people, the occurrence of a great miracle, in that the heart of the ram of Anion, that had been torn by wolves, had been found again within the breast of the dead prophet Rui.

Ani at once descended from his chariot, knelt down before all the people, who followed his example, lifted his arms to heaven, and praised the Gods in a loud voice. When, after some minutes, he rose and entered the palace, slaves came out and distributed bread to the crowd in Ameni's name.

"The Regent has an open hand," said a joiner to his neighbor; "only look how white the bread is. I will put it in my pocket and take it to the children."

"Give me a bit!" cried a naked little scamp, snatching the cake of bread from the joiner's hand and running away, slipping between the legs of the people as lithe as a snake.

"You crocodile's brat!" cried his victim. "The insolence of boys gets worse and worse every day."

"They are hungry," said the woman apologetically. "Their fathers are gone to the war, and the mothers have nothing for their children but papyrus-pith and lotus-seeds."

"I hope they enjoy it," laughed the joiner. "Let us push to the left; there is a man with some more bread."

"The Regent must rejoice greatly over the miracle," said a shoemaker. "It is costing him something."

"Nothing like it has happened for a long time," said a basket-maker. "And he is particularly glad it should be precisely Rui's body, which the sacred heart should have blessed. You ask why? —Hatasu is Ani's ancestress, blockhead!"

"And Rui was prophet of the temple of Hatasu," added the joiner.

"The priests over there are all hangers-on of the old royal house, that I know," asserted a baker.

"That's no secret!" cried the cobbler. "The old times were better than these too. The war upsets everything, and quite respectable people go barefoot because they cannot pay for shoe-leather. Rameses is a great warrior, and the son of Ra, but what can he do without the Gods; and they don't seem to like to stay in Thebes any longer; else why should the heart of the sacred ram seek a new dwelling in the Necropolis, and in the breast of an adherent of the old —"

"Hold your tongue," warned the basket-maker. "Here comes one of the watch."

"I must go back to work," said the baker. "I have my hands quite full for the feast to-morrow."

"And I too," said the shoemaker with a sigh, "for who would follow the king of the Gods through the Necropolis barefoot."

"You must earn a good deal," cried the basket-maker. "We should do better if we had better workmen," replied the shoemaker, "but all the good hands are gone to the war. One has to put up with stupid youngsters. And as for the women! My wife must needs have a new gown for the procession, and bought necklets for the children. Of course we must honor the dead, and they repay it often by standing by us when we want it-but what I pay for sacrifices no one can tell. More than half of what I earn goes in them —"

"In the first grief of losing my poor wife," said the baker, "I promised a small offering every new moon, and a greater one every year. The priests will not release us from our vows, and times get harder and harder. And my dead wife owes me a grudge, and is as thankless as she was is her lifetime; for when she appears to me in a dream she does not give me a good word, and often torments me."

"She is now a glorified all-seeing spirit," said the basket-maker's wife, "and no doubt you were faithless to her. The glorified souls know all that happens, and that has happened on earth."

The baker cleared his throat, having no answer ready; but the shoemaker exclaimed:

"By Anubis, the lord of the under-world, I hope I may die before my old woman! for if she finds out down there all I have done in this world, and if she may be changed into any shape she pleases, she will come to me every night, and nip me like a crab, and sit on me like a mountain."

"And if you die first," said the woman, "she will follow you afterwards to the under-world, and see through you there."

"That will be less dangerous," said the shoemaker laughing, "for then I shall be glorified too, and shall know all about her past life. That will not all be white paper either, and if she throws a shoe at me I will fling the last at her."

"Come home," said the basket-maker's wife, pulling her husband away. "You are getting no good by hearing this talk."

The bystanders laughed, and the baker exclaimed:

"It is high time I should be in the Necropolis before it gets dark, and see to the tables being laid for to-morrow's festival. My trucks are close to the narrow entrance to the valley. Send your little ones to me, and I will give them something nice. Are you coming over with me?"

"My younger brother is gone over with the goods," replied the shoemaker. "We have plenty to do still for the customers in Thebes, and here am I standing gossiping. Will the wonderful heart of the sacred ram be exhibited to-morrow do you know?"

"Of course-no doubt," said the baker, "good-bye, there go my cases!"

CHAPTER XXVI.

Notwithstanding the advanced hour, hundreds of people were crossing over to the Necropolis at the same time as the baker. They were permitted to linger late on into the evening, under the inspection of the watch, because it was the eve of the great feast, and they had to set out their counters and awnings, to pitch their tents, and to spread out their wares; for as soon as the sun rose next day all business traffic would be stopped, none but festal barges might cross from Thebes, or such boats as ferried over pilgrims-men, women, and children whether natives or foreigners, who were to take part in the great procession.

In the halls and work-rooms of the House of Seti there was unusual stir. The great miracle of the wonderful heart had left but a short time for the preparations for the festival. Here a chorus was being practised, there on the sacred lake a scenic representation was being rehearsed; here the statues of the Gods were being cleaned and dressed,[98] and the colors of the sacred emblems were being revived, there the panther-skins and other parts of the ceremonial vestments of the priests were being aired and set out; here sceptres, censers and other metal-vessels were being cleaned, and there the sacred bark which was to be carried in the procession was being decorated. In the sacred groves of the temple the school-boys, under the direction of the gardeners, wove garlands and wreaths to decorate the landing-places, the sphinxes, the temple, and the statues of the Gods. Flags were hoisted on the brass-tipped masts in front of the pylon, and purple sails were spread to give shadow to the court.

The inspector of sacrifices was already receiving at a side-door the cattle, corn and fruit, offerings which were brought as tribute to the House of Seti, by citizens from all parts of the country, on the occasion of the festival of the Valley, and he was assisted by scribes, who kept an account of all that was brought in by the able-bodied temple-servants and laboring serfs.

Ameni was everywhere: now with the singers, now with the magicians, who were to effect wonderful transformations before the astonished multitude; now with the workmen, who were erecting thrones for the Regent, the emissaries from other collegiate foundations-even from so far as the Delta-and the prophets from Thebes; now with the priests, who were preparing the incense, now with the servants, who were trimming the thousand lamps for the illumination at night-in short everywhere; here inciting, there praising. When he had convinced himself that all was going on well he desired one of the priests to call Pentaur.

After the departure of the exiled prince Rameri, the young priest had gone to the work-room of his friend Nebsecht.

The leech went uneasily from his phials to his cages, and from his cages back to his flasks. While he told Pentaur of the state he had found his room in on his return home, he wandered about in feverish excitement, unable to keep still, now kicking over a bundle of plants, now thumping down his fist on the table; his favorite birds were starved to death, his snakes had escaped, and his ape had followed their example, apparently in his fear of them.

"The brute, the monster!" cried Nebsecht in a rage. "He has thrown over the jars with the beetles in them, opened the chest of meal that I feed the birds and insects upon, and rolled about in it; he has thrown my knives, prickers, and forceps, my pins, compasses, and reed pens all out of window; and when I came in he was sitting on the cupboard up there, looking just like a black slave that works night and day in a corn-mill; he had got hold of the roll which contained all my observations on the structure of animals-the result of years of study-and was looking at it gravely with his head on one side. I wanted to take the book from him, but he fled with the roll, sprang out of window, let himself down to the edge of the well, and tore and rubbed the manuscript to pieces in a rage. I leaped out after him, but he jumped into the bucket, took hold of the chain, and let himself down, grinning at me in mockery, and when I drew him up again he jumped into the water with the remains of the book."

"And the poor wretch is drowned?" asked Pentaur.

"I fished him up with the bucket, and laid him to dry in the sun; but he had been tasting all sorts of medicines, and he died at noon. My observations are gone! Some of them certainly are still left; however, I must begin again at the beginning. You see apes object as much to my labors as sages; there lies the beast on the shelf."

Pentaur had laughed at his friend's story, and then lamented his loss; but now he said anxiously:

"He is lying there on the shelf? But you forget that he ought to have been kept in the little oratory of Toth near the library. He belongs to the sacred dogfaced apes,[99] and all the sacred marks were found upon him. The librarian gave him into your charge to have his bad eye cured."

"That was quite well," answered Nebsecht carelessly.

"But they will require the uninjured corpse of you, to embalm it," said Pentaur.

"Will they?" muttered Nebsecht; and he looked at his friend like a boy who is asked for an apple that has long been eaten.

"And you have already been doing something with it," said Pentaur, in a tone of friendly vexation.

The leech nodded. "I have opened him, and examined his heart.'

"You are as much set on hearts as a coquette!" said Pentaur. "What is become of the human heart that the old paraschites was to get for you?"

Nebsecht related without reserve what the old man had done for him, and said that he had investigated the human heart, and had found nothing in it different from what he had discovered in the heart of beasts.

"But I must see it in connection with the other organs of the human body," cried he; "and my decision is made. I shall leave the House of Seti, and ask the kolchytes to take me into their guild. If it is necessary I will first perform the duties of the lowest paraschites."

Pentaur pointed out to the leech what a bad exchange he would be making, and at last exclaimed, when Nebsecht eagerly contradicted him, "This dissecting of the heart does not please me. You say yourself that you learned nothing by it. Do you still think it a right thing, a fine thing—or even useful?"

"I do not trouble myself about it," replied Nebsecht. "Whether my observations seem good or evil, right or heinous, useful or useless, I want to know how things are, nothing more."

"And so for mere curiosity," cried Pentaur, "you would endanger the blissful future of thousands of your fellow-men, take upon yourself the most abject duties, and leave this noble scene of your labors, where we all strive for enlightenment, for inward knowledge and truth."

The naturalist laughed scornfully; the veins swelled angrily in Pentaur's forehead, and his voice took a threatening tone as he asked:

"And do you believe that your finger and your eyes have lighted on the truth, when the noblest souls have striven in vain for thousands of years to find it out? You descend beneath the level of human understanding by madly wallowing in the mire; and the more clearly you are convinced that you have seized the truth, the more utterly you are involved in the toils of a miserable delusion."

"If I believed I knew the truth should I so eagerly seek it?" asked Nebsecht. "The more I observe and learn, the more deeply I feel my want of knowledge and power."

"That sounds modest enough," said the poet, "but I know the arrogance to which your labors are leading you. Everything that you see with your own eyes and touch with your own hand, you think infallible, and everything that escapes your observation you secretly regard as untrue, and pass by with a smile of superiority. But you cannot carry your experiments beyond the external world, and you forget that there are things which lie in a different realm."

"I know nothing of those things," answered Nebsecht quietly.

"But we—the Initiated," cried Pentaur, "turn our attention to them also. Thoughts—traditions—as to their conditions and agency have existed among us for a thousand years; hundreds of generations of men have examined these traditions, have approved them, and have handed them down to us. All our knowledge, it is true, is defective, and yet prophets have been favored with the gift of looking into the future, magic powers have been vouchsafed to mortals. All this is contrary to the laws of the external world, which are all that you recognize, and yet it can easily be explained if we accept the idea of a higher order of things. The spirit of the Divinity dwells in each of us, as in nature. The natural man can only attain to such knowledge as is common to all; but it is the divine capacity for serene discernment-which is omniscience-that works in the seer; it is the divine and unlimited power-which is omnipotence-that from time to time enables the magician to produce supernatural effects!"

"Away with prophets and marvels!" cried Nebsecht.

"I should have thought," said Pentaur, "that even the laws of nature which you recognize presented the greatest marvels daily to your eyes; nay the Supreme One does not disdain sometimes to break through the common order of things, in order to reveal to that portion of Himself which we call our soul, the sublime Whole of which we form part-Himself. Only today you have seen how the heart of the sacred ram —"

"Man, man!" Nebsecht interrupted, "the sacred heart is the heart of a hapless sheep that a sot of a soldier sold for a trifle to a haggling grazier, and that was slaughtered in a common herd. A proscribed paraschites put it into the body of Rui, and-and —" he opened the cupboard, threw the carcase of the ape and some clothes on to the floor, and took out an alabaster bowl which he held before the poet —"the muscles you see here in brine, this machine, once beat in the breast of the prophet Rui. My sheep's heart wilt be carried to-morrow in the procession! I would have told you all about it if I had not promised the old man to hold my tongue, and then-But what ails you, man?" Pentaur had turned away from his friend, and covered his face with his hands, and he groaned as if he were suffering some frightful physical pain. Nebsecht divined what was passing in the mind of his friend. Like a child that has to ask forgiveness of its mother for some misdeed, he went close up to Pentaur, but stood trembling behind him not daring to speak to him.

Several minutes passed. Suddenly Pentaur raised his head, lifted his hands to heaven, and cried:

"O Thou! the One! —though stars may fall from the heavens in summer nights, still Thy eternal and immutable laws guide the never-resting planets in their paths. Thou pure and all-prevading Spirit, that dwellest in me, as I know by my horror of a lie, manifest Thyself in me-as light when I think, as mercy when I act, and when I speak, as truth-always as truth!"

The poet spoke these words with absorbed fervor, and Nebsecht heard them as if they were speech from some distant and beautiful world. He went affectionately up to his friend, and eagerly held out his hand. Pentaur grasped it, pressed it warmly, and said:

"That was a fearful moment! You do not know what Ameni has been to me, and now, now!"

He hardly had ceased speaking when steps were heard approaching the physician's room, and a young priest requested the friends to appear at once in the meeting-room of the Initiated. In a few moments they both entered the great hall, which was brilliantly lighted.

Not one of the chiefs of the House of Seti was absent.

Ameni sat on a raised seat at a long table; on his right hand was old Gagabu, on his left the third Prophet of the temple. The principals of the different orders of priests had also found places at the table, and among them the chief of the haruspices, while the rest of the priests, all in snow-white linen robes, sat, with much dignity, in a large semicircle, two rows deep. In the midst stood a statue of the Goddess of truth and justice.

Behind Ameni's throne was the many-colored image of the ibis-headed Toth, who presided over the measure and method of things, who counselled the Gods as well as men, and presided over learning and the arts. In a niche at the farther end of the hall were painted the divine Triad of Thebes, with Rameses I. and his son Seti, who approached them with offerings. The priests were placed with strict regard to their rank, and the order of initiation. Pentaur's was the lowest place of all.

No discussion of any importance had as yet taken place, for Ameni was making enquiries, receiving information, and giving orders with reference to the next day's festival. All seemed to be well arranged, and promised a magnificent solemnity; although the scribes complained of the scarce influx of beasts from the peasants, who were so heavily taxed for the war, and although that feature would be wanting in the procession which was wont to give it the greatest splendor-the presence of the king and the royal family.

This circumstance aroused the disapprobation of some of the priests, who were of opinion that it would be hazardous to exclude the two children of Rameses, who remained in Thebes, from any share in the solemnities of the feast.

Ameni then rose.

"We have sent the boy Rameri," he said, "away from this house. Bent-Anat must be purged of her uncleanness, and if the weak superior of the temple of Anion absolves her, she may pass for purified over there, where they live for this world only, but not here, where it is our duty to prepare the soul for death. The Regent, a descendant of the great deposed race of kings, will appear in the procession with all the splendor of his rank. I see you are surprised, my friends. Only he! Aye! Great things are stirring, and it may happen that soon the mild sun of peace may rise upon our war-ridden people."

"Miracles are happening," he continued, "and in a dream I saw a gentle and pious man on the throne of the earthly vicar of Ra. He listened to our counsel, he gave us our due, and led back to our fields our serfs that had been sent to the war; he overthrew the altars of the strange gods, and drove the unclean stranger out from this holy land."

"The Regent Ani!" exclaimed Septah.

An eager movement stirred the assembly, but Ameni went on:

"Perhaps it was not unlike him, but he certainly was the One; he had the features of the true and legitimate descendants of Ra, to whom Rui was faithful, in whose breast the heart of the sacred ram found a refuge. To-morrow this pledge of the divine grace shall be shown to the people, and another mercy will also be announced to them. Hear and praise the dispensations of the Most High! An hour ago I received the news that a new Apis, with all the sacred marks upon him, has been found in the herds of Ani at Hermonthis."

Fresh excitement was shown by the listening conclave. Ameni let their astonishment express itself freely, but at last he exclaimed:

"And now to settle the last question. The priest Pentaur, who is now present, has been appointed speaker at the festival to-morrow. He has erred greatly, yet I think we need not judge him till after the holy day, and, in consideration of his former innocence, need not deprive him of the honorable office. Do you share my wishes? Is there no dissentient voice? Then come forward, you, the youngest of us all, who are so highly trusted by this holy assembly."

Pentaur rose and placed himself opposite to Ameni, in order to give, as he was required to do, a broad outline of the speech he proposed to deliver next day to the nobles and the people.

The whole assembly, even his opponents, listened to him with approbation. Ameni, too, praised him, but added:

"I miss only one thing on which you must dwell at greater length, and treat with warmer feeling—I mean the miracle which has stirred our souls to-day. We must show that the Gods brought the sacred heart—"

"Allow me," said Pentaur, interrupting the high-priest, and looking earnestly into those eyes which long since he had sung of—"Allow me to entreat you not to select me to declare this new marvel to the people."

Astonishment was stamped on the face of every member of the assembly. Each looked at his neighbor, then at Pentaur, and at last enquiringly at Ameni. The superior knew Pentaur, and saw that no mere whimsical fancy, but some serious motive had given rise to this refusal. Horror, almost aversion, had rung in his tone as he said the words 'new marvel.' He doubted the genuineness of this divine manifestation!

Ameni gazed long and enquiringly into Pentaur's eyes, and then said: "You are right, my friend. Before judgment has been passed on you, before you are reinstated in your old position, your lips are not worthy to announce this divine wonder to the multitude. Look into your own soul, and teach the devout a horror of sin, and show them the way, which you must now tread, of purification of the heart. I myself will announce the miracle."

The white-robed audience hailed this decision of their master with satisfaction. Ameni enjoined this thing on one, on another, that; and on all, perfect silence as to the dream which he had related to them, and then he dissolved the meeting. He begged only Gagabu and Pentaur to remain.

As soon as they were alone Ameni asked the poet "Why did you refuse to announce to the people the miracle, which has filled all the priests of the Necropolis with joy?"

"Because thou hast taught me," replied Pentaur, "that truth is the highest aim we can have, and that there is nothing higher."

"I tell you so again now," said Ameni. "And as you recognize this doctrine, I ask you, in the name of the fair daughter of Ra. Do you doubt the genuineness of the miracle that took place under our very eyes?"

"I doubt it," replied Pentaur.

"Remain on the high stand-point of veracity," continued Ameni, "and tell us further, that we may learn, what are the scruples that shake thy faith?"

"I know," replied the poet with a dark expression, "that the heart which the crowd will approach and bow to, before which even the Initiated prostrate themselves as if it had been the incarnation of Ra, was torn from the bleeding carcass of a common sheep, and smuggled into the kanopus which contained the entrails of Rui."

Ameni drew back a step, and Gagabu cried out "Who says so? Who can prove it? As I grow older I hear more and more frightful things!"

"I know it," said Pentaur decidedly. "But I can, not reveal the name of him from whom I learned it."

"Then we may believe that you are mistaken, and that some impostor is fooling you. We will enquire who has devised such a trick, and he shall be punished! To scorn the voice of the Divinity is a sin, and he who lends his ear to a lie is far from the truth. Sacred and thrice sacred is the heart, blind fool, that I purpose to-morrow to show to the people, and before which you yourself-if not with good will, then by compulsion-shall fall, prostrate in the dust.

"Go now, and reflect on the words with which you will stir the souls of the people to-morrow morning; but know one thing-Truth has many forms, and her aspects are as manifold as those of the Godhead. As the sun does not travel over a level plain or by a straight path-as the stars follow a circuitous course, which we compare with the windings of the snake Mehen-so the elect, who look out over time and space, and on whom the conduct of human life devolves, are not only permitted, but commanded, to follow indirect ways in order to reach the highest aims, ways that you do not understand, and which you may fancy deviate widely from the path of truth. You look only at to-day, we look forward to the morrow, and what we announce as truth you must needs believe. And mark my words: A lie stains the soul, but doubt eats into it."

Ameni had spoken with strong excitement; when Pentaur had left the room, and he was alone with Gagabu, he exclaimed:

"What things are these? Who is ruining the innocent child-like spirit of this highly favored youth?"

"He is ruining it himself," replied Gagabu. "He is putting aside the old law, for he feels a new one growing up in his own breast."

"But the laws," exclaimed Ameni, "grow and spread like shadowy woods; they are made by no one. I loved the poet, yet I must restrain him, else he will break down all barriers, like the Nile when it swells too high. And what he says of the miracle —"

"Did you devise it?"

"By the Holy One-no!" cried Ameni.

"And yet Pentaur is sincere, and inclined to faith," said the old man doubtfully.

"I know it," returned Ameni. "It happened as he said. But who did it, and who told him of the shameful deed?"

Both the priests stood thoughtfully gazing at the floor.

Ameni first broke the silence.

"Pentaur came in with Nebsecht," he exclaimed, "and they are intimate friends. Where was the leech while I was staying in Thebes?"

"He was taking care of the child hurt by Bent-Anat —the child of the paraschites Pinem, and he stayed there three days," replied Gagabu.

"And it was Pinem," said Ameni, "that opened the body of Rui! Now I know who has dimmed Pentaur's faith. It was that inquisitive stutterer, and he shall be made to repent of it. For the present let us think of to-morrow's feast, but the day after I will examine that nice couple, and will act with iron severity."

"First let us examine the naturalist in private," said Gagabu. "He is an ornament to the temple, for he has investigated many matters, and his dexterity is wonderful."

"All that may be considered Ameni said, interrupting the old enough to think of at present."

"And even more to consider later," retorted Gagabu. "We have entered on a dangerous path. You know very well I am still hot-headed, though I am old in years, and alas! timidity was never my weakness; but Rameses is a powerful man, and duty compels me to ask you: Is it mere hatred for the king that has led you to take these hasty and imprudent steps?"

"I have no hatred for Rameses," answered Ameni gravely. "If he did not wear the crown I could love him; I know him too, as well as if I were his brother, and value all that is great in him; nay I will admit that he is disfigured by no littleness. If I did not know how strong the enemy is, we might try to overthrow him with smaller means. You know as well as I do that he is our enemy. Not yours, nor mine, nor the enemy of the Gods; but the enemy of the old and reverend ordinances by which this people and this country must be governed, and above all of those who are required to protect the wisdom of the fathers, and to point out the right way to the sovereign —I mean the priesthood, whom it is my duty to lead, and for whose rights I will fight with every weapon of the spirit. In this contest, as you know, all that otherwise would be falsehood, treachery, and cunning, puts on the bright aspect of light and truth. As the physician needs the knife and fire to heal the sick, we must do fearful things to save the community when it is in danger. Now you will see me fight with every weapon, for if we remain idle, we shall soon cease to be the leaders of the state, and become the slaves of the king."

Gagabu nodded assent, but Ameni went on with increasing warmth, and in that rhythmical accent in which, when he came out of the holy of holies, he was accustomed to declare the will of the Divinity, "You were my teacher, and I value you, and so you now shall be told everything that stirred my soul, and made me first resolve upon this fearful struggle. I was, as you know, brought up in this temple with Rameses-and it was very wise of Seti to let his son grow up here with other boys. At work and at play the heir to the throne and I won every prize. He was quite my superior in swift apprehension-in keen perception-but I had greater caution, and deeper purpose. Often he laughed at my laborious efforts, but his brilliant powers appeared to me a vain delusion. I became one of the initiated, he ruled the state in partnership with his father, and, when Seti died, by himself. We both grew older, but the foundation of our characters remained the same. He rushed to splendid victories, overthrew nations, and raised the glory of the Egyptian name to a giddy height, though stained with the blood of his people; I passed my life in industry and labor, in teaching the young, and in guarding the laws which regulate the intercourse of men and bind the people to the Divinity. I compared the present with the past: What were the priests? How had they come to be what they are? What would Egypt be without them? There is not an art, not a science, not a faculty that is not thought out, constructed, and practised by us. We crown the kings, we named the Gods, and taught the people to honor them as divine-for the crowd needs a hand to lead it, and under which it shall tremble as under the mighty hand of Fate. We are the willing ministers of the divine representative of Ra on the throne, so long as he rules in accordance with our institutions-as the One God reigns, subject to eternal laws. He used to choose his counsellors from among us; we told him what would benefit the country, he heard us willingly, and executed our plans. The old kings were the hands, but we, the priests, were the head. And now, my father, what has become of us? We are made use of to keep the people in the faith, for if they cease to honor the Gods how will they submit to kings? Seti ventured much, his son risks still more, and therefore both have required much succor from the Immortals. Rameses is pious, he sacrifices frequently, and loves prayer: we are necessary to him, to waft incense, to slaughter hecatombs, to offer prayers, and to interpret dreams-but we are no longer his advisers. My father, now in Osiris, a worthier high-priest than I, was charged by the Prophets to entreat his father to give up the guilty project of connecting the north sea by a navigable channel with the unclean waters of the Red Sea.[100]

"Such things can only benefit the Asiatics. But Seti would not listen to our counsel. We desired to preserve the old division of the land, but Rameses introduced the new to the disadvantage of the priests; we warned him against fresh wars, and the king again and again has taken the field; we had the ancient sacred documents which exempted our peasantry from military service, and, as you know, he outrageously defies them. From the most ancient times no one has been permitted to raise temples in this land to strange Gods, and Rameses favors the son of the stranger, and, not only in the north country, but in the reverend city of Memphis and here in Thebes, he has raised altars and magnificent sanctuaries, in the strangers' quarter, to the sanguinary false Gods of the East."[101]

"You speak like a Seer," cried old Gagabu, "and what you say is perfectly true. We are still called priests, but alas! our counsel is little asked. 'You have to prepare men for a happy lot in the other world,' Rameses once said; 'I alone can guide their destinies in this.'"

"He did say so," answered Ameni, "and if he had said no more than that he would have been doomed. He and his house are the enemies of our rights and of our noble country. Need I tell you from whom the race of the Pharaoh is descended? Formerly the hosts who came from the east, and fell on our land like swarms of locusts, robbing and destroying it, were spoken of as 'a curse' and a 'pest.' Rameses' father was of that race. When Ani's ancestors expelled the Hyksos, the bold chief, whose children now govern Egypt, obtained the favor of being allowed to remain on the banks of the Nile; they served in the armies, they distinguished themselves, and, at last, the first Rameses succeeded in gaining the troops over to himself, and in pushing the old race of the legitimate sons of Ra, weakened as they were by heresy, from the throne. I must confess, however unwillingly, that some priests of the true faith-among them your grandfather, and mine-supported the daring usurper who clung faithfully to the old traditions. Not less than a hundred generations of my ancestors, and of yours, and of many other priestly families, have lived and died here by the banks of the Nile-of Rameses race we have seen ten, and only know of them that they descend from strangers, from the caste of Amu! He is like all the Semitic race; they love to wander, they call us ploughmen—[The word Fellah (pl. Fellahin) means ploughman] —and laugh to scorn the sober regularity with which we, tilling the dark soil, live through our lives to a tardy death, in honest labor both of mind and body. They sweep round on foraying excursions, ride the salt waves in ships, and know no loved and fixed home; they settle down wherever they are tempted by rapine, and when there is nothing more to be got they build a house in another spot. Such was Seti, such is Rameses! For a year he will stop in Thebes, then he must set out for wars in strange lands. He does not know how to yield piously, or to take advice of wise counsellors, and he will not learn. And such as the father is, so are the children! Think of the criminal behavior of Bent-Anat!"

"I said the kings liked foreigners. Have you duly considered the importance of that to us? We strive for high and noble aims, and have wrenched off the shackles of the flesh in order to guard our souls. The poorest man lives secure under the shelter of the law, and through us participates in the gifts of the spirit; to the rich are offered the priceless treasures of art and learning. Now look abroad: east and west wandering tribes roam over the desert with wretched tents; in the south a debased populace prays to feathers, and to abject idols, who are beaten if the worshipper is not satisfied. In the north certainly there are well regulated states, but the best part of the arts and sciences which they possess they owe to us, and their altars still reek with the loathsome sacrifice of human blood. Only backsliding from the right is possible under the stranger, and therefore it is prudent to withdraw from him; therefore he is hateful to our

Gods. And Rameses, the king, is a stranger, by blood and by nature, in his affections, and in his appearance; his thoughts are always abroad-this country is too small for him-and he will never perceive what is really best for him, clear as his intellect is. He will listen to no guidance, he does mischief to Egypt, and therefore I say: Down with him from the throne!"

"Down with him!" —Gagabu eagerly echoed the words. Ameni gave the old man his hand, which trembled with excitement, and went on more calmly.

"The Regent Ani is a legitimate child of the soil, by his father and mother both. I know him well, and I am sure that though he is cunning indeed, he is full of true veneration, and will righteously establish us in the rights which we have inherited. The choice is easy: I have chosen, and I always carry through what I have once begun! Now you know all, and you will second me."

"With body and soul!" cried Gagabu.

"Strengthen the hearts of the brethren," said Ameni, preparing to go. "The initiated may all guess what is going on, but it must never be spoken of."

CHAPTER XXVII.

The sun was up on the twenty-ninth morning of the second month of the over-flow of the Nile,[102] and citizens and their wives, old men and children, freemen and slaves, led by priests, did homage to the rising day-star before the door of the temple to which the quarter of the town belonged where each one dwelt.

The Thebans stood together like Huge families before the pylons, waiting for the processions of priests, which they intended to join in order to march in their train round the great temple of the city, and thence to cross with the festal barks to the Necropolis.

To-day was the Feast of the Valley, and Anion, the great God of Thebes, was carried over in solemn pomp to the City of the Dead, in order that he-as the priests said-might sacrifice to his fathers in the other world. The train marched westward; for there, where the earthly remains of man also found rest, the millions of suns had disappeared, each of which was succeeded daily by a new one, born of the night. The young luminary, the priests said, did not forget those that had been extinguished, and from whom he was descended; and Anion paid them this mark of respect to warn the devout not to forget those who were passed away, and to whom they owed their existence.

"Bring offerings," says a pious text, "to thy father and thy mother who rest in the valley of the tombs; for such gifts are pleasing to the Gods, who will receive them as if brought to themselves. Often visit thy dead, so that what thou dost for them, thy son may do for thee."

The Feast of the Valley was a feast of the dead; but it was not a melancholy solemnity, observed with lamentation and wailing; on the contrary, it was a cheerful festival, devoted to pious and sentimental memories of those whom we cease not to love after death, whom we esteem happy and blest, and of whom we think with affection; to whom too the throng from Thebes brought offerings, forming groups in the chapel-like tombs, or in front of the graves, to eat and drink.

Father, mother and children clung together; the house-slaves followed with provisions, and with torches, which would light up the darkness of the tomb and show the way home at night.

Even the poorest had taken care to secure beforehand a place in one of the large boats which conveyed the people across the stream; the barges of the rich, dressed in the gayest colors, awaited their owners with their households, and the children had dreamed all night of the sacred bark of Anion, whose splendor, as their mothers told them, was hardly less than that of the golden boat in which the Sun-God and his companions make their daily voyage across the ocean of heaven. The broad landing place of the temple of Anion was already crowded with priests, the shore with citizens, and the river with boats; already loud music drowned the din of the crowds, who thronged and pushed, enveloped in clouds of dust, to reach the boats; the houses and hovels of Thebes were all empty, and the advent of the God through the temple-gates was eagerly expected; but still the members of the royal family had not appeared, who were wont on this solemn day to go on foot to the great temple of Anion; and, in the crowd, many a one asked his neighbor why Bent-Anat, the fair daughter of Rameses, lingered so long, and delayed the starting of the procession.

The priests had begun their chant within the walls, which debarred the outer world from any glimpse into the bright precincts of the temple; the Regent with his brilliant train had entered the sanctuary; the gates were thrown open; the youths in their short-aprons, who threw flowers in the path of the God, had come out; clouds of incense announced the approach of Anion-and still the daughter of Rameses appeared not.

Many rumors were afloat, most of them contradictory; but one was accurate, and confirmed by the temple servants, to the great regret of the crowd-Bent-Anat was excluded from the Feast of the Valley.

She stood on her balcony with her brother Rameri and her friend Nefert, and looked down on the river, and on the approaching God.

Early in the previous morning Bek-en-Chunsu, the old high-priest of the temple of An-ion had pronounced her clean, but in the evening he had come to communicate to her the intelligence that Ameni prohibited her entering the Necropolis before she had obtained the forgiveness of the Gods of the West for her offence.

While still under the ban of uncleanness she had visited the temple of Hathor, and had defiled it by her presence; and the stern Superior of the City of the Dead was in the right-that Bek-en-Chunsu himself admitted-in closing the western shore against her. Bent-Anat then had recourse to Ani; but, though he promised to mediate for her, he came late in the evening to tell her that Ameni was inexorable. The Regent at the same time, with every appearance of regret, advised her to avoid an open quarrel, and not to defy Ameni's lofty severity, but to remain absent from the festival.

Katuti at the same time sent the dwarf to Nefert, to desire her to join her mother, in taking part in the procession, and in sacrificing in her father's tomb; but Nefert replied that she neither could nor would leave her royal friend and mistress.

Bent-Anat had given leave of absence to the highest members of her household, and had prayed them to think of her at the splendid solemnity.

When, from her balcony, she saw the mob of people and the crowd of boats, she went back into her room, called Rameri, who was angrily declaiming at what he called Ameni's insolence, took his hands in hers, and said:

"We have both done wrong, brother; let us patiently submit to the consequences of our faults, and conduct ourselves as if our father were with us."

"He would tear the panther-skin from the haughty priest's shoulders," cried Rameri, "if he dared to humiliate you so in his presence;" and tears of rage ran down his smooth cheeks as he spoke.

"Put anger aside," said Bent-Anat. "You were still quite little the last time my father took part in this festival."

"Oh! I remember that morning well," exclaimed Rameri, "and shall never forget it."

"So I should think," said the princess. "Do not leave us, Nefert-you are now my sister. It was a glorious morning; we children were collected in the great hall of the King, all in festival dresses; he had us called into this room, which had been inhabited by my mother, who then had been dead only a few months. He took each of us by the hand, and said he forgave us everything we might have done wrong if only we were sincerely penitent, and gave us each a kiss on our forehead. Then he beckoned us all to him, and said, as humbly as if he were one of us instead of the great king, 'Perhaps I may have done one of you some injustice, or have kept you out of some right; I am not conscious of such a thing, but if it has occurred I am very sorry' —we all rushed upon him, and wanted to kiss him, but he put us aside smiling, and said, 'Each of you has enjoyed an equal share of one thing, that you may be sure —I mean your father's love; and I see now that you return what I have given you.' Then he spoke of our mother, and said that even the tenderest father could not fill the place of a mother. He drew a lovely picture of the unselfish devotion of the dead mother, and desired us to pray and to sacrifice with him at her resting-place, and to resolve to be worthy of her; not only in great things but in trifles too, for they make up the sum of life, as hours make the days, and the years. We elder ones clasped each other's hands, and I never felt happier than in that moment, and afterwards by my mother's grave." Nefert raised her eyes that were wet with tears.

"With such a father it must be easy to be good," she said.

"Did your mother never speak good words that went to your heart on the morning of this festival?" asked Bent-Anat.

Nefert colored, and answered: "We were always late in dressing, and then had to hurry to be at the temple in time."

"Then let me be your mother to-day," cried the princess, "and yours too, Rameri. Do you not remember how my father offered forgiveness to the officers of the court, and to all the servants, and how he enjoined us to root out every grudge from our hearts on this day? 'Only stainless garments,' he said, 'befit this feast; only hearts without spot.' So, brother, I will not hear an evil word about Ameni, who is most likely forced to be severe by the law; my father will enquire into it all and decide. My heart is so full, it must overflow. Come, Nefert, give me a kiss, and you too, Rameri. Now I will go into my little temple, in which the images of our ancestors stand, and think of my mother and the blessed spirits of those loved ones to whom I may not sacrifice to-day."

"I will go with you," said Rameri.

"You, Nefert-stay here," said Bent-Anat, "and cut as many flowers as you like; take the best and finest, and make a wreath, and when it is ready we will send a messenger across to lay it, with other gifts, on the grave of your Mena's mother."

When, half-an-hour later, the brother and sister returned to the young wife, two graceful garlands hung in Nefert's bands, one for the grave of the dead queen, and one for Mena's mother.

"I will carry over the wreaths, and lay them in the tombs," cried the prince.

"Ani thought it would be better that we should not show ourselves to the people," said his sister. "They will scarcely notice that you are not among the school-boys, but —"

"But I will not go over as the king's son, but as a gardener's boy —" interrupted the prince. "Listen to the flourish of trumpets! the God has now passed through the gates."

Rameri stepped out into the balcony, and the two women followed him, and looked down on the scene of the embarkation which they could easily see with their sharp young eyes.

"It will be a thinner and poorer procession without either my father or us, that is one comfort," said Rameri. "The chorus is magnificent; here come the plume-bearers and singers; there is the chief prophet at the great temple, old Bek-en-Chunsu. How dignified he looks, but he will not like going. Now the God is coming, for I smell the incense."

With these words the prince fell on his knees, and the women followed his example-when they saw first a noble bull in whose shining skin the sun was reflected, and who bore between his horns a golden disk, above which stood white ostrich-feathers; and then, divided from the bull only by a few fan-bearers, the God himself, sometimes visible, but more often hidden from sight by great semi-circular screens of black and white ostrich-feathers, which were fixed on long poles, and with which the priests shaded the God.

His mode of progress was as mysterious as his name, for he seemed to float slowly on his gorgeous throne from the temple-gates towards the stream. His seat was placed on a platform, magnificently decorated with bunches and garlands of flowers, and covered with hangings of purple and gold brocade, which concealed the priests who bore it along with a slow and even pace.

As soon as the God had been placed on board his barge, Bent-Anat and her companions rose from their knees.

Then came some priests, who carried a box with the sacred evergreen tree of Amon; and when a fresh outburst of music fell on her ear, and a cloud of incense was wafted up to her, Bent-Anat said: "Now my father should be coming."

"And you," cried Rameri, "and close behind, Nefert's husband, Mena, with the guards. Uncle Ani comes on foot. How strangely he has dressed himself like a sphinx hind-part before!"

"How so?" asked Nefert.

"A sphinx," said Rameri laughing, it has the body of a lion, and the head of a man,[103] and my uncle has a peaceful priest's robe, and on his head the helmet of a warrior."

"If the king were here, the distributor of life," said Nefert, "you would not be missing from among his supporters."

"No indeed!" replied the prince, "and the whole thing is altogether different when my father is here. His heroic form is splendid on his golden throne; the statues of Truth and justice spread their wings behind him as if to protect him; his mighty representative in fight, the lion, lies peacefully before him, and over him spreads the canopy with the Urmus snake at the top. There is hardly any end to the haruspices, the pastophori with the standards, the images of the Gods, and the flocks and herds for sacrifice. Only think, even the North has sent representatives to the feast, as if my father were here. I know all the different signs on the standards. Do you recognize the images of the king's ancestors, Nefert? No? no more do I; but it seemed to me that Ahmes I., who expelled the Hyksos-from whom our grandmother was descended-headed the procession, and not my grandfather Seti, as he should have done. Here come the soldiers; they are the legions which Ani equipped, and who returned victorious from Ethiopia only last night. How the people cheer them! and indeed they have behaved valiantly. Only think, Bent-Anat and Nefert, what it will be when my father comes home, with a hundred captive princes, who will humbly follow his chariot, which your Mena will drive, with our brothers and all the nobles of the land, and the guards in their splendid chariots."

"They do not think of returning yet!" sighed Nefert. While more and more troops of the Regent's soldiers, more companies of musicians, and rare animals, followed in procession, the festal bark of Amon started from the shore.

It was a large and gorgeous barge of wood, polished all over and overlaid with gold, and its edge was decorated with glittering glass-beads, which imitated rubies and emeralds; the masts and yards were gilt, and purple sails floated from them. The seats for the priests were of ivory, and garlands of lilies and roses hung round the vessel, from its masts and ropes.

The Regent's Nile-boat was not less splendid; the wood-work shone with gilding, the cabin was furnished with gay Babylonian carpets; a lion's-head formed the prow, as formerly in Hatasu's sea-going vessels, and two large rubies shone in it, for eyes. After the priests had embarked, and the sacred barge had reached the opposite shore, the people pressed into the boats, which, filled almost to sinking, soon so covered the whole breadth of the river that there was hardly a spot where the sun was mirrored in the yellow waters.

"Now I will put on the dress of a gardener," cried Rameri, "and cross over with the wreaths."

"You will leave us alone?" asked Bent-Anat.

"Do not make me anxious," said Rameri.

"Go then," said the princess. "If my father were here how willingly I would go too."

"Come with me," cried the boy. "We can easily find a disguise for you too."

"Folly!" said Bent-Anat; but she looked enquiringly at Nefert, who shrugged her shoulders, as much as to say: "Your will is my law."

Rameri was too sharp for the glances of the friends to have escaped him, and he exclaimed eagerly:

"You will come with me, I see you will! Every beggar to-day flings his flower into the common grave, which contains the black mummy of his father-and shall the daughter of Rameses, and the wife of the chief charioteer, be excluded from bringing garlands to their dead?"

"I shall defile the tomb by my presence," said Bent-Anat coloring.

"You-you!" exclaimed Rameri, throwing his arms round his sister's neck, and kissing her. "You, a noble generous creature, who live only to ease sorrow and to wipe away tears; you, the very image of my father-unclean! sooner would I believe that the swans down there are as black as crows, and the rose-wreaths on the balcony rank hemlock branches. Bek-en-Chunsu pronounced you clean, and if Ameni —"

"Ameni only exercises his rights," said Bent-Anat gently, "and you know what we have resolved. I will not hear one hard word about him to-day."

"Very well! he has graciously and mercifully kept us from the feast," said Rameri ironically, and he bowed low in the direction of the Necropolis, "and you are unclean. Do not enter the tombs and the temples on my account; let us stay outside among the people. The roads over there are not so very sensitive; paraschites and other unclean folks pass over them every day. Be sensible, Bent-Anat, and come. We will disguise ourselves; I will conduct you; I will lay the garlands in the tombs, we will pray together outside, we will see the sacred procession and the feats of the magicians, and hear the festive discourse. Only think! Pentaur, in spite of all they have said against him, is to deliver it. The temple of Seti wants to do its best to-day, and Ameni knows very well that Pentaur, when he opens his mouth, stirs the hearts of the people more than all the sages together if they were to sing in chorus! Come with me, sister."

"So be it then," said Bent-Anat with sudden decision.

Rameri was surprised at this quick resolve, at which however he was delighted; but Nefert looked anxiously at her friend. In a moment her eyes fell; she knew now who it was that her friend loved, and the fearful thought —"How will it end?" flashed through her mind.

CHAPTER XXVIII.

An hour later a tall, plainly dressed woman crossed the Nile, with a dark-skinned boy and a slender youth by her side. The wrinkles on her brow and cheeks agreed little with her youthful features; but it would have been difficult to recognize in these three the proud princess, the fair young prince, and the graceful Nefert, who looked as charming as ever in the long white robe of a temple-student.

They were followed by two faithful and sturdy head-servants from among the litter-bearers of the princess, who were however commanded to appear as though they were not in any way connected with their mistress and her companions.

The passage across the Nile had been accomplished but slowly, and thus the royal personages had experienced for the first time some of the many difficulties and delays which ordinary mortals must conquer to attain objects which almost fly to meet their rulers. No one preceded them to clear the river, no other vessel made way for them; on the contrary, all tried to take place ahead of them, and to reach the opposite shore before them.

When at last they reached the landing-place, the procession had already passed on to the temple of Seti; Ameni had met it with his chorus of singers, and had received the God on the shore of the Nile; the prophets of the Necropolis had with their own hands placed him in the sacred Sam-bark of the House of Seti, which was artistically constructed of cedar wood and electrum set with jewels; thirty pastophori took the precious burden on their shoulders, and bore it up the avenue of Sphinxes-which led from the river to the temple-into the sanctuary of Seti, where Amon remained while the emissaries from the different provinces deposited their offerings in the forecourt. On his road from the shore kolchytes had run before him, in accordance with ancient custom, strewing sand in his path.

In the course of an hour the procession once more emerged into the open air, and turning to the south, rested first in the enormous temple of Anienophis III., in front of which the two giant statues stood as sentinels-they still remain, the colossi of the Nile valley. Farther to the south it reached the temple of Thotmes the Great, then, turning round, it clung to the eastern face of the Libyan hills-pierced with tombs and catacombs; it mounted the terraces of the temple of Hatasu, and paused by the tombs of the oldest kings which are in the immediate neighborhood; thus by sunset it had reached the scene of the festival itself, at the entrance of the valley in which the tomb of Setitt had been made, and in whose westernmost recesses were some of the graves of the Pharaohs of the deposed race.

This part of the Necropolis was usually visited by lamp-light, and under the flare of torches, before the return of the God to his own temple and the mystery-play on the sacred lake, which did not begin till midnight.

Behind the God, in a vase of transparent crystal, and borne high on a pole that all the multitude might see it, was the heart of the sacred ram.

Our friends, after they had laid their wreaths on the magnificent altars of their royal ancestors without being recognized, late in the afternoon joined the throng who followed the procession. They mounted the eastern cliff of the hills close by the tomb of Mena's forefathers, which a prophet of Amon, named Neferhotep-Mena's great-grandfather —had constructed. Its narrow doorway was besieged by a crowd, for within the first of the rock-chambers of which it consisted, a harper was singing a dirge for the long-since buried prophet, his wife and his sister. The song had been composed by the poet attached to his house; it was graven in the stone of the second rock-room of the tomb, and Neferhotep had left a plot of ground in trust to the Necropolis, with the charge of administering its revenues for the payment of a minstrel, who every-year at the feast of the dead should sing the monody to the accompaniment of his lute.[104]

The charioteer well knew this dirge for his ancestor, and had often sung it to Nefert, who had accompanied him on her lute; for in their hours of joy also-nay especially-the Egyptians were wont to remember their dead.

Now the three companions listened to the minstrel as he sang:

"Now the great man is at rest,
Gone to practise sweeter duties.
Those that die are the elect
Since the Gods have left the earth.
Old men pass and young men come;
Yea, a new Sun rises daily
When the old sun has found rest
In the bosom of the night.

"Hail, O Prophet! on this feast day
Odorous balsams, fragrant resins
Here we bring-and offer garlands,
Throwing flowers down before thee,
And before thy much-loved sister,
Who has found her rest beside thee.

"Songs we sing, and strike the lyre
To thy memory, and thine honor.
All our cares are now forgotten,
Joy and hope our breasts are filling;
For the day of our departure
Now draws near, and in the silence
Of the farther shore is rest."

When the song ceased, several people pressed into the little oratory to express their gratitude to the deceased prophet by laying a few flowers on his altar. Nefert and Rameri also went in, and when Nefert had offered a long and silent prayer to the glorified spirits of her dead, that they might watch over Mena, she laid her garland beside the grave in which her husband's mother rested.

Many members of the court circle passed close to the royal party without recognizing them; they made every effort to reach the scene of the festival, but the crowd was so great that the ladies had several times to get into a tomb to avoid it. In each they found the altar loaded with offerings, and, in most, family-parties, who here remembered their dead, with meat and fruits, beer and wine, as though they were departed travellers who had found some far off rest, and whom they hoped sooner or later to see again.

The sun was near setting when at last the princess and her companions reached the spot where the feast was being held. Here stood numbers of stalls and booths, with eatables of every sort, particularly sweet cakes for the children, dates, figs, pomegranates, and other fruits. Under light awnings, which kept off the sun, were sold sandals and kerchiefs of every material and hue, ornaments, amulets, fans, and sun-shades, sweet essences of every kind, and other gifts for offerings or for the toilet. The baskets of the gardeners and flower-girls were already empty, but the money-changers were full of business, and the tavern and gambling booths were driving a brisk trade.

Friends and acquaintances greeted each other kindly, while the children showed each other their new sandals, the cakes they had won at the games, or the little copper rings they had had given to them, and which must now be laid out. The largest crowd was gathered to see the magicians from the House of Seti, round which the mob squatted on the ground in a compact circle, and the children were good-naturedly placed in the front row.

When Bent-Anat reached the place all the religious solemnity was ended.

There stood the canopy under which the king and his family were used to listen to the festal discourse, and under its shade sat to-day the Regent Ani. They could see too the seats of the grandees, and the barriers which kept the people at a distance from the Regent, the priests, and the nobles.

Here Ameni himself had announced to the multitude the miracle of the sacred heart, and had proclaimed that a new Apis had been found among the herds of the Regent Ani.

His announcement of these divine tokens had been repeated from mouth to mouth; they were omens of peace and happiness for the country through the means of a favorite of the Gods; and though no one said it, the dullest could not fail to see that this favorite was none other than Ani, the descendant of the great Hatasu, whose prophet had been graced by the transfer to him of the heart of the sacred rain. All eyes were fixed on Ani, who had sacrificed before all the people to the sacred heart, and received the high-priest's blessing.

Pentaur, too, had ended his discourse when Bent-Anat reached the scene of the festival. She heard an old man say to his son:

"Life is hard. It often seems to me like a heavy burden laid on our poor backs by the cruel Gods; but when I heard the young priest from the House of Seti, I felt that, after all, the Immortals are good, and we have much to thank them for."

In another place a priest's wife said to her son:

"Could you see Pentaur well, Hor-Uza? He is of humble birth, but he stands above the greatest in genius and gifts, and will rise to high things."

Two girls were speaking together, and one said to the other:

"The speaker is the handsomest man I ever saw, and his voice sounds like soft music."

"And how his eyes shone when he spoke of truth as the highest of all virtues!" replied the other. "All the Gods, I believe, must dwell in him."

Bent-Anat colored as these words fell on her ear. It was growing dark, and she wished to return home but Rameri wished to follow the procession as it marched through the western valley by torch-light, so that the grave of his grandfather Seti should also be visited. The princess unwillingly yielded, but it would in any case have been difficult to reach the river while every one was rushing in the opposite direction; so the two ladies, and Rameri, let themselves be carried along by the crowd, and by the time the daylight was gone, they found themselves in the western valley, where to-night no beasts of prey dared show themselves; jackals and hyenas had fled before the glare of the torches, and the lanterns made of colored papyrus.

The smoke of the torches mingled with the dust stirred by a thousand feet, and the procession moved along, as it were, in a cloud, which also shrouded the multitude that followed.

The three companions had labored on as far as the hovel of the paraschites Pinem, but here they were forced to pause, for guards drove back the crowd to the right and left with long staves, to clear a passage for the procession as it approached.

"See, Rameri," said Bent-Anat, pointing out the little yard of the hut which stood only a few paces from them. "That is where the fair, white girl lives, whom I ran over. But she is much better. Turn round; there, behind the thorn-hedge, by the little fire which shines full in your (her? D.W.) face-there she sits, with her grandfather."

The prince stood on tip-toe, looked into the humble plot of ground, and then said in a subdued voice "What a lovely creature! But what is she doing with the old man? He seems to be praying, and she first holds a handkerchief before his mouth, and then rubs his temples. And how unhappy she looks!"

"The paraschites must be ill," replied Bent-Anat. "He must have had too much wine down at the feast," said Rameri laughing. "No doubt of it! Only look how his lips tremble, and his eyes roll. It is hideous-he looks like one possessed."[105]

"He is unclean too!" said Nefert.

"But he is a good, kind man, with a tender heart," exclaimed the princess eagerly. "I have enquired about him. He is honest and sober, and I am sure he is ill and not drunk."

"Now she is standing up," said Rameri, and he dropped the paper-lantern which he had bought at a booth. "Step back, Bent-Anat, she must be expecting some one. Did you ever see any one so very fair, and with such a pretty little head. Even her red hair becomes her wonderfully; but she staggers as she stands-she must be very weak. Now she has sat down again by the old man, and is rubbing his forehead. Poor souls! look how she is sobbing. I will throw my purse over to them."

"No, no!" exclaimed Bent-Anat. "I gave them plenty of money, and the tears which are shed there cannot be staunched with gold. I will send old Asnath over to-morrow to ask how we can help them. Look, here comes the procession, Nefert. How rudely the people press! As soon as the God is gone by we will go home."

"Pray do," said Nefert. "I am so frightened!" and she pressed trembling to the side of the princess.

"I wish we were at home, too," replied Bent-Anat.

"Only look!" said Rameri. "There they are. Is it not splendid? And how the heart shines, as if it were a star!"

All the crowd, and with them our three friends, fell on their knees.

The procession paused opposite to them, as it did at every thousand paces; a herald came forward, and glorified, in a loud voice, the great miracle, to which now another was added-the sacred heart since the night had come on had begun to give out light.

Since his return home from the embalming house, the paraschites had taken no nourishment, and had not answered a word to the anxious questions of the two frightened women. He stared blindly, muttered a few unintelligible words, and often clasped his forehead in his hand. A few hours before he had laughed loud and suddenly, and his wife, greatly alarmed, had gone at once to fetch the physician Nebsecht.

During her absence Uarda was to rub her grandfather's temples with the leaves which the witch Hekt had laid on her bruises, for as they had once proved efficacious they might perhaps a second time scare away the demon of sickness.

When the procession, with its thousand lamps and torches, paused before the hovel, which was almost invisible in the dusk, and one citizen said to another: "Here comes the sacred heart!" the old man started, and stood up. His eyes stared fixedly at the gleaming relic in its crystal case; slowly, trembling in every limb, and with outstretched neck he stood up.

The herald began his eulogy of the miracle.

Then, while all the people were prostrate in adoration, listening motionless to the loud voice of the speaker, the paraschites rushed out of his gate, striking his forehead with his fists, and opposite the sacred heart, he broke out into a mad, loud fit of scornful laughter, which re-echoed from the bare cliffs that closed in the valley.

Horror full on the crowd, who rose timidly from their knees.

Ameni, who too, was close behind the heart, started too and looked round on the author of this hideous laugh. He had never seen the paraschites, but he perceived the glimmer of his little fire through the dust and gloom, and he knew that he lived in this place. The whole case struck him at once; he whispered a few significant words to one of the officers who marched with the troops on each side of the procession; then he gave the signal, and the procession moved on as if nothing had happened.

The old man tried with still more loud and crazy laughter to reach and seize the heart, but the crowd kept him back; and while the last groups passed on after the priests, he contrived to slip back as far as the door of his hovel, though much damaged and hurt.

There he fell, and Uarda rushed out and threw herself over the old man, who lay on the earth, scarcely recognizable in the dust and darkness.

"Crush the scoffer!"

"Tear him in pieces!"

"Burn down the foul den!"

"Throw him and the wench into the fire!" shouted the people who had been disturbed in their devotions, with wild fury.

Two old women snatched the lanterns froth the posts, and flung them at the unfortunate creatures, while an Ethiopian soldier seized Uarda by the hair, and tore her away from her grandfather.

At this moment Pinem's wife appeared, and with her Pentaur. She had found not Nebsecht, but Pentaur, who had returned to the temple after his speech. She had told him of the demon who had fallen upon her husband, and implored him to come with her. Pentaur immediately followed her in his working dress, just as he was, without putting on the white priest's robe, which he did not wish to wear on this expedition.

When they drew near to the paraschites' hovel, he perceived the tumult among the people, and, loud above all the noise, heard Uarda's shrill cry of terror. He hurried forward, and in the dull light of the scattered fire-brands and colored lanterns, he saw the black hand of the soldier clutching the hair of the helpless child; quick as thought he gripped the soldier's throat with his iron fingers, seized him round the body, swung him in the air, and flung him like a block of stone right into the little yard of the hut.

The people threw themselves on the champion in a frenzy of rage, but he felt a sudden warlike impulse surging up in him, which he had never felt before. With one wrench he pulled out the heavy wooden pole, which supported the awning which the old paraschites had put up for his sick grandchild; he swung it round his head, as if it were a reed, driving back the crowd, while he called to Uarda to keep close to him.

"He who touches the child is a dead man!" he cried. "Shame on you! —falling on a feeble old man and a helpless child in the middle of a holy festival!"

For a moment the crowd was silent, but immediately after rushed forward with fresh impetus, and wilder than ever rose the shouts of:

"Tear him to pieces! burn his house down!"

A few artisans from Thebes closed round the poet, who was not recognizable as a priest. He, however, wielding his tent-pole, felled them before they could reach him with their fists or cudgels, and down went every man on whom it fell. But the struggle could not last long, for some of his assailants sprang over the fence, and attacked him in the rear. And now Pentaur was distinctly visible against a background of flaring light, for some fire-brands had fallen on the dry palm-thatch of the hovel behind him, and roaring flames rose up to the dark heavens.

The poet heard the threatening blaze behind him. He put his left hand round the head of the trembling girl, who crouched beside him, and feeling that now they both were lost, but that to his latest breath he must protect the innocence and life of this frail creature, with his right hand he once more desperately swung the heavy stake.

But it was for the last time; for two men succeeded in clutching the weapon, others came to their support, and wrenched it from his hand, while the mob closed upon him, furious but unarmed, and not without great fear of the enormous strength of their opponent.

Uarda clung to her protector with shortened breath, and trembling like a hunted antelope. Pentaur groaned when he felt himself disarmed, but at that instant a youth stood by his side, as if he had sprung from the earth, who put into his hand the sword of the fallen soldier-who lay near his feet-and who then, leaning his back against Pentaur's, faced the foe on the other side. Pentaur pulled himself together, sent out a battle-cry like some fighting hero who is defending his last stronghold, and brandished his new weapon. He stood with flaming eyes, like a lion at bay, and for a moment the enemy gave way, for his young ally Rameri, had taken a hatchet, and held it up in a threatening manner.

"The cowardly murderers are flinging fire-brands," cried the prince. "Come here, girl, and I will put out the pitch on your dress."

He seized Uarda's hand, drew her to him, and hastily put out the flame, while Pentaur protected them with his sword.

The prince and the poet stood thus back to back for a few moments, when a stone struck Pentaur's head; he staggered, and the crowd were rushing upon him, when the little fence was torn away by a determined hand, a tall womanly form appeared on the scene of combat, and cried to the astonished mob:

"Have done with this! I command you! I am Bent-Anat, the daughter of Rameses."

The angry crowd gave way in sheer astonishment. Pentaur had recovered from the stunning blow, but he thought he must be under some illusion. He felt as if he must throw himself on his knees before Bent-Anat, but his mind had been trained under Ameni to rapid reflection; he realized, in a flash of thought, the princess's position, and instead of bowing before her he exclaimed:

"Whoever this woman may be, good folks, she is not Bent-Anat the princess, but I, though I have no white robe on, am a priest of Seti, named Pentaur, and the Cherheb of to-day's festival. Leave this spot, woman, I command you, in right of my sacred office."

And Bent-Anat obeyed.

Pentaur was saved; for just as the people began to recover from their astonishment just as those whom he had hurt were once more inciting the mob to fight just as a boy, whose hand he had crushed, was crying out: "He is not a priest, he is a sword's-man. Down with the liar!"

A voice from the crowd exclaimed:

"Make way for my white robe, and leave the preacher Pentaur alone, he is my friend. You most of you know me."

"You are Nebsecht the leech, who set my broken leg," cried a sailor.

"And cured my bad eye," said a weaver.

"That tall handsome man is Pentaur, I know him well," cried the girl, whose opinion had been overheard by Bent-Anat.

"Preacher this, preacher that!" shouted the boy, and he would have rushed forward, but the people held him back, and divided respectfully at Nebsecht's command to make way for him to get at those who had been hurt.

First he stooped over the old paraschites.

"Shame upon you!" he exclaimed. —"You have killed the old man."

"And I," said Pentaur, "Have dipped my peaceful hand in blood to save his innocent and suffering grandchild from a like fate."

"Scorpions, vipers, venomous reptiles, scum of men!" shrieked Nebsecht, and he sprang wildly forward, seeking Uarda. When he saw her sitting safe at the feet of old Hekt, who had made her way into the courtyard, he drew a deep breath of relief, and turned his attention to the wounded.

"Did you knock down all that are lying here?" he whispered to his friend.

Pentaur nodded assent and smiled; but not in triumph, rather in shame; like a boy, who has unintentionally squeezed to death in his hand a bird he has caught.

Nebsecht looked round astonished and anxious. "Why did you not say who you were?" he asked. "Because the spirit of the God Menth possessed me," answered Pentaur. "When I saw that accursed villain there with his hand in the girl's hair, I heard and saw nothing, I—"

"You did right," interrupted Nebsecht. "But where will all this end?"

At this moment a flourish of trumpets rang through the little valley. The officer sent by Ameni to apprehend the paraschites came up with his soldiers.

Before he entered the court-yard he ordered the crowd to disperse; the refractory were driven away by force, and in a few minutes the valley was cleared of the howling and shouting mob, and the burning house was surrounded by soldiers. Bent-Anat, Rameri, and Nefert were obliged to quit their places by the fence; Rameri, so soon as he saw that Uarda was safe, had rejoined his sister.

Nefert was almost fainting with fear and excitement. The two servants, who had kept near them, knit their hands together, and thus carried her in advance of the princess. Not one of them spoke a word, not even Rameri, who could not forget Uarda, and the look of gratitude she bid sent after him. Once only Bent-Anat said:

"The hovel is burnt down. Where will the poor souls sleep to-night?"

When the valley was clear, the officer entered the yard, and found there, besides Uarda and the witch Hekt, the poet, and Nebsecht, who was engaged in tending the wounded.

Pentaur shortly narrated the affair to the captain, and named himself to him.

The soldier offered him his hand.

"If there were many men in Rameses' army," said he, "who could strike such a blow as you, the war with the Cheta would soon be at an end. But you have struck down, not Asiatics, but citizens of Thebes, and, much as I regret it, I must take you as a prisoner to Ameni."

"You only do your duty," replied Pentaur, bowing to the captain, who ordered his men to take up the body of the paraschites, and to bear it to the temple of Seti.

"I ought to take the girl in charge too," he added, turning to Pentaur.

"She is ill," replied the poet.

"And if she does not get some rest," added Nebsecht, "she will be dead. Leave her alone; she is under the particular protection of the princess Bent-Anat, who ran over her not long ago."

"I will take her into my house," said Hekt, "and will take care of her. Her grandmother is lying there; she was half choked by the flames, but she will soon come to herself—and I have room for both."

"Till to-morrow," replied the surgeon. "Then I will provide another shelter for her."

The old woman laughed and muttered: "There are plenty of folks to take care of her, it seems."

The soldiers obeyed the command of their leader, took up the wounded, and went away with Pentaur, and the body of Pinem.

Meanwhile, Bent-Anat and her party had with much difficulty reached the river-bank. One of the bearers was sent to find the boat which was waiting for them, and he was enjoined to make haste, for already they could see the approach of the procession, which escorted the God on his return journey. If they could not succeed in finding their boat without delay, they must wait at least an hour, for, at night, not a boat that did not belong to the train of Amon-not even the barge of a noble-might venture from shore till the whole procession was safe across.

They awaited the messenger's signal in the greatest anxiety, for Nefert was perfectly exhausted, and Bent-Anat, on whom she leaned, felt her trembling in every limb.

At last the bearer gave the signal; the swift, almost invisible bark, which was generally used for wild fowl shooting, shot by-Rameri seized one end of an oar that the rower held out to him, and drew the little boat up to the landing-place.

The captain of the watch passed at the same moment, and shouting out, "This is the last boat that can put off before the passage of the God!"

Bent-Anat descended the steps as quickly as Nefert's exhausted state permitted. The landing-place was now only dimly lighted by dull lanterns, though, when the God embarked, it would be as light as day with cressets and torches. Before she could reach the bottom step, with Nefert still clinging heavily to her arm, a hard hand was laid on her shoulder, and the rough voice of Paaker exclaimed:

"Stand back, you rabble! We are going first." The captain of the watch did not stop him, for he knew the chief pioneer and his overbearing ways. Paaker put his finger to his lips, and gave a shrill whistle that sounded like a yell in the silence.

The stroke of oars responded to the call, and Paaker called out to his boatmen:

"Bring the boat up here! these people can wait!" The pioneer's boat was larger and better manned than that of the princess.

"Jump into the boat!" cried Rameri.

Bent-Anat went forward without speaking, for she did not wish to make herself known again for the sake of the people, and for Nefert's; but Paaker put himself in her way.

"Did I not tell you that you common people must wait till we are gone. Push these people's boat out into the stream, you men."

Bent-Anat felt her blood chill, for a loud squabble at once began on the landing-steps.

Rameri's voice sounded louder than all the rest; but the pioneer exclaimed:

"The low brutes dare to resist? I will teach them manners! Here, Descher, look after the woman and these boys!"

At his call his great red hound barked and sprang forward, which, as it had belonged to his father, always accompanied him when he went with his mother to visit the ancestral tomb. Nefert shrieked with fright, but the dog at once knew her, and crouched against her with whines of recognition.

Paaker, who had gone down to his boat, turned round in astonishment, and saw his dog fawning at the feet of a boy whom he could not possibly recognize as Nefert; he sprang back, and cried out:

"I will teach you, you young scoundrel, to spoil my dog with spells-or poison!"

He raised his whip, and struck it across the shoulders of Nefert, who, with one scream of terror and anguish, fell to the ground.

The lash of the whip only whistled close by the cheek of the poor fainting woman, for Bent-Anat had seized Paaker's arm with all her might.

Rage, disgust, and scorn stopped her utterance; but Rameri had heard Nefert's shriek, and in two steps stood by the women.

"Cowardly scoundrel!" he cried, and lifted the oar in his hand. Paaker evaded the blow, and called to the dog with a peculiar hiss:

"Pull him down, Descher."

The hound flew at the prince; but Rameri, who from his childhood, had been his father's companion in many hunts and field sports, gave the furious brute such a mighty blow on the muzzle that he rolled over with a snort.

Paaker believed that he possessed in the whole world no more faithful friend than this dog, his companion on all his marches across desert tracts or through the enemy's country, and when he saw him writhing on the ground his rage knew no bounds, and he flew at the youngster with his whip; but Rameri-madly excited by all the events of the night, full of the warlike spirit of his fathers, worked up to the highest pitch by the insults to the two ladies, and seeing that he was their only protector-suddenly felt himself endowed with the strength of a man; he dealt the pioneer such a heavy blow on the left hand, that he dropped his whip, and now seized the dagger in his girdle with his right.

Bent-Anat threw herself between the man and the stripling, who was hardly more than a boy, once more declared her name, and this time her brother's also, and commanded Paaker to make peace among the boatmen. Then she led Nefert, who remained unrecognized, into the boat, entered it herself with her companions, and shortly after landed at the palace, while Paaker's mother, for whom he had called his boat, had yet a long time to wait before it could start. Setchem had seen the struggle from her litter at the top of the landing steps, but without understanding its origin, and without recognizing the chief actors.

The dog was dead. Paaker's hand was very painful, and fresh rage was seething in his soul.

"That brood of Rameses!" he muttered. "Adventurers! They shall learn to know me. Mena and Rameses are closely connected —I will sacrifice them both."

CHAPTER XXIX.

At last the pioneer's boat got off with his mother and the body of the dog, which he intended to send to be embalmed at Kynopolis, the city in which the dog was held sacred above all animals;[106] Paaker himself returned to the House of Seti, where, in the night which closed the feast day, there was always a grand banquet for the superior priests of the Necropolis and of the temples of eastern Thebes, for the representatives of other foundations, and for select dignitaries of the state.

His father had never failed to attend this entertainment when he was in Thebes, but he himself had to-day for the first time received the much-coveted honor of an invitation, which-Ameni told him when he gave it-he entirely owed to the Regent.

His mother had tied up his hand, which Rameri had severely hurt; it was extremely painful, but he would not have missed the banquet at any cost, although he felt some alarm of the solemn ceremony. His family was as old as any in Egypt, his blood purer than the king's, and nevertheless he never felt thoroughly at home in the company of superior people. He was no priest, although a scribe; he was a warrior, and yet he did not rank with royal heroes.

He had been brought up to a strict fulfilment of his duty, and he devoted himself zealously to his calling; but his habits of life were widely different from those of the society in which he had been brought up —a society of which his handsome, brave, and magnanimous father had been a chief ornament. He did not cling covetously to his inherited wealth, and the noble attribute of liberality was not strange to him, but the coarseness of his nature showed itself most when he was most lavish, for he was never tired of exacting gratitude from those whom he had attached to him by his gifts, and he thought he had earned the right by his liberality to meet the recipient with roughness or arrogance, according to his humor. Thus it happened that his best actions procured him not friends but enemies.

Paaker's was, in fact, an ignoble, that is to say, a selfish nature; to shorten his road he trod down flowers as readily as he marched over the sand of the desert. This characteristic marked him in all things, even in his outward demeanor; in the sound of his voice, in his broad features, in the swaggering gait of his stumpy figure.

In camp he could conduct himself as he pleased; but this was not permissible in the society of his equals in rank; for this reason, and because those faculties of quick remark and repartee, which distinguished them, had been denied to him, he felt uneasy and out of his element when he mixed with them, and he would hardly have accepted Ameni's invitation, if it had not so greatly flattered his vanity.

It was already late; but the banquet did not begin till midnight, for the guests, before it began, assisted at the play which was performed by lamp and torch-light on the sacred lake in the south of the Necropolis, and which represented the history of Isis and Osiris.

When he entered the decorated hall in which the tables were prepared, he found all the guests assembled. The Regent Ani was present, and sat on Ameni's right at the top of the centre high-table at which several places were unoccupied; for the prophets and the initiated of the temple of Amon had excused themselves from being present. They were faithful to Rameses and his house; their grey-haired Superior disapproved of Ameni's severity towards the prince and princess, and they regarded the miracle of the sacred heart as a malicious trick of the chiefs of the Necropolis against the great temple of the capital for which Rameses had always shown a preference.

The pioneer went up to the table, where sat the general of the troops that had just returned victorious from Ethiopia, and several other officers of high rank, There was a place vacant next to the general. Paaker fixed his eyes upon this, but when he observed that the officer signed to the one next to him to come a little nearer, the pioneer imagined that each would endeavor to avoid having him for his neighbor, and with an angry glance he turned his back on the table where the warriors sat.

The Mohar was not, in fact, a welcome boon-companion. "The wine turns sour when that churl looks at it," said the general.

The eyes of all the guests turned on Paaker, who looked round for a seat, and when no one beckoned him to one he felt his blood begin to boil. He would have liked to leave the banqueting hall at once with a swingeing curse. He had indeed turned towards the door, when the Regent, who had exchanged a few whispered words with Ameni, called to him, requested him to take the place that had been reserved for him, and pointed to the seat by his side, which had in fact been intended for the high-priest of the temple of Amon.

Paaker bowed low, and took the place of honor, hardly daring to look round the table, lest he should encounter looks of surprise or of mockery. And yet he had pictured to himself his grandfather Assa, and his father, as somewhere near this place of honor, which had actually often enough been given up to them. And was he not their descendant and heir? Was not his mother Setchem of royal race? Was not the temple of Seti more indebted to him than to any one?

A servant laid a garland of flowers round his shoulders, and another handed him wine and food. Then he raised his eyes, and met the bright and sparkling glance of Gagabu; he looked quickly down again at the table.

Then the Regent spoke to him, and turning to the other guests mentioned that Paaker was on the point of starting next day for Syria, and resuming his arduous labors as Mohar. It seemed to Paaker that the Regent was excusing himself for having given him so high a place of honor.

Presently Ani raised his wine-cup, and drank to the happy issue of his reconnoitring-expedition, and a victorious conclusion to every struggle in which the Mohar might engage. The high-priest then pledged him, and thanked him emphatically in the name of the brethren of the temple, for the noble tract of arable land which he had that morning given them as a votive offering. A murmur of approbation ran round the tables, and Paaker's timidity began to diminish.

He had kept the wrappings that his mother had applied round his still aching hand.

"Are you wounded?" asked the Regent.

"Nothing of importance," answered the pioneer. "I was helping my mother into the boat, and it happened —"

"It happened," interrupted an old school-fellow of the Mohar's, who himself held a high appointment as officer of the city-watch of Thebes —"It happened that an oar or a stake fell on his fingers."

"Is it possible!" cried the Regent.

"And quite a youngster laid hands on him," continued the officer. "My people told me every detail. First the boy killed his dog —"

"That noble Descher?" asked the master of the hunt in a tone of regret. "Your father was often by my side with that dog at a boar-hunt."

Paaker bowed his head; but the officer of the watch, secure in his position and dignity, and taking no notice of the glow of anger which flushed Paaker's face, began again:

"When the hound lay on the ground, the foolhardy boy struck your dagger out of your hand."

"And did this squabble lead to any disturbance?" asked Ameni earnestly.

"No," replied the officer. "The feast has passed off to-day with unusual quiet. If the unlucky interruption to the procession by that crazy paraschites had not occurred, we should have nothing but praise for the populace. Besides the fighting priest, whom we have handed over to you, only a few thieves have been apprehended, and they belong exclusively to the caste,[107] so we simply take their booty from them, and let them go. But say, Paaker, what devil of amiability took possession of you down by the river, that you let the rascal escape unpunished."

"Did you do that?" exclaimed Gagabu. "Revenge is usually your —"

Ameni threw so warning a glance at the old man, that he suddenly broke off, and then asked the pioneer: "How did the struggle begin, and who was the fellow?"

"Some insolent people," said Paaker, "wanted to push in front of the boat that was waiting for my mother, and I asserted my rights. The rascal fell upon me, and killed my dog and-by my Osirian father! —the crocodiles would long since have eaten him if a woman had not come between us, and made herself known to me as Bent-Anat, the daughter of Rameses. It was she herself, and the rascal was the young prince Rameri, who was yesterday forbidden this temple."

"Oho!" cried the old master of the hunt. "Oho! my lord! Is this the way to speak of the children of the king?"

Others of the company who were attached to Pharaoh's family expressed their indignation; but Ameni whispered to Paaker —"Say no more!" then he continued aloud:

"You never were careful in weighing your words, my friend, and now, as it seems to me, you are speaking in the heat of fever. Come here, Gagabu, and examine Paaker's wound, which is no disgrace to him-for it was inflicted by a prince."

The old man loosened the bandage from the pioneer's swollen hand.

"That was a bad blow," he exclaimed; "three fingers are broken, and-do you see? —the emerald too in your signet ring."

Paaker looked down at his aching fingers, and uttered a sigh of rehef, for it was not the oracular ring with the name of Thotmes III., but the valuable one given to his father by the reigning king that had been crushed. Only a few solitary fragments of the splintered stone remained in the setting; the king's name had fallen to pieces, and disappeared. Paaker's bloodless lips moved silently, and an inner voice cried out to him: "The Gods point out the way! The name is gone, the bearer of the name must follow."

"It is a pity about the ring," said Gagabu. "And if the hand is not to follow it-luckily it is your left hand-leave off drinking, let yourself be taken to Nebsecht the surgeon, and get him to set the joints neatly, and bind them up."

Paaker rose, and went away after Ameni had appointed to meet him on the following day at the Temple of Seti, and the Regent at the palace.

When the door had closed behind him, the treasurer of the temple said:

"This has been a bad day for the Mohar, and perhaps it will teach him that here in Thebes he cannot swagger as he does in the field. Another adventure occurred to him to-day; would you like to hear it?"

"Yes; tell it!" cried the guests.

"You all knew old Seni," began the treasurer. "He was a rich man, but he gave away all his goods to the poor, after his seven blooming sons, one after another, had died in the war, or of illness. He only kept a small house with a little garden, and said that as the Gods had taken his children to themselves in the other world he would take pity on the forlorn in this. 'Feed the hungry, give drink to the thirsty, clothe the naked' says the law; and now that Seni has nothing more to give away, he goes through the city, as you know, hungry and thirsty himself, and scarcely clothed, and begging for his adopted children, the poor. We have all given to him, for we all know for whom he humbles himself, and holds out his hand. To-day he went round with his little bag, and begged, with his kind good eyes, for alms. Paaker has given us a good piece of arable land, and thinks, perhaps with reason, that he has done his part. When Seni addressed him, he told him to go; but the old man did not give up asking him, he followed him persistently to the grave of his father, and a great many people with him. Then the pioneer pushed him angrily back, and when at last the beggar clutched his garment, he raised his whip, and struck him two or three times, crying out: 'There-that is your portion!' The good old man bore it quite patiently, while he untied the bag, and said with tears in his eyes: 'My portion-yes-but not the portion of the poor!'

"I was standing near, and I saw how Paaker hastily withdrew into the tomb, and how his mother Setchem threw her full purse to Seni. Others followed her example, and the old man never had a richer harvest. The poor may thank the Mohar! A crowd of people collected in front of the tomb, and he would have fared badly if it had not been for the police guard who drove them away."

During this narrative, which was heard with much approval-for no one is more secure of his result than he who can tell of the downfall of a man who is disliked for his arrogance-the Regent and the high-priest had been eagerly whispering to each other.

"There can be no doubt," said Ameni, "that Bent-Anat did actually come to the festival."

"And had also dealings with the priest whom you so warmly defend," whispered the other.

"Pentaur shall be questioned this very night," returned the high-priest. "The dishes will soon be taken away, and the drinking will begin. Let us go and hear what the poet says."

"But there are now no witnesses," replied Ani.

"We do not need them," said Ameni. "He is incapable of a lie."

"Let us go then," said the Regent smiling, "for I am really curious about this white negro, and how he will come to terms with the truth. You have forgotten that there is a woman in the case."

"That there always is!" answered Ameni; he called Gagabu to him, gave him his seat, begged him to keep up the flow of cheerful conversation, to encourage the guests to drink, and to interrupt all talk of the king, the state, or the war.

"You know," he concluded, "that we are not by ourselves this evening. Wine has, before this, betrayed everything! Remember this-the mother of foresight looks backwards!"

Ani clapped his hand on the old man's shoulder. "There will be a space cleared to-night in your winelofts. It is said of you that you cannot bear to see either a full glass or an empty one; to-night give your aversion to both free play. And when you think it is the right moment, give a sign to my steward, who is sitting there in the corner. He has a few jars of the best liquor from Byblos, that he brought over with him, and he will bring it to you. I will come in again and bid you good-night." Ameni was accustomed to leave the hall at the beginning of the drinking.

When the door was closed behind him and his companion, when fresh rose-garlands had been brought for the necks of the company, when lotus blossoms decorated their heads, and the beakers were refilled, a choir of musicians came in, who played on harps, lutes, flutes, and small drums. The conductor beat the time by clapping his hands, and when the music had raised the spirits of the drinkers, they seconded his efforts by rhythmical clippings. The jolly old Gagabu kept up his character as a stout drinker, and leader of the feast.

The most priestly countenances soon beamed with cheerfulness, and the officers and courtiers outdid each other in audacious jokes. Then the old man signed to a young temple-servant, who wore a costly wreath; he came forward with a small gilt image of a mummy, carried it round the circle and cried:

"Look at this, be merry and drink so long as you are on earth, for soon you must be like this."[108]

Gagabu gave another signal, and the Regent's steward brought in the wine from Byblos. Ani was much lauded for the wonderful choiceness of the liquor.

"Such wine," exclaimed the usually grave chief of the pastophori, "is like soap."[109]

"What a simile!" cried Gagabu. "You must explain it."

"It cleanses the soul of sorrow," answered the other. "Good, friend!" they all exclaimed. "Now every one in turn shall praise the noble juice in some worthy saying."

"You begin-the chief prophet of the temple of Atnenophis."

"Sorrow is a poison," said the priest, "and wine is the antidote."

"Well said! —go on; it is your turn, my lord privy councillor."

"Every thing has its secret spring," said the official, "and wine is the secret of joy."

"Now you, my lord keeper of the seal."

"Wine seals the door on discontent, and locks the gates on sorrow."

"That it does, that it certainly does! —Now the governor of Hermothis, the oldest of all the company."

"Wine ripens especially for us old folks, and not for you young people."

"That you must explain," cried a voice from the table of the military officers.

"It makes young men of the old," laughed the octogenarian, "and children of the young."

"He has you there, you youngsters," cried Gagabu. "What have you to say, Septah?"

"Wine is a poison," said the morose haruspex, "for it makes fools of wise men."

"Then you have little to fear from it, alas!" said Gagabu laughing. "Proceed, my lord of the chase."

"The rim of the beaker," was the answer, "is like the lip of the woman you love. Touch it, and taste it, and it is as good as the kiss of a bride."

"General-the turn is yours."

"I wish the Nile ran with such wine instead of with water," cried the soldier, "and that I were as big as the colossus of Atnenophis, and that the biggest obelisk of Hatasu were my drinking vessel, and that I might drink as much as I would! But now-what have you to say of this noble liquor, excellent Gagabu?"

The second prophet raised his beaker, and gazed lovingly at the golden fluid; he tasted it slowly, and then said with his eyes turned to heaven:

"I only fear that I am unworthy to thank the Gods for such a divine blessing."

"Well said!" exclaimed the Regent Ani, who had re-entered the room unobserved. "If my wine could speak, it would thank you for such a speech."

"Hail to the Regent Ani!" shouted the guests, and they all rose with their cups filled with his noble present.

He pledged them and then rose.

"Those," said he, "who have appreciated this wine, I now invite to dine with me to-morrow. You will then meet with it again, and if you still find it to your liking, you will be heartily welcome any evening. Now, good night, friends."

A thunder of applause followed him, as he quitted the room.

The morning was already grey, when the carousing-party broke up; few of the guests could find their way unassisted through the courtyard; most of them had already been carried away by the slaves, who had waited for them-and who took them on their heads, like bales of goods-and had been borne home in their litters; but for those who remained to the end, couches were prepared in the House of Seti, for a terrific storm was now raging.

While the company were filling and refilling the beakers, which raised their spirits to so wild a pitch, the prisoner Pentaur had been examined in the presence of the Regent. Ameni's messenger had found the poet on his knees, so absorbed in meditation that he did not perceive his approach. All his peace of mind had deserted him, his soul was in a tumult, and he could not succeed in obtaining any calm and clear control over the new life-pulses which were throbbing in his heart.

He had hitherto never gone to rest at night without requiring of himself an account of the past day, and he had always been able to detect the most subtle line that divided right from wrong in his actions. But to-night he looked back on a perplexing confusion of ideas and events, and when he endeavored to sort them and arrange them, he could see nothing clearly but the image of Bent-Anat, which enthralled his heart and intellect.

He had raised his hand against his fellow-men, and dipped it in blood, he desired to convince himself of his sin, and to repent but he could not; for each time he recalled it, to blame and condemn himself, he saw the soldier's hand twisted in Uarda's hair, and the princess's eyes beaming with approbation, nay with admiration, and he said to himself that he had acted rightly, and in the same position would do the same again to-morrow. Still he felt that he had broken through all the conditions with which fate had surrounded his existence, and it seemed to him that he could never succeed in recovering the still, narrow, but peaceful life of the past.

His soul went up in prayer to the Almighty One, and to the spirit of the sweet humble woman whom he had called his mother, imploring for peace of mind and modest content; but in vain-for the longer he remained prostrate, flinging up his arms in passionate entreaty, the keener grew his longings, the less he felt able to repent or to recognize his guilt. Ameni's order to appear before him came almost as a deliverance, and he followed the messenger prepared for a severe punishment; but not afraid-almost joyful.

In obedience to the command of the grave high-priest, Pentaur related the whole occurrence-how, as there was no leech in the house, he had gone with the old wife of the paraschites to visit her possessed husband; how, to save the unhappy girl from ill-usage by the mob, he had raised his hand in fight, and dealt indeed some heavy blows.

"You have killed four men," said Ameni, "and severely wounded twice as many. Why did you not reveal yourself as a priest, as the speaker of the morning's discourse? Why did you not endeavor to persuade the people with words of warning, rather than with brute force?"

"I had no priest's garment," replied Pentaur. "There again you did wrong," said Ameni, "for you know that the law requires of each of us never to leave this house without our white robes. But you cannot pretend not to know your own powers of speech, nor to contradict me when I assert that, even in the plainest working-dress, you were perfectly able to produce as much effect with words as by deadly blows!" "I might very likely have succeeded," answered Pentaur, "but the most savage temper ruled the crowd; there was no time for reflection, and when I struck down the villain, like some reptile, who had seized the innocent girl, the lust of fighting took possession of me. I cared no more for my own life, and to save the child I would have slain thousands."

"Your eyes sparkle," said Ameni, "as if you had performed some heroic feat; and yet the men you killed were only unarmed and pious citizens, who were roused to indignation by a gross and shameless outrage. I cannot conceive whence the warrior-spirit should have fallen on a gardener's son-and a minister of the Gods."

"It is true," answered Pentaur, "when the crowd rushed upon me, and I drove them back, putting out all my strength, I felt something of the warlike rage of the soldier, who repulses the pressing foe from the standard committed to his charge. It was sinful in a priest, no doubt, and I will repent of it-but I felt it."

"You felt it-and you will repent of it, well and good," replied Ameni. "But you have not given a true account of all that happened. Why have you concealed that Bent-Anat —Rameses' daughter-was mixed up in the fray, and that she saved you by announcing her name to the people, and commanding them to leave you alone? When you gave her the lie before all the people, was it because you did not believe that it was Bent-Anat? Now, you who stand so firmly on so high a platform-now you standard-bearer of the truth answer me."

Pentaur had turned pale at his master's words, and said, as he looked at the Regent:

"We are not alone."

"Truth is one!" said Ameni coolly. "What you can reveal to me, can also be heard by this noble lord, the Regent of the king himself. Did you recognize Bent-Anat, or not?"

"The lady who rescued me was like her, and yet unlike," answered the poet, whose blood was roused by the subtle irony of his Superior's words. "And if I had been as sure that she was the princess, as I am that you are the man who once held me in honor, and who are now trying to humiliate me, I would all the more have acted as I did to spare a lady who is more like a goddess than a woman, and who, to save an unworthy wretch like me, stooped from a throne to the dust."

"Still the poet-the preacher!" said Ameni. Then he added severely. "I beg for a short and clear answer. We know for certain that the princess took part in the festival in the disguise of a woman of low rank, for she again declared herself to Paaker; and we know that it was she who saved you. But did you know that she meant to come across the Nile?"

"How should I?" asked Pentaur.

"Well, did you believe that it was Bent-Anat whom you saw before you when she ventured on to the scene of conflict?"

"I did believe it," replied Pentaur; he shuddered and cast down his eyes.

"Then it was most audacious to drive away the king's daughter as an impostor."

"It was," said Pentaur. "But for my sake she had risked the honor of her name, and that of her royal father, and I —I should not have risked my life and freedom for —"

"We have heard enough," interrupted Ameni.

"Not so," the Regent interposed. "What became of the girl you had saved?"

"An old witch, Hekt by name, a neighbor of Pinem's, took her and her grandmother into her cave," answered the poet; who was then, by the high-priest's order, taken back to the temple-prison.

Scarcely had he disappeared when the Regent exclaimed:

"A dangerous man! an enthusiast! an ardent worshipper of Rameses!"

"And of his daughter," laughed Ameni, "but only a worshipper. Thou hast nothing to fear from him —I will answer for the purity of his motives."

"But he is handsome and of powerful speech," replied Ani. "I claim him as my prisoner, for he has killed one of my soldiers."

Ameni's countenance darkened, and he answered very sternly:

"It is the exclusive right of our conclave, as established by our charter, to judge any member of this fraternity. You, the future king, have freely promised to secure our privileges to us, the champions of your own ancient and sacred rights."

"And you shall have them," answered the Regent with a persuasive smile. "But this man is dangerous, and you would not have him go unpunished."

"He shall be severely judged," said Ameni, "but by us and in this house."

"He has committed murder!" cried Ani. "More than one murder. He is worthy of death."

"He acted under pressure of necessity," replied Ameni. "And a man so favored by the Gods as he, is not to be lightly given up because an untimely impulse of generosity prompted him to rash conduct. I know —I can see that you wish him ill. Promise me, as you value me as an ally, that you will not attempt his life."

"Oh, willingly!" smiled the Regent, giving the high-priest his hand.

"Accept my sincere thanks," said Ameni. "Pentaur was the most promising of my disciples, and in spite of many aberrations I still esteem him highly. When he was telling us of what had occurred to-day, did he not remind you of the great Assa, or of his gallant son, the Osirian father of the pioneer Paaker?"

"The likeness is extraordinary," answered Ani, "and yet he is of quite humble birth. Who was his mother?"

"Our gate-keeper's daughter, a plain, pious, simple creature."

"Now I will return to the banqueting hall," said Ani, after a fete moments of reflection. "But I must ask you one thing more. I spoke to you of a secret that will put Paaker into our power. The old sorceress Hekt, who has taken charge of the paraschites' wife and grandchild, knows all about it. Send some policeguards over there, and let her be brought over here as a prisoner; I will examine her myself, and so can question her without exciting observation."

Ameni at once sent off a party of soldiers, and then quietly ordered a faithful attendant to light up the so-called audience-chamber, and to put a seat for him in an adjoining room.

CHAPTER XXX.

While the banquet was going forward at the temple, and Ameni's messengers were on their way to the valley of the kings' tombs, to waken up old Hekt, a furious storm of hot wind came up from the southwest, sweeping black clouds across the sky, and brown clouds of dust across the earth. It bowed the slender palm-trees as an archer bends his bow, tore the tentpegs up on the scene of the festival, whirled the light tent-cloths up in the air, drove them like white witches through the dark night, and thrashed the still surface of the Nile till its yellow waters swirled and tossed in waves like a restless sea.

Paaker had compelled his trembling slaves to row him across the stream; several times the boat was near being swamped, but he had seized the helm himself with his uninjured hand, and guided it firmly and surely, though the rocking of the boat kept his broken hand in great and constant pain. After a few ineffectual attempts he succeeded in landing. The storm had blown out the lanterns at the masts-the signal lights for which his people looked-and he found neither servants nor torch-bearers on the bank, so he struggled through the scorching wind as far as the gate of his house. His big dog had always been wont to announce his return home to the door-keeper with joyful barking; but to-night the boatmen long knocked in vain at the heavy doer. When at last he entered the court-yard, he found all dark, for the wind had extinguished the lanterns and torches, and there were no lights but in the windows of his mother's rooms.

The dogs in their open kennels now began to make themselves heard, but their tones were plaintive and whining, for the storm had frightened the beasts; their howling cut the pioneer to the heart, for it reminded him of the poor slain Descher, whose deep voice he sadly missed; and when he went into his own room he was met by a wild cry of lamentation from the Ethiopian slave, for the dog which he had trained for Paaker's father, and which he had loved.

The pioneer threw himself on a seat, and ordered some water to be brought, that he might cool his aching hand in it, according to the prescription of Nebsecht.

As soon as the old man saw the broken fingers, he gave another yell of woe, and when Paaker ordered him to cease he asked:

"And is the man still alive who did that, and who killed Descher?"

Paaker nodded, and while he held his hand in the cooling water he looked sullenly at the ground. He felt miserable, and he asked himself why the storm had not swamped the boat, and the Nile had not swallowed him. Bitterness and rage filled his breast, and he wished he were a child, and might cry. But his mood soon changed, his breath came quickly, his breast heaved, and an ominous light glowed in his eyes. He was not thinking of his love, but of the revenge that was even dearer to him.

"That brood of Rameses!" he muttered. "I will sweep them all away together-the king, and Mena, and those haughty princes, and many more —I know how. Only wait, only wait!" and he flung up his right fist with a threatening gesture.

The door opened at this instant, and his mother entered the room; the raging of the storm had drowned the sound of her steps, and as she approached her revengeful son, she called his name in horror at the mad wrath which was depicted in his countenance. Paaker started, and then said with apparent composure:

"Is it you, mother? It is near morning, and it is better to be asleep than awake in such an hour."

"I could not rest in my rooms," answered Setchem. "The storm howled so wildly, and I am so anxious, so frightfully unhappy-as I was before your father died."

"Then stay with me," said Paaker affectionately, "and lie down on my couch."

"I did not come here to sleep," replied Setchem. "I am too unhappy at all that happened to you on the larding-steps, it is frightful! No, no, my son, it is not about your smashed hand, though it grieves me to see you in pain; it is about the king, and his anger when he hears of the quarrel. He favors you less than he did your lost father, I know it well. But how wildly you smile, how wild you looked when I came in! It went through my bones and marrow."

Both were silent for a time, and listened to the furious raging of the storm. At last Setchem spoke. "There is something else," she said, "which disturbs my mind. I cannot forget the poet who spoke at the festival to-day, young Pentaur. His figure, his face, his movements, nay his very voice, are exactly like those of your father at the time when he was young, and courted me. It is as if the Gods were fain to see the best man that they ever took to themselves, walk before them a second time upon earth."

"Yes, my lady," said the black slave; "no mortal eye ever saw such a likeness. I saw him fighting in front of the paraschites' cottage, and he was more like my dead master than ever. He swung the tent-post over his head, as my lord used to swing his battle-axe."

"Be silent," cried Paaker, "and get out-idiot! The priest is like my father; I grant it, mother; but he is an insolent fellow, who offended me grossly, and with whom I have to reckon-as with many others."

"How violent you are!" interrupted his mother, "and how full of bitterness and hatred. Your father was so sweet-tempered, and kind to everybody."

"Perhaps they are kind to me?" retorted Paaker with a short laugh. "Even the Immortals spite me, and throw thorns in my path. But I will push them aside with my own hand, and will attain what I desire without the help of the Gods and overthrow all that oppose me."

"We cannot blow away a feather without the help of the Immortals," answered Setchem. "So your father used to say, who was a very different man both in body and mind from you! I tremble before you this evening, and at the curses you have uttered against the children of your lord and sovereign, your father's best friend."

"But my enemy," shouted Paaker. "You will get nothing from me but curses. And the brood of Rameses shall learn whether your husband's son will let himself be ill-used and scorned without revenging him self. I will fling them into an abyss, and I will laugh when I see them writhing in the sand at my feet!"

"Fool!" cried Setchem, beside herself. "I am but a woman, and have often blamed myself for being soft and weak; but as sure as I am faithful to your dead father-who you are no more like than a bramble is like a palm-tree —so surely will I tear my love for you out of my heart if you-if you-Now I see! now I know! Answer me-murderer! Where are the seven arrows with the wicked words which used to hang here? Where are the arrows on which you had scrawled 'Death to Mena?'"

With these words Setchem breathlessly started forward, but the pioneer drew back as she confronted him, as in his youthful days when she threatened to punish him for some misdemeanor. She followed him up, caught him by the girdle, and in a hoarse voice repeated her question. He stood still, snatched her hand angrily from his belt, and said defiantly:

"I have put them in my quiver-and not for mere play. Now you know."

Incapable of words, the maddened woman once more raised her hand against her degenerate son, but he put back her arm.

"I am no longer a child," he said, "and I am master of this house. I will do what I will, if a hundred women hindered me!" and with these words he pointed to the door. Setchem broke into loud sobs, and turned her back upon him; but at the door once more she turned to look at him. He had seated himself, and was resting his forehead on the table on which the bowl of cold water stood.

Setchem fought a hard battle. At last once more through her choking tears she called his name, opened her arms wide and exclaimed:

"Here I am-here I am! Come to my heart, only give up these hideous thoughts of revenge."

But Paaker did not move, he did not look up at her, he did not speak, he only shook his head in negation. Setchem's hands fell, and she said softly:

"What did your father teach you out of the scriptures? 'Your highest praise consists in this, to reward your mother for what she has done for you, in bringing you up, so that she may not raise her hands to God, nor He hear her lamentation.'"

At these words, Paaker sobbed aloud, but he did not look at his mother. She called him tenderly by his name; then her eyes fell on his quiver, which lay on a bench with other arms. Her heart shrunk within her, and with a trembling voice she exclaimed:

"I forbid this mad vengeance-do you hear? Will you give it up? You do not move? No! you will not! Ye Gods, what can I do?"

She wrung her hands in despair; then she hastily crossed the room, snatched out one of the arrows, and strove to break it. Paaker sprang from his seat, and wrenched the weapon from her hand; the sharp point slightly scratched the skin, and dark drops of blood flowed from it, and dropped upon the floor.

The Mohar would have taken the wounded hand, for Setchem, who had the weakness of never being able to see blood flow-neither her own nor anybody's else-had turned as pale as death; but she pushed him from her, and as she spoke her gentle voice had a dull estranged tone.

"This hand," she said —"a mother's hand wounded by her son-shall never again grasp yours till you have sworn a solemn oath to put away from you all thoughts of revenge and murder, and not to disgrace your father's name. I have said it, and may his glorified spirit be my witness, and give me strength to keep my word!"

Paaker had fallen on his knees, and was engaged in a terrible mental struggle, while his mother slowly went towards the door. There again she stood still for a moment; she did not speak, but her eyes appealed to him once more.

In vain. At last she left the room, and the wind slammed the door violently behind her. Paaker groaned, and pressed his hand over his eyes.

"Mother, mother!" he cried. "I cannot go back —I cannot."

A fearful gust of wind howled round the house, and drowned his voice, and then he heard two tremendous claps, as if rocks had been hurled from heaven. He started up and went to the window, where the melancholy grey dawn was showing, in order to call the slaves. Soon they came trooping out, and the steward called out as soon as he saw him:

"The storm has blown down the masts at the great gate!"

"Impossible!" cried Paaker.

"Yes, indeed!" answered the servant. "They have been sawn through close to the ground. The matmaker no doubt did it, whose collar-bone was broken. He has escaped in this fearful night."

"Let out the dogs," cried the Mohar. "All who have legs run after the blackguard! Freedom, and five handfuls of gold for the man who brings him back."

The guests at the House of Seti had already gone to rest, when Ameni was informed of the arrival of the sorceress, and he at once went into the hall, where Ani was waiting to see her; the Regent roused himself from a deep reverie when he heard the high-priest's steps.

"Is she come?" he asked hastily; when Ameni answered in the affirmative Ani went on meanwhile carefully disentangling the disordered curls of his wig, and arranging his broad, collar-shaped necklace:

"The witch may exercise some influence over me; will you not give me your blessing to preserve me from her spells? It is true, I have on me this Houss'-eye, and this Isis-charm, but one never knows."

"My presence will be your safe-guard," said Ameni. "But-no, of course you wish to speak with her alone. You shall be conducted to a room, which is protected against all witchcraft by sacred texts. My brother," he continued to one of the serving-priests, "let the witch be taken into one of the consecrated rooms, and then, when you have sprinkled the threshold, lead my lord Ani thither."

The high-priest went away, and into a small room which adjoined the hall where the interview between the Regent and the old woman was about to take place, and where the softest whisper spoken in the larger room could be heard by means of an ingeniously contrived and invisible tube.

When Ani saw the old woman, he started back is horror; her appearance at this moment was, in fact, frightful. The storm had tossed and torn her garment and tumbled all her thick, white hair, so that locks of it fell over her face. She leaned on a staff, and bending far forward looked steadily at the Regent; and her eyes, red and smarting from the sand which the wind had flung in her face, seemed to glow as she fixed them on his. She looked as a hyaena might when creeping to seize its prey, and Ani felt a cold shiver and he heard her hoarse voice addressing him to greet him and to represent that he had chosen a strange hour for requiring her to speak with him.

When she had thanked him for his promise of renewing her letter of freedom, and had confirmed the statement that Paaker had had a love-philter from her, she parted her hair from off her face-it occurred to her that she was a woman.

The Regent sat in an arm-chair, she stood before him; but the struggle with the storm had tired her old limbs, and she begged Ani to permit her to be seated, as she had a long story to tell, which would put Paaker into his power, so that he would find him as yielding as wax. The Regent signed her to a corner of the room, and she squatted down on the pavement.

When he desired her to proceed with her story, she looked at the floor for some time in silence, and then began, as if half to herself:

"I will tell thee, that I may find peace —I do not want, when I die, to be buried unembalmed. Who knows but perhaps strange things may happen in the other world, and I would not wish to miss them. I want to see him again down there, even if it were in the seventh limbo of the damned. Listen to me! But, before I speak, promise me that whatever I tell thee, thou wilt leave me in peace, and will see that I am embalmed when I am dead. Else I will not speak."

Ani bowed consent.

"No-no," she said. "I will tell thee what to swear 'If I do not keep my word to Hekt-who gives the Mohar into my power-may the Spirits whom she rules, annihilate me before I mount the throne.' Do not be vexed, my lord-and say only 'Yes.' What I can tell, is worth more than a mere word."

"Well then-yes!" cried the Regent, eager for the mighty revelation.

The old woman muttered a few unintelligible words; then she collected herself, stretched out her lean neck, and asked, as she fixed her sparkling eyes on the man before her:

"Did'st thou ever, when thou wert young, hear of the singer Beki? Well, look at me, I am she."

She laughed loud and hoarsely, and drew her tattered robe across her bosom, as if half ashamed of her unpleasing person.

"Ay!" she continued. "Men find pleasure in grapes by treading them down, and when the must is drunk the skins are thrown on the dung-hill. Grape-skins, that is what I am-but you need not look at me so pitifully; I was grapes once, and poor and despised as I am now, no one can take from me what I have had and have been. Mine has been a life out of a thousand, a complete life, full to overflowing of joy and suffering, of love and hate, of delight, despair, and revenge. Only to talk of it raises me to a seat by thy throne there. No, let me be, I am used now to squatting on the ground; but I knew thou wouldst hear me to the end, for once I too was one of you. Extremes meet in all things —I know it by experience. The greatest men will hold out a hand to a beautiful woman, and time was when I could lead you all as with a rope. Shall I begin at the beginning? Well —I seldom am in the mood for it now-a-days. Fifty years ago I sang a song with this voice of mine; an old crow like me? sing! But so it was. My father was a man of rank, the governor of Abydos; when the first Rameses took possession of the throne my father was faithful to the house of thy fathers, so the new king sent us all to the gold mines, and there they all died-my parents, brothers, and sisters. I only survived by some miracle. As I was handsome and sang well, a music master took me into his band, brought me to Thebes, and wherever there was a feast given in any great house, Beki was in request. Of flowers and money and tender looks I had a plentiful harvest; but I was proud and cold, and the misery of my people had made me bitter at an age when usually even bad liquor tastes of honey. Not one of all the gay young fellows, princes' sons, and nobles, dared to touch my hand. But my hour was to come; the handsomest and noblest man of them all, and grave and dignified too-was Assa, the old Mohar's father, and grandfather of Pentaur-no, I should say of Paaker,

189

the pioneer; thou hast known him. Well, wherever I sang, he sat opposite me, and gazed at me, and I could not take my eyes off him, and-thou canst tell the rest! no! Well, no woman before or after me can ever love a man as I loved Assa. Why dost thou not laugh? It must seem odd, too, to hear such a thing from the toothless mouth of an old witch. He is dead, long since dead. I hate him! and yet-wild as it sounds —I believe I love him yet. And he loved me-for two years; then he went to the war with Seti, and remained a long time away, and when I saw him again he had courted the daughter of some rich and noble house. I was handsome enough still, but he never looked at me at the banquets. I came across him at least twenty times, but he avoided me as if I were tainted with leprosy, and I began to fret, and fell ill of a fever. The doctors said it was all over with me, so I sent him a letter in which there was nothing but these words: 'Beki is dying, and would like to see Assa once more,' and in the papyrus I put his first present —a plain ring. And what was the answer? a handful of gold! Gold-gold! Thou may'st believe me, when I say that the sight of it was more torturing to my eyes than the iron with which they put out the eyes of criminals. Even now, when I think of it-But what do you men, you lords of rank and wealth, know of a breaking heart? When two or three of you happen to meet, and if thou should'st tell the story, the most respectable will say in a pompous voice: 'The man acted nobly indeed; he was married, and his wife would have complained with justice if he had gone to see the singer.' Am I right or wrong? I know; not one will remember that the other was a woman, a feeling human being; it will occur to no one that his deed on the one hand saved an hour of discomfort, and on the other wrought half a century of despair. Assa escaped his wife's scolding, but a thousand curses have fallen on him and on his house. How virtuous he felt himself when he had crushed and poisoned a passionate heart that had never ceased to love him! Ay, and he would have come if he had not still felt some love for me, if he had not misdoubted himself, and feared that the dying woman might once more light up the fire he had so carefully smothered and crushed out. I would have grieved for him-but that he should send me money, money! —that I have never forgiven; that he shall atone for in his grandchild." The old woman spoke the last words as if in a dream, and without seeming to remember her hearer. Ani shuddered, as if he were in the presence of a mad woman, and he involuntarily drew his chair back a little way.

The witch observed this; she took breath and went on: "You lords, who walk in high places, do not know how things go on in the depths beneath you; you do not choose to know.

"But I will shorten my story. I got well, but I got out of my bed thin and voiceless. I had plenty of money, and I spent it in buying of everyone who professed magic in Thebes, potions to recover Assa's love for me, or in paying for spells to be cast on him, or for magic drinks to destroy him. I tried too to recover my voice, but the medicines I took for it made it rougher not sweeter. Then an excommunicated priest, who was famous among the magicians, took me into his house, and there I learned many things; his old companions afterwards turned upon him, he came over here into the Necropolis, and I came with him. When at last he was taken and hanged, I remained in his cave, and myself took to witchcraft. Children point their fingers at me, honest men and women avoid me, I am an abomination to all men, nay to myself. And one only is guilty of all this ruin-the noblest gentleman in Thebes-the pious Assa.

"I had practised magic for several years, and had become learned in many arts, when one day the gardener Sent, from whom I was accustomed to buy plants for my mixtures-he rents a plot of ground from the temple of Seti-Sent brought me a new-born child that had been born with six toes; I was to remove the supernumerary toe by my art. The pious mother of the child was lying ill of fever, or she never would have allowed it; I took the screaming little wretch-for such things are sometimes curable. The next morning, a few hours after sunrise, there was a bustle in front of my cave; a maid, evidently belonging to a noble house, was calling me. Her mistress, she said, had come with her to visit the tomb of her fathers, and there had been taken ill, and had given birth to a child. Her mistress was lying senseless —I must go at once, and help her. I took the little six-toed brat in my cloak, told my slavegirl to follow me with water, and soon found myself-as thou canst guess-at the tomb of Assa's ancestors. The poor woman, who lay there in convulsions, was his daughter-in-law Setchem. The baby, a boy, was as sound as a nut, but she was evidently in great danger. I sent the maid with the litter, which was waiting outside, to the temple here for help; the girl said that her master, the father of the child, was at the war, but that the grandfather, the noble Assa, had promised to meet the lady Setchem at the tomb, and would shortly be coming; then she disappeared with the litter. I washed the child, and kissed it as if it were my own. Then I heard distant steps in the valley, and the recollection of the moment when I, lying at the point of death, had received that gift of money from Assa came over me, and then I do not know myself how it happened —I gave the new-born grandchild of Assa to my slave-girl, and told her to carry it quickly to the cave, and I wrapped the little six-toed baby in my rags and held it in my lap. There I sat-and the minutes seemed hours, till Assa came up; and when he stood before me, grown grey, it is true, but still handsome and upright —I put the gardener's boy, the six-toed brat, into his very arms, and a thousand demons seemed to laugh hoarsely within me. He thanked me, he did not know me, and once more he offered me a handful of gold. I took it, and I listened as the priest, who had come from the temple, prophesied all sorts of fine things for the little one, who was born in so fortunate an hour; and then I went back into my cave, and there I laughed till I cried, though I do not know that the tears sprang from the laughter.

"A few days after I gave Assa's grandchild to the gardener, and told him the sixth toe had come off; I had made a little wound on his foot to take in the bumpkin. So Assa's grandchild, the son of the Mohar, grew up as the gardener's child, and received the name of Pentaur, and he was brought up in the temple here, and is wonderfully like Assa; but the gardener's monstrous brat is the pioneer Paaker. That is the whole secret."

Ani had listened in silence to the terrible old woman.

We are involuntarily committed to any one who can inform us of some absorbing fact, and who knows how to make the information valuable. It did not occur to the Regent to punish the witch for her crimes; he thought rather of his older friends' rapture when they talked of the singer Beki's songs and beauty. He looked at the woman, and a cold shiver ran through all his limbs.

"You may live in peace," he said at last; "and when you die I will see to your being embalmed; but give up your black arts. You must be rich, and, if you are not, say what you need. Indeed, I scarcely dare offer you gold-it excites your hatred, as I understand."

"I could take thine-but now let me go!"

She got up, and went towards the door, but the Regent called to her to stop, and asked:

"Is Assa the father of your son, the little Nemu, the dwarf of the lady Katuti?"

The witch laughed loudly. "Is the little wretch like Assa or like Beki? I picked him up like many other children."

"But he is clever!" said Ani.

"Ay-that he is. He has planned many a shrewd stroke, and is devoted to his mistress. He will help thee to thy purpose, for he himself has one too."

"And that is —?"

"Katuti will rise to greatness with thee, and to riches through Paaker, who sets out to-morrow to make the woman he loves a widow."

"You know a great deal," said Ani meditatively, "and I would ask you one thing more; though indeed your story has supplied the answer-but perhaps you know more now than you did in your youth. Is there in truth any effectual love-philter?"

"I will not deceive thee, for I desire that thou should'st keep thy word to me," replied Hekt. "A love potion rarely has any effect, and never but on women who have never before loved. If it is given to a woman whose heart is filled with the image of another man her passion for him only will grow the stronger."

"Yet another," said Ani. "Is there any way of destroying an enemy at a distance?"

"Certainly," said the witch. "Little people may do mean things, and great people can let others do things that they cannot do themselves. My story has stirred thy gall, and it seems to me that thou dost not love the poet Pentaur. A smile! Well then —I have not lost sight of him, and I know he is grown up as proud and as handsome as Assa. He is wonderfully like him, and I could have loved him-have loved as this foolish heart had better never have loved. It is strange! In many women, who come to me, I see how their hearts cling to the children of men who have abandoned them, and we women are all alike, in most things. But I will not let myself love Assa's grandchild —I must not. I will injure him, and help everyone that persecutes him; for though Assa is dead, the wrongs he did me live in me so long as I live myself. Pentaur's destiny must go on its course. If thou wilt have his life, consult with Nemu, for he hates him too, and he will serve thee more effectually than I can with my vain spells and silly harmless brews. Now let me go home!"

A few hours later Ameni sent to invite the Regent to breakfast.

"Do you know who the witch Hekt is?" asked Ani.

"Certainly-how should I not know? She is the singer Beki-the former enchantress of Thebes. May I ask what her communications were?"

Ani thought it best not to confide the secret of Pentaur's birth to the high-priest, and answered evasively. Then Ameni begged to be allowed to give him some information about the old woman, and how she had had a hand in the game; and he related to his hearer, with some omissions and variations-as if it were a fact he had long known-the very story which a few hours since he had overheard, and learned for the first time. Ani feigned great astonishment, and agreed with the high-priest that Paaker should not for the present be informed of his true origin.

"He is a strangely constituted man," said Ameni, "and he is not incapable of playing us some unforeseen trick before he has done his part, if he is told who he is."

The storm had exhausted itself, and the sky, though covered still with torn and flying clouds, cleared by degrees, as the morning went on; a sharp coolness succeeded the hot blast, but the sun as it mounted higher and higher soon heated the air. On the roads and in the gardens lay uprooted trees and many slightly-built houses which had been blown down, while the tents in the strangers' quarter, and hundreds of light palm-thatched roofs, had been swept away.

The Regent was returning to Thebes, and with him went Ameni, who desired to ascertain by his own eyes what mischief the whirlwind had done to his garden in the city. On the Nile they met Paaker's boat, and Ani caused it and his own to be stopped, while he requested Paaker to visit him shortly at the palace.

The high-priest's garden was in no respect inferior in beauty and extent to that of the Mohar. The ground had belonged to his family from the remotest generations, and his house was large and magnificent. He seated himself in a shady arbor, to take a repast with his still handsome wife and his young and pretty daughters.

He consoled his wife for the various damage done by the hurricane, promised the girls to build a new and handsomer clove-cot in the place of the one which had been blown down, and laughed and joked with them all; for here the severe head of the House of Seti, the grave Superior of the Necropolis, became a simple man, an affectionate husband, a tender father, a judicious friend, among his children, his flowers, and his birds. His youngest daughter clung to his right arm, and an older one to his left, when he rose from table to go with them to the poultry-yard.

On the way thither a servant announced to him that the Lady Setchem wished to see him.

"Take her to your mistress," he said.

But the slave-who held in his hand a handsome gift in money-explained that the widow wished to speak with him alone.

"Can I never enjoy an hour's peace like other men?" exclaimed Ameni annoyed. "Your mistress can receive her, and she can wait with her till I come. It is true, girls-is it not? —that I belong to you just now, and to the fowls, and ducks, and pigeons?"

His youngest daughter kissed him, the second patted him affectionately, and they all three went gaily forward. An hour later he requested the Lady Setchem to accompany him into the garden.

The poor, anxious, and frightened woman had resolved on this step with much difficulty; tears filled her kind eyes, as she communicated her troubles to the high-priest.

"Thou art a wise counsellor," she said, "and thou knowest well how my son honors the Gods of the temple of Seti with gifts and offerings. He will not listen to his mother, but thou hast influence with him. He meditates frightful things, and if he cannot be terrified by threats of punishment from the Immortals, he will raise his hand against Mena, and perhaps—"

"Against the king," interrupted Ameni gravely. "I know it, and I will speak to him."

"Thanks, oh a thousand thanks!" cried the widow, and she seized the high-priests robe to kiss it. "It was thou who soon after his birth didst tell my husband that he was born under a lucky star, and would grow to be an honor and an ornament to his house and to his country. And now-now he will ruin himself in this world, and the next."

"What I foretold of your son," said Ameni, "shall assuredly be fulfilled, for the ways of the Gods are not as the ways of men."

"Thy words do me good!" cried Setchem. "None can tell what fearful terror weighed upon my heart, when I made up my mind to come here. But thou dost not yet know all. The great masts of cedar, which Paaker sent from Lebanon to Thebes to bear our banners, and ornament our gateway, were thrown to the ground at sunrise by the frightful wind."

"Thus shall your son's defiant spirit be broken," said Ameni; "But for you, if you have patience, new joys shall arise."

"I thank thee again," said Setchem. "But something yet remains to be said. I know that I am wasting the time that thou dost devote to thy family, and I remember thy saying once that here in Thebes thou wert like a pack-Horse with his load taken off, and free to wander over a green meadow. I will not disturb thee much longer-but the Gods sent me such a wonderful vision. Paaker would not listen to me, and I went back into my room full of sorrow; and when at last, after the sun had risen, I fell asleep for a few minutes, I dreamed I saw before me the poet Pentaur, who is wonderfully like my dead husband in appearance and in voice. Paaker went up to him, and abused him violently, and threatened him with his fist; the priest raised his arms in prayer, just as I saw him yesterday at the festival-but not in devotion, but to seize Paaker, and wrestle with him. The struggle did not last long, for Paaker seemed to shrink up, and lost his human form, and fell at the poet's feet-not my son, but a shapeless lump of clay such as the potter uses to make jars of."

"A strange dream!" exclaimed Ameni, not without agitation. "A very strange dream, but it bodes you good. Clay, Setchem, is yielding, and clearly indicates that which the Gods prepare for you. The Immortals will give you a new and a better son instead of the old one, but it is not revealed to me by what means. Go now, and sacrifice to the Gods, and trust to the wisdom of those who guide the life of the universe, and of all mortal creatures. Yet—I would give you one more word of advice. If Paaker comes to you repentant, receive him kindly, and let me know; but if he will not yield, close your rooms against him, and let him depart without taking leave of you."

When Setchem, much encouraged, was gone away, Ameni said to himself:

"She will find splendid compensation for this coarse scoundrel, and she shall not spoil the tool we need to strike our blow. I have often doubted how far dreams do, indeed, foretell the future, but to-day my faith in them is increased. Certainly a mother's heart sees farther than that of any other human being."

At the door of her house Setchem came up with her son's chariot. They saw each other, but both looked away, for they could not meet affectionately, and would not meet coldly. As the horses outran the litter-bearers, the mother and son looked round at each other, their eyes met, and each felt a stab in the heart.

In the evening the pioneer, after he had had an interview with the Regent, went to the temple of Seti to receive Ameni's blessing on all his undertakings. Then, after sacrificing in the tomb of his ancestors, he set out for Syria.

Just as he was getting into his chariot, news was brought him that the mat-maker, who had sawn through the masts at the gate, had been caught.

"Put out his eyes!" he cried; and these were the last words he spoke as he quitted his home.

Setchem looked after him for a long time; she had refused to bid him farewell, and now she implored the Gods to turn his heart, and to preserve him from malice and crime.

CHAPTER XXXI.

Three days had passed since the pioneer's departure, and although it was still early, busy occupation was astir in Bent-Anat's work-rooms.

The ladies had passed the stormy night, which had succeeded the exciting evening of the festival, without sleep.

Nefert felt tired and sleepy the next morning, and begged the princess to introduce her to her new duties for the first time next day; but the princess spoke to her encouragingly, told her that no man should put off doing right till the morrow, and urged her to follow her into her workshop.

"We must both come to different minds," said she. "I often shudder involuntarily, and feel as if I bore a brand-as if I had a stain here on my shoulder where it was touched by Paaker's rough hand."

The first day of labor gave Nefert a good many difficulties to overcome; on the second day the work she had begun already had a charm for her, and by the third she rejoiced in the little results of her care.

Bent-Anat had put her in the right place, for she had the direction of a large number of young girls and women, the daughters, wives, and widows of those Thebans who were at the war, or who had fallen in the field, who sorted and arranged the healing herbs. Her helpers sat in little circles on the ground; in the midst of each lay a great heap of fresh and dry plants, and in front of each work-woman a number of parcels of the selected roots, leaves, and flowers.

An old physician presided over the whole, and had shown Nefert the first day the particular plants which he needed.

The wife of Mena, who was fond of flowers, had soon learnt them all, and she taught willingly, for she loved children.

She soon had favorites among the children, and knew some as being industrious and careful, others as idle and heedless:

"Ay! ay!" she exclaimed, bending over a little half-naked maiden with great almond-shaped eyes. "You are mixing them all together. Your father, as you tell me, is at the war. Suppose, now, an arrow were to strike him, and this plant, which would hurt him, were laid on the burning wound instead of this other, which would do him good-that would be very sad."

The child nodded her head, and looked her work through again. Nefert turned to a little idler, and said: "You are chattering again, and doing nothing, and yet your father is in the field. If he were ill now, and has no medicine, and if at night when he is asleep he dreams of you, and sees you sitting idle, he may say to himself: 'Now I might get well, but my little girl at home does not love me, for she would rather sit with her hands in her lap than sort herbs for her sick father.'"

Then Nefert turned to a large group of the girls, who were sorting plants, and said: "Do you, children, know the origin of all these wholesome, healing herbs? The good Horus went out to fight against Seth, the murderer of his father, and the horrible enemy wounded Horus in the eye in the struggle; but the son of Osiris conquered, for good always conquers evil. But when Isis saw the bad wound, she pressed her son's head to her bosom, and her heart was as sad as that of any poor human mother that holds her suffering child in her arms. And she thought: 'How easy it is to give wounds, and how hard it is to heal them!' and so she wept; one tear after another fell on the earth, and wherever they wetted the ground there sprang up a kindly healing plant."

"Isis is good!" cried a little girl opposite to her. "Mother says Isis loves children when they are good."

"Your mother is right," replied Nefert. "Isis herself has her dear little son Horus; and every human being that dies, and that was good, becomes a child again, and the Goddess makes it her own, and takes it to her breast, and nurses it with her sister Nephthys till he grows up and can fight for his father."

Nefert observed that while she spoke one of the women was crying. She went up to her, and learned that her husband and her son were both dead, the former in Syria, and the latter after his return to Egypt. "Poor soul!" said Nefert. "Now you will be very careful, that the wounds of others may be healed. I will tell you something more about Isis. She loved her husband Osiris dearly, as you did your dead husband, and I my husband Mena, but he fell a victim to the cunning of Seth, and she could not tell where to find the body that had been carried away, while you can visit your husband in his grave. Then Isis went through the land lamenting, and ah! what was to become of Egypt, which received all its fruitfulness from Osiris. The sacred Nile was dried up, and not a blade of verdure was green on its banks. The Goddess grieved over this beyond words, and one of her tears fell in the bed of the river, and immediately it began to rise. You know, of course, that each inundation arises from a tear of Isis. Thus a widow's sorrow may bring blessing to millions of human beings."

The woman had listened to her attentively, and when Nefert ceased speaking she said:

"But I have still three little brats of my son's to feed, for his wife, who was a washerwoman, was eaten by a crocodile while she was at work. Poor folks must work for themselves, and not for others. If the princess did not pay us, I could not think of the wounds of the soldiers, who do not belong to me. I am no longer strong, and four mouths to fill —"

Nefert was shocked-as she often was in the course of her new duties-and begged Bent-Gnat to raise the wages of the woman.

"Willingly," said the princess. "How could I beat down such an assistant. Come now with me into the kitchen. I am having some fruit packed for my father and brothers; there must be a box for Mena too." Nefert followed her royal friend, found them packing in one case the golden dates of the oasis of Amon, and in another the dark dates of Nubia, the king's favorite sort. "Let me pack them!" cried Nefert; she made the servants empty the box again, and re-arranged the various-colored dates in graceful patterns, with other fruits preserved in sugar.

Bent-Anat looked on, and when she had finished she took her hand. "Whatever your fingers have touched," she exclaimed, "takes some pretty aspect. Give me that scrap of papyrus; I shall put it in the case, and write upon it:

"'These were packed for king Rameses by his daughter's clever helpmate, the wife of Mena.'"

After the mid-day rest the princess was called away, and Nefert remained for some hours alone with the work-women.

When the sun went down, and the busy crowd were about to leave, Nefert detained them, and said: "The Sun-bark is sinking behind the western hills; come, let us pray together for the king and for those we love in the field. Each of you think of her own: you children of your fathers, you women of your sons, and we wives of our distant husbands, and let us entreat Amon that they may return to us as certainly as the sun, which now leaves us, will rise again to-morrow morning."

Nefert knelt down, and with her the women and the children.

When they rose, a little girl went up to Nefert, and said, pulling her dress: "Thou madest us kneel here yesterday, and already my mother is better, because I prayed for her."

"No doubt," said Nefert, stroking the child's black hair.

She found Bent-Anat on the terrace meditatively gazing across to the Necropolis, which was fading into darkness before her eyes. She started when she heard the light footsteps of her friend.

"I am disturbing thee," said Nefert, about to retire.

"No, stay," said Bent-Anat. "I thank the Gods that I have you, for my heart is sad-pitifully sad."

"I know where your thoughts were," said Nefert softly. "Well?" asked the princess.

"With Pentaur."

"I think of him-always of him," replied the princess, "and nothing else occupies my heart. I am no longer myself. What I think I ought not to think, what I feel I ought not to feel, and yet, I cannot command it, and I think my heart would bleed to death if I tried to cut out

196

those thoughts and feelings. I have behaved strangely, nay unbecomingly, and now that which is hard to endure is hanging over me, something strange-which will perhaps drive you from me back to your mother."

"I will share everything with you," cried Nefert. "What is going to happen? Are you then no longer the daughter of Rameses?"

"I showed myself to the people as a woman of the people," answered Bent-Anat, "and I must take the consequences. Bek en Chunsu, the high-priest of Amon, has been with me, and I have had a long conversation with him. The worthy man is good to me, I know, and my father ordered me to follow his advice before any one's. He showed me that I have erred deeply. In a state of uncleanness I went into one of the temples of the Necropolis, and after I had once been into the paraschites' house and incurred Ameni's displeasure, I did it a second time. They know over there all that took place at the festival. Now I must undergo purification, either with great solemnity at the hands of Ameni himself, before all the priests and nobles in the House of Seti, or by performing a pilgrimage to the Emerald-Hathor, under whose influence the precious stones are hewn from the rocks, metals dug out, and purified by fire. The Goddess shall purge me from my uncleanness as metal is purged from the dross. At a day's journey and more from the mines, an abundant stream flows from 'the holy mountain-Sinai,' as it is called by the Mentut-and near it stands the sanctuary of the Goddess, in which priests grant purification. The journey is a long one, through the desert, and over the sea; But Bek en Chunsu advises me to venture it. Ameni, he says, is not amiably disposed towards me, because I infringed the ordinance which he values above all others. I must submit to double severity, he says, because the people look first to those of the highest rank; and if I went unpunished for contempt of the sacred institutions there might be imitators among the crowd. He speaks in the name of the Gods, and they measure hearts with an equal measure. The ell-measure is the symbol of the Goddess of Truth. I feel that it is all not unjust; and yet I find it hard to submit to the priest's decree, for I am the daughter of Rameses!"

"Aye, indeed!" exclaimed Nefert, "and he is himself a God!"

"But he taught me to respect the laws!" interrupted the princess. "I discussed another thing with Bek en Chunsu. You know I rejected the suit of the Regent. He must secretly be much vexed with me. That indeed would not alarm me, but he is the guardian and protector appointed over me by my father, and yet can I turn to him in confidence for counsel, and help? No! I am still a woman, and Rameses' daughter! Sooner will I travel through a thousand deserts than humiliate my father through his child. By to-morrow I shall have decided; but, indeed, I have already decided to make the journey, hard as it is to leave much that is here. Do not fear, dear! but you are too tender for such a journey, and to such a distance; I might —"

"No, no," cried Nefert. "I am going, too, if you were going to the four pillars of heaven, at the limits of the earth. You have given me a new life, and the little sprout that is green within me would wither again if I had to return to my mother. Only she or I can be in our house, and I will re-enter it only with Mena."

"It is settled —I must go," said the princess. "Oh! if only my father were not so far off, and that I could consult him!"

"Yes! the war, and always the war!" sighed Nefert. "Why do not men rest content with what they have, and prefer the quiet peace, which makes life lovely, to idle fame?"

"Would they be men? should we love them?" cried Bent-Anat eagerly. "Is not the mind of the Gods, too, bent on war? Did you ever see a more sublime sight than Pentaur, on that evening when he brandished the stake he had pulled up, and exposed his life to protect an innocent girl who was in danger?"

"I dared not once look down into the court," said Nefert. "I was in such an agony of mind. But his loud cry still rings in my ears."

"So rings the war cry of heroes before whom the enemy quails!" exclaimed Bent-Anat.

"Aye, truly so rings the war cry!" said prince Rameri, who had entered his sister's half-dark room unperceived by the two women.

The princess turned to the boy. "How you frightened me!" she said.

"You!" said Rameri astonished.

"Yes, me. I used to have a stout heart, but since that evening I frequently tremble, and an agony of terror comes over me, I do not know why. I believe some demon commands me."

"You command, wherever you go; and no one commands you," cried Rameri. "The excitement and tumult in the valley, and on the quay, still agitate you. I grind my teeth myself when I remember how they turned me out of the school, and how Paaker set the dog at us. I have gone through a great deal today too."

"Where were you so long?" asked Bent-Anat. "My uncle Ani commanded that you should not leave the palace."

"I shall be eighteen years old next month," said the prince, "and need no tutor."

"But your father —" said Bent-Anat.

"My father" —interrupted the boy, "he little knows the Regent. But I shall write to him what I have today heard said by different people. They were to have sworn allegiance to Ani at that very feast in the valley, and it is quite openly said that Ani is aiming at the throne, and intends to depose the king. You are right, it is madness-but there must be something behind it all."

Nefert turned pale, and Bent-Anat asked for particulars. The prince repeated all he had gathered, and added laughing: "Ani depose my father! It is as if I tried to snatch the star of Isis from the sky to light the lamps-which are much wanted here."

"It is more comfortable in the dark," said Nefert. "No, let us have lights," said Bent-Anat. "It is better to talk when we can see each other face to face. I have no belief in the foolish talk of the people; but you are right-we must bring it to my fathers knowledge."

"I heard the wildest gossip in the City of the Dead," said Rameri.

"You ventured over there? How very wrong!"

"I disguised myself a little, and I have good news for you. Pretty Uarda is much better. She received your present, and they have a house of their own again. Close to the one that was burnt down, there was a tumbled-down hovel, which her father soon put together again; he is a bearded soldier, who is as much like her as a hedgehog is like a white dove. I offered her to work in the palace for you with the other girls, for good wages, but she would not; for she has to wait on her sick grandmother, and she is proud, and will not serve any one."

"It seems you were a long time with the paraschites' people," said Bent-Anat reprovingly. "I should have thought that what has happened to me might have served you as a warning."

"I will not be better than you!" cried the boy. "Besides, the paraschites is dead, and Uarda's father is a respectable soldier, who can defile no one. I kept a long way from the old woman. To-morrow I am going again. I promised her."

"Promised who?" asked his sister.

"Who but Uarda? She loves flowers, and since the rose which you gave her she has not seen one. I have ordered the gardener to cut me a basket full of roses to-morrow morning, and shall take them to her myself."

"That you will not!" cried Bent-Anat. "You are still but half a child-and, for the girl's sake too, you must give it up."

"We only gossip together," said the prince coloring, "and no one shall recognize me. But certainly, if you mean that, I will leave the basket of roses, and go to her alone. No-sister, I will not be forbidden this; she is so charming, so white, so gentle, and her voice is so soft and sweet! And she has little feet, as small as-what shall I say? —as small and graceful as Nefert's hand. We talked most about Pentaur. She knows his father, who is a gardener, and knows a great deal about him. Only think! she says the poet cannot be the son of his parents, but a good spirit that has come down on earth-perhaps a God. At first she was very timid, but when I spoke of Pentaur she grew eager; her reverence for him is almost idolatry-and that vexed me."

"You would rather she should reverence you so," said Nefert smiling.

"Not at all," cried Rameri. "But I helped to save her, and I am so happy when I am sitting with her, that to-morrow, I am resolved, I will put a flower in her hair. It is red certainly, but as thick as yours, Bent-Anat, and it must be delightful to unfasten it and stroke it."

The ladies exchanged a glance of intelligence, and the princess said decidedly:

"You will not go to the City of the Dead to-morrow, my little son!"

"That we will see, my little mother!" He answered laughing; then he turned grave.

"I saw my school-friend Anana too," he said. "Injustice reigns in the House of Seti! Pentaur is in prison, and yesterday evening they sat in judgment upon him. My uncle was present, and would have pounced upon the poet, but Ameni took him under his protection. What was finally decided, the pupils could not learn, but it must have been something bad, for the son of the Treasurer heard Ameni saying, after the sitting, to old Gagabu: 'Punishment he deserves, but I will not let him be overwhelmed;' and he can have meant no one but Pentaur. To-morrow I will go over, and learn more; something frightful, I am afraid-several years of imprisonment is the least that will happen to him."

Bent-Anat had turned very pale.

"And whatever they do to him," she cried, "he will suffer for my sake! Oh, ye omnipotent Gods, help him-help me, be merciful to us both!"

She covered her face with her hands, and left the room. Rameri asked Nefert:

"What can have come to my sister? she seems quite strange to me; and you too are not the same as you used to be."

"We both have to find our way in new circumstances."

"What are they?"

"That I cannot explain to you! —but it appears to me that you soon may experience something of the same kind. Rumeri, do not go again to the paraschites."

CHAPTER XXXII.

Early on the following clay the dwarf Nemu went past the restored hut of Uarda's father-in which he had formerly lived with his wife-with a man in a long coarse robe, the steward of some noble family. They went towards old Hekt's cave-dwelling.

"I would beg thee to wait down here a moment, noble lord," said the dwarf, "while I announce thee to my mother."

"That sounds very grand," said the other. "However, so be it. But stay! The old woman is not to call me by my name or by my title. She is to call me 'steward' —that no one may know. But, indeed, no one would recognize me in this dress."

Nemu hastened to the cave, but before he reached his mother she called out: "Do not keep my lord waiting —I know him well."

Nemu laid his finger to his lips.

"You are to call him steward," said he.

"Good," muttered the old woman. "The ostrich puts his head under his feathers when he does not want to be seen."

"Was the young prince long with Uarda yesterday?"

"No, you fool," laughed the witch, "the children play together. Rameri is a kid without horns, but who fancies he knows where they ought to grow. Pentaur is a more dangerous rival with the red-headed girl. Make haste, now; these stewards must not be kept waiting!"

The old woman gave the dwarf a push, and he hurried back to Ani, while she carried the child, tied to his board, into the cave, and threw the sack over him.

A few minutes later the Regent stood before her. She bowed before him with a demeanor that was more like the singer Beki than the sorceress Hekt, and begged him to take the only seat she possessed.

When, with a wave of his hand, he declined to sit down, she said:

"Yes-yes-be seated! then thou wilt not be seen from the valley, but be screened by the rocks close by. Why hast thou chosen this hour for thy visit?"

"Because the matter presses of which I wish to speak," answered Ani; "and in the evening I might easily be challenged by the watch. My disguise is good. Under this robe I wear my usual dress. From this I shall go to the tomb of my father, where I shall take off this coarse thing, and these other disfigurements, and shall wait for my chariot, which is already ordered. I shall tell people I had made a vow to visit the grave humbly, and on foot, which I have now fulfilled."

"Well planned," muttered the old woman.

Ani pointed to the dwarf, and said politely: "Your pupil."

Since her narrative the sorceress was no longer a mere witch in his eyes. The old woman understood this, and saluted him with a curtsey of such courtly formality, that a tame raven at her feet opened his black beak wide, and uttered a loud scream. She threw a bit of cheese within the cave, and the bird hopped after it, flapping his clipped wings, and was silent.

"I have to speak to you about Pentaur," said Ani. The old woman's eyes flashed, and she eagerly asked, "What of him?"

"I have reasons," answered the Regent, "for regarding him as dangerous to me. He stands in my way. He has committed many crimes, even murder; but he is in favor at the House of Seti, and they would willingly let him go unpunished. They have the right of sitting in judgment on each other, and I cannot interfere with their decisions; the day before yesterday they pronounced their sentence. They would send him to the quarries of Chennu.[110]

"All my objections were disregarded, and now Nemu, go over to the grave of Anienophis, and wait there for me —I wish to speak to your mother alone."

Nemu bowed, and then went down the slope, disappointed, it is true, but sure of learning later what the two had discussed together.

When the little man had disappeared, Ani asked:

"Have you still a heart true to the old royal house, to which your parents were so faithfully attached?" The old woman nodded.

"Then you will not refuse your help towards its restoration. You understand how necessary the priesthood is to me, and I have sworn not to make any attempt on Pentaur's life; but, I repeat it, he stands in my way. I have my spies in the House of Seti, and I know through them what the sending of the poet to Chennu really means. For a time they will let him hew sandstone, and that will only improve his health, for he is as sturdy as a tree. In Chennu, as you know, besides the quarries there is the great college of priests, which is in close alliance with the temple of Seti. When the flood begins to rise, and they hold the great Nile-festival in Chennu, the priests there have the right of taking three of the criminals who are working in the quarries into their house as servants. Naturally they will, next year, choose Pentaur, set him at liberty-and I shall be laughed at."

"Well considered!" said aid Hekt.

"I have taken counsel with myself, with Katuti, and even with Nemu," continued Ani, "but all that they have suggested, though certainly practicable, was unadvisable, and at any rate must have led to conjectures which I must now avoid. What is your opinion?"

"Assa's race must be exterminated!" muttered the old woman hoarsely.

She gazed at the ground, reflecting.

"Let the boat be scuttled," she said at last, "and sink with the chained prisoners before it reaches Chennu."

"No-no; I thought of that myself, and Nemu too advised it," cried Ani. "That has been done a hundred times, and Ameni will regard me as a perjurer, for I have sworn not to attempt Pentaur's life."

"To be sure, thou hast sworn that, and men keep their word-to each other. Wait a moment, how would this do? Let the ship reach Chennu with the prisoners, but, by a secret order to the captain, pass the quarries in the night, and hasten on as fast as possible as far as Ethiopia. From Suan —[The modern Assuan at the first cataract.] —the prisoners may be conducted through the desert to the gold workings. Four weeks or even eight may pass before it is known here what has happened. If Ameni attacks thee about it, thou wilt be very angry at this oversight, and canst swear by all the Gods of the heavens and of the abyss, that thou hast not attempted Pentaur's life. More weeks will pass in enquiries. Meanwhile do thy best, and Paaker do his, and thou art king. An oath is easily broken by a sceptre, and if thou wilt positively keep thy word leave Pentaur at the gold mines. None have yet returned from thence. My father's and my brother's bones have bleached there."

"But Ameni will never believe in the mistake," cried Ani, anxiously interrupting the witch.

"Then admit that thou gavest the order," exclaimed Hekt. "Explain that thou hadst learned what they proposed doing with Pentaur at Chennu, and that thy word indeed was kept, but that a criminal could not be left unpunished. They will make further enquiries, and if Assa's grandson is found still living thou wilt be justified. Follow my advice, if thou wilt prove thyself a good steward of thy house, and master of its inheritance."

"It will not do," said the Regent. "I need Ameni's support-not for to-day and to-morrow only. I will not become his blind tool; but he must believe that I am."

The old woman shrugged her shoulders, rose, went into her cave, and brought out a phial.

"Take this," she said. "Four drops of it in his wine infallibly destroys the drinker's senses; try the drink on a slave, and thou wilt see how effectual it is."

"What shall I do with it?" asked Ani.

"Justify thyself to Ameni," said the witch laughing. "Order the ship's captain to come to thee as soon as he returns; entertain him with wine-and when Ameni sees the distracted wretch, why should he not believe that in a fit of craziness he sailed past Chennu?"

"That is clever! that is splendid!" exclaimed Ani. "What is once remarkable never becomes common. You were the greatest of singers-you are now the wisest of women-my lady Beki."

"I am no longer Beki, I am Hekt," said the old woman shortly.

"As you will! In truth, if I had ever heard Beki's singing, I should be bound to still greater gratitude to her than I now am to Hekt," said Ani smiling. "Still, I cannot quit the wisest woman in Thebes without asking her one serious question. Is it given to you to read the future? Have you means at your command whereby you can see whether the great stake-you know which I mean-shall be won or lost?"

Hekt looked at the ground, and said after reflecting a short time:

"I cannot decide with certainty, but thy affair stands well. Look at these two hawks with the chain on their feet. They take their food from no one but me. The one that is moulting, with closed, grey eyelids, is Rameses; the smart, smooth one, with shining eyes, is thyself. It comes to this-which of you lives the longest. So far, thou hast the advantage."

Ani cast an evil glance at the king's sick hawk; but Hekt said: "Both must be treated exactly alike. Fate will not be done violence to."

"Feed them well," exclaimed the Regent; he threw a purse into Hekt's lap, and added, as he prepared to leave her: "If anything happens to either of the birds let me know at once by Nemu."

Ani went down the hill, and walked towards the neighboring tomb of his father; but Hekt laughed as she looked after him, and muttered to herself:

"Now the fool will take care of me for the sake of his bird! That smiling, spiritless, indolent-minded man would rule Egypt! Am I then so much wiser than other folks, or do none but fools come to consult Hekt? But Rameses chose Ani to represent him! perhaps because he thinks that those who are not particularly clever are not particularly dangerous. If that is what he thought, he was not wise, for no one usually is so self-confident and insolent as just such an idiot."

CHAPTER XXXIII.

An hour later, Ani, in rich attire, left his father's tomb, and drove his brilliant chariot past the witch's cave, and the little cottage of Uarda's father.

Nemu squatted on the step, the dwarf's usual place. The little man looked down at the lately rebuilt hut, and ground his teeth, when, through an opening in the hedge, he saw the white robe of a man, who was sitting by Uarda.

The pretty child's visitor was prince Rameri, who had crossed the Nile in the early morning, dressed as a young scribe of the treasury, to obtain news of Pentaur-and to stick a rose into Uarda's hair.

This purpose was, indeed, the more important of the two, for the other must, in point of time at any rate, be the second.

He found it necessary to excuse himself to his own conscience with a variety of cogent reasons. In the first place the rose, which lay carefully secured in a fold of his robe, ran great danger of fading if he first waited for his companions near the temple of Seti; next, a hasty return from thence to Thebes might prove necessary; and finally, it seemed to him not impossible that Bent-Anat might send a master of the ceremonies after him, and if that happened any delay might frustrate his purpose.

His heart beat loud and violently, not for love of the maiden, but because he felt he was doing wrong. The spot that he must tread was unclean, and he had, for the first time, told a lie. He had given himself out to Uarda to be a noble youth of Bent-Anat's train, and, as one falsehood usually entails another, in answer to her questions he had given her false information as to his parents and his life.

Had evil more power over him in this unclean spot than in the House of Seti, and at his father's? It might very well be so, for all disturbance in nature and men was the work of Seth, and how wild was the storm in his breast! And yet! He wished nothing but good to come of it to Uarda. She was so fair and sweet-like some child of the Gods: and certainly the white maiden must have been stolen from some one, and could not possibly belong to the unclean people.

When the prince entered the court of the hut, Uarda was not to be seen, but he soon heard her voice singing out through the open door. She came out into the air, for the dog barked furiously at Rameri. When she saw the prince, she started, and said:

"You are here already again, and yet I warned you. My grandmother in there is the wife of a paraschites."

"I am not come to visit her," retorted the prince, "but you only; and you do not belong to them, of that I am convinced. No roses grow in the desert."

"And yet: am my father's child," said Uarda decidedly, "and my poor dead grandfather's grandchild. Certainly I belong to them, and those that do not think me good enough for them may keep away."

With these words she turned to re-enter the house; but Rameri seized her hand, and held her back, saying:

"How cruel you are! I tried to save you, and came to see you before I thought that you might-and, indeed, you are quite unlike the people whom you call your relations. You must not misunderstand me; but it would be horrible to me to believe that you, who are so beautiful, and as white as a lily, have any part in the hideous curse. You charm every one, even my mistress, Bent-Anat, and it seems to me impossible —"

"That I should belong to the unclean! —say it out," said Uarda softly, and casting down her eyes.

Then she continued more excitedly: "But I tell you, the curse is unjust, for a better man never lived than my grandfather was."

Tears sprang from her eyes, and Rameri said: "I fully believe it; and it must be very difficult to continue good when every one despises and scorns one; I at least can be brought to no good by blame, though I can by praise. Certainly people are obliged to meet me and mine with respect."

"And us with contempt!" exclaimed Uarda. "But I will tell you something. If a man is sure that he is good, it is all the same to him whether he be despised or honored by other people. Nay-we may be prouder than you; for you great folks must often say to yourselves that you are worth less than men value you at, and we know that we are worth more."

"I have often thought that of you," exclaimed Rameri, "and there is one who recognizes your worth; and that is I. Even if it were otherwise, I must always-always think of you."

"I have thought of you too," said Uarda. "Just now, when I was sitting with my sick grandmother, it passed through my mind how nice it would be if I had a brother just like you. Do you know what I should do if you were my brother?"

"Well?"

"I should buy you a chariot and horse, and you should go away to the king's war."

"Are you so rich?" asked Rameri smiling.

"Oh yes!" answered Uarda. "To be sure, I have not been rich for more than an hour. Can you read?"

"Yes."

"Only think, when I was ill they sent a doctor to me from the House of Seti. He was very clever, but a strange man. He often looked into my eyes like a drunken man, and he stammered when he spoke."

"Is his name Nebsecht?" asked the prince.

"Yes, Nebsecht. He planned strange things with grandfather, and after Pentaur and you had saved us in the frightful attack upon us he interceded for us. Since then he has not come again, for I was already much better. Now to-day, about two hours ago, the dog barked, and an old man, a stranger, came up to me, and said he was Nebsecht's brother, and had a great deal of money in his charge for me. He gave me a ring too, and said that he would pay the money to him, who took the ring to him from me. Then he read this letter to me."

Rameri took the letter and read. "Nebsecht to the fair Uarda."

"Nebsecht greets Uarda, and informs her that he owed her grandfather in Osiris, Pinem-whose body the kolchytes are embalming like that of a noble —a sum of a thousand gold rings. These he has entrusted to his brother Teta to hold ready for her at any moment. She may trust Teta entirely, for he is honest, and ask him for money whenever she needs it. It would be best that she should ask Teta to take care of the money for her, and to buy her a house and field; then she could remove into it, and live in it free from care with her grandmother. She may wait a year, and then she may choose a husband. Nebsecht loves Uarda much. If at the end of thirteen months he has not been to see her, she had better marry whom she will; but not before she has shown the jewel left her by her mother to the king's interpreter."

"How strange!" exclaimed Rameri. "Who would have given the singular physician, who always wore such dirty clothes, credit for such generosity? But what is this jewel that you have?"

Uarda opened her shirt, and showed the prince the sparkling ornament.

"Those are diamonds-it is very valuable!" cried the prince; "and there in the middle on the onyx there are sharply engraved signs. I cannot read them, but I will show them to the interpreter. Did your mother wear that?"

"My father found it on her when she died," said Uarda. "She came to Egypt as a prisoner of war, and was as white as I am, but dumb, so she could not tell us the name of her home."

"She belonged to some great house among the foreigners, and the children inherit from the mother," cried the prince joyfully. "You are a princess, Uarda! Oh! how glad I am, and how much I love you!"

The girl smiled and said, "Now you will not be afraid to touch the daughter of the unclean."

"You are cruel," replied the prince. "Shall I tell you what I determined on yesterday-what would not let me sleep last night-and for what I came here today?"

"Well?"

Rameri took a most beautiful white rose out of his robe and said:

"It is very childish, but I thought how it would be if I might put this flower with my own hands into your shining hair. May I?"

"It is a splendid rose! I never saw such a fine one."

"It is for my haughty princess. Do pray let me dress your hair! It is like silk from Tyre, like a swan's breast, like golden star-beams —there, it is fixed safely! Nay, leave it so. If the seven Hathors could see you, they would be jealous, for you are fairer than all of them."

"How you flatter!" said Uarda, shyly blushing, and looking into his sparkling eyes.

"Uarda," said the prince, pressing her hand to his heart. "I have now but one wish. Feel how my heart hammers and beats. I believe it will never rest again till you-yes, Uarda-till you let me give you one, only one, kiss."

The girl drew back.

"Now," she said seriously. "Now I see what you want. Old Hekt knows men, and she warned me."

"Who is Hekt, and what can she know of me?"

"She told me that the time would come when a man would try to make friends with me. He would look into my eyes, and if mine met his, then he would ask to kiss me. But I must refuse him, because if I liked him to kiss me he would seize my soul, and take it from me, and I must wander, like the restless ghosts, which the abyss rejects, and the storm whirls before it, and the sea will not cover, and the sky will not receive, soulless to the end of my days. Go away-for I cannot refuse you the kiss, and yet I would not wander restless, and without a soul!"

"Is the old woman who told you that a good woman?" asked Rameri.

Uarda shook her head.

"She cannot be good," cried the prince. "For she has spoken a falsehood. I will not seize your soul; I will give you mine to be yours, and you shall give me yours to be mine, and so we shall neither of us be poorer-but both richer!"

"I should like to believe it," said Uarda thoughtfully, "and I have thought the same kind of thing. When I was strong, I often had to go late in the evening to fetch water from the landing-place where the great water-wheel stands. Thousands of drops fall from the earthenware pails as it turns, and in each you can see the reflection of a moon, yet there is only one in the sky. Then I thought to myself, so it must be with the love in our hearts. We have but one heart, and yet we pour it out into other hearts without its losing in strength or in warmth. I thought of my grandmother, of my father, of little Scherau, of the Gods, and of Pentaur. Now I should like to give you a part of it too."

"Only a part?" asked Rameri.

"Well, the whole will be reflected in you, you know," said Uarda, "as the whole moon is reflected in each drop."

"It shall!" cried the prince, clasping the trembling girl in his arms, and the two young souls were united in their first kiss.

"Now do go!" Uarda entreated.

"Let me stay a little while," said Rameri. "Sit down here by me on the bench in front of the house. The hedge shelters us, and besides this valley is now deserted, and there are no passers by."

"We are doing what is not right," said Uarda. "If it were right we should not want to hide ourselves."

"Do you call that wrong which the priests perform in the Holy of Holies?" asked the prince. "And yet it is concealed from all eyes."

"How you can argue!" laughed Uarda. "That shows you can write, and are one of his disciples."

"His, his!" exclaimed Rameri. "You mean Pentaur. He was always the dearest to me of all my teachers, but it vexes me when you speak of him as if he were more to you than I and every one else. The poet, you said, was one of the drops in which the moon of your soul finds a reflection-and I will not divide it with many."

"How you are talking!" said Uarda. "Do you not honor your father, and the Gods? I love no one else as I do you-and what I felt when you kissed me-that was not like moon-light, but like this hot mid-day sun. When I thought of you I had no peace. I will confess to you now, that twenty times I looked out of the door, and asked whether my preserver-the kind, curly-headed boy-would really come again, or whether he despised a poor girl like me? You came, and I am so happy, and I could enjoy myself with you to my heart's content. Be kind again-or I will pull your hair!"

"You!" cried Rameri. "You cannot hurt with your little hands, though you can with your tongue. Pentaur is much wiser and better than I, you owe much to him, and nevertheless I —"

"Let that rest," interrupted the girl, growing grave. "He is not a man like other men. If he asked to kiss me, I should crumble into dust, as ashes dried in the sun crumble if you touch them with a finger, and I should be as much afraid of his lips as of a lion's. Though you may laugh at it, I shall always believe that he is one of the Immortals. His own father told me that a great wonder was shown to him the very day after his birth. Old Hekt has often sent me to the gardener with a message to enquire after his son, and though the man is rough he is kind. At first he was not friendly, but when he saw how much I liked his flowers he grew fond of me, and set me to work to tie wreaths and bunches, and to carry them to his customers. As we sat together, laying the flowers side by side, he constantly told me something about his son, and his beauty and goodness and wisdom. When he was quite a little boy he could write poems, and he learned to read before any one had shown him how. The high-priest Ameni heard of it and took him to the House of Seti, and there he improved, to the astonishment of the gardener; not long ago I went through the garden with the old man. He talked of Pentaur as usual, and then stood still before a noble shrub with broad leaves, and said, My son is like this plant, which has grown up close to me, and I know not how. I laid the seed in the soil, with others that I bought over there in Thebes; no one knows where it came from, and yet it is my own. It certainly is not a native of Egypt; and is not Pentaur as high above me and his mother and his brothers, as this shrub is above the other flowers? We are all small and bony, and he is tall and slim; our skin is dark and his is rosy; our speech is hoarse, his as sweet as a song. I believe he is a child of the Gods that the Immortals have laid in my homely house. Who knows their decrees?' And then I often saw Pentaur at the festivals, and asked myself which of the other priests of the temple came near him in height and dignity? I took him for a God, and when I saw him who saved my life overcome a whole mob with superhuman strength must I not regard him as a superior Being? I look up to him as to one of them; but I could never look in his eyes as I do in yours. It would not make my blood flow faster, it would freeze it in my veins. How can I say what I mean! my soul looks straight out, and it finds you; but to find him it must look up to the heavens. You are a fresh rose-garland with which I crown myself-he is a sacred persea-tree before which I bow."

Rameri listened to her in silence, and then said, "I am still young, and have done nothing yet, but the time shall come in which you shall look up to me too as to a tree, not perhaps a sacred tree, but as to a sycamore under whose shade we love to rest. I am no longer gay; I will leave you for I have a serious duty to fulfil. Pentaur is a complete man, and I will be one too. But you shall be the rose-garland to grace me. Men who can be compared to flowers disgust me!"

The prince rose, and offered Uarda his hand.

"You have a strong hand," said the girl. "You will be a noble man, and work for good and great ends; only look, my fingers are quite red with being held so tightly. But they too are not quite useless. They have never done anything very hard certainly, but what they tend flourishes, and grandmother says they are 'lucky.' Look at the lovely lilies and the pomegranate bush in that corner. Grandfather brought the earth here from the Nile, Pentaur's father gave me the seeds, and each little plant that ventured to show a green shoot through the soil I sheltered and nursed and watered, though I had to fetch the water in my little pitcher, till it was vigorous, and thanked me with flowers. Take this pomegranate flower. It is the first my tree has borne; and it is very strange, when the bud first began to lengthen and swell my grandmother said,

'Now your heart will soon begin to bud and love.' I know now what she meant, and both the first flowers belong to you-the red one here off the tree, and the other, which you cannot see, but which glows as brightly as this does."

Rameri pressed the scarlet blossom to his lips, and stretched out his hand toward Uarda; but she shrank back, for a little figure slipped through an opening in the hedge.

It was Scherau.

His pretty little face glowed with his quick run, and his breath was gone. For a few minutes he tried in vain for words, and looked anxiously at the prince.

Uarda saw that something unusual agitated him; she spoke to him kindly, saying that if he wished to speak to her alone he need not be afraid of Rameri, for he was her best friend.

"But it does not concern you and me," replied the child, "but the good, holy father Pentaur, who was so kind to me, and who saved your life."

"I am a great friend of Pentaur," said the prince. "Is it not true, Uarda? He may speak with confidence before me."

"I may?" said Scherau, "that is well. I have slipped away; Hekt may come back at any moment, and if she sees that I have taken myself off I shall get a beating and nothing to eat."

"Who is this horrible Hekt?" asked Rameri indignantly.

"That Uarda can tell you by and by," said the little one hurriedly. "Now only listen. She laid me on my board in the cave, and threw a sack over me, and first came Nemu, and then another man, whom she spoke to as Steward. She talked to him a long time. At first I did not listen, but then I caught the name of Pentaur, and I got my head out, and now I understand it all. The steward declared that the good Pentaur was wicked, and stood in his way, and he said that Ameni was going to send him to the quarries at Chennu, but that that was much too small a punishment. Then Hekt advised him to give a secret commission to the captain of the ship to go beyond Chennu, to the frightful mountain-mines, of which she has often told me, for her father and her brother were tormented to death there."

"None ever return from thence," said the prince. "But go on."

"What came next, I only half understood, but they spoke of some drink that makes people mad. Oh! what I see and hear! —I would he contentedly on my board all my life long, but all else is too horrible —I wish that I were dead."

And the child began to cry bitterly.

Uarda, whose cheeks had turned pale, patted him affectionately; but Rameri exclaimed:

"It is frightful! unheard of! But who was the steward? did you not hear his name? Collect yourself, little man, and stop crying. It is a case of life and death. Who was the scoundrel? Did she not name him? Try to remember."

Scherau bit his red lips, and tried for composure. His tears ceased, and suddenly he exclaimed, as he put his hand into the breast of his ragged little garment: "Stay, perhaps you will know him again —I made him!"

"You did what?" asked the prince.

"I made him," repeated the little artist, and he carefully brought out an object wrapped up in a scrap of rag, "I could just see his head quite clearly from one side all the time he was speaking, and my clay lay by me. I always must model something when my mind is excited, and this time I quickly made his face, and as the image was successful, I kept it about me to show to the master when Hekt was out."

While he spoke he had carefully unwrapped the figure with trembling fingers, and had given it to Uarda.

"Ani!" cried the prince. "He, and no other! Who could have thought it! What spite has he against Pentaur? What is the priest to him?"

For a moment he reflected, then he struck his hand against his forehead.

"Fool that I am!" he exclaimed vehemently. "Child that I am! of course, of course; I see it all. Ani asked for Bent-Anat's hand, and she-now that I love you, Uarda, I understand what ails her. Away with deceit! I will tell you no more lies, Uarda. I am no page of honor to Bent-Anat;

I am her brother, and king Rameses' own son. Do not cover your face with your hands, Uarda, for if I had not seen your mother's jewel, and if I were not only a prince, but Horus himself, the son of Isis, I must have loved you, and would not have given you up. But now other things have to be done besides lingering with you; now I will show you that I am a man, now that Pentaur is to be saved. Farewell, Uarda, and think of me!"

He would have hurried off, but Scherau held him by the robe, and said timidly: "Thou sayst thou art Rameses' son. Hekt spoke of him too. She compared him to our moulting hawk."

"She shall soon feel the talons of the royal eagle," cried Rameri. "Once more, farewell!"

He gave Uarda his hand, she pressed it passionately to her lips, but he drew it away, kissed her forehead, and was gone.

The maiden looked after him pale and speechless. She saw another man hastening towards her, and recognizing him as her father, she went quickly to meet him. The soldier had come to take leave of her, he had to escort some prisoners.

"To Chennu?" asked Uarda.

"No, to the north," replied the man.

His daughter now related what she had heard, and asked whether he could help the priest, who had saved her.

"If I had money, if I had money!" muttered the soldier to himself.

"We have some," cried Uarda; she told him of Nebsecht's gift, and said: "Take me over the Nile, and in two hours you will have enough to make a man rich.[111]

But no; I cannot leave my sick grandmother. You yourself take the ring, and remember that Pentaur is being punished for having dared to protect us."

"I remember it," said the soldier. "I have but one life, but I will willingly give it to save his. I cannot devise schemes, but I know something, and if it succeeds he need not go to the gold-mines. I will put the wine-flask aside-give me a drink of water, for the next few hours I must keep a sober head."

"There is the water, and I will pour in a mouthful of wine. Will you come back and bring me news?"

"That will not do, for we set sail at midnight, but if some one returns to you with the ring you will know that what I propose has succeeded."

Uarda went into the hut, her father followed her; he took leave of his sick mother and of his daughter. When they went out of doors again, he said: "You have to live on the princess's gift till I return, and I do not want half of the physician's present. But where is your pomegranate blossom?"

"I have picked it and preserved it in a safe place."

"Strange things are women!" muttered the bearded man; he tenderly kissed his child's forehead, and returned to the Nile down the road by which he had come.

The prince meanwhile had hurried on, and enquired in the harbor of the Necropolis where the vessel destined for Chennu was lying-for the ships loaded with prisoners were accustomed to sail from this side of the river, starting at night. Then he was ferried over the river, and hastened to Bent-Anat. He found her and Nefert in unusual excitement, for the faithful chamberlain had learned-through some friends of the king in Ani's suite-that the Regent had kept back all the letters intended for Syria, and among them those of the royal family.

A lord in waiting, who was devoted to the king, had been encouraged by the chamberlain to communicate to Bent-Anat other things, which hardly allowed any doubts as to the ambitious projects of her uncle; she was also exhorted to be on her guard with Nefert, whose mother was the confidential adviser of the Regent.

Bent-Anat smiled at this warning, and sent at once a message to Ani to inform him that she was ready to undertake the pilgrimage to the "Emerald-Hathor," and to be purified in the sanctuary of that Goddess.

She purposed sending a message to her father from thence, and if he permitted it, joining him at the camp.

She imparted this plan to her friend, and Nefert thought any road best that would take her to her husband.

Rameri was soon initiated into all this, and in return he told them all he had learned, and let Bent-Anat guess that he had read her secret.

So dignified, so grave, were the conduct and the speech of the boy who had so lately been an overhearing mad-cap, that Bent-Anat thought to herself that the danger of their house had suddenly ripened a boy into a man.

She had in fact no objection to raise to his arrangements. He proposed to travel after sunset, with a few faithful servants on swift horses as far as Keft, and from thence ride fast across the desert to the Red Sea, where they could take a Phoenician ship, and sail to Aila. From thence they would cross the peninsula of Sinai, and strive to reach the Egyptian army by forced marches, and make the king acquainted with Ani's criminal attempts.

To Bent-Anat was given the task of rescuing Pentaur, with the help of the faithful chamberlain.

Money was fortunately not wanting, as the high treasurer was on their side. All depended on their inducing the captain to stop at Chennu; the poet's fate would there, at the worst, be endurable. At the same time, a trustworthy messenger was to be sent to the governor of Chennu, commanding him in the name of the king to detain every ship that might pass the narrows of Chennu by night, and to prevent any of the prisoners that had been condemned to the quarries from being smuggled on to Ethiopia.

Rameri took leave of the two women, and he succeeded in leaving Thebes unobserved.

Bent-Anat knelt in prayer before the images of her mother in Osiris, of Hathor, and of the guardian Gods of her house, till the chamberlain returned, and told her that he had persuaded the captain of the ship to stop at Chennu, and to conceal from Ani that he had betrayed his charge.

The princess breathed more freely, for she had come to a resolution that if the chamberlain had failed in his mission, she would cross over to the Necropolis forbid the departure of the vessel, and in the last extremity rouse the people, who were devoted to her, against Ani.

The following morning the Lady Katuti craved permission of the princess to see her daughter. Bent-Anat did not show herself to the widow, whose efforts failed to keep her daughter from accompanying the princess on her journey, or to induce her to return home. Angry and uneasy, the indignant mother hastened to Ani, and implored him to keep Nefert at home by force; but the Regent wished to avoid attracting attention, and to let Bent-Anat set out with a feeling of complete security.

"Do not be uneasy," he said. "I will give the ladies a trustworthy escort, who will keep them at the Sanctuary of the 'Emerald-Hathor' till all is settled. There you can deliver Nefert to Paaker, if you still like to have him for a son-in-law after hearing several things that I have learned. As for me, in the end I may induce my haughty niece to look up instead of down; I may be her second love, though for that matter she certainly is not my first."

On the following day the princess set out.

Ani took leave of her with kindly formality, which she returned with coolness. The priesthood of the temple of Amon, with old Bek en Chunsu at their head, escorted her to the harbor. The people on the banks shouted Bent-Anat's name with a thousand blessings, but many insulting words were to be heard also.

The pilgrim's Nile-boat was followed by two others, full of soldiers, who accompanied the ladies "to protect them."

The south-wind filled the sails, and carried the little procession swiftly down the stream. The princess looked now towards the palace of her fathers, now towards the tombs and temples of the Necropolis. At last even the colossus of Anienophis disappeared, and the last houses of Thebes. The brave maiden sighed deeply, and tears rolled down her checks. She felt as if she were flying after a lost battle, and yet not wholly discouraged, but hoping for future victory. As she turned to go to the cabin, a veiled girl stepped up to her, took the veil from her face, and said: "Pardon me, princess; I am Uarda, whom thou didst run over, and to whom thou hast since been so good. My grandmother is dead, and I am quite alone. I slipped in among thy maid-servants, for I wish to follow thee, and to obey all thy commands. Only do not send me away."

"Stay, dear child," said the princess, laying her hand on her hair.

Then, struck by its wonderful beauty, she remembered her brother, and his wish to place a rose in Uarda's shining tresses.

CHAPTER XXXIV.

Two months had past since Bent-Anat's departure from Thebes, and the imprisonment of Pentaur. Ant-Baba is the name of the valley, in the western half of the peninsula of Sinai,[112] through which a long procession of human beings, and of beasts of burden, wended their way.

It was winter, and yet the mid-day sun sent down glowing rays, which were reflected from the naked rocks. In front of the caravan marched a company of Libyan soldiers, and another brought up the rear. Each man was armed with a dagger and battle-axe, a shield and a lance, and was ready to use his weapons; for those whom they were escorting were prisoners from the emerald-mines, who had been convoyed to the shores of the Red Sea to carry thither the produce of the mines, and had received, as a return-load, provisions which had arrived from Egypt, and which were to be carried to the storehouses of the mountain mines. Bent and panting, they made their way along. Each prisoner had a copper chain riveted round his ankles, and torn rags hanging round their loins, were the only clothing of these unhappy beings, who, gasping under the weight of the sacks they had to carry, kept their staring eyes fixed on the ground. If one of them threatened to sink altogether under his burden, he was refreshed by the whip of one of the horsemen, who accompanied the caravan. Many a one found it hard to choose whether he could best endure the suffering of mere endurance, or the torture of the lash.

No one spoke a word, neither the prisoners nor their guards; and even those who were flogged did not cry out, for their powers were exhausted, and in the souls of their drivers there was no more impulse of pity than there was a green herb on the rocks by the way. This melancholy procession moved silently onwards, like a procession of phantoms, and the ear was only made aware of it when now and then a low groan broke from one of the victims.

The sandy path, trodden by their naked feet, gave no sound, the mountains seemed to withhold their shade, the light of clay was a torment-every thing far and near seemed inimical to the living. Not a plant, not a creeping thing, showed itself against the weird forms of the barren grey and brown rocks, and no soaring bird tempted the oppressed wretches to raise their eyes to heaven.

In the noontide heat of the previous day they had started with their loads from the harbor-creek. For two hours they had followed the shore of the glistening, blue-green sea,[113] then they had climbed a rocky shoulder and crossed a small plateau. They had paused for their night's rest in the gorge which led to the mines; the guides and soldiers lighted fires, grouped themselves round them, and lay down to sleep under the shelter of a cleft in the rocks; the prisoners stretched themselves on the earth in the middle of the valley without any shelter, and shivering with the cold which suddenly succeeded the glowing heat of the day. The benumbed wretches now looked forward to the crushing misery of the morning's labor as eagerly as, a few hours since, they had longed for the night, and for rest.

Lentil-broth and hard bread in abundance, but a very small quantity of water was given to them before they started; then they set out through the gorge, which grew hotter and hotter, and through ravines where they could pass only one by one. Every now and then it seemed as if the path came to an end, but each time it found an outlet, and went on-as endless as the torment of the wayfarers.

Mighty walls of rock composed the view, looking as if they were formed of angular masses of hewn stone piled up in rows; and of all the miners one, and one only, had eyes for these curious structures of the ever-various hand of Nature.

This one had broader shoulders than his companions, and his burden weighed on him comparatively lightly. "In this solitude," thought he, "which repels man, and forbids his passing his life here, the Chnemu, the laborers who form the world, have spared themselves the trouble of filling up the seams, and rounding off the corners. How is it that Man should have dedicated this hideous land-in which even the human heart seems to be hardened against all pity-to the merciful Hathor? Perhaps because it so sorely stands in need of the joy and peace which the loving goddess alone can bestow."

"Keep the line, Huni!" shouted a driver.

The man thus addressed, closed up to the next man, the panting leech Nebsecht. We know the other stronger prisoner. It is Pentaur, who had been entered as Huni on the lists of mine-laborers, and was called by that name. The file moved on; at every step the ascent grew more rugged. Red and black fragments of stone, broken as small as if by the hand of man, lay in great heaps, or strewed the path which led up the almost perpendicular cliff by imperceptible degrees. Here another gorge opened before them, and this time there seemed to be no outlet.

"Load the asses less!" cried the captain of the escort to the prisoners. Then he turned to the soldiers, and ordered them, when the beasts were eased, to put the extra burthens on the men. Putting forth their utmost strength, the overloaded men labored up the steep and hardly distinguishable mountain path.

The man in front of Pentaur, a lean old man, when half way up the hill-side, fell in a heap under his load, and a driver, who in a narrow defile could not reach the bearers, threw a stone at him to urge him to a renewed effort.

The old man cried out at the blow, and at the cry-the paraschites stricken down with stones-his own struggle with the mob-and the appearance of Bent Anat flashed into Pentaur's memory. Pity and a sense of his own healthy vigor prompted him to energy; he hastily snatched the sack from the shoulders of the old man, threw it over his own, helped up the fallen wretch, and finally men and beasts succeeded in mounting the rocky wall.

The pulses throbbed in Pentaur's temples, and he shuddered with horror, as he looked down from the height of the pass into the abyss below, and round upon the countless pinnacles and peaks, cliffs and precipices, in many-colored rocks-white and grey, sulphurous yellow, blood-red and ominous black. He recalled the sacred lake of Muth in Thebes, round which sat a hundred statues of the lion-headed Goddess in black basalt, each on a pedestal; and the rocky peaks, which surrounded the valley at his feet, seemed to put on a semblance of life and to move and open their yawning jaws; through the wild rush of blood in his ears he fancied he heard them roar, and the load beyond his strength which he carried gave him a sensation as though their clutch was on his breast.

Nevertheless he reached the goal.

The other prisoners flung their loads from their shoulders, and threw themselves down to rest. Mechanically he did the same: his pulses beat more calmly, by degrees the visions faded from his senses, he saw and heard once more, and his brain recovered its balance. The old man and Nebsecht were lying beside him.

His grey-haired companion rubbed the swollen veins in his neck, and called down all the blessings of the Gods upon his head; but the captain of the caravan cut him short, exclaiming:

"You have strength for three, Huni; farther on, we will load you more heavily."

"How much the kindly Gods care for our prayers for the blessing of others!" exclaimed Nebsecht. "How well they know how to reward a good action!"

"I am rewarded enough," said Pentaur, looking kindly at the old man. "But you, you ever-lasting scoffer-you look pale. How do you feel?"

"As if I were one of those donkeys there," replied the naturalist. "My knees shake like theirs, and I think and I wish neither more nor less than they do; that is to say —I would we were in our stalls."

"If you can think," said Pentaur smiling, "you are not so very bad."

"I had a good thought just now, when you were staring up into the sky. The intellect, say the priestly sages, is a vivifying breath of the eternal spirit, and our soul is the mould or core for the mass of matter which we call a human being. I sought the spirit at first in the heart, then in the brain; but now I know that it resides in the arms and legs, for when I have strained them I find thought is impossible. I am too tired to enter on further evidence, but for the future I shall treat my legs with the utmost consideration."

"Quarrelling again you two? On again, men!" cried the driver.

The weary wretches rose slowly, the beasts were loaded, and on went the pitiable procession, so as to reach the mines before sunset.

The destination of the travellers was a wide valley, closed in by two high and rocky mountain-slopes; it was called Ta Mafka by the Egyptians, Dophka by the Hebrews. The southern cliff-wall consisted of dark granite, the northern of red sandstone; in a distant branch of the valley lay the mines in which copper was found. In the midst of the valley rose a hill, surrounded by a wall, and crowned with small stone houses, for the guard, the officers, and the overseers. According to the old regulations, they were without roofs, but as many deaths and much sickness had occurred among the workmen in consequence of the cold nights, they had been slightly sheltered with palm-branches brought from the oasis of the Alnalckites, at no great distance.

On the uttermost peak of the hill, where it was most exposed to the wind, were the smelting furnaces, and a manufactory where a peculiar green glass was prepared, which was brought into the market under the name of Mafkat, that is to say, emerald. The genuine precious stone was found farther to the south, on the western shore of the Red Sea, and was highly prized in Egypt.

Our friends had already for more than a month belonged to the mining-community of the Mafkat valley, and Pentaur had never learned how it was that he had been brought hither with his companion Nebsecht, instead of going to the sandstone quarries of Chennu.

That Uarda's father had effected this change was beyond a doubt, and the poet trusted the rough but honest soldier who still kept near him, and gave him credit for the best intentions, although he had only spoken to him once since their departure from Thebes.

That was the first night, when he had come up to Pentaur, and whispered: "I am looking after you. You will find the physician Nebsecht here; but treat each other as enemies rather than as friends, if you do not wish to be parted."

Pentaur had communicated the soldier's advice to Nebsecht, and he had followed it in his own way.

It afforded him a secret pleasure to see how Pentaur's life contradicted the belief in a just and beneficent ordering of the destinies of men; and the more he and the poet were oppressed, the more bitter was the irony, often amounting to extravagance, with which the mocking sceptic attacked him.

He loved Pentaur, for the poet had in his keeping the key which alone could give admission to the beautiful world which lay locked up in his own soul; but yet it was easy to him, if he thought they were observed, to play his part, and to overwhelm Pentaur with words which, to the drivers, were devoid of meaning, and which made them laugh by the strange blundering fashion in which he stammered them out.

"A belabored husk of the divine self-consciousness." "An advocate of righteousness hit on the mouth." "A juggler who makes as much of this worst of all possible worlds as if it were the best." "An admirer of the lovely color of his blue bruises." These and other terms of invective, intelligible only to himself and his butt, he could always pour out in new combinations, exciting Pentaur to sharp and often witty rejoinders, equally unintelligible to the uninitiated.

Frequently their sparring took the form of a serious discussion, which served a double purpose; first their minds, accustomed to serious thought, found exercise in spite of the murderous pressure of the burden of forced labor, and secondly, they were supposed really to be enemies. They slept in the same court-yard, and contrived, now and then, to exchange a few words in secret; but by day Nebsecht worked in the turquoise-diggings, and Pentaur in the mines, for the careful chipping out of the precious stones from their stony matrix was the work best suited to the slight physician, while Pentaur's giant-strength was fitted for hewing the ore out of the hard rock. The drivers often looked in surprise at his powerful strokes, as he flung his pick against the stone.

The stupendous images that in such moments of wild energy rose before the poet's soul, the fearful or enchanting tones that rang in his spirit's ear-none could guess at.

Usually his excited fancy showed him the form of Bent-Anat, surrounded by a host of men-and these he seemed to fell to the earth, one-by-one, as-he hewed the rock. Often in the middle of his work he would stop, throw down his pick-axe, and spread out his arms-but only to drop them with a deep groan, and wipe the sweat from his brow.

The overseers did not know what to think of this powerful youth, who often was as gentle as a child, and then seemed possessed of that demon to which so many of the convicts fell victims. He had indeed become a riddle to himself; for how was it that he-the gardener's son, brought up in the peaceful temple of Seti-ever since that night by the house of the paraschites had had such a perpetual craving for conflict and struggle?

The weary gangs were gone to rest; a bright fire still blazed in front of the house of the superintendent of the mines, and round it squatted in a circle the overseers and the subalterns of the troops.

"Put the wine-jar round again," said the captain, "for we must hold grave council. Yesterday I had orders from the Regent to send half the guard to Pelusium. He requires soldiers, but we are so few in number that if the convicts knew it they might make short work of us, even without arms. There are stones enough hereabouts, and by day they have their hammer and chisel. Things are worst among the Hebrews in the copper-mines; they are a refractory crew that must be held tight. You know me well, fear is unknown to me-but I feel great anxiety. The last fuel is now burning in this fire, and the smelting furnaces and the glass-foundry must not stand idle. Tomorrow we must send men to Raphidim[114] to obtain charcoal from the Amalekites. They owe us a hundred loads still. Load the prisoners with some copper, to make them tired and the natives civil. What can we do to procure what we want, and yet not to weaken the forces here too much?"

Various opinions were given, and at last it was settled that a small division, guarded by a few soldiers, should be sent out every day to supply only the daily need for charcoal.

It was suggested that the most dangerous of the convicts should be fettered together in pairs to perform their duties.

The superintendent was of opinion that two strong men fettered together would be more to be feared if only they acted in concert.

"Then chain a strong one to a weak one," said the chief accountant of the mines, whom the Egyptians called the 'scribe of the metals.' "And fetter those together who are enemies."

"The colossal Huni, for instance, to that puny spat row, the stuttering Nebsecht," said a subaltern.

"I was thinking of that very couple," said the accountant laughing.

Three other couples were selected, at first with some laughter, but finally with serious consideration, and Uarda's father was sent with the drivers as an escort.

On the following morning Pentaur and Nebsecht were fettered together with a copper chain, and when the sun was at its height four pairs of prisoners, heavily loaded with copper, set out for the Oasis of the Amalekites, accompanied by six soldiers and the son of the paraschites, to fetch fuel for the smelting furnaces.

They rested near the town of Alus, and then went forward again between bare walls of greyish-green and red porphyry. These cliffs rose higher and higher, but from time to time, above the lower range, they could see the rugged summit of some giant of the range, though, bowed under their heavy loads, they paid small heed to it.

The sun was near setting when they reached the little sanctuary of the 'Emerald-Hathor.'

A few grey and black birds here flew towards them, and Pentaur gazed at them with delight.

How long he had missed the sight of a bird, and the sound of their chirp and song! Nebsecht said: "There are some birds-we must be near water."

And there stood the first palm-tree!

Now the murmur of the brook was perceptible, and its tiny sound touched the thirsty souls of the travellers as rain falls on dry grass.

On the left bank of the stream an encampment of Egyptian soldiers formed a large semicircle, enclosing three large tents made of costly material striped with blue and white, and woven with gold thread. Nothing was to be seen of the inhabitants of these tents, but when the prisoners had passed them, and the drivers were exchanging greetings with the out-posts, a girl, in the long robe of an Egyptian, came towards them, and looked at them.

Pentaur started as if he had seen a ghost; but Nebsecht gave expression to his astonishment in a loud cry.

At the same instant a driver laid his whip across their shoulders, and cried laughing:

"You may hit each other as hard as you like with words, but not with your hands."

Then he turned to his companions, and said: "Did you see the pretty girl there, in front of the tent?"

"It is nothing to us!" answered the man he addressed. "She belongs to the princess's train. She has been three weeks here on a visit to the holy shrine of Hathor."

"She must have committed some heavy sin," replied the other. "If she were one of us, she would have been set to sift sand in the diggings, or grind colors, and not be living here in a gilt tent. Where is our red-beard?"

Uarda's father had lingered a little behind the party, for the girl had signed to him, and exchanged a few words with him.

"Have you still an eye for the fair ones?" asked the youngest of the drivers when he rejoined the gang.

"She is a waiting maid of the princess," replied the soldier not without embarrassment. "To-morrow morning we are to carry a letter from her to the scribe of the mines, and if we encamp in the neighborhood she will send us some wine for carrying it."

"The old red-beard scents wine as a fox scents a goose. Let us encamp here; one never knows what may be picked up among the Mentu, and the superintendent said we were to encamp outside the oasis. Put down your sacks, men! Here there is fresh water, and perhaps a few dates and sweet Manna for you to eat with it.[115]

But keep the peace, you two quarrelsome fellows-Huni and Nebsecht."

Bent-Anat's journey to the Emerald-Hathor was long since ended. As far as Keft she had sailed down the Nile with her escort, from thence she had crossed the desert by easy marches, and she had been obliged to wait a full week in the port on the Red Sea, which was chiefly inhabited by Phoenicians, for a ship which had finally brought her to the little seaport of Pharan. From Pharan she had crossed the mountains to the oasis, where the sanctuary she was to visit stood on the northern side.

The old priests, who conducted the service of the Goddess, had received the daughter of Rameses with respect, and undertook to restore her to cleanness by degrees with the help of the water from the mountain-stream which watered the palm-grove of the Amalekites, of in-cense-burning, of pious sentences, and of a hundred other ceremonies. At last the Goddess declared herself satisfied, and Bent-Anat wished to start for the north and join her father, but the commander of the escort, a grey-headed Ethiopian field officer-who had been promoted to a high grade by Ani-explained to the Chamberlain that he had orders to detain the princess in the oasis until her departure was authorized by the Regent himself.

Bent-Anat now hoped for the support of her father, for her brother Rameri, if no accident had occurred to him, might arrive any day. But in vain.

The position of the ladies was particularly unpleasant, for they felt that they had been caught in a trap, and were in fact prisoners. In addition to this their Ethiopian escort had quarrelled with the natives of the oasis, and every day skirmishes took place under their eyes-indeed lately one of these fights had ended in bloodshed.

Bent-Anat was sick at heart. The two strong pinions of her soul, which had always borne her so high above other women-her princely pride and her bright frankness-seemed quite broken; she felt that she had loved once, never to love again, and that she, who had sought none of her happiness in dreams, but all in work, had bestowed the best half of her identity on a vision. Pentaur's image took a more and more vivid, and at the same time nobler and loftier, aspect in her mind; but he himself had died for her, for only once had a letter reached them from Egypt, and that was from Katuti to Nefert. After telling her that late intelligence established the statement that her husband had taken a prince's daughter, who had been made prisoner, to his tent as his share of the booty, she added the information that the poet Pentaur, who had been condemned to forced labor, had not reached the mountain mines, but, as was supposed, had perished on the road.

Nefert still held to her immovable belief that her husband was faithful to his love for her, and the magic charm of a nature made beautiful by its perfect mastery over a deep and pure passion made itself felt in these sad and heavy days.

It seemed as though she had changed parts with Bent-Anat. Always hopeful, every day she foretold help from the king for the next; in truth she was ready to believe that, when Mena learned from Rameri that she was with the princess, he himself would come to fetch them if his duties allowed it. In her hours of most lively expectation she could go so far as to picture how the party in the tents would be divided, and who would bear Bent-Anat company if Mena took her with him to his camp, on what spot of the oasis it would be best to pitch it, and much more in the same vein.

Uarda could very well take her place with Bent-Anat, for the child had developed and improved on the journey. The rich clothes which the princess had given her became her as if she had never worn any others; she could obey discreetly, disappear at the right moment, and, when she was invited, chatter delightfully. Her laugh was silvery, and nothing consoled Bent-Anat so much as to hear it.

Her songs too pleased the two friends, though the few that she knew were grave and sorrowful. She had learned them by listening to old Hekt, who often used to play on a lute in the dusk, and who, when she perceived that Uarda caught the melodies, had pointed out her faults, and given her advice.

"She may some day come into my hands," thought the witch, "and the better she sings, the better she will be paid."

Bent-Anat too tried to teach Uarda, but learning to read was not easy to the girl, however much pains she might take. Nevertheless, the princess would not give up the spelling, for here, at the foot of the immense sacred mountain at whose summit she gazed with mixed horror and longing, she was condemned to inactivity, which weighed the more heavily on her in proportion as those feelings had to be kept to herself which she longed to escape from in work. Uarda knew the origin of her mistress's deep grief, and revered her for it, as if it were something sacred. Often she would speak of Pentaur and of his father, and always in such a manner that the princess could not guess that she knew of their love.

When the prisoners were passing Bent-Anat's tent, she was sitting within with Nefert, and talking, as had become habitual in the hours of dusk, of her father, of Mena, Rameri, and Pentaur.

"He is still alive," asserted Nefert. "My mother, you see, says that no one knows with certainty what became of him. If he escaped, he beyond a doubt tried to reach the king's camp, and when we get there you will find him with your father."

The princess looked sadly at the ground. Nefert looked affectionately at her, and asked:

"Are you thinking of the difference in rank which parts you from the man you have chosen?"

"The man to whom I offer my hand, I put in the rank of a prince," said Bent-Anat. "But if I could set Pentaur on a throne, as master of the world, he would still be greater and better than I."

"But your father?" asked Nefert doubtfully.

"He is my friend, he will listen to me and understand me. He shall know everything when I see him; I know his noble and loving heart."

Both were silent for some time; then Bent-Anat spoke:

"Pray have lights brought, I want to finish my weaving."

Nefert rose, went to the door of the tent, and there met Uarda; she seized Nefert's hand, and silently drew her out into the air.

"What is the matter, child? you are trembling," Nefert exclaimed.

"My father is here," answered Uarda hastily. "He is escorting some prisoners from the mines of Mafkat. Among them there are two chained together, and one of them-do not be startled-one of them is the poet Pentaur. Stop, for God's sake, stop, and hear me. Twice before I have seen my father when he has been here with convicts. To-day we must rescue Pentaur; but the princess must know nothing of it, for if my plan fails —"

"Child! girl!" interrupted Nefert eagerly. "How can I help you?"

"Order the steward to give the drivers of the gang a skin of wine in the name of the princess, and out of Bent-Anat's case of medicines take the phial which contains the sleeping draught, which, in spite of your wish, she will not take. I will wait here, and I know how to use it."

Nefert immediately found the steward, and ordered him to follow Uarda with a skin of wine. Then she went back to the princess's tent, and opened the medicine case.[116]

"What do you want?" asked Bent-Anat.

"A remedy for palpitation," replied Nefert; she quietly took the flask she needed, and in a few minutes put it into Uarda's hand.

The girl asked the steward to open the wine-skin, and let her taste the liquor. While she pretended to drink it, she poured the whole contents of the phial into the wine, and then let Bent-Anat's bountiful present be carried to the thirsty drivers.

She herself went towards the kitchen tent, and found a young Amalekite sitting on the ground with the princess's servants. He sprang up as soon as he saw the damsel.

"I have brought four fine partridges,"[117] he said, "which I snared myself, and I have brought this turquoise for you-my brother found it in a rock. This stone brings good luck, and is good for the eyes; it gives victory over our enemies, and keeps away bad dreams."

"Thank you!" said Uarda, and taking the boy's hand, as he gave her the sky-blue stone, she led him forward into the dusk.

"Listen, Salich" she said softly, as soon as she thought they were far enough from the others. "You are a good boy, and the maids told me that you said I was a star that had come down from the sky to become a woman. No one says such a thing as that of any one they do not like very much; and I know you like me, for you show me that you do every day by bringing me flowers, when you carry the game that your father gets to the steward. Tell me, will you do me and the princess too a very great service? Yes? —and willingly? Yes? I knew you would! Now listen. A friend of the great lady Bent-Anat, who will come here to-night, must be hidden for a day, perhaps several days, from his pursuers. Can he, or rather can they, for there will probably be two, find shelter and protection in your father's house, which lies high up there on the sacred mountain?"

"Whoever I take to my father," said the boy, "will be made welcome; and we defend our guests first, and then ourselves. Where are the strangers?"

"They will arrive in a few hours. Will you wait here till the moon is well up?"

"Till the last of all the thousand moons that vanish behind the hills is set."

"Well then, wait on the other side of the stream, and conduct the man to your house, who repeats my name three times. You know my name?"

"I call you Silver-star, but the others call you Uarda."

"Lead the strangers to your hut, and, if they are received there by your father, come back and tell me. I will watch for you here at the door of the tent. I am poor, alas! and cannot reward you, but the princess will thank your father as a princess should. Be watchful, Salich!"

The girl vanished, and went to the drivers of the gang of prisoners, wished them a merry and pleasant evening, and then hastened to Bent-Anat, who anxiously stroked her abundant hair, and asked her why she was so pale.

"Lie down," said the princess kindly, "you are feverish. Only look, Nefert, I can see the blood coursing through the blue veins in her forehead."

Meanwhile the drivers drank, praised the royal wine, and the lucky day on which they drank it; and when Uarda's father suggested that the prisoners too should have a mouthful one of his fellow soldiers cried: "Aye, let the poor beasts be jolly too for once."

217

The red-beard filled a large beaker, and offered it first to a forger and his fettered companion, then he approached Pentaur, and whispered:

"Do not drink any-keep awake!"

As he was going to warn the physician too, one of his companions came between them, and offering his tankard to Nebsecht said:

"Here mumbler, drink; see him pull! His stuttering mouth is spry enough for drinking!"

CHAPTER XXXV.

The hours passed gaily with the drinkers, then they grew more and more sleepy.

Ere the moon was high in the heavens, while they were all sleeping, with the exception of Kaschta and Pentaur, the soldier rose softly. He listened to the breathing of his companions, then he approached the poet, unfastened the ring which fettered his ankle to that of Nebsecht, and endeavored to wake the physician, but in vain.

"Follow me!" cried he to the poet; he took Nebsecht on his shoulders, and went towards the spot near the stream which Uarda had indicated. Three times he called his daughter's name, the young Amalekite appeared, and the soldier said decidedly: "Follow this man, I will take care of Nebsecht."

"I will not leave him," said Pentaur. "Perhaps water will wake him." They plunged him in the brook, which half woke him, and by the help of his companions, who now pushed and now dragged him, he staggered and stumbled up the rugged mountain path, and before midnight they reached their destination, the hut of the Amalekite.

The old hunter was asleep, but his son aroused him, and told him what Uarda had ordered and promised.

But no promises were needed to incite the worthy mountaineer to hospitality. He received the poet with genuine friendliness, laid the sleeping leech on a mat, prepared a couch for Pentaur of leaves and skins, called his daughter to wash his feet, and offered him his own holiday garment in the place of the rags that covered his body.

Pentaur stretched himself out on the humble couch, which to him seemed softer than the silken bed of a queen, but on which nevertheless he could not sleep, for the thoughts and fancies that filled his heart were too overpowering and bewildering.

The stars still sparkled in the heavens when he sprang from his bed of skins, lifted Nebsecht on to it, and rushed out into the open air. A fresh mountain spring flowed close to the hunter's hut. He went to it, and bathed his face in the ice-cold water, and let it flow over his body and limbs. He felt as if he must cleanse himself to his very soul, not only from the dust of many weeks, but from the rebellion and despondency, the ignominy and bitterness, and the contact with vice and degradation. When at last he left the spring, and returned to the little house, he felt clean and fresh as on the morning of a feast-day at the temple of Seti, when he had bathed and dressed himself in robes of snow-white linen. He took the hunter's holiday dress, put it on, and went out of doors again.

The enormous masses of rock lay dimly before him, like storm-clouds, and over his head spread the blue heavens with their thousand stars.

The soothing sense of freedom and purity raised his soul, and the air that he breathed was so fresh and light, that he sprang up the path to the summit of the peak as if he were borne on wings or carried by invisible hands.

A mountain goat which met him, turned from him, and fled bleating, with his mate, to a steep peak of rock, but Pentaur said to the frightened beasts:

"I shall do nothing to you-not I!"

He paused on a little plateau at the foot of the jagged granite peak of the mountain. Here again he heard the murmur of a spring, the grass under his feet was damp, and covered with a film of ice, in which were mirrored the stars, now gradually fading. He looked up at the lights in the sky, those never-tarrying, and yet motionless wanderers-away, to the mountain heights around him-down, into the gorge below-and far off, into the distance.

The dusk slowly grew into light, the mysterious forms of the mountain-chain took shape and stood up with their shining points, the light clouds were swept away like smoke. Thin vapors rose from the oasis and the other valleys at his feet, at first in heavy masses, then they parted and were wafted, as if in sport, above and beyond him to the sky. Far below him soared a large eagle, the only living creature far or near.

A solemn and utter silence surrounded him, and when the eagle swooped down and vanished from his sight, and the mist rolled lower into the valley, he felt that here, alone, he was high above all other living beings, and standing nearer to the Divinity.

He drew his breath fully and deeply, he felt as he had felt in the first hours after his initiation, when for the first time he was admitted to the holy of holies-and yet quite different.

Instead of the atmosphere loaded with incense, he breathed a light pure air; and the deep stillness of the mountain solitude possessed his soul more strongly than the chant of the priests.

Here, it seemed to him, that the Divine being would hear the lightest murmur of his lips, though indeed his heart was so full of gratitude and devotion that his impulse was to give expression to his mighty flow of feelings in jubilant song. But his tongue seemed tied; he knelt down in silence, to pray and to praise.

Then he looked at the panorama round him. Where was the east which in Egypt was clearly defined by the long Nile range? Down there where it was beginning to be light over the oasis. To his right hand lay the south, the sacred birth-place of the Nile, the home of the Gods of the Cataracts; but here flowed no mighty stream, and where was there a shrine for the visible manifestation of Osiris and Isis; of Horns, born of a lotus flower in a thicket of papyrus; of Rennut, the Goddess of blessings, and of Zeta? To which of them could he here lift his hands in prayer?

A faint breeze swept by, the mist vanished like a restless shade at the word of the exorcist, the many-pointed crown of Sinai stood out in sharp relief, and below them the winding valleys, and the dark colored rippling surface of the lake, became distinctly visible.

All was silent, all untouched by the hand of man yet harmonized to one great and glorious whole, subject to all the laws of the universe, pervaded and filled by the Divinity.

He would fain have raised his hand in thanksgiving to Apheru, "the Guide on the way;" but he dared not; and how infinitely small did the Gods now seem to him, the Gods he had so often glorified to the multitude in inspired words, the Gods that had no meaning, no dwelling-place, no dominion but by the Nile.

"To ye," he murmured, "I cannot pray! Here where my eye can pierce the distance, as if I myself were a god-here I feel the presence of the One, here He is near me and with me —I will call upon Him and praise him!"

And throwing up his arms he cried aloud: "Thou only One! Thou only One! Thou only One!" He said no more; but a tide of song welled up in his breast as he spoke —a flood of thankfulness and praise.

When he rose from his knees, a man was standing by him; his eyes were piercing and his tall figure had the dignity of a king, in spite of his herdsman's dress.

"It is well for you!" said the stranger in deep slow accents. "You seek the true God."

Pentaur looked steadily into the face of the bearded man before him.

"I know you now," he said. "You are Mesu. —[Moses] —I was but a boy when you left the temple of Seti, but your features are stamped on my soul. Ameni initiated me, as well as you, into the knowledge of the One God."

"He knows Him not," answered the other, looking thoughtfully to the eastern horizon, which every moment grew brighter.

The heavens glowed with purple, and the granite peaks, each sheathed in a film of ice, sparkled and shone like dark diamonds that had been dipped in light.

The day-star rose, and Pentaur turned to it, and prostrated himself as his custom was. When he rose, Mesu also was kneeling on the earth, but his back was turned to the sun.

When he had ended his prayer, Pentaur said, "Why do you turn your back on the manifestation of the Sun-god? We were taught to look towards him when he approaches."

"Because I," said his grave companion, "pray to another God than yours. The sun and stars are but as toys in his hand, the earth is his foot-stool, the storm is his breath, and the sea is in his sight as the drops on the grass."

"Teach me to know the Mighty One whom you worship!" exclaimed Pentaur.

"Seek him," said Mesu, "and you will find him; for you have passed through misery and suffering, and on this spot on such a morning as this was He revealed to me."

The stranger turned away, and disappeared behind a rock from the enquiring gaze of Pentaur, who fixed his eyes on the distance.

Then he thoughtfully descended the valley, and went towards the hut of the hunter. He stayed his steps when he heard men's voices, but the rocks hid the speakers from his sight.

Presently he saw the party approaching; the son of his host, a man in Egyptian dress, a lady of tall stature, near whom a girl tripped lightly, and another carried in a litter by slaves.

Pentaur's heart beat wildly, for he recognized Bent-Anat and her companions. They disappeared in the hunter's cottage, but he stood still, breathing painfully, spell-bound to the cliff by which he stood —a long, long time-and did not stir.

He did not hear a light step, that came near to him, and died away again, he did not feel that the sun began to cast fierce beams on him, and on the porphyry cliff behind him, he did not see a woman now coming quickly towards him; but, like a deaf man who has suddenly acquired the sense of hearing, he started when he heard his name spoken-by whose lips?

"Pentaur!" she said again; the poet opened his arms, and Bent-Anat fell upon his breast; and he held her to him, clasped, as though he must hold her there and never part from her all his life long.

Meanwhile the princess's companions were resting by the hunter's little house.

"She flew into his arms —I saw it," said Uarda. "Never shall I forget it. It was as if the bright lake there had risen up to embrace the mountain."

"Where do you find such fancies, child?" cried Nefert.

"In my heart, deep in my heart!" cried Uarda. "I am so unspeakably happy."

"You saved him and rewarded him for his goodness; you may well be happy."

"It is not only that," said Uarda. "I was in despair, and now I see that the Gods are righteous and loving."

Mena's wife nodded to her, and said with a sigh:

"They are both happy!"

"And they deserve to be!" exclaimed Uarda. "I fancy the Goddess of Truth is like Bent-Anat, and there is not another man in Egypt like Pentaur."

Nefert was silent for awhile; then she asked softly: "Did you ever see Mena?"

"How should I?" replied the girl. "Wait a little while, and your turn will come. I believe that to-day I can read the future like a prophetess. But let us see if Nebsecht lies there, and is still asleep. The draught I put into the wine must have been strong."

"It was," answered Nefert, following her into the hut.

The physician was still lying on the bed, and sleeping with his mouth wide open. Uarda knelt down by his side, looked in his face, and said:

"He is clever and knows everything, but how silly he looks now! I will wake him."

She pulled a blade of grass out of the heap on which he was lying, and saucily tickled his nose.

Nebsecht raised himself, sneezed, but fell back asleep again; Uarda laughed out with her clear silvery tones. Then she blushed —"That is not right," she said, "for he is good and generous."

She took the sleeper's hand, pressed it to her lips, and wiped the drops from his brow. Then he awoke, opened his eyes, and muttered half in a dream still:

"Uarda-sweet Uarda."

The girl started up and fled, and Nefert followed her.

When Nebsecht at last got upon his feet and looked round him, he found himself alone in a strange house. He went out of doors, where he found Bent-Anat's little train anxiously discussing things past and to come.

CHAPTER XXXVI.

The inhabitants of the oasis had for centuries been subject to the Pharaohs, and paid them tribute; and among the rights granted to them in return, no Egyptian soldier might cross their border and territory without their permission.

The Ethiopians had therefore pitched Bent-Anat's tents and their own camp outside these limits; but various transactions soon took place between the idle warriors and the Amalekites, which now and then led to quarrels, and which one evening threatened serious consequences, when some drunken soldiers had annoyed the Amalekite women while they were drawing water.

This morning early one of the drivers on awaking had missed Pentaur and Nebsecht, and he roused his comrades, who had been rejoined by Uarda's father. The enraged guard of the gang of prisoners hastened to the commandant of the Ethiopians, and informed him that two of his prisoners had escaped, and were no doubt being kept in concealment by the Amalekites.

The Amalekites met the requisition to surrender the fugitives, of whom they knew nothing, with words of mockery, which so enraged the officer that he determined to search the oasis throughout by force, and when he found his emissaries treated with scorn he advanced with the larger part of his troops on to the free territory of the Amalekites.

The sons of the desert flew to arms; they retired before the close order of the Egyptian troops, who followed them, confident of victory, to a point where the valley widens and divides on each side of a rocky hill. Behind this the larger part of the Amalekite forces were lying in ambush, and as soon as the unsuspicious Ethiopians had marched past the hill, they threw themselves on the rear of the astonished invaders, while those in front turned upon them, and flung lances and arrows at the soldiers, of whom very few escaped.

Among them, however, was the commanding officer, who, foaming with rage and only slightly wounded, put himself at the head of the remainder of Bent-Anat's body-guard, ordered the escort of the prisoners also to follow him, and once more advanced into the oasis.

That the princess might escape him had never for an instant occurred to him, but as soon as the last of her keepers had disappeared, Bent-Anat explained to her chamberlain and her companions that now or never was the moment to fly.

All her people were devoted to her; they loaded themselves with the most necessary things for daily use, took the litters and beasts of burden with them, and while the battle was raging in the valley, Salich guided them up the heights of Sinai to his father's house.

It was on the way thither that Uarda had prepared the princess for the meeting she might expect at the hunter's cottage, and we have seen how and where the princess found the poet.

Hand in hand they wandered together along the mountain path till they came to a spot shaded by a projection of the rock, Pentaur pulled some moss to make a seat, they reclined on it side by side, and there opened their hearts, and told each other of their love and of their sufferings, their wanderings and escapes.

At noonday the hunter's daughter came to offer them a pitcher full of goat's milk, and Bent-Anat filled the gourd again and again for the man she loved; and waiting upon him thus, her heart overflowed with pride, and his with the humble desire to be permitted to sacrifice his blood and life for her.

Hitherto they had been so absorbed in the present and the past, that they had not given a thought to the future, and while they repeated a hundred times what each had long since known, and yet could never tire of hearing, they forgot the immediate changes which was hanging over them.

After their humble meal, the surging flood of feeling which, ever since his morning devotions, had overwhelmed the poet's soul, grew calmer; he had felt as if borne through the air, but now he set foot, so to speak, on the earth again, and seriously considered with Bent-Anat what steps they must take in the immediate future.

The light of joy, which beamed in their eyes, was little in accordance with the grave consultation they held, as, hand in hand, they descended to the hut of their humble host.

The hunter, guided by his daughter, met them half way, and with him a tall and dignified man in the full armor of a chief of the Amalekites.

Both bowed and kissed the earth before Bent-Anat and Pentaur. They had heard that the princess was detained in the oasis by force by the Ethiopian troops, and the desert-prince, Abocharabos, now informed them, not without pride, that the Ethiopian soldiers, all but a few who were his prisoners, had been exterminated by his people; at the same time he assured Pentaur, whom he supposed to be a son of the king, and Bent-Anat, that he and his were entirely devoted to the Pharaoh Rameses, who had always respected their rights.

"They are accustomed," he added, "to fight against the cowardly dogs of Kush; but we are men, and we can fight like the lions of our wilds. If we are outnumbered we hide like the goats in clefts of the rocks."

Bent-Anat, who was pleased with the daring man, his flashing eyes, his aquiline nose, and his brown face which bore the mark of a bloody sword-cut, promised him to commend him and his people to her father's favor, and told him of her desire to proceed as soon as possible to the king's camp under the protection of Pentaur, her future husband.

The mountain chief had gazed attentively at Pentaur and at Bent-Anat while she spoke; then he said: "Thou, princess, art like the moon, and thy companion is like the Sun-god Dusare. Besides Abocharabos," and he struck his breast, "and his wife, I know no pair that are like you two. I myself will conduct you to Hebron with some of my best men of war. But haste will be necessary, for I must be back before the traitor who now rules over Mizraim —[The Semitic name of Egypt] —and who persecutes you, can send fresh forces against us. Now you can go down again to the tents, not a hen is missing. To-morrow before daybreak we will be off."

At the door of the hut Pentaur was greeted by the princess's companions.

The chamberlain looked at him not without anxious misgiving.

The king, when he departed, had, it is true, given him orders to obey Bent-Anat in every particular, as if she were the queen herself; but her choice of such a husband was a thing unheard of, and how would the king take it?

Nefert rejoiced in the splendid person of the poet, and frequently repeated that he was as like her dead uncle-the father of Paaker, the chief-pioneer —as if he were his younger brother.

Uarda never wearied of contemplating him and her beloved princess. She no longer looked upon him as a being of a higher order; but the happiness of the noble pair seemed to her an embodied omen of happiness for Nefert's love-perhaps too for her own.

Nebsecht kept modestly in the background. The headache, from which he had long been suffering, had disappeared in the fresh mountain air. When Pentaur offered him his hand he exclaimed:

"Here is an end to all my jokes and abuse! A strange thing is this fate of men. Henceforth I shall always have the worst of it in any dispute with you, for all the discords of your life have been very prettily resolved by the great master of harmony, to whom you pray."

"You speak almost as if you were sorry; but every thing will turn out happily for you too."

"Hardly!" replied the surgeon, "for now I see it clearly. Every man is a separate instrument, formed even before his birth, in an occult workshop, of good or bad wood, skilfully or unskilfully made, of this shape or the other; every thing in his life, no matter what we call it, plays upon him, and the instrument sounds for good or evil, as it is well or ill made. You are an AEolian harp-the sound is delightful, whatever breath of fate may touch it; I am a weather-cock —I turn whichever way the wind blows, and try to point right, but at the same time I creak, so that it hurts my own ears and those of other people. I am content if now and then a steersman may set his sails rightly by my indication; though after all, it is all the same to me. I will turn round and round, whether others look at me or no-What does it signify?"

When Pentaur and the princess took leave of the hunter with many gifts, the sun was sinking, and the toothed peaks of Sinai glowed like rubies, through which shone the glow of half a world on fire.

The journey to the royal camp was begun the next morning. Abocharabos, the Amalekite chief, accompanied the caravan, to which Uarda's father also attached himself; he had been taken prisoner in the struggle with the natives, but at Bent-Anat's request was set at liberty.

At their first halting place he was commanded to explain how he had succeeded in having Pentaur taken to the mines, instead of to the quarries of Chennu.

"I knew," said the soldier in his homely way, "from Uarda where this man, who had risked his life for us poor folks, was to be taken, and I said to myself—I must save him. But thinking is not my trade, and I never can lay a plot. It would very likely have come to some violent act, that would have ended badly, if I had not had a hint from another person, even before Uarda told me of what threatened Pentaur. This is how it was.

"I was to convoy the prisoners, who were condemned to work in the Mafkat mines, across the river to the place they start from. In the harbor of Thebes, on the other side, the poor wretches were to take leave of their friends; I have seen it a hundred times, and I never can get used to it, and yet one can get hardened to most things! Their loud cries, and wild howls are not the worst-those that scream the most I have always found are the first to get used to their fate; but the pale ones, whose lips turn white, and whose teeth chatter as if they were freezing, and whose eyes stare out into vacancy without any tears-those go to my heart. There was all the usual misery, both noisy and silent. But the man I was most sorry for was one I had known for a long time; his name was Huni, and he belonged to the temple of Amon, where he held the place of overseer of the attendants on the sacred goat. I had often met him when I was on duty to watch the laborers who were completing the great pillared hall, and he was respected by every one, and never failed in his duty. Once, however, he had neglected it; it was that very night which you all will remember when the wolves broke into the temple, and tore the rams, and the sacred heart was laid in the breast of the prophet Rui. Some one, of course, must be punished, and it fell on poor Huni, who for his carelessness was condemned to forced labor in the mines of Mafkat. His successor will keep a sharp look out! No one came to see him off, though I know he had a wife and several children. He was as pale as this cloth, and was one of the sort whose grief eats into their heart. I went up to him, and asked him why no one came with him. He had taken leave of them at home, he answered, that his children might not see him mixed up with forgers and murderers. Eight poor little brats were left unprovided for with their mother, and a little while before a fire had destroyed everything they possessed. There was not a crumb to stop their little squalling mouths. He did not tell me all this straight out; a word fell from him now and then, like dates from a torn sack. I picked it up bit by bit, and when he saw I felt for him he grew fierce and said: 'They may send me to the gold mines or cut me to pieces, as far as I am concerned, but that the little ones should starve that-that,' and he struck his forehead. Then I left him to say good bye to Uarda, and on the way I kept repeating to myself 'that-that,' and saw before me the man and his eight brats. If I were rich, thought I, there is a man I would help. When I got to the little one there, she told me how much money the leech Nebsecht had given her, and offered to give it me to save Pentaur; then it passed through my mind-that may go to Hum's children, and in return he will let himself be shipped off to Ethiopia. I ran to the harbor, spoke to the man, found him ready and willing, gave the money to his wife, and at night when the prisoners were shipped I contrived the exchange Pentaur came with me on my boat under the name of the other, and Huni went to the south, and was called Pentaur. I had not deceived the man into thinking he would stop at Chennu. I told him he would be taken on to Ethiopia, for it is always impossible to play a man false when you know it is quite easy to do it. It is very strange! It is a real pleasure to cheat a cunning fellow or a sturdy man, but who would take in a child or a sick person? Huni certainly would have gone into the fire-pots of hell without complaining, and he left me quite cheerfully. The rest, and how we got here, you yourselves know. In Syria at this time of year you will suffer a good deal from rain. I know the country, for I have escorted many prisoners of war into Egypt, and I was there five years with the troops of the great Mohar, father of the chief pioneer Paaker."

Bent-Anat thanked the brave fellow, and Pentaur and Nebsecht continued the narrative.

"During the voyage," said Nebsecht, "I was uneasy about Pentaur, for I saw how he was pining, but in the desert he seemed to rouse himself, and often whispered sweet little songs that he had composed while we marched."

"That is strange," said Bent-Anat, "for I also got better in the desert."

"Repeat the verses on the Beytharan plant," said Nebsecht.

"Do you know the plant?" asked the poet. "It grows here in many places; here it is. Only smell how sweet it is if you bruise the fleshy stem and leaves. My little verse is simple enough; it occurred to me like many other songs of which you know all the best."

"They all praise the same Goddess," said Nebsecht laughing.

"But let us have the verses," said Bent-Anat. The poet repeated in a low voice:

> "How often in the desert I have seen
> The small herb, Beytharan, in modest green!
> In every tiny leaf and gland and hair
> Sweet perfume is distilled, and scents the air.
> How is it that in barren sandy ground
> This little plant so sweet a gift has found?
> And that in me, in this vast desert plain,
> The sleeping gift of song awakes again?"

"Do you not ascribe to the desert what is due to love?" said Nefert.

"I owe it to both; but I must acknowledge that the desert is a wonderful physician for a sick soul. We take refuge from the monotony that surrounds us in our own reflections; the senses are at rest; and here, undisturbed and uninfluenced from without, it is given to the mind to think out every train of thought to the end, to examine and exhaust every feeling to its finest shades. In the city, one is always a mere particle in a great whole, on which one is dependent, to which one must contribute, and from which one must accept something. The solitary wanderer in the desert stands quite alone; he is in a manner freed from the ties which bind him to any great human community; he must fill up the void by his own identity, and seek in it that which may give his existence significance and consistency. Here, where the present retires into the background, the thoughtful spirit finds no limits however remote."

"Yes; one can think well in the desert," said Nebsecht. "Much has become clear to me here that in Egypt I only guessed at."

"What may that be?" asked Pentaur.

"In the first place," replied Nebsecht, "that we none of us really know anything rightly; secondly that the ass may love the rose, but the rose will not love the ass; and the third thing I will keep to myself, because it is my secret, and though it concerns all the world no one would trouble himself about it. My lord chamberlain, how is this? You know exactly how low people must bow before the princess in proportion to their rank, and have no idea how a back-bone is made."

"Why should I?" asked the chamberlain. "I have to attend to outward things, while you are contemplating inward things; else your hair might be smoother, and your dress less stained."

The travellers reached the old Cheta city of Hebron without accident; there they took leave of Abocharabos, and under the safe escort of Egyptian troops started again for the north. At Hebron Pentaur parted from the princess, and Bent-Anat bid him farewell without complaining.

Uarda's father, who had learned every path and bridge in Syria, accompanied the poet, while the physician Nebsecht remained with the ladies, whose good star seemed to have deserted them with Pentaur's departure, for the violent winter rains which fell in the mountains of Samaria destroyed the roads, soaked through the tents, and condemned them frequently to undesirable delays. At Megiddo they were received with high honors by the commandant of the Egyptian garrison, and they were compelled to linger here some days, for Nefert, who had been particularly eager to hurry forward, was taken ill, and Nebsecht was obliged to forbid her proceeding at this season.

Uarda grew pale and thoughtful, and Bent-Anat saw with anxiety that the tender roses were fading from the cheeks of her pretty favorite; but when she questioned her as to what ailed her she gave an evasive answer. She had never either mentioned Rameri's name before the princess, nor shown her her mother's jewel, for she felt as if all that had passed between her and the prince was a secret which did not belong to her alone. Yet another reason sealed her lips. She was passionately devoted to Bent-Anat, and she told herself that if the princess heard it all, she would either blame her brother or laugh at his affection as at a child's play, and she felt as if in that case she could not love Rameri's sister any more.

A messenger had been sent on from the first frontier station to the king's camp to enquire by which road the princess, and her party should leave Megiddo. But the emissary returned with a short and decided though affectionate letter written by the king's own hand, to his daughter, desiring her not to quit Megiddo, which was a safe magazine and arsenal for the army, strongly fortified and garrisoned, as it commanded the roads from the sea into North and Central Palestine. Decisive encounters, he said, were impending, and she knew that the Egyptians always excluded their wives and daughters from their war train, and regarded them as the best reward of victory when peace was obtained.

While the ladies were waiting in Megiddo, Pentaur and his red-bearded guide proceeded northwards with a small mounted escort, with which they were supplied by the commandant of Hebron.

He himself rode with dignity, though this journey was the first occasion on which he had sat on horseback. He seemed to have come into the world with the art of riding born with him. As soon as he had learned from his companions how to grasp the bridle, and had made himself familiar with the nature of the horse, it gave him the greatest delight to tame and subdue a fiery steed.

He had left his priest's robes in Egypt. Here he wore a coat of mail, a sword, and battle-axe like a warrior, and his long beard, which had grown during his captivity, now flowed down over his breast. Uarda's father often looked at him with admiration, and said:

"One might think the Mohar, with whom I often travelled these roads, had risen from the dead. He looked like you, he spoke like you, he called the men as you do, nay he sat as you do when the road was too bad for his chariot,[118] and he got on horseback, and held the reins."

None of Pentaur's men, except his red-bearded friend, was more to him than a mere hired servant, and he usually preferred to ride alone, apart from the little troop, musing on the past-seldom on the future-and generally observing all that lay on his way with a keen eye. They soon reached Lebanon; between it and Lebanon a road led through the great Syrian valley. It rejoiced him to see with his own eyes the distant shimmer of the white snow-capped peaks, of which he had often heard warriors talk.

The country between the two mountain ranges was rich and fruitful, and from the heights waterfalls and torrents rushed into the valley. Many villages and towns lay on his road, but most of them had been damaged in the war. The peasants had been robbed of their teams of cattle, the flocks had been driven off from the shepherds, and when a vine-dresser, who was training his vine saw the little troop approaching, he fled to the ravines and forests.

The traces of the plough and the spade were everywhere visible, but the fields were for the most part not sown; the young peasants were under arms, the gardens and meadows were trodden down by soldiers, the houses and cottages plundered and destroyed, or burnt. Everything bore the trace of the devastation of the war, only the oak and cedar forests lorded it proudly over the mountain-slopes, planes and locust-trees grew in groves, and the gorges and rifts of the thinly-wooded limestone hills, which bordered the fertile low-land, were filled with evergreen brushwood.

At this time of year everything was moist and well-watered, and Pentaur compared the country with Egypt, and observed how the same results were attained here as there, but by different agencies. He remembered that morning on Sinai, and said to himself again: "Another God than ours rules here, and the old masters were not wrong who reviled godless strangers, and warned the uninitiated, to whom the secret of the One must remain unrevealed, to quit their home."

The nearer he approached the king's camp, the more vividly he thought of Bent-Anat, and the faster his heart beat from time to time when he thought of his meeting with the king. On the whole he was full of cheerful confidence, which he felt to be folly, and which nevertheless he could not repress.

Ameni had often blamed him for his too great diffidence and his want of ambition, when he had willingly let others pass him by. He remembered this now, and smiled and understood himself less than ever, for though he resolutely repeated to himself a hundred times that he was a low-born, poor, and excommunicated priest, the feeling would not be smothered that he had a right to claim Bent-Anat for his own.

And if the king refused him his daughter-if he made him pay for his audacity with his life?

Not an eyelash, he well knew, would tremble under the blow of the axe, and he would die content; for that which she had granted him was his, and no God could take it from him!

CHAPTER XXXVII.

Once or twice Pentaur and his companions had had to defend themselves against hostile mountaineers, who rushed suddenly upon them out of the woods. When they were about two days' journey still from the end of their march, they had a bloody skirmish with a roving band of men that seemed to belong to a larger detachment of troops.

The nearer they got to Kadesh, the more familiar Kaschta showed himself with every stock and stone, and he went forward to obtain information; he returned somewhat anxious, for he had perceived the main body of the Cheta army on the road which they must cross. How came the enemy here in the rear of the Egyptian army? Could Rameses have sustained a defeat?

Only the day before they had met some Egyptian soldiers, who had told them that the king was staying in the camp, and a great battle was impending. This however could not have by this time been decided, and they had met no flying Egyptians.

"If we can only get two miles farther without having to fight," said Uarda's father. "I know what to do. Down below, there is a ravine, and from it a path leads over hill and vale to the plain of Kadesh. No one ever knew it but the Mohar and his most confidential servants. About half-way there is a hidden cave, in which we have often stayed the whole day long. The Cheta used to believe that the Mohar possessed magic powers, and could make himself invisible, for when they lay in wait for us on the way we used suddenly to vanish; but certainly not into the clouds, only into the cave, which the Mohar used to call his Tuat. If you are not afraid of a climb, and will lead your horse behind you for a mile or two, I can show you the way, and to-morrow evening we will be at the camp."

Pentaur let his guide lead the way; they came, without having occasion to fight, as far as the gorge between the hills, through which a full and foaming mountain torrent rushed to the valley. Kaschta dropped from his horse, and the others did the same. After the horses had passed through the water, he carefully effaced their tracks as far as the road, then for about half a mile he ascended the valley against the stream. At last he stopped in front of a thick oleander-bush, looked carefully about, and lightly pushed it aside; when he had found an entrance, his companions and their weary scrambling beasts followed him without difficulty, and they presently found themselves in a grove of lofty cedars. Now they had to squeeze themselves between masses of rock, now they labored up and down over smooth pebbles, which offered scarcely any footing to the horses' hoofs; now they had to push their way through thick brushwood, and now to cross little brooks swelled by the winter-rains.

The road became more difficult at every step, then it began to grow dark, and heavy drops of rain fell from the clouded sky.

"Make haste, and keep close to me," cried Kaschta. "Half an hour more, and we shall be under shelter, if I do not lose my way."

Then a horse broke down, and with great difficulty was got up again; the rain fell with increased violence, the night grew darker, and the soldier often found himself brought to a stand-still, feeling for the path with his hands; twice he thought he had lost it, but he would not give in till he had recovered the track. At last he stood still, and called Pentaur to come to him.

"Hereabouts," said he, "the cave must be; keep close to me-it is possible that we may come upon some of the pioneer's people. Provisions and fuel were always kept here in his father's time. Can you see me? Hold on to my girdle, and bend your head low till I tell you you may stand upright again. Keep your axe ready, we may find some of the Cheta or bandits roosting there. You people must wait, we will soon call you to come under shelter."

Pentaur closely followed his guide, pushing his way through the dripping brushwood, crawling through a low passage in the rock, and at last emerging on a small rocky plateau.

"Take care where you are going!" cried Kaschta. "Keep to the left, to the right there is a deep abyss. I smell smoke! Keep your hand on your axe, there must be some one in the cave. Wait! I will fetch the men as far as this."

The soldier went back, and Pentaur listened for any sounds that might come from the same direction as the smoke. He fancied he could perceive a small gleam of light, and he certainly heard quite plainly, first a tone of complaint, then an angry voice; he went towards the light, feeling his way by the wall on his left; the light shone broader and brighter, and seemed to issue from a crack in a door.

By this time the soldier had rejoined Pentaur, and both listened for a few minutes; then the poet whispered to his guide:

"They are speaking Egyptian, I caught a few words."

"All the better," said Kaschta. "Paaker or some of his people are in there; the door is there still, and shut. If we give four hard and three gentle knocks, it will be opened. Can you understand what they are saying?"

"Some one is begging to be set free," replied Pentaur, "and speaks of some traitor. The other has a rough voice, and says he must follow his master's orders. Now the one who spoke before is crying; do you hear? He is entreating him by the soul of his father to take his fetters off. How despairing his voice is! Knock, Kaschta-it strikes me we are come at the right moment-knock, I say."

The soldier knocked first four times, then three times. A shriek rang through the cave, and they could hear a heavy, rusty bolt drawn back, the roughly hewn door was opened, and a hoarse voice asked:

"Is that Paaker?"

"No," answered the soldier, "I am Kaschta. Do not you know me again, Nubi?"

The man thus addressed, who was Paaker's Ethiopian slave, drew back in surprise.

"Are you still alive?" he exclaimed. "What brings you here?"

"My lord here will tell you," answered Kaschta as he made way for Pentaur to enter the cave. The poet went up to the black man, and the light of the fire which burned in the cave fell full on his face.

The old slave stared at him, and drew back in astonishment and terror. He threw himself on the earth, howled like a dog that fawns at the feet of his angry master, and cried out:

"He ordered it-Spirit of my master! he ordered it." Pentaur stood still, astounded and incapable of speech, till he perceived a young man, who crept up to him on his hands and feet, which were bound with thongs, and who cried to him in a tone, in which terror was mingled with a tenderness which touched Pentaur's very soul.

"Save me-Spirit of the Mohar! save me, father!" Then the poet spoke.

"I am no spirit of the dead," said he. "I am the priest Pentaur; and I know you, boy; you are Horus, Paaker's brother, who was brought up with me in the temple of Seti."

The prisoner approached him trembling, looked at him enquiringly and exclaimed:

"Be you who you may, you are exactly like my father in person and in voice. Loosen my bonds, and listen to me, for the most hideous, atrocious, and accursed treachery threatens us the king and all."

Pentaur drew his sword, and cut the leather thongs which bound the young man's hands and feet. He stretched his released limbs, uttering thanks to the Gods, then he cried:

"If you love Egypt and the king follow me; perhaps there is yet time to hinder the hideous deed, and to frustrate this treachery."

"The night is dark," said Kaschita, "and the road to the valley is dangerous."

"You must follow me if it is to your death!" cried the youth, and, seizing Pentaur's hand, he dragged him with him out of the cave.

As soon as the black slave had satisfied himself that Pentaur was the priest whom he had seen fighting in front of the paraschites' hovel, and not the ghost of his dead master, he endeavored to slip past Paaker's brother, but Horus observed the manoeuvre, and seized him by his woolly hair. The slave cried out loudly, and whimpered out:

"If thou dost escape, Paaker will kill me; he swore he would."

"Wait!" said the youth. He dragged the slave back, flung him into the cave, and blocked up the door with a huge log which lay near it for that purpose.

When the three men had crept back through the low passage in the rocks, and found themselves once more in the open air, they found a high wind was blowing.

"The storm will soon be over," said Horus. "See how the clouds are driving! Let us have horses, Pentaur, for there is not a minute to be lost."

The poet ordered Kaschta to summon the people to start but the soldier advised differently.

"Men and horses are exhausted," he said, "and we shall get on very slowly in the dark. Let the beasts feed for an hour, and the men get rested and warm; by that time the moon will be up, and we shall make up for the delay by having fresh horses, and light enough to see the road."

"The man is right," said Horus; and he led Kaschta to a cave in the rocks, where barley and dates for the horses, and a few jars of wine, had been preserved. They soon had lighted a fire, and while some of the men took care of the horses, and others cooked a warm mess of victuals, Horus and Pentaur walked up and down impatiently.

"Had you been long bound in those thongs when we came?" asked Pentaur.

"Yesterday my brother fell upon me," replied Horus. "He is by this time a long way ahead of us, and if he joins the Cheta, and we do not reach the Egyptian camp before daybreak, all is lost."

"Paaker, then, is plotting treason?"

"Treason, the foulest, blackest treason!" exclaimed the young man. "Oh, my lost father! —"

"Confide in me," said Pentaur going up to the unhappy youth who had hidden his face in his hands. "What is Paaker plotting? How is it that your brother is your enemy?"

"He is the elder of us two," said Horus with a trembling voice. "When my father died I had only a short time before left the school of Seti, and with his last words my father enjoined me to respect Paaker as the head of our family. He is domineering and violent, and will allow no one's will to cross his; but I bore everything, and always obeyed him, often against my better judgment. I remained with him two years, then I went to Thebes, and there I married, and my wife and child are now living there with my mother. About sixteen months afterwards I came back to Syria, and we travelled through the country together; but by this time I did not choose to be the mere tool of my brother's will, for I had grown prouder, and it seemed to me that the father of my child ought not to be subservient, even to his own brother. We often quarrelled, and had a bad time together, and life became quite unendurable, when—about eight weeks since—Paaker came back from Thebes, and the king gave him to understand that he approved more of my reports than of his. From my childhood I have always been softhearted and patient; every one says I am like my mother; but what Paaker made me suffer by words and deeds, that is —I could not —" His voice broke, and Pentaur felt how cruelly he had suffered; then he went on again:

"What happened to my brother in Egypt, I do not know, for he is very reserved, and asks for no sympathy, either in joy or in sorrow; but from words he has dropped now and then I gather that he not only bitterly hates Mena, the charioteer-who certainly did him an injury-but has some grudge against the king too. I spoke to him of it at once, but only once, for his rage is unbounded when he is provoked, and after all he is my elder brother.

"For some days they have been preparing in the camp for a decisive battle, and it was our duty to ascertain the position and strength of the enemy; the king gave me, and not Paaker, the commission to prepare the report. Early yesterday morning I drew it out and wrote it; then my brother said he would carry it to the camp, and I was to wait here. I positively refused, as Rameses had required the report at my hands, and not at his. Well, he raved like a madman, declared that I had taken advantage of his absence to insinuate myself into the king's favor, and commanded me to obey him as the head of the house, in the name of my father.

"I was sitting irresolute, when he went out of the cavern to call his horses; then my eyes fell on the things which the old black slave was tying together to load on a pack-horse —among them was a roll of writing. I fancied it was my own, and took it up to look at it, when-what should I find? At the risk of my life I had gone among the Cheta, and had found that the main body of their army is collected in a cross-valley of the Orontes, quite hidden in the mountains to the north-east of Kadesh; and in the roll it was stated, in Paaker's own hand-writing, that that valley is clear, and the way through it open, and well suited for the passage of the Egyptian war-chariots; various other false details were given, and when I looked further among his things, I found between the arrows in his quiver, on which he had written 'death to Mena,' another little roll of writing. I tore it open, and my blood ran cold when I saw to whom it was addressed."

"To the king of the Cheta?" cried Pentaur in excitement.

"To his chief officer, Titure," continued Horus. "I was holding both the rolls in my hand, when Paaker came back into the cave. 'Traitor!' I cried out to him; but he flung the lasso, with which he had been catching the stray horses, threw it round my neck, and as I fell choking on the ground, he and the black man, who obeys him like a dog, bound me hand and foot; he left the old negro to keep guard over me, took the rolls and rode away. Look, there are the stars, and the moon will soon be up."

"Make haste, men!" cried Pentaur. "The three best horses for me, Horus, and Kaschta; the rest remain here."

As the red-bearded soldier led the horses forward, the moon shone forth, and within an hour the travellers had reached the plain; they sprang on to the beasts and rode madly on towards the lake, which, when the sun rose, gleamed before them in silvery green. As they drew near to it they could discern, on its treeless western shore, black masses moving hither and thither; clouds of dust rose up from the plain, pierced by flashes of light, like the rays of the sun reflected from a moving mirror.

"The battle is begun!" cried Horus; and he fell sobbing on his horse's neck.

"But all is not lost yet!" exclaimed the poet, spurring his horse to a final effort of strength. His companions did the same, but first Kaschta's horse fell under him, then Horus's broke down.

"Help may be given by the left wing!" cried Horus. "I will run as fast as I can on foot, I know where to find them. You will easily find the king if you follow the stream to the stone bridge. In the cross-valley about a thousand paces farther north-to the northwest of our stronghold-the surprise is to be effected. Try to get through, and warn Rameses; the Egyptian pass-word is 'Bent-Anat,' the name of the king's favorite daughter. But even if you had wings, and could fly straight to him, they would overpower him if I cannot succeed in turning the left wing on the rear of the enemy."

Pentaur galloped onwards; but it was not long before his horse too gave way, and he ran forward like a man who runs a race, and shouted the pass-word "Bent-Anat" —for the ring of her name seemed to give him vigor. Presently he came upon a mounted messenger of the enemy; he struck him down from his horse, flung himself into the saddle, and rushed on towards the camp; as if he were riding to his wedding.

CHAPTER XXXVIII.

During the night which had proved so eventful to our friends, much had occurred in the king's camp, for the troops were to advance to the long-anticipated battle before sunrise.

Paaker had given his false report of the enemy's movements to the Pharaoh with his own hand; a council of war had been held, and each division had received instructions as to where it was to take up its position. The corps, which bore the name of the Sungod Ra, advanced from the south towards Schabatun,[119] so as to surround the lake on the east, and fall on the enemy's flank; the corps of Seth, composed of men from lower Egypt, was sent on to Arnam to form the centre; the king himself, with the flower of the chariot-guard, proposed to follow the road through the valley, which Paaker's report represented as a safe and open passage to the plain of the Orontes. Thus, while the other divisions occupied the enemy, he could cross the Orontes by a ford, and fall on the rear of the fortress of Kadesh from the north-west. The corps of Amon, with the Ethiopian mercenaries, were to support him, joining him by another route, which the pioneer's false indications represented as connecting the line of operations. The corps of Ptah remained as a reserve behind the left wing.

The soldiers had not gone to rest as usual; heavily, armed troops, who bore in one hand a shield of half a man's height, and in the other a scimitar, or a short, pointed sword, guarded the camp,[120] where numerous fires burned, round which crowded the resting warriors. Here a wine-skin was passed from hand to hand, there a joint was roasting on a wooden spit; farther on a party were throwing dice for the booty they had won, or playing at morra. All was in eager activity, and many a scuffle occurred amoung the excited soldiers, and had to be settled by the camp-watch.

Near the enclosed plots, where the horses were tethered, the smiths were busily engaged in shoeing the beasts which needed it, and in sharpening the points of the lances; the servants of the chariot-guard were also fully occupied, as the chariots had for the most part been brought over the mountains in detached pieces on the backs of pack-horses and asses, and now had to be put together again, and to have their wheels greased. On the eastern side of the camp stood a canopy, under which the standards were kept, and there numbers of priests were occupied in their office of blessing the warriors, offering sacrifices, and singing hymns and litanies. But these pious sounds were frequently overpowered by the loud voices of the gamblers and revellers, by the blows of the hammers, the hoarse braying of the asses, and the neighing of the horses. From time to time also the deep roar of the king's war-lions[121] might be heard; these beasts followed him into the fight, and were now howling for food, as they had been kept fasting to excite their fury.

In the midst of the camp stood the king's tent, surrounded by foot and chariot-guards. The auxiliary troops were encamped in divisions according to their nationality, and between them the Egyptian legions of heavy-armed soldiers and archers. Here might be seen the black Ethiopian with wooly matted hair, in which a few feathers were stuck-the handsome, well pro- portioned "Son of the desert" from the sandy Arabian shore of the Red Sea, who performed his wild war-dance flourishing his lance, with a peculiar wriggle of his-hips pale Sardinians, with metal helmets and heavy swords-light colored Libyans, with tattooed arms and ostrich-feathers on their heads-brown, bearded Arabs, worshippers of the stars, inseparable from their horses, and armed, some with lances, and some with bows and arrows. And not less various than their aspect were the tongues of the allied troops-but all obedient to the king's word of command.

In the midst of the royal tents was a lightly constructed temple with the statues of the Gods of Thebes, and of the king's forefathers; clouds of incense rose in front of it, for the priests were engaged from the eve of the battle until it was over, in prayers, and offerings to Amon, the king of the Gods, to Necheb, the Goddess of victory, and to Menth, the God of war.

The keeper of the lions stood by the Pharaoh's sleeping-tent, and the tent, which served as a council chamber, was distinguished by the standards in front of it; but the council-tent was empty and still, while in the kitchen-tent, as well as in the wine-store close by, all was in a bustle. The large pavilion, in which Rameses and his suite were taking their evening meal, was more brilliantly lighted than all the others; it was a covered tent, a long square in shape, and all round it were colored lamps, which made it as light as day; a body-guard of Sardinians, Libyans, and Egyptians guarded it with drawn swords, and seemed too wholly absorbed with the importance of their office even to notice the dishes and wine-jars, which the king's pages-the sons of the highest families in Egypt-took at the tent-door from the cooks and butlers.

The walls and slanting roof of this quickly-built and movable banqueting-hall, consisted of a strong, impenetrable carpet-stuff, woven at Thebes, and afterwards dyed purple at Tanis by the Phoenicians. Saitic artists had embroidered the vulture, one of the forms in which Necheb appears, a hundred times on the costly material with threads of silver. The cedar-wood pillars of the tent were covered with gold, and the ropes, which secured the light erection to the tent-pegs, were twisted of silk, and thin threads of silver. Seated round four tables, more than a hundred men were taking their evening meal; at three of them the generals of the army, the chief priests, and councillors, sat on light stools; at the fourth, and at some distance from the others, were the princes of the blood; and the king himself sat apart at a high table, on a throne supported by gilt figures of Asiatic prisoners in chains. His table and throne stood on a low dais covered with panther-skin; but even without that Rameses would have towered above his companions. His form was powerful, and there was a commanding aspect in his bearded face, and in the high brow, crowned with a golden diadem adorned with the heads of two Uraeus-snakes, wearing the crowns of Upper and Lower Egypt. A broad collar of precious stones covered half his breast, the lower half was concealed by a scarf or belt, and his bare arms were adorned with bracelets. His finely-proportioned limbs looked as if moulded in bronze, so smoothly were the powerful muscles covered with the shining copper-colored skin. Sitting here among those who were devoted to him, he looked with kind and fatherly pride at his blooming sons.

The lion was at rest-but nevertheless he was a lion, and terrible things might be looked for when he should rouse himself, and when the mighty hand, which now dispensed bread, should be clenched for the fight. There was nothing mean in this man, and yet nothing alarming; for, if his eye had a commanding sparkle, the expression of his mouth was particularly gentle; and the deep voice which could make itself heard above the clash of fighting men, could also assume the sweetest and most winning tones. His education had not only made him well aware of his greatness and power, but had left him also a genuine man, a stranger to none of the emotions of the human soul.

Behind Pharaoh stood a man, younger than himself, who gave him his wine-cup after first touching it with his own lips; this was Mena, the king's charioteer and favorite companion. His figure was slight and yet vigorous, supple and yet dignified, and his finely-formed features and frank bright eyes were full at once of self-respect and of benevolence. Such a man might fail in reflection and counsel, but would be admirable as an honorable, staunch, and faithful friend.

Among the princes, Chamus sat nearest to the king;[122] he was the eldest of his sons, and while still young had been invested with the dignity of high-priest of Memphis. The curly-haired Rameri, who had been rescued from imprisonment-into which he had fallen on his journey from Egypt-had been assigned a place with the younger princes at the lowest end of the table.

"It all sounds very threatening!" said the king. "But though each of you croakers speaks the truth, your love for me dims your sight. In fact, all that Rameri has told me, that Bent-Anat writes, that Mena's stud-keeper says of Ani, and that comes through other channels-amounts to nothing that need disturb us. I know your uncle —I know that he will make his borrowed throne as wide as he possibly can; but when we return home he will be quite content to sit on a narrow seat again. Great enterprises and daring deeds are not what he excels in; but he is very apt at carrying out a ready-made system, and therefore I choose him to be my Regent."

"But Ameni," said Chamus, bowing respectfully to his father, "seems to have stirred up his ambition, and to support him with his advice. The chief of the House of Seti is a man of great ability, and at least half of the priesthood are his adherents."

"I know it," replied the king. "Their lordships owe me a grudge because I have called their serfs to arms, and they want them to till their acres. A pretty sort of people they have sent me! their courage flies with the first arrow. They shall guard the camp tomorrow; they will be equal to that when it is made clear to their understanding that, if they let the tents be taken, the bread, meat and wines-skins will also fall into the hands of the enemy. If Kadesh is taken by storm, the temples of the Nile shall have the greater part of the spoil, and you yourself, my young high-priest of Memphis, shall show your colleagues that Rameses repays in bushels that which he has taken in handfuls from the ministers of the Gods."

"Ameni's disaffection," replied Chamus, "has a deeper root; thy mighty spirit seeks and finds its own way —"

"But their lordships," interrupted Rameses, "are accustomed to govern the king too, and I —I do not do them credit. I rule as vicar of the Lord of the Gods, but —I myself am no God, though they attribute to me the honors of a divinity; and in all humility of heart I willingly leave it to them to be the mediators between the Immortals and me or my people. Human affairs certainly I choose to manage in my own way. And now no more of them. I cannot bear to doubt my friends, and trustfulness is so dear, so essential to me, that I must indulge in it even if my confidence results in my being deceived."

The king glanced at Mena, who handed him a golden cup-which he emptied. He looked at the glittering beaker, and then, with a flash of his grave, bright eyes, he added:

"And if I am betrayed-if ten such as Ameni and Ani entice my people into a snare —I shall return home, and will tread the reptiles into dust."

His deep voice rang out the words, as if he were a herald proclaiming a victorious deed of arms. Not a word was spoken, not a hand moved, when he ceased speaking. Then he raised his cup, and said:

"It is well before the battle to uplift our hearts! We have done great deeds; distant nations have felt our hand; we have planted our pillars of conquest by their rivers, and graven the record of our deeds on their rocks.[123]

Your king is great above all kings, and it is through the might of the Gods, and your valor my brave comrades. May to-morrow's fight bring us new glory! May the Immortals soon bring this war to a close! Empty your wine cups with me-To victory and a speedy return home in peace!"

"Victory! Victory! Long life to the Pharaoh! Strength and health!" cried the guests of the king, who, as he descended from his throne, cried to the drinkers:

"Now, rest till the star of Isis sets. Then follow me to prayer at the altar of Amon, and then-to battle."

Fresh cries of triumph sounded through the room, while Rameses gave his hand with a few words of encouragement to each of his sons in turn. He desired the two youngest, Mernephtah and Rameri to follow him, and quitting the banquet with them and Mena, he proceeded, under the escort of his officers and guards, who bore staves before him with golden lilies and ostrich-feathers, to his sleeping-tent, which was surrounded by a corps d'elite under the command of his sons. Before entering the tent he asked for some pieces of meat, and gave them with his own hand to his lions, who let him stroke them like tame cats.

Then he glanced round the stable, patted the sleek necks and shoulders of his favorite horses, and decided that 'Nura' and 'Victory to Thebes' should bear him into the battle on the morrow.[124]

When he had gone into the sleeping-tent, he desired his attendants to leave him; he signed Mena to divest him of his ornaments and his arms, and called to him his youngest sons, who were waiting respectfully at the door of the tent.

"Why did I desire you to accompany me?" he asked them gravely. Both were silent, and he repeated his question.

"Because," said Rameri at length, "you observed that all was not quite right between us two."

"And because," continued the king, "I desire that unity should exist between my children. You will have enemies enough to fight with to-morrow, but friends are not often to be found, and are too often taken from us by the fortune of war. We ought to feel no anger towards the friend we may lose, but expect to meet him lovingly in the other world. Speak, Rameri, what has caused a division between you?"

"I bear him no ill-will," answered Rameri. "You lately gave me the sword which Mernephtah has there stuck in his belt, because I did my duty well in the last skirmish with the enemy. You know we both sleep in the same tent, and yesterday, when I drew my sword out of its sheath to admire the fine work of the blade, I found that another, not so sharp, had been put in its place."

"I had only exchanged my sword for his in fun," interrupted Mernephtah. "But he can never take a joke, and declared I want to wear a prize that I had not earned; he would try, he said, to win another and then —"

"I have heard enough; you have both done wrong," said the King. "Even in fun, Mernephtah, you should never cheat or deceive. I did so once, and I will tell you what happened, as a warning.

"My noble mother, Tuaa, desired me, the first time I went into Fenchu —[Phoenicia: on monuments of the 18th dynasty.] —to bring her a pebble from the shore near Byblos, where the body of Osiris was washed. As we returned to Thebes, my mother's request returned to my mind; I was young and thoughtless —I picked up a stone by the way-side, took it with me, and when she asked me for the remembrance from Byblos I silently gave her the pebble from Thebes. She was delighted, she showed it to her brothers and sisters, and laid it by the statues of her ancestors; but I was miserable with shame and penitence, and at last I secretly took away the stone, and threw it into the water. All the servants were called together, and strict enquiry was made as to the theft of the stone; then I could hold out no longer, and confessed everything. No one punished me, and yet I never suffered more severely; from that time I have never deviated from the exact truth even in jest. Take the lesson to heart, Mernephtah-you, Rameri, take back your sword, and, believe me, life brings us so many real causes of vexation, that it is well to learn early to pass lightly over little things if you do not wish to become a surly fellow like the pioneer Paaker; and that seems far from likely with a gay, reckless temper like yours. Now shake hands with each other."

The young princes went up to each other, and Rameri fell on his brother's neck and kissed him. The king stroked their heads. "Now go in peace," he said, "and to-morrow you shall both strive to win a fresh mark of honor."

When his sons had left the tent, Rameses turned to his charioteer and said: "I have to speak to you too before the battle. I can read your soul through your eyes, and it seems to me that things have gone wrong with you since the keeper of your stud arrived here. What has happened in Thebes?" Mena looked frankly, but sadly at the king:

"My mother-in-law Katuti," he said, "is managing my estate very badly, pledging the land, and selling the cattle."

"That can be remedied," said Rameses kindly. "You know I promised to grant you the fulfilment of a wish, if Nefert trusted you as perfectly as you believe. But it appears to me as if something more nearly concerning you than this were wrong, for I never knew you anxious about money and lands. Speak openly! you know I am your father, and the heart and the eye of the man who guides my horses in battle, must be open without reserve to my gaze."

Mena kissed the king's robe; then he said:

"Nefert has left Katuti's house, and as thou knowest has followed thy daughter, Bent-Anat, to the sacred mountain, and to Megiddo."

"I thought the change was a good one," replied Rameses. "I leave Bent-Anat in the care of Bent-Anat, for she needs no other guardianship, and your wife can have no better protector than Bent-Anat."

"Certainly not!" exclaimed Mena with sincere emphasis. "But before they started, miserable things occurred. Thou knowest that before she married me she was betrothed to her cousin, the pioneer Paaker, and he, during his stay in Thebes, has gone in and out of my house, has helped Katuti with an enormous sum to pay the debts of my wild brother-in-law, and-as my stud-keeper saw with his own eyes-has made presents of flowers to Nefert."

The king smiled, laid his hand on Mena's shoulder, and said, as he looked in his face: "Your wife will trust you, although you take a strange woman into your tent, and you allow yourself to doubt her because her cousin gives her some flowers! Is that wise or just? I believe you are jealous of the broad-shouldered ruffian that some spiteful Wight laid in the nest of the noble Mohar, his father."

"No, that I am not," replied Mena, "nor does any doubt of Nefert disturb my soul; but it torments me, it nettles me, it disgusts me, that Paaker of all men, whom I loathe as a venomous spider, should look at her and make her presents under my very roof."

"He who looks for faith must give faith," said the king. "And must not I myself submit to accept songs of praise from the most contemptible wretches? Come-smooth your brow; think of the approaching victory, of our return home, and remember that you have less to forgive Paaker than he to forgive you. Now, pray go and see to the horses, and to-morrow morning let me see you on my chariot full of cheerful courage-as I love to see you."

Mena left the tent, and went to the stables; there he met Rameri, who was waiting to speak to him. The eager boy said that he had always looked up to him and loved him as a brilliant example, but that lately he had been perplexed as to his virtuous fidelity, for he had been informed that Mena had taken a strange woman into his tent-he who was married to the fairest and sweetest woman in Thebes.

"I have known her," he concluded, "as well as if I were her brother; and I know that she would die if she heard that you had insulted and disgraced her. Yes, insulted her; for such a public breach of faith is an insult to the wife of an Egyptian. Forgive my freedom of speech, but who knows what to-morrow may bring forth-and I would not for worlds go out to battle, thinking evil of you."

Mena let Rameri speak without interruption, and then answered:

"You are as frank as your father, and have learned from him to hear the defendant before you condemn him. A strange maiden, the daughter of the king of the Danaids,[125] lives in my tent, but I for months have slept at the door of your father's, and I have not once entered my own since she has been there. Now sit down by me, and let me tell you how it all happened. We had pitched the camp before Kadesh, and there was very little for me to do, as Rameses was still laid up with his wound, so I often passed my time in hunting on the shores of the lake. One day I went as usual, armed only with my bow and arrow, and, accompanied by my grey-hounds, heedlessly followed a hare; a troop of Danaids fell upon me, bound me with cords, and led me into their camp.[126]

There I was led before the judges as a spy, and they had actually condemned me, and the rope was round my neck, when their king came up, saw me, and subjected me to a fresh examination. I told him the facts at full length-how I had fallen into the hands of his people while following up my game, and not as an enemy, and he heard me favorably, and granted me not only life but freedom. He knew me for a noble, and treated me as one, inviting me to feed at his own table, and I swore in my heart, when he let me go, that I would make him some return for his generous conduct.

"About a month after, we succeeded in surprising the Cheta position, and the Libyan soldiers, among other spoil, brought away the Danaid king's only daughter. I had behaved valiantly, and when we came to the division of the spoils Rameses allowed me to choose first. I laid my hand on the maid, the daughter of my deliverer and host, I led her to my tent, and left her there with her waiting-women till peace is concluded, and I can restore her to her father."

"Forgive my doubts!" cried Rameri holding out his hand. "Now I understand why the king so particularly enquired whether Nefert believed in your constancy to her."

"And what was your answer?" asked Mena.

"That she thinks of you day and night, and never for an instant doubted you. My father seemed delighted too, and he said to Chamus: 'He has won there!'"

"He will grant me some great favor," said Mena in explanation, "if, when she hears I have taken a strange maiden to my tent her confidence in me is not shaken, Rameses considers it simply impossible, but I know that I shall win. Why! she must trust me."

CHAPTER XXXIX.

Before the battle[127] prayers were offered and victims sacrificed for each division of the army. Images of the Gods were borne through the ranks in their festal barks, and miraculous relics were exhibited to the soldiers; heralds announced that the high-priest had found favorable omens in the victims offered by the king, and that the haruspices foretold a glorious victory. Each Egyptian legion turned with particular faith to the standard which bore the image of the sacred animal or symbol of the province where it had been levied, but each soldier was also provided with charms and amulets of various kinds; one had tied to his neck or arm a magical text in a little bag, another the mystic preservative eye, and most of them wore a scarabaeus in a finger ring. Many believed themselves protected by having a few hairs or feathers of some sacred animal, and not a few put themselves under the protection of a living snake or beetle carefully concealed in a pocket of their apron or in their little provision-sack.

When the king, before whom were carried the images of the divine Triad of Thebes, of Menth, the God of War and of Necheb, the Goddess of Victory, reviewed the ranks, he was borne in a litter on the shoulders of twenty-four noble youths; at his approach the whole host fell on their knees, and did not rise till Rameses, descending from his position, had, in the presence of them all, burned incense, and made a libation to the Gods, and his son Chamus had delivered to him, in the name of the Immortals, the symbols of life and power. Finally, the priests sang a choral hymn to the Sun-god Ra, and to his son and vicar on earth, the king.

Just as the troops were put in motion, the paling stars appeared in the sky, which had hitherto been covered with thick clouds; and this occurrence was regarded as a favorable omen, the priests declaring to the army that, as the coming Ra had dispersed the clouds, so the Pharaoh would scatter his enemies.

With no sound of trumpet or drum, so as not to arouse the enemy, the foot-soldiers went forward in close order, the chariot-warriors, each in his light two-wheeled chariot drawn by two horses, formed their ranks, and the king placed himself at their head. On each side of the gilt chariot in which he stood, a case was fixed, glittering with precious stones, in which were his bows and arrows. His noble horses were richly caparisoned; purple housings, embroidered with turquoise beads, covered their backs and necks, and a crown-shaped ornament was fixed on their heads, from which fluttered a bunch of white ostrich-feathers. At the end of the ebony pole of the chariot, were two small padded yokes, which rested on the necks of the horses, who pranced in front as if playing with the light vehicle, pawed the earth with their small hoofs, and tossed and curved their slender necks.

The king wore a shirt of mail,[128] over which lay the broad purple girdle of his apron, and on his head was the crown of Upper and Lower Egypt; behind him stood Mena, who, with his left hand, tightly held the reins, and with his right the shield which was to protect his sovereign in the fight.

The king stood like a storm-proof oak, and Mena by his side like a sapling ash.

The eastern horizon was rosy with the approaching sun-rise when they quitted the precincts of the camp; at this moment the pioneer Paaker advanced to meet the king, threw himself on the ground before him, kissed the earth, and, in answer to the king's question as to why he had come without his brother, told him that Horus was taken suddenly ill. The shades of dawn concealed from the king the guilty color, which changed to sallow paleness, on the face of the pioneer-unaccustomed hitherto to lying and treason.

"How is it with the enemy?" asked Rameses.

"He is aware," replied Paaker, "that a fight is impending, and is collecting numberless hosts in the camps to the south and east of the city. If thou could'st succeed in falling on the rear from the north of Kadesh, while the foot soldiers seize the camp of the Asiatics from the south, the fortress will be thine before night. The mountain path that thou must follow, so as not to be discovered, is not a bad one."

"Are you ill as well as your brother, man?" asked the king. "Your voice trembles."

"I was never better," answered the Mohar.

"Lead the way," commanded the king, and Paaker obeyed. They went on in silence, followed by the vast troop of chariots through the dewy morning air, first across the plain, and then into the mountain range. The corps of Ra, armed with bows and arrows, preceeded them to clear the way; they crossed the narrow bed of a dry torrent, and then a broad valley opened before them, extending to the right and left and enclosed by ranges of mountains.

"The road is good," said Rameses, turning to Mena. "The Mohar has learned his duties from his father, and his horses are capital. Now he leads the way, and points it out to the guards, and then in a moment he is close to us again."

"They are the golden-bays of my breed," said Mena, and the veins started angrily in his forehead. "My stud-master tells me that Katuti sent them to him before his departure. They were intended for Nefert's chariot, and he drives them to-day to defy and spite me."

"You have the wife-let the horses go," said Rameses soothingly.

Suddenly a blast of trumpets rang through the morning air; whence it came could not be seen, and yet it sounded close at hand.

Rameses started up and took his battle-axe from his girdle, the horses pricked their ears, and Mena exclaimed:

"Those are the trumpets of the Cheta! I know the sound."

A closed wagon with four wheels in which the king's lions were conveyed, followed the royal chariot. "Let loose the lions!" cried the king, who heard an echoing war cry, and soon after saw the vanguard which had preceded him, and which was broken up by the chariots of the enemy, flying towards him down the valley again.

The wild beasts shook their manes and sprang in front of their master's chariot with loud roars. Mena lashed his whip, the horses started forward and rushed with frantic plunges towards the fugitives, who however could not be brought to a standstill, or rallied by the king's voice-the enemy were close upon them, cutting them down.

"Where is Paaker?" asked the king. But the pioneer had vanished as completely as if the earth had swallowed him and his chariot.

The flying Egyptians and the death-dealing chariots of the enemy came nearer and nearer, the ground trembled, the tramp of hoofs and the roar of wheels sounded louder and louder, like the roll of a rapidly approaching storm.

Then Rameses gave out a war cry, that rang back from the cliffs on the right hand and on the left like the blast of a trumpet; his chariot-guard joined in the shout-for an instant the flying Egyptians paused, but only to rush on again with double haste, in hope of escape and safety: suddenly the war-cry of the enemy was heard behind the king, mingling with the trumpet-call of the Cheta, and out from a cross valley, which the king had passed unheeded by-and into which Paaker had disappeared-came an innumerable host of chariots which, before the king could retreat, had broken through the Egyptian ranks, and cut him off from the body of his army. Behind him he could hear the roar and shock of the battle, in front of him he saw the fugitives, the fallen, and the enemy growing each instant in numbers and fury. He saw the whole danger, and drew up his powerful form as if to prove whether it were an equal match for such a foe. Then, raising his voice to such a pitch, that it sounded above the cries and groans of the fighting men, the words of command, the neighing of the horses, the crash of overthrown chariots, the dull whirr of lances and swords, their heavy blows on shields and helmets, and the whole bewildering tumult of the battle-with a loud shout he drew his bow, and his first arrow pierced a Cheta chief.

His lions sprang forward, and carried confusion into the hosts that were crowding down upon him, for many of their horses became unmanageable at the roar of the furious brutes, overthrew the chariots, and so hemmed the advance of the troops in the rear. Rameses sent arrow after arrow, while Mena covered him with the shield from the shots of the enemy. His horses meanwhile had carried him forward, and he could fell the foremost of the Asiatics with his battle-axe; close by his side fought Rameri and three other princes; in front of him were the lions.

The press was fearful, and the raging of the battle wild and deafening, like the roar of the surging ocean when it is hurled by a hurricane against a rocky coast.

Mena seemed to be in two places at once, for, while he guided the horses forwards, backwards, or to either hand, as the exigences of the position demanded, not one of the arrows shot at the king touched him. His eye was everywhere, the shield always ready, and not an eyelash of the young hero trembled, while Rameses, each moment more infuriated, incited his lions with wild war-cries, and with flashing eyes advanced farther and farther into the enemy's ranks.

Three arrows aimed, not at the king but at Mena himself, were sticking in the charioteer's shield, and by chance he saw written on the shaft of one of them the words "Death to Mena."

A fourth arrow whizzed past him. His eye followed its flight, and as he marked the spot whence it had come, a fifth wounded his shoulder, and he cried out to the king:

"We are betrayed! Look over there! Paaker is fighting with the Cheta."

Once more the Mohar had bent his bow, and came so near to the king's chariot that he could be heard exclaiming in a hoarse voice, as he let the bowstring snap, "Now I will reckon with you-thief! robber! My bride is your wife, but with this arrow I will win Mena's widow."

The arrow cut through the air, and fell with fearful force on the charioteer's helmet; the shield fell from his grasp, and he put his hand to his head, feeling stunned; he heard Paaker's laugh of triumph, he felt another of his enemy's arrows cut his wrist, and, beside himself with rage, he flung away the reins, brandished his battle-axe, and forgetting himself and his duty, sprang from the chariot and rushed upon Paaker. The Mohar awaited him with uplifted sword; his lips were white, his eyes bloodshot, his wide nostrils trembled like those of an over-driven horse, and foaming and hissing he flew at his mortal foe. The king saw the two engaged in a struggle, but he could not interfere, for the reins which Mena had dropped were dragging on the ground, and his ungoverned horses, following the lions, carried him madly onwards.

Most of his comrades had fallen, the battle raged all round him, but Rameses stood as firm as a rock, held the shield in front of him, and swung the deadly battle-axe; he saw Rameri hastening towards him with his horses, the youth was fighting like a hero, and Rameses called out to encourage him: "Well done! a worthy grandson of Seti!"

"I will win a new sword!" cried the boy, and he cleft the skull of one of his antagonists. But he was soon surrounded by the chariots of the enemy; the king saw the enemy pull down the young prince's horses, and all his comrades-among whom were many of the best warriors-turn their horses in flight.

Then one of the lions was pierced by a lance, and sank with a dying roar of rage and pain that was heard above all the tumult. The king himself had been grazed by an arrow, a sword stroke had shivered his shield, and his last arrow had been shot away.

Still spreading death around him, he saw death closing in upon him, and, without giving up the struggle, he lifted up his voice in fervent prayer, calling on Amon for support and rescue.

While thus in the sorest need he was addressing himself to the Lords of Heaven, a tall Egyptian suddenly appeared in the midst of the struggle and turmoil of the battle, seized the reins, and sprang into the chariot behind the king, to whom he bowed respectfully. For the first time Rameses felt a thrill of fear. Was this a miracle? Had Amon heard his prayer?

He looked half fearfully round at his new charioteer, and when he fancied he recognized the features of the deceased Mohar, the father of the traitor Paaker, he believed that Amon had assumed this aspect, and had come himself to save him.

"Help is at hand!" cried his new companion. "If we hold our own for only a short time longer, thou art saved, and victory is ours."

Then once more Rameses raised his war-cry, felled a Cheta, who was standing close to him to the ground, with a blow on his skull, while the mysterious supporter by his side, who covered him with the shield, on his part also dealt many terrible strokes.

Thus some long minutes passed in renewed strife; then a trumpet sounded above the roar of the battle, and this time Rameses recognized the call of the Egyptians; from behind a low ridge on his right rushed some thousands of men of the foot-legion of Ptah who, under the command of Horus, fell upon the enemy's flank. They saw their king, and the danger he was in. They flung themselves with fury on the foes that surrounded him, dealing death as they advanced, and putting the Cheta to flight, and soon Rameses saw himself safe, and protected by his followers.

But his mysterious friend in need had vanished. He had been hit by an arrow, and had fallen to the earth —a quite mortal catastrophe; but Rameses still believed that one of the Immortals had come to his rescue.

But the king granted no long respite to his horses and his fighting-men; he turned to go back by the way by which he had come, fell upon the forces which divided him from the main army, took them in the rear while they were still occupied with his chariot-brigade which was already giving way, and took most of the Asiatics prisoners who escaped the arrows and swords of the Egyptians. Having rejoined the main body of the troops, he pushed forwards across the plain where the Asiatic horse and chariot-legions were engaged with the Egyptian swordsmen, and forced the enemy back upon the river Orontes and the lake of Kadesh. Night-fall put an end to the battle, though early next morning the struggle was renewed.

Utter discouragement had fallen upon the Asiatic allies, who had gone into battle in full security of victory; for the pioneer Paaker had betrayed his king into their hands.

When the Pharaoh had set out, the best chariot-warriors of the Cheta were drawn up in a spot concealed by the city, and sent forward against Rameses through the northern opening of the valley by which he was to pass, while other troops of approved valor, in all two thousand five hundred chariots, were to fall upon him from a cross valley where they took up their position during the night.

These tactics had been successfully carried out, and notwithstanding the Asiatics had suffered a severe defeat-besides losing some of their noblest heroes, among them Titure their Chancellor, and Chiropasar, the chronicler of the Cheta king, who could wield the sword as effectively as the pen, and who, it was intended, should celebrate the victory of the allies, and perpetuate its glory to succeeding generations. Rameses had killed one of these with his own hands, and his unknown companion the other, and besides these many other brave captains of the enemy's troops. The king was greeted as a god, when he returned to the camp, with shouts of triumph and hymns of praise.

Even the temple-servants, and the miserable troops from Upper Egypt-ground down by the long war, and bought over by Ani-were carried away by the universal enthusiasm, and joyfully hailed the hero and king who had successfully broken the stiff necks of his enemies.

The next duty was to seek out the dead and wounded; among the latter was Mena; Rameri also was missing, but news was brought next day that he had fallen into the hands of the enemy, and he was immediately exchanged for the princess who had been sheltered in Mena's tent.

Paaker had disappeared; but the bays which he had driven into the battle were found unhurt in front of his ruined and blood-sprinkled chariot.

The Egyptians were masters of Kadesh, and Chetasar, the king of the Cheta, sued to be allowed to treat for peace, in his own name and in that of his allies; but Rameses refused to grant any terms till he had returned to the frontier of Egypt. The conquered peoples had no choice, and the representative of the Cheta king-who himself was wounded-and twelve princes of the principal nations who had fought against Rameses, were forced to follow his victorious train. Every respect was shown them, and they were treated as the king himself, but they were none the less his prisoners. The king was anxious to lose no time, for sad suspicion filled his heart; a shadow hitherto unknown to his bright and genial nature had fallen upon his spirit.

This was the first occasion on which one of his own people had betrayed him to the enemy. Paaker's deed had shaken his friendly confidence, and in his petition for peace the Cheta prince had intimated that Rameses might find much in his household to be set to rights-perhaps with a strong hand.

The king felt himself more than equal to cope with Ani, the priests, and all whom he had left in Egypt; but it grieved him to be obliged to feel any loss of confidence, and it was harder to him to bear than any reverse of fortune. It urged him to hasten his return to Egypt.

There was another thing which embittered his victory. Mena, whom he loved as his own son, who understood his lightest sign, who, as soon as he mounted his chariot, was there by his side like a part of himself-had been dismissed from his office by the judgment of the commander-in-chief, and no longer drove his horses. He himself had been obliged to confirm this decision as just and even mild, for that man was worthy of death who exposed his king to danger for the gratification of his own revenge.

Rameses had not seen Mena since his struggle with Paaker, but he listened anxiously to the news which was brought him of the progress of his sorely wounded officer.

The cheerful, decided, and practical nature of Rameses was averse to every kind of dreaminess or self-absorption, and no one had ever seen him, even in hours of extreme weariness, give himself up to vague and melancholy brooding; but now he would often sit gazing at the ground in wrapt meditation, and start like an awakened sleeper when his reverie was disturbed by the requirements of the outer world around him. A hundred times before he had looked death in the face, and defied it as he would any other enemy, but now it seemed as though he felt the cold hand of the mighty adversary on his heart. He could not forget the oppressive sense of helplessness which had seized him when he had felt himself at the mercy of the unrestrained horses, like a leaf driven by the wind, and then suddenly saved by a miracle.

A miracle? Was it really Amon who had appeared in human form at his call? Was he indeed a son of the Gods, and did their blood flow in his veins?

The Immortals had shown him peculiar favor, but still he was but a man; that he realized from the pain in his wound, and the treason to which he had been a victim. He felt as if he had been respited on the very scaffold. Yes; he was a man like all other men, and so he would still be. He rejoiced in the obscurity that veiled his future, in the many weaknesses which he had in common with those whom he loved, and even in the feeling that he, under the same conditions of life as his contemporaries, had more responsibilities than they.

Shortly after his victory, after all the important passes and strongholds had been conquered by his troops, he set out for Egypt with his train and the vanquished princes. He sent two of his sons to Bent-Anat at Megiddo, to escort her by sea to Pelusium; he knew that the commandant of the harbor of that frontier fortress, at the easternmost limit of his kingdom, was faithful to him, and he ordered that his daughter should not quit the ship till he arrived, to secure her against any attempt on the part of the Regent. A large part of the material of war, and most of the wounded, were also sent to Egypt by sea.

CHAPTER XL.

Nearly three months had passed since the battle of Kadesh, and to-day the king was expected, on his way home with his victorious army, at Pelusium, the strong hold and key of Egyptian dominion in the east. Splendid preparations had been made for his reception, and the man who took the lead in the festive arrangements with a zeal that was doubly effective from his composed demeanor was no less a person than the Regent Ani.

His chariot was to be seen everywhere: now he was with the workmen, who were to decorate triumphal arches with fresh flowers; now with the slaves, who were hanging garlands on the wooden lions erected on the road for this great occasion; now-and this detained him longest-he watched the progress of the immense palace which was being rapidly constructed of wood on the site where formerly the camp of the Hyksos had stood, in which the actual ceremony of receiving the king was to take place, and where the Pharaoh and his immediate followers were to reside. It had been found possible, by employing several thousand laborers, to erect this magnificent structure, in a few weeks, and nothing was lacking to it that could be desired, even by a king so accustomed as Rameses to luxury and splendor. A high exterior flight of steps led from the garden-which had been created out of a waste-to the vestibule, out of which the banqueting hall opened.

This was of unusual height, and had a vaulted wooden ceiling, which was painted blue and sprinkled with stars, to represent the night heavens, and which was supported on pillars carved, some in the form of date-palms, and some like cedars of Lebanon; the leaves and twigs consisted of artfully fastened and colored tissue; elegant festoons of bluish gauze were stretched from pillar to pillar across the hall, and in the centre of the eastern wall they were attached to a large shell-shaped canopy extending over the throne of the king, which was decorated with pieces of green and blue glass, of mother of pearl, of shining plates of mica, and other sparkling objects.

The throne itself had the shape of a buckler, guarded by two lions, which rested on each side of it and formed the arms, and supported on the backs of four Asiatic captives who crouched beneath its weight. Thick carpets, which seemed to have transported the sea-shore on to the dry land-for their pale blue ground was strewn with a variety of shells, fishes, and water plants-covered the floor of the banqueting hall, in which three hundred seats were placed by the tables, for the nobles of the kingdom and the officers of the troops.

Above all this splendor hung a thousand lamps, shaped like lilies and tulips, and in the entrance hall stood a huge basket of roses to be strewn before the king when he should arrive.

Even the bed-rooms for the king and his suite were splendidly decorated; finely embroidered purple stuffs covered the walls, a light cloud of pale blue gauze hung across the ceiling, and giraffe skins were laid instead of carpets on the floors.

The barracks intended for the soldiers and bodyguard stood nearer to the city, as well as the stable buildings, which were divided from the palace by the garden which surrounded it. A separate pavilion, gilt and wreathed with flowers, was erected to receive the horses which had carried the king through the battle, and which he had dedicated to the Sun-God.

The Regent Ani, accompanied by Katuti, was going through the whole of these slightly built structures.

"It seems to me all quite complete," said the widow.

"Only one thing I cannot make up my mind about," replied Ani, "whether most to admire your inventive genius or your exquisite taste."

"Oh! let that pass," said Katuti smiling. "If any thing deserves your praise it is my anxiety to serve you. How many things had to be considered before this structure at last stood complete on this marshy spot where the air seemed alive with disgusting insects and now it is finished how long will it last?"

Ani looked down. "How long?" he repeated. Then he continued: "There is great risk already of the plot miscarrying. Ameni has grown cool, and will stir no further in the matter; the troops on which I counted are perhaps still faithful to me, but much too weak; the Hebrews, who tend their flocks here, and whom I gained over by liberating them from forced labor, have never borne arms. And you know the people. They will kiss the feet of the conqueror if they have to wade up to there through the blood of their children. Besides-as it happens-the hawk which old Hekt keeps as representing me is to-day pining and sick —"

"It will be all the prouder and brighter to-morrow if you are a man!" exclaimed Katuti, and her eyes sparkled with scorn. "You cannot now retreat. Here in Pelusium you welcome Rameses as if he were a God, and he accepts the honor. I know the king, he is too proud to be distrustful, and so conceited that he can never believe himself deceived in any man, either friend or foe. The man whom he appointed to be his Regent, whom he designated as the worthiest in the land, he will most unwillingly condemn. Today you still have the car of the king; to-morrow he will listen to your enemies, and too much has occurred in Thebes to be blotted out. You are in the position of a lion who has his keeper on one side, and the bars of his cage on the other. If you let the moment pass without striking you will remain in the cage; but if you act and show yourself a lion your keepers are done for!"

"You urge me on and on," said Ani. "But supposing your plan were to fail, as Paaker's well considered plot failed?"

"Then you are no worse off than you are now," answered Katuti. "The Gods rule the elements, not men. Is it likely that you should finish so beautiful a structure with such care only to destroy it? And we have no accomplices, and need none."

"But who shall set the brand to the room which Nemu and the slave have filled with straw and pitch?" asked Ani.

"I," said Katuti decidedly. "And one who has nothing to look for from Rameses."

"Who is that?"

"Paaker."

"Is the Mohar here?" asked the Regent surprised.

"You yourself have seen him."

"You are mistaken," said Ani. "I should —"

"Do you recollect the one-eyed, grey-haired, blackman, who yesterday brought me a letter? That was my sister's son."

The Regent struck his forehead —"Poor wretch" he muttered.

"He is frightfully altered," said Katuti. "He need not have blackened his face, for his own mother would not know him again: He lost an eye in his fight with Mena, who also wounded him in the lungs with a thrust of his sword, so that he breathes and speaks with difficulty, his broad shoulders have lost their flesh, and the fine legs he swaggered about on have shrunk as thin as a negro's. I let him pass as my servant without any hesitation or misgiving. He does not yet know of my purpose, but I am sure that he would help us if a thousand deaths threatened him. For God's sake put aside all doubts and fears! We will shake the tree for you, if you will only hold out your hand to-morrow to pick up the fruit. Only one thing I must beg. Command the head butler not to stint the wine, so that the guards may give us no trouble. I know that you gave the order that only three of the five ships which brought the contents of your winelofts should be unloaded. I should have thought that the future king of Egypt might have been less anxious to save!"

Katuti's lips curled with contempt as she spoke the last words. Ani observed this and said:

"You think I am timid! Well, I confess I would far rather that much which I have done at your instigation could be undone. I would willingly renounce this new plot, though we so carefully planned it when we built and decorated this palace. I will sacrifice the wine; there are jars of wine there that were old in my father's time-but it must be so! You are right! Many things have occurred which the king will not forgive! You are right, you are right-do what seems good to you. I will retire after the feast to the Ethiopian camp."

"They will hail you as king as soon as the usurpers have fallen in the flames," cried Katuti. "If only a few set the example, the others will take up the cry, and even though you have offended

Ameni he will attach himself to you rather than to Rameses. Here he comes, and I already see the standards in the distance."

"They are coming!" said the Regent. "One thing more! Pray see yourself that the princess Bent-Anat goes to the rooms intended for her; she must not be injured."

"Still Bent-Anat?" said Katuti with a smile full of meaning but without bitterness. "Be easy, her rooms are on the ground floor, and she shall be warned in time."

Ani turned to leave her; he glanced once more at the great hall, and said with a sigh. "My heart is heavy —I wish this day and this night were over!"

"You are like this grand hall," said Katuti smiling, "which is now empty, almost dismal; but this evening, when it is crowded with guests, it will look very different. You were born to be a king, and yet are not a king; you will not be quite yourself till the crown and sceptre are your own."

Ani smiled too, thanked her, and left her; but Katuti said to herself:

"Bent-Anat may burn with the rest: I have no intention of sharing my power with her!"

Crowds of men and women from all parts had thronged to Pelusium, to welcome the conqueror and his victorious army on the frontier. Every great temple-college had sent a deputation to meet Rameses, that from the Necropolis consisting of five members, with Ameni and old Gagabu at their head. The white-robed ministers of the Gods marched in solemn procession towards the bridge which lay across the eastern-Pelusiac-arm of the Nile, and led to Egypt proper-the land fertilized by the waters of the sacred stream.

The deputation from the temple of Memphis led the procession; this temple had been founded by Mena, the first king who wore the united crowns of Upper and Lower Egypt, and Chamus, the king's son, was the high-priest. The deputation from the not less important temple of Heliopolis came next, and was followed by the representatives of the Necropolis of Thebes.

A few only of the members of these deputations wore the modest white robe of the simple priest; most of them were invested with the panther-skin which was worn by the prophets. Each bore a staff decorated with roses, lilies, and green branches, and many carried censers in the form of a golden arm with incense in the hollow of the hand, to be burnt before the king. Among the deputies from the priesthood at Thebes were several women of high rank, who served in the worship of this God, and among them was Katuti, who by the particular desire of the Regent had lately been admitted to this noble sisterhood.

Ameni walked thoughtfully by the side of the prophet Gagabu.

"How differently everything has happened from what we hoped and intended!" said Gagabu in a low voice. "We are like ambassadors with sealed credentials-who can tell their contents?"

"I welcome Rameses heartily and joyfully," said Ameni. "After that which happened to him at Kadesh he will come home a very different man to what he was when he set out. He knows now what he owes to Amon. His favorite son was already at the head of the ministers of the temple at Memphis, and he has vowed to build magnificent temples and to bring splendid offerings to the Immortals. And Rameses keeps his word better than that smiling simpleton in the chariot yonder."

"Still I am sorry for Ani," said Gagabu.

"The Pharaoh will not punish him-certainly not," replied the high-priest. "And he will have nothing to fear from Ani; he is a feeble reed, the powerless sport of every wind."

"And yet you hoped for great things from him!"

"Not from him, but through him-with us for his guides," replied Ameni in a low voice but with emphasis. "It is his own fault that I have abandoned his cause. Our first wish-to spare the poet Pentaur-he would not respect, and he did not hesitate to break his oath, to betray us, and to sacrifice one of the noblest of God's creatures, as the poet was, to gratify a petty grudge. It is harder to fight against cunning weakness than against honest enmity. Shall we reward the man who has deprived the world of Pentaur by giving him a crown? It is hard to quit the trodden way, and seek a better-to give up a half-executed plan and take a more promising one; it is hard,

I say, for the individual man, and makes him seem fickle in the eyes of others; but we cannot see to the right hand and the left, and if we pursue a great end we cannot remain within the narrow limits which are set by law and custom to the actions of private individuals. We draw back just as we seem to have reached the goal, we let him fall whom we had raised, and lift him, whom we had stricken to the earth, to the pinnacle of glory, in short we profess-and for thousands of years have professed-the doctrine that every path is a right one that leads to the great end of securing to the priesthood the supreme power in the land. Rameses, saved by a miracle, vowing temples to the Gods, will for the future exhaust his restless spirit not in battle as a warrior, but in building as an architect. He will make use of us, and we can always lead the man who needs us. So I now hail the son of Seti with sincere joy."

Ameni was still speaking when the flags were hoisted on the standards by the triumphal arches, clouds of dust rolled up on the farther shore of the Nile, and the blare of trumpets was heard.

First came the horses which had carried Rameses through the fight, with the king himself, who drove them. His eyes sparkled with joyful triumph as the people on the farther side of the bridge received him with shouts of joy, and the vast multitude hailed him with wild enthusiasm and tears of emotion, strewing in his path the spoils of their gardens-flowers, garlands, and palm-branches.

Ani marched at the head of the procession that went forth to meet him; he humbly threw himself in the dust before the horses, kissed the ground, and then presented to the king the sceptre that had been entrusted to him, lying on a silk cushion. The king received it graciously, and when Ani took his robe to kiss it, the king bent down towards him, and touching the Regent's forehead with his lips, desired him to take the place by his side in the chariot, and fill the office of charioteer.

The king's eyes were moist with grateful emotion. He had not been deceived, and he could re-enter the country for whose greatness and welfare alone he lived, as a father, loving and beloved, and not as a master to judge and punish. He was deeply moved as he accepted the greetings of the priests, and with them offered up a public prayer. Then he was conducted to the splendid structure which had been prepared for him gaily mounted the outside steps, and from the top-most stair bowed to his innumerable crowd of subjects; and while he awaited the procession from the harbor which escorted Bent-Anat in her litter, he inspected the thousand decorated bulls and antelopes which were to be slaughtered as a thank-offering to the Gods, the tame lions and leopards, the rare trees in whose branches perched gaily-colored birds, the giraffes, and chariots to which ostriches were harnessed, which all marched past him in a long array.[129]

Rameses embraced his daughter before all the people; he felt as if he must admit his subjects to the fullest sympathy in the happiness and deep thankfulness which filled his soul. His favorite child had never seemed to him so beautiful as this day, and he realized with deep emotion her strong resemblance to his lost wife. —[Her name was Isis Nefert.]

Nefert had accompanied her royal friend as fanbearer, and she knelt before the king while he gave himself up to the delight of meeting his daughter. Then he observed her, and kindly desired her to rise. "How much," he said, "I am feeling to-day for the first time! I have already learned that what I formerly thought of as the highest happiness is capable of a yet higher pitch, and I now perceive that the most beautiful is capable of growing to greater beauty! A sun has grown from Mena's star."

Rameses, as he spoke, remembered his charioteer; for a moment his brow was clouded, and he cast down his eyes, and bent his head in thought.

Bent-Anat well knew this gesture of her father's; it was the omen of some kindly, often sportive suggestion, such as he loved to surprise his friends with.

He reflected longer than usual; at last he looked up, and his full eyes rested lovingly on his daughter as he asked her:

"What did your friend say when she heard that her husband had taken a pretty stranger into his tent, and harbored her there for months? Tell me the whole truth of it, Bent-Anat."

"I am indebted to this deed of Mena's, which must certainly be quite excusable if you can smile when you speak of it," said the princess, "for it was the cause of his wife's coming to me. Her mother blamed her husband with bitter severity, but she would not cease to believe in him, and left her house because it was impossible for her to endure to hear him blamed."

"Is this the fact?" asked Rameses.

Nefert bowed her pretty head, and two tears ran down her blushing cheeks.

"How good a man must be," cried the king, "on whom the Gods bestow such happiness! My lord Chamberlain, inform Mena that I require his services at dinner to-day —as before the battle at Kadesh. He flung away the reins in the fight when he saw his enemy, and we shall see if he can keep from flinging down the beaker when, with his own eyes, he sees his beloved wife sitting at the table. —You ladies will join me at the banquet."

Nefert sank on her knees before the king; but he turned from her to speak to the nobles and officers who had come to meet him, and then proceeded to the temple to assist at the slaughter of the victims, and to solemnly renew his vow in the presence of the priests and the people, to erect a magnificent temple in Thebes as a thank-offering for his preservation from death. He was received with rapturous enthusiasm; his road led to the harbor, past the tents in which lay the wounded, who had been brought home to Egypt by ship, and he greeted them graciously from his chariot.

Ani again acted as his charioteer; they drove slowly through the long ranks of invalids and convalescents, but suddenly Ani gave the reins an involuntary pull, the horses reared, and it was with difficulty that he soothed them to a steady pace again.

Rameses looked round in anxious surprise, for at the moment when the horses had started, he too had felt an agitating thrill-he thought he had caught sight of his preserver at Kadesh.

Had the sight of a God struck terror into the horses? Was he the victim of a delusion? or was his preserver a man of flesh and blood, who had come home from the battle-field among the wounded!

The man who stood by his side, and held the reins, could have informed him, for Ani had recognized Pentaur, and in his horror had given the reins a perilous jerk.

CHAPTER XLI.

The king did not return to the great pavilion till after sun-down; the banqueting hall, illuminated with a thousand lamps, was now filled with the gay crowd of guests who awaited the arrival of the king. All bowed before him, as he entered, more or less low, each according to his rank; he immediately seated himself on his throne, surrounded by his children in a wide semicircle, and his officers and retainers all passed before him; for each he had a kindly word or glance, winning respect from all, and filling every one with joy and hope.

"The only really divine attribute of my royal condition," said he to himself, "is that it is so easy to a king to make men happy. My predecessors chose the poisonous Uraeus as the emblem of their authority, for we can cause death as quickly and certainly as the venomous snake; but the power of giving happiness dwells on our own lips, and in our own eyes, and we need some instrument when we decree death."

"Take the Uraeus crown from my head," he continued aloud, as he seated himself at the feast. "Today I will wear a wreath of flowers."

During the ceremony of bowing to the king, two men had quitted the hall-the Regent Ani, and the high-priest Ameni.

Ani ordered a small party of the watch to go and seek out the priest Pentaur in the tents of the wounded by the harbor, to bring the poet quietly to his tent, and to guard him there till his return. He still had in his possession the maddening potion, which he was to have given to the captain of the transport-boat, and it was open to him still to receive Pentaur either as a guest or as a prisoner. Pentaur might injure him, whether Katuti's project failed or succeeded.

Ameni left the pavilion to go to see old Gagabu, who had stood so long in the heat of the sun during the ceremony of receiving the conqueror, that he had been at last carried fainting to the tent which he shared with the high-priest, and which was not far from that of the Regent. He found the old man much revived, and was preparing to mount his chariot to go to the banquet, when the Regent's myrmidons led Pentaur past in front of him. Ameni looked doubtfully at the tall and noble figure of the prisoner, but Pentaur recognized him, called him by his name, and in a moment they stood together, hand clasped in hand. The guards showed some uneasiness, but Ameni explained who he was.

The high-priest was sincerely rejoiced at the preservation and restoration of his favorite disciple, whom for many months he had mourned as dead; he looked at his manly figure with fatherly tenderness, and desired the guards, who bowed to his superior dignity, to conduct his friend, on his responsibility; to his tent instead of to Ani's.

There Pentaur found his old friend Gagabu, who wept with delight at his safety. All that his master had accused him of seemed to be forgotten. Ameni had him clothed in a fresh white robe, he was never tired of looking at him, and over and over again clapped his hand upon his shoulder, as if he were his own son that had been lost and found again.

Pentaur was at once required to relate all that had happened to him, and the poet told the story of his captivity and liberation at Mount Sinai, his meeting with Bent-Anat, and how he had fought in the battle of Kadesh, had been wounded by an arrow, and found and rescued by the faithful Kaschta. He concealed only his passion for Bent-Anat, and the fact that he had preserved the king's life.

"About an hour ago," he added, "I was sitting alone in my tent, watching the lights in the palace yonder, when the watch who are outside brought me an order from the Regent to accompany them to his tent. What can he want with me? I always thought he owed me a grudge."

Gagabu and Ameni glanced meaningly at each other, and the high-priest then hastened away, as already he had remained too long away from the banquet. Before he got into his chariot he commanded the guard to return to their posts, and took it upon himself to inform the Regent that his guest would remain in his tent till the festival was over; the soldiers unhesitatingly obeyed him.

Ameni arrived at the palace before them, and entered the banqueting-hall just as Ani was assigning a place to each of his guests. The high-priest went straight up to him, and said, as he bowed before him:

"Pardon my long delay, but I was detained by a great surprise. The poet Pentaur is living-as you know. I have invited him to remain in my tent as my guest, and to tend the prophet Gagabu."

The Regent turned pale, he remained speechless and looked at Ameni with a cold ghastly smile; but he soon recovered himself.

"You see," he said, "how you have injured me by your unworthy suspicions; I meant to have restored your favorite to you myself to-morrow."

"Forgive me, then, for having anticipated your plan," said Ameni, taking his seat near the king. Hundreds of slaves hurried to and fro loaded with costly dishes. Large vessels of richly wrought gold and silver were brought into the hall on wheels, and set on the side-boards. Children were perched in the shells and lotus-flowers that hung from the painted rafters; and from between the pillars, that were hung with cloudy transparent tissues, they threw roses and violets down on the company. The sounds of harps and songs issued from concealed rooms, and from an altar, six ells high, in the middle of the hall, clouds of incense were wafted into space.

The king-one of whose titles was "Son of the Sun," —was as radiant as the sun himself. His children were once more around him, Mena was his cupbearer as in former times, and all that was best and noblest in the land were gathered round him to rejoice with him in his triumph and his return. Opposite to him sat the ladies, and exactly in front of him, a delight to his eyes, Bent-Anat and Nefert. His injunction to Mena to hold the wine cup steadily seemed by no means superfluous, for his looks constantly wandered from the king's goblet to his fair wife, from whose lips he as yet had heard no word of welcome, whose hand he had not yet been so happy as to touch.

All the guests were in the most joyful excitement. Rameses related the tale of his fight at Kadesh, and the high-priest of Heliopolis observed, "In later times the poets will sing of thy deeds."

"Their songs will not be of my achievements," exclaimed the king, "but of the grace of the Divinity, who so miraculously rescued your sovereign, and gave the victory to the Egyptians over an innumerable enemy."

"Did you see the God with your own eyes? and in what form did he appear to you?" asked Bent-Anat. "It is most extraordinary," said the king, "but he exactly resembled the dead father of the traitor Paaker. My preserver was of tall stature, and had a beautiful countenance; his voice was deep and thrilling, and he swung his battle-axe as if it were a mere plaything."

Ameni had listened eagerly to the king's words, now he bowed low before him and said humbly: "If I were younger I myself would endeavor, as was the custom with our fathers, to celebrate this glorious deed of a God and of his sublime son in a song worthy of this festival; but melting tones are no longer mine, they vanish with years, and the car of the listener lends itself only to the young. Nothing is wanting to thy feast, most lordly Ani, but a poet, who might sing the glorious deeds of our monarch to the sound of his lute, and yet-we have at hand the gifted Pentaur, the noblest disciple of the House of Seti."

Bent-Anat turned perfectly white, and the priests who were present expressed the utmost joy and astonishment, for they had long thought the young poet, who was highly esteemed throughout Egypt, to be dead.

The king had often heard of the fame of Pentaur from his sons and especially from Rameri, and he willingly consented that Ameni should send for the poet, who had himself borne arms at Kadesh, in order that he should sing a song of triumph. The Regent gazed blankly and uneasily into his wine cup, and the high-priest rose to fetch Pentaur himself into the presence of the king.

During the high-priest's absence, more and more dishes were served to the company; behind each guest stood a silver bowl with rose water, in which from time to time he could dip his fingers to cool and clean them; the slaves in waiting were constantly at hand with embroidered napkins to wipe them, and others frequently changed the faded wreaths, round the heads and shoulders of the feasters, for fresh ones.

"How pale you are, my child!" said Rameses turning to Bent-Anat. "If you are tired, your uncle will no doubt allow you to leave the hall; though I think you should stay to hear the performance of this much-lauded poet. After having been so highly praised he will find it difficult to satisfy his hearers. But indeed I am uneasy about you, my child-would you rather go?" The Regent had risen and said earnestly, "Your presence has done me honor, but if you are fatigued I beg you to allow me to conduct you and your ladies to the apartments intended for you."

"I will stay," said Bent-Anat in a low but decided tone, and she kept her eyes on the floor, while her heart beat violently, for the murmur of voices told her that Pentaur was entering the hall. He wore the long white robe of a priest of the temple of Seti, and on his forehead the ostrich-feather which marked him as one of the initiated. He did not raise his eyes till he stood close before the king; then he prostrated himself before him, and awaited a sign from the Pharaoh before he rose again.

But Rameses hesitated a long time, for the youthful figure before him, and the glance that met his own, moved him strangely. Was not this the divinity of the fight? Was not this his preserver? Was he again deluded by a resemblance, or was he in a dream?

The guests gazed in silence at the spellbound king, and at the poet; at last Rameses bowed his head,

Pentaur rose to his feet, and the bright color flew to his face as close to him he perceived Bent-Anat.

"You fought at Kadesh?" asked the king. "As thou sayest," replied Pentaur.

"You are well spoken of as a poet," said Rameses, "and we desire to hear the wonderful tale of my preservation celebrated in song. If you will attempt it, let a lute be brought and sing."

The poet bowed. "My gifts are modest," he said, "but I will endeavor to sing of the glorious deed, in the presence of the hero who achieved it, with the aid of the Gods."

Rameses gave a signal, and Ameni caused a large golden harp to be brought in for his disciple. Pentaur lightly touched the strings, leaned his head against the top of the tall bow of the harp, for some time lest in meditation; then he drew himself up boldly, and struck the chords, bringing out a strong and warlike music in broad heroic rhythm.

Then he began the narrative: how Rameses had pitched his camp before Kadesh, how he ordered his troops, and how he had taken the field against the Cheta, and their Asiatic allies. Louder and stronger rose his tones when he reached the turning-point of the battle, and began to celebrate the rescue of the king; and the Pharaoh listened with eager attention as Pentaur sang: —[A literal translation of the ancient Egyptian poem called "The Epos of Pentaur"]

"Then the king stood forth, and, radiant with courage,
He looked like the Sun-god armed and eager for battle.
The noble steeds that bore him into the struggle
'Victory to Thebes' was the name of one, and the other
Was called 'contented Nura' —were foaled in the stables
Of him we call 'the elect,' 'the beloved of Amon,'
'Lord of truth,' the chosen vicar of Ra.

Up sprang the king and threw himself on the foe,
The swaying ranks of the contemptible Cheta.
He stood alone-alone, and no man with him.
As thus the king stood forth all eyes were upon him,
And soon he was enmeshed by men and horses,
And by the enemy's chariots: two thousand five hundred.
The foe behind hemmed him in and enclosed him.
Dense the array of the contemptible Cheta,

Dense the swarm of warriors out of Arad,
Dense the Mysian host, the Pisidian legions.
Every chariot carried three bold warriors,
All his foes, and all allied like brothers.

"Not a prince is with me, not a captain,
Not an archer, none to guide my horses!
Fled the riders! fled my troops and horse
By my side not one is now left standing."
Thus the king, and raised his voice in prayer.
"Great father Amon, I have known Thee well.
And can the father thus forget his son?
Have I in any deed forgotten Thee?
Have I done aught without Thy high behest
Or moved or staid against Thy sovereign will?
Great am I —mighty are Egyptian kings
But in the sight of Thy commanding might,
Small as the chieftain of a wandering tribe.
Immortal Lord, crush Thou this unclean people;
Break Thou their necks, annihilate the heathen.

And I —have I not brought Thee many victims,
And filled Thy temple with the captive folk?
And for thy presence built a dwelling place
That shall endure for countless years to come?
Thy garners overflow with gifts from me.
I offered Thee the world to swell Thy glory,
And thirty thousand mighty steers have shed
Their smoking blood on fragrant cedar piles.
Tall gateways, flag-decked masts, I raised to Thee,
And obelisks from Abu I have brought,
And built Thee temples of eternal stone.
For Thee my ships have brought across the sea
The tribute of the nations. This I did —
When were such things done in the former time?

For dark the fate of him who would rebel
Against Thee: though Thy sway is just and mild.
My father, Amon-as an earthly son
His earthly father-so I call on Thee.
Look down from heaven on me, beset by foes,
By heathen foes-the folk that know Thee not.
The nations have combined against Thy son;
I stand alone-alone, and no man with me.
My foot and horse are fled, I called aloud
And no one heard-in vain I called to them.
And yet I say: the sheltering care of Amon
Is better succor than a million men,
Or than ten thousand knights, or than a thousand
Brothers and sons though gathered into one.
And yet I say: the bulwarks raised by men
However strong, compared to Thy great works

Are but vain shadows, and no human aid
Avails against the foe-but Thy strong hand.
The counsel of Thy lips shall guide my way;
I have obeyed whenever Thou hast ruled;
I call on Thee-and, with my fame, Thy glory
Shall fill the world, from farthest east to west."

Yea, his cry rang forth even far as Hermonthis,
And Amon himself appeared at his call; and gave him
His hand and shouted in triumph, saying to the Pharaoh:
"Help is at hand, O Rameses. I will uphold thee —
I thy father am he who now is thy succor,
Bearing thee in my hands. For stronger and readier
I than a hundred thousand mortal retainers;
I am the Lord of victory loving valor?
I rejoice in the brave and give them good counsel,
And he whom I counsel certainly shall not miscarry."

Then like Menth, with his right he scattered the arrows,
And with his left he swung his deadly weapon,
Felling the foe-as his foes are felled by Baal.
The chariots were broken and the drivers scattered,
Then was the foe overthrown before his horses.
None found a hand to fight: they could not shoot
Nor dared they hurl the spear but fled at his coming
Headlong into the river."[130]

A silence as of the grave reigned in the vast hall, Rameses fixed his eyes on the poet, as though he would engrave his features on his very soul, and compare them with those of another which had dwelt there unforgotten since the day of Kadesh. Beyond a doubt his preserver stood before him.

Seized by a sudden impulse, he interrupted the poet in the midst of his stirring song, and cried out to the assembled guests:

"Pay honor to this man! for the Divinity chose to appear under his form to save your king when he 'alone, and no man with him,' struggled with a thousand."

"Hail to Pentaur!" rang through the hall from the vast assembly, and Nefert rose and gave the poet the bunch of flowers she had been wearing on her bosom.

The king nodded approval, and looked enquiringly at his daughter; Bent-Anat's eyes met his with a glance of intelligence, and with all the simplicity of an impulsive child, she took from her head the wreath that had decorated her beautiful hair, went up to Pentaur, and crowned him with it, as it was customary for a bride to crown her lover before the wedding.

Rameses observed his daughter's action with some surprise, and the guests responded to it with loud cheering.

The king looked gravely at Bent-Anat and the young priest; the eyes of all the company were eagerly fixed on the princess and the poet. The king seemed to have forgotten the presence of strangers, and to be wholly absorbed in thought, but by degrees a change came over his face, it cleared, as a landscape is cleared from the morning mists under the influence of the spring sunshine. When he looked up again his glance was bright and satisfied, and Bent-Anat knew what it promised when it lingered lovingly first on her, and then on her friend, whose head was still graced by the wreath that had crowned hers.

At last Rameses turned from the lovers, and said to the guests:

"It is past midnight, and I will now leave you. To-morrow evening I bid you all-and you especially, Pentaur-to be my guests in this banqueting hall. Once more fill your cups, and let us empty them-to a long time of peace after the victory which, by the help of the Gods, we have won. And at the same time let us express our thanks to my friend Ani, who has entertained us so magnificently, and who has so faithfully and zealously administered the affairs of the kingdom during my absence."

The company pledged the king, who warmly shook hands with the Regent, and then, escorted by his wandbearers and lords in waiting, quitted the hall, after he had signed to Mena, Ameni, and the ladies to follow him.

Nefert greeted her husband, but she immediately parted from the royal party, as she had yielded to the urgent entreaty of Katuti that she should for this night go to her mother, to whom she had so much to tell, instead of remaining with the princess. Her mother's chariot soon took her to her tent.

Rameses dismissed his attendants in the ante-room of his apartments; when they were alone he turned to Bent-Anat and said affectionately.

"What was in your mind when you laid your wreath on the poet's brow?"

"What is in every maiden's mind when she does the like," replied Bent-Anat with trustful frankness.

"And your father?" asked the king.

"My father knows that I will obey him even if he demands of me the hardest thing-the sacrifice of all my-happiness; but I believe that he-that you love me fondly, and I do not forget the hour in which you said to me that now my mother was dead you would be father and mother both to me, and you would try to understand me as she certainly would have understood me. But what need between us of so many words. I love Pentaur-with a love that is not of yesterday-with the first perfect love of my heart and he has proved himself worthy of that high honor. But were he ever so humble, the hand of your daughter has the power to raise him above every prince in the land."

"It has such power, and you shall exercise it," cried the king. "You have been true and faithful to yourself, while your father and protector left you to yourself. In you I love the image of your mother, and I learned from her that a true woman's heart can find the right path better than a man's wisdom. Now go to rest, and to-morrow morning put on a fresh wreath, for you will have need of it, my noble daughter."

CHAPTER XLII

The cloudless vault of heaven spread over the plain of Pelusium, the stars were bright, the moon threw her calm light over the thousands of tents which shone as white as little hillocks of snow. All was silent, the soldiers and the Egyptians, who had assembled to welcome the king, were now all gone to rest.

There had been great rejoicing and jollity in the camp; three enormous vats, garlanded with flowers and overflowing with wine, which spilt with every movement of the trucks on which they were drawn by thirty oxen, were sent up and down the little streets of tents, and as the evening closed in tavern-booths were erected in many spots in the camp, at which the Regent's servants supplied the soldiers with red and white wine. The tents of the populace were only divided from the pavilion of the Pharaoh by the hastily-constructed garden in the midst of which it stood, and the hedge which enclosed it.

The tent of the Regent himself was distinguished from all the others by its size and magnificence; to the right of it was the encampment of the different priestly deputations, to the left that of his suite; among the latter were the tents of his friend Katuti, a large one for her own use, and some smaller ones for her servants. Behind Ani's pavilion stood a tent, enclosed in a wall or screen of canvas, within which old Hekt was lodged; Ani had secretly conveyed her hither on board his own boat. Only Katuti and his confidential servants knew who it was that lay concealed in the mysteriously shrouded abode.

While the banquet was proceeding in the great pavilion, the witch was sitting in a heap on the sandy earth of her conical canvas dwelling; she breathed with difficulty, for a weakness of the heart, against which she had long struggled, now oppressed her more frequently and severely; a little lamp of clay burned before her, and on her lap crouched a sick and ruffled hawk; the creature shivered from time to time, closing the filmy lids of his keen eyes, which glowed with a dull fire when Hekt took him up in her withered hand, and tried to blow some air into his hooked beak, still ever ready to peck and tear her.

At her feet little Scherau lay asleep. Presently she pushed the child with her foot. "Wake up," she said, as he raised himself still half asleep. "You have young ears-it seemed to me that I heard a woman scream in Ani's tent. Do you hear any thing?"

"Yes, indeed," exclaimed the little one. "There is a noise like crying, and that-that was a scream! It came from out there, from Nemu's tent."

"Creep through there," said the witch, "and see what is happening!"

The child obeyed: Hekt turned her attention again to the bird, which no longer perched in her lap, but lay on one side, though it still tried to use its talons, when she took him up in her hand.

"It is all over with him," muttered the old woman, "and the one I called Rameses is sleeker than ever. It is all folly and yet-and yet! the Regent's game is over, and he has lost it. The creature is stretching itself-its head drops-it draws itself up-one more clutch at my dress-now it is dead!"

She contemplated the dead hawk in her lap for some minutes, then she took it up, flung it into a corner of the tent, and exclaimed:

"Good-bye, King Ani. The crown is not for you!" Then she went on: "What project has he in hand now, I wonder? Twenty times he has asked me whether the great enterprise will succeed; as if I knew any more than he! And Nemu too has hinted all kinds of things, though he would not speak out. Something is going on, and I —and I? There it comes again."

The old woman pressed her hand to her heart and closed her eyes, her features were distorted with pain; she did not perceive Scherau's return, she did not hear him call her name, or see that, when she did not answer him, he left her again. For an hour or more she remained unconscious, then her senses returned, but she felt as if some ice-cold fluid slowly ran through her veins instead of the warm blood.

"If I had kept a hawk for myself too," she muttered, "it would soon follow the other one in the corner! If only Ani keeps his word, and has me embalmed!

"But how can he when he too is so near his end. They will let me rot and disappear, and there will be no future for me, no meeting with Assa."

The old woman remained silent for a long time; at last she murmured hoarsely with her eyes fixed on the ground:

"Death brings release, if only from the torment of remembrance. But there is a life beyond the grave. I do not, I will not cease to hope. The dead shall all be equally judged, and subject to the inscrutable decrees. —Where shall I find him? Among the blest, or among the damned? And I? It matters not! The deeper the abyss into which they fling me the better. Can Assa, if he is among the blest, remain in bliss, when he sees to what he has brought me? Oh! they must embalm me —I cannot bear to vanish, and rot and evaporate into nothingness!"

While she was still speaking, the dwarf Nemu had come into the tent; Scherau, seeing the old woman senseless, had run to tell him that his mother was lying on the earth with her eyes shut, and was dying. The witch perceived the little man.

"It is well," she said, "that you have come; I shall be dead before sunrise."

"Mother!" cried the dwarf horrified, "you shall live, and live better than you have done till now! Great things are happening, and for us!"

"I know, I know," said Hekt. "Go away, Scherau-now, Nemu, whisper in my ear what is doing?" The dwarf felt as if he could not avoid the influence of her eye, he went up to her, and said softly —"The pavilion, in which the king and his people are sleeping, is constructed of wood; straw and pitch are built into the walls, and laid under the boards. As soon as they are gone to rest we shall set the tinder thing on fire. The guards are drunk and sleeping."

"Well thought of," said Hekt. "Did you plan it?" "I and my mistress," said the dwarf not without pride. "You can devise a plot," said the old woman, "but you are feeble in the working out. Is your plan a secret? Have you clever assistants?"

"No one knows of it," replied the dwarf, "but Katuti, Paaker, and I; we three shall lay the brands to the spots we have fixed upon. I am going to the rooms of Bent-Anat; Katuti, who can go in and out as she pleases, will set fire to the stairs, which lead to the upper story, and which fall by touching a spring; and Paaker to the king's apartments."

"Good-good, it may succeed," gasped the old woman. "But what was the scream in your tent?" The dwarf seemed doubtful about answering; but Hekt went on:

"Speak without fear-the dead are sure to be silent." The dwarf, trembling with agitation, shook off his hesitation, and said:

"I have found Uarda, the grandchild of Pinem, who had disappeared, and I decoyed her here, for she and no other shall be my wife, if Ani is king, and if Katuti makes me rich and free. She is in the service of the Princess Bent-Anat, and sleeps in her anteroom, and she must not be burnt with her mistress. She insisted on going back to the palace, so, as she would fly to the fire like a gnat, and I would not have her risk being burnt, I tied her up fast."

"Did she not struggle?" said Hekt.

"Like a mad thing," said the dwarf. "But the Regent's dumb slave, who was ordered by his master to obey me in everything to-day, helped me. We tied up her mouth that she might not be heard screaming!"

"Will you leave her alone when you go to do your errand?"

"Her father is with her!"

"Kaschta, the red-beard?" asked the old woman in surprise. "And did he not break you in pieces like an earthenware pot?"

"He will not stir," said Nemu laughing. "For when I found him, I made him so drunk with Ani's old wine that he lies there like a mummy. It was from him that I learned where Uarda was, and I went to her, and got her to come with me by telling her that her father was very ill, and begged her to go to see him once more. She flew after me like a gazelle, and when she saw the soldier lying there senseless she threw herself upon him, and called for water to cool his

255

head, for he was raving in his dreams of rats and mice that had fallen upon him. As it grew late she wanted to return to her mistress, and we were obliged to prevent her. How handsome she has grown, mother; you cannot imagine how pretty she is."

"Aye, aye!" said Hekt. "You will have to keep an eye upon her when she is your wife."

"I will treat her like the wife of a noble," said Nemu. "And pay a real lady to guard her. But by this time Katuti has brought home her daughter, Mena's wife; the stars are sinking and-there-that was the first signal. When Katuti whistles the third time we are to go to work. Lend me your fire-box, mother."

"Take it," said Hekt. "I shall never need it again. It is all over with me! How your hand shakes! Hold the wood firmly, or you will drop it before you have brought the fire."

The dwarf bid the old woman farewell, and she let him kiss her without moving. When he was gone, she listened eagerly for any sound that might pierce the silence of the night, her eyes shone with a keen light, and a thousand thoughts flew through her restless brain. When she heard the second signal on Katuti's silver whistle, she sat upright and muttered:

"That gallows-bird Paaker, his vain aunt and that villain Ani, are no match for Rameses, even when he is asleep. Ani's hawk is dead; he has nothing to hope for from Fortune, and I nothing to hope for from him. But if Rameses-if the real king would promise me-then my poor old body-Yes, that is the thing, that is what I will do."

She painfully raised herself on her feet with the help of her stick, she found a knife and a small flask which she slipped into her dress, and then, bent and trembling, with a last effort of her remaining strength she dragged herself as far as Nemu's tent. Here she found Uarda bound hand and foot, and Kaschta lying on the ground in a heavy drunken slumber.

The girl shrank together in alarm when she saw the old woman, and Scherau, who crouched at her side, raised his hands imploringly to the witch.

"Take this knife, boy," she said to the little one. "Cut the ropes the poor thing is tied with. The papyrus cords are strong, saw them with the blade."[131]

While the boy eagerly followed her instructions with all his little might, she rubbed the soldier's temples with an essence which she had in the bottle, and poured a few drops of it between his lips. Kaschta came to himself, stretched his limbs, and stared in astonishment at the place in which he found himself. She gave him some water, and desired him to drink it, saying, as Uarda shook herself free from the bonds:

"The Gods have predestined you to great things, you white maiden. Listen to what I, old Hekt, am telling you. The king's life is threatened, his and his children's; I purpose to save them, and I ask no reward but this-that he should have my body embalmed and interred at Thebes. Swear to me that you will require this of him when you have saved him."

"In God's name what is happening?" cried Uarda. "Swear that you will provide for my burial," said the old woman.

"I swear it!" cried the girl. "But for God's sake —"

"Katuti, Paaker, and Nemu are gone to set fire to the palace when Rameses is sleeping, in three places. Do you hear, Kaschta! Now hasten, fly after the incendiaries, rouse the servants, and try to rescue the king."

"Oh fly, father," cried the girl, and they both rushed away in the darkness.

"She is honest and will keep her word," muttered Hekt, and she tried to drag herself back to her own tent; but her strength failed her half-way. Little Scherau tried to support her, but he was too weak; she sank down on the sand, and looked out into the distance. There she saw the dark mass of the palace, from which rose a light that grew broader and broader, then clouds of black smoke, then up flew the soaring flame, and a swarm of glowing sparks.

"Run into the camp, child," she cried, "cry fire, and wake the sleepers."

Scherau ran off shouting as loud as he could.

The old woman pressed her hand to her side, she muttered: "There it is again."

"In the other world-Assa-Assa," and her trembling lips were silent for ever.

CHAPTER XLIII.

Katuti had kept her unfortunate nephew Paaker concealed in one of her servants' tents. He had escaped wounded from the battle at Kadesh, and in terrible pain he had succeeded, by the help of an ass which he had purchased from a peasant, in reaching by paths known to hardly any one but himself, the cave where he had previously left his brother. Here he found his faithful Ethiopian slave, who nursed him till he was strong enough to set out on his journey to Egypt. He reached Pelusium, after many privations, disguised as an Ismaelite camel-driver; he left his servant, who might have betrayed him, behind in the cave.

Before he was permitted to pass the fortifications, which lay across the isthmus which parts the Mediterranean from the Red Sea, and which were intended to protect Egypt from the incursions of the nomad tribes of the Chasu, he was subjected to a strict interrogatory, and among other questions was asked whether he had nowhere met with the traitor Paaker, who was minutely described to him. No one recognized in the shrunken, grey-haired, one-eyed camel-driver, the broad-shouldered, muscular and thick-legged pioneer. To disguise himself the more effectually, he procured some hair-dye —a cosmetic known in all ages-and blackened himself.[132]

Katuti had arrived at Pelusium with Ani some time before, to superintend the construction of the royal pavilion. He ventured to approach her disguised as a negro beggar, with a palm-branch in his hand. She gave him some money and questioned him concerning his native country, for she made it her business to secure the favor even of the meanest; but though she appeared to take an interest in his answers, she did not recognize him; now for the first time he felt secure, and the next day he went up to her again, and told her who he was.

The widow was not unmoved by the frightful alteration in her nephew, and although she knew that even Ani had decreed that any intercourse with the traitor was to be punished by death, she took him at once into her service, for she had never had greater need than now to employ the desperate enemy of the king and of her son-in-law.

The mutilated, despised, and hunted man kept himself far from the other servants, regarding the meaner folk with undiminished scorn. He thought seldom, and only vaguely of Katuti's daughter, for love had quite given place to hatred, and only one thing now seemed to him worth living for-the hope of working with others to cause his enemies' downfall, and of being the instrument of their death; so he offered himself to the widow a willing and welcome tool, and the dull flash in his uninjured eye when she set him the task of setting fire to the king's apartments, showed her that in the Mohar she had found an ally she might depend on to the uttermost.

Paaker had carefully examined the scene of his exploit before the king's arrival. Under the windows of the king's rooms, at least forty feet from the ground, was a narrow parapet resting on the ends of the beams which supported the rafters on which lay the floor of the upper story in which the king slept. These rafters had been smeared with pitch, and straw had been laid between them, and the pioneer would have known how to find the opening where he was to put in the brand even if he had been blind of both eyes.

When Katuti first sounded her whistle he slunk to his post; he was challenged by no watchman, for the few guards who had been placed in the immediate vicinity of the pavilion, had all gone to sleep under the influence of the Regent's wine. Paaker climbed up to about the height of two men from the ground by the help of the ornamental carving on the outside wall of the palace; there a rope ladder was attached, he clambered up this, and soon stood on the parapet, above which were the windows of the king's rooms, and below which the fire was to be laid.

Rameses' room was brightly illuminated. Paaker could see into it without being seen, and could hear every word that was spoken within. The king was sitting in an arm-chair, and looked thoughtfully at the ground; before him stood the Regent, and Mena stood by his couch, holding in his hand the king's sleeping-robe.

Presently Rameses raised his head, and said, as he offered his hand with frank affection to Ani:

"Let me bring this glorious day to a worthy end, cousin. I have found you my true and faithful friend, and I had been in danger of believing those over-anxious counsellors who spoke evil of you. I am never prone to distrust, but a number of things occurred together that clouded my judgment, and I did you injustice. I am sorry, sincerely sorry; nor am I ashamed to apologize to you for having for an instant doubted your good intentions. You are my good friend-and I will prove to you that I am yours. There is my hand-take it; and all Egypt shall know that Rameses trusts no man more implicitly than his Regent Ani. I will ask you to undertake to be my guard of honor to-night —we will share this room. I sleep here; when I lie down on my couch take your place on the divan yonder." Ani had taken Rameses' offered hand, but now he turned pale as he looked down. Paaker could see straight into his face, and it was not without difficulty that he suppressed a scornful laugh.

Rameses did not observe the Regent's dismay, for he had signed to Mena to come closer to him.

"Before I sleep," said the king, "I will bring matters to an end with you too. You have put your wife's constancy to a severe test, and she has trusted you with a childlike simplicity that is often wiser than the arguments of sages, because she loved you honestly, and is herself incapable of guile. I promised you that I would grant you a wish if your faith in her was justified. Now tell me what is your will?"

Mena fell on his knees, and covered the king's robe with kisses.

"Pardon!" he exclaimed. "Nothing but pardon. My crime was a heavy one, I know; but I was driven to it by scorn and fury-it was as if I saw the dishonoring hand of Paaker stretched out to seize my innocent wife, who, as I now know, loathes him as a toad —"

"What was that?" exclaimed the king. "I thought I heard a groan outside."

He went up to the window and looked out, but he did not see the pioneer, who watched every motion of the king, and who, as soon as he perceived that his involuntary sigh of anguish had been heard, stretched himself close under the balustrade. Mena had not risen from his knees when the king once more turned to him.

"Pardon me," he said again. "Let me be near thee again as before, and drive thy chariot. I live only through thee, I am of no worth but through thee, and by thy favor, my king, my lord, my father!"

Rameses signed to his favorite to rise. "Your request was granted," said he, "before you made it. I am still in your debt on your fair wife's account. Thank Nefert-not me, and let us give thanks to the Immortals this day with especial fervor. What has it not brought forth for us! It has restored to me you two friends, whom I regarded as lost to me, and has given me in Pentaur another son."

A low whistle sounded through the night air; it was Katuti's last signal.

Paaker blew up the tinder, laid it in the bole under the parapet, and then, unmindful of his own danger, raised himself to listen for any further words.

"I entreat thee," said the Regent, approaching Rameses, "to excuse me. I fully appreciate thy favors, but the labors of the last few days have been too much for me; I can hardly stand on my feet, and the guard of honor —"

"Mena will watch," said the king. "Sleep in all security, cousin. I will have it known to all men that I have put away from me all distrust of you. Give the my night-robe, Mena. Nay-one thing more I must tell you. Youth smiles on the young, Ani. Bent-Anat has chosen a worthy husband, my preserver, the poet Pentaur. He was said to be a man of humble origin, the son of a gardener of the House of Seti; and now what do I learn through Ameni? He is the true son of the dead Mohar, and the foul traitor Paaker is the gardener's son. A witch in the Necropolis changed the children. That is the best news of all that has reached me on this propitious day, for the Mohar's widow, the noble Setchem, has been brought here, and I should have been obliged to choose between two sentences on her as the mother of the villain who has escaped us. Either I must have sent her to the quarries, or have had her beheaded before all the people-In the name of the Gods, what is that?"

They heard a loud cry in a man's voice, and at the same instant a noise as if some heavy mass had fallen to the ground from a great height. Rameses and Mena hastened to the window, but started back, for they were met by a cloud of smoke.

"Call the watch!" cried the king.

"Go, you," exclaimed Mena to Ani. "I will not leave the king again in danger."

Ani fled away like an escaped prisoner, but he could not get far, for, before he could descend the stairs to the lower story, they fell in before his very eyes; Katuti, after she had set fire to the interior of the palace, had made them fall by one blow of a hammer. Ani saw her robe as she herself fled, clenched his fist with rage as he shouted her name, and then, not knowing what he did, rushed headlong through the corridor into which the different royal apartments opened.

The fearful crash of the falling stairs brought the King and Mena also out of the sleeping-room.

"There lie the stairs! that is serious!" said the king cooly; then he went back into his room, and looked out of a window to estimate the danger. Bright flames were already bursting from the northern end of the palace, and gave the grey dawn the brightness of day; the southern wing or the pavilion was not yet on fire. Mena observed the parapet from which Paaker had fallen to the ground, tested its strength, and found it firm enough to bear several persons. He looked round, particularly at the wing not yet gained by the flames, and exclaimed in a loud voice:

"The fire is intentional! it is done on purpose. See there! a man is squatting down and pushing a brand into the woodwork."

He leaped back into the room, which was now filling with smoke, snatched the king's bow and quiver, which he himself had hung up at the bed-head, took careful aim, and with one cry the incendiary fell dead.

A few hours later the dwarf Nemu was found with the charioteer's arrow through his heart. After setting fire to Bent-Anat's rooms, he had determined to lay a brand to the wing of the palace where, with the other princes, Uarda's friend Rameri was sleeping.

Mena had again leaped out of window, and was estimating the height of the leap to the ground; the Pharaoh's room was getting more and more filled with smoke, and flames began to break through the seams of the boards. Outside the palace as well as within every one was waking up to terror and excitement.

"Fire! fire! an incendiary! Help! Save the king!" cried Kaschta, who rushed on, followed by a crowd of guards whom he had roused; Uarda had flown to call Bent-Anat, as she knew the way to her room. The king had got on to the parapet outside the window with Mena, and was calling to the soldiers.

"Half of you get into the house, and first save the princess; the other half keep the fire from catching the south wing. I will try to get there."

But Nemu's brand had been effectual, the flames flared up, and the soldiers strained every nerve to conquer them. Their cries mingled with the crackling and snapping of the dry wood, and the roar of the flames, with the trumpet calls of the awakening troops, and the beating of drums. The young princes appeared at a window; they had tied their clothes together to form a rope, and one by one escaped down it.

Rameses called to them with words of encouragement, but he himself was unable to take any means of escape, for though the parapet on which he stood was tolerably wide, and ran round the whole of the building, at about every six feet it was broken by spaces of about ten paces. The fire was spreading and growing, and glowing sparks flew round him and his companion like chaff from the winnowing fan.

"Bring some straw and make a heap below!" shouted Rameses, above the roar of the conflagration. "There is no escape but by a leap down."

The flames rushed out of the windows of the king's room; it was impossible to return to it, but neither the king nor Mena lost his self-possession. When Mena saw the twelve princes descending to the ground, he shouted through his hands, using them as a speaking trumpet, and called to Rameri, who was about to slip down the rope they had contrived, the last of them all.

"Pull up the rope, and keep it from injury till I come."

Rameri obeyed the order, and before Rameses could interfere, Mena had sprung across the space which divided one piece of the balustrade from another. The king's blood ran cold as Mena, a second time, ventured the frightful leap; one false step, and he must meet with the same fearful death as his enemy Paaker.

While the bystanders watched him in breathless silence-while the crackling of the wood, the roar of the flames, and the dull thump of falling timber mingled with the distant chant of a procession of priests who were now approaching the burning pile, Nefert roused by little Scherau knelt on the bare ground in fervent and passionate prayer to the saving Gods. She watched every movement of her husband, and she bit her lips till they bled not to cry out. She felt that he was acting bravely and nobly, and that he was lost if even for an instant his attention were distracted from his perilous footing. Now he had reached Rameri, and bound one end of the rope made out of cloaks and handkerchiefs, round his body; then he gave the other end to Rameri, who held fast to the window-sill, and prepared once more to spring. Nefert saw him ready to leap, she pressed her hands upon her lips to repress a scream, she shut her eyes, and when she opened them again he had accomplished the first leap, and at the second the Gods preserved him from falling; at the third the king held out his hand to him, and saved him from a fall. Then Rameses helped him to unfasten the rope from round his waist to fasten it to the end of a beam.

Rameri now loosened the other end, and followed Mena's example; he too, practised in athletic exercises in the school of the House of Seti, succeeded in accomplishing the three tremendous leaps, and soon the king stood in safety on the ground. Rameri followed him, and then Mena, whose faithful wife went to meet him, and wiped the sweat from his throbbing temples.

Rameses hurried to the north wing, where Bent-Anat had her apartments; he found her safe indeed, but wringing her hands, for her young favorite Uarda had disappeared in the flames after she had roused her and saved her with her father's assistance. Kaschta ran up and down in front of the burning pavilion, tearing his hair; now calling his child in tones of anguish, now holding his breath to listen for an answer. To rush at random into the immense-burning building would have been madness. The king observed the unhappy man, and set him to lead the soldiers, whom he had commanded to hew down the wall of Bent-Anat's rooms, so as to rescue the girl who might be within. Kaschta seized an axe, and raised it to strike.

But he thought that he heard blows from within against one of the shutters of the ground-floor, which by Katuti's orders had been securely closed; he followed the sound-he was not mistaken, the knocking could be distinctly heard.

With all his might he struck the edge of the axe between the shutter and the wall, and a stream of smoke poured out of the new outlet, and before him, enveloped in its black clouds, stood a staggering man who held Uarda in his arms. Kaschta sprang forward into the midst of the smoke and sparks, and snatched his daughter from the arms of her preserver, who fell half smothered on his knees. He rushed out into the air with his light and precious burden, and as he pressed his lips to her closed eyelids his eyes were wet, and there rose up before him the image of the woman who bore her, the wife that had stood as the solitary green palm-tree in the desert waste of his life. But only for a few seconds-Bent-Anat herself took Uarda into her care, and he hastened back to the burning house.

He had recognized his daughter's preserver; it was the physician Nebsecht, who had not quitted the princess since their meeting on Sinai, and had found a place among her suite as her personal physician.

The fresh air had rushed into the room through the opening of the shutter, the broad flames streamed out of the window, but still Nebsecht was alive, for his groans could be heard through the smoke. Once more Kaschta rushed towards the window, the bystanders could see that the ceiling of the room was about to fail, and called out to warn him, but he was already astride the sill.

"I signed myself his slave with my blood," he cried, "Twice he has saved my child, and now I will pay my debt," and he disappeared into the burning room.

He soon reappeared with Nebsecht in his arms, whose robe was already scorched by the flames. He could be seen approaching the window with his heavy burden; a hundred soldiers, and with them Pentaur, pressed forward to help him, and took the senseless leech out of the arms of the soldier, who lifted him over the window sill.

Kaschta was on the point of following him, but before he could swing himself over, the beams above gave way and fell, burying the brave son of the paraschites.

Pentaur had his insensible friend carried to his tent, and helped the physicians to bind up his burns. When the cry of fire had been first raised, Pentaur was sitting in earnest conversation with the high-priest; he had learned that he was not the son of a gardener, but a descendant of one of the noblest families in the land. The foundations of life seemed to be subverted under his feet, Ameni's revelation lifted him out of the dust and set him on the marble floor of a palace; and yet Pentaur was neither excessively surprised nor inordinately rejoiced; he was so well used to find his joys and sufferings depend on the man within him, and not on the circumstances without.

As soon as he heard the cry of fire, he hastened to the burning pavilion, and when he saw the king's danger, he set himself at the head of a number of soldiers who had hurried up from the camp, intending to venture an attempt to save Rameses from the inside of the house. Among those who followed him in this hopeless effort was Katuti's reckless son, who had distinguished himself by his valor before Kadesh, and who hailed this opportunity of again proving his courage. Falling walls choked up the way in front of these brave adventurers; but it was not till several had fallen choked or struck down by burning logs, that they made up their minds to retire-one of the first that was killed was Katuti's son, Nefert's brother.

Uarda had been carried into the nearest tent. Her pretty head lay in Bent-Anat's lap, and Nefert tried to restore her to animation by rubbing her temples with strong essences. Presently the girl's lips moved: with returning consciousness all she had seen and suffered during the last hour or two recurred to her mind; she felt herself rushing through the camp with her father, hurrying through the corridor to the princess's rooms, while he broke in the doors closed by Katuti's orders; she saw Bent-Anat as she roused her, and conducted her to safety; she remembered her horror when, just as she reached the door, she discovered that she had left in her chest her jewel, the only relic of her lost mother, and her rapid return which was observed by no one but by the leech Nebsecht.

Again she seemed to live through the anguish she had felt till she once more had the trinket safe in her bosom, the horror that fell upon her when she found her escape impeded by smoke and flames, and the weakness which overcame her; and she felt as if the strange white-robed priest once more raised her in his arms. She remembered the tenderness of his eyes as he looked into hers, and she smiled half gratefully but half displeased at the tender kiss which had been pressed on her lips before she found herself in her father's strong arms.

"How sweet she is!" said Bent-Anat. "I believe poor Nebsecht is right in saying that her mother was the daughter of some great man among the foreign people. Look what pretty little hands and feet, and her skin is as clear as Phoenician glass."

CHAPTER XLIV.

While the friends were occupied in restoring Uarda to animation, and in taking affectionate care of her, Katuti was walking restlessly backwards and forwards in her tent.

Soon after she had slipped out for the purpose of setting fire to the palace, Scherau's cry had waked up Nefert, and Katuti found her daughter's bed empty when, with blackened hands and limbs trembling with agitation, she came back from her criminal task.

Now she waited in vain for Nemu and Paaker.

Her steward, whom she sent on repeated messages of enquiry whether the Regent had returned, constantly brought back a negative answer, and added the information that he had found the body of old Hekt lying on the open ground. The widow's heart sank with fear; she was full of dark forebodings while she listened to the shouts of the people engaged in putting out the fire, the roll of drums, and the trumpets of the soldiers calling each other to the help of the king.

To these sounds now was added the dull crash of falling timbers and walls.

A faint smile played upon her thin lips, and she thought to herself: "There–that perhaps fell on the king, and my precious son-in-law, who does not deserve such a fate–if we had not fallen into disgrace, and if since the occurrences before Kadesh he did not cling to his indulgent lord as a calf follows a cow."

She gathered fresh courage, and fancied she could hear the voice of Ethiopian troops hailing the Regent as king–could see Ani decorated with the crown of Upper and Lower Egypt, seated on Rameses' throne, and herself by his side in rich though unpretending splendor. She pictured herself with her son and daughter as enjoying Mena's estate, freed from debt and increased by Ani's generosity, and then a new, intoxicating hope came into her mind. Perhaps already at this moment her daughter was a widow, and why should she not be so fortunate as to induce Ani to select her child, the prettiest woman in Thebes, for his wife? Then she, the mother of the queen, would be indeed unimpeachable, and all-powerful. She had long since come to regard the pioneer as a tool to be cast aside, nay soon to be utterly destroyed; his wealth might probably at some future time be bestowed upon her son, who had distinguished himself at Kadesh, and whom Ani must before long promote to be his charioteer or the commander of the chariot warriors.

Flattered by these fancies, she forgot every care as she walked faster and faster to and fro in her tent. Suddenly the steward, whom she had this time sent to the very scene of the fire, rushed into the tent, and with every token of terror broke to her the news that the king and his charioteer were hanging in mid air on a narrow wooden parapet, and that unless some miracle happened they must inevitably be killed. It was said that incendiaries had occasioned the fire, and he, the steward, had hastened forward to prepare her for evil news as the mangled body of the pioneer, which had been identified by the ring on his finger, and the poor little corpse of Nemu, pierced through by an arrow, had been carried past him.

Katuti was silent for a moment.

"And the king's sons?" she asked with an anxious sigh.

"The Gods be praised," replied the steward, "they succeeded in letting themselves down to the ground by a rope made of their garments knotted together, and some were already safe when I came away."

Katuti's face clouded darkly; once more she sent forth her messenger. The minutes of his absence seemed like days; her bosom heaved in stormy agitation, then for a moment she controlled herself, and again her heart seemed to cease beating–she closed her eyes as if her anguish of anxiety was too much for her strength. At last, long after sunrise, the steward reappeared.

Pale, trembling, hardly able to control his voice, he threw himself on the ground at her feet crying out:

"Alas! this night! prepare for the worst, mistress! May Isis comfort thee, who saw thy son fall in the service of his king and father! May Amon, the great God of Thebes, give thee strength! Our pride, our hope, thy son is slain, killed by a falling beam."

Pale and still as if frozen, Katuti shed not a tear; for a minute she did not speak, then she asked in a dull tone:

"And Rameses?"

"The Gods be praised!" answered the servant, "he is safe-rescued by Mena!"

"And Ani?"

"Burnt! —they found his body disfigured out of all recognition; they knew him again by the jewels he wore at the banquet."

Katuti gazed into vacancy, and the steward started back as from a mad woman when, instead of bursting into tears, she clenched her small jewelled hands, shook her fists in the air, and broke into loud, wild laughter; then, startled at the sound of her own voice, she suddenly became silent and fixed her eyes vacantly on the ground. She neither saw nor heard that the captain of the watch, who was called "the eyes and ears of the king," had come in through the door of her tent followed by several officers and a scribe; he came up to her, and called her by her name. Not till the steward timidly touched her did she collect her senses like one suddenly roused from deep sleep.

"What are you doing in my tent?" she asked the officer, drawing herself up haughtily.

"In the name of the chief judge of Thebes," said the captain of the watch solemnly. "I arrest you, and hail you before the high court of justice, to defend yourself against the grave and capital charges of high treason, attempted regicide, and incendiarism."

"I am ready," said the widow, and a scornful smile curled her lips. Then with her usual dignity she pointed to a seat and said:

"Be seated while I dress."

The officer bowed, but remained standing at the door of the tent while she arranged her black hair, set her diadem on her brow, opened her little ointment chest, and took from it a small phial of the rapid poison strychnine, which some months before she had procured through Nemu from the old witch Hekt.

"My mirror!" she called to a maid servant, who squatted in a corner of the tent. She held the metal mirror so as to conceal her face from the captain of the watch, put the little flask to her lips and emptied it at one mouthful. The mirror fell from her hand, she staggered, a deadly convulsion seized her-the officer rushed forward, and while she fixed her dying look upon him she said:

"My game is lost, but Ameni-tell Ameni that he will not win either."

She fell forward, murmured Nefert's name, struggled convulsively and was dead.

When the draught of happiness which the Gods prepare for some few men, seems to flow clearest and purest, Fate rarely fails to infuse into it some drop of bitterness. And yet we should not therefore disdain it, for it is that very drop of bitterness which warns us to drink of the joys of life thankfully, and in moderation.

The perfect happiness of Mena and Nefert was troubled by the fearful death of Katuti, but both felt as if they now for the first time knew the full strength of their love for each other. Mena had to make up to his wife for the loss of mother and brother, and Nefert to restore to her husband much that he had been robbed of by her relatives, and they felt that they had met again not merely for pleasure but to be to each other a support and a consolation.

Rameses quitted the scene of the fire full of gratitude to the Gods who had shown such grace to him and his. He ordered numberless steers to be sacrificed, and thanksgiving festivals to be held throughout the land; but he was cut to the heart by the betrayal to which he had fallen a victim. He longed-as he always did in moments when the balance of his mind had been disturbed-for an hour of solitude, and retired to the tent which had been hastily erected for him. He could not bear to enter the splendid pavilion which had been Ani's; it seemed to him infested with the leprosy of falsehood and treason.

For an hour he remained alone, and weighed the worst he had suffered at the hands of men against that which was good and cheering, and he found that the good far outweighed the evil.

He vividly realized the magnitude of his debt of gratitude, not to the Immortals only, but also to his earthly friends, as he recalled every moment of this morning's experience.

"Gratitude," he said to himself, "was impressed on you by your mother; you yourself have taught your children to be grateful. Piety is gratitude to the Gods, and he only is really generous who does not forget the gratitude he owes to men."

He had thrown off all bitterness of feeling when he sent for Bent-Anat and Pentaur to be brought to his tent. He made his daughter relate at full length how the poet had won her love, and though he frequently interrupted her with blame as well as praise, his heart was full of fatherly joy when he laid his darling's hand in that of the poet.

Bent-Anat laid her head in full content on the breast of the noble Assa's grandson, but she would have clung not less fondly to Pentaur the gardener's son.

"Now you are one of my own children," said Rameses; and he desired the poet to remain with him while he commanded the heralds, ambassadors, and interpreters to bring to him the Asiatic princes, who were detained in their own tents on the farther side of the Nile, that he might conclude with them such a treaty of peace as might continue valid for generations to come. Before they arrived, the young princes came to their father's tent, and learned from his own lips the noble birth of Pentaur, and that they owed it to their sister that in him they saw another brother; they welcomed him with sincere affection, and all, especially Rameri, warmly congratulated the handsome and worthy couple.

The king then called Rameri forward from among his brothers, and thanked him before them all for his brave conduct during the fire. He had already been invested with the robe of manhood after the battle of Kadesh; he was now appointed to the command of a legion of chariot-warriors, and the order of the lion to wear round his neck was bestowed on him for his bravery. The prince knelt, and thanked his father; but Rameses took the curly head in his hands and said:

"You have won praise and reward by your splendid deeds from the father whom you have saved and filled with pride. But the king watches over the laws, and guides the destiny of this land, the king must blame you, nay perhaps punish you. You could not yield to the discipline of school, where we all must learn to obey if we would afterwards exercise our authority with moderation, and without any orders you left Egypt and joined the army. You showed the courage and strength of a man, but the folly of a boy in all that regards prudence and foresight-things harder to learn for the son of a race of heroes than mere hitting and slashing at random; you, without experience, measured yourself against masters of the art of war, and what was the consequence? Twice you fell a prisoner into the hands of the enemy, and I had to ransom you.

"The king of the Danaids gave you up in exchange for his daughter, and he rejoices long since in the restoration of his child; but we, in losing her, lost the most powerful means of coercing the seafaring nations of the islands and northern coasts of the great sea who are constantly increasing in might and daring, and so diminished our chances of securing a solid and abiding peace.

"Thus-through the careless wilfulness of a boy, the great work is endangered which I had hoped to have achieved. It grieves me particularly to humiliate your spirit to-day, when I have had so much reason to encourage you with praise. Nor will I punish you, only warn you and teach you. The mechanism of the state is like the working of the cogged wheels which move the water-works on the shore of the Nile-if one tooth is missing the whole comes to a stand-still however strong the beasts that labor to turn it. Each of you-bear this in mind-is a main-wheel in the great machine of the state, and can serve an end only by acting unresistingly in obedience to the motive power. Now rise! we may perhaps succeed in obtaining good security from the Asiatic king, though we have lost our hostage."

Heralds at this moment marched into the tent, and announced that the representative of the Cheta king and the allied princes were in attendance in the council tent; Rameses put on the crown of Upper and Lower Egypt and all his royal adornments; the chamberlain who carried the insignia of his power, and his head scribe with his decoration of plumes marched before him, while his sons, the commanders in chief, and the interpreters followed him. Rameses took his seat on his throne with great dignity, and the sternest gravity marked his demeanor while he received the homage of the conquered and fettered kings.

The Asiatics kissed the earth at his feet, only the king of the Danaids did no more than bow before him. Rameses looked wrathfully at him, and ordered the interpreter to ask him whether he considered himself conquered or no, and the answer was given that he had not come before the Pharaoh as a prisoner, and that the obeisance which Rameses required of him was regarded as a degradation according to the customs of his free-born people, who prostrated them selves only before the Gods. He hoped to become an ally of the king of Egypt, and he asked would he desire to call a degraded man his friend?

Rameses measured the proud and noble figure before him with a glance, and said severely:

"I am prepared to treat for peace only with such of my enemies as are willing to bow to the double crown that I wear. If you persist in your refusal, you and your people will have no part in the favorable conditions that I am prepared to grant to these, your allies."

The captive prince preserved his dignified demeanor, which was nevertheless free from insolence, when these words of the king were interpreted to him, and replied that he had come intending to procure peace at any cost, but that he never could nor would grovel in the dust at any man's feet nor before any crown. He would depart on the following day; one favor, however, he requested in his daughter's name and his own-and he had heard that the Egyptians respected women. The king knew, of course, that his charioteer Mena had treated his daughter, not as a prisoner but as a sister, and Praxilla now felt a wish, which he himself shared, to bid farewell to the noble Mena, and his wife, and to thank him for his magnanimous generosity. Would Rameses permit him once more to cross the Nile before his departure, and with his daughter to visit Mena in his tent.

Rameses granted his prayer: the prince left the tent, and the negotiations began.

In a few hours they were brought to a close, for the Asiatic and Egyptian scribes had agreed, in the course of the long march southwards, on the stipulations to be signed; the treaty itself was to be drawn up after the articles had been carefully considered, and to be signed in the city of Rameses called Tanis-or, by the numerous settlers in its neighborhood, Zoan. The Asiatic princes were to dine as guests with the king; but they sat at a separate table, as the Egyptians would have been defiled by sitting at the same table with strangers.

Rameses was not perfectly satisfied. If the Danaids went away without concluding a treaty with him, it was to be expected that the peace which he was so earnestly striving for would before long be again disturbed; and he nevertheless felt that, out of regard for the other conquered princes, he could not forego any jot of the humiliation which he had required of their king, and which he believed to be due to himself-though he had been greatly impressed by his dignified manliness and by the bravery of the troops that had followed him into the field.

The sun was sinking when Mena, who that day had leave of absence from the king, came in great excitement up to the table where the princes were sitting and craved the king's permission to make an important communication. Rameses signed consent; the charioteer went close up to him, and they held a short but eager conversation in a low voice.

Presently the king stood up and said, speaking to his daughter:

"This day which began so horribly will end joyfully. The fair child who saved you to-day, but who so nearly fell a victim to the flames, is of noble origin."

"She cones of a royal house," said Rameri, disrespectfully interrupting his father. Rameses looked at him reprovingly. "My sons are silent," he said, "till I ask them to speak."

The prince colored and looked down; the king signed to Bent-Anat and Pentaur, begged his guests to excuse him for a short time, and was about to leave the tent; but Bent-Anat went up to him, and whispered a few words to him with reference to her brother. Not in vain: the king paused, and reflected for a few moments; then he looked at Rameri, who stood abashed, and as if rooted to the spot where he stood. The king called his name, and beckoned him to follow him.

CHAPTER XLV.

Rameri had rushed off to summon the physicians, while Bent-Anat was endeavoring to restore the rescued Uarda to consciousness, and he followed them into his sister's tent. He gazed with tender anxiety into the face of the half suffocated girl, who, though uninjured, still remained unconscious, and took her hand to press his lips to her slender fingers, but Bent-Anat pushed him gently away; then in low tones that trembled with emotion he implored her not to send him away, and told her how dear the girl whose life he had saved in the fight in the Necropolis had become to him-how, since his departure for Syria, he had never ceased to think of her night and day, and that he desired to make her his wife.

Bent-Anat was startled; she reminded her brother of the stain that lay on the child of the paraschites and through which she herself had suffered so much; but Rameri answered eagerly:

"In Egypt rank and birth are derived through the mother and Kaschta's dead wife —"

"I know," interrupted Bent-Anat. "Nebsecht has already told us that she was a dumb woman, a prisoner of war, and I myself believe that she was of no mean house, for Uarda is nobly formed in face and figure."

"And her skin is as fine as the petal of a flower," cried Rameri. "Her voice is like the ring of pure gold, and-Oh! look, she is moving. Uarda, open your eyes, Uarda! When the sun rises we praise the Gods. Open your eyes! how thankful, how joyful I shall be if those two suns only rise again."

Bent-Anat smiled, and drew her brother away from the heavily-breathing girl, for a leech came into the tent to say that a warm medicated bath had been prepared and was ready for Uarda. The princess ordered her waiting-women to help lift the senseless girl, and was preparing to follow her when a message from her father required her presence in his tent. She could guess at the significance of this command, and desired Rameri to leave her that she might dress in festal garments; she could entrust Uarda to the care of Nefert during her absence.

"She is kind and gentle, and she knows Uarda so well," said the princess, "and the necessity of caring for this dear little creature will do her good. Her heart is torn between sorrow for her lost relations, and joy at being united again to her love. My father has given Mena leave of absence from his office for several days, and I have excused her from her attendance on me, for the time during which we were so necessary to each other really came to an end yesterday. I feel, Rameri, as if we, after our escape, were like the sacred phoenix which comes to Heliopolis and burns itself to death only to soar again from its ashes young and radiant-blessed and blessing!"

When her brother had left her, she threw herself before the image of her mother and prayed long and earnestly; she poured an offering of sweet perfume on the little altar of the Goddess Hathor, which always accompanied her, had herself dressed in happy preparation for meeting her father, and-she did not conceal it from herself-Pentaur, then she went for a moment to Nefert's tent to beg her to take good care of Uarda, and finally obeyed the summons of the king, who, as we know, fulfilled her utmost hopes.

As Rameri quitted his sister's tent he saw the watch seize and lead away a little boy; the child cried bitterly, and the prince in a moment recognized the little sculptor Scherau, who had betrayed the Regent's plot to him and to Uarda, and whom he had already fancied he had seen about the place. The guards had driven him away several times from the princess's tent, but he had persisted in returning, and this obstinate waiting in the neighborhood had aroused the suspicions of an officer; for since the fire a thousand rumors of conspiracies and plots against the king had been flying about the camp. Rameri at once freed the little prisoner, and heard from him that it was old Hekt who, before her death, had sent Kaschta and his daughter to the rescue of the king, that he himself had helped to rouse the troops, that now he had no home and wished to go to Uarda.

The prince himself led the child to Nefert, and begged her to allow him to see Uarda, and to let him stay with her servants till he himself returned from his father's tent.

The leeches had treated Uarda with judgment, for under the influence of the bath she recovered her senses; when she had been dressed again in fresh garments and refreshed by the essences and medicines which they gave her to inhale and to drink, she was led back into Nefert's tent, where Mena, who had never before seen her, was astonished at her peculiar and touching beauty.

"She is very like my Danaid princess," he said to his wife; "only she is younger and much prettier than she."

Little Scherau came in to pay his respects to her, and she was delighted to see the boy; still she was sad, and however kindly Nefert spoke to her she remained in silent reverie, while from time to time a large tear rolled down her cheek.

"You have lost your father!" said Nefert, trying to comfort her. "And I, my mother and brother both in one day."

"Kaschta was rough but, oh! so kind," replied Uarda. "He was always so fond of me; he was like the fruit of the doom palm; its husk is hard and rough, but he who knows how to open it finds the sweet pulp within. Now he is dead, and my grandfather and grandmother are gone before him, and I am like the green leaf that I saw floating on the waters when we were crossing the sea; anything so forlorn I never saw, abandoned by all it belonged to or had ever loved, the sport of a strange element in which nothing resembling itself ever grew or ever can grow."

Nefert kissed her forehead. "You have friends," she said, "who will never abandon you."

"I know, I know!" said Uarda thoughtfully, "and yet I am alone-for the first time really alone. In Thebes I have often looked after the wild swans as they passed across the sky; one flies in front, then comes the body of the wandering party, and very often, far behind, a solitary straggler; and even this last one I do not call lonely, for he can still see his brethren in front of him. But when the hunters have shot down all the low-flying loiterers, and the last one has lost sight of the flock, and knows that he never again can find them or follow them he is indeed to be pitied. I am as unhappy as the abandoned bird, for I have lost sight to-day of all that I belong to, and I am alone, and can never find them again."

"You will be welcomed into some more noble house than that to which you belong by birth," said Nefert, to comfort her.

Uarda's eyes flashed, and she said proudly, almost defiantly:

"My race is that of my mother, who was a daughter of no mean house; the reason I turned back this morning and went into the smoke and fire again after I had escaped once into the open air-what I went back for, because I felt it was worth dying for, was my mother's legacy, which I had put away with my holiday dress when I followed the wretched Nemu to his tent. I threw myself into the jaws of death to save the jewel, but certainly not because it is made of gold and precious stones-for I do not care to be rich, and I want no better fare than a bit of bread and a few dates and a cup of water-but because it has a name on it in strange characters, and because I believe it will serve to discover the people from whom my mother was carried off; and now I have lost the jewel, and with it my identity and my hopes and happiness."

Uarda wept aloud; Nefert put her arm around her affectionately.

"Poor child!" she said, "was your treasure destroyed in the flames?"

"No, no," cried Uarda eagerly. "I snatched it out of my chest and held it in my hand when Nebsecht took me in his arms, and I still had it in my hand when I was lying safe on the ground outside the burning house, and Bent-Anat was close to me, and Rameri came up. I remember seeing him as if I were in a dream, and I revived a little, and I felt the jewel in my fingers then."

"Then it was dropped on the way to the tent?" said Nefert.

Uarda nodded; little Scherau, who had been crouching on the floor beside her, gave Uarda a loving glance, dimmed with tears, and quietly slipped out of the tent.

Time went by in silence; Uarda sat looking at the ground, Nefert and Mena held each other's hands, but the thoughts of all three were with the dead. A perfect stillness reigned, and the happiness of the reunited couple was darkly overshadowed by their sorrow. From time to time the silence was broken by a trumpet-blast from the royal tent; first when the Asiatic princes were introduced into the Council-tent, then when the Danaid king departed, and lastly when the Pharaoh preceded the conquered princes to the banquet.

The charioteer remembered how his master had restored him to dignity and honor, for the sake of his faithful wife; and gratefully pressed her hand.

Suddenly there was a noise in front of the tent, and an officer entered to announce to Mena that the Danaid king and his daughter, accompanied by body-guard, requested to see and speak with him and Nefert.

The entrance to the tent was thrown wide open. Uarda retired modestly into the background, and Mena and Nefert went forward hand in hand to meet their unexpected guests.

The Greek prince was an old man, his beard and thick hair were grey, but his movements were youthful and light, though dignified and deliberate. His even, well-formed features were deeply furrowed, he had large, bright, clear blue eyes, but round his fine lips were lines of care. Close to him walked his daughter; her long white robe striped with purple was held round her hips by a golden girdle, and her sunny yellow hair fell in waving locks over her neck and shoulders, while it was confined by a diadem which encircled her head; she was of middle height, and her motions were measured and calm like her father's. Her brow was narrow, and in one line with her straight nose, her rosy mouth was sweet and kind, and beyond everything beautiful were the lines of her oval face and the turn of her snow-white throat. By their side stood the interpreter who translated every word of the conversation on both sides. Behind them came two men and two women, who carried gifts for Mena and his wife.

The prince praised Mena's magnanimity in the warmest terms.

"You have proved to me," he said, "that the virtues of gratitude, of constancy, and of faith are practised by the Egyptians; although your merit certainly appears less to me now that I see your wife, for he who owns the fairest may easily forego any taste for the fair."

Nefert blushed.

"Your generosity," she answered, "does me more than justice at your daughter's expense, and love moved my husband to the same injustice, but your beautiful daughter must forgive you and me also."

Praxilla went towards her and expressed her thanks; then she offered her the costly coronet, the golden clasps and strings of rare pearls which her women carried; her father begged Mena to accept a coat of mail and a shield of fine silver work. The strangers were then led into the tent, and were there welcomed and entertained with all honor, and offered bread and wine. While Mena pledged her father, Praxilla related to Nefert, with the help of the interpreter, what hours of terror she had lived through after she had been taken prisoner by the Egyptians, and was brought into the camp with the other spoils of war; how an older commander had asserted his claim to her, how Mena had given her his hand, had led her to his tent, and had treated her like his own daughter. Her voice shook with emotion, and even the interpreter was moved as she concluded her story with these words: "How grateful I am to him, you will fully understand when I tell you that the man who was to have been my husband fell wounded before my eyes while defending our camp; but he has recovered, and now only awaits my return for our wedding."

"May the Gods only grant it!" cried the king, "for Praxilla is the last child of my house. The murderous war robbed me of my four fair sons before they had taken wives, my son-in-law was slain by the Egyptians at the taking of our camp, and his wife and new-born son fell into their hands, and Praxilla is my youngest child, the only one left to me by the envious Gods."

While he was still speaking, they heard the guards call out and a child's loud cry, and at the same instant little Scherau rushed into the tent holding up his hand exclaiming.

"I have it! I have found it!"

Uarda, who had remained behind the curtain which screened the sleeping room of the tent-but who had listened with breathless attention to every word of the foreigners, and who had never taken her eyes off the fair Praxilla-now came forward, emboldened by her agitation, into the midst of the tent, and took the jewel from the child's hand to show it to the Greek king;

for while she stood gazing at Praxilla it seemed to her that she was looking at herself in a mirror, and the idea had rapidly grown to conviction that her mother had been a daughter of the Danaids. Her heart beat violently as she went up to the king with a modest demeanor, her head bent down, but holding her jewel up for him to see.

The bystanders all gazed in astonishment at the veteran chief, for he staggered as she came up to him, stretched out his hands as if in terror towards the girl, and drew back crying out:

"Xanthe, Xanthe! Is your spirit freed from Hades? Are you come to summon me?"

Praxilla looked at her father in alarm, but suddenly she, too, gave a piercing cry, snatched a chain from her neck, hurried towards Uarda, and seizing the jewel she held, exclaimed:

"Here is the other half of the ornament, it belonged to my poor sister Xanthe!"

The old Greek was a pathetic sight, he struggled hard to collect himself, looking with tender delight at Uarda, his sinewy hands trembled as he compared the two pieces of the necklet; they matched precisely-each represented the wing of an eagle which was attached to half an oval covered with an inscription; when they were laid together they formed the complete figure of a bird with out-spread wings, on whose breast the lines exactly matched of the following oracular verse:

"Alone each is a trifling thing, a woman's useless toy
But with its counterpart behold! the favorite bird of Zeus."

A glance at the inscription convinced the king that he held in his hand the very jewel which he had put with his own hands round the neck of his daughter Xanthe on her marriage-day, and of which the other half had been preserved by her mother, from whom it had descended to Praxilla. It had originally been made for his wife and her twin sister who had died young. Before he made any enquiries, or asked for any explanations, he took Uarda's head between his hands, and turning her face close to his he gazed at her features, as if he were reading a book in which he expected to find a memorial of all the blissful hours of his youth, and the girl felt no fear; nor did she shrink when he pressed his lips to her forehead, for she felt that this man's blood ran in her own veins. At last the king signed to the interpreter; Uarda was asked to tell all she knew of her mother, and when she said that she had come a captive to Thebes with an infant that had soon after died, that her father had bought her and had loved her in spite of her being dumb, the prince's conviction became certainty; he acknowledged Uarda as his grandchild, and Praxilla clasped her in her arms.

Then he told Mena that it was now twenty years since his son-in-law had been killed, and his daughter Xanthe, whom Uarda exactly resembled, had been carried into captivity. Praxilla was then only just born, and his wife died of the shock of such terrible news. All his enquiries for Xanthe and her child had been fruitless, but he now remembered that once, when he had offered a large ransom for his daughter if she could be found, the Egyptians had enquired whether she were dumb, and that he had answered "no." No doubt Xanthe had lost the power of speech through grief, terror, and suffering.

The joy of the king was unspeakable, and Uarda was never tired of gazing at his daughter and holding her hand.

Then she turned to the interpreter.

"Tell me," she said. "How do I say 'I am so very happy?'"

He told her, and she smilingly repeated his words. "Now 'Uarda will love you with all her heart?'" and she said it after him in broken accents that sounded so sweet and so heart-felt, that the old man clasped her to his breast.

Tears of emotion stood in Nefert's eyes, and when Uarda flung herself into her arms she said:

"The forlorn swan has found its kindred, the floating leaf has reached the shore, and must be happy now!" Thus passed an hour of the purest happiness; at last the Greek king prepared to leave, and the wished to take Uarda with him; but Mena begged his permission to communicate all that had occurred to the Pharaoh and Bent-Anat, for Uarda was attached to the princess's train, and had been left in his charge, and he dared not trust her in any other hands without Bent-Anat's permission. Without waiting for the king's reply he left the tent, hastened to the banqueting tent, and, as we know, Rameses and the princess had at once attended to his summons.

On the way Mena gave them a vivid description of the exciting events that had taken place, and Rameses, with a side glance at Bent-Anat, asked Rameri:

"Would you be prepared to repair your errors, and to win the friendship of the Greek king by being betrothed to his granddaughter?"

The prince could not answer a word, but he clasped his father's hand, and kissed it so warmly that Rameses, as he drew it away, said:

"I really believe that you have stolen a march on me, and have been studying diplomacy behind my back!"

Rameses met his noble opponent outside Mena's tent, and was about to offer him his hand, but the Danaid chief had sunk on his knees before him as the other princes had done.

"Regard me not as a king and a warrior," he exclaimed, "only as a suppliant father; let us conclude a peace, and permit me to take this maiden, my grandchild, home with me to my own country."

Rameses raised the old man from the ground, gave him his hand, and said kindly:

"I can only grant the half of what you ask. I, as king of Egypt, am most willing to grant you a faithful compact for a sound and lasting peace; as regards this maiden, you must treat with my children, first with my daughter Bent-Anat, one of whose ladies she is, and then with your released prisoner there, who wishes to make Uarda his wife."

"I will resign my share in the matter to my brother," said Bent-Anat, "and I only ask you, maiden, whether you are inclined to acknowledge him as your lord and master?"

Uarda bowed assent, and looked at her grandfather with an expression which he understood without any interpreter.

"I know you well," he said, turning to Rameri. "We stood face to face in the fight, and I took you prisoner as you fell stunned by a blow from my sword. You are still too rash, but that is a fault which time will amend in a youth of your heroic temper. Listen to me now, and you too, noble Pharaoh, permit me these few words; let us betroth these two, and may their union be the bond of ours, but first grant me for a year to take my long-lost child home with me that she may rejoice my old heart, and that I may hear from her lips the accents of her mother, whom you took from me. They are both young; according to the usages of our country, where both men and women ripen later than in your country, they are almost too young for the solemn tie of marriage. But one thing above all will determine you to favor my wishes; this daughter of a royal house has grown up amid the humblest surroundings; here she has no home, no family-ties. The prince has wooed her, so to speak, on the highway, but if she now comes with me he can enter the palace of kings as suitor to a princess, and the marriage feast I will provide shall be a right royal one."

"What you demand is just and wise," replied Rameses. "Take your grand-child with you as my son's betrothed bride-my future daughter. Give me your hands, my children. The delay will teach you patience, for Rameri must remain a full year from to-day in Egypt, and it will be to your profit, sweet child, for the obedience which he will learn through his training in the army will temper the nature of your future husband. You, Rameri, shall in a year from to-day —and I think you will not forget the date-find at your service a ship in the harbor of Pelusium, fitted and manned with Phoenicians, to convey you to your wedding."

"So be it!" exclaimed the old man. "And by Zeus who hears me swear —I will not withhold Xanthe's daughter from your son when he comes to claim her!"

When Rameri returned to the princes' tent he threw himself on their necks in turn, and when he found himself alone with their surly old house-steward, he snatched his wig from his head, flung it in the air, and then coaxingly stroked the worthy officer's cheeks as he set it on his head again.

270

CHAPTER XLVI.

Uarda accompanied her grandfather and Praxilla to their tent on the farther side of the Nile, but she was to return next morning to the Egyptian camp to take leave of all her friends, and to provide for her father's internment. Nor did she delay attending to the last wishes of old Hekt, and Bent-Anat easily persuaded her father, when he learnt how greatly he had been indebted to her, to have her embalmed like a lady of rank.

Before Uarda left the Egyptian camp, Pentaur came to entreat her to afford her dying preserver Nebsecht the last happiness of seeing her once more; Uarda acceded with a blush, and the poet, who had watched all night by his friend, went forward to prepare him for her visit.

Nebsecht's burns and a severe wound on his head caused him great suffering; his cheeks glowed with fever, and the physicians told Pentaur that he probably could not live more than a few hours.

The poet laid his cool hand on his friend's brow, and spoke to him encouragingly; but Nebsecht smiled at his words with the peculiar expression of a man who knows that his end is near, and said in a low voice and with a visible effort:

"A few breaths more and here, and here, will be peace." He laid his hand on his head and on his heart.

"We all attain to peace," said Pentaur. "But perhaps only to labor more earnestly and unweariedly in the land beyond the grave. If the Gods reward any thing it is the honest struggle, the earnest seeking after truth; if any spirit can be made one with the great Soul of the world it will be yours, and if any eye may see the Godhead through the veil which here shrouds the mystery of His existence yours will have earned the privilege."

"I have pushed and pulled," sighed Nebsecht, "with all my might, and now when I thought I had caught a glimpse of the truth the heavy fist of death comes down upon me and shuts my eyes. What good will it do me to see with the eye of the Divinity or to share in his omniscience? It is not seeing, it is seeking that is delightful-so delightful that I would willingly set my life there against another life here for the sake of it." He was silent, for his strength failed, and Pentaur begged him to keep quiet, and to occupy his mind in recalling all the hours of joy which life had given him.

"They have been few," said the leech. "When my mother kissed me and gave me dates, when I could work and observe in peace, when you opened my eyes to the beautiful world of poetry-that was good!"

And you have soothed the sufferings of many men, added Pentaur, "and never caused pain to any one."

Nebsecht shook his head.

"I drove the old paraschites," he muttered, "to madness and to death."

He was silent for a long time, then he looked up eagerly and said: "But not intentionally-and not in vain! In Syria, at Megiddo I could work undisturbed; now I know what the organ is that thinks. The heart! What is the heart? A ram's heart or a man's heart, they serve the same end; they turn the wheel of animal life, they both beat quicker in terror or in joy, for we feel fear or pleasure just as animals do. But Thought, the divine power that flies to the infinite, and enables us to form and prove our opinions, has its seat here-Here in the brain, behind the brow."

He paused exhausted and overcome with pain. Pentaur thought he was wandering in his fever, and offered him a cooling drink while two physicians walked round his bed singing litanies; then, as Nebsecht raised himself in bed with renewed energy, the poet said to him:

"The fairest memory of your life must surely be that of the sweet child whose face, as you once confessed to me, first opened your soul to the sense of beauty, and whom with your own hands you snatched from death at the cost of your own life. You know Uarda has found her own relatives and is happy, and she is very grateful to her preserver, and would like to see him once more before she goes far away with her grandfather."

The sick man hesitated before he answered softly:

"Let her come-but I will look at her from a distance."

Pentaur went out and soon returned with Uarda, who remained standing with glowing cheeks and tears in her eyes at the door of the tent. The leech looked at her a long time with an imploring and tender expression, then he said:

"Accept my thanks-and be happy."

The girl would have gone up to him to take his hand, but he waved her off with his right hand enveloped in wrappings.

"Come no nearer," he said, "but stay a moment longer. You have tears in your eyes; are they for me or only for my pain?"

"For you, good noble man! my friend and my preserver!" said Uarda. "For you dear, poor Nebsecht!" The leech closed his eyes as she spoke these words with earnest feeling, but he looked up once more as she ceased speaking, and gazed at her with tender admiration; then he said softly:

"It is enough-now I can die."

Uarda left the tent, Pentaur remained with him listening to his hoarse and difficult breathing; suddenly:

Nebsecht raised himself, and said: "Farewell, my friend-my journey is beginning, who knows whither?"

"Only not into vacancy, not to end in nothingness!" cried Pentaur warmly.

The leech shook his head. "I have been something," he said, "and being something I cannot become nothing. Nature is a good economist, and utilizes the smallest trifle; she will use me too according to her need. She brings everything to its end and purpose in obedience to some rule and measure, and will so deal with me after I am dead; there is no waste. Each thing results in being that which it is its function to become; our wish or will is not asked-my head! when the pain is in my head I cannot think-if only I could prove-could prove — —"

The last words were less and less audible, his breath was choked, and in a few seconds Pentaur with deep regret closed his eyes.

Pentaur, as he quitted the tent where the dead man lay, met the high-priest Ameni, who had gone to seek him by his friend's bed-side, and they returned together to gaze on the dead. Ameni, with much emotion, put up a few earnest prayers for the salvation of his soul, and then requested Pentaur to follow him without delay to his tent. On the way he prepared the poet, with the polite delicacy which was peculiar to him, for a meeting which might be more painful than joyful to him, and must in any case bring him many hours of anxiety and agitation.

The judges in Thebes, who had been compelled to sentence the lady Setchem, as the mother of a traitor, to banishment to the mines had, without any demand on her part, granted leave to the noble and most respectable matron to go under an escort of guards to meet the king on his return into Egypt, in order to petition for mercy for herself, but not, as it was expressly added-for Paaker; and she had set out, but with the secret resolution to obtain the king's grace not for herself but for her son.[133]

Ameni had already left Thebes for the north when this sentence was pronounced, or he would have reversed it by declaring the true origin of Paaker; for after he had given up his participation in the Regent's conspiracy, he no longer had any motive for keeping old Hekt's secret.

Setchem's journey was lengthened by a storm which wrecked the ship in which she was descending the Nile, and she did not reach Pelusium till after the king. The canal which formed the mouth of the Nile close to this fortress and joined the river to the Mediterranean, was so over-crowded with the boats of the Regent and his followers, of the ambassadors, nobles, citizens, and troops which had met from all parts of the country, that the lady's boat could find anchorage only at a great distance from the city, and accompanied by her faithful steward she had succeeded only a few hours before in speaking to the high-priest.

Setchem was terribly changed; her eyes, which only a few months since had kept an efficient watch over the wealthy Theban household, were now dim and weary, and although her figure had not grown thin it had lost its dignity and energy, and seemed inert and feeble. Her lips, so

272

ready for a wise or sprightly saying, were closely shut, and moved only in silent prayer or when some friend spoke to her of her unhappy son. His deed she well knew was that of a reprobate, and she sought no excuse or defence; her mother's heart forgave it without any. Whenever she thought of him-and she thought of him incessantly all through the day and through her sleepless nights-her eyes overflowed with tears.

Her boat had reached Pelusium just as the flames were breaking out in the palace; the broad flare of light and the cries from the various vessels in the harbor brought her on deck. She heard that the burning house was the pavilion erected by Ani for the king's residence; Rameses she was told was in the utmost danger, and the fire had beyond a doubt been laid by traitors.

As day broke and further news reached her, the names of her son and of her sister came to her ear; she asked no questions-she would not hear the truth-but she knew it all the same; as often as the word "traitor" caught her ear in her cabin, to which she had retreated, she felt as if some keen pain shot through her bewildered brain, and shuddered as if from a cold chill.

All through that day she could neither eat nor drink, but lay with closed eyes on her couch, while her steward-who had soon learnt what a terrible share his former master had taken in the incendiarism, and who now gave up his lady's cause for lost-sought every where for the high-priest Ameni; but as he was among the persons nearest to the king it was impossible to see him that day, and it was not till the next morning that he was able to speak with him. Ameni inspired the anxious and sorrowful old retainer with, fresh courage, returned with him in his own chariot to the harbor, and accompanied him to Setchem's boat to prepare her for the happiness which awaited her after her terrible troubles. But he came too late, the spirit of the poor lady was quite clouded, and she listened to him without any interest while he strove to restore her to courage and to recall her wandering mind. She only interrupted him over and over again with the questions: "Did he do it?" or "Is he alive?"

At last Ameni succeeded in persuading her to accompany him in her litter to his tent, where she would find her son. Pentaur was wonderfully like her lost husband, and the priest, experienced in humanity, thought that the sight of him would rouse the dormant powers of her mind. When she had arrived at his tent, he told her with kind precaution the whole history of the exchange of Paaker for Pentaur, and she followed the story with attention but with indifference, as if she were hearing of the adventures of others who did not concern her. When Ameni enlarged on the genius of the poet and on his perfect resemblance to his dead father she muttered:

"I know —I know. You mean the speaker at the Feast of the Valley," and then although she had been told several times that Paaker had been killed, she asked again if her son was alive.

Ameni decided at last to fetch Pentaur himself,

When he came back with him, fully prepared to meet his heavily-stricken mother, the tent was empty. The high-priest's servants told him that Setchem had persuaded the easily-moved old prophet Gagabu to conduct her to the place where the body of Paaker lay. Ameni was very much vexed, for he feared that Setchem was now lost indeed, and he desired the poet to follow him at once.

The mortal remains of the pioneer had been laid in a tent not far from the scene of the fire; his body was covered with a cloth, but his pale face, which had not been injured in his fall, remained uncovered; by his side knelt the unhappy mother.

She paid no heed to Ameni when he spoke to her, and he laid his hand on her shoulder and said as he pointed to the body:

"This was the son of a gardener. You brought him up faithfully as if he were your own; but your noble husband's true heir, the son you bore him, is Pentaur, to whom the Gods have given not only the form and features but the noble qualities of his father. The dead man may be forgiven-for the sake of your virtues; but your love is due to this nobler soul-the real son of your husband, the poet of Egypt, the preserver of the king's life."

Setchem rose and went up to Pentaur, she smiled at him and stroked his face and breast.

"It is he," she said. "May the Immortals bless him!"

Pentaur would have clasped her in his arms, but she pushed him away as if she feared to commit some breach of faith, and turning hastily to the bier she said softly:

"Poor Paaker-poor, poor Paaker!"

"Mother, mother, do you not know your son?" cried Pentaur deeply moved.

She turned to him again: "It is his voice," she said. "It is he."

She went up to Pentaur, clung to him, clasped her arm around his neck as he bent over her, then kissing him fondly:

"The Gods will bless you!" she said once more. She tore herself from him and threw herself down by the body of Paaker, as if she had done him some injustice and robbed him of his rights.

Thus she remained, speechless and motionless, till they carried her back to her boat, there she lay down, and refused to take any nourishment; from time to time she whispered "Poor Paaker!" She no longer repelled Pentaur, for she did not again recognize him, and before he left her she had followed the rough-natured son of her adoption to the other world.

CHAPTER XLVII.

The king had left the camp, and had settled in the neighboring city of Rameses' Tanis, with the greater part of his army. The Hebrews, who were settled in immense numbers in the province of Goshen, and whom Ani had attached to his cause by remitting their task-work, were now driven to labor at the palaces and fortifications which Rameses had begun to build.

At Tanis, too, the treaty of peace was signed and was presented to Rameses inscribed on a silver tablet by Tarthisebu, the representative of the Cheta king, in the name of his lord and master.

Pentaur followed the king as soon as he had closed his mother's eyes, and accompanied her body to Heliopolis, there to have it embalmed; from thence the mummy was to be sent to Thebes, and solemnly placed in the grave of her ancestors. This duty of children towards their parents, and indeed all care for the dead, was regarded as so sacred by the Egyptians, that neither Pentaur nor Bent-Anat would have thought of being united before it was accomplished.

On the 21st day of the month Tybi, of the 21st year of the reign of Rameses, the day on which the peace was signed, the poet returned to Tanis, sad at heart, for the old gardener, whom he had regarded and loved as his father, had died before his return home; the good old man had not long survived the false intelligence of the death of the poet, whom he had not only loved but reverenced as a superior being bestowed upon his house as a special grace from the Gods.

It was not till seven months after the fire at Pelusium that Pentaur's marriage with Bent-Anat was solemnized in the palace of the Pharaohs at Thebes; but time and the sorrows he had suffered had only united their hearts more closely. She felt that though he was the stronger she was the giver and the helper, and realized with delight that like the sun, which when it rises invites a thousand flowers to open and unfold, the glow of her presence raised the poet's oppressed soul to fresh life and beauty. They had given each other up for lost through strife and suffering, and now had found each other again; each knew how precious the other was. To make each other happy, and prove their affection, was now the aim of their lives, and as they each had proved that they prized honor and right-doing above happiness their union was a true marriage, ennobling and purifying their souls. She could share his deepest thoughts and his most difficult undertakings, and if their house were filled with children she would know how to give him the fullest enjoyment of those small blessings which at the same time are the greatest joys of life.

Pentaur finding himself endowed by the king with superabundant wealth, gave up the inheritance of his fathers to his brother Horus, who was raised to the rank of chief pioneer as a reward for his interposition at the battle of Kadesh; Horus replaced the fallen cedar-trees which had stood at the door of his house by masts of more moderate dimensions.

The hapless Huni, under whose name Pentaur had been transferred to the mines of Sinai, was released from the quarries of Chennu, and restored to his children enriched by gifts from the poet.

The Pharaoh fully recognized the splendid talents of his daughter's husband; she to his latest days remained his favorite child, even after he had consolidated the peace by marrying the daughter of the Cheta king, and Pentaur became his most trusted adviser, and responsible for the weightiest affairs in the state. Rameses learned from the papers found in Ani's tent, and from other evidence which was only too abundant, that the superior of the House of Seti, and with him the greater part of the priesthood, had for a long time been making common cause with the traitor; in the first instance he determined on the severest, nay bloodiest punishment, but he was persuaded by Pentaur and by his son Chamus to assert and support the principles of his government by milder and yet thorough measures. Rameses desired to be a defender of religion–of the religion which could carry consolation into the life of the lowly and over-burdened, and give their existence a higher and fuller meaning–the religion which to him, as king, appeared the indispensable means of keeping the grand significance of human life ever present to his mind–sacred as the inheritance of his fathers, and useful as the school where the people, who needed leading, might learn to follow and obey.

But nevertheless no one, not even the priests, the guardians of souls, could be permitted to resist the laws of which he was the bulwark, to which he himself was subject, and which enjoined obedience to his authority; and before he left Tanis he had given Ameni and his followers to understand that he alone was master in Egypt.

The God Seth, who had been honored by the Semite races since the time of the Hyksos, and whom they called upon under the name of Baal, had from the earliest times never been allowed a temple on the Nile, as being the God of the stranger; but Rameses-in spite of the bold remonstrances of the priestly party who called themselves the 'true believers' —raised a magnificent temple to this God in the city of Tanis to supply the religious needs of the immigrant foreigners. In the same spirit of toleration he would not allow the worship of strange Gods to be interfered with, though on the other hand he was jealous in honoring the Egyptian Gods with unexampled liberality. He caused temples to be erected in most of the great cities of the kingdom, he added to the temple of Ptah at Memphis, and erected immense colossi in front of its pylons in memory of his deliverance from the fire.[134]

In the Necropolis of Thebes he had a splendid edifice constructed-which to this day delights the beholder by the symmetry of its proportions in memory of the hour when he escaped death as by a miracle; on its pylon he caused the battle of Kadesh to be represented in beautiful pictures in relief, and there, as well as on the architrave of the great banqueting-hall, he had the history inscribed of the danger he had run when he stood "alone and no man with him!"

By his order Pentaur rewrote the song he had sung at Pelusium; it is preserved in three temples, and, in fragments, on several papyrus-rolls which can be made to complete each other. It was destined to become the national epic-the Iliad of Egypt.

Pentaur was commissioned to transfer the school of the House of Seti to the new votive temple, which was called the House of Rameses, and arrange it on a different plan, for the Pharaoh felt that it was requisite to form a new order of priests, and to accustom the ministers of the Gods to subordinate their own designs to the laws of the country, and to the decrees of their guardian and ruler, the king. Pentaur was made the superior of the new college, and its library, which was called "the hospital for the soul," was without an equal; in this academy, which was the prototype of the later-formed museum and library of Alexandria, sages and poets grew up whose works endured for thousands of years-and fragments of their writings have even come down to us. The most famous are the hymns of Anana, Pentaur's favorite disciple, and the tale of the two Brothers, composed by Gagabu, the grandson of the old Prophet.

Ameni did not remain in Thebes. Rameses had been informed of the way in which he had turned the death of the ram to account, and the use he had made of the heart, as he had supposed it, of the sacred animal, and he translated him without depriving him of his dignity or revenues to Mendes, the city of the holy rams in the Delta, where, as he observed not without satirical meaning, he would be particularly intimate with these sacred beasts; in Mendes Ameni exerted great influence, and in spite of many differences of opinion which threatened to sever them, he and Pentaur remained fast friends to the day of his death.

In the first court of the House of Rameses there stands-now broken across the middle-the wonder of the traveller, the grandest colossus in Egypt, made of the hardest granite, and exceeding even the well-known statue of Memnon in the extent of its base. It represents Rameses the Great. Little Scherau, whom Pentaur had educated to be a sculptor, executed it, as well as many other statues of the great sovereign of Egypt.

A year after the burning of the pavilion at Pelusium Rameri sailed to the land of the Danaids, was married to Uarda, and then remained in his wife's native country, where, after the death of her grandfather, he ruled over many islands of the Mediterranean and became the founder of a great and famous race. Uarda's name was long held in tender remembrance by their subjects, for having grown up in misery she understood the secret of alleviating sorrow and relieving want, and of doing good and giving happiness without humiliating those she benefitted.

Footnotes

1. The course of the Sun was compared to that of the life of Man. He rose as the child Horns, grew by midday to the hero Ra, who conquered the Uraeus snake for his diadem, and by evening was an old Man, Tum. Light had been born of darkness, hence Tum was regarded as older than Horns and the other gods of light.

2. The jackal-headed god Anubis was the son of Osiris and Nephthys, and the jackal was sacred to him. In the earliest ages even he is prominent in the nether world. He conducts the mummifying process, preserves the corpse, guards the Necropolis, and, as Hermes Psychopompos (Hermanubis), opens the way for the souls. According to Plutarch "He is the watch of the gods as the dog is the watch of men."

3. The two pyramidal towers joined by a gateway which formed the entrance to an Egyptian temple were called the Pylon.

4. Hathor was Isis under a substantial form. She is the goddess of the pure, light heaven, and bears the Sun-disk between cow-horns on a cow's head or on a human head with cow's ears. She was named the Fair, and all the pure joys of life are in her gift. Later she was regarded as a Muse who beautifies life with enjoyment, love, song, and the dance. She appears as a good fairy by the cradle of children and decides their lot in life. She bears many names: and several, generally seven, Hathors were represented, who personified the attributes and influence of the goddess.

5. The title here rendered pioneer was that of an officer whose duties were those at once of a scout and of a Quarter-Master General. In unknown and comparatively savage countries it was an onerous post. —Translator.

6. The Typhon of the Greeks. The enemy of Osiris, of truth, good and purity. Discord and strife in nature. Horns who fights against him for his father Osiris, can throw him and stun him, but never annihilate him.

7. Every detail of this description of an Egyptian school is derived from sources dating from the reign of Rameses II. and his successor, Merneptah.

8. Pharaoh is the Hebrew form of the Egyptian Peraa-or Phrah. "The great house," "sublime house," or "high gate" is the literal meaning.

9. A support of crescent form on which the Egyptians rested their heads. Many specimens were found in the catacombs, and similar objects are still used in Nubia

10. Egyptians belonging to the higher classes wore wigs on their shaven heads. Several are preserved in museums.

11. What is here stated with regard to the medical schools is principally derived from the medical writings of the Egyptians themselves, among which the "Ebers Papyrus" holds the first place, "Medical Papyrus I." of Berlin the second, and a hieratic MS. in London which, like the first mentioned, has come down to us from the 18th dynasty, takes the third. Also see Herodotus II. 84. Diodorus I. 82.

12. Among the six hermetic books of medicine mentioned by Clement of Alexandria, was one devoted to surgical instruments: otherwise the very badly-set fractures found in some of the mummies do little honor to the Egyptian surgeons.

13. The Egyptians seem to have preferred to use flint instruments for surgical purposes, at any rate for the opening of bodies and for circumcision. Many flint instruments have been found and preserved in museums.

14. Small statuettes, placed in graves to help the dead in the work performed in the under-world. They have axes and ploughs in their hands, and seed-bags on their backs. The sixth chapter of the Book of the Dead is inscribed on nearly all.

15. Toth is the god of the learned and of physicians. The Ibis was sacred to him, and he was usually represented as Ibis-headed. Ra created him "a beautiful light to show the name of his evil enemy." Originally the Dfoon-god, he became the lord of time and measure. He is the weigher, the philosopher among the gods, the lord of writing, of art and of learning. The Greeks called him Hermes Trismegistus, i.e. threefold or "very great" which was, in fact, in imitation of the Egyptians, whose name Toth or Techud signified twofold, in the same way "very great"

16. Besa, the god of the toilet of the Egyptians. He was represented as a deformed pigmy. He led the women to conquest in love, and the men in war. He was probably of Arab origin.

17. In Egypt, as in Palestine, beasts trod out the corn, as we learn from many pictures in the catacombs, even in the remotest ages; often with the addition of a weighted sledge, to the runners of which rollers are attached. It is now called noreg.

18. Calendars have been preserved, the completest is the papyrus Sallier IV., which has been admirably treated by F. Chabas. Many days are noted as lucky, unlucky, etc. In the temples many Calendars of feasts have been found, the most perfect at Medinet Abu, deciphered by Dumich.

19. The Pastophori were an order of priests to which the physicians belonged.

20. Chennu was situated on a bend of the Nile, not far from the Nubian frontier; it is now called Gebel Silsilch; it was in very ancient times the seat of a celebrated seminary.

21. Gazelles were tamed for domestic animals: we find them in the representations of the herds of the wealthy Egyptians and as slaughtered for food. The banquet is described from the pictures of feasts which have been found in the tombs.

22. Cellars maintain the mean temperature of the climate, and in Egypt are hot Wine was best preserved in shady and airy lofts.

23. Hymn to Amon preserved in a papyrus roll at Bulaq, and deciphered by Grehaut and L. Stern.

24. A particularly solemn festival in honor of Amon-Chem, held in the temple of Medinet-Abu.

25. At no period Egyptian writers use more Semitic words than during the reigns of Rame-ses II. and his son Mernephtah.

26. The severe duties of the Mohar are well known from the papyrus of Anastasi I. in the Brit. Mus., which has been ably treated by F. Chabas, Voyage d'un Egyptien.

27. Corresponding to our minister of war. A person of the highest importance even in the earliest times.

28. In the demotic papyrus preserved at Bulaq (novel by Setnau) first treated by H. Brugsch, the following words occur: "Is it not the law, which unites one to another?" Betrothed brides are mentioned, for instance on the sarcophagus of Unnefer at Bulaq.

29. Red was the color of Seth and Typhon. The evil one is named the Red, as for instance in the papyrus of fibers. Red-haired men were typhonic.

30. In Latin "micare digitis." A game still constantly played in the south of Europe, and frequently represented by the Egyptians. The games depicted in the monuments are collected by Minutoli, in the Leipziger Illustrirte Zeitung, 1852.

31. The Syene of the Greeks, non, called Assouan at the first cataract.

32. Many portraits have come down to us of Rameses: the finest is the noble statue preserved at Turin. A likeness has been detected between its profile, with its slightly aquiline nose, and that of Napoleon I.

33. A venomous Egyptian serpent which was adopted as the symbol of sovereign power, in consequence of its swift effects for life or death. It is never wanting to the diadem of the Pharaohs.

34. She formed a triad with Anion and Chunsu under the name of Muth. The great "Sanctuary of the kingdom" —the temple of Karnak-was dedicated to them.

35. The paraschites, with an Ethiopian knife, cuts the flesh of the corpse as deeply as the law requires: but instantly takes to flight, while the relatives of the deceased pursue him with stones, and curses, as if they wished to throw the blame on him.

36. Literally the "cutting" which, under Seti I., the father of Rameses, was the first Suez Canal; a representation of it is found on the northern outer wall of the temple of Karnak. It followed nearly the same direction as the Fresh-water canal of Lesseps, and fertilized the land of Goshen.

37. The Egyptian mestem, that is stibium or antimony, which was introduced into Egypt by the Asiatics at a very early period and universally used.

38. At the present day the Egyptian women are fond of chewing them, on account of their pleasant taste. The ancient Egyptians used various pills. Receipts for such things are found in the Ebers Papyrus.

39. A goddess with the head of a lioness or a cat, over which the Sun- disk is usually found. She was the daughter of Ra, and in the form of the Uraeus on her father's crown personified the murderous heat of the star of day. She incites man to the hot and wild passion of love, and as a cat or lioness tears burning wounds in the limbs of the guilty in the nether world; drunkenness and pleasure are her gifts She was also named Bast and Astarte after her sister-divinity among the Phoenicians.

40. The fields of the blest, which were opened to glorified souls. In the Book of the Dead it is shown that in them men linger, and sow and reap by cool waters.

41. An Aramaean race, according to Schrader's excellent judgment. At the time of our story the peoples of western Asia had allied themselves to them.

42. The sentences and mediums employed by the witches, according to papyrus-rolls which remain. I have availed myself of the Magic papyrus of Harris, and of two in the Berlin collection, one of which is in Greek.

43. The Egyptians had no coins before Alexander and the Ptolemies, but used metals for exchange, usually in the form of rings.

44. Kyphi was a celebrated Egyptian incense. Recipes for its preparation have been preserved in the papyrus of Ebers, in the laboratories of the temples, and elsewhere. Parthey had three different varieties prepared by the chemist, L. Voigt, in Berlin. Kyphi after the formula of Dioskorides was the best. It consisted of rosin, wine, rad, galangae, juniper berries, the root of the aromatic rush, asphalte, mastic, myrrh, Burgundy grapes, and honey.

45.   A rattling metal instrument used by the Egyptians in the service of the Gods. Many specimens are extant in Museums. Plutarch describes it correctly, thus: "The Sistrum is rounded above, and the loop holds the four bars which are shaken." On the bend of the Sistrum they often set the head of a cat with a human face.

46.   Amon, that is to say, "the hidden one." He was the God of Thebes, which was under his aegis, and after the Hykssos were expelled from the Nile-valley, he was united with Ra of Heliopolis and endowed with the attributes of all the remaining Gods. His nature was more and more spiritualized, till in the esoteric philosophy of the time of the Rameses he is compared to the All filling and All guiding intelligence. He is "the husband of his mother, his own father, and his own son," As the living Osiris, he is the soul and spirit of all creation.

47.   Ra, originally the Sun-God; later his name was introduced into the pantheistic mystic philosophy for that of the God who is the Universe.

48.   Ptah is the Greek Henhaistas, the oldest of the Gods, the great maker of the material for the creation, the "first beginner," by whose side the seven Chnemu stand, as architects, to help him, and who was named "the lord of truth," because the laws and conditions of being proceeded from him. He created also the germ of light, he stood therefore at the head of the solar Gods, and was called the creator of ice, from which, when he had cleft it, the sun and the moan came forth. Hence his name "the opener."

49.   The holy star of Isis, Sirius or the dog star, whose course in the time of the Pharaohs coincided with the exact Solar year, and served at a very early date as a foundation for the reckoning of time among the Egyptians.

50.   Mesu is the Egyptian name of Moses, whom we may consider as a contemporary of Rameses, under whose successor the exodus of the Jews from Egypt took place.

51.   The justified dead became Osiris; that is to say, attained to the fullest union (Henosis) with the divinity.

52.   The Greeks and Romans report that the Egyptians were so addicted to satire and pungent witticisms that they would hazard property and life to gratify their love of mockery. The scandalous pictures in the so-called kiosk of Medinet Habu, the caricatures in an indescribable papyrus at Turin, confirm these statements. There is a noteworthy passage in Flavius Vopiscus, that compares the Egyptians to the French.

53.   The Egyptians were great letter-writers, and many of their letters have come down to us, they also had established postmen, and had a word for them in their language "fai chat."

54.   These were an eastern race who migrated from Asia into Egypt, conquered the lower Nile-valley, and ruled over it for nearly 500 years, till they were driven out by the successors of the old legitimate Pharaohs, whose dominion had been confined to upper Egypt.

55.   "With good management," said the first Napoleon, "the Nile encroaches upon the desert, with bad management the desert encroaches upon the Nile."

56.   Two recipes for pills are found in the papyri, one with honey for women, and one without for men.

57.   Marriages between brothers and sisters were allowed in ancient Egypt. The Ptolemaic princes adopted this, which was contrary to the Macedonian customs. When Ptolemy II. Philadelphus married his sister Arsinoe, it seems to have been thought necessary

to excuse it by the relative positions of Venus and Saturn at that period, and the constraining influences of these planets.

58. In Egypt, where there is so little wood, to this day the dried dung of beasts is the commonest kind of fuel.

59. Among the Orientals-and even the Spaniards-it was and is common to give the name of uncle to a parent's cousin.

60. The lock of youth was a curl of hair which all the younger members of princely families wore at the side of the head. The young Horus is represented with it.

61. It was a king of the fourth dynasty, named Asychis by Herodotus, who it is admitted was the first to pledge the mummies of his ancestors. "He who stakes this pledge and fails to redeem the debt shall, after his death, rest neither in his father's tomb nor in any other, and sepulture shall be denied to his descendants." Herod. 11. 136.

62. When Apis (the sacred bull) died under Ptolemy I. Soter, his keepers spent not only the money which they had received for his maintenance, in his obsequies but borrowed 50 talents of silver from the king. In the time of Diodurus 100 talents were spent for the same purpose.

63. This is the beginning of November. The Nile begins slowly to rise early in June; between the 15th and 20th of July it suddenly swells rapidly, and in the first half of October, not, as was formerly supposed, at the end of September, the inundation reaches its highest level. Heinrich Barth established these data beyond dispute. After the water has begun to sink it rises once more in October and to a higher level than before. Then it soon falls, at first slowly, but by degrees quicker and quicker.

64. Dolls belonging to the time of the Pharaohs are preserved in the museums, for instance, the jointed ones at Leyden.

65. Hogs were sacrificed at the feasts of Selene (the Egyptian Nechebt). The poor offer pigs made of dough. Herodotus II., 47. Various kinds of cakes baked in the form of animals are represented on the monuments.

66. Hathor is frequently called "the golden," particularly at Dendera She has much in common with the "golden Aphrodite."

67. This temple is well proportioned, and remains in good preservation. Copies of the interesting pictures discovered in it are to be found in the "Fleet of an Egyptian queen" by Dutnichen. Other details may be found in Lepsius' Monuments of Egypt, and a plan of the place has recently been published by Mariette.

68. The daughter of Thotmes I., wife of her brother Thotmes II., and predecessor of her second brother Thotmes III. An energetic woman who executed great works, and caused herself to be represented with the helmet and beard-case of a man.

69. Polygonal pillars, which were used first in tomb-building under the 12th dynasty, and after the expulsion of the Hyksos under the kings of the 17th and 18th, in public buildings; but under the subsequent races of kings they ceased to be employed.

70. Arabia; apparently also the coast of east Africa south of Egypt as far as Somali. The latest of the lists published by Mariette, of the southern nations conquered by Thotmes III., mentions it. This list was found on the pylon of the temple of Karnak.

71. "To be full (meh) of any one" is used in the Egyptian language for "to be in love with any one."

72.   Vases of clay, limestone, or alabaster, which were used for the preservation of the intestines of the embalmed Egyptians, and represented the four genii of death, Amset, Hapi, Tuamutef, and Khebsennuf. Instead of the cover, the head of the genius to which it was dedicated, was placed on each kanopus. Amset (tinder the protection of Isis) has a human head, Hapi (protected by Nephthys) an ape's head, Tuamutef (protected by Neith) a jackal's head, and Khebsennuf (protected by Selk) a sparrow-hawk's head. In one of the Christian Coptic Manuscripts, the four archangels are invoked in the place of these genii.

73.   The Books of the Dead are often found amongst the cloths, (by the leg or under the arm), or else in the coffin trader, or near, the mummy.

74.   The vignettes of Chapter 125 of the Book of the Dead represent the Last Judgment of the Egyptians. Under a canopy Osiris sits enthroned as Chief Judge, 42 assessors assist him. In the hall stand the scales; the dog headed ape, the animal sacred to Toth, guides the balance. In one scale lies the heart of the dead man, in the other the image of the goddess of Truth, who introduces the soul into the hall of justice Toth writs the record. The soul affirms that it has not committed 42 deadly sins, and if it obtains credit, it is named "maa cheru," i.e. "the truth-speaker," and is therewith declared blessed. It now receives its heart back, and grows into a new and divine life.

75.   For an account of the traces of the Jews in Egypt, see Chabas, Melanges, and Ebers, AEgypten und die Bucher Moses

76.   "The priests," says Clement of Alexandria, "allow none to be participators in their mysteries, except kings or such amongst themselves as are distinguished for virtue or wisdom." The same thing is shown by the monuments in many places

77.   In Sais the statue of Athene (Neith) has the following, inscription: "I am the All, the Past, the Present, and the Future, my veil has no mortal yet lifted." Plutarch, Isis and Osiris 9, a similar quotation by Proclus, in Plato's Timaeus.

78.   Begun by Rameses I. continued by Seti I., completed by Rameses II. The remains of this immense hall, with its 134 columns, have not their equal in the world.

79.   According to the inscription accompanying the famous representations of the four nations (Egyptians, Semites, Libyans, and Ethiopians) in the tomb of Seti I.

80.   Called by the Greeks "Hermetic Books." The Papyrus Ebers is the work called by Clemens of Alexandria "the Book of Remedies."

81.   Human brains are prescribed for a malady of the eyes in the Ebers papyrus. Herophilus, one of the first scholars of the Alexandrine Museum, studied not only the bodies of executed criminals, but made his experiments also on living malefactors. He maintained that the four cavities of the human brain are the seat of the soul.

82.   At the time of our narrative the Egyptians had two kinds of writing-the hieroglyphic, which was generally used for monumental inscriptions, and in which the letters consisted of conventional representations of various objects, mathematical and arbitrary symbols, and the hieratic, used for writing on papyrus, and in which, with the view of saving time, the written pictures underwent so many alterations and abbreviations that the originals could hardly be recognized. In the 8th century there was a further abridgment of the hieratic writing, which was called the demotic, or people's writing, and was used in commerce. Whilst the hieroglyphic and hieratic writings laid the foundations of the old sacred dialect, the demotic letters were only used to write the spoken language of the people. E. de Rouge's Chrestomathie Egyptienne. H. Brugsch's Hieroglyphische Grammatik. Le Page Renouf's shorter hieroglyphical

grammar. Ebers' Ueber das Hieroglyphische Schriftsystem, 2nd edition, 1875, in the lectures of Virchow Holtzendorff.

83. In the streets of modern Egyptian towns asses stand saddled for hire. On the monuments only foreigners are represented as riding on asses, but these beasts are mentioned in almost every list of the possessions of the nobles, even in very early times, and the number is often considerable. There is a picture extant of a rich old man who rides on a seat supported on the backs of two donkeys. Lepsius, Denkmaler, part ii. 126.

84. Recipes for exterminating noxious creatures are found in the papyrus in my possession.

85. At Medinet Habu a picture represents Rameses the Third, not Rameses the Second, playing at draughts with his daughter.

86. The hieroglyphic sign Sam seems to me to represent the wooden stick used to produce fire (as among some savage tribes) by rapid friction in a hollow piece of wood.

87. Radishes, onions, and garlic were the hors-d'oeuvre of an Egyptian dinner. 1600 talents worth were consumed, according to Herodotus. during the building of the pyramid of Cheops —£360,000 (in 1881.)

88. This vase was called canopus at a later date. There were four of them for each mummy.

89. Seb is the earth; Plutarch calls Seb Chronos. He is often spoken of as the "father of the gods" on the monuments. He is the god of time, and as the Egyptians regarded matter as eternal, it is not by accident that the sign which represented the earth was also used for eternity.

90. Imitations of the sacred beetle Scarabaeus made of various materials were frequently put into the mummies in the place of the heart. Large specimens have often the 26th, 30th, and 64th chapters of the Book of the Dead engraved on them, as they treat of the heart.

91. The brains of corpses were drawn out of the nose with a hook. Herodotus II. 87.

92. Wolves have now disappeared from Egypt; they were sacred animals, and were worshipped and buried at Lykopolis, the present Siut, where mummies of wolves have been found. Herodotus says that if a wolf was found dead he was buried, and Aelian states that the herb Lykoktonon, which was poisonous to wolves, might on no account be brought into the city, where they were held sacred. The wolf numbered among the sacral animals is the canis lupaster, which exists in Egypt at the present day. Besides this species there are three varieties of wild dogs, the jackal, fox, and fenek, canis cerda.

93. One of the mummies of Prague which were dissected by Czermak, had the soles of the feet removed and laid on the breast. We learn from Chapter 125 of the Book of the Dead that this was done that the sacred floor of the hall of judgment might not be defiled when the dead were summoned before Osiris.

94. Cherheb was the title of the speaker or reciter at a festival. We cannot agree with those who confuse this personage with the chief of the Kolchytes.

95. Asparagus was known to the Egyptians. Pliny says they held in their mouths, as a remedy for toothache, wine in which asparagus had been cooked.] —not peas," said another looking over his shoulder, and pretending to be flogging. They all shouted again with laughter, but it was hushed as soon as they heard Ameni's well-known footstep.

96. Pictures on the monuments show that in ancient Egypt, as at the present time, bouquets of flowers were bestowed as tokens of friendly feeling.

97. Ibis religiosa. It has disappeared from Egypt There were two varieties of this bird, which was sacred to Toth, and mummies of both have been found in various places. Elian states that an immortal Ibis was shown at Hermopolis. Plutarch says, the ibis destroys poisonous reptiles, and that priests draw the water for their purifications where the Ibis has drunk, as it will never touch unwholesome water.

98. The dressing and undressing of the holy images was conducted in strict accordance with a prescribed ritual. The inscriptions in the seven sanctuaries of Abydos, published by Alariette, are full of instruction as to these ordinances, which were significant in every detail.

99. The dog faced baboon, Kynokephalos, was sacred to Toth as the Moongod. Mummies of these apes have been found at Thebes and Hermopolis, and they are often represented as reading with much gravity. Statues of them have been found to great quantities, and there is a particularly life-like picture of a Kynokephalos in relief on the left wall of the library of the temple of Isis at Philoe.

100. The harbors of the Red Sea were in the hands of the Phoenicians, who sailed from thence southwards to enrich themselves with the produce of Arabia and Ophir. Pharaoh Necho also projected a Suez canal, but does not appear to have carried it out, as the oracle declared that the utility of the undertaking would be greatest to foreigners.

101. Human sacrifices, which had been introduced into Egypt by the Phoenicians, were very early abolished.

102. The 29th Phaophi. The Egyptians divided the year into three seasons of four months each. Flood-time, seed-time and Harvest. (Scha, per and schemu.) The 29th Phaophi corresponds to the 8th November.

103. There were no female sphinxes in Egypt. The sphinx was called Neb, i.e., the lord. The lion-couchant had either a man's or a rams head.

104. The tomb of Neferhotep is well preserved, and in it the inscription from which the monody is translated.

105. It was thought that the insane were possessed by demons. A stele admirably treated by F. de Rouge exists at Paris, which relates that the sister-in law of Rameses III., who was possessed by devils, had them driven out by the statue of Chunsu, which was sent to her in Asia.

106. Kynopolis, or in old Egyptian Saka, is now Samalut; Anubis was the chief divinity worshipped there. Plutarch relates a quarrel between the inhabitants of this city, and the neighboring one of Oxyrynchos, where the fish called Oxyrynchos was worshipped. It began because the Kynopolitans eat the fish, and in revenge the Oxyrynchites caught and killed dogs, and consumed them in sacrifices. Juvenal relates a similar story of the Ombites-perhaps Koptites-and Pentyrites in the 15th Satire.

107. According to Diodorous (I. 80) there was a cast of thieves in Thebes. All citizens were obliged to enter their names in a register, and state where they lived, and the thieves did the same. The names were enrolled by the "chief of the thieves," and all stolen goods had to be given up to him. The person robbed had to give a written description of the object he had lost, and a declaration as to when and where he had lost it. The stolen property was then easily recovered, and restored to the owner on

the payment of one fourth of its value, which was given to the thief. A similar state of things existed at Cairo within a comparatively short time.

108. A custom mentioned by Herodotus. Lucian saw such an image brought in at a feast. The Greeks adopted the idea, but beautified it, using a winged Genius of death instead of a mummy. The Romans also had their "larva."

109. This comparison is genuinely Eastern. Kisra called wine "the soap of sorrow." The Mohammedans, to whom wine is forbidden, have praised it like the guests of the House of Seti. Thus Abdelmalik ibn Salih Haschimi says: "The best thing the world enjoys is wine." Gahiz says: "When wine enters thy bones and flows through thy limbs it bestows truth of feeling, and perfects the soul; it removes sorrow, elevates the mood, etc., etc." When Ibn 'Aischah was told that some one drank no wine, he said: "He has thrice disowned the world." Ibn el Mu'tazz sang: "Heed not time, how it may linger, or how swiftly take its flight, Wail thy sorrows only to the wine before thee gleaming bright. But when thrice thou st drained the beaker watch and ward keep o'er thy heart. Lest the foam of joy should vanish, and thy soul with anguish smart, This for every earthly trouble is a sovereign remedy, Therefore listen to my counsel, knowing what will profit thee, Heed not time, for ah, how many a man has longed in pain Tale of evil days to lighten-and found all his longing vain." —Translated by Mary J. Safford.

110. Chennu is now Gebel Silsileh; the quarries there are of enormous extent, and almost all the sandstone used for building the temples of Upper Egypt was brought from thence. The Nile is narrower there than above, and large stela, were erected there by Rameses II. his successor Mernephtah, on which were inscribed beautiful hymns to the Nile, and lists of the sacrifices to be offered at the Nile- festivals. These inscriptions can be restored by comparison, and my friend Stern and I had the satisfaction of doing this on the spot (Zeitschrift fur Agyptishe Sprache, 1873, p. 129.)

111. It may be observed that among the Egyptian women were qualified to own and dispose of property. For example a papyrus (vii) in the Louvre contains an agreement between Asklepias (called Semmuthis), the daughter or maid-servant of a corpse-dresser of Thebes, who is the debtor, and Arsiesis, the creditor, the son of a kolchytes; both therefore are of the same rank as Uarda.

112. I have described in detail the peninsula of Sinai, its history, and the sacred places on it, in my book "Durch Gosen zum Sinai," published in 1872. In depicting this scenery in the present romance, I have endeavored to reproduce the reality as closely as possible. He who has wandered through this wonderful mountain wilderness can never forget it. The valley now called "Laba," bore the same name in the time of the Pharaohs.

113. The Red Sea-in Hebrew and Coptic the reedy sea-is of a lovely blue green color. According to the Ancients it was named red either from its red banks or from the Erythraeans, who were called the red people. On an early inscription it is called "the water of the Red country." See "Durch Gosen zum Sinai."

114. The oasis at the foot of Horeb, where the Jews under Joshua's command conquered the Amalekites, while Aaron and Hur held up Moses' arms. Exodus 17, 8.

115. "Man" is the name still given by the Bedouins of Sinai to the sweet gum which exudes from the Tamarix mannifera. It is the result of the puncture of an insect, and occurs chiefly in May. By many it is supposed to be the Manna of the Bible.

116. A medicine case, belonging to a more ancient period than the reign of Rameses, is preserved in the Berlin Museum.

117. A brook springs on the peak called by the Sinaitic monks Mr. St. Katherine, which is called the partridge's spring, and of which many legends are told. For instance, God created it for the partridges which accompanied the angels who carried St. Katharine of Alexandria to her tomb on Sinai.

118. The Mohars used chariots in their journeys. This is positively known from the papyrus Anastasi I. which vividly describes the hardships experienced by a Mohar while travelling through Syria.

119. Kadesh was the chief city of the Cheta, i.e. Aramaans, round which the united forces of all the peoples of western Asia had collected. There were several cities called Kadesh. That which frequently checked the forces of Thotmes III. may have been situated farther to the south; but the Cheta city of Kadesh, where Rameses II. fought so hard a battle, was undoubtedly on the Orontes, for the river which is depicted on the pylon of the Ramesseum as parting into two streams which wash the walls of the fortress, is called Aruntha, and in the Epos of Pentaur it is stated that this battle took place at Kadesh by the Orontes. The name of the city survives, at a spot just three miles north of the lake of Riblah. The battle itself I have described from the Epos of Pentaur, the national epic of Egypt. It ends with these words: "This was written and made by the scribe Pentaur." It was so highly esteemed that it is engraved in stone twice at Luqsor, and once at Karnak. Copies of it on papyrus are frequent; for instance, papyrus Sallier III. and papyrus Raifet-unfortunately much injured-in the Louvre. The principal incident, the rescue of the king from the enemy, is repeated at the Ramessetun at Thebes, and at Abu Simbel. It was translated into French by Vicomte E. de Rouge. The camp of Rameses is depicted on the pylons of Luqsor and the Ramesseum.

120. Representations of Rameses' camp are preserved on the pylons of the temple of Luxor and the Ramesseum.

121. See Diodorus, 1. 47. Also the pictures of the king rushing to the fight.

122. He is named Cha-em-Us on the monuments, i.e., 'splendor in Thebes.' He became the Sam, or high-priest of Memphis. His mummy was discovered by Mariette in the tomb of Apis at Saqqarah during ha excavations of the Serapeum at Memphis.

123. Herodotus speaks of the pictures graven on the rocks in the provinces conquered by Rameses II., in memory of his achievements. He saw two, one of which remains on a rock near Beyrut.

124. The horses driven by Rameses at the battle of Kadesh were in fact thus named.

125. A people of the Greeks at the time of the Trojan war. They are mentioned among the nations of the Mediterranean allied against Rameses III. The Dardaneans were inhabitants of the Trojan provinces of Dardanin, and whose name was used for the Trojans generally.

126. Grey-hounds, trained to hunt hares, are represented in the most ancient tombs, for instance, the Mastaba at Meydum, belonging to the time of Snefru (four centuries BC).

127. The battle about to be described is taken entirely from the epos of Pentaur.

128. The remains of a shirt of mail, dating from the time of Scheschenk I. (Sesonchis), who belonged to the 22d dynasty, is in the British Museum. It is made of leather, on which bronze scales are fastened.

129.   The splendor of the festivities I make Ani prepare seems pitiful compared with those Ptolemy Philadelphus, according to the report of an eye witness, Callexenus, displayed to the Alexandrians on a festal occasion.

130.   I have availed myself of the help of Prof. Lushington's translation in "Records of the past," edited by Dr. S. Birch. Translator.

131.   Papyrus was used not only for writing on, but also for ropes. The bridge of boats on which Xerxes crossed the Hellespont was fastened with cables of papyrus.

132.   In my papyrus there are several recipes for the preparation of hair-dye; one is ascribed to the Lady Schesch, the mother of Teta, wife of the first king of Egypt. The earliest of all the recipes preserved to us is a prescription for dyeing the hair.

133.   Agatharchides, in Diodorus III. 12, says that in many cases not only the criminal but his relations also were condemned to labor in the mines. In the convention signed between Rameses and the Cheta king it is expressly provided that the deserter restored to Egypt shall go unpunished, that no injury shall be done "to his house, his wife or his children, nor shall his mother be put to death."

134.   One of these is still in existence. It lies on the ground among the ruins of ancient Memphis.

Made in United States
North Haven, CT
15 June 2024

53689541R00163